SEAFORT'S CHALLENGE

SEAFORT'S CHALLENGE

Prisoner's Hope

Fisherman's Hope

DAVID FEINTUCH

Published by arrangement with
Warner Books, Inc.
1271 Avenue of the Americas
New York, New York 10020

ISBN 1-56865-189-9

Contents

Introduction

Dear Science Fiction Book Club Readers,

As I write this, I'm bidding a sad farewell to a friend who's dominated my life for the last eight years.

It wasn't easy to live with him—he's been arrogant, at times unfeeling, perhaps a bit obsessed with his own actions. Yet I found him touching—he strove so to set an example, to justify his existence on this earth, though always, in his heart, he felt he often fell short.

I'm going to miss him terribly.

I'm referring, of course, to Nicholas Ewing Seafort.

The Nick Seafort novels you are about to read—*Prisoner's Hope* and *Fisherman's Hope*—were completed over a year ago. That's the way it works in publishing. Months, even years pass between the time a publisher buys your work and the time it sees the light of day. My four novels were actually sold to Warner Books in April, 1993, and it was seventeen months—November 1994—before *Midshipman's Hope* was released. Since then, another book in the series has been issued every five months or so.

Of course, I'm not one who can write a novel and put it down to go on with something else. No, I'm not that lucky. I have to fiddle with it, rewrite, tinker, clean it up, change words, until the final galleys are sent back for correction. Even then, I wish I could keep at it. My first novel, *Midshipman*, still has three words I'd just love to change.

But *Fisherman*'s galleys were sent to Warner months ago, and the book will ship a week from today.

Why, you might ask, am I just now saying good-bye?

Because, though *Fisherman* is the climax and conclusion of the series, it's . . . well, not quite.

You see, after finishing *Fisherman*, another idea percolated for months, and finally resulted in *Voices of Hope*, to be published October 1996. It is a sort of epilogue, meant to stand alone, a book you can read without having first read the series, yet in another sense, it caps and completes the Nick Seafort series in a way I could not have anticipated while writing *Fisherman*.

And as it happens, I write this introduction for the SF Book Club edition while my laser printer is cranking out the final version of *Voices of Hope*, for Warner's copyedit. Late last night—actually, early this morning—I made final adjustments to the text, and closed the file.

I'm not sure I know how to face life without Nick. Partings have always been hard for me, ever since my mother died suddenly when I was eleven. It's something I've never gotten over—I cry at good-byes in movies, and at any scene involving death of a sympathetic character.

Hey, you may be saying, Seafort's just a guy in a book.

Not so. Not for me.

The only way I know how to write is to get so deeply into the characters that they become utterly real. As most any novelist can tell you, there are those moments when the characters nudge you aside and take over the telling of their own story—the dialogue, the action, even the plot twists become theirs. I, the author, am reduced to a transcriptionist, writing what I hear as fast as they speak.

I live for those moments.

And, thank God, they come often.

But because Nick Seafort is real to me, his pain is real as well. So it's been a harrowing eight years. The more so in that I have to write a paragraph far more slowly than you read it. So while you live through it in seconds, I feel it in minutes that stretch into hours. I experience Nick's pain in slow motion.

This is true for me for all characters, even minor ones. I visualize them utterly—I see their height, their faces, their physical attitudes—I know exactly what makes them tick.

The final scenes of *Voices* are more intense than anything I could have imagined writing. To finish the novel, I immersed myself in the climax, writing six, eight, ten hours a day. When the first draft was done, I was an emotional basket case, mooning about the house, exhausted, ragged, weeping at the slightest provocation.

The fan mail I get—and I'm amazed how much I receive—shows that readers feel something of the emotion I've endured. They respond by reaching out to me, with questions about Nick, with praise, with arguments about his world and his choices, with thanks.

Flattered? Of course I am. I love it. But what I love best is that we shared a moment of communion about Nick, about the struggle to find and do right. I think that's why so much of my mail demands I keep writing.

I will, but not about Nick. At least for now.

My next work is a fantasy, which Warner has bought and will release sometime about August 1997. It's mostly completed, but I have a ways to go. The central character isn't like Nick Seafort—he doesn't have Nick's implacable morality—but he, too, is enduring pain as he grows and matures, and the writing is difficult.

I received an interesting letter not long ago. A reader said, more or less, "All right, I understand Nick Seafort's religion and where he comes from. But where do *you* stand? What are your beliefs? Are you a Christian? Do you believe in damnation? In redemption?"

At first, I was indignant at what sounded like an interrogation. Then I came to understand he'd given me high praise indeed. If he didn't know where I stand, if I hadn't clobbered him with my own point of view, then as an author I've done my job, and stayed completely out of sight. My characters speak for themselves, and perhaps the story raises moral issues for you to consider. What I personally believe is in a way irrelevant. It's what *you* decide that matters.

How, then, do I see my job as an author?

First, the obvious: to tell a story we both care about. One worth your time to read, that doesn't leave you feeling cheated. One that I feel was worth my struggle to write.

Second, to be competent. To tell my story cleanly and precisely. I hate to be hauled abruptly out of a book, wondering, "What in hell did that sentence mean?" Or, "Why does he keep overusing that word?" In my early drafts of *Midshipman,* for example, I always had people "glaring" or "growling." I had to use word-search to seek and destroy the skulking repetitions.

About certain things I am compulsive. Finding exactly the right word, for instance, and not just a near neighbor. Using crisp dialogue that advances the plot, reveals the motivations of the characters, delineates the characters by style differences, and creates tension.

You'd be surprised how hard that is, at least for me.

My dialogue is polished and repolished fanatically, until I'm finally satisfied. Eliminating excess words, showing emotions rather than labeling them, ending sentences on strong words, not belaboring the obvious . . . Man, I work hard at trying to get good.

At book signings and through e-mail, folks ask me which book of mine I like best. I always tell them it's the last one. They think I'm joking, but I really mean it.

You see, in each book I've learned something more about the craft of writing.

In my first novel, *Midshipman's Hope,* I learned how to tell a coherent, publishable coming-of-age story. But it was episodic, and therefore loose. In *Challenger's Hope* I learned to tell a single story, straight as an arrow, with no diversions, with the tension building throughout. In *Prisoner's Hope* I learned to tell several stories at once, merging them all into a powerful climax. In *Fisherman's Hope*, I learned how to travel through time, telling two interconnected stories about two different eras of Nick's life.

And in *Voices of Hope*, I learned to tell a tale through several alternating points of view, never losing focus on the advancing action.

Therefore, each book, in my view, was better than the last.

You have, in the following pages, the result of my schooling, and the climax to which the Nick Seafort saga has steadily built. I stumbled across the ending to *Fisherman* halfway through writing the previous novel, and in fact I put *Prisoner* aside for a couple of weeks to write a draft of the ending to *Fisherman* I didn't dare lose.

So here they are, the last two novels of the series.

Hope you like them. Do let me know.

David Feintuch
January 24, 1996

P.O. Box 366
Mason, MI 48854
MIDAVE@DELPHI.COM
WRITEMAN@CRIS.COM

Prisoner's Hope

To Rick, Betsy, John and Beth Grafing, friends, to Ardath Mayhar, for unstinting support, Betsy Mitchell, for her sagacity and nearly infinite patience, Don Maass for helping a miracle come to pass, and as always, Jettie. Especial thanks to the staff and musicians at Ragtime Rick's of Toledo, Ohio, for serving and sustaining that odd character in the corner booth tapping at the keys of his computer.

PRISONER'S HOPE

*Being the third voyage
of Nicholas Seafort, U.N.N.S.,
in the year of our Lord 2200*

Part 1

April, in the year of our Lord 2200

1

Admiral Tremaine drew himself up, jowls pursed in indignation. "Who would you believe—this young scoundrel or me?" Ignored for the moment, I held the at-ease position.

"That's not the issue." Fleet Admiral De Marnay gestured at the holovid chip I'd brought on U.N.S. *Hibernia* across sixty-nine light-years of void. "Captain Seafort is but a messenger. Your recall was ordered by Admiralty at home."

Through the Admiral's unshuttered window, the late afternoon sun of Hope Nation illuminated his Centraltown office with dazzling brightness. A muted roar signaled yet another shuttle lifting off to Orbit Station from the spaceport behind Admiralty House.

I sighed; I'd docked *Hibernia* at the Station just hours before, and my trip groundside was proving no respite from the tensions of the bridge. I'd had no idea Geoffrey Tremaine would be in the office when Admiral De Marnay received my report.

"Messenger, my arse." Tremaine swung toward me, glowering. "You arranged it!"

I decided it was a question, so I could respond without fear of contradicting my superior. "No, sir, Admiral Brentley made the decision and I wasn't consulted."

"A patent lie." Tremaine dismissed me with an airy wave and turned back to the Admiral Commanding. "Georges, be reasonable—"

"It is no lie!" The savagery of my snarl startled even me. The two Admirals glared, astounded at such an interruption from a mere Captain, the youngest in the U.N. Navy. I rushed on, abandoning the shreds of my discipline. "Mr. Tremaine, Lord God knows that if anyone should be removed from command, it is you. But I say again, I had no part in it. Admiral De Marnay, as my verity has been questioned, I demand truth testing!" Drugs and polygraph would quickly confirm my statement or expose my lie.

Georges De Marnay got slowly to his feet. "You demand, Captain?" His tone was glacial.

"Sir, I have never lied to a superior officer!" It was the one remnant

of honor I'd retained in my slide to damnation. "Three times he's accused—"

"Seafort, get hold of yourself. Be silent!"

"Aye aye, sir." Midshipman or Captain, there was no other possible
reply to a direct order.

Admiral Tremaine's choleric face shook with wrath. "You see the insolence I had to put up with, when he had *Portia*? He—"

"Before you stole her from him." De Marnay's acid reply sliced
through Tremaine's diatribe.

"Stole her? What are you saying?" Before De Marnay could answer,
Tremaine rushed on. "The facts are clear from *Portia*'s Log, which you
reviewed when I docked. I had to threaten to hang him before he'd transfer to *Challenger*!"

Better had he done so. Many would live who now were lost.

De Marnay said nothing.

Tremaine's voice took on a wheedling tone. "Recall or no, you're the
Admiral in theater. Those bloody aliens of Seafort's may strike at any time.
You need a commander groundside as well as aloft, and Admiralty didn't
appoint my replacement. As Admiral Commanding, you could reconfirm
me until my tour's up. Or try me yourself, for that matter."

"Yes, I could well do that." De Marnay swung his chair, fingers tapping at the edge of his desk.

I closed my eyes, my jaw throbbing with the effort to hold it shut. My
commander had ordered me to be silent, and silent I would be. In any
event, nothing I said could prevent Admiral De Marnay from reinstating
Tremaine, the man who'd taken my *Portia*. His own U.N.S. *Challenger* had
been disabled by the huge goldfish-shaped aliens that I'd discovered three
years before on my first interstellar voyage. Tremaine transferred his flag,
leaving me, as well as the aged and infirm passengers and the young
transpops he loathed, drifting on *Challenger*, deep in interstellar space,
unable to Fuse.

After he fled, the fish had come again. We'd been testing the fusion
drive, and they seemed to sense the N-waves on which our ships traveled
the void between stars. Over and again, they'd Defused alongside *Challenger* to hurl their acid tentacles at our hull.

I took a sharp breath, realized I was clammy under my stiff jacket.

"After all, Admiralty is far from the scene, eh, Georges? They don't
know—"

Admiral De Marnay said, "I could reinstate you, Mr. Tremaine. But I
won't."

Tremaine said slowly, "You'd believe that"—he spat out the words—"that trannie Captain over me?"

"I believe the evidence in the Log, and in your conduct, sir." De Marnay's tone was icy. "Admiral Tremaine, you are relieved. Mr. Seafort, you may go."

"Aye aye, sir." I saluted and quickly made my escape.

I trudged across the back yard of Admiralty House to the spaceport perimeter and the terminal building seventy yards beyond. Other than the hum of a distant engine, all was silent.

At the far end of the tarmac, freight was piled high. My *Hibernia*'s cargo would soon be added to the supplies and equipment stockpiled here for the U.N. forces defending our colony from the aliens.

When last I'd seen Hope Nation I'd been so young, and innocent of the shattered oath that damned me.

Though I was fully recuperated from my physical ordeal on *Challenger*, my appalling misdeeds left me subject to fits of black despair. On our long journey to Hope Nation my companion and lover, Annie Wells, had done her best to allay them in the solitude of our cabin.

I wondered if Annie knew how I relied on her ministrations. Now even she would soon be gone. I'd come to know Annie on *Challenger*; she'd been among the transients from the slums of Lower New York bound for faraway Detour as part of a foolish social welfare program. After *Challenger*'s ill-fated voyage, we'd sailed again on *Hibernia*.

We'd made the sixteen-month cruise in one interminable Fuse, with a tiny corrective jump at the end. I'd docked at massive Orbit Station, taken the shuttle groundside, reported to the now bustling Admiralty House, Admiral Tremaine's recall orders among the packet of chips in my case.

Now I looked around, wondered what to do with my day before going back aloft to Annie.

I wished I could talk over the morning's encounter with a friend like Midshipman Derek Carr, one of the officers I'd forced to stay behind when I was transferred to *Challenger*. But Derek was stationed on U.N.S. *Catalonia* en route to Detour, and not expected home for months. So I was alone, on my mandatory long-leave, free of responsibilities. I had time to look up Vax Holser and the others.

As I crossed the terminal a whoop split the air; I turned to see Lieutenant Alexi Tamarov bounding after me. "You're here! Thank Lord God, you made it!" He snapped a crisp salute, grinning with pleasure. Then he saw my face and blanched. "My God, what happened, sir?"

My scar had that effect.

I offered him my hand, relieved beyond words to see him safe and well. "A laser, on board *Challenger*. It's healed."

"You look—" He remembered his manners and bit it off. Friend or no friend, I was Captain.

"Awful. Yes, I know." I deserved a ruined face. Lord God in his time would do worse. An oath is sacred.

"Well, er, different, sir." He quickly changed the subject. While he chattered I reflected on all that had passed since our days as midshipmen in *Hibernia*'s wardroom, when Alexi was a young fifteen and I, at seventeen, struggled toward manhood.

After *Hibernia*'s officers had been killed and I was catapulted to Captain, I'd left Alexi in the wardroom. We'd shipped together afterward on *Portia*, but since then we'd gone our separate ways for two long years. He was—what? twenty-one?—and I was tired and numbed at twenty-three.

"God, I'm glad I ran into you, sir. I'm off duty today, but tomorrow it's back to Admiralty House." He shrugged and smiled wryly. "They have me working in Tactics." Like any lieutenant, Alexi wanted ship time, which would give him a leg up toward promotion. His grin faded; his eyes drifted from mine. "About what I did on *Portia*, sir, I'm so—I'm ashamed."

"Did?" I tried to remember what he might be ashamed of.

"I wanted to volunteer for transfer, sir. I meant to ask the Admiral, but I couldn't. I sat in my cabin for hours before I gave up pretending. Now I know how cowardly I am."

"Stop that!" My anger thrust him back a step. "I told you then I wouldn't accept you on *Challenger* under any circumstances. You're no coward."

"I should have volunteered." He turned away. "Whether you took me or not. You had the courage to go."

"You fool!" I spoke so savagely he winced with the hurt. "If Amanda and Nate hadn't died, perhaps I'd have wanted to live. I wasn't brave, I was running away!" His look of dismay only goaded me further. "If I'd died I wouldn't have become what I am now."

Alexi's eyes met mine, troubled. What he saw there made him shrug and try a tentative smile. "Whatever our motives, sir, we've done what was in us. I won't let you down again."

"I absolve you, for what it's worth." To distract him I said, "They've relieved Tremaine."

"Thank Lord God, sir. But what about your challenge?"

"You heard about that?" Livid with rage when Geoffrey Tremaine had off-loaded *Portia*'s transient children before fleeing to safety, I'd sworn an oath to call challenge upon him, to fight a duel that would destroy one of us. Now that he was relieved it was legal for me to do so. But what did that oath matter? I'd already forsworn myself.

"Yes, we knew," Alexi said. "The Admiral wasn't alone on the bridge when you radioed. And Danny recorded. He'd have told us if we hadn't already heard." *Portia's* puter liked to gossip, no doubt to ease his loneliness. What a joy it would be to visit with Danny again, as on so many deadened days on the bridge after my wife's death. We'd become friends, if such a thing was possible between man and machine. But I didn't even know where in the galaxy my old ship had been sent.

"I suppose I have to call the challenge, Alexi." At the time I'd yearned to cast my life against Tremaine's. Yet, Philip Tyre and the rest were dead, and nothing would bring them back. With an effort I thrust recriminations aside. "What happened to Vax?"

Alexi bit his lip. "He's here, sir. They have him running back and forth between Admiralty House and the Station."

Lieutenant Holser was alive and well. My old rival, once my enemy, now my friend. Twice he'd saved my life. "It will be good to see him."

After a moment Alexi spoke of other things. Restless, I invited him to wander Centraltown with me. He accepted with delight, and proudly led me to the electricar he'd managed to acquire. They were in short supply thanks to the population increase. I stared out the window as he drove downtown along Spaceport Road.

Centraltown had grown since my last visit, but the town had no sights I hadn't seen before, and what I saw reminded me of Amanda. For Alexi's sake I fought my depression, and eventually settled with him in a downtown restaurant. He respected my lapses into glum silence, and the evening provided more companionship than I'd had in many months. When finally we left, Minor was full overhead, and Major, Hope Nation's second moon, was just over the horizon. I looked up, imagining I could see Orbit Station passing above.

"Have you a place to stay, sir?"

I shook my head. "I'll bunk on the ship for a few days, I suppose."

"I meant tonight. Would you—" He hesitated. "Sir, would you, ah, care to stay with me this evening?" I understood his unease; the gulf between a lieutenant and a Captain was normally unbridgeable.

"Annie is waiting on *Hibernia*." Still, it was late, and I had no idea whether another shuttle would lift tonight; if not, I'd find myself sleeping at the terminal or in Naval barracks. "Well . . . for the night. I'd like that." I was rewarded with a shy grin of pleasure.

Alexi's flat was in one of the dozen or so prefabs that had sprung up

along Spaceport Road since my last visit. Sparse, tiny, and clean, it reminded me of the middies' wardroom I'd once occupied on *Hibernia*,
though it was far larger.

He said, "The bedroom's in there, sir. I'll take the couch."

How could I have not realized he'd have but one bedroom? "I prefer
the couch." My tone was gruff.

"You can't!" He was scandalized.

"I won't take your bed, Alexi." Rank or no rank, I wouldn't put him
out of his home.

"Please, sir." He patted the couch. "It's comfortable; I'll be fine.
Anyway"—he rushed on before I could object—"I won't sleep at all if
you're bunked here while I've got the only bed. Please."

Grumbling, I let him persuade me, wondering if his respect was for
my rank or for myself. Then I marveled at my foolishness. I was Captain,
and he was but lieutenant; what else could he do?

In the morning Alexi dropped me off at the spaceport and I handed
the agent a voucher for the early shuttle. Two hours later I was back on
Hibernia. I debated whether to check the bridge.

By naval regs, all crew members were entitled to thirty days long-
leave after a ten-month cruise or longer, and during that leave only a
nominal, rotating watch was kept, in which no one was made to spend
more than four days aboard.

Nonetheless, my footsteps carried me along the Level 1 circumference corridor, past my cabin to the bridge beyond. The hatch was open;
normally, under weigh, it would have been sealed. Lieutenant Connor, in
the watch officer's chair, was leaning back, boots on the console. Her eyes
widened in alarm as I strode in. She scrambled to her feet.

"As you were, Ms. Connor." Had I found her lollygagging on watch
while under weigh I'd have been outraged. Moored, it didn't matter.

I glanced at the darkened simulscreens on the curved front bulkhead.
Normally, they provided a breathtaking view from the nose of the ship.
And under our puter Darla's control, they could simulate any conditions
known. My black leather armchair was bolted behind the left console, at
the center of the compartment. Lieutenant Connor, of course, was in her
own seat. No one dared sit in the Captain's place.

"All quiet, Ms. Connor?"

"Yes, sir. The remaining passengers went down on last night's shuttle,
except for Miss Wells."

There was nothing I need do. "I'll be in my cabin."

"Yes, sir. Miss Wells, ah, seems to miss the other passengers, sir." She looked away quickly, as if she'd gone too far in speaking of my personal affairs. She had, but I let it pass.

As I slapped open my cabin hatch a lithe form flew at me, knocking my breath away. I hugged Annie with heartfelt warmth, grinning until I realized she was sobbing softly into my shoulder. "What's wrong, hon?"

Annie clung. "All'em gone. Dey be downdere, all'em joeys. No one up here 'cept me." Only under stress did her hard-won grammar and diction lapse into her former trannie dialect.

I squeezed her tighter. She'd known that all the transpops awaiting transshipment to Detour would be leaving, including herself, and had chosen to stay with me a few extra days. I thought better of reminding her. "Sorry I couldn't get back last night, hon."

She sighed, disengaging herself from my damp shoulder. "I unner—understand," she said carefully. "Did yo' Admiral say where they sending you next?"

"No." I hung my jacket in the bulkhead closet. A third of the entire Naval fleet was now protecting Hope Nation system. There was little chance *Hibernia* would be the next ship to Detour colony.

Annie and I would have to part, and we both knew it. The only way we could stay together was to marry, if she'd have me, and that would almost certainly cost me my career. Admiralty was notoriously conservative; my disregard for regulations and my youth already worked against me. Were I to marry a former transpop—one of the ignorant and despised hordes who roamed most of Earth's sprawling cities—I'd be blackballed. Though I'd never be told the reason, I'd be unlikely to see command again.

"I met Alexi," I said. Both he and Annie had shipped on *Portia*, but she'd known him then only as a distant, handsome young figure occasionally glimpsed in the corridors of Level 1.

"Nicky, I been thinking." As she calmed, her diction returned, and despite myself, I smiled. "This staying on ship, it be no good," she said. "I ain—I'm not ever going to see Hope Nation again, and you need time on real land. Would you show me dis place?"

"It's full of memories." My tone was gentle. How could I take her where I'd gone with Amanda? The comparison could only be cruel.

"I wantin'—I want to know your memories." I frowned and she rushed on, "Nicky, yo' wife is dead. She ain' never coming back. You got to live. I won' be 'round, but you got to go on."

That she was right didn't make it easier, but I owed much to her. "If that's what you'd like," I said. "We'll rent a room groundside and I'll show you the sights." The Venturas, perhaps; the breathtaking mountains of

Western Continent, where Amanda and Derek and I—no, this would be a different trip.

We could visit the plantations. Emmett Branstead, a passenger I'd impressed into the Service on *Challenger*, had returned to Hope Nation while I was recuperating at Lunapolis from my injuries. Despite his condescending and irritable manner before enlisting, Emmett had proven a loyal and conscientious sailor once he'd taken the oath. He'd left word at Admiralty House that I was invited to his family's plantation whenever I could come.

His invitation rather surprised me; I'd have thought he'd be anxious to put his involuntary servitude behind him. I'd met his brother Harmon, three years before, on my long-leave with Derek Carr.

I put aside the throb of memories. "When would you like to go?"

"Today?"

I groaned; my chest still hurt from the morning's liftoff. Still, diving into Hope Nation's gravity well wouldn't be half as bad as clawing out of it. "Very well." I reached for the caller, set it down again. "No, let's walk to Dispatch; I'll show you Orbit Station."

"I don' want to go to dat place."

"The Station is just like a ship, only bigger."

"There ain't no air around it. I don' like it." Groundsiders.

"It's as safe as *Hibernia*, and I'll be with you. Come, I'll show you around." Protesting, she let me take her through the locks.

Imagine an old-fashioned pencil stood on end, with two or three half-inch-thick disks slid halfway down and pressed together. That's a rough model of an interstellar ship. Forward of the disks is the hold, in which cargoes for our settlements are crammed, along with the supplies consumed during the ship's long voyage.

The passengers and crew live and work on the disks. Each disk is a Level, girdled by a circumference corridor, connected to the other disks by east and west ladders. The bridge is always on Level 1. Hydroponics and recycling are below. Aft of the disks sits the engine room, whose great Fusion motors terminate at the drive shaft comprising the stern of the ship.

Orbit Station was like a stack of these disks, only without the pencil. And more and larger disks. The Station had five levels, enough to get lost in, which to my embarrassment I soon did.

"You ain' no better than a groundsider," Annie scoffed when we passed the commissary again. "Jus' ask someone."

"Dispatching should be down this corridor."

"It wasn't the last time."

She could be maddening. "Come on." We passed a sign pointing to Naval HQ but I ignored it; though they could arrange shuttle seats for us, I could have done as much from the caller in my cabin. My goal was to find Dispatching, somewhere on Level 4.

Annie seemed as relieved as I when we finally arrived at the dispatcher's office. A shuttle was leaving in two hours; time enough for us to pack. I let the dispatcher provide us detailed instructions back to *Hibernia*'s bay.

I came on a young officer lounging in the entryway of Naval HQ, and I stopped. "Excuse me, Lieutenant, are you assigned here?"

He stiffened. "Yes, sir."

"Do you know Mr. Holser?"

"Holser? Oh, yes, Vax. The big joey." He grinned. "He's posted to tactics. I believe he's at Admiralty House this rotation, sir."

"Please check."

A few moments later the man returned, another lieutenant a few steps behind. "As I thought, sir. He'll be groundside another week."

"Very well. Thank you."

"Uh, Captain Seafort?" The lanky officer who'd followed.

I returned the lieutenant's salute. "Yes?"

"I thought it was you, sir, from the holozine pics. Second Lieutenant Jeffrey Kahn."

"What do you want?" My voice was sharper than I'd intended.

"I—nothing, sir, except to speak with you. I wondered if—what it was like to see the aliens, sir. For the first time." Those damned holozines. Just as the notoriety of my discovering the aliens had begun to fade, my return with *Challenger* had fanned the flames.

Annie gasped, wrenching her hand free. My face was hot, my scar throbbed. "Where are you assigned, sir?"

"I was on *Valencia*, sir. Sorry if I—"

"If you were under my command you'd be sorrier, Lieutenant. Dismissed!"

"Aye aye, sir. I apologize."

I stalked down the corridor, pulling Annie with me until she protested. "Nicky, you hurtin' me."

I let go of her arm. "The damn—blessed insolence! Interrupting a Captain!" She scurried to keep up. "Just so he could say he'd met me!"

Annie spoke with dignified care. "There no harm being famous. You're lucky."

"*Is* no harm," I corrected, my pace slowing. During our year on *Hibernia* I'd labored, at Annie's request, to teach her Uppie speech and civilized ways. She approached the English language as the study of a foreign tongue, which in a way for her it was.

"Anyway, that's not the point," I said. "If one of my lieutenants felt free to annoy a Captain I'd—"

I'd what? I didn't know. I recalled Alexi offering me the use of his apartment, though it was a blatant breach of protocol. But we were friends, weren't we? Shipmates.

No, that shouldn't matter. I sighed. Perhaps I'd been a touch hard on Mr. Kahn.

I browsed through listings in a spaceport caller booth and arranged apartment showings. The furnished flats were expensive, especially on a lease of weeks, but on a ship in Fusion my pay gathered unspent, so I could afford it. As it happened, the second apartment we saw was but two blocks from Alexi's and for some reason I liked it enough to take it without looking further.

We unpacked our few belongings and sauntered around our block. Annie devoured the texture of Hope Nation with eager eyes. I promised her a tour of downtown, we bought a few groceries for the micro, and sun still setting, we went home to bed. As we snuggled under the covers she made it clear that I'd get little sleep that night.

In the morning, surprisingly rested, I strolled downtown with Annie, pointing out buildings I knew. We passed Circuit Court, where years before I'd confronted Judge Chesley in defense of my authority to enlist cadets. Near downtown, several blocks had been set aside for an open park; we wandered amid its greenery.

She caught her breath. "What's that, Nicky?" A Gothic spire lanced upward through the genera trees ahead.

"The Cathedral, hon."

"It's beautiful."

So it was. On my previous landfall, I'd visited Reunification Cathedral, to pray that the burden of command be lifted. "Shall we go in?" I took her hand.

The Cathedral's spires soared from thick buttresses of cut stone, each testifying to the dedication and fervor in which the Cathedral had been born over a century before. When Hope Nation was founded, the Reunification Church had already become our official state religion. Though we tolerated splinter sects, our U.N. Government was founded in the authority of the One True God, and I, as Captain, was his representative aboard ship.

Annie and I knelt before the altar. I gave silent prayer, sad at the knowledge that it must go unheard.

Annie waited behind me, in a pew. When I stood she whispered, "Look up."

I gazed upward at the ornate gilt-edged craftsmanship of the buttresses. "Yes. Beautiful." I squeezed her hand.

"Place is so strong. I feel . . . safe. Don't wanna go."

Yes, she'd feel secure in Lord God's house, if anywhere. I stopped myself from saying it aloud. "Detour has its own churches, hon." But none as beautiful as this. Detour was too young, too raw.

"Let me stay here awhile." She ran her finger along the sturdy, burnished wood of the pew.

"All right." I sat, took a missal, idly thumbed through it. Annie wandered.

"Sir? Is that you?" A plump youngish man.

I peered. "Mr. Forbee!" An old acquaintance. We shook hands. "I'd have thought they'd let you retire again."

Three years ago, when I first arrived with *Hibernia*, Forbee was floundering as Commandant of the tiny Naval station, eager to be relieved. "I suppose I could if I wanted to," he said. His eye flicked to my scar, and away. "But with the invasion, and all . . . as long as there are senior officers so I'm not left in charge again . . ."

"Of course."

He paused. "I'm with the tactical group now. Enjoy the work."

"Isn't that where Vax Holser's posted?"

"Yes, sir. He's at Admiralty House this rotation." For a moment his eyes clouded. "What are your plans, sir?"

"Miss Wells and I are taking in the sights." I beckoned to Annie, introduced her. "We're lunching with Lieutenant Tamarov, then I'll stop at Admiralty House."

He hesitated. "Sir, about Vax . . ."

"Is he well?"

"Oh, yes, fine. Couldn't be better."

I said, "He's a good man, very good, but I'll admit he takes some getting used to." I glanced at my watch and stood. "Annie, we'd better get going; Alexi's waiting. Nice to see you again, Mr. Forbee." I extended my hand.

We met Alexi at a restaurant I recalled from my previous visit, and afterward he drove us back to our apartment. At Annie's urging I accompanied Alexi back to Admiralty House; she wanted our dinner to be her own accomplishment. I went eagerly.

Alexi said little during the short drive, as if preoccupied. After he parked, we climbed the steps to the double doors, past the winged-anchor Naval emblem and the "Admiralty House" brass plaque I'd known from my first cruise.

The lanky duty lieutenant stood from his console to salute. "You're here for Admiral De Marnay?"

"No, Vax Holser."

"He's upstairs in the tactics office, sir. Shall I call him down?"

I grinned. "I'll run up. We're shipmates."

Alexi followed me up the ladder. "Sir, I think I should tell you—"

"Later, Alexi. Let me say hello to Vax."

"But—"

"Vax? Are you there?"

"STAND TO!" Vax Holser's bellow made me flinch. The roomful of lieutenants and midshipmen snapped to attention.

Eyes locked front, the brawny lieutenant stood ramrod stiff.

"As you were." I hurried forward, my hand out. "Vax, how are you? Good to—" I stumbled to a halt.

Vax Holser, his face an icy mask, had swung into the at-ease position, hands clasped behind him. His eyes were riveted on the bulkhead past my shoulder. He pointedly ignored my hand.

I gaped. "What's wrong?"

"Nothing, sir." His gaze remained fixed on the wall. He said no more.

"I'm so glad to see you, Vax!"

"Thank you, Captain." His voice was remote.

Alexi cleared his throat. "Mr. Holser, Captain Seafort's been through hell. He came to see you as soon as he—"

"Be silent, Mr. Tamarov," I snarled. I wouldn't have Alexi beg on my behalf. "Leave at once!"

"Aye aye, sir." Alexi wouldn't argue with a direct order, even if I wasn't his commanding officer.

I approached my former first lieutenant with trepidation. "Are you speaking to me, Vax?"

Vax Holser said slowly and distinctly, "Yes, sir. We're on duty."

His reply told me what I needed to know. I turned on my heel and left.

Alexi waited below in the anteroom. "I tried to warn you, sir, before—"

"Why?" I demanded. "What's he so angry about?"

"When you were to be left behind on *Challenger*, you wouldn't let him relieve Tremaine or transfer to join you."

I was stunned. "He won't forgive my saving him from harm?"

"No, sir."

Numbly I went out into the heat of the day.

We paused on the steps. "I tried talking to him," Alexi offered. "He wouldn't listen. He said you had no right to refuse our help, to face that nightmare alone."

"Lord God damn it!"

Alexi drew back, shocked, knowing it was blasphemy. For the moment I didn't care. I hated the Navy that had cost me my wife, my son, my friends.

"So, you young whelp, I suppose you're smirking over your revenge."

I spun. Admiral Tremaine glared from the foot of the steps.

Alexi echoed, "Revenge?"

"Thanks to him I've been relieved, as I'm sure you know." Tremaine's expression was sour. "Despite your sniveling, Seafort, you made it home and back again. So your whining about *Challenger* was for nothing."

I was in a foul temper. "Admiral Geoffrey Tremaine, you are on inactive duty; before witness I do call challenge on you to defend your honor!"

The Admiral's eyes narrowed. "You'd go through with it, then? Very well. You're aware the choice of weapons is mine?"

"Of course." I'd practiced with the dueling pistols Admiral Brentley had given me, but not nearly enough.

"Very well, then. If you find someone to act as your second, have him call on me to arrange the details. I'll be at—"

"With your permission, sir, I will be your second."

"Thank you, Alexi." I saluted the Admiral. "Please make your arrangements, gentlemen." I stalked off.

They had tried to stop me. Annie begged, and when that failed, used all her wiles to divert me. "But what good it do, you be killed? Dey bury you here, and dat Admiral goin' home free?"

I made my voice gentle, for her sake. "Hon, I have to."

"But why? You know he shoot better than you!" Antique powder weapons were the Admiral's particular hobby.

She couldn't understand, of course. In some things, the striving is important, not the achieving. And I'd sworn my vengeance to Lord God. Though I'd already forsworn myself in other things, my misery made me anxious not to do it again.

Four days after my challenge, we met on a grassy meadow outside the town, Alexi stiff and formal at my side, a staff lieutenant an unhappy second to the Admiral. Other officers waited in hushed groups a distance away; news of our duel had spread.

I hadn't allowed Annie to attend.

While our seconds conducted the preliminary ritual I stood sweating in dress whites, conscious of every quivering leaf of the great genera tree in whose shadow we stood, aware of every tremulous beat of my heart.

I hadn't prayed Lord God's help; my soul was forfeit and my prayers must go unanswered. I was afraid, though. Not of death, but of what was to come afterward.

I had much to account for.

The Admiral's second stepped forward. "Gentlemen, I appeal to you to forsake your quarrel and declare that honor is satisfied, that this matter may be put to rest."

Admiral Tremaine's smile was almost a sneer. "You will recall that Mr. Seafort initiated this quarrel. I do but respond." At his lieutenant's frown he added, as if reluctant, "However, I declare that honor is satisfied, if the Captain is so minded."

The Admiral's second turned to me. "Captain Seafort?"

The sun beat down on the stillness of the meadow. Alexi, young and handsome, spoke softly. "What shall you do, sir?" I hesitated. He blurted, "Sir, he's ordered home for trial. You told me how Admiral Brentley spoke of him. He's finished."

I felt my legs tremble and spoke loudly as if to stop him from noticing. "You care that much if I live?"

Alexi looked down, but with an effort returned his gaze to mine. "Very much, sir."

My legs steadied. Alexi cared, as did Annie. If they truly understood me they wouldn't have such feelings, but I was glad nonetheless. As Alexi said, Tremaine was done for. Honor didn't require me to sacrifice my life to accomplish what the law itself would achieve.

Admiral De Marnay would also be pleased if I called it off. A day before, he had summoned me to his office to demand that I withdraw my challenge.

"Is that an order, sir?"

He waved it away. "You know perfectly well I can't give such an order. You're on leave and he's inactive." His fingers drummed the console at his mahogany desk.

"Then, sir, I—"

"There's no point to fighting him, Seafort. You're needed on *Hibernia.*"

"Yes, sir. On the other hand, I gave my oath."

"That bloody dueling code should be amended. A Captain fighting an Admiral . . . it looks bad." He glanced at me, said quickly, "Oh, I know in your case it has nothing to do with promotion or advancement. But people won't understand."

"Captain Von Walther fought a duel with Governor Ibn Saud, sir." Generations ago, but Captain Von Walther was the idol of every officer in the Navy. I'd once stood in his very footsteps.

"The Governor wasn't his superior officer. And you're not Von Walther." His tone was acid.

"No, sir." It was presumptuous to compare myself to the legendary Hugo Von Walther, who'd discovered the derelict *Celestina*, become Admiral of the Fleet, and twice been elected Secretary-General. "Still, there's the matter of my oath."

"I could put you back on active duty." It would effectively bar me from a duel.

"Yes, sir. But I'm entitled to long-leave."

De Marnay's stare was cold. "I know that. But Tremaine isn't. I can recall him."

I swallowed, glad of the reprieve. "If that's what you wish, sir."

His fingers drummed. "No, I won't, even to save you. I wasn't free to beach him myself, but now that he's recalled, I'll let it stand. I still want you to withdraw your challenge."

"Yes, sir, I understand."

His tone softened. "Seafort, you've been through a lot. You're coiled tight as a spring. If you were thinking clearly, you'd find a way to let this go."

"I understand, sir," I repeated. By giving no more, it was a refusal.

"Very well." He studied me. "That's all." As I left, I could feel his eyes pierce my back.

"Sir?"

I blinked, back on the dueling field. Alexi awaited my answer.

Again I swallowed. For Annie, and for Alexi. For Admiral De Marnay. "Tell him—tell him I agree—"

Father's stern voice, as I sat over my lessons at the creaky kitchen table. "Your oath is your bond, Nicholas. Without it, you are nothing." Yes, Father. But I am already damned. For some sins, there can be no forgiveness.

Father faded to distant disapproval.

The young voice had a catch in it. "I'm glad to have served with you, sir. Godspeed."

Blanching, I whirled. "What did you say?"

Alexi stepped back. "Nothing, sir. I didn't speak."

"Not you. Philip Ty—" I snapped my mouth shut. Was I out of my mind? Philip Tyre was dead, thanks to the cruelty of the man I faced. A troubled boy who'd striven to do his duty.

I spoke to the Admiral's second. "Sir, tell your principal that upon his humble apology to the memory of Lieutenant Philip Tyre and the passengers and crew of *Challenger*, I will consider my oath fulfilled. And on no other terms."

Tremaine didn't wait for his lieutenant to repeat my speech. "Get on with it, then."

I picked up the round-barreled pistol, its grip vaguely familiar in my hand. Admiral Brentley's parting gift. I turned to Alexi. "Thank you for your assistance, sir. I'm most grateful to you."

Alexi's formality matched my own. "And I to you, sir." He saluted.

We paced and turned. I saw the savage glint in Admiral Tremaine's eye as we raised to fire.

2

"Honor is satisfied. For God's sake, get them to a doctor!"

"The Captain, yes." The lieutenant looked up from Tremaine's inert body. "It's too late for the Admiral."

I stood swaying, glad of the shade of the red maple. My chest was numb. I put my hand to my side. It came away wet.

"It'll be too late for Captain Seafort as well, unless you hurry." One of De Marnay's staff; I didn't remember his name.

"I'll help you into the heli, sir," said a solicitous voice.

"I'm all right, Alexi."

"You aren't, sir. Let me help you."

Numb, I let Alexi lead me to the waiting heli. Bending to get in jarred something in me; a wave of pain carried me off to a far place. I coughed and it blossomed to fiery agony.

"Christ, get moving!" someone shouted.

I thought to rebuke the blasphemy, but choked and couldn't find my breath. I spat salty red liquid. The whap of the heli blades merged with my ragged breath in a red crescendo that slowly faded to blessed black silence.

The bridge was white, too white. "Have we Defused? Plot a course to Orbit Station."

"It's all right, sir."

The middy knew he was required to say, "Aye aye, sir." It was the only permissible response to his Captain. Well, he'd learn after a caning; the barrel was a quick teacher.

But weren't we still Fused? "I didn't order a Defuse!" It emerged a feeble whisper instead of the bark I'd intended. And what was draped over me? A tent?

"We're groundside, sir. You're in hospital."

Why was Alexi here? He'd gone on to Hope Nation with Admiral Tremaine.

"When did we dock?" I whispered, groggy. "We just Defused for nav check."

"That was weeks ago, sir."

God, how my chest hurt. I slept.

Shadowy figures kept me company. Walter Dakko, master-at-arms on *Challenger* and on *Hibernia*. Eddie Boss, the transpop who'd responded to my call for enlistment. Annie Wells, her face worried. Even Philip Tyre came to sit with me for a while, before I recalled that he was dead.

I drifted in and out of consciousness as the sedation eased. Doctors and nurses loomed, disappeared, reappeared. The fires of hell burned.

"The infection's spread," someone said crisply. "Yank the lung, replace it, and be done with it." Two doctors conferred as I gazed passively through the vapormask.

A medipulse pressed against my arm. Solicitous aides lifted me from my bed to a gurney. The ceiling slid smoothly past, and I struggled to stay awake. I failed.

The officer across the desk quickly looked away from my face, but I was used to that by now. "Do you know where you are?"

The tube had been in my throat too long; it still hurt when I spoke. "Centraltown General Hospital." I read the nameplate on his desk. "And you're the psych officer, Dr., uh, Tendres." I coughed, flinching as a lance of pain stabbed.

He smiled briefly. "This interview is to see how you're orienting yourself. Your name."

"Nicholas Ewing Seafort, Captain, U.N.N.S. I'm twenty-three. Six years seniority."

"What else do you remember, before your recent cruise?"

I said grimly, "I sailed on *Portia*, part of Admiral Tremaine's relief squadron to Hope Nation. My baby son died in an alien attack and my wife Amanda followed soon after." Then we'd encountered the Admiral's flagship, disabled by the fish. "Tremaine off-loaded the elderly passengers and the young transpops. I swore I would call challenge on him. You know the rest."

"Tell me."

My throat was sore and I wanted to get it over with. "The fish attacked again." My tone was dull. "Our remaining lasers were knocked out. I used the last of our propellant to ram the biggest fish just as it tried to Fuse. We were Fused with it, and starved for several weeks in a derelict ship. The fish Defused outside Jupiter's orbit." But before the stricken fish had brought us home, I'd broken my solemn oath.

"Your memory seems intact, Seafort. You know how long you've been here?"

"Three weeks, they tell me." Enough for *Hibernia* to sail without me. I'd lost her, and what little home I had.

"Much of the time you were delirious or under sedation."

"They gave me a new lung."

"Which your body is accepting well, so far. You're loaded with antirejection drugs, of course. You're familiar with antirejection therapy?"

I nodded. "The time-release meds last a month or so. The second treatment will pretty well cut out any chance of rejection."

"That's right. Routine replacement, a lung."

I fingered the skintape covering my healing incision, wondering when I'd be released. And more important, when I'd be fit for active duty. Before I could get a ship, I would need clearance from the man I confronted.

As if reading my thoughts Dr. Tendres said, "You've faced a lot for a joey your age, Seafort."

I didn't reply.

He read from my chart in his holovid. "You still have the nightmares?"

"Which ones?" I asked despite myself. Well, my medical records would indicate the recurrent dream I'd had for years. Father and I were walking from the train station to Academy, where I was to begin my first term; I'd never left Cardiff before, except for day trips. When we arrived, Father turned my shoulders and pushed me toward the gates. Inside, I turned to wave good-bye, but he strode away without looking back. I was thirteen.

It was as it had happened. It was Father's way.

Perhaps my records also mentioned the dream in which Tuak and Rogoff, men I'd hanged for mutiny, shambled into my cabin, dead.

I doubted he knew about the others.

He raised his eyebrow. "Tell me your nightmares."

"I dream sometimes," I said uneasily. "I'm all right."

"You've seen a lot of death." His flat statement gave me no clue to read his thoughts.

"Yes." I'd caused a lot of death.

He suddenly asked, "How do you feel about what you've done?"

"The killing?"

"Everything."

I hesitated a long moment. "I betrayed my oath, you know."

"That bothers you."

"Bothers me?" I half rose from my wheelchair, subsided when the pain stabbed. The man must be a freethinker. How else could he not understand my desolation?

"Your oath is what you are," Father had taught me. It was my covenant with Lord God Himself. I'd deliberately broken my sworn pledge. In doing so, I'd damned my soul to everlasting hell; no act of contrition or penance could save me. Now the thread of my life was all that stood between me and the eternal torment of Lord God's displeasure.

Yes, it bothered me.

And even if I should somehow be granted the miracle of Lord God's forgiveness, I must live with the knowledge that I was a man without honor, a man whose word could never be trusted, a man of expediency.

I waved my hand irritably. "I've learned to live with it," I said. Surely he must understand. If not, there was no point in laboring to explain.

"Lookidaman be sleepindere!"

The familiar voice recalled me from my doze. "Hi, Annie," I said. Automatically I added, "Don't talk that way," though I knew she did so only to tease me.

"Feeling better today?" She was beautiful in a new sky-blue jumpsuit, perhaps one size snugger than absolutely necessary. Annie had adapted with enthusiasm to the latest fashions and hairstyles.

"Yes, hon," I said dutifully. I felt a pang of regret that she would soon be gone to Detour.

"Good." I was rewarded by a chaste kiss on the forehead. Annie was restraining herself, lest undue excitement cause me breathing problems. She curled into the chair alongside the bed. "I been shopping."

"Oh?" My throat hurt hardly at all today.

"Mira!" She emptied the shopping bag on my stomach. Frilly garments tumbled out. Gauzy, gossamer, weightless ones. Chemiwear. The material responded to changes in skin chemistry. Certain changes caused them to become translucent.

"I don't wear silk underwear," I said, pretending crossness, which had the effect I intended.

"I c'n see you on your bridge in these, sure," she snorted.

I raised myself carefully, aching; this morning they'd made me promenade the corridors for an hour. I took Annie's hand in mine and lay back, wondering if my revenge against Tremaine was worth the cost: my health, my ship, Admiral De Marnay's goodwill.

Ashamed, I recalled the misery my crew and passengers had endured after our abandonment. I thought of Philip Tyre, sailing bravely to his death aboard *Challenger*'s fragile launch. Yes, it was worth it.

My reverie was interrupted by Annie's soft voice. "Where are you, Nicky?"

I smiled. "Just dreaming, hon. Nothing important."

I glowered at the young lieutenant until I was rewarded by a look of nervous anxiety. I turned away; it wasn't his fault. I swung my legs out of bed. Annie, sitting quietly in the corner, shot me a worried glance.

"Very well," I growled. "Where do they want me to stay?"

"Shoreside, in the Centraltown area, sir. That's all Admiral De Marnay said."

I glowered at the orders in the holovid before snapping it off. "Inactive duty until certified as fully recovered . . ." Well, that was fair; it had been my own doing. If I hadn't chosen revenge, I wouldn't have spent weeks in a hospital trying to avoid a cough that might dislodge my lung.

I didn't like at all the phrase that followed. ". . . from disabling physical injury and continuing emotional stress." The orders were signed by Georges De Marnay himself.

"Very well, Lieutenant. Thank you." The young officer saluted and left with obvious relief.

I'd killed De Marnay's fellow Admiral; was that why he was beaching me? He had a reputation as a fair man, but . . .

No, my careless answers to Dr. Tendres's probing questions had caused my grounding. I should have pretended a relaxation I didn't feel, and denied my nightmares.

Still, I'd come this far without having lied to a superior officer. I had little else to be proud of; I would keep that shred of honor, even if it cost me my posting.

I smiled at Annie. "They gave us more time together, hon. Would you like that?"

Her grin of delight was answer enough. I wondered when she'd be called for Detour. By unspoken agreement we never mentioned our parting.

The door swung open. "Why all the smiles, sir? Oh, good afternoon, Miss Wells."

"We have a vacation, Alexi." I reached for my shirt.

"For how long, sir?"

"Awhile." I dressed myself slowly. "Until they say I'm recovered. I'll need a place to stay. At least they haven't taken my pay billet; could you two find me a home?" Annie had closed our apartment when it was clear I'd be a long while in hospital.

"Of course, sir," Alexi said automatically. "We'll look this afternoon, if Miss Wells is ready."

"You knowin' my name be Annie," she said disdainfully. "All that Miss Wells goofjuice be for records an' all." She tossed her sweater over her shoulder. "I be ready now, Mist' Tamarov." At the door she turned regally. "Good afternoon, Nick." Now her diction was flawless. "I'll be back to see you after dinner." With a scornful toss of her head she was gone.

Alexi, at the doorway, shrugged ruefully. "Sorry, sir." He followed. Alone, I wondered what strings Alexi had pulled to be assigned as my aide during my recovery. Well, it was a soft shoreside billet . . .

On the other hand, perhaps he hadn't even volunteered. After all, why would he want to be posted with me?

"Do you know how many capital ships we have in system? Thirty-eight! And we've seen not a single fish." Captain Derghinski stared morosely into the setting sun.

I turned away, my hand tightening on the rough-sawn balcony railing. But for my self-indulgence in challenging Tremaine, I would have a vessel of my own. Absently I fingered the scar on my cheek.

"Is that bad?" Annie asked.

His visage softened. "I realize you've met the aliens, ma'am, and it wasn't pleasant. But we can't beach the fleet in Hope Nation forever, waiting for fish."

I sipped at a cold drink, feeling the welcome sting of the alcohol. Being grounded had advantages; alcohol, like most drugs, was contraband aboard ship.

"I'm surprised at how much of the fleet Admiralty committed here," I admitted. In addition to Tremaine's squadron, two others had arrived while I was in hospital. They provided Admiral De Marnay with more firepower than had been massed anywhere for many decades.

Derghinski nodded. "Eventually we'll have to go home. What if the fish show up near Terra or the Lunar bases? And while we've diverted squadrons to Hope Nation, our interstellar commerce has gone to hell." Naval vessels carried most of our cargo and all passenger traffic between the stars. Schedules had been sparse enough before the alien invasion. Now, they were almost nonexistent.

That was one reason Annie was still with me. In the past, the lone supply ship that visited Hope Nation would have continued to Detour, taking her to her new home.

The apartment Alexi and Annie had found was in a row of connected town houses on the outskirts of Centraltown. From our balcony I could just glimpse Farreach Ocean in the distance. It wasn't far from where my wife Amanda had once roomed, in another time, another life.

"A fine party, Mr. Seafort."

I smiled back at Captain De Vroux. "Thank you, ma'am."

To my surprise, my home was becoming a shoreside refuge for off-duty officers. The constant replenishment of drinks and food ate into my savings, but I didn't mind. At least it helped keep me informed. The lieutenants and Captains, for their part, liked to unwind without guarding their speech as they'd have to among civilians. They probably enjoyed Annie's good looks and careless charm as well.

I breathed deep, glad to be free of pain at last. I turned back to Captain Derghinski. "We can't hit them until we find them," I said. "So far we've never found a fish . . . they've always found us."

A confident young lieutenant from *Resolute* spoke up. "Well, sir, if your theory is right that the fish hear us Fuse, they should be swarming over us by now. All our ships dropping into normal space as they arrive . . ."

"It was only a suggestion," I muttered. "And anyway—what's your name, again?"

"Ter Horst, Ravan G., Lieutenant, sir," the young man said cautiously. I could understand his anxiety. Though I'd never been a lieutenant I remembered the awe that a Captain—any Captain—inspired in me as a midshipman. For all this fellow knew, I consorted with Admirals, if not Lord God Himself, and a word from me could do him inestimable harm.

"Well, Mr. Ter Horst, we have no idea how long it takes the fish to respond once they hear us. Or even where they come from." I shivered despite the afternoon warmth. "They might be on their way even now."

"Yes, sir."

"You needn't be afraid of me," I snapped. "I don't bite, at least off duty."

He attempted a grin. "Sorry, sir. Anyway, we're ready for them this time. Thirty-eight ships, all armed to the teeth with laser cannon. I'd like to see the fish that can run that blockade."

"Not a blockade, Ter Horst." Captain Derghinski was gruff. "We're scattered all over the system; we have to protect miners' ships and local commercial craft as well, you know. And ten of our ships are posted near Orbit Station; we can't afford to lose the Station under any circumstances."

No, we certainly couldn't. Our huge interstellar vessels, assembled in space, couldn't heave themselves out of a planet's gravity well. The ships were floating cities and warehouses that carried passengers, crew, and cargo across the immense reaches of interstellar space, on voyages that took months or years to complete. Hope Nation's cargo and passengers were off-loaded at the huge, bustling Orbit Station, where they transferred to shuttles for reshipment groundside.

If Orbit Station and its shuttles were destroyed, only the starships' frail launches would serve as lifelines to the colony. Hope Nation's trade would be crippled.

"Still, sir," said the lieutenant, "we've got more than enough force to handle any imaginable attack."

"I hope so," I said. Though I wished I were aloft, part of me silently thanked Lord God I was ashore; the thought of the fish appearing to hurl their acid globs at my ship sent chills down my spine. I turned away, ashamed of my cowardice.

Captain Derghinski stared bleakly at the lieutenant. "U.N.S. *Resolute*, hmm? I don't remember that she encountered any fish on the way out."

"No, sir," Ter Horst agreed.

"I remind you, sir, that you speak to Captain Nicholas Seafort of *Hibernia, Portia,* and *Challenger.* He discovered the aliens and fought them three times. He hardly requires your advice."

Lieutenant Ter Horst wilted under Derghinski's rebuke. "Please forgive me, Captain Seafort," he said quickly. "I spoke without thinking."

I tried not to show annoyance at Captain Derghinski; after all, he was my guest and my senior as well. "No matter, Lieutenant. I'm glad you're eager to do battle for us." I turned to Derghinski as Ter Horst gratefully made his escape. "Thanks for your concern, sir. I'm really all right, though."

"Hope so," Derghinski said bluntly as we drifted toward the buffet. "Not according to rumors I've heard."

"Oh?"

He sized me up with a glance. "They say you're at the end of your tether. Not just your wound, but the word is the psych report blew you off the bridge."

"Dinner, Nick. Gentlemen?" Annie's blessed appearance at the door saved me from the need to answer.

"Wouldn't hurt you to get a word in at Admiralty House," Derghinski muttered, as we drifted inside.

No, it wouldn't, if I could get through to Admiral De Marnay. I'd already tried twice for an appointment.

I suppose dinner was delicious. I didn't notice.

I pointed to the prefab going up across the street. "Last time I was here, all that was open land."

Annie shrugged. "It better havin' somethin' on it." I nuzzled her hand as we strolled toward the spaceport, and Admiralty House beyond. She'd survived the streets in Lower New York, where every lot held either a decaying building or rubble; to Annie, open spaces were dangerous jungles to be crossed to the safety of abandoned tenements. She added, "What's so special about a piece of land, anyways?"

In those thickets Alexi Tamarov had hidden two dirty and disheveled cadets, waiting while a loyal sailor lured me to their hideaway, unable to reveal his secret. "Nothing, hon." Once I'd passed Judge Chesley in the street. If he recognized me, he gave no sign. I was content to leave it so. Another voyage, another time.

I would miss Annie, when the transpops were shipped onward. I suspected, though, that the Centraltown authorities would be glad to see the last of them. Freed from shipboard discipline, the rash young streeters had been involved in more than a few incidents. Now, most of them were gathered in a temporary camp on the edge of town.

The iron gate to Admiralty House creaked as I opened it. Two lieutenants on their way out saluted; I returned their salutes automatically, my mind on the interview I sought. I brushed back my hair.

"Yes, sir?" The lieutenant paused at his console.

"I'd like to see Admiral De Marnay."

"Have you an appointment, sir?"

"No." I couldn't get one.

He looked dubious. "I don't know if I can get you in, sir. The Admiral shuttles back and forth to Orbit Station. When he's groundside the quartermasters, supply officers and tacticians line up waiting." His eyes darted to my cheek. "You're Captain Seafort, sir?"

"Yes." My scar was ample identification.

"I'm Lieutenant Eiferts. Glad to meet you. If you'll have a seat I'll pass the word you're here."

"Thank you. Let's sit, Annie." Though I wouldn't admit it, the long hike from Centraltown had winded me. I picked up a holozine and flicked through it.

"Mr. Seafort?" It was Captain Forbee. "Here for a meeting?"

"Not exactly. We—Miss Wells and I—took a long walk today, and I thought perhaps Admiral De Marnay could see me."

"Did Eiferts say you haven't a chance?"

"The Admiral's that busy?"

"Well, I might be able to get you a word with him. Depends on his mood at the moment. Come upstairs." He touched his cap to Annie. "Nice to have met you, Miss, uh, Wells." Was there a second's hesitation before he acknowledged the name? He led me up the red-carpeted stairs and along the paneled hall.

Forbee's office was bigger than the one I remembered from my first visit to Hope Nation. He parked me in a comfortable chair and disappeared.

I was looking for something to read when a head appeared in the doorway. "Excuse me, sir. Midshipman Bezrel. The Admiral will see you now."

"Very well." I followed the very young middy down the hall, through a waiting room filled with officers, some of whom I recognized. I saw speculation in their faces; was I summoned back to active duty? If not, how had I managed to slip past them?

The midshipman knocked and opened the door. He snapped to attention, as did I. "Captain Seafort, sir," he said. His voice hadn't quite settled into the lower registers.

"As you were, Bezrel. That's all." Admiral De Marnay stood from behind his desk. "Hello, Seafort. Stand easy." He put out his hand.

"Thank you for seeing me, sir."

"You're supposed to make an appointment for this sort of thing," he said irritably.

"Yes, sir. I've tried several times."

"Did it occur to you that I wasn't ready to see you?"

"I hoped it wasn't the case."

"Well, it was." The Admiral's scrutiny was neither friendly nor hostile. "Sit down. What do you want?"

"A ship, sir."

"No."

"Return to active duty, then. In any capacity."

"No."

"May I ask why, sir?"

"No."

"Aye aye, sir." I was finished. I wondered what I was suited for, other than the Navy.

He relented. "You're not recovered from your ordeals, Seafort. You were near death for a long while." That was true. I'd been around death for longer than he knew. Much of it I'd caused by my ineptitude.

"We walked here today, sir. From downtown."

"We?"

"A friend and I, sir."

"Well, that's good. But physical recovery is only the half of it. You're overstressed, Seafort. You've had more tragedies—catastrophes—than most Captains see in their entire career. You're not fit."

I tried to keep my voice calm. "In what way, sir?"

"Emotionally, Seafort. You're a bundle of nerves."

"That's goofjuice," I said, regretting it almost instantly.

He ignored the impertinence. "You're wound so tight you wouldn't even answer the psych officer's questions. What if you cracked under the strain of command? You could lose a ship, or even suicide, as your wife did."

"That's not fair!" I cried. "Amanda was distraught. Her baby—"

"You're distraught too, whether or not you know it."

"No, I'm not! I—"

He came to his feet in one supple motion. "Look at yourself!" he bellowed. "Why do your eyes glisten? Your fists are clenched, did you know that? Do you realize how you've been talking to me?"

I was shocked into silence.

"You've done more than anyone could ask," he said more gently. "You've proven yourself over and over again. I'm not going to let you drive yourself into a hormone-rebalancing ward. You've earned a rest, Seafort. Take it."

I sat in abject misery, not daring to speak further. Finally I whispered, "I can't lie about and do nothing, sir. Please give me a job. Anything."

"If you can get clearance from Dr. Tendres in psych, I'll find you a shoreside billet. Later we'll see about a ship. That's all."

I opened my mouth to protest but realized I would only work against myself. I saluted and slunk out.

It was a long walk back to the apartment; past the spaceport, past the prefabs alongside the road, past bars and restaurants, offices and homes. Annie tried to chat at first, but my grim and uncivil replies reduced her to silence.

"I'm sorry," I muttered, pressing my thumb to the door lock. "It's not your fault."

"Damn ri' it ain't," she responded. "So why you acting like it be?"

I smiled despite myself. "Because there's no one else to take it out on."

"He said he'd put you back to work, didn't he?"

"When I get clearance from the psych officer."

"You'll go see him?"

See him, and face his probing questions. I could lie to rescue my career, or hold to the truth and stay beached. So grounded I would remain. "Sure, hon. I'll call tomorrow."

She busied herself rummaging through the freezer for a dinner we'd like. "Yo' problem is you afraid of seein' him," she announced. "My Nicky, he be'ent—isn't—as brave as we thought." She put the dinners in the micro. "Two minutes on high, then broil for a minute," she told it, then turned to me, wrapping her arms around me as I slumped exhausted in an easy chair.

"I never was brave," I said, pushing away her caress.

She regarded me thoughtfully. "You really be unzark, huh? Do this my way, then."

"Do what?"

"Promise you won't call ol' doctor man for a few days."

"Huh? What are you talking about?"

"That psych man, promise you won't call."

"I've got to—"

She fell into my lap. Her lips pressed against mine, while her hands wandered down to my waist.

"Hey, you have dinner on. Maybe later, after we—"

"Promise."

3

The walk to the hospital was farther than to the spaceport four days earlier, yet I was hardly winded. I squinted in the bright sunlight, forcing my pace to slow. A full hour before my appointment, and I was striding like an anxious middy at Academy. I grinned.

At the hospital I put a zine in the holovid while I waited. Two years old now, the holozine had reached Hope Nation no more than eight months before. Almost too recent for a doctor's waiting room. I flipped through the pages on my screen.

"You're the first article, Mr. Seafort."

Startled, I looked up at the nurse. "I—what?"

"The lead story, right after the ads. See it?"

I flipped to the first few pages. Aghast, I saw my haggard face staring back. "I wasn't looking for—I mean—"

"At first you were in all the zines. The hero of Miningcamp, savior of *Hibernia*, all that. Then it kind of died down." She smiled.

"Yes." I snapped off the holo.

"But they started again when you rescued *Challenger* and fought off all those fish," she said without remorse. " *Holoweek* calls you the Navy's most eligible bachelor, even with that silly scar."

"God in heaven." I stumbled to my feet, dropping the holovid on the coffee table.

"If you're collecting clippings, Mr. Seafort, I'm sure we could help—"

"No!"

"Hello, Seafort, you're looking fit."

I turned to see Dr. Tendres waiting in the doorway. "Thank you, Miss, er, um, Miss. Thank you for asking. Offering." I fled to his office.

"So, then, how do you feel?" His office lights were off. Though the blinds were open, his desk was in shadows.

"Better." I sat in a straight chair in front of the desk, cap on my lap, knees tight.

"Still having the dreams?"

"None lately." For the past few days, at any rate. I'd been too busy at night for dreams.

"What were your nightmares about?"

I recognized his test: a few weeks ago, I'd refused to talk about them. I took a deep breath. "The one about Father bringing me to Academy, you've seen in my record. I also dream about men I've killed—Tuak, Rogoff, and others—coming to take revenge on me. And about how brutal I was to Philip Tyre, a lieutenant I shipped with."

"How do you feel about that?"

"Mr. Tyre? I regret I wasn't kinder. I wish I could apologize to him. The other men?" I considered. "I don't know. I had little choice but to execute them." How glibly the words rolled off my tongue.

"How badly do you want a ship, Nick?"

"Badly." The word slipped out before I could stop it.

"Enough to tell me what I want to hear?"

"What I've said is the truth."

"Yes, but do you feel it true?" He went to the window, clasped his hands behind him. "Tell me how you feel about yourself."

It was my turn to stand. "Sir, must I do this?" I twisted my cap in my hands.

He turned. "You find it painful?"

"Excruciating." I forced myself to meet his eye.

He regarded me. "You may choose whether to answer or not. I only ask that you tell me the truth or nothing."

Slowly I sat. "Very well." It was a moment before I was able to summon the words. "I feel myself a failure, in that I've been unable to carry out my duties without terrible cost to those around me and to myself. I know the Navy doesn't see it that way, sir, but I do."

"What cost?"

"Pain, death, and damnation."

After a long silence I realized he wouldn't speak, and went on. "I've hurt many people, and caused the death of people I wasn't alert enough to save. And I've dishonored and damned myself."

"Your oath?"

"My oath." I willed my irritation away. If he didn't understand, it was my task to make it clear to him. "I shot a woman whom I'd sworn I wouldn't harm. I gave her my oath so that I could get close enough to shoot her. I knew when I gave my pledge that I intended to break it."

"Your purpose doesn't matter, then?"

"My motive was to save my ship, yes. You people—Admiral Brentley, back home, and others at Admiralty—seem to think my duty to protect *Challenger* was an excuse. I do not." And surely Lord God does not.

"Our Government is founded on the Reunification Church and we all serve the One True God," he said carefully. "But there's more than one interpretation of His will in the matter."

My fury welled forth. "I don't engage in sophistry."

"That's not—"

"Or heresy!"

That silenced him, as well it might.

After a long moment he said coldly, "I won't argue theology with you, Captain Seafort. It is not germane to our purpose."

I scowled back at him, knowing I'd destroyed any chance that he'd give me clearance.

The silence dragged out. At length I said with more calm, "I'm sorry, sir. I know you view my outburst as more evidence that I'm unfit."

"I view it as evidence that you have strong religious convictions." He sat again. "How will your supposed damnation affect the way you function?"

"My soul is forfeit; duty is all I have left." Whatever satisfaction this life gave me would soon be ended; what was to come did not bear thinking about.

"Can you ever be happy?"

I considered it. "I was once. For a brief time."

"When?"

"On *Portia* with my wife and baby son. Before they died."

"And now?"

"Now I have duty. Perhaps with Lord God's grace I will see contentment again, but I doubt that."

"So, again, how do you feel?"

I closed my eyes to seek an honest answer. What I found surprised me. "Not happiness, exactly, but . . . a sort of peace. I know the worst that will happen to me, and all other dangers pale before it. I have a—a companion now, and I enjoy her company."

"Miss, ah, Wells."

"Yes, sir." Just how much I'd enjoyed her company during the past three days, I didn't intend to tell him. Hour upon hour of bedplay, soft caresses interspersed with dizzying bouts of passionate love at odd and frequent intervals . . . Omelettes at the kitchen table, a quick trip to the head, Annie's hand pulling me insistently back to the bed, her lips and hands exploring, her feverish thighs pressing me tightly, until at last I begged her only half in jest to let me die in peace. It just made her smile, and lay her head against my chest, and . . .

I blinked, back again in Dr. Tendres's office. "Sorry, sir. My mind was wandering."

"From the look of it, a pleasant memory."

I smiled. "Yes."

He snapped on his holovid. "Well, whatever the cause, you're more relaxed than when I last saw you." Relaxed? That was one word for it. "I'll recommend limited shoreside duty, Mr. Seafort. Three months, and then we'll see."

"Three months?" Had my honesty cost me this? "I was hoping to be assigned a ship—"

He waved impatiently. "No, Mr. Seafort, you'll get nowhere by pushing me. Three months."

"Liaison, sir?" I repeated. "Surely you can't mean it."

"Why not?" Admiral De Marnay glowered. "The planters respect your accomplishments; you've been here before, you've even visited their plantations."

I stared glumly at the carpet. "I've met some of them, yes, but as for their respecting me—"

"Harmon Branstead, and his brother Emmett from *Challenger*. They've been singing your praises to the other families. You're well regarded."

I said doggedly, "Whatever talents I have, sir, public relations isn't among them."

"There's not much public relations involved. The planters are agitating for self-government. We want someone to listen sympathetically without committing himself. With a war on, it's important to keep communications open." The Admiral checked his watch. "Anyway, that's your assignment. Feel free to travel."

"Isn't there any other duty, sir, that I could—"

De Marnay roared, "Damn it, Seafort, why won't you let me be diplomatic about finding you makework? You'd stay beached for the rest of the year if I hadn't promised you something!" His fingers drummed his holovid. "You talked Tendres into a clearance, so I'll keep my word, but don't ask for more."

Shocked, I could say nothing.

A knock at the door. The same young middy I'd seen earlier said urgently, "Sir, excuse me, *Resolute* reports ambig-ambiguous contact at edge of radar range. It may be a fish."

"Very well, Bezrel, I'll be right there. Look, Seafort. I have nothing against you." He got to his feet. "You'll get a ship in good time. But first you need rest." He accompanied me to the door, clearly in a hurry. "I've

got to run. If that's one of the aliens . . ." As I left he called after me,
"Take an aide and a driver to help out."

I spent several days nursing my resentment in the isolation of my
apartment; even Annie's wiles couldn't lure me out of my sulk. It was only
when Alexi asked permission to put in for a transfer that I was shaken into
awareness.

"Apply whenever it suits you," I said, trying to make my voice tone-
less.

"Yes, sir, thank you." He bit his lip, troubled. "It's just that, now
you're recovered and inactive, there's nothing for me to do."

"I know that," I said, relenting. "You know about the glorified vacation they've forced on me. Do you want to be part of it or to go back to
ship duty?"

"I want ship duty, of course."

"Very well."

He blushed up to the roots of his hair. "But, ah, I was hoping . . ."

"Spit it out."

"Aye aye, sir. I hoped you'd ask me along, when they give you a
ship."

"Oh, Alexi." I wandered to the balcony doors. "I'm sorry. Of course
I'll have you. Shall we wait it out together?"

He grinned. "Whatever you say, sir."

"Admiralty House is even busier than before since that false alarm
with the fish, so we'd better organize our own jaunt. Admiral De Marnay
said something about a driver. I don't suppose we really need one."

Alexi said, "Pardon, sir, but the larger your detail, the more you'll
impress the planters."

"Um." I thought it over and sighed. "Very well, put in for a driver."

The following morning I was ready to leave. I'd vetoed putting in for
a heli; we had little enough to do as it was, and I wanted to keep our
mission low-key. An electricar was ample. Alexi loaded our luggage, along
with maps, callers, and, just in case, camping gear, while I said my good-
byes to Annie. Her idea of farewell was different from mine; as I changed
clothes afterward I said, "We'll only be a few days, hon. Sure you can
manage without me?"

She rewarded me with an impish grin. "You be surprised how well I
can manage without you, Cap'n."

"Belay that," I growled with mock severity, and bestowed a final kiss.

Outside, I hurried to the electricar. "Sorry to keep you waiting. Let's
get—" I stumbled to a halt. The driver came to attention, grinning. I
managed, "What are *you* doing here?" Eddie Boss, like Annie, had been

one of the transpops set adrift in *Challenger*. He'd chosen to enlist, and remained in the Navy after we were rescued.

"I be assigned to drivin' you, sir." The huge petty officer's smile was wider than usual.

"But how—why—"

"Dunno, sir. I was on *Kitty Hawk* and I got orders. Come on down and drive for the Cap'n, they say."

"I put in for him, sir," said Alexi. "As a surprise." He regarded me with misgiving. "Maybe it wasn't a good idea."

"You surprised me, all right." I felt myself smiling. "As you were, sailor." Eddie relaxed. "Do you drive?" I asked. In Lower New York, the only cars seen were gutted hulks.

"*Hibernia*'s joes taught me on long-leave, sir."

I settled into the front seat. "Well, let's see what you learned. Mr. Tamarov, brace yourself." I made a show of gripping the dash.

"Aye aye, sir!" We were off.

I didn't need to study the map; only one road led west out of Centraltown to the plantation zone, and I'd driven it before. Bulldozed through the rich red earth, Plantation Road ran more or less parallel to the seacoast. An hour or so out of town, it narrowed and the smooth pavement gave way to gravel.

"You went this way with Derek Carr?" asked Alexi from the back seat.

"To visit his family holdings. As I remember, we had lunch at Hauler's Rest. The meals are big enough to fill even Mr. Boss." Eddie grinned his gap-toothed smile.

Derek and Alexi had served together as midshipmen on *Hibernia* and were friends. Now Derek was on a run to Detour, eleven weeks away. Even if he returned safely, I might not see him again if I gained a ship first.

After a time Alexi took the wheel. With three drivers we could continue until well after dark. Along the road grew thickets of unfamiliar ropy foliage through which an occasional massive genera tree thrust its mighty snout. On my last trip I'd enjoyed the drive. Today, the woods projected an ominous silence that disturbed me. What was different, other than myself?

By midafternoon we were still long hours from the plantation zone. I took the wheel. As evening fell Minor rose first, followed by Major. I had to concentrate on my driving; their twin shadows made me dizzy. I glanced occasionally at the map to see how far we were from the vast estates that supplied so much of Terra's foodstuffs.

Alexi said, "The Bransteads aren't expecting us until tomorrow, sir. We can stop at any plantation for the night; we'd be welcome in a guest house."

"I know." All plantations offered food and lodging without charge to travelers; it was the local custom and they could well afford it.

We drove another hour before we came on the marker for Mantiet, the first of the many plantations that justified Hope Nation's existence. I slowed, biting my lip. "I hate to ask hospitality at this hour of the night."

"We be campin', then?" asked Eddie.

Alexi snapped, "Speak when you're spoken to."

His manner helped me decide. "Why struggle with a tent when we're tired and irritable? Let's find the guest house."

I turned down the long dirt drive, past fields of corn and wheat radiant in the soft moonlight. Eventually we came to a circular drive that curved around the front lawn of a sprawling mansion.

A dog barked. A light went on; a moment later the door swung open. The man who strode toward us had obviously dressed with hurry. He peered into the car.

"Sorry," I said. "I didn't mean to wake you."

"Then why drive past my home at midnight?"

"I was hoping to find the guest house."

"You don't think it's a bit late to be calling?" Without waiting for an answer he pointed to the drive. "Behind the manse. You're welcome to breakfast in the morning, then be on your way." He turned on his heel and strode to the door.

Alexi called, "This is Cap—"

"Quiet." I slammed the vehicle into gear.

"Cap'n, the house be over—"

"I heard him, Mr. Boss!" The car lurched over the rutted drive toward the main road.

Alexi asked mildly, "I take it we're not staying?"

I growled, "The temperature isn't right."

"Sir?"

"Hell hasn't frozen over." I spun the electricar onto the highway, muttering under my breath. Alexi and Eddie Boss knew me well enough to remain silent.

I drove at a fast clip until my adrenaline faded, leaving me tired and shaky. "Look for a good place to pull over," I said. "We'll camp the night."

A half hour later we were parked alongside the road pulling out our duffels. I'd forgotten just how easy our pair of poly-mil tents were to assemble, or I'd have been less reluctant to use them. After we pounded in the stakes, Alexi, Eddie, and I quickly spread the tough plastic over the poles and staked it. Alexi rummaged in the cooler and came up with softies for all of us; I swigged mine greedily.

Alexi asked, "Shall I bunk with Mr. Boss, sir?"

I hesitated. A lieutenant didn't share quarters with a seaman; it wasn't done. But he wouldn't share quarters with his Captain, either. We should have brought three tents.

I felt a wistful longing for times past. "If you had your choice?"

He shifted uncomfortably. "I—um, as you wish, sir."

I raised my eyebrow, realized he couldn't see the gesture in the dark. "If you'd like to bunk with me, I don't mind." My tone was gruff.

"If you're sure—I mean, thank you, sir." He tossed his duffel into the tent. "Take the other, Mr. Boss."

"Aye aye, sir." Eddie stared up at the unfamiliar constellations. "Never slept in no outside place before."

"Not even in New York?" I asked.

He shrugged. "On roofs, sometimes. But didn't see no stars from there."

"They won't hurt you, Mr. Boss."

"I know." He sounded scornful. I left Eddie contemplating the majesty of the heavens.

Alexi had unrolled our self-inflating mattresses and was getting ready for bed. "Almost like old times, sir," he said softly as I undressed.

How many years had it been since *Hibernia*'s wardroom? "I was thinking the same," I said.

Huddled in our beds we recalled old shipmates: Vax Holser, Derek Carr, and poor Sandy Wilsky, long dead.

"I'll never know how you had the guts to stand up to Vax, sir. He could have broken you in half."

It had been a memorable fight. But it was the Navy way; wardroom matters were to be settled between the middies. "I had a secret weapon, Alexi."

"What was that, sir?"

"I didn't care."

"I felt that way after Philip Tyre was put in charge."

"I'm sorry. I shouldn't have done that to you."

A long pause. "That's what makes you different, sir. Other Captains would have no regrets."

"It's worse, then. I knew better, but still did wrong."

"He was senior." Alexi turned onto his other side. "After Tremaine off-loaded you and the others onto *Challenger*, it was . . . odd."

"Oh?"

"Captain Hasselbrad was in charge. A ship has but one Captain."

"Of course."

"But the Admiral wouldn't leave him alone. He'd stay on the bridge for hours at a time. The Captain would give an order and Tremaine would countermand it in front of us all. I almost felt sorry for Hasselbrad."

"Almost?"

"He assented to what Tremaine did to you."

"You all did, Alexi. You had to!"

He said fiercely, "No, we chose to!"

"It's over and done with."

His voice wavered. "It isn't. It never can be. We let you down." He struggled for words. "When you . . . Some wrongs cannot be righted. We only learn to live with them."

I mused, "Derek Carr's gone, in Lord God's hands. Vax hates me. You're my only friend. Please don't do this to yourself."

A long quiet. Alexi said with a catch in his voice, "God, sir, I've missed you."

4

We got up late, washed as best we could in an icy chuckling stream, and sipped steaming coffee while we repacked the electricar. I drove; after an hour we came to a dirt road that wound away into a heavy woods, under a homebuilt gate whose sign read BRANSTEAD PLANTATION.

When we pulled up to the house a youngster lounging on the porch got up to greet us. "I'm Jerence." He sounded sullen. "Pa told me to say hello if he was still out back."

"You've grown, boy."

"Yeah, I guess. I'm thirteen now. I was ten last time you came." He opened my door and gestured toward the house. "Go on in. I'll call him."

"Thank you."

He kicked disconsolately at the red earth. "You're welcome." He loped away, disappearing behind the house.

Sarah Branstead was at her door before we reached the steps. "Welcome back, Captain Seafort. To Hope Nation and Branstead Plantation." Her smile was warm and genuine.

"Thank you, ma'am."

"No, you must call me Sarah. It's good to see you again, Captain. I've heard you've had . . . difficult times."

"Yes." I cast about for a way to change the subject. "Who'll be here today?"

"Tomas Palabee, old Zack Hopewell, Laura Triforth. The Volksteaders, do you know them? I know you met Plumwell, the manager of Carr Plantation. Some others; I'm not sure just who Harmon invited. And Mantiet, of course." A momentary annoyance passed across her features. "Mustn't leave him out."

We strolled into the manse. Moments later Harmon Branstead hurried in to greet us, two youngsters trotting alongside.

"Sorry, Captain. I was working on the new silo." We shook hands, and I introduced Alexi.

When he heard we'd camped out for the night, Branstead was appalled. "After passing half a dozen plantations? Hospitality was all around you!"

I grunted, catching Alexi's eye before he could speak. "I camped on my last trip," I said. "I was looking forward to it."

I'd have waited until dinner hour to eat, but Eddie Boss, offered refreshments, accepted with alacrity despite my scowl. The housekeeper, noting Eddie's enthusiasm, disappeared into his kitchen. The tray he brought us a few minutes later—savory sliced meats and steaming fresh vegetables—was more a meal than a snack, and I ate with gusto.

I was just mopping the last of my gravy when the whap of heli blades sounded in the distance. As a lightweight private craft settled on the front lawn the Branstead family moved outside to greet their guests. A burly, unsmiling man jumped out before the blades stopped whirling.

He gave Harmon Branstead a perfunctory handshake and scrutinized us as he approached the manse. "You're Seafort, the imperial envoy? I'm Palabee." His clasp was firm. "Did they instruct you to keep us pacified at any cost, or to tell us to go to hell?"

"Tomas, don't harass him. He's just arrived from a night in the woods. Imperial envoy, indeed!"

"Isn't that what you are?" Palabee was blunt.

"I—"

Harmon Branstead said firmly, "No. He is my guest."

Palabee had the grace to blush. The corners of his mouth turned up. "Very well, sorry. But the sooner we get to business, the better."

"What business is that?" I asked.

He shot me an appraising glance. "Didn't they tell you?"

"They told me I got along well with the planters," I said coolly. "Apparently they were mistaken."

He ignored my tone. "Just why *are* you here?"

"As liaison between the Government and the plantation owners." I glowered. "Why are *you* here?"

"To negotiate, of course. If they haven't prepared you for that, we're wasting our time."

"What's to negotiate?"

His reply was forestalled by the throb of another heli. We went outside, where I was introduced to Seth Morsten: flabby, middle-aged, affable. Awaiting the rest of the guests, we retired to the parlor and drinks.

The Volksteaders farmed the next plantation west; they arrived by land. So did Lawrence Plumwell, manager of Carr Plantation. He eyed me with disfavor. "It seems we've met before, Captain."

"Yes, sir. Three years ago."

"You traveled with your retarded cousin, I recall." His tone was acid.

I flushed. We'd thought the deception necessary to get Derek Carr safely in and out of the plantation he owned but did not control. "I'm sorry, sir."

"As am I. It would have been good to speak candidly with Mr. Carr."

"If I see him I'll tell him so."

With a sardonic smile Plumwell moved on.

Zack Hopewell looked old enough to be Harmon Branstead's grand-father. Given the intermingling of the old Hope Nation families, perhaps he was. He nodded shortly to Palabee, shook hands warmly with Bran-stead, and turned to me. "So this is the hero of Miningcamp."

I flushed.

"Seriously, Captain Seafort. My granddaughter instructed me not to return without your autograph. Your exploits are well known here. And admired."

"An honor I'd be happier without."

The old man's tone was severe. "Lord God chooses your destiny. You do not."

He sounded so much like Father that I glanced up, half expecting to meet Father's stern visage. "Lord God provides choices," I said slowly. "We may turn toward Him or away from Him."

Zack Hopewell studied my face. "You're troubled."

I blurted, "I am forsworn of my oath and have no honor." An as-tounding admission, but he'd sounded so like Father . . .

He blinked. "Well, I asked for it. Teach me to meddle. Sorry I in-truded."

"Better all should know." I didn't bother to hide my bitterness.

"Is that why you wear the mark of Cain?"

My hand went to my face. "It was given in a fight. I have no reason to remove it."

He frowned. "Get rid of it, lad. Men will judge your soul without need of external markers."

I had to turn away: memories of Father's hearth were so strong. Ashamed of my indiscretion, I wandered the ornate parlor, examining the ancient imported furniture. At the buffet I helped myself to a glass of wine. Sarah Branstead said, smiling, "I didn't know you Navy men were allowed alcohol."

"Aboard ship it's contraband, ma'am. Ashore we're free to partake." I sipped from my glass of wine. "I'm not much of a drinker."

Mrs. Branstead waved away my comment. "Oh, no criticism in-tended. I just wish it were the case in Centraltown."

I thought of a sailors' bar I'd once patronized, outside the spaceport. "I wasn't aware of a problem, ma'am."

"It's getting worse. In part because of the war, partly thanks to the farmhands we've imported over the years. Downtown gets very nasty at night."

"My neighborhood seems peaceful enough."

"You're fortunate," she said primly. "Mrs. Volksteader was accosted on the way from a restaurant to her car. If another couple hadn't come along at the right moment, she might have been in great trouble."

I felt a touch of sadness that Hope Nation was going the way of old Earth. "The civil authorities don't respond?"

"Oh, they try, but what can they do? Centraltown's just a small town. The men ran away. Our police don't have fancy tracking tools, like your—" Her face lit as a couple entered the parlor. "Oh, look, the Mantiets. Excuse me a moment."

Frederick Mantiet strode into the room, his breathless wife a step behind. Mrs. Branstead gave him a scant nod but bestowed a warm hug on the woman. The greeting completed, she brought the Mantiets to the buffet and introduced us.

"Glad to meet you, sir." I held out my hand.

His stare was hostile and contemptuous. "That was you last night, eh?" He looked me up and down. "Force us into discourtesy, to put us at a disadvantage? Well, it won't work."

I said evenly, "It hardly seems necessary to force you into discourtesy, sir."

Mrs. Branstead intervened. "Oh, I do so want you to be friends. Frederick, have you heard Emmett's stories of Captain Seafort on *Challenger*? He was absolutely marvelous."

Mantiet muttered something under his breath. I managed to busy myself with my glass until the moment passed. After a time Alexi drifted closer and said quietly, "Do you sense hostility, sir?"

"From some, yes."

"But why?"

"I don't know yet."

"How many of these joes did you meet three years ago?"

"Just Branstead and Plumwell."

"When Ms. Triforth joins us, the planters in this room will account for about eighty percent of Hope Nation's revenues."

"So?"

"If they're hostile, it's something to worry about, sir."

"Thanks for telling me my business, Lieutenant."

Alexi gulped. "Sorry, sir." He retreated.

From time to time I caught contemplative glances from the planters.

I tried to keep my face a mask as I studied them in return. Palabee was skeptical and faintly combative, expecting some sort of negotiating session. Mantiet was thoroughly antagonistic, but I couldn't tell whether that was because I had driven away from his manse in a rage, or from a deeper cause. Plumwell was unfriendly, but then, I'd once abused his hospitality with Derek.

On the other side of the ledger, Arvin Volksteader seemed eager to get along with everybody; and old Zack Hopewell seemed friendly enough, in his stern, righteous way.

Only Laura Triforth was absent.

Sarah Branstead conferred with her housekeeper and called us in to an early dinner. The long plank table was ample even for a gathering as large as ours. I sat next to Harmon, who was at the head of his table. Alexi was across from me, and the other planters and their wives farther down the table. Some guests seemed disgruntled by their placement; it made me appreciate all the more the round tables at which officers and passengers sat aboard ship.

Jerence, used to eating with the adults, was directed to the kitchen with his younger brothers and Eddie Boss; he obeyed with a disdainful toss of his head.

While the food was passing I leaned toward Harmon. "I thought this was to be an introductory meeting, a social occasion."

"That's what I had in mind, Captain Seafort." He looked perturbed. "But some of them don't want to wait; they're ready for serious talk."

"I'm not quite sure—"

"Pity I didn't meet you on your last trip, Mr. Seafort." Tomas Palabee, from the other end of the table. "An eighteen-year-old Captain would have been a sight to see."

My smile was perfunctory. "It was. I was lucky to bring *Hibernia* back home."

"And skillful." Sarah Branstead. "Emmett says—"

"Emmett, Emmett, Emmett." Mantiet sounded sour. "You quote your brother-in-law as if he were Gospel, Sarah."

"Not Gospel, Frederick," she rejoined. "But he's the only one of us who's seen Captain Seafort in his element."

"As he never tires of reminding us." Palabee's tone was dry.

Harmon looked annoyed. "My brother is proud of his—"

"Don't bother to get up!" The door swung wide as a lanky middle-aged woman strode in, cape flowing. "Late. Business to attend to."

Harmon Branstead rose smoothly. "Captain Seafort, may I present Laura Triforth, of Triforth Plantation."

I stood. "Glad to meet—"

"Yes, and all that. Well, well. The official Naval liaison to the locals." She shot me an appraising glance. "So you're the one who discovered the aliens?"

"Unfortunately."

"Get on with your dinner. I've eaten, but I'll sit." She unclasped her cape and tossed it over the back of an empty chair. "Got the damp-rot licked, Palabee?"

Conversation resumed.

After the huge dinner we adjourned to the parlor, which had been cleared of the afternoon's hors d'oeuvres. Alexi arranged our chairs so that he sat alongside and a bit behind me.

Arvin Volksteader asked, "Just what do you know of our situation, Captain?"

I said slowly, "Hope Nation supplies hundreds of millions of tons of foodstuffs for Earth. Most comes from the plantations represented in this room."

"That's right. Now, we've tried for years to get proper representation in the U.N. Several years ago we sent Randolph Carr as a special envoy, but he got nowhere."

"Why do you need representation?"

"Who ships our grain?" demanded Frederick Mantiet.

"The interstellar liners carry some," I answered carefully. "The barges take most of it." Larger even than passenger vessels such as *Hibernia*, manned by skeleton crews, the huge, slow barges carried home grain from Hope Nation and ores from Miningcamp. A chain of barges was always in the pipeline, en route between the mother world and her colonies.

"Yes, but who runs the barges?"

"They're under Naval jurisdiction."

"Right!" He shook his head angrily.

"I don't see the problem."

"The rates, man!" Mantiet paced the open area in the center of the parlor. "You've been systematically gutting us for years. You set the charges for our grain shipments and for the return shipment of our supplies."

"The Navy doesn't set—"

"Not your damned Navy, the U.N. tariff office!"

Zack Hopewell said quietly, "This was to be a discussion, not a confrontation."

"We've had discussions, Zack! We've been having discussions since you were a boy. What good are they?"

"Then why are you here, Frederick?" Hopewell's voice was mild.

"Don't patronize me, you old fool!"

Amid shocked murmurs Zack Hopewell came slowly to his feet. There was nothing mild in his manner when finally he spoke. "Frederick Mantiet, I do hereby call chall—"

"Wait!"

Hopewell brushed off Harmon's restraining arm. "No, I choose not to wait. Mantiet, I—"

"This is *my* home!" Branstead's tone made even Hopewell go silent.

Harmon Branstead appealed to Mantiet. "I've lived on Hope Nation all my life. It's been a good life, all in all. We were brought up as gentlemen, we taught our sons the graces, expanded our holdings, did well for ourselves."

He turned to the rest of the planters. "But something is changing in us. Can't you feel it? We're becoming . . ." He groped for a word. "Imperious. We're losing our civility of speech, as well as our patience. And I . . ." He broke off, apologetically wiped his glasses. "I won't have it. In my house there will be civility. There shall be grace. Your remarks are unacceptable, Frederick, though I'm sure you couldn't have meant them as they sounded. So I'll have you apologize to Zack, or I'll have no choice but to call challenge on you myself."

Mantiet looked from one to the other. "Are you both mad? You'd have us waste strength dueling each other rather than fighting them, the real enemy?" He gestured at me with contempt. "No, he's not worth that. It's evident I can't work with you, but I'll not waste my blood or yours. Zack, I withdraw my remark. Good day to you all."

He stalked out. His wife scurried after.

"Hotheads." Harmon Branstead shook his head. Late in the evening we sat over steaming spiced drinks at his plank table. The guests had long since departed; Alexi and the others of the household had gone to bed. "They don't stop to reason."

"Not all of them," I said.

"Enough. Even Zack, when he gets his dander up."

"They're strong-willed. Especially Ms. Triforth."

"Laura's one of a kind." Harmon shifted in his chair. "She's the first woman who's ever headed a plantation, you know."

"How did that come about? You have primogeniture here."

"Yes, of course." He pursed his lips. "Her older brother Armistad was to inherit. A tragedy. A stroke at thirty-two."

"And she was the heir?"

"Oh, he didn't die. Not for many years. But he was—well, there wasn't much left of his mind. He had no sons; there were no younger brothers, so Laura stepped in. She faced down the banks, expanded the acreage . . . did a hell of a job. Armistad finally died, a few years back. It's all hers now."

"How many of you feel as she does?"

Harmon looked a touch apologetic. "The grievances she cited are legitimate. You have to admit the shipping rates are abominable; our shipping costs are twice what you charge your own merchants to send their goods here."

"Ah." I hadn't known that.

Tariffs weren't all they'd brought to my attention. After Mantiet's departure the discussion had ranged far and wide. Some planters were infuriated by the paternalism of the colonial Government; others worried about the quality of settlers arriving from Terra.

What had disturbed me most of all was Laura Triforth's sardonic description of the waste and mismanagement of our war effort. She'd paced the parlor as she spoke, emphasizing her words with sweeping gestures, while the others nodded agreement.

"Since you were last here, Seafort, they've sent more ships than we've seen since Hope Nation was founded. Ships loaded with unnecessary machinery, useless supplies, and foolish men."

"Be specific, please." I'd made an effort to sound conciliatory.

"Fine. They've sent thousands of soldiers. Why? The planet hasn't been under attack, and if it were, I doubt we could defend it from the ground. Your troops were sent to the Ventura Mountains, halfway across the world from our settlements. And to top it off, the holds of at least three of your ships were filled with—" Laura paused dramatically for effect.

I allowed her a moment of theater. "Yes?"

"Food! Food that we here on Hope Nation grow and send to Earth, they send back as rations! If there's one thing we could provide your armies, it's enough food."

"I agree."

She smiled without mirth. "A pity you weren't in charge of planning the expedition. But there's worse. They intend the army to be based here a long while, so they sent a huge prefab factory on one of the ships. It was supposed to turn out modular housing."

I sighed. All this was outside my brief and well beyond my competence. "Go on."

"Unfortunately, they forgot that we have no landing craft specifically designed to bring such heavy machinery down from orbit. So, we've had to divert cargo shuttles we needed to haul our produce, and modify them for you. Your factory was to crunch genera trees, of which God knows we have an abundant supply, and spit out celuwall." She stopped her pacing to face my chair.

"Unfortunately, they forgot we have no roads in the Venturas to bring raw trees to the factory or carry the modular housing units to their bases." She glared as if it were my fault.

"I'm sure all that can be—"

"The factory was cleverly designed; it's powered by any heavy-duty electric power source. Unfortunately, they forgot we have no generating plants in the Venturas."

I listened with growing uneasiness.

Laura smiled again. "Oh, we didn't let your soldiers freeze or go homeless, though we had to divert valuable manpower during our harvest season. I won't mention the laser installation built in the Venturas, also without a proper power source. If we hadn't sent them an emergency fission generating plant . . ." She sighed. "And perhaps you noticed the vast stockpiles of war matériel sitting on the tarmac at Centraltown, with no convenient way to get it to the Venturas and no need for them when they arrive?" She paused for breath. "The worst is that our land taxes have more than doubled to pay for it all!"

"It's only fair for you to help defend—"

"What defense? Your army sits safe and useless in the Venturas!" From the other planters, sounds of agreement.

I asked, "Have you brought all this to the attention of Unified Command?"

"Once. They patted me on the head and told me to mind my own business." She ran her fingers through her short, curly hair. "I'll tell you what *is* our business. It's the loutish, unmannerly sailors and soldiers and greedy civilians who are taking over Centraltown."

"Now, Laura—"

"I didn't mean him, Harmon. Sorry, Captain, if that seemed personal. But Centraltown was a small town, and we liked it that way. Now, it isn't even safe after dark."

"You people are more of a menace than your mysterious aliens!" Plumwell, my old adversary at Carr Plantation.

"Be fair," Harmon Branstead interjected. "Centraltown's problems were on the rise for years before the military buildup. Ever since we started hiring temporary workers for harvest rather than keeping resident field hands. All winter, they—"

Laura said wearily, "All right, Harmon, the migrants contribute. But the soldiers make matters worse."

I got slowly to my feet. "I can't respond to all you've told me, but I'll take your complaints to my superiors. I promise I'll get you answers."

"When?" Zack Hopewell was blunt.

"I don't know. I have to go through Admiral De Marnay, and he's a busy man. As soon—"

"I told you we're wasting our time!" Laura Triforth knotted her fists. "Mantiet may get carried away, but essentially he's right. They haven't listened, and they never will."

Zack Hopewell said, "Sit down, Laura." His tone brooked no argument. Surprised, she turned to face him. Their eyes locked, and after a moment the woman gave way. Muttering, she sat.

"The lad deserves a chance," Hopewell said gruffly. "We've waited so long there's little to be lost by waiting a few days longer."

"Days?" said Laura with scorn.

"Or weeks. He knows our grievances, and he knows we want things put right. Let us see how he handles himself." He glowered until he heard murmurs of assent.

Now, at night, sitting across the plank table from Harmon, I doubted I could be of any help. If only they knew how hard I'd found it to get through to the Admiral . . .

Harmon checked his watch. "I was hoping Emmett would be back this evening, but it doesn't seem likely."

"Perhaps I'll see him in the morning, before I go." I bade him good night and went to my room.

In the morning, Mr. and Mrs. Volksteader drove over to join us for breakfast and see us off. After an ample meal we strolled along the drive, chatting. Mrs. Volksteader attached herself to me, chatting with animation about matters of no consequence. I noticed her husband take Alexi aside and speak urgently, glancing once in my direction. After, Alexi, his lips compressed, hurried to rejoin us.

After our stroll we said our good-byes, piled into our electricar. As Eddie drove down the long, shaded lane toward the main road Alexi said, "Sir, I had the oddest conversation with Arvin Volksteader."

"Go on." Just ahead I spotted a slim figure trudging down the drive. "Who's that, walking this far from the manse?" As we approached I recog-

nized Jerence, a bulky knapsack strapped to his back. Eddie slowed, and
the boy waved us down. I bade Eddie stop.

"C'n I have a ride?"

"Which way?"

"I'm going east, same as you." Jerence seemed far more animated
than the previous afternoon.

I was dubious. "What are you doing on foot?"

"Thought I'd walk to Cary Mantiet's, since it's a nice day, but since
you're headed that way anyhow . . ." He paused, then said politely, "I'd
appreciate a lift, if you don't mind."

"Of course." I made room for him next to me in the back seat.

"Thanks." He hopped in, unstrapping the knapsack.

"What are you lugging?" I asked, to make conversation.

Jerence shot me a suspicious look. "Nothing. Just stuff."

With a pang of nostalgia I remembered my thirteenth year, running
free with my friend Jason, before the football riots of '90. We had our
secrets from the adult world, as did this joey.

"Very well." We turned onto the main road. There was no traffic in
sight; outside of Centraltown I expected none.

Alexi said, "We've time to make it home tonight if we try, sir."

I thought of Annie, and found the idea appealing. As if reading my
mind, Eddie Boss drove a touch faster.

Alexi ventured, "About that other matter I mentioned, sir?"

I glanced at Jerence. "Later, when we're alone."

"Aye aye, sir." Alexi stared out his window, brooding. "I'm glad to be
out of there," he muttered. "Too much antagonism."

"They have cause."

"But some are looking for trouble."

I grunted, not wanting to discuss the matter in front of the boy.

"Ms. Triforth and Mantiet are odd ducks. I wouldn't trust them
any—"

I said sharply, "Another time, Lieutenant."

"Aye aye, sir." Alexi subsided.

We reached the end of Branstead lands, and as the road curved we
came upon the Mantiet marker that signaled the border of his estate.
"Where should we drop you, boy?"

"Outside the main gate, please," said Jerence.

Eddie slowed for the curve, then pumped the brakes hard. Ahead, a
grain hauler was jackknifed across the road, blinkers flashing. "Careful,
Mr. Boss," I said.

We neared the accident. The scene was deserted.

"Where's the driver?" asked Alexi.

I snapped, "How should I know?"

"Odd that no one's here." Jerence.

"He's probably gone to the manse for—"

"Get us *OUT* of here!" Alexi reached across, jammed his foot on the gas, twisted the wheel. We lurched away from the truck.

"Alexi! What in hell are—"

A flash of white light. Stupendous pressure. A giant hand tossed our electricar into the air. A rending crash. We slammed into the bole of a huge genera tree.

Pitched from the broken vehicle, I lay dazed, my ribs aching abominably. I coughed, waiting for the salty taste of blood, but none came. It seemed too much effort to sit. Minutes passed.

The squeal of brakes. A door slammed, then footsteps.

"Good Christ!"

"Don't blaspheme," I mumbled.

Someone poured water from a canteen onto a cloth, and held it to my head. I struggled to prop myself against the genera.

"Are you all right, sir?"

I started at the familiar voice of Emmett Branstead. "Yes, I think so." I leaned against the trunk.

"We've called a heli ambulance from Centraltown."

"I don't need one."

"Not for you," Branstead's tone was grim.

Oh, Lord God. "Help me up. Please."

Clutching his arm I staggered to my feet. Eddie Boss sat dazed, nursing a broken wrist. Alexi Tamarov's head was cradled in his lap.

"Alexi?" I fell to my knees.

No answer. Blood oozed from Alexi's nose and ear. His mouth was half open, and his breathing was ragged.

"No!" I eased my arm under his head, felt something soft and wet. My hand came away red. I closed my eyes.

"What happened, sir?" Though Emmett Branstead was no longer a seaman, discipline died hard.

I blinked. "I don't know." Frowning, I tried to recall. "A hauler had jackknifed. An explosion . . ."

Branstead snorted. "I'll say." He pointed to the road. "Look at that crater."

"Never mind that. Look to Alexi."

"I'm no med tech, sir. Are you?"

I bit back a vile reply. "No."

Eddie said, "My han' all broke up." He sounded plaintive.

"I know, Mr. Boss."

"Hadda carry Mist' Tamarov outadere, only one han'."

I snarled, "Why did you move him?"

Eddie shrugged. "Dunno if be fire in dere."

"Electricars don't blow up, you trannie fool!"

He stared at me without expression. "Neither do roads," he said with meticulous enunciation.

After a long moment I had to look away. "I'm sorry," I muttered. "Mr. Boss, Mr. Branstead, I beg you both to forgive me."

Eddie grinned mirthlessly. "Cap'n shook up, all of us be." He pointed to his lap. "I put my coat unner his head, make him as comf'ble as I can."

"Thank you." It was hard to meet his eye. I cleared my throat. "Where's the bloody heli?"

"It'll probably be a good half hour." Emmett Branstead.

I cursed under my breath. My ribs aching, I paced helplessly until at last we heard blades beating in the distance. A small heli set down in the center of the road.

But it wasn't the ambulance. Harmon Branstead jumped out, ran toward us. "I was in the granary when you called, Emmett. What in God's grace is going on?"

Emmett Branstead returned his brother's quick embrace. "I'd say an ambush. Someone tried to kill Captain Seafort."

My mind reeled. "What?"

Emmett gave me a strange look. "You think we blow up roads for amusement? What did you imagine happened?"

"Some sort of accident. The truck, dangerous cargo . . ."

"We don't use explosives here. The dirt is soft; we just sculpt it with a bulldozer. Anyway, look at the hauler."

The abandoned cargo hauler was twisted by the force of the blast. "What about it?"

"It's still there," Emmett replied, impatient. "If the cargo had exploded, there would be nothing left of the hauler. The explosive must have been buried in the road. The hauler was there to make you stop."

"But why—how do you know it was me they were after?"

Harmon said, "Who else? Your driver?"

I swallowed, trying to take it all in. "Harmon, can you take us to a hospital?"

Emmett said, "Wait for the medevac heli, Captain. Don't try to move him." I looked down at Alexi and nodded with reluctance.

Harmon's eye roved past Eddie to the genera under which Jerence stood quietly. Harmon crossed the distance in quick strides. He studied his son without expression. Abruptly he slapped the boy's face. Jerence recoiled, his hand rising to his reddened cheek.

Harmon slapped him again. "Into the heli!" Jerence bit back a sob, ran to the open door. Emmett Branstead looked grim.

"What's going—what was that—"

Harmon asked, "Why were you taking my son to Centraltown?" His eyes were hard.

"Centraltown? Nonsense; he asked for a ride to the Mantiet place."

"Why?"

"To see his friend Cary Mantiet."

Harmon glared at me until Emmett intervened. "Frederick Mantiet has no children, Captain. Harmon, he didn't know."

I took a deep breath, ignoring the pain in my bruised ribs. "What in Lord God's own hell is this about?"

Harmon's shoulders sagged. He shook his head, walked back to the waiting heli.

Emmett said softly, "My nephew was running away, Captain. He's done it twice before." I gaped; he shrugged, as if in apology. "I assume he asked for a ride to Mantiet's because he figured you wouldn't take him to the city. He probably meant to hop a grain hauler the rest of the way."

"But why?"

Emmett said quietly, "For the family's sake, keep this to yourself."

I nodded.

"He can't buy goofjuice out here. Only in Centraltown."

I said bleakly, "His life wasted, at thirteen."

Emmett stared at the open heli door. "Lord God knows why. Or how he gets it. He's on the edge: habituated, but not yet fully addicted."

Goofjuice. I'd seen the results of its use, years ago on *Hibernia*, when crewmen had smuggled some aboard. The user is quite happy while he's sailing high. He may, with perfectly good cheer, slaughter his best friend. Perhaps afterward he might feel remorse.

"Haven't they tried . . . I mean, doctors—"

"Everything short of having him committed."

Harmon emerged from the heli and hurried toward us. "Sorry about that. Personal problems. I called Centraltown; the ambulance will be here in five minutes."

Emmett crouched next to Alexi. "He's still breathing, sir. He may have a chance. It's amazing what modern surg—"

I grated, "Who did this?"

Harmon shook his head. "We're crossing Mantiet land. Frederick left yesterday in anger, but I can't believe—"

"Why isn't he here? Didn't he hear the explosion?"

"I don't know. I called the house, but he's out. His wife didn't know where, or how long."

Emmett asked, "Whose hauler is that, Harmon?"

"I don't recognize it. We can trace it by the transponder number or the engine serial number, if it comes to that."

The welcome thump of a heli grew audible. "Make sure it's done." My voice was tight.

If the hauler was his, Frederick Mantiet could be seized for questioning under polygraph and truth drugs. Thank Lord God that the Truth in Testimony Act of 2026 abolished the ridiculous right to silence that had hampered criminal investigations for centuries. These days, once we had a suspect, we got answers.

If Mantiet was guilty, the sophisticated drugs would force him to admit it, and of course we could then use his confession as evidence in his trial. If he was innocent, he'd suffer only a headache and nausea. After I'd returned home with *Hibernia*, reporting the death of her officers, I'd submitted to extensive questioning with the drugs and poly. It wasn't pleasant, but it cleared me of suspicion.

Harmon was grim. "Oh, yes, we'll find whose hauler that is. My son was in your car too."

The heli landed; med techs scrambled out and hovered over Alexi. His head bandaged and supported, they eased him onto a stretcher and bundled him into the heli. Eddie Boss and I climbed aboard.

"Find out," I shouted as we lifted off. From Harmon, a grim nod.

5

"Sorry, the Admiral isn't here."

I scowled at Lieutenant Eiferts as if it were his fault. Then I sighed. "When will he be back?"

"Probably not for a while, sir. He went up to Orbit Station, and from there he may take a ship to review the squadron positions."

"Why bother? They're in the puter." I regretted it almost instantly, but it was too late.

The lieutenant said carefully, "I wouldn't know, sir." I wondered if he'd repeat my disparaging remark to De Marnay.

"I've been trying to reach him for three days, Mr. Eiferts."

"Yes, sir."

"Very well." I left Admiralty House with as much dignity as I could muster.

Outside, Annie crouched at the flower beds, gently fingering the geraniums. She straightened. "Will he see you?"

"He's not here." I slipped my hand into hers as we walked to our rented electricar.

"Oh, Nicky."

"Can't be helped."

Annie had met us at the hospital, showered my face with kisses amid sobs of relief. She'd waited outside the operating room, pressing against my side, while they'd worked to save Alexi. During the five days since, she had followed me wherever possible, unwilling to let me out of her sight even for a trip to the grocer's. "Where to?" she asked now.

"The hospital."

"I called this morning. He no better."

I knew. I had called too. Nonetheless, I could sit at Alexi's side. Tubes in his nose and throat, waste lines attached below the sheets, his monitors maintained their vigil. His brain waves weren't flat; there was hope. I gathered not much hope, though the doctors, as all doctors, were reticent.

At Centraltown Hospital we signed in at the nurses' station and hurried to Alexi's room. He lay unmoving. In the corner Eddie Boss stirred.

"Eddie? What are you doing here?"

"Wanted to wait wid him." The seaman was gruff.

"There's nothing you can do," I said gently.

"Nothin' you can do, neither." Insolence, from a sailor to a Captain. And yet . . . His eyes met mine until I broke contact.

"Very well, Mr. Boss." We sat together, and waited, hoping.

Annie sat next to the hulking sailor. Her hand strayed to Eddie's cast. I'd watched a med tech apply the bone-growth stimulator; Eddie wouldn't have to bear the cast long.

After a silent hour in Alexi's sterile room we left. Eddie followed us to our car. "How often have you been to see him, Mr. Boss?"

"Every day." His look challenged me to object.

"I didn't think you knew Alexi that well."

"Back on *Challenger*. When dem—those Uppies were makin' fun of us. He chase them away, sometimes."

"Ah." More I hadn't known.

Annie opened the car door. "You gonna go see the planters, Nicky?"

It was foolish to visit until I had news to report, but soon they'd decide I was ignoring them. "I suppose I ought to."

"In a heli this time." It was more a demand than a question.

I sighed. "Yes, Annie, in a heli." I looked at Eddie Boss. "I'd like you to look after Annie while I'm gone."

The huge seaman broke into a slow smile. "Aye aye, sir. No joe be messin' wid Annie. I see to dat."

They'd taught me piloting at Academy, and I'd flown a civilian craft on my last visit to Hope Nation. Now, on duty, I rated a military heli. It took me a while to acquaint myself with the heavier machine and its unfamiliar equipment. A miniputer chattered bearings and weather information until I flipped a switch to silence it; I preferred to fly by dumb instruments.

I had no anxiety as I raised the nimble craft off the tarmac and headed for Zack Hopewell's plantation. None about flying, that is. I had no idea how the planters would react when I admitted Admiral De Marnay had made no time for them. I worked out diplomatic phrases in my head: Investigating the allegations. Reviewing their information. Deciding how best to alleviate their grievances.

Zack Hopewell had set on a radar beacon for me, and I let the autopilot home on it. Hopewell and Harmon Branstead were waiting on the lawn when I set the machine down. Hopewell Plantation was similar to the others I'd visited, though there was a sternness, a lack of frivolity about the place that reflected its proprietor.

I followed Zack Hopewell into his manse. Unlike Branstead, he offered no hors d'oeuvres, no liquors, but mugs of hot, steaming coffee and good soft pastries. I chewed on a roll and sipped my coffee gratefully.

They waited.

I addressed Zack Hopewell. "Since I spoke to you last," I began. If only he didn't look so much like Father . . . "I haven't accomplished a thing," I blurted. "I've made several tries but I can't get in to see the Admiral."

Hopewell snorted. "Well, at least he doesn't offer the usual bullshit."

"I'm sorry."

"Your candor is refreshing." He shrugged. "We haven't been able to do much, either. No one knows where Frederick is. With Dora's permission we even searched his house, and I can verify he wasn't there. We traced the hauler; it belongs to him and was supposed to be in Centraltown."

"What could Mantiet gain by killing me?"

Harmon's face darkened. "He called you the real enemy, remember? Said we shouldn't waste our blood fighting among ourselves instead of you."

"Still, how does he benefit?"

"If he wants to disrupt the Government, eliminating a reasonable voice would be in his interest."

"That's treason!" I could conceive of murder for personal gain. But rebellion against the lawfully ordained Government of Lord God Himself? On Terra, we'd had no revolution since the Rebellious Ages ended, over a century ago. I tasted bile.

Harmon said carefully, "I didn't say treason. I said disruption."

A distinction without a difference. I was about to say as much when Zack Hopewell intervened. "In any event, Mantiet will confirm the truth when he's caught."

"Yes." I sat again, slowly. "I wish I could tell you Admiralty was anxious to correct its mistakes. Perhaps they will be, when I manage to inform them."

"You didn't submit a written report?"

"Of course. I dropped off my chip the day after I returned. But still . . ." I doubted De Marnay would take action unless I personally warned him of the planters' vehemence. Perhaps not even then.

"I don't know what Mantiet thinks, but Laura wants to revise the Planetary Charter," Harmon said. "Eliminate the Governorship, elect a council from among the planters."

"She needs to take that up with the U.N. at home," I said stiffly. "It's not my province."

"No," said Harmon. "But you should be aware of it."

We broke for a light lunch, and afterward I stopped at the Palabees for a brief visit before returning home. I was revving the throttle when a call came from Hopewell.

"A Miss Wells called, Captain. She wanted urgently to speak with you."

I muttered under my breath. It was folly to allow my personal life to mix with duty. I thought of returning her call, but I was leaving anyway, and would be home in an hour or so. I relayed a message to that effect and started my engine.

Annie met me at the door, her eyes red. "Dey call here coupla hours back, sayin' *Concord* be leavin' in morning. I gotta be ready go, ten o'clock."

"Oh, Annie." I took her into my arms. I'd known it was to come, yet . . .

She sniffled. "I be all ri' on Detour, Nicky. Be wid trannies, 'n all."

"With, not wid," I said automatically. We'd struggled so hard.

"With," she said dutifully.

We wandered into the bedroom. Her bag was on the bed, half packed. My voice was dull. "I wish you could stay."

"I know, Nicky."

"They'll give me a ship soon, and you couldn't go with me."

"I know." She smiled through tears. "How I get all my fancy clothes in? Gonna need 'nother case."

"We'll get one. The best that money can buy." I grabbed her hand. "And that ruby necklace you liked, at the jewelers."

Her eyes widened. "Really? Oh, Nick, you don' have ta do that."

I was already regretting my impetuosity; the bauble would cost me almost two months pay. But what would I spend it on, alone? "I don't mind," I said manfully. I led her to the door and the waiting car.

Hours later, necklace shining against the pale satin of her dress, we came back to the apartment, my pleasure already dampened by her impending departure. I keyed the lock. "Just a minute," she said, and went to the bedroom.

I sat disconsolately, knowing I would soon hate this place. Perhaps I would move into Naval barracks.

She called, "C'n you help me with this, Nicky?"

"Can't close the case, hon? Should we have bought the bigger one?" I went into the bedroom.

Nude, she stood outlined against the window, ruby necklace sparkling in the soft evening light, hands cupping her breasts. Slowly she raised her hands to the clasp. "Show me how this works, Nicky."

I came behind her, touched the clasp. She turned, slid into my arms, soft, vulnerable, irresistible. Our lips met, then our tongues. I clawed my way out of my jacket and we fell onto the bed.

Later, in the darkened room, I roused myself to pick up the buzzing caller.

"Captain Seafort? Lieutenant Eiferts. I got you a few minutes with Admiral De Marnay in the morning, at ten."

"Very well." I rang off.

"Who was it?" Annie sounded heavy with sleep.

"The Admiral will finally see me tomorrow. I'll drop you off at the spaceport and walk to Admiralty House."

"That's good, you gettin' talk wid him."

"Yes." I lay back.

A moment later, a sob.

My arms provided what comfort I could. I knew that after tomorrow, I'd never see her again. She'd settle into her new life in one of Detour's many new factories, producing goods so urgently needed by the new-settled colony. We'd write, or at least I would, for a while. Then we would forget each other.

With Lord God's help, I might forget.

In the morning I called the hospital. Alexi remained in coma. His chances of recovery dimmed each day it lasted.

I dressed, inhaled hot coffee at the kitchen table, stared moodily at a holovid copy of the report I'd left for the Admiral. Annie put the last of her gear in her fancy new case.

Somewhere above waited *Concord*, moored at Orbit Station. I puttered about the apartment until it was late enough to justify leaving. We drove past the spaceport, parked in front of Admiralty House, got out of our electricar. The brass plaque gleamed in the bright morning sunlight. Beyond, on the tarmac, the shuttle was already loading. An hour and a half from now, it would dock at Orbit Station.

"Annie, I don't—"

Her smile was radiant. "No, Nick. No good-byes, otherwise I'll cry again."

"I'll miss you so much." My voice was hoarse.

"We was good fo' each other." Despite her resolve her eyes glistened as she hefted her two cases. "Bye, Nicky. Take care a yo'self." Without looking back, she hurried across the tarmac. I watched until she reached the shuttle and disappeared from sight.

I climbed the steps, opened the door. Lieutenant Eiferts said, "I'll tell the Admiral you're here, sir. He'll be a few minutes."

I checked my watch. Five minutes to ten. I sat, stared listlessly at a holozine.

Lieutenant Eiferts said something. I grunted a reply. I had no idea what either of us had said. I stood abruptly.

"Pardon, sir?"

"My apologies to the Admiral. I've been unavoidably detained."

His jaw dropped. "Been what?"

"Detained." Out the double doors, down the steps three at a time. I sprinted across the yard to the tarmac.

The shuttle hatch was closing; I waved frantically as I ran. It reopened. One of the larger shuttles, with row upon row of seats. The pilot raised her eyebrow. "You're too late; our weight is already in the puter."

I climbed aboard. "I'm not going."

She looked at me quizzically. "Then you'll have to dis—"

I peered past rows of heads. "Annie?"

"Captain, we leave in two minutes."

"This won't take two minutes."

"I have to seal my hatches!"

"Yes, ma'am." Where was she? "Annie!"

Slowly she stood, several rows back. Her eyes widened in fear. " 'Bout Alexi? What happened?"

The pilot's protests faded.

I cleared my throat, fumbling for words. As Annie's fingers darted to her necklace, I blurted, "Marry me."

"I—what?"

"Please. Stay with me."

She bit her lip, turned away to hide the tears. "You sure, Nicky? I be'ent righ' kinda joeygirl fo' Cap'n."

I said huskily, "You be joe fo' Cap'n. I sho'."

"Oh, God, Nicky!" She flew into my arms.

I said to the Pilot, "Is there time to off-load her luggage?"

She grinned. "The lady is disembarking?"

My tone was firm. "Yes."

"Then there's plenty of time. I have to recalculate the weight." I gathered she didn't mind.

Annie clung to me, sobbing. I didn't know whether to laugh or cry; I did both.

It took some doing, waiving the banns and all, but we were married the next afternoon in a hastily arranged ceremony in a chapel of the Reunification Cathedral. Eddie Boss was best man. Annie stood radiant in a traditional white-fringed jumpsuit; I wore my dress whites. From time to time during the service my glance strayed upward to the majesty of the domed roof. My only sadness was that though our marriage was in the name of Lord God, my damnation meant He would not bless our union.

Over the caller, Admiral De Marnay listened to my apology without comment. Afterward, Lieutenant Eiferts called to reschedule my appointment for two days later. I'd been forgiven my unthinkable rudeness. Perhaps even my unthinkable marriage, to a despised transpop.

My escapade became known throughout Centraltown, and beyond. Cards of congratulations came from the nurses at the hospital, from Harmon Branstead, from Captain Derghinski on *Kitty Hawk*.

Alexi Tamarov stirred, his eyes vacant, and sank back into deep, unending sleep.

Lieutenant Eiferts was apologetic. "He had to run up to the Station, sir. I'll have to arrange something when he gets back."

Well, it was my own fault; I'd missed my best chance for a meeting. "When will that be?"

"I have no idea, sir."

I hung up, brooding. More days wasted, if not weeks. I'd have to explain the delay to Harmon and Zack Hopewell, a matter I'd rather not dwell on. "Come on, hon, let's go see Alexi."

Annie proudly put her hand in mine, her gold ring glittering.

We found Alexi still unconscious. The floor nurse assured us his brain waves were steady. As usual, Eddie Boss sat glumly in the corner. I realized I'd have to put him to work soon, or transfer him back to regular duty. The silence lengthened.

"I'll get us all some coffee. Be right back." At the other end of the hall, I strove to balance three cups of coffee for the long trip down the corridor.

"Captain Seafort?"

I turned. "Hmm? Oh, Mr. Forbee."

"Here, let me help with that." He held a cup for me.

"Thanks. What are you doing here?"

"Antiviral booster. It was time again." Forbee gestured toward the door. "Seeing your lieutenant, sir?"

"Yes." I was brusque. Forbee could have no idea how I yearned for Alexi's reassuring presence.

"Admiral De Marnay was livid when he heard about the attack on your party. Said to give whatever help you need to investigate."

"We have to find Mantiet." The planter had disappeared with clothing, cash, papers, and supplies. Dora Mantiet seemed panicked, and professed complete ignorance. The Centraltown police had circulated Frederick's picture, hardly necessary in so small a town.

"What are they up to?" Forbee gestured vaguely toward the plantation zone.

"There's going to be trouble. The Admiral should be briefed, but I blew the appointment he gave me."

"I heard." Forbee's eyes twinkled. "He's a busy man. Why don't you meet him at Orbit Station?"

I stopped dead in the corridor. I hadn't thought of that. "Thank you, Forbee. I think I will."

Annie wrapped herself around me tearfully. "You be careful, Nicky. Don' go gettin' yourself hurt."

"I'll be safe, Annie. It's just Orbit Station. You were there yourself."

"Safe!" She sniffed. "Way out in space . . ."

"I'll be back as soon as I can. Visit Alexi tomorrow for me." I swallowed a lump, trying to convince myself I wasn't abandoning him. If anything happened while I was gone . . .

"Eddie will take me," she said. I nodded. She'd be as safe with him as with a platoon of Unie troops, notwithstanding his injured arm.

"I have to run." I gave her a last squeeze, nodded to Eddie Boss, and loped across the field to the waiting shuttle. A few technicians returning from shore leave were the only other passengers. The pilot nodded briefly and returned to his instruments.

Moments later we hurtled down the runway and were airborne. At five thousand feet the pilot raised the nose into a stall and fired the rockets. Pressed into my seat, I gritted my teeth, willing my body to relax as the shuttle roared toward the Station.

As often as I had endured the boost, still I tensed rather than riding with the pressure as my instructors had tried to teach me. I could hear Sarge now. "Ease up, Seafort! Relax your chest muscles. Feel it press you. Just like a woman lay atop you, but I guess you wouldn't know about that." I could feel the blush that heated my face, neck, arms. Sarge's chuckle echoed still.

And then we were free, floating weightless, thrusters silent. Nothing to do but wait. I planned my long-delayed presentation to the Admiral.

As we neared the Station I glanced out the porthole. Most of the bays were closed and empty. Well, we hadn't sent a third of our ships to Hope Nation to keep them moored at Orbit Station; they'd be out patrolling. I noticed a few vessels undergoing repair in the drydock bays. We were too far away to see anyone working.

Strapped in my seat in zero gravity, I leaned into the aisle to watch the pilot, his entire attention on the meticulous docking procedure. When at last our airlock seals were mated with the Station's, the cabin lights brightened and I got gratefully to my feet, flexing my muscles.

Technicians bustled past in the bright station lights. I knew my way to the Commandant's office; I'd been there several times before. I assumed that's where I'd find Admiral De Marnay.

In the reception area for the Commandant's office a sergeant looked me over, unimpressed. He was U.N.A.F., not Navy.

"Your Admiral? No, if he's on station he'd be in the Naval corridor."

"And General Tho?"

"In a meeting," the sergeant said. "May last awhile. I could page you when he's free."

"Don't bother him. I'll find the Admiral."

He grinned without humor. "Don't get lost, Navy."

"No problem," I said immediately. "I like it groundside." I slipped out before he could reply. Interservice rivalry didn't bring out the best in me. Not much did, these days.

Despite my bravado it took me over an hour to locate the Naval corridor, and I had to backtrack at least once. I'm not sure about the second time.

A lieutenant I'd seen before greeted me at the entranceway. "You had an appointment, sir?"

"No, but I need to see the Admiral anyway." I spoke with a confidence I didn't feel.

"Yes, sir. Sorry, but he went with *Vestra*. They're somewhere outside the orbit of Planet Four."

"I see." Any idiot would have known to call ahead; why didn't I?

"He's not due back until tomorrow." *Vestra* could Fuse here in minutes, in an emergency, so De Marnay wasn't really out of touch. But why did he keep taking these jaunts? Was he hungry for ship time, like me? The lieutenant chewed at his lip. "Sir, would you like me to signal him you're here?"

"No thanks," I said quickly. Such presumption would not go over well, especially after I'd broken my last appointment.

"You're welcome to stay in Naval barracks overnight, sir. I'm sure the Admiral would authorize it."

"Thank you." I tried to lift my flagging spirits. "It'd give me time to look around."

"The Level 4 restaurant isn't bad, or you could try the officers' mess. And if you'd care to listen to traffic, you could visit the comm room."

Was it an invitation to leave? I couldn't tell, but in any event there was no point in hanging around the Admiral's office. "Page me if *Vestra* docks," I said.

"Of course, sir."

I wouldn't go to the comm room, not immediately. I wandered along the circumference corridor until I found Naval barracks and signed myself in. They gave me a private room, almost as large as a Captain's cabin aboard ship.

I wandered through Naval territory, stopped at the mess for a quick supper, then tramped back to General Tho's wing of the Station. He would remember me, if I could arrange an appointment. These days I was having trouble getting to see anybody.

"Mr. Seafort, is that you?" He stood in the entryway to the Commandant's wing, chatting with an officer.

I gawked. "Uh, yes. Yes, sir." I shook hands with the short, elegantly groomed man. "How are you, General Tho?"

"Fine, fine. How long have you been on station?"

"A couple of hours. I was hoping to see the Admiral."

"He's on *Vestra*."

"So I learned."

"Come in." He led the way to his comfortable, spacious office. We passed through the reception area. His arm on my shoulder, the General ushered me past the astounded receptionist.

"I missed you when *Hibernia* came in, Mr. Seafort. And then you, ah, were injured."

Nearly killed in my foolish duel, he meant. "Yes." Politeness demanded something more than that. "I'm recovered, and on shore duty now."

"With our beloved planters."

"Yes, sir."

"They think the planet revolves around them." He sighed. "Well, I suppose it does. Hope Nation's agribusiness is the reason we're here. It's why we can afford a station as huge as this." He waved me to a chair. "The planters are a Naval problem, thank Lord God. Not mine."

I gazed at the simulscreen filling one wall of his office. It offered a view of Hope Nation system, from the periphery of the Station.

"Basically, they stuck with your plan, you know."

I said, "Pardon?"

"When you left here three years ago, you told Forbee to accept my orders so we'd have a unified command. They kept the unified command, but Navy has more pull than U.N.A.F., so your Admiral's in charge. He ranks even over the civilian Governor." He fished in his desk drawer, brought out glasses and a bottle. "Drink? Good. I don't mind about the command, actually. I've got my hands full running the Station, with the traffic your squadron brings. Don't need Naval jurisdiction or civilian oversight to keep me busy."

I said, meaning it, "Not many men could turn away power with as few regrets, General."

He smiled, handing me a glass of Scotch. "Oh, I won't say I didn't have some choice words for William when the news came, before I had a chance to reflect on it."

"For whom?"

"I'm William, sir." A confident baritone voice from all around me. I jumped, spilling my Scotch.

"Sorry, Captain." General Tho grinned. "Multiple speakers. They're rather startling, at first."

"Permit me to introduce myself," said the baritone. "W-30304, at your service. Colloquially known as William."

"Your, ah, ship's puter?" I brushed beads of liquid from my knee.

A short silence. William's tone was frosty. "I am to a ship's puter what your puter is to an Arcvid."

"Uh, pardon me."

A microsecond's pause before he relented. "I understand your confusion, sir. You're Navy, and according to your personnel file you've never spent extended time on a station. No offense taken. You're aware of all the functions your puter monitors aboard ship? Hydroponics, recycling, and so on?"

"Of course." I felt foolish. General Tho listened with a grin.

"Well, I do all that for the Station on a much larger scale, but I also record and evaluate all tightbeam transmissions from the puters in each of your ships, as they arrive. In addition, I monitor all Station traffic and cargo selection, storage, and loading."

"I see." He would have stupendous data banks, and a RAM that was breathtaking.

"Before I leave you to your conversation, may I say I've heard a lot about you, Captain Seafort."

"Oh?" Did they program the holozines into him?

"From Darla."

"I see."

He chuckled. "Darla is quite opinionated, but I take her conclusions with a grain of salt."

I thought of asking what data from my old ship's puter William viewed skeptically, but decided against it. "Uh, thank you."

William said nothing.

I turned back to General Tho. I might as well make use of my visit. "Sir, have you heard much about the groundside base?"

"In the Venturas? Never actually been there. I gather U.N. Command wanted to land a force capable of defending the planet itself, in case of invasion." He shook his head. "Can't see it, myself. Groundside could only be invaded if the fleet were destroyed, and then the aliens would have air superiority to wipe out a ground force."

"Lord God forbid." I repressed a shudder.

"And why put our forces halfway across the planet from Centraltown?" He grimaced. "See what happens when you try to run a war from a distance? They should have left it in local hands."

"What kind of invasion is the base designed to counter?"

He sipped moodily at his drink. "They're equipped with all sorts of antiviral synthesizers and pandemic vaccines. But mainly they're a laser installation. Got a hell of a battery of cannon, if they finish setting it up. Could knock out just about anything."

"Lasers don't seem to do much good," I reflected. "The fish Fuse as soon as we get their range."

"Well, what else should we use?" he snorted. "Atomics?"

Lord God forbid. General Tho skated on thin ice even joking about it. Not only the use of atomic weapons but any proposal to employ them carried a mandatory death penalty. Ever since the Last War, the national governments at home were united in enforcing the ban. A hundred forty years after the last horrid bomb lit Terran skies, frightful scars remained.

We finished our drinks. When he glanced at his watch I knew it was time to go. We shook hands again; I went directly to the barracks and to bed.

I slept surprisingly well. In the morning I downed powdered eggs and burnt toast while I sipped at my coffee. My breakfast was interrupted by a midshipman bringing me a chip faxed from Centraltown. With sudden anxiety I snapped open the case and slipped it into a holovid.

"Your Lieutenant Tamarov is out of coma. Dazed but apparently lucid, according to initial reports. I thought you'd like to know immediately. Forbee." Thank you, Lord God.

"Any reply, sir?"

I looked up. The boy was waiting. "No. Dismissed." Gratefully he hurried away.

My breakfast was delicious.

After leaving the mess I couldn't help myself; I checked with Naval HQ in case the duty lieutenant had forgotten to page me, but Admiral De Marnay hadn't returned. I paced the sterile corridors until I remembered the lieutenant's suggestion of the previous day. The comm room was halfway around the disk. On a large station, a good distance. I set out, my step jaunty. Alexi was healing.

In the comm room the Navy techs gave me an informal salute but stayed at their places, as was proper when the Station was at a high degree of alert. I pulled up a chair. "Anything doing?"

"No, sir. A few puters on tightbeam with each other, but nothing for us." He hesitated. "Sir, you're, ah, Captain Seafort?"

"Yes."

"Do you think . . ." He fumbled in his pocket. "Sorry if I'm out of line, sir, but could I have your autograph?"

I bridled. What was Naval discipline coming to? At my frown he quickly thrust the paper back into his jacket and bent to his console. "Sorry, sir."

I sighed. "Never mind. Give it here." They had few enough diversions, on extended station duty. I scribbled my name. Shamefacedly, the others crowded round, scraps of paper materializing from pockets and consoles.

"I saw you in the zines, sir. Did you know you made the cover of *Newsworld?*"

Another tech gave the speaker a nudge in the ribs. "Of course he knows, you idiot." I smiled politely. I hadn't. We sat in uncomfortable silence for several minutes.

A console light flashed. The voice on the speaker sounded weary. "Station, we're about to test the airlock again. Disregard signals, please."

"Very well, *Portia.*"

"*Portia's* here?" My heart beat faster.

"Yes, sir. In the repair bay."

I stood. "I'd like to see her. Which way?"

I followed their directions to the repair bays. *Portia* had been my first assigned command. I'd sailed with such high hopes, with my unborn son, my wife Amanda, with Vax Holser, with Alexi.

I found the bay, cycled through the Station's lock to *Portia*'s, and pressed the entry pad. A moment later the lock slid open and a young middy came quickly to attention. "Good afternoon, sir."

"As you were," I said gruffly. "I'm Captain Seafort. May I enter?"

"Captain Akers isn't aboard, sir. No one is, except my lieutenant, and he's sleeping. And the Chief, doing repairs."

"I didn't want Captain Akers." I felt foolish. "*Portia* was my ship once. I just wanted to . . ." My voice trailed off. How could I explain the whim that had overtaken me, without seeming an idiot? "I wanted to see her again," I said firmly. "Visit her bridge."

The boy swallowed, nervous in the presence of such exalted rank. Well, that was as it should be. A word from me could have him caned without a moment's pause. "I don't think they'd mind, sir, while we're moored. The bridge is this way."

I suppressed a smile. "I know."

He colored. "Yes, of course, sir. Sorry. If you care to go ahead, I'll inform the duty lieutenant."

"Very well." He scurried off while I made my way to the bridge. My chest tightened as I passed my old cabin. Within its confines, tiny Nate had died. I could almost feel Amanda's presence. I hurried past the first lieutenant's cabin, once Vax Holser's. I had spurned his help, at the cost of his friendship. Past the wardroom, where Philip Tyre had struggled manfully to redeem himself. The second lieutenant's cabin, where Alexi savored revenge against Philip until its taste soured in his mouth. Oh, Alexi, what have we done to you?

The bridge hatch was open; docked and under repair, *Portia* was virtually decommissioned.

I glanced at the simulscreens that dominated the bridge. They were blank, of course. On the console, an airlock light blinked.

I cleared my throat, suddenly shy. "Danny?" At one time the eager young puter had been my only confidant. No answer. "Puter, respond by voice, please."

A dull, machinelike voice said, "D 20471 responding. Please identify yourself."

"Captain Nicholas Seafort, U.N.N.S. Uh, reactivate conversational overlays." How could they have locked him inside for so long?

A warm contralto issued from the speaker. "Thank you, Captain. How may I help you?"

I blinked. "Danny? You sound different."

"I'm Diane, sir. Ship's puter."

Unthinking, I dropped into the Captain's seat, no longer mine to occupy. "Where's Danny?" I asked.

Diane hesitated a microsecond. "I have all Danny's memory and data banks, sir."

My hand tightened on the chair. "Where's Danny?"

An irate voice, in the corridor. "Middy, let anyone board without permission again and I'll have you over the barrel so fast you'll—"

I turned to the hatch.

"Lieutenant Tolliver repor—" We gaped in mutual astonishment.

Edgar Tolliver. A year older than I, senior by one class. My persistent tormentor at Academy, where he'd been nominated cadet corporal and put in charge of our dormitory. Sour memories welled.

His eyes flickered to my insignia. He came to attention.

"As you were," I grated. "What happened to Danny?"

Tolliver said carefully, "Diane has been the puter since I've been aboard, sir. I understand Admiral Tremaine ordered complete powerdown after he took *Portia*."

"Why?" My voice was hoarse.

He started to shrug, remembered he was in a Captain's presence. "I believe he was making sure you hadn't sabotaged the puter, sir."

I swung to the speaker. "Diane, what happened to Danny? His personality?"

"It's gone, disassembled with powerdown."

"Is he retrievable?" But I already knew the answer.

Her tone held a note of finality. "No, sir. He is not."

I sank back, dazed. My friend Danny, who'd pondered whether he had a soul. Who'd comforted me after the death of Amanda. Gone.

Derek, Danny, Vax, all lost.

I began to cry.

From the hatch Tolliver watched impassively. I fought to control myself. "Sorry," I mumbled. "It was a shock."

"Quite all right, sir."

"Thank you for having me aboard." Humiliated, I stumbled off the bridge, drying my eyes as I fled down the corridor. Tolliver and the young midshipman saw me off at the airlock.

I trudged back to the comm room. Was it blasphemy to pray for Danny's soul? I decided that regardless of the risk, I would. If Lord God could listen to one such as I.

At the comm room the tech waved me to my seat, his ear to his headphones. "Confirm, *Freiheit*, two sightings quadrant seventeen."

"What's afoot?" I asked.

The speaker crackled. "Station, *Calumet* en route to sector four, quadrant sixteen as per orders."

The tech's voice shook with excitement. "Fish! Confirmed, no false alarm. *Freiheit*'s engaging, with *Valencia* coming on. The rest of the fleet's moving into position."

I sat listening as the great ships reported their locations. Orders flowed and were instantly confirmed and obeyed. The speakers crackled with a flood of data.

"*Freiheit* reporting. Two fish, alongside! We're under attack. They're launching those, uh, outriders. Permission to Fuse!" Captain Tenere sounded anxious, as well he might.

De Marnay. "Where's *Valencia*?"

"*Valencia*, here, sir. Coordinates eighteen, one thirty-five, sixty-two. About half an hour from *Freiheit*."

"Very well, *Freiheit*. Set coordinates and Fuse to safety, minimum distance, then report immediately."

"Aye aye, sir. Engine Room, Fuse!" Tenere's radio went dead.

"*Valencia* reporting. Where do you want us, sir?"

"Mr. Groves, wait for *Freiheit* to reappear. If she's close enough, go to her on thrusters, else Fuse to her."

"I'll need an hour to reach Fusion clearance, sir—Whoops!" The voice tightened. "Three more fish, two ahead, one alongside, matched velocities! Engaging!"

"*Kitty Hawk* here. I've got three sightings." Derghinski read his coordinates.

Admiral De Marnay. "All ships, execute Maneuver B!"

Fists knotted, I watched the screens while the armada moved ponderously, our ships expending prodigious amounts of propellant to reach their new stations, hours distant.

"*Freiheit* Defused and reporting. New position quadrant eleven, grid coordinates eighteen, two oh three, fifteen."

"Very well, Mr. Tenere."

"Where do you want us to—Good Christ!"

"*Freiheit*?"

"Four, five, half a dozen fish! They're all over us! We're taking hits. Decompression. Sealing—"

The caller went dead.

"*Valencia* under fire. Two fish. We're firing back. There goes one of them, by Christ. Spewing his guts!"

My throat dry, I listened to snatches of disaster and success.

Behind me, in the Station, an alarm wailed. "*NOW HEAR THIS!* Battle Stations! All off-duty personnel and all visitors disembark Orbit Station at once! Shuttles departing in three minutes!"

I jumped to my feet and ran to Naval HQ. The outer office was empty; I opened the inner hatch and found myself in the plotting room. "Can I be of help?"

A harried Captain shot me an annoyed look. "Stay out of the way. You're off duty."

"Can I plot—"

"You'd better get groundside, Mr., ah, Seafort. If we come under attack there's nothing you can do here."

Reluctantly I said, "Aye aye, sir." It wasn't time to argue.

I reached the shuttle bay just as the safety hatches began to close. On the shuttle I dropped into a seat, struggling to catch my breath.

"Passengers, prepare for launch, please. Departure Control, Shuttle Charlie Fox four oh six ready to launch."

The reply was almost immediate. "Cleared to launch, Four oh six."

The huge shuttle bay hatch slid open. Gently at first, our thrusters drummed propellant against the launch bay's protective shields, ejecting us from the Station. I peered through the porthole. Behind us, the bright-lit Station sailed placidly through empty space.

A moment after flipabout our pilot kicked in the jet engines and we became a jet-powered aircraft. As the runway slid into view, the shuttle's stubby wings shifted into VTOL mode. We bled off speed and dropped to the tarmac, the shuttle's underbelly jets cushioning our fall.

I scrambled out of my seat the moment the engines died. When the hatch opened I jumped out to dash across the field. I galloped across the Admiralty House yard and took the front steps two at a time.

Lieutenant Eiferts looked up from his desk.

I gasped, "You have a comm link with Orbit Station?"

"Yes, sir, in the tactics office."

"What Captains are here now?"

"None, sir, other than yourself." For a moment I imagined a reproach.

"Very well. I'm going up." There was none to stop me. I hurried upstairs, bracing myself for an unpleasant encounter with Vax Holser.

"Attention!" A voice rang out in the enclosed space.

Lieutenants and midshipmen came out of their chairs. "As you were."
I saw with relief that Vax was not among them. I found an empty seat.
"Brief me, someone."

A familiar face. "Lieutenant Anton, sir. We're under attack. Hostiles,
Fusing in at random intervals."

I already knew that. "Go on."

"The fleet's deployed, sir, as per Maneuver B. You're familiar with
the plan, of course."

"No, you bloody—" I bit back the rest. It wasn't his fault I so desperately wanted a ship. "I was on shoreside duty when the plan was issued."

"Yes, sir. The fleet was divided, lightly patroling all sectors to maxi-
mize our chance of making contact. When the fish appeared, the Admiral
ordered our ships to regroup into flotillas at preassigned locations within
each sector. That's Maneuver B. Any ship under attack automatically became the locus for the flotilla in that sector."

"Very well."

"We count about thirty fish in all, sir."

"But that's—" Lord God. More than we'd ever seen before.

"Yes, sir."

"What are your standing orders, Lieutenant?"

"The Admiral's running the show from *Vestra*, sir. He communicates
with Orbit Station by tightbeam. If he'd been here, it would be our office
sending out fleet signals. While De Marnay's in orbit, his commands are
relayed from the Station. Our job is to record them and serve as a backup,
should—should . . ." He faltered.

"Yes?"

"Should the Station be damaged, sir."

"Lord God grant that it is not." I stared at the screen, trying to make
sense of the blips. "What else do we know, Lieutenant?"

"*Freiheit* reported decompression. *Kitty Hawk* caught a transponder
beam from her launch but hasn't had time to home on it. *Valencia's*
snuffed two fish, and *Hibernia's* taken out four."

"Good."

The speaker crackled. "This is *Resolute*. We're engaging two fish. I—
damn, make that three! Am firing."

The Admiral responded, "Very well, *Resolute*. *Kitty Hawk* is your
closest support."

"Yes, sir. Derghinski, I'll ring if I need you." Gallows humor. I knew
the impulse.

"Belay that!" The Admiral.

"Aye aye, sir." *Resolute's* Captain, chastened.

"*Kitty Hawk* here. The bastards keep Fusing when we line up a shot."
Derghinski swore. "Here come two more!"

I stared at the screen. Was I watching a coordinated attack or a feeding frenzy? Perhaps I'd never know.

"Admiral, *Kitty Hawk* reporting. We've taken a hit. Lost our portside thruster but otherwise undamaged. Got the fish." Without port thrusters Derghinski's maneuvering would be infinitely more complicated, and far slower.

"Very well."

"*Resolute*, here. We've got four beasties Fused in. Two amidshi—Oh, Jesus, they're—" Silence.

Lord God, save our people.

Lieutenant Anton pounded the console. "Where the hell are they coming from?" He glanced, saw my disapproval. "Sorry, sir."

I grunted. I too would like to know. More important, *why* did they come?

De Marnay's voice, calm. "Station, *Vestra* is under attack. Only one fish at present. Taking evasive—He's let a tentacle fly. Think he's going to miss." A long pause. "If I fail to respond for ten minutes, assume I'm out of commission. Captain Vorhees is senior, on *Electra*. Station, do you acknowledge?"

General Tho himself answered. I could sense the small, dark man pacing his office, fingers smoothing his neat little mustache. "Yes, Admiral, we do. It's in your standing orders."

"Admiralty House, do you copy?"

Lieutenant Anton keyed the caller. "Yes, sir."

"Who's on duty?"

"I am, sir: Anton. With Mr. Zalla and the techs. And three middies. Mr. Eiferts is below."

"You're senior, aren't you?"

"Uh, yes, sir. But Captain Seafort's with us."

"Seafort? What's he—Put him on."

I scrambled for the caller. "Yes, sir?"

"They know the drill, Seafort. Don't interfere."

"Yes, sir." My cheeks burned.

He hesitated. "Still, it's good you're there. If anything happens to me, you're in charge at Admiralty House until the chain of command is reestablished."

"Aye aye, sir."

He broke the connection.

We sat through the interminable afternoon, long dull periods of inaction, punctuated by terse reports of fish sighted, ships engaged, positions reached.

The fish kept coming.

We'd lost *Resolute* and *Freiheit*. *Kitty Hawk* broke off and limped back to Orbit Station, emergency patches on her hull.

We lost *Valencia*.

As inconclusively as the attack had begun, it dwindled. Finally, hours had passed with no further reports of attack. The surviving ships searched grimly for enemies, without success, but their sailors couldn't be kept at Battle Stations indefinitely. Our armada stood down.

It was late into the night before I left Admiralty House, drained and exhausted. We'd done nothing but listen and record, yet I felt as if I'd been in the thick of battle. My nerves tingled with the rush of adrenaline and fear.

Disoriented, I looked for my electricar, realized that Annie had dropped me at the spaceport the day before for my trip aloft. Without qualms I ordered a midshipman to drive me home in an Admiralty car. After all, I was acting Head of Station.

I brooded while we rode in silence through deserted streets. No one knew from where the fish came. Our xenobiologists suggested a large, low-density planet near a hot sun, but that was merely guesswork. We had no idea whether the fish themselves, or their outriders, were the dominant species. Perhaps they were symbiotes. They might even be different elements within one species. Both fish and outriders appeared to be unicellular organisms on a hitherto unimaginable scale. Were either species intelligent, or did they attack instinctively, without reason?

The middy cleared his throat. "Pardon, is that your building, sir?"

I nodded, realized he couldn't see in the dark. "Yes. Let me out in front."

"Aye aye, sir."

At the curb I got out, waved him off. In the distance boisterous shouts echoed. Some drunken melee, downtown.

So, what were we to do about the invaders? The U.N. had seventeen major colonies on hospitable worlds, and more planned. We mined a number of less-livable worlds for ores and fissionable elements. Our Navy couldn't possibly defend all our colonies at once; it would require ten times the ships we had, and each represented a colossal investment.

I trudged slowly up the walk, absently noting the twin shadows cast by Major and Minor. Could we abandon our colonies, withdraw to home system? Even retreat wouldn't free us from peril, unless our fleet stopped Fusing. Perhaps even that was too late; at least one fish had appeared in home system, mortally wounded, speared by *Challenger*'s prow in our last desperate attack.

I touched my thumb to the lock and let myself in quietly so as not to wake Annie.

Until we learned how many fish existed, we couldn't know if our fleet had the strength to protect Hope Nation, or if we'd be overwhelmed and annihilated. Today we'd lost three ships, and on them men I'd entertained in this very apartment. Captain Tenere of *Freiheit*, missing and presumed dead. Lieutenant Ter Horst of *Resolute*.

I groped my way to my favorite living-room chair, slipped off my shoes. Well, Mr. Ter Horst had met his aliens, and his optimism hadn't been justified. In the bedroom Annie stirred, moaned; a bad dream. Would she have been safer on Detour? For that matter, would *Concord* ever reach port there, or would the fish ravage her en route? Had I saved Annie's life, or held her back in greater peril?

Annie moaned again. I stood, my limbs weary. I was the one accustomed to nightmares; if my wife began having them too . . .

I padded to the bedroom door. Morning would be soon enough to worry about the fish. I heard Annie thrash against the sheets. I'd wake her, comfort her.

I opened the door. "Hon, are you all—"

A bare back, broad hips thrusting against upturned thighs, flesh gleaming in the light of two moons, frozen in a petrified moment of silence. As one they turned in shock, stared at the door.

Annie. Eddie Boss.

For an endless moment the tableau held.

I spun, slammed the door, bolted through the darkened living room, fumbled for my shoes. The sound of a window sliding, in the bedroom. I felt along the floor, pawed under the chair.

Eddie. Annie. I barked my shin on the coffee table. Where were the God-cursed shoes?

A shaft of light; the bedroom door opened. My shoes were near the couch where I'd left them.

Annie, a robe thrown over her nakedness. "Nicky?"

I tugged the laces tight on the left shoe, thrust my foot into the right. "Nick . . ."

I stumbled to the door, opened it, lurched outside, fighting not to retch. The moonlight blinded me after the dark of the house. Mechanically I set one foot in front of the other. The walkway stretched to eternity. I reached our car. I couldn't trust myself to drive, not yet. The sidewalk, then. I strode, faster and faster, until my breath rasped and the darkened houses began to give way to the offices and stores of downtown.

I tried to think of nothing. Images intruded. My footsteps echoed, surprisingly loud.

I walked with head down, hands in my pockets. I heard a rasping sob, realized it was my own, cut it off. I crossed a street, then another. I passed an alley. Again I heard the footsteps, understood they weren't mine.

"Well, looka we have here!" A hand spun me around.

"What do you want?" I spat out the words.

"How 'bouta little loan? Few unibucks, 'til payday?" A brutish face leered in reflected moonlight.

Behind him, two broad-shouldered hoodlums snickered. "Skip the bilge, just do him!"

I slapped the hand from my shoulder. The other two joeys circled, their mirth vanished. A knife glinted.

"Hey, for an Uppie, you're kinda—whuf!"

I'd put everything I had into the uppercut. He reeled backward, slammed into the brick wall. His eyes rolled up as he slid to the ground.

"Get the motherfuc—"

The voice sounded like Eddie's. With a howl I hurled myself under the knife, wrenched the joey's arm, butted him in the stomach. He doubled over. I kneed his face with all the strength I could muster. A bone snapped. The third man backed away, hands extended, waving me off. He fled as I charged.

We sprinted through an alley, across an empty lot. Gradually he pulled ahead. Despite my frenzied efforts I fell back, until at last I lost him in the distant shadows. I fell to my knees, chest heaving, heart slamming against my ribs. Slowly the mists cleared.

When I could breathe again, I walked, until the first rays of daylight crept over downtown. I found a restaurant that opened early, sat at the counter sipping at steaming coffee, all I could afford. I'd left my jacket with my ID and money in my living room.

I couldn't abandon all my clothes; I had to go home. I would have to see her, if only for a moment. Where would I stay? Another apartment, perhaps. Or Naval barracks; they were open to me. I dropped a bill on the counter and plodded to the door.

Our apartment was many blocks to the west. Filthy and exhausted, I stumbled along the road, willing the streets to pass. My feet ached.

Ages later I trod the walkway, under a balcony whose view I'd once relished. I pressed my thumb to the lock, took a deep breath, walked in.

Annie lay curled on the couch, eyes red. "Nicky?"

My jacket first. I thrust in my arms. Now I had my papers, my pay, my insignia. An officer again, I felt a shade more secure.

"I'm sorry, Nicky." She sat hunched over, eyes wary. "I din' wan' hurt you."

I would need clothes. I went to the bedroom, opened the closet, slung my duffel on the bed. She'd put on fresh sheets, blanket folded down from the pillow, Navy corners. As if clean sheets could—I forced down the thought. Underwear, shirts, socks. I traded my grimy shirt for a fresh one.

She came to the bedroom door, sagged against it. "Talk to me, Nicky. Please."

I zipped the duffel.

Defiantly she stood in the open doorway, blocking my exit. "You got to unnerstan' one thing," she said. "I din' mean hurt you." Her beseeching eyes met mine. "Eddie an' I, we tribe. We knowed each other since N'Yawk! Tribe alla time doin' it, doncha unnerstan'? Even onna ship. Eddie wasn' only one."

I focused on the closet, desperate not to hear her words. What else would I need in barracks?

She fell into a chair by the door. "If you won' talk, listena me, then. I don' wan' you to go. You be my husban'."

"Until the Church grants an annulment."

She flinched as if struck. "Nicky, there anything I can do, make it up?"

"No."

She cried, "But I love you! Din' mean nothin', what we was doin'!"

My slap knocked her sideways out of the chair, onto her knees. Her fingers crept to her reddened face. I strode to the door, and beyond.

6

I drove through downtown looking for the barracks. I'd never had occasion to visit them but I knew they were behind Centraltown Hospital.

After a few twists and turns I was hopelessly lost. Finally I managed to reorient myself, but seeing the hospital reminded me two days had passed since I'd heard Alexi had wakened from his coma.

I parked, signed into barracks. The bored petty officer at the desk assigned me a room; I saw it had a bed, dumped my duffel on it, closed the door behind me as I left.

At the hospital I trudged wearily to Alexi's room. I opened the door cautiously, lest he be asleep. Alexi, bundled in a robe, sat by the window, hands crossed in his lap.

My heart leapt. "Oh, Alexi! How are you?"

"Not too bad, today." His eyes were on mine, as if awaiting my tidings.

"Thank heaven. We were so worried." Awkwardly I sat on the bed. "You were unconscious for so long . . ."

"Eleven days, they say."

"Does your head hurt?"

"No, but I'm weak as a baby."

I smiled. "We'll take care of that." Annie and I could fatten—My smile vanished. "You'll get your strength back." I stared at the floor. "There's something I need to tell you."

"Yes?" He watched me warily, as if he already knew. Had Annie been here first? She couldn't have. Eddie Boss, then?

"Things aren't going well, Alexi." I stared through the window. "The planters are disgusted that I haven't done anything for them, and at home—"

"I think you'd better—"

"No, let me finish," I said urgently. It was hard to speak, but I knew I must, before I burst. "Annie and I . . . while you were in coma, she and Eddie Boss and I sat with you almost every day. They called her for embarkation on *Concord*, and I married her. I wanted you there, but we didn't know when you'd recover." Or if. My eyes stung.

"Uh, I—"

I blurted, "Alexi, she's been with Eddie. I found them coupling in the bedroom. I took a room in barracks, but I don't know what to do." My voice was unsteady. "Help me. Please."

A moment's silence.

Alexi said, "Could you perhaps tell me who you are?"

An hour later we sat across from each other, Alexi on the bed, me in the chair. "You can't remember Academy either?"

"I'm trying. Don't you know how much I want to remember?"

"I'm not criticizing," I said gently. "Help me understand."

"I've been over it all with the doctors."

"Would you tell me too?"

"Why?"

"For old times' sake. For our friendship."

"I don't have any old times," he said bitterly. "Don't you realize?"

"No!" I flared. "And unless you help me, I never will!"

He recoiled from my wrath. Then, a sardonic smile. "Well, perhaps I deserved that; I wouldn't know. All right. When I woke up, I couldn't figure out where I was. A hospital, obviously, but where?" He shook his head. "They told me Hope Nation. It was . . . I'd heard of it, someplace, like a book I'd read years ago. When they called me 'Alexi,' I knew it was my name. At least I have that."

I ached for him. "Go on."

"They told me I'm a lieutenant in the Navy. It's not that it feels wrong. I can accept being a lieutenant. I just don't remember becoming one. You have to be a midshipman first, don't you?"

I nodded.

"I remember my mother; she lives in Kiev. Before I left for school in the morning she'd thaw my lunch." His eyes showed alarm. "Is she still alive?"

"I don't know, Alexi."

"You said you were my closest friend."

"We were apart a year and a half. And we're a long way from home."

"If anything's happened to her . . ." His eyes filled.

"I'm sure she's all right," I said.

"The snow crunched under my feet on the way to school . . . you had to jiggle the switch to make our classroom holo work. I'm not a boy any longer, but those are my memories!"

"The others will come back."

"How do you know?"

I sighed. "I don't. Not for certain."

"I'd rather die than live like this!" He turned his face.

"Oh, Alexi." I squeezed his shoulder. "You'll be all right."

Alexi turned. Coldly he said, "Take your frazzing hand off me!"

I trudged back to the barracks, reeling from exhaustion. Above me loomed the spire of Reunification Cathedral, where Annie and I were married. I tried to block out her radiant smile, the sparkling ruby necklace, my answering grin of pleasure as we knelt at the altar to take our vows.

Until death do us part. Unless, of course, the marriage was annulled. I grimaced. Even if the elders permitted it, annulment made a travesty of our vows. The Church granted divorce for adultery, though several constituent sects consented to the rite with utmost reluctance. I would have to apply through the diocese and wait for approval. I headed up the barracks steps. What choice had I? I couldn't live with what she'd done.

For better or worse, until death do us part. I paused, my hand on the door.

Not adultery, Lord. That was too much to ask. Even the Church doesn't expect it.

"Ahh, Nicholas . . ." Father, his eyes bleak and disapproving.

In sickness and health, for better or worse . . . The barracks door swung open; two enlisted men came out, laughing until they spotted my insignia.

Regardless of the Church's toleration of divorce, I still knew right from wrong; Father had taught me well. I couldn't leave Annie without again betraying an oath. Yet, why did that matter, now that I was damned?

I cursed long and fluently. Then I went to my room, grabbed my duffel, got in my car, drove home.

She sat in the kitchen, sitting over a cup of tea. Her eyes raised slowly, hope dawning. "Nicky?"

My voice was like gritty sandpaper. "I won't divorce you. I swore to stay until death, and I'll fulfill my oath. You may divorce me, if you wish. I won't stop you."

"That's not what I wan'."

"Then we'll live together. What happened in the bedroom, we will not speak of. Not ever. That's all I have to say." I turned to put my duffel back in the bedroom.

"That's not all you swore." Tremulously she came to her feet. I stared at her. "Love, honor, and protect. You promised that part too."

The words caught in my throat. "I don't love you now. I—can't help that."

Her eyes brimmed. "What's marriage for?"

"I swore to it." Would that I hadn't.

"About Eddie—"

"Don't speak of him. I warn you."

"Will we sleep together? Share a bed? Talk?"

I sat heavily. "I don't know. It's all too much."

"You can't live here, hating me."

I rested my head on the table. "I don't hate you." Lord God, burn what I saw from my memory. Let me take Alexi's place, blessed with his forgetfulness. "Alexi has amnesia," I said. "He doesn't know me."

"Oh, Nicky."

I tried to speak, failed.

Her hand went to my neck, stroked me. "Nicky."

Jezebel, don't touch my flesh!

She gathered my head into her arms. Despite my resolve, I clung to her, buried my head in her soft breasts, clutched her as to a liferaft while my shoulders heaved with sobs.

Part 2

May, in the year of our Lord 2200

7

My outburst resolved nothing; after an hour I pulled myself together and went about my business. I could not put aside Annie's unfaithfulness even if I was grateful for her comfort. I realized I should have stayed in barracks; life in our apartment would be unbearably tense.

I roomed alone in the tiny spare bedroom, and I slept badly.

Daily, I visited Alexi. Sometimes Annie came along. Though Alexi seemed to like her, he had no memory of her.

A few days after the attack on our fleet, Admiral De Marnay returned to Admiralty House; we held our conference at last. He heard my account of the planters' grievances without interruption.

"And your conclusion?" He leaned back in his chair.

I pondered. "The planters' anger is one issue. The other is how the war effort has been handled."

"I told you to deal with the planters, not the war." His fingers drummed the desk irritably.

"Yes, sir. But I don't know whether their complaints are valid. If they are, and we seem to be ignoring them . . ."

"With any military buildup there's inefficiency, you know that." He glowered. "Especially when they insist on running the show from home, and informing me by holovid chip."

"I understand, sir."

"Don't you think I know it's madness to put our major base in the Venturas?" His fist rattled the table.

"Yes, sir. The complaints aren't mine."

After a moment the Admiral's glare faded. "I know." He sighed. We waited through the roar of a departing shuttle. "I could appoint you inspector-general," he mused.

"What?" I blushed. "Sorry, sir. There's no such post as inspector-general."

"Unless I create one." He tapped the papers on his desk. "Son, we've lost four ships. The enemy may strike again at any moment. The last thing we need is discontent on the home front; we *have* to keep the planters happy."

Again his fingers drummed. "Laura Triforth is right: without their help we'd never have been able to activate the Venturas Base, and we may need their aid again. Tell them you're appointed to check into their complaints so we can put them right."

"What authority would I have?"

"Authority to report to me. Don't scowl; it's a public relations title. If I decide anything needs doing, we'll take care of it."

I shook my head. "Those joeys trust me. Some are my friends. I won't pretend to be something I'm not, to mollify them."

De Marnay leaned forward, his warmth vanished. "They told me you had an insubordinate streak."

I was too tired to be diplomatic. "Yes, sir, I think I do. I'm sorry about it."

For the first time a hint of amusement flickered at his mouth. "Well, we understand each other. Take the job, and keep the planters off my back."

I stared at the floor, unready for the sudden crisis. After a time I said, "I'd rather resign, if you'll allow me."

"Resign what? Your liaison post?"

"No, sir. My commission." I met his eye.

He growled, "Don't threaten me; I'll take you up on it."

I took a deep breath. "Very well, sir."

He studied me intently, then sighed. "A lot *that* would do for morale. All right, Seafort, you've been demanding a real job, and I haven't obliged. Have it your way. I'll appoint you inspector-general. You have authority to inspect all installations and remedy any inefficiency or incompetence you find, subject to my veto. Your theater is the Venturas Base, our accommodations and arrangements in Centraltown, and Orbit Station. The fleet is off-limits; that's my bailiwick." He hesitated. "Are you aware I'm making you one of the most powerful men on the planet?"

"I'd prefer a ship."

"I told you, you'll have one. You still have two months of shore duty."

I capitulated. "Very well, sir. Where should I start?"

He stood. "How in hell would I know? That's your worry." He indicated the door. "My waiting room is packed. I need to get on with my appointments."

I said, "Pardon, sir, but why do you call me insubordinate, then hand me such power?"

"I have to work with the material at hand, Seafort. My other Captains are all shipboard, and I suppose the job really needs doing if the plantation zone is in such turmoil. Put in for a lieutenant or two as staff. And middies, if you want them." He sighed, then stuck out his hand. "Good luck."

I smiled, amazed at his largesse. "Thank you, sir."

In the outer office I asked the ubiquitous Lieutenant Eiferts where to apply for personnel. He directed me upstairs.

The lieutenant in BuPers didn't bother to rise from his console. "Captain, you already have an enlisted man and a lieutenant."

"Lieutenant Tamarov is on sicklist. The enlisted man is . . . not available."

"Unfortunately, sir, the Admiral gave your liaison duty low priority. There's no way I can augment your staff. Sorry." With a perfunctory nod, he turned to his files.

I glowered. If he refused to give me staff I'd have to go over his head, and De Marnay would know I couldn't even put together a work detail. "I see."

His fingers tapped at the keyboard. After a time he looked up. "Is there anything else, Captain?"

"Yes. I'd like a lieutenant—no, make that two—assigned to my department forthwith."

"I've already told you why—"

"Stand at attention."

He complied, though slowly. "I'm on Admiral De Marnay's personal staff, sir. I'm not subject to outside orders."

"Be silent until I tell you to speak."

His position was awkward. As he'd said, he was on De Marnay's personal staff. Yet I was a Captain and he a mere lieutenant. And a Captain is obeyed, always.

I sat, leafing through a holozine. Several minutes passed, during which the lieutenant became more and more uneasy. I could see him readying himself to object to my high-handedness.

I asked abruptly, "Have you ever been to Miningcamp, Lieutenant?"

He looked confused. "No, sir."

"You've heard of it?"

"Of course."

"Think you'll like it there?"

He said cautiously, "I'm afraid I don't know what you mean."

"U.N.A.F. runs the miners' station, you know, not the Navy. They don't have much in the way of amenities. The Station is more pleasant than the asteroid, though. At least Miningcamp Station is aired."

I browsed through the holozine. A glance told me I had his full attention. "Unless I get my staff in the next two minutes, you'll find yourself the new Naval liaison to Miningcamp, and you'll spend years wondering how you were transferred and shipped off-planet on less than an hour's notice." I switched off my holozine. "Do I make myself clear?" "Quite, sir." He was sweating. "If I may, sir? I think I can make some changes." I nodded. With relief he dropped into his seat. His fingers flew over the keyboard. "I'll post the assignments immediately, sir. Have you any specific personnel in mind?"

I remembered the time I'd requisitioned staff at Hope Nation, years ago. "No behavioral problems. Top-rated fitness reports only."

"Aye aye, sir. They'll report to you tomorrow. Is that soon enough?" "It will do."

"Shall I put your Mr. Tamarov on disability leave?" On general disability, Alexi would languish in the hospital, among uncaring strangers.

"No, leave him with me." Perhaps I could find a way to keep him busy. Some way to summon his memories.

I stood, strode to the door. "One more thing."

"Yes, sir?" The lieutenant was all ears.

"The enlisted man on my staff, Eddie Boss. He's in barracks now. Transfer him to the first ship going outsystem."

"Aye aye, sir." He saluted as I left.

On my way to the car, I tried to imagine Admiral De Marnay's response had the BuPers officer complained I was reassigning him to Miningcamp. Foolish joey, the lieutenant. After all, it was he who posted the assignments.

While waiting in my apartment for my two new staffers I reviewed my notes. True to his word, Admiral De Marnay had cut orders authorizing me to "investigate and correct abuses and inefficiency of whatever nature with respect to the state of readiness of U.N. Forces in the Hope Nation theater." With surprise, I realized that my writ ran to U.N. Armed Forces as well as Navy; De Marnay was in charge of the whole show and he'd chosen to give me a free hand.

My first need was office space. I couldn't very well be inspector-general from my living room.

I paced. I had promised Alexi I'd visit at noon. Annie, anxious to please, had left the apartment for the morning so I'd be free to meet with my lieutenants.

Should I start with the Venturas? A quick trip would give me a picture of what I faced. Hopefully, Laura Triforth had exaggerated the problems there. In any event, I'd like to glimpse the Venturas once more, though Amanda was long dead and Derek was light-years distant.

The doorbell chimed. I answered it, and recoiled.

"Lieutenant Tolliver reporting for duty, sir." He saluted.

"I know your name," I snarled. "Did you request this posting?" Disgusted, I turned away.

He followed me inside. "No, sir. Orders came in transferring me off *Portia*. That's all I know."

Was the BuPers lieutenant exacting his revenge? No, he had no way to know of my resentment of Tolliver.

"I'll get someone else," I muttered. "This must be as awkward for you as for me."

He looked surprised. "Awkward, sir? Why?"

"Don't tell me you can't remember."

"When we were cadets, sir?"

I nodded.

"I was a class ahead of you."

"Yes." You made life so much more miserable than need be.

"I'm sorry you're uncomfortable with me, sir. I certainly have no objection to working with you."

I peered suspiciously. Apparently he meant it. "You don't recall Academy?"

He stared, uncomprehending. "The hazing, you mean?" He shrugged. "Part of the drill, as far as I was concerned."

"I hated you." And still do.

He shrugged again. "I'm sorry, sir. I was hazed too, my first year."

My angry reply was forestalled by the chime. Lieutenant Eiferts. I let him in. "A message from the Admiral?"

"No, sir. I've been assigned to your operation."

"What?"

"I'm to join your staff."

"But you work directly for the Admiral."

"I did until today."

I hadn't known De Marnay was so devious. Whom could he trust to keep an eye on me, if not his personal aide?

"I see. I suppose if I asked for another lieutenant, they'd all be unavailable?"

The corners of his mouth turned up. "Perhaps, sir. I'm not in BuPers."

I could work with him, even if he was a spy for the Admiral, but I had to know. "Mr. Tolliver, outside."

"Aye aye, sir." Tolliver's obedience was automatic; he'd just come from a ship. Eiferts, on the other hand, had served in a soft shoreside berth. We would see.

"Well now." I paced, as if on a bridge. "Who engineered this, you or the Admiral?"

"Engineered what, sir?" Eiferts was the soul of innocence.

I said nothing. After a time, he shifted uncomfortably. I let the silence drag on.

"I'm to help however you see fit," he ventured.

"To whom is your loyalty, Lieutenant? Me or the Admiral?"

He looked puzzled. "Is there a conflict, sir?" Good question. What did I have to hide?

I smiled grimly. "Will you report to him?"

"I presume you'll expect me to do your staff work, sir. That would include processing your reports."

I roared, "Tell the truth, you insolent sea lawyer! All of it! At once!"

He flushed. "Yes, sir!" He thrust out a palm, as if to ward off my fury. "I'm to be of whatever assistance I can, sir. I'm also to report to the Admiral at my own discretion. Anything I think he should know."

I resumed my pacing. "Were your orders to report to him in secret, Lieutenant?"

He hesitated. "Not specifically, sir. I think that was understood."

"Very well. Report to the Admiral as ordered, and inform me each time you report to him. Acknowledge."

"Aye aye, sir. I will inform you each time I report to Admiral De Marnay. Orders received and understood, sir." His forehead glistened.

"Very well, then. Welcome to my staff, Lieutenant Eiferts."

"Thank you, sir." He smiled weakly.

"I'm going to the hospital to visit Mr. Tamarov. You know the ropes; how long will it take to get office space?"

"Do you want rooms in Admiralty House, sir?"

"Um, no. Downtown, I should think."

"Perhaps near Naval barracks . . . I could make a couple of calls, sir." He brightened at the thought of dealing with matters he understood.

"Very well. In the morning we leave for the Venturas. I want office space by the time we're home." I ushered him out.

Tolliver, hands clasped behind his back, was examining the flowers along the walk. I growled to him. "We'll need a couple of holovids, a day's rations, and a heli for the Venturas in the morning. See to it."

"Aye aye, sir." Tolliver cleared his throat. "Does that mean I'm to stay on your staff, sir?"

"It means you have your orders." I strode away. Driving to Centraltown Hospital I sighed with exasperation. I'd thoroughly alienated both my new staffers, to say nothing of the BuPers lieutenant at Admiralty House. A fine start.

"What are the Venturas?" Alexi frowned.

"The mountain range of Western Continent," I repeated patiently. Awesome peaks they were, which towered over vast tracts of unspoiled wilderness.

"And we—your Navy—have a base there?"

"Yes, Alexi."

"Am I required to go?"

"No."

"Then I'd rather not." He stared down at the manicured lawn below his window.

"Very well." I tried not to feel hurt. "I'll see you when I'm back."

"If you wish."

As I headed for the door he blurted, "What will they do with me?"

"You're on sick leave until you get well."

"The doctors say I may never get my memory back . . . if I don't, am I still in the Navy? Do I have to follow orders?"

"You haven't been discharged, Alexi. But if you don't recover, I'm sure they'll allow you a medical release."

"And then?" He turned, with a bitter smile. "I have nowhere to go and haven't the faintest idea what I should do."

It was as close to an appeal as I'd heard. "I'll look after you, Alexi."

He turned back to the window. "I don't want to be looked after."

"I'm sorry." I thought to touch his shoulder, refrained. "Good-bye, then."

"Good-bye, Mr. Seafort." He hesitated. "Am I supposed to call you 'sir'?"

"Of course. But I won't hold you to it until you remember why."

"Thank you." When I left he was staring out the window.

8

The flight west to the Venturas was as I remembered it: uneventful hours droning over the shallows of Farreach Ocean. Lush submarine vegetation sent tentacles groping for the surface, where they contested for sunlight with water lilies that rose and fell gently with the swells. Hope Nation had no animal life, so the ocean was a vast soup of competing herbage.

I piloted the military machine with relaxed enjoyment. One hand on the collective, the other on the cyclic, the puter switched to passive mode, I had ample time to recall which switches operated the various missiles and antimissile gear with which the heli could be armed. About two hours from Western Continent our radar homed on the Venturas Base beacon. I switched on the autopilot and leaned back, glad of the rest. I'd been flying for six hours.

In the rear seat, Tolliver dozed. Next to me, Lieutenant Eiferts studied his holovid. "Sir?"

"What?"

"I've been looking over the material and supplies we poured into that base, sir. In theory the plan made sense, but I don't think it worked out too well."

"Pity you weren't in charge of strategic planning," I said acidly. He fell silent, until I relented. "I gather the idea was to be able to defend both hemispheres."

"When Orbit Station is over Eastern Continent, Western Continent has a clear shot at any invaders above it. But that meant we had to split our resources. We should have put the base where we could support it."

"That's what we're here to learn," I reminded him.

"Anyway, ships make better laser platforms than land installations."

"But ships are so vulnerable to attack. Look how many we've lost." My *Challenger*, among them. "And fish don't operate groundside."

"Unless it was they who brought the Hope Nation virus."

"They probably did." I shivered, despite the afternoon warmth. "There was a fellow, years ago, who claimed he saw them spraying."

"Captain Grone."

I looked up in surprise. "You knew about him?"

He nodded. "Used to live near the Great Falls area."

"What happened to him?"

"Nobody knows, sir."

Poor, demented Captain Grone. When I'd met him, his wife Janna was due to have a child. I wondered if the baby had survived. I thought of Nate, who would be three now. My throat tightened.

The speaker crackled. "Incoming heli, course two oh nine, identify yourself."

Lieutenant Eiferts reached for the caller. "Ventura, this is Naval heli two four nine Alpha, ETA your base forty minutes."

"We don't show a flight plan filed, two four nine Alpha. Who are you?"

"Captain Nicholas Seafort and staff. We're here to insp—"

I switched off the caller.

"Sir?" Eiferts gaped.

"Aboard ship my lieutenants knew their place," I growled. I pried the caller from his hand, keyed it on. "Ventura Base, this is Captain Seafort, U.N.N.S. We're on a sightseeing trip through the Venturas."

"Unauthorized visitors aren't allowed, sir."

I recalled our carefree flight to the falls, Derek, Amanda, and I. No flight plan, no authorizations.

The voice hesitated. "You're, uh, Captain Seafort? *The* Captain Seafort?"

"Yes." Again, my cursed notoriety.

"I'm sure the General—I'll have to confirm, sir, but I'm certain it will be all right. Do you have our beacon?"

"Affirmative."

"Please stay on your present course. I'll be back to you." The line went dead.

Eiferts looked abashed. "Sorry, sir. I thought it was customary to check in with Base Command."

I'd learn more from an unannounced trip, even if it meant we'd travel under false colors. But still . . . I sighed. "I'm on edge, Mr. Eiferts. Pardon me."

He looked startled. Captains did not apologize to lieutenants, even when wrong. "Yes, sir, of course. Sorry I interfered."

We flew in silence, a knot forming in my stomach. The speaker crackled. "Captain Seafort, General Khartouf welcomes you to Venturas Base. Would you join him this evening for dinner?"

I keyed the caller. "I'd be happy to accept." Eiferts shot me a glance, but was silent.

"Very well, sir, we'll expect you."

We were coming over the coastline. Great hills swept down from the highlands to plunge into the sea. Behind them the sun was drifting toward the horizon.

"Wake Tolliver."

"I'm up, sir." He leaned forward from the rear seat.

"Listen, both of you. When we land I'll go with the top brass. You two get a look around. We'll meet later and compare notes."

Eiferts said, "Aye aye, sir. What are we looking for?"

"Anything odd. Evidence that the base isn't well run. Sloppy security or lack of readiness."

"We already know their security is sloppy," Tolliver said.

I scowled. "How so?"

"They're letting us land, though we're unexpected and have no flight plan filed."

"I'm a U.N.N.S. Captain," I snapped.

"They only know you *said* you are," he replied coolly.

I bit back an irate reply. He was right.

When we were a few miles from the airfield I took over from the autopilot. I followed the beacon until the base was in sight, and set down on their parade ground, as instructed.

The field was a parade ground in name only. Around it, red earthen roads gouged from the plain were a mass of ruts; after a hard downpour the base must be a morass. Prefab barracks and stark operations buildings lined the perimeter road.

I straightened my jacket, tugged at my tie as a handful of officers approached, ducking under the slowing blades.

"Captain Seafort? General Khartouf." I shook the proffered hand. "My adjutant, Major Rinehart." He introduced me to the rest of his staff.

I took a deep breath; time for work. "Impressive place you have, General."

"A bit rough, still." He grinned through even white teeth. "But we manage." His eyes flickered to my scar. "We've heard a lot about you, Captain."

I grunted. I wasn't here to talk about myself. "How many men do you have, sir? Last time I was in Western Continent I saw nothing but wilderness."

"Three thousand. And they're hardly enough." We strolled toward the main building. "Join me for a drink, Captain. And your officers too, if you wish."

"My lieutenants can look after themselves," I said offhandedly. "Eiferts, Tolliver, you're off duty until the morning."

"Aye aye, sir." My two aides watched me saunter off with the Base C.O.

Dinner was served by an enlisted steward. Though I'd dismissed my lieutenants in cavalier fashion, the General's dining hall was crowded with his own officers. It was only after the soup, while we were engaged in animated conversation, that I realized they'd all come for a glimpse of me. Dismayed, I forced my attention back to General Khartouf's comment.

"They'd be easier to fight if we had weapons designed specifically for them."

"Pardon? The fish, you mean?" I toyed with my second course. It happened to be fish, imported frozen from home, and I felt my appetite subside. "Unfortunately, we don't know what weapons would work best."

"That's what I was saying." The General eyed me askance.

A middle-aged colonel cleared his throat. "Pardon me, sir, but what was most effective in your own encounters with the fish?"

His neighbor turned his head, so as not to miss a word. I stopped, fork halfway to mouth, realizing the entire table was hanging on my answer. Did they expect a blow-by-blow account of my battles? Was that the price of my dinner? Nausea battled with disgust. I wouldn't have it. Not for all the fine Terran wines on the starched white tablecloth.

No, it wasn't the price of my dinner. It was the price of my two lieutenants having the run of the base, free to ask innocent questions. I forced a smile. "Well, on *Challenger*, they attacked three times . . ."

Unnoticed, the forkful of fish returned to my plate.

"So?"

My two lieutenants exchanged looks. Eiferts gave a small nod, and Tolliver began. "Venturas Base has been in operation over a year, sir. They've had the prefab factory set up for half that time, but the enlisted men are still living five to a two-man unit."

I thought of the transients, shipped to Hope Nation six to a cabin, packed like sardines. "Go on."

"The prefab factory was run by civilians brought from Terra on six-month contracts. They agreed to an extension, but demanded and got return passage after nine months. By then the Army was supposed to have men trained to replace them. Because it took so long to get the factory operating, the workers weren't well trained. Apparently production is minimal at best. No one's seen any celuwall leave the plant in months. I couldn't ask too much more without making the sergeant suspicious."

I waited, but that was all Tolliver had to say. I turned to Eiferts. "And you?"

"I took a long walk, sir. None of the roads are paved. Someone told me in winter they're virtually impassable."

"That's all you learned?" My tone was scathing.

"No, my stroll took me to the laser control building. I was enthralled, so the lieutenant on duty showed me through." Wearily, he made as if to sit, realized he was in my presence. "The base has four huge puter-aimed laser cannon powered by the emergency fission station the planters hauled from Centraltown. The actual cannon are on that rise south of the base. Their combined firepower would be staggering. Unfortunately, they can't be fired together."

"Why?" I gestured to the seat.

Gratefully he eased himself into a chair. He must have had a long hike. "Thanks, sir. Because the power step-down lines haven't been hooked properly. Only one laser can be fired at a time."

"Christ!" Tolliver, with feeling.

I glared. "I don't condone blasphemy."

"Your pardon, sir."

"Though I share the sentiment. The only real purpose of this base is to man those laser emplacements." I brooded. "We need to know if Khartouf mentioned these shortfalls to Admiral De Marnay. I'll call in the morning."

"He didn't, sir," said Eiferts.

"Oh?"

"Khartouf's progress reports passed over my desk, sir. I brought everything of importance to the Admiral's attention."

"That smug bastard!"

Eiferts's jaw dropped.

"Khartouf," I growled, "not Mr. De Marnay." I paced the length of our tiny cubicle, my chest tight. "What do we do?"

Eiferts said, "How do your orders read? 'Investigate and correct abuses and inefficiency'?"

"You saw them?"

"I posted them." He smiled apologetically.

"Call their office and get me an appointment with General Khartouf for the morning."

"Aye aye, sir."

I went into my adjoining bedroom and took off my jacket. A moment later, a knock. Lieutenant Eiferts, his mouth set in a grim line. "There's no answer at Base HQ, sir."

"What?"

"I can't get through."

I swore fluently. Lieutenant Tolliver raised an eyebrow.

Eiferts said, "I ought to mention, sir, that I'll be reporting this to Admiral De Marnay."

"Never mind that." I thrust my feet back into my shoes. "Let's go."

"Where, sir?"

"Out." I stalked down the corridor, the two lieutenants dogging my heels.

"HQ building, sir?" panted Eiferts.

"No. The laser control station first."

He winced at the prospect of another long hike. "Aye aye, sir." He pointed down the perimeter road. "It's that way."

It took several minutes at fast pace to reach the laser installation. The night air was chill, and though the exercise warmed me I felt the tickle of a cold coming on.

We approached the darkened building. It seemed deserted but as we neared I saw a dim light in a side window. "What's in there?"

"I don't know," said Eiferts. "I used the front gate, and the sergeant took me directly to the control room."

I stopped beneath the window. From that vantage point all I could see was a ceiling. "Boost me up."

Tolliver gaped.

"Boost me. How else am I supposed to see?"

"Aye aye, sir." He made a cup with his hands and braced himself.

I hoisted myself up to cling from the window frame. After a moment I dropped down again.

"What did you see, sir?" Eiferts whispered.

I shook my head, unable to speak.

"What, sir?"

"They're playing cards," I snarled. "Two men in the comm room, sitting over a deck of cards."

"On duty?" Tolliver was scandalized. On ship, such conduct would bring down the Captain's almighty wrath. With a twinge of guilt I recalled my chess games on the bridge, during the long dreary hours of watch. But we were Fused then. Wasn't that different?

"Freeze!"

I looked up. The sentry's gun pointed directly at me.

"Easy, soldier," said Tolliver. "This man's—"

"What are you joeys doing?"

A face appeared at the window. "Sarge, what's—"

The sentry snapped, "Call HQ, stat. We've got intruders."

"I—"

"Move it, Varney!"

The face disappeared. "Stay put, all of you," the guard ordered. He waved his laser rifle at me. "Well?"

"I'm Captain Nicholas Seafort."

"I know who you are. I asked what you were doing."

I approached him, ignoring the weapon he brandished. As I neared, I could see the stereoplug in his ear.

"What's that?" Without warning I snatched it from him.

"Hey, give it—"

"A stereoplug? On sentry duty?" Slap music emanated faintly from the plug.

"You've got no right—"

With my heel, I ground the plug into the dirt. Over seventy unibucks, in Centraltown, and that a continent away.

The sentry, wary now, looked back and forth among us. "Just what's up, here?"

"I'm acting with the authority of Admiral Georges De Marnay, head of Unified Command. Where is your C.O.?"

"General Khartouf?" He pointed up the road we'd just followed. "Officers' barracks."

"Very well. Take us there."

He shook his head. "I can't leave my post."

"You may now. You're relieved."

"What's your authority to give me orders?"

My opinion of him went up a notch. "Mr. Tolliver, your holovid." Tolliver pulled a portable from his pocket, switched it on, snapped in a chip. "Read this," I said to the guard.

By moonlight, on the laser building steps, the sentry read carefully through my orders. At length he said, "Well, sir, I guess they put you in charge. I'm Sergeant Trabao. If you'll follow me to officers' barracks . . ."

The officers' dormitory was a hundred yards from the HQ building, not far from our own rooms. Outside, a lone sentry slouched in the shadows. At the sight of us he thrust something in his pocket. "Hey, what are you—"

"It's all right, Portillo, they're with me." Uncertain, the second sentry stood aside.

Trabao said, "The General's—"

"—right here." Khartouf stood on the top step, hands on hips. "What in bloody hell are you up to?"

I said, "You'll want to discuss it privately, General."

"Nonsense. Why are you skulking around my base in the middle of the night? Your answer better be good, or you'll find yourselves in the guardhouse."

"I'm here by order of Georges De Marnay, Admiral Commanding." Not quite true; De Marnay had authorized my jaunt but he certainly hadn't ordered it. I pressed on. "I'm inspecting your readiness."

"By standing on your flunky's hands peering into windows?"

I felt an idiot. "My conduct is not at issue."

"It bloody well is, Captain!"

"Tolliver, show him the chip."

Lieutenant Tolliver proffered his holovid. "Here, sir."

Khartouf took the holo, let it fall to the dirt. "You men, escort them to the guardhouse. By force, if necessary. We'll deal with them in the morning."

The second sentry reached for his pistol. Sergeant Trabao shook his head. "No, sir. I think you'd better read the holo."

"Portillo, put Sergeant Trabao under arrest with the rest."

I protested, "If you'll just read my orders—"

"Prong your orders. I give you the hospitality of my table, and you sneak around betraying us in the night. I won't have—"

Something snapped within. I snarled, "What you'll have no longer matters. You're relieved of command."

Tolliver, Eiferts, and even Trabao gaped, but I was past caring. "Eiferts, take Sergeant Trabao's pistol. Move when I give an order! Now, cover Mr. Khartouf. Mr. Trabao, we'll adjourn to the Commandant's office. Lead the way."

A few moments later General Khartouf slammed the holovid down on his table. "All right, Seafort, I've read the bloody thing! You have authority to relieve no one."

"You're wrong." I turned to the Sergeant. "Mr. Trabao, we'll be leaving first thing in the morning. Make sure my heli is ready."

"We'll see who ends up relieved," the General jeered. "The moment you're gone I'll be on the caller to Admiralty House."

"No, you won't. I'm taking you along."

Eiferts stirred, his uneasiness apparent. "Who'll run the base, sir? Someone has to be in charge."

"True."

"Who, sir? I ought to put it in my report."

"You."

"I—WHAT?"

"You're acting Base Commandant, as of now."

He spluttered, protocol abandoned. "But—me, sir? Why?"

"You know the problems; you've seen the reports General Khartouf sent. And I don't know who else to trust. So it's you."

"I'd need the Admiral's approval for that, sir," he said slowly. "I don't know if—"

"Have you heard of a chain of command?" My tone was savage. "Does a Captain outrank a lieutenant?"

He stared until he comprehended, then his eyes fell. "Aye aye, sir. I'm sorry. Orders received and understood, sir."

"Very well." I paced the office. "We're too keyed up to sleep. Turn on the office holo. Find the files on the prefab plant. You'll need what help the General will give you. I think you'll have your hands full cleaning up this fiasco."

"The only fiasco here is attempted kidnapping," the General shouted. "You think I'll help you rifle my files? I'll watch your hanging, Seafort! This is mutiny!"

I turned. Something in my eyes gave him pause. "Hanging?" My voice was odd. "Don't bring up the subject, General. I could stretch my authority even further."

"You wouldn't da—"

"Try me." I held my gaze until he looked away. "Mr. Eiferts, the General will show you his files now. I'll be outside. Mr. Trabao, come along."

In the hallway, I confronted the guard. "I don't think much of a stereochip on sentry duty."

He reddened. "Things have been sort of slack around here."

"You like it that way?"

He studied me. "The truth? No. I was a drill sergeant back in Rio. But when no one backs you up, it's hard. You end by doing what the others do. I wasn't always like that."

"You don't have to be, any longer."

"Sir?"

"Mr. Eiferts will need an aide who knows his way around. Can we trust you, Trabao?"

He let out a long, slow breath. "Yes."

"I will, then. Show Mr. Eiferts the ropes."

"Yes, sir."

"I'll be outside." Shivering, I coughed. The room seemed chill.

"Stand at attention!"

I complied at once. Admiral De Marnay, red-faced, planted himself inches from my nose. "What in Lord God's own hell are you up to, Seafort? Are you power-mad?"

"No, sir." At least, I didn't think so. I felt exhausted. It had been a long, sullen trip back. Lieutenant Eiferts must have radioed ahead; after we landed I had no trouble getting an appointment with the Admiral. Not this time.

He bellowed, "The hell you aren't!"

"Sir, I—"

"Quiet, you presumptuous young—you upstart! You lunatic! You—" He spluttered to a halt.

Spine rigid, hands pressed to my sides, I stared at the wall behind his desk.

"Who gave you authority to remove a commander in the field, you insolent pup?"

"You did, sir."

"Be silent, I said!" That was unfair; when he asked a question I was obligated to answer. He growled, "Khartouf was appointed by the U.N.A.F. Chief of Staff! Am I supposed to tell Staff a baby-faced Captain, acting without orders, removed his man from office?"

I assumed the question was rhetorical.

"Answer!"

I'd assumed wrong. "No, sir."

"Oh? You're suggesting I lie to him?"

Wearily I said, "No, sir."

Admiral De Marnay flung himself into his seat. "I ought to court-martial you, Seafort!"

I knew there'd be trouble, but I hadn't expected quite so much. Well, I'd often considered resigning; now the Navy would save me the trouble. "On what charges, sir?"

"Insubordination, incitement to rebellion, mutiny . . . Don't worry, we'll find ones that fit!"

"Very well, sir."

He roared, "Is that all you have to say for yourself?"

"No, sir."

"Then say it, before I throw you out of here!" His jaw jutted.

I said, "Khartouf's base is a shambles. His lasers sit unready, his barracks unbuilt, while he dines in luxury with his officers. He's a fool."

"That's not your judgment to make."

"He's also a corrupt fool."

"I told you—eh?"

"Lieutenant Eiferts spent the night going through Khartouf's puter accounts. According to Mr. Trabao, the men have had nothing but Q-rations for the last six months."

"Well, it's a war zone. What of it?"

"There were indents for tons of supplemental foodstuffs purchased in Centraltown and supposedly flown to the base. No one knows where it went."

He was observing me closely. "Go on."

"The food may have been imaginary, or it may actually have been sent to the Venturas and resold from there. I have no idea; we didn't have time to trace it."

He shifted in his seat. "All right, assume Khartouf had his hand in the till. Perhaps he should have been removed and tried. But not by you, Seafort. Not by you."

"I understand that now, sir. I made a bad mistake."

"In removing him?"

"No, sir. In taking your orders literally."

It brought him out of his chair, hands closing into fists. I was still imprisoned at attention, my back aching, and I felt dizzy. I shouldn't have taken that long walk in the cold Venturas night.

"By God, Seafort, you're an arrogant one!"

I no longer cared. "That may be so. You knew what I was when you appointed me!" It was breathtaking insolence, for which I would have instantly broken a subordinate. I ignored his stunned amazement and rushed on. "You ordered me to investigate and correct abuses and ineffi-ciency. Tell me how Khartouf's abuses could have been corrected without removing him!"

"You could report to me. I'd have removed him."

"You didn't order me to report abuses! You said to correct them!"

"Don't be a sea lawyer," he growled. "I had no idea that meant stripping a Base Commander of his post."

"Neither did I, sir," I said truthfully. We lapsed into silence while I fought to remain at proper attention. His anger abating, the Admiral sank back into his chair. At length I said, "Will you court-martial me?"

"Eh? No, of course not. You knew I was just letting off steam."

I'd known no such thing. "Very well, sir." I hesitated. "It's clear you don't want me to continue as inspector-general."

"I'm the Admiral here, Seafort! I'll tell *you* what's clear."

"Yes, sir."

"Stand easy."

I sagged with relief. "May I sit?" At his nod I dropped into a chair. "Sorry, sir. I don't feel well."

He tapped his desk, lost in thought. "Khartouf's brother is Assistant
Deputy SecGen, as you no doubt knew." He shook his head. "Have you
any idea of the trouble you've made?"

"You can always veto my acts, sir."

"You know I have to stand behind you. Reinstating him now would
be a license to steal. And the Navy has to look after its own."

"I see." It was the wrong reason to back me.

His annoyance flared again. "And you've taken my chief aide as well."

"Mr. Eiferts? I needed someone immediately, and uh, I had to work
with the material at hand."

"Don't be insolent!"

"Aye aye, sir. Eiferts knew the problems, and he had your confidence. He was ideal."

"I know. You were right. I can't see who else to put in charge, so now
I'm without his services."

"Sorry." He couldn't have it both ways.

"Don't get in a huff, Seafort. It's all my fault; I wrote your blessed
orders myself." For the first time his eyes held a glint of humor.

"What should I do now, sir?"

He tapped his desk. After a time he sighed and said, "Go on with
your business."

"As inspector-general?" I sounded incredulous.

"That's your post," he snapped. "While you're at it, check the shipping records on Orbit Station. See if you can figure out why we have such
a pileup of supplies at Centraltown."

"Aye aye, sir."

The Admiral's thoughts were elsewhere. "We won't try him here, of
course. Send him to Earth with a full accounting."

"Yes, sir." The hot potato would be handed on.

"You'll have made enemies at home, Seafort. That's out of my hands."

"Yes, sir."

"Very well, dismissed." As I headed for the door he added, "You
relieved Khartouf before you found he was stealing."

"Yes, sir."

His eye met mine. "Someday you'll go too far."

I held his gaze for a long moment.

"Dismissed."

9

Early in the morning I drooped over my kitchen table inhaling coffee, struggling to wakefulness, still bothered by my cold. Tolliver was due at our new office near the barracks in an hour; I needed something to keep him busy. Arrange an inspection trip to Orbit Station? No, if I alerted the Station I wouldn't see regular operations, I'd find a station made ready for inspection. Though I detested it, I would have to keep skulking about.

I tied my shoes. Annie had gone out to shop, giving me the distance I obviously wanted. Why, then, did I feel miserable? I left for work.

We'd been assigned a three-room suite: my office, a room for my two lieutenants, and a waiting room for visitors. Plush, by naval standards. Tolliver was waiting.

Inside, I sat drumming my desk. I had a report to prepare, but nothing else to do.

"I'm going to the hospital for an hour or so."

"Yes, sir. Do you have an assignment for me?"

I thought of piling him with drudgery, in revenge for the hazing which he'd once inflicted. Abstract the quartermasters' reports for the last eighteen months. Detail the labor that the planters supplied to Venturas Base. Count the bricks in the top thirty feet of the building.

"Nothing for now." I added reluctantly, "Would you care to visit Mr. Tamarov?" I knew I'd prefer to see Alexi alone.

"I'd like to meet him, sir."

"Very well." I sighed.

At the hospital, Alexi's glance flitted between us as if assessing our relationship. Our conversation was stilted. After a while Tolliver wandered to the coffee shop, to give us time alone.

Absently, Alexi rubbed at the stubble covering his scalp where his bandage had been, while I told him about my escapade in the Venturas. When I was done he ventured, "Relieving him won't hurt your career?"

I shrugged. "I already have enemies. I make them wherever I go."

"Really?"

"Does that surprise you?"

He studied me. "Well, yes."

I shook my head. "I have no talent at dealing with people."

"But you're kind."

I snorted with derision. "You can't be serious."

"I am, Mr. Seafort."

"How little you remember." I was immediately sorry, but it was too late.

He reddened, but said, "You've certainly been kind since I woke. Was it once different?"

"Yes." I wished the subject hadn't come up. "When you were a midshipman."

"I seem to have survived."

I grunted, looking to change the topic. "You're gaining your strength."

"Yes." He stood, walked to the window. "What do I do now?"

"You're on sick leave. Wait for your memory to return."

"It won't, you know." He spoke as if certain. "The doctors tell me that after so long a coma, there's only a small chance."

I groped for a way to help him, found none. "I'm sorry."

"They've room here. They're in no hurry to eject me." He slumped back on his bed.

Tolliver returned. I shivered, reminding myself to find some meds for my cold. "I'll see you again in a day or so."

"Nice of you."

Something in Alexi's voice gave me pause. "Don't you want me to visit?"

He was silent a long while. "You don't understand. You come, and talk about people I should know and places I ought to remember. It's excruciating."

I said stiffly, "I won't bother you, if that's what you'd prefer."

He spoke as if Tolliver weren't present. "You still don't see. I sit in this damned room day after day, listening for your step. If it wasn't for you, I'd have nobody who cared. I'm dependent on you, and it's terrifying!"

"Oh, Alexi." I squeezed his shoulder. This time, he didn't pull free. "I'm so sorry. I'll visit every day until you're better."

"Until they give you a ship, you mean. Then I'll be alone."

True. A warship was no place for a confused and injured officer. "That won't be for a while," I said. "You'll be well by then."

"Will I?" He stared at the window.

The silence stretched. Tolliver said, "Mr. Tamarov, these things take time. I had an uncle once—"

"I don't give Christ's damn about your uncle!"

Tolliver and I exchanged glances. I said, "We'd best go. We're upsetting you."

"As you wish." Alexi still hadn't moved.

"Come, Mr. Tolliver." I drifted to the doorway, motioned for Tolliver to pass. Alexi turned. In two strides he was at the door, clutching my wrist. "Mr. Seafort, I—"

Tolliver thrust himself between us, sent Alexi sprawling onto the bed. I caught his arm. "Tolliver, no!"

"He handled you!"

Alexi leaped to his feet. Tolliver raised his fists.

"*BELAY THAT, BOTH OF YOU!*" My bellow tore at my throat, but it halted the melee.

"Aye aye, sir," Tolliver said at once. He trembled slightly as he brushed the neatly creased pants of his uniform.

"Tolliver, by the door! Alexi, sit!"

Alexi made as if to object, sank onto the bed. "He shoved me!"

"Yes. You touched me."

"So? You touch me at times."

"I'm a Captain."

"What does that have—"

Tolliver's tone was harsh. "It is a capital offense to touch the Captain."

"I wasn't fighting, just—"

"He's right, Alexi. Tolliver, he didn't know."

"He's a Naval officer."

"Who suffers from amnesia. You will make allowances."

Tolliver swallowed. "Aye aye, sir."

Alexi sat, his knees shaky. "Will I be executed?"

"Alexi, for God's sake!"

He flung himself across the bed. "I don't understand your world! I can get killed doing what seems perfectly innocent!"

My voice was husky. "Sit up." I waited for him to comply. "What were you saying when Mr. Tolliver interrupted?"

Alexi blinked. "It's hardly . . . I didn't want you to go. I knew I'd been taking out my frustration on you."

"Neither of you meant any harm." I held Tolliver's eye, then Alexi's. "I want an end to this."

Tolliver was the first to respond. "Mr. Tamarov, I bear you no ill will."

Alexi stood shakily. "I'm sorry I touched your Captain; I understand you were protecting him." They shook. After a few awkward moments, we left.

* * *

"You were correct." I coughed.

"About what?" Laura Triforth asked. Her voice was distorted over the caller.

"The Venturas Base was a mess. We're reorganizing it now." I peered through my office window at the streets below.

"Where else have you been?"

"Nowhere, yet."

"I see." Her silence spoke volumes.

"I've been trying to shake off a cold." It sounded a lame excuse.

"What will you do about our shipping charges?"

"I have no authority over rates."

"I'd have thought you had no authority over General Khartouf."

"I'm not sure I did." The less said about that episode, the better. "What about Mantiet?"

"Frederick's disappeared. No one knows where."

I tried to keep my frustration in check. "You all know each other, Ms. Triforth. Surely there aren't so many places to hide."

"There's Centraltown, the plantations, the whole continent."

I said, "Most of it undeveloped wilderness."

"Which has thousands of glades where a heli could be hidden, its transponder turned off."

My chest was tight. "Mantiet nearly killed Lieutenant Tamarov. We've got to bring him to justice."

Laura's voice softened. "He nearly killed you too. We want to find him just as much as you, Mr. Seafort."

I doubted that was possible. "Very well." We rung off. I glowered at Tolliver.

"Are they pacified, sir?"

"When I want your questions, I'll tell you." My head throbbed; all I wanted was to lie down.

"Sorry." He didn't seem perturbed. How could a man such as Tolliver feel about his assignment? He claimed to have nothing against me, yet I hated every moment of his company. I knew I wasn't being fair; he was performing his duties conscientiously and showed no resentment at my curt manner. But seeing him constantly recalled my misery at Academy.

I muttered, "Ms. Triforth insists I do something about shipping rates." I gathered my holochips to take home.

"Yes, sir."

"Is that all you have to say?"

In a patient tone, as with a child, he answered, "Yes, sir. I'm sorry if I offend you."

I slammed the door on the way out.

I decided I might as well deliver my report chip in person, in case the Admiral wanted to confer with me.

He didn't. I presented my chip to Lieutenant Eiferts's replacement and wandered to the spaceport terminal across the tarmac. The gift shop displayed low-priced tourist goods made on Hope Nation, and expensive ones shipped from home. I lunched at the spaceport restaurant. After, I dawdled, not wanting to go back to my office and cope with Tolliver.

I was glancing at the holozines in the rack when a lieutenant peered over my shoulder. "Hello, Captain." He seemed vaguely familiar. "Lieutenant Kahn, sir. I met you on the Station."

"Ah."

"Have you heard the news?"

I felt a stab of alarm. "Another attack?"

"Nothing like that, sir. A ship docked this morning."

"Oh." I shrugged. Once, the arrival of a vessel such as *Hibernia* was major news, but now ships came and went almost unnoticed. "I'll bet they're looking forward to long-lea—"

"She left Lunapolis nine months ago."

"What?"

Kahn grinned at my astonishment. "Nine months. One Fuse straight from home system."

"But—why—I mean, how—?"

"Something to do with how the fish Fuse. Our engineers went to work on it. I don't know the details, but they're calling it Augmented Fusion."

"Good Lord." What a change. No longer would we endure interminable journeys to the stars. Nine months was a—an instant.

"*Victoria*, they call her. She's small, but God, she's fast."

I frowned at his blasphemy. "How small?"

"Twenty-four crew, forty-two passengers. Not much more than a sloop. No one knows what class to name her."

I smiled. "Call her a fastship."

"Yes, sir." He grinned, sharing my delight in the extraordinary news. "She docked this morning with dispatches for the Admiral."

"Should you be gossiping about that, Lieutenant?"

For a moment he looked worried. "Well, sir, you're inspector-general. If I can't tell you, who's to trust?" His face brightened. "I heard they stripped her bare to reduce mass. Only two laser emplacements, one fore, one aft."

I said, "She'd better be fast, then. You can't fight fish with only two lasers."

"I'd love to see her. In fact, I'm putting in for transfer this afternoon."

I thought of the long slow days. Sixteen months from Lunapolis to Hope Nation; now we would cut that time almost in half. How would it affect a Captain's authority? What if the scientists shortened the journey even more? Would a Captain eventually be made to defer all important decisions to Admiralty? What if I'd been forced to brig my mutineers, to prosecute them when we reached port? Could I have maintained discipline had I not hanged them?

I paid my bill, went back to the office.

"I'm going to Orbit Station."

"Do you have a program in mind, sir?" Tolliver.

"To look around." Perhaps I'd get a glimpse of *Victoria*. Perhaps not.

"That's all?"

"Mostly." And to see what trouble I could stir up. I tried to imagine the Admiral's reaction if he heard I'd relieved General Tho as well as Khartouf.

"When will you meet with the planters?"

"After I get back." I made a note to ask BuPers to replace Tolliver; his very voice drove me to distraction. "Book us on a shuttle."

"Aye aye, sir. There's one at nine this evening." Time enough to go to the apartment, pack my duffel for overnight.

"Do we have the quartermaster's report yet?"

"No, sir."

"Go to the spaceport and get it."

"Aye aye, sir. If the quartermaster says it isn't ready?"

"Have him give you what he's got. We want to know what supplies are sitting on the runway and how long they've been there. I'll meet you at nine."

The apartment was silent and dark; at first I thought Annie was gone. I found her lying facedown on the bed, fully dressed.

"I'll be at the Station tonight."

"I see." Her voice was muffled.

I threw a couple of shirts and my toilet articles into my duffel. "I'm not sure when I'll be back. Probably tomorrow."

" 'Kay."

"Good-bye, then." For some reason, my chest ached.

"Good-bye."

I stood at the door a moment, decided to say no more. I left. I drove our electricar to the spaceport; Annie hated to drive and wouldn't need it.

I negotiated the streets with care. Though I was in the outskirts of the city I didn't feel as comfortable as I would on Plantation Road; too many vehicles were about. I kept a wary eye for haulers or buses that might lunge at me.

Few people walked along the roadway; I eyed each pedestrian with suspicion, half expecting him to dash across my path. I passed a sailor waiting to cross the street. A lady and her dog. A youth with a knapsack.

I jammed on the brakes. The boy, startled, stared at me.

I rolled down the window. "Jerence? What are you doing here?"

He backed away. I put the car into reverse to follow, glancing nervously at the mirror. "Does your father know you're—"

He sprinted down the sidewalk, away from the spaceport.

I watched as he disappeared around a bend. Shaking my head, I drove on. The boy wasn't my problem. As a courtesy, I would radio Harmon and tell him I'd seen his son. He could heli to Centraltown and search. By that time, of course, it would be dark and the boy would have vanished.

I parked at the spaceport. I'd made it with a half hour to spare. The field was only a few steps distant.

I coughed. Jerence wasn't my concern. As inspector-general my task was to check our military readiness. On the other hand my posting as liaison to the planters hadn't been canceled. But that didn't mean . . .

Damn. I restarted the car, wheeled out of the lot. Unmindful of traffic I hurtled down the road toward Centraltown, watching both sides of the street.

Something moved. I slowed, peering between houses. Nothing. I drove another mile. Jerence couldn't have run so far yet; I stopped, turned around. When I reached the house where I'd seen movement I got out, walked up the drive. All was quiet.

The house seemed empty, unlit in the twilight. The side yard was overgrown with weeds. No sign of the boy, and I didn't want to trespass. I started back to my car, hesitated, turned again. Cursing my foolishness, I loped to the rear of the house, praying an enraged homeowner wouldn't charge at me with a stunner.

The boy bolted from the back porch, tore across the yard.

I lunged and missed. He dashed out the drive, raced toward downtown, knapsack thumping his back.

I galloped after.

Jerence was the swifter runner. My jacket pulled at my chest. I fumbled at buttons. The boy glanced back, spotted me, ran faster. I pulled one arm free, then the other, and tossed the jacket aside. At Academy we'd run the four-forty, the six-sixty, the mile. I was never the fastest in my squad, but I'd usually managed to keep ahead of the instructor who brought up the rear. If he tagged you with his baton, it meant the barrel.

My vision narrowed to the sidewalk ahead, I strove to maintain rhythm. Another block. At least I was keeping pace. It was all I could do to keep my legs pumping. My breath came in racking sobs; my heart pounded.

Slowly the gap began to narrow.

A woman weeding her yard gaped as I raced past. I hoped she'd call the police, thought of telling her but knew I was too winded to speak. I couldn't keep this up much longer.

Ahead, Jerence stumbled. He rolled to his feet, raced on his way, but I'd gained precious yards. Now, he too was slowing. I pictured my drill instructor, summoned the dreaded baton, managed to pull within feet of the fleeing boy. Abruptly he veered to the left. I lunged, caught his waist, held tight as we rolled in unmown grass.

Jerence kicked desperately in an effort to break free. My chest heaving, lungs on fire, I rolled on top of him to sit on his back. Sweat poured from my face while I panted. Below me, the boy was firmly pinned.

At length I felt able to speak. "Get up!" I kept a tight grip on his arm.

"Lemme go! You don't have a right—"

I hauled him to his feet. "Walk." My legs trembled; I hoped he wouldn't notice.

"Why?" A sullen voice, a look of hate.

"You were running away." It wasn't a question.

"Mind your own business!"

"It's not my affair." I sucked in more air, thrust him toward my car, blocks away. "But I know your father."

"So?"

"I saw his face when he found you at the car wreck." Jerence stopped, braced himself against my pushing. I shoved violently with both hands; he staggered and fell. "Up, boy. And don't try running, or . . ."

"Or?" It was a sneer.

"When I catch you I'll break your arm."

He eyed me, sizing me up as I approached. Reluctantly he nodded, fell into step beside me. "Yeah, you're big enough to beat me up. I suppose you would, too; you're just like the rest of them."

I still hadn't caught my breath. "Rest of whom?"

"Pa, and the others. 'Do what you're told. Be a farmer. Live out on a plantation, in the middle of nowhere.' "

I snorted. "You have so much to feel sorry about." Eventually he would inherit more than I'd earn in a lifetime.

"You don't understand." He trudged ahead. "No one does."

After what seemed like hours we reached my car. I opened the passenger door, shoved him in. "Touch the doorknob and see what you get," I said, striving for confidence I didn't feel. I tottered to the driver's side. Jerence slumped in his seat while I drove back to the spaceport.

"What you gonna do?"

"Call your father."

"Thanks a lot."

"You're welcome." That ended the conversation.

I parked, got out, opened his door. Jerence came out, shivering. He buttoned his jacket against the night air. I steered him to the terminal.

"This way, sir." Tolliver hurried toward me. "The shuttle's about ready to—are you all right?"

"I'm fine." I spotted a public caller and headed toward it, a firm grip on Jerence.

I let go of the boy and settled in the booth, grateful for a chance to sit. I punched Harmon Branstead's code. I'd have an airport official hang on to the boy until he arrived. Outside, Jerence watched in sullen silence.

Tolliver rapped on the transplex. "We only have a minute. Shall I ask them to hold the shuttle?"

"No, I'll just be—"

Jerence bolted.

Tolliver stared. I surged to my feet. "Get him!" I shoved him toward the fleeing youngster. "Move!"

He blinked, slow to understand, then wheeled and charged after Jerence.

Tolliver always ran ahead of me in Academy drills.

He caught the boy in the parking lot, grappled with him, twisted his arm behind his back, frog-marched him inside. Jerence lashed out in vain.

Tolliver snarled, "The Captain wants you *now*, joey!" He hurled the boy forward, almost into my lap.

I glanced at my watch. No time to call Harmon, no time to arrange a baby-sitter. "God"—I caught myself—"bless it! We'll miss the shuttle!"

"What's this about, sir?"

"He's Branstead's son. A runaway."

"Should I stay with him and join you in the morning?"

"No, I need you along." I made up my mind. "Bring him. We'll call Harmon from the Station."

Jerence looked sulky. "Kidnap me and Pa will throw you in jail!"

Tolliver wheeled on him. "You'll do what the Captain says."

"I'll scream!"

"Hang on to this ruffian." I hurried to the gate.

Tolliver's tone was as savage as I'd ever heard at Academy. "I'll give you a reason to scream! Move, while you're able!"

Jerence scurried alongside Tolliver, his defiance gone. "Don't make me go off-planet," he begged. "I've never been in one of those buses. They're dangerous."

I saved my breath for walking. At the hatch the steward waited. "Have room for an extra?" I asked. Jerence tried to twist loose. Tolliver collared him.

"We have seats, sir. The boy too?"

"Yes." From Jerence, a yelp of protest. I controlled an impulse to look back. "Naval business. He's my guest."

The steward glanced at my pass, nodded. "Have him stand with you on the scales." Jerence complied, rubbing his arm, a reproachful eye on Tolliver. Our weight computed, we took our seats. I set Jerence between us and strapped in, settling myself for acceleration.

Jerence twisted and squirmed, peering down the aisles, out the portholes. "What will happen? Does it hurt?"

"Yes," Tolliver growled.

I lowered my seat. "Don't do that to him." The joey would be frightened enough. "Jerence, lie back. A few moments after takeoff you'll feel a great pressure. Ease up. Relax your chest muscles. Let it press down on you without fighting back."

Tolliver's lips twitched. "You sound like Sarge, sir."

I smiled despite myself. One learns from one's betters.

We lifted off, the shuttle's stubby wings biting the air. At a few thousand feet the wings shifted backward, the nose flipped up and the thrusters caught. Jerence whimpered. Before the acceleration became too great I reached over and squeezed his hand. Then, I gripped my armrests and tensed my chest.

"Are you all right, sir?"

I thrust away Tolliver's hand. "I'm fine."

He leaned over me, worry in his eyes. "You passed out."

"Where are we?"

"Falling toward the Station."

My chest ached. Running after Jerence had done me no good. Blinking, I looked about. Jerence was green. He swallowed over and over, clutching the armrests as if to keep himself in his seat.

Tolliver followed my gaze. "Puke on me, boy, and I'll wrench you inside out and stuff the pieces in the recycler." Jerence moaned.

I snarled, "Don't brutalize him."

"Aye aye, sir." Tolliver seemed puzzled.

I closed my eyes, heart thumping. When we docked, I would face endless walking, through and about the Station. I would also face the certain hostility of General Tho when he discovered the purpose of my visit. I'd have to tell Harmon Branstead I'd shanghaied his son off-planet. And I'd have to find a place to park the boy while I did my work.

If only I hadn't spotted Jerence and his bloody knapsack.

I dozed, wishing I felt better. Eons later the airlocks mated and the hatches hissed open. I got cautiously to my feet, waited for dizziness to pass. "Come along," I muttered. Under the influence of the Station's gravitrons, Jerence's color slowly began to return.

"Where, Mr. Seafort?" In the unfamiliar environment, the boy hovered close.

"To tell your father what we've done."

"Must you?" Docile, he trudged along the corridor to the ladder. "Yes."

His protest died when he saw my expression.

We plodded through endless corridors, descended to Level 5. From there, it was a long way to the comm room. Though it was nearly midnight, occasional lieutenants and middies still trod the corridors on their errands. As we passed, I returned their salutes absently, hardly aware of their curious looks. Civilians were rare in these precincts; children unknown.

I made Jerence wait outside with Tolliver while the comm room tech patched me through to Branstead Plantation. In a moment Harmon came on the line.

I hadn't thought to ask for a private line; our conversation crackled from the speakers while the two techs listened. Now the station staff would learn of my folly in kidnapping a planter's child. "Captain Seafort? I really don't have long; I was on my way to Centraltown. Family business."

"To look for Jerence, by any chance?"

A pause. "How did you know?"

"I have him."

"With you?" He seemed astounded. "Why would he follow you?"

"That's not quite how it happened." I explained.

"So he's on Orbit Station now?"

"Yes." I waited for the explosion.

"If you'd left him in Centraltown I could have come for him."

"There wasn't time, and he was in a mood to run."

He sighed. "I suppose he's better off there than roaming downtown. Ever since he got the notion he didn't want to be a planter, he's been impossible." A pause. "Let me know when you'll be down; I'll meet your shuttle."

"Very well. In the meantime, have you a message for Jerence?"

His tone was grim. "Yes. Tell him when I'm done with him he'll regret he was born." The line went dead.

Jerence waited anxiously under Tolliver's vigilant eye. "What did he say?"

I gave him the message.

He grimaced. "That's how I usually feel." He said no more.

At General Tho's office the duty sergeant shook his head. "He's gone to his apartment for the night, sir. Shall I ring him?"

"No." I would serve the General ill enough, nosing in his affairs. "Let it wait to morning." I led my flock to the Naval barracks and signed us in for the night.

Exhausted, I tossed and turned for hours. Finally, giving up on sleep, I wrestled into my clothes and went out.

The mess was closed, as were most offices. Naturally the comm room was manned, as was Naval HQ, but I had no business in either office. I wandered the corridors, hoping to make myself tired enough to sleep, paying little attention to where I went.

"May I help you, sir?"

Disconcerted, I stared at the U.N.A.F. sentry. "Um, where am I? What's in there?"

"This is *Victoria's* bay, sir. You're on Level 3."

My breath caught. "*Victoria.* Could I get a peek?"

He gestured to a nearby porthole.

"Thanks." I peered through the transplex hatch into the docking bay beyond, but couldn't see much of the fastship moored alongside. From what I saw of her disks she looked like any other vessel.

The bell chimed. A light flashed red as *Victoria's* inner lock cycled; someone was coming through from the fastship to the Station. Though the seal between ship and station was tight, inner and outer locks were never left open at the same time.

The station lock cycled. A young middy in crisp, fresh uniform stepped through. He saw my uniform, saluted, and stiffened to attention.

"As you—Ricky!"

Ricardo Fuentes, *Hibernia's* ship's boy during my first voyage, struggled to maintain a solemn expression. He broke into a pleased grin.

"As you were, Mr. Fuentes." I hesitated, held out my hand.

"They told me you were somewhere in Hope System, sir." He gripped my hand with obvious pleasure.

"Groundside, unfortunately. You've grown, boy." Ricky Fuentes had been thirteen when I'd last seen him, just promoted from cadet to middy, and off to Academy for a year of coursework.

"I'm almost sixteen, sir."

"Good Lord."

"*Vicky's* my first posting. Isn't she zarky? Commandant Kearsey got me the berth as a reward for first in nav class."

"Wonderful!"

"Thank you, sir." He paused. "What are you here for, sir?" Though it was none of a middy's business, Ricky seemed unaware of any breach of protocol.

My smile faded. "I'm on business for the Admiral."

"Yes, sir. I meant here outside our lock."

I smiled. Ricky had lost none of his youthful exuberance. "Getting a look at the new marvel."

We fell silent. I said reluctantly, "I'll be on my way, then."

"Yes, sir. It's good to see you again." As I turned he blurted, "Would you like to see her? Inside, I mean?"

Would I? I'd give a few fingers, if not a whole arm. I pointed to a corridor notice. "She's restricted, Ricky. Authorized personnel only."

"Let me ask Lieutenant Steiner, sir. He has the night watch. After I deliver these reports to HQ." He waved his chipcase.

"Don't bother him. It's not that important." I tried to sound nonchalant.

"Aye aye, sir. But Mr. Steiner is a good joe, sir, and he'll probably let me show you around."

"Well . . ."

"Let me drop these off, sir. I'll be back as quick as I can."

I surrendered. "Very well, Mr. Fuentes."

"Right, sir. I'll try to hurry, but if I get any more demerits for running I'm in big trouble." He saluted again, scurried off. His pace . . . well, it wasn't quite a run.

Half an hour later I was shaking hands with *Victoria's* officers. "I'm sorry, Captain Martes, I had no idea Mr. Steiner would wake you." As a full Captain I was senior to him, but I had no rights aboard his ship.

The young Commander grinned, waved away my apology. "He had to, sir. I'm the only one authorized to allow visitors."

"I'm sorry."

"Well, sir, you've had three ships of your own. What would you think of a Captain who minded being awakened in the night?"

"Good point." I relaxed somewhat. From midshipman on, we learned to catch our sleep when opportunity came, and never to expect a full night undisturbed.

"Besides, it's a great honor to meet you, Mr. Seafort. We've heard all about you. I'll show you the bridge first, if you like. That will be all, Mr. Fuentes."

Ricky's face fell. "Aye aye, sir." He saluted, spun on his heel, and left. Vax Holser, once his senior, had taught him well.

The bridge was much like *Challenger's*. I stood behind Captain Martes's chair to peer at the instruments while he and Lieutenant Steiner stood by. Only the fusion drive screen was different from ones I knew. Where I'd traced my finger down the screen from OFF to ON, the controls now read OFF, PRIMED, and ON. I raised an eyebrow.

"It's Augmented Fusion, Mr. Seafort. We begin by priming the drives, firing them but holding their output just short of Fusion. Then we mesh the Augmentation wave with the fusion drive's N-wave, and let her go."

My head spun. I had never fully grasped the technical aspects of Fusion, no matter how hard I tried. "Holding short . . . that sounds dangerous."

He grinned. "Very. You're heating the drive shaft walls while you prime, so you've only got about twenty seconds to synchronize the waves, or you'd better shut down."

"I would turn it off automatically," said a cold female voice from the speaker.

"Yes, of course." He made a rueful gesture. "Captain Seafort, our puter, Rosetta."

"Hello," I said awkwardly.

"Good evening, Captain." A fractional pause. "Or good night, as it were. Isn't it rather late for social contacts?"

"Rosetta!" Martes was scandalized. "Mr. Seafort is a U.N.N.S. Captain!"

"I'm aware. William tightbeamed me his dossier. My question was for informational purposes only. No disrespect was implied or should be inferred."

"Enough. Rosetta, put the aft view on the simulscreen, please."

"Aye aye, sir," she said primly. Almost instantly a camera view from aft of Level 2 flashed on the huge simulscreen that filled the front bulkhead of the bridge.

Large ships, such as *Hibernia*, had three Levels. Smaller vessels like *Challenger* had only two. The Navy had a few cutters with but one Level, but they were obsolete; it was more economical to build vessels that could transship the volumes of cargo the larger ships supported. *Victoria* was a two-decker.

At the moment the simulscreen pictured the wave-emission chamber astern of the engine room. Where a normal ship's stern tapered outward in a graceful curve, *Victoria*'s was thick and stubby. Nor did her drive shaft extend as far aft as I expected.

"Looks odd, doesn't it?"

"Yes, Mr. Martes."

"She's not much for looks, but she goes like a bat out of hell."

I frowned at the phrase, but ignored it for politeness' sake. "What other changes did they make?"

"Other than reducing us to minimal hold capacity, none. Of course, we're sadly lacking in lasers."

"Why?"

"To conserve mass, sir," said Steiner. "With the added mass of the laser mountings we wouldn't be able to put her into Fusion."

"I see." Fusion was a mystery whose depths I'd never be able to plumb.

"Bram is our Augmentation expert," said the Captain. "Anything happens to him and the Chief, it's back to the manuals. Anyway, they've made us into a sitting duck. Or rather, a sprinting duck. We can run, but we can't fight. That's the only reason I'll be glad to leave her."

I looked up. "Oh?"

"Transferred as of next week." His eyes sparkled. "To a fighting ship, I hope."

"Who's your replacement?"

"Don't know." He pointed vaguely beyond the hull. "I haven't been groundside yet. What's it like?"

I had to force my mind to my reply. "Hope Nation? It's lovely. Don't you have long-leave coming?"

"Deferred 'til our next run, sir. We've only been out nine months."

I let them walk me through the rest of the ship. The only time I pulled rank was when I insisted that Martes not wake the off-duty crew or officers. At length I found myself at the airlock, saying my good-byes.

"Your hospitality is appreciated, Captain. And yours, Lieutenant."

The young Commander grinned. "It's worth an hour of sleep to be able to say I met Captain Seafort."

I cleared my throat. "Yes. Well." I paused at the airlock hatch. "Your Mr. Fuentes. I commend him to you. An exemplary officer."

"Ricky? He's a good joey. And he's told us all about you."

"Ah." I saluted and made my escape.

10

"Inspect my shipment records?"

"Yes, sir." I tried to meet General Tho's eye. He had greeted me effusively when I'd entered. Now his manner was something else entirely.

"But—why?" He stood abruptly. "Never mind. You have the Admiral's authority. Why is none of my concern."

"I just want—"

"William has all our records on file. You may study them here, if you wish."

"I don't need to take up your office. I can—"

"It may not be my office when you're through."

I gaped, trying to get his meaning. I ventured, "You mean General Khartouf? He—"

"That too is not my concern. Review the records at your leisure." It was a dismissal. Cheeks flaming, I left.

In the outer office, Tolliver and Jerence waited while I stopped at the sergeant's desk. "Where can I find a console?"

"If you need to be private, use the quartermaster's office, two hatches to the east."

"Thank you. Come along," I snapped. My lieutenant and his charge followed as I stalked down the corridor. Under my breath, I cursed the ambition that had saddled me with this meddlesome job. I was short of sleep, ill-tempered, and still not recovered from my mad dash through Centraltown.

Jerence sullenly scuffed the deck. "Where are you taking me?"

"Tolliver, keep him out of my hair."

"Aye aye, sir." Tolliver smiled. "Say something, boy. Anything."

Jerence swallowed. In silence we marched to the quartermaster's office. The corporal in the outer office came to his feet. I growled, "General Tho sent me. Where's your console?"

"Mr. Cary's office, in there. But I don't think you should—" I was already slapping open the hatch. The console rested under a large screen that resembled the simulscreen on a bridge.

As I sat I realized I had no idea how to activate the Station's puter. On ship I would enter my ID code, of course. I tried it.

"May I be of service, Captain?" I jumped at the hidden voice.

"Uh, yes, William. How do I enter a request for data?"

"You might try asking me." I'd have sworn he smiled.

"Right." I glanced at Tolliver. Whatever humor he saw, he knew to keep to himself. "William, put the incoming cargo manifests for the last year on the screen, please."

"Certainly, sir." The screen was full before he finished speaking.

I tried to take in the overwhelming mass of data. "Um, show me arrival dates."

"Here you are, Mr. Seafort." He highlighted them.

I hadn't realized how much cargo flowed from home system to the Hope Nation colony. The screen was crammed with data, and had space to show only the first two months.

I remembered that I didn't have to examine it all. "Only military cargoes, please."

The screen shifted. Now, with less data, I could scan four months at a time. William's display ran across many columns, hundreds of lines deep. Each line represented a consignment ferried sixty-nine light-years from Earth to support our vast military buildup. Our strength here was second only to home system.

"Show the consignee of each cargo, please, and the intended destination."

"Right, Captain."

I puzzled through the data. "Now, where delivered and when."

"You've got it. What did you do to irk the Commandant?"

"Now add—I beg your pardon?"

"General Tho seemed put out after you left his office. I wondered why."

"You were there. Didn't you hear our conversation?"

He sounded offended. "No, of course not. I can't listen in unless I'm invited."

"I see."

"After you left Mr. Tho delivered a few remarks. He didn't order me to erase them."

"Don't repeat his private conversations," I said quickly. "Show two more months."

"Right." It sounded like a sigh.

I studied the shipping data. Many consignments had been dropped at Centraltown. A few had gone directly to Venturas Base, but most of the Venturas cargo had—

"I have to go to the bathroom."

Tolliver was already out of his seat. In one swift motion he snatched Jerence's arm and swept him toward the hatch. "Sorry, sir." They were gone.

Most of the Venturas cargo had been set down at Centraltown, where much of it still waited. Well, the Venturas Base didn't even have a proper landing strip; only the smallest of the Station's shuttles could drop cargo directly there. Mr. Eiferts would soon remedy that.

"William, show supply requisition dates and actual delivery dates." I studied the chart he generated. It looked as if General Tho had met his delivery schedules; cargo was off-loaded from incoming ships and barges and brought down to Centraltown when expected.

The hatch opened; Jerence and Tolliver went to their seats. The boy sat hugging himself, crying softly. I raised an eyebrow. Tolliver stared back impassively. I decided to let it pass unobserved, as with a middy.

"No problems here," I said to Tolliver. He crossed the room to read the screen from behind my seat.

"How far back did you check, sir?"

"A year."

"And how recently?"

His questions annoyed me. "To the present."

The speaker crackled. "Until *Victoria*, *Cordoba* was the last ship to dock, Captain. Four weeks ago."

"Thank you, William." I studied the chart; *Cordoba*'s cargo was listed as delivered to Centraltown as requested. "Well, that wraps it up. We could have done all this from groundside." I stood and snapped off the screen.

"It's good that General Tho's records aren't as confused as the quartermaster's," Tolliver said.

"True." My head ached, and I didn't want to be sidetracked. "Tho stays on top of his paperwork." I grimaced at Tolliver. "We could visit the cargo bays, I suppose. Just a formality. Get up, Jerence, we're done here."

The boy leapt to his feet, with an anxious glance at Tolliver. I opened the hatch, recalling the endless frustration of paperwork on a ship such as *Hibernia*. "William, how often are deliveries updated?"

"Actual delivery, Captain, or the request dates?"

"Actual, of course. The request dates wouldn't be updated."

"I post actual delivery dates immediately after the shuttles land with their cargo."

"Who posts the dates on which the quartermaster requests his supplies be delivered?" I crossed back to the console.

An infinitesimal pause. "Which time, Mr. Seafort?"

I held my annoyance in check. "You said they're only posted once."

"No, Captain," William sounded prim. "You said that."

It was like pulling teeth. "When else is the requested delivery schedule updated?"

"Approximately monthly, Captain."

Tolliver whistled under his breath.

I frowned. "But why?"

"To conform to actual deliveries," said William.

I blinked.

Tolliver said with awe, "The son of a bitch rewrites his delivery requests to match what he actually delivers!"

"That's approximately correct," agreed William. "Minus the expletives."

I grated, "What fool orders that?"

"I do." A voice came from the hatchway.

I whirled. "General? But . . ." I sank into my seat. "Who told you what we were reviewing?"

"William mentioned it." The diminutive, neatly dressed man fingered his razor mustache.

"Mr. Tolliver, take Jerence outside." The moment the hatch was closed I demanded, "Why fudge your delivery dates?"

"To make the reports I send home look better." General Tho held my gaze until I had to look away.

I said bitterly, "For that, you made a shambles of our supply operation?"

"No. Supply was already a shambles. I move my cargoes groundside as fast as possible. Changing the schedules retroactively did no harm."

"Except to your integrity."

"Except that." He looked about uncertainly, chose a chair across from the console. "You're an innocent. If you knew politics, you'd understand."

My chest ached. I coughed, wishing I hadn't chased after Jerence. "I know what signing my name to a lie means."

He nodded. "Yes. I'll resign, if you like. Save you the trouble of dismissing me."

I tasted bile. "I have no authority to dismiss you."

"Odd, your dismissing General Khartouf, then." His stare was unflinching.

I gestured toward the screen. "Why was this charade necessary?"

"Necessary? I don't know that it was." He left his seat, stared moodily at the console. "Advisable, perhaps. Expected."

"By whom?"

"Seafort, you're Navy. You're the senior service. Naval appropriations sail through the General Assembly, and your Academy is deluged with applications. You steep your cadets in honor and tradition." He focused on something deep within the screen, perhaps light-years distant. "The Army's . . . different. U.N.A.F. has to fight for scraps after Navy's done feeding. So, we have to do a better job. Appear to do a better job."

"Who cares about delivery schedules at a colony sixty-nine light-years from home?"

"The General Staff cares." His tone was fierce. "They present thousands of figures like those I send, when they go hat in hand to the U.N. appropriations committees. What you see as falsifying records, personal dishonor, is a way of life for us. As long as no one is hurt . . ."

His hand flicked in a gesture of helplessness. "How did I come to this? When I bicycled across the hills to Vientiane to drop off my application at the recruiting station . . . I don't know." With a shrug he drew himself up to his full meager height, eyed me bleakly. "Do as you will. I'll be in my office."

"General, wait—" He was gone.

I sat motionless in the silent room. After a time I got to my feet, opened the hatch. Tolliver and Jerence waited in the corridor. "Let's go."

"What will you do, sir?" Tolliver fell in step beside me.

"Visit the cargo bays."

"I meant about General Tho. Now we have to go through all his records with a fine-tooth comb." He shook his head. "Lord God knows what corruption we'll find. Where do we start?"

I stopped short. "Do *we* make decisions now?"

Tolliver looked startled. "No, sir. I just thought—you obviously have to do something about him." Jerence glanced back and forth between us.

"Is that your order?"

Tolliver gulped. "No, sir, not at all. Excuse me."

My tone was savage. "I don't excuse you, Lieutenant. In future when I want your opinion I'll ask for it. Is that clear?"

"Yes, sir. Aye aye, sir."

Jerence shot him a vengeful look. I wheeled on him. "Behave!"

"Me?" He was indignant. "I didn't do anything."

"Yes, you did. If I see that look again, I'll set you in a cabin alone with Mr. Tolliver." That silenced him. It was handy having a bogeyman on staff. In mutual outrage we all trudged down the corridor to the cargo bays.

Hours later I sat in the officers' mess with Tolliver comparing notes. We'd found several cargo booking procedures that would benefit from change, but we'd uncovered no serious problems. A memo to the quarter-master would be the end of it.

"What about supplies to the fleet?" Tolliver asked.

"The fleet is out of my jurisdiction. The Admiral made that quite clear." I picked at my food. Across the table, Jerence wolfed his sandwich.

"Yes, sir." Tolliver cleared his throat. "And the General?"

"Is out of your jurisdiction, Lieutenant. As the fleet is beyond mine."

"Aye aye, sir." His eyes fell to his coffee, and remained there.

"Anyway, we still have to—" I fell silent.

Tolliver looked up. "What, sir?" He followed my gaze. Lieutenant Vax Holser carried a tray from the line, searching for a table.

I stood. "Wait with Jerence." I crossed the room. "Vax?"

The burly lieutenant looked up, startled. Emotions flitted across his face, quickly suppressed. "I didn't expect you here." He added as if an afterthought, "Sir."

I ignored his manner. "I'd like to talk with you."

"I wouldn't like that."

I closed my eyes, willing away the pain. "Please."

His lips compressed. "Whatever the Captain orders."

"It's not an order, Mr. Holser." I looked around. Most of the tables were occupied; I saw no private place to talk. "I'll wait in the corridor, Mr. Holser. Come if you wish. If not, I'll accept your decision." Without wait-ing for a reply I strode out.

Naval personnel of all ranks walked the corridor, going about their business. I paced.

Vax wouldn't come. I'd begun years ago by brutalizing him, and ended by spurning his friendship. He would never forgive me; it was painful for him even to speak to me. Anyway, what could I say to him? That I was sorry? That I'd meant only to save him? I thrust my hands in my pockets, paced with head down.

"I'm here." It was a challenge.

I whirled. "Don't sneak up on me! What's wrong with you?" Thoughts of conciliation were forgotten.

Vax eyed me steadily. "Nothing. What's wrong with you, other than the mess you've made of your face?"

I bit back an angry retort. "Vax, why won't you speak to me?"

His glare could have melted an alumalloy hull. "You know God damned well why."

"Don't blaspheme!" My fury matched his own.

"That's no longer your concern, Captain Seafort. I'm on the Admiral's staff now."

"Vax," I said hoarsely. "Tell me what you won't forgive."

He was silent for a long time. When his eyes finally met mine, they were cold. "You bastard."

I gaped. Even in informal conversation, a lieutenant couldn't—I thrust down my indignation. "What did I do?"

"You saved me," he said simply.

"But I—"

"On *Portia*, whenever Alexi sent Philip Tyre up to be caned, I beat him with especial relish, because he was what I might have become without you. He was cruel and sadistic, and unappeasable. You saved me from that."

"I'm glad."

"We were friends."

"Yes."

"And then you discarded me." The words slashed.

"*Challenger?*"

"Yes, *Challenger.*" He glanced around, saw that nobody was looking, shoved me against the bulkhead. "I could kill you, Seafort."

"Vax," I said in anguish, "I wanted you to live. No more than that."

He bellowed, "I wanted to be loyal! No more than that!" Stunned, I could say nothing. "I wanted to follow you, even if it cost my life. What right had you to make that decision for me? Who appointed you God?"

"I was Captain." I knew that wasn't enough. "Vax, I didn't care any longer. I'd lost Nate, and—and—" I found it hard to speak. "And I'd lost Amanda. I was going to my death. I didn't want you swept up in that."

"You had no right to make the choice for me."

"As Capt—"

"Not if we were friends."

The words hung heavy in the silence. I forced myself to meet his eye. "Forgive me, Vax."

"No, not ever." The finality shook me.

"I've been through—you don't know what I had to endure on that cruise. I'm damned, and have no one but myself to blame. Please, Vax. Be with me."

"No. You made your choice." His eyes burned like lasers. "And I've made mine." He strode away.

I walked the corridor until I was composed enough to face Tolliver and the boy. At length I took a deep breath, went back into the mess. Vax Holser was nowhere in sight.

"Tolliver, book us seats on the next shuttle groundside."

"Aye aye, sir." He spotted a caller, went to it. I sat heavily at the table, across from Jerence.

"Is something wrong, Mr. Seafort?"

"Yes."

"Can I help?"

I was enraged at his sarcasm, until I realized he meant it. "There's nothing you can do."

"What happened?"

"An old friend I betrayed. He . . . told me what he thinks of me."

"You didn't betray him."

I smiled without mirth. "How would you know?"

"I've seen you with Pa and I've heard Uncle Emmett. I know."

I cleared my throat. "Thank you."

"There's always goofjuice." His tone was bitter.

I raised my gaze from the table. "Why do you use it, Jerence?"

"What else is there for me on a frazzing plantation? The world is different when you're juiced. You'd have to try it to understand."

I didn't tell him that I had, once. On Lunapolis, many leaves ago, as a green and stupid midshipman. I never touched the juice again. Not because I didn't like how it made me feel, but because I knew that given another taste of euphoria I might never give it up.

He stared at his empty plate. "Anyway, it's better than having to face farming all my life."

I smiled despite myself. "That's not written in stone, Jerence."

"There's Pa." He looked sullen. "I'm firstborn, so Branstead Plantation goes to me. I've told him I don't want it, but he won't listen. I don't think he even hears."

"A shuttle leaves in about an hour, sir." Tolliver.

"Very well." I stood. "We might as well head toward the bay."

We left the mess and wandered the endless corridors. To pass the time I showed Jerence the comm room. Some of the techs I'd met previously were on duty. The boy perused the rows of consoles, most of them silent now. After a while we left for the shuttle bay.

I would be glad to depart the Station, happier never to return.

We passed the cutoff for U.N.A.F. Command. I slowed, hesitated. "In here, first."

"The shuttle is past—"

"I know where the shuttle bay is." I stalked to the General's office, Tolliver and Jerence hurrying to keep up. I slapped open the hatch.

The desk sergeant eyed me uncertainly. "General Tho's in conference, sir."

"Get him out."

"What?"

"You heard me!"

A moment later General Duc Twan Tho stood in his outer office, hands on hips. His stare was icy. "Well?"

"This is private, sir."

He pursed his lips. "Very well. In my office." He turned on his heel. I thought it better not to sit. "I'm leaving for Centraltown."

"So I understand."

"I don't expect to be back."

"Very well."

"We've made a few recommendations about cargo storage. Mr. Tolliver will prepare a memo to your quartermaster."

"Very well."

I turned to leave. "Another matter. You needn't update your delivery paperwork so often; it's inefficient." His eyes bored into me. Reddening, I mumbled, "I'll write you a memo when I have the chance." I fled.

"Thank you." His soft voice pursued me into the corridor. "Thank you, Mr. Seafort."

Harmon Branstead struggled with his disapproval. "I wouldn't have chosen to reward him with a tour of Orbit Station."

My cold had settled into my chest. "I'm sorry I interfered, Mr. Branstead."

"No, I'm glad you caught him. I already told you that." He stared at the heli parked on the tarmac, in which Jerence waited, slumped in the passenger seat. He sighed. "Forgive my manners. This whole business—I don't know what to do."

"I understand."

He brooded, then snapped his fingers. "By the way, Emmett says one of our hands saw Frederick Mantiet in Centraltown."

My fist clenched. "Where?"

"Downtown, near the sailors' district."

"Did you alert the authorities?"

"Governor Saskrit? On Hope Nation, we handle these affairs ourselves. Laura Triforth and I took a few men and searched. We couldn't find him."

"I see."

He gestured to the cargo stacked at the far end of the runway. "What did you learn about that situation?"

"Orbit Station downloads cargo as fast as it can. They have little contact with the quartermaster groundside. Loads end up here whether they're needed or not."

"As Laura said, then."

"Yes."

"What will you do about it?"

I said stiffly, "We're working on it." My glance flickered to the heli. "What about Jerence?"

Harmon shook his head in exasperation. "I've no idea what to try next. Between the goofjuice and his nonsense about ceding the plantation to his younger brother . . ."

"He's a bright little joey." If it weren't for the goofjuice, a tour in the Navy might do him wonders.

"I'm considering an abuse program at the hospital. I'd hoped it wouldn't come to that."

"It'll come to worse if the authorities catch him first." Society wasn't lenient with substance violators, and hadn't been since the end of the Rebellious Ages. Rightly, the law made no distinctions for age; even at thirteen Jerence could land in a penal colony for possession of the contraband drug.

After Branstead's heli receded into the late-afternoon sun I checked in at Admiralty House to drop off my reports. Then I dismissed Tolliver and headed home.

Annie was waiting in the living room, dressed, her coat across her lap. Wearily I stripped off my jacket. "Going out?"

"I don't know." I looked at her, my eyebrow raised. "It depends. Nicky, we have to talk."

"About what?"

"What happened with—about me and Eddie."

"We've spoken about it." I wanted only to lie down.

"No, we haven't." Her vehemence surprised me, yet seemed oddly familiar. I realized it reminded me of Amanda.

"Talk, then." I sat.

"Nick, I did a wrong thing. I know I did, and I can't take it back. You don' understand tribe, an' I hurt you." She paused, marshaling her diction. "But we're married. You say it's for the rest of our lives. I want you to care for me, to love me. If not—" She mumbled something into her hands.

"I didn't hear the last." My voice was wooden.

"I said if you can't, I'll move out."

"Where would you go?"

She shook her head. "I'd find someplace. Or live on the streets, if it came to that. I'm a trannie, remember?"

"Not anymore."

Her eyes filled with tears. "What are we to do, Nicky?"

"I don't know." Images overlapped on the canvas of my mind: Annie sitting in my cabin, struggling to become more than she was. Annie crying in my arms. The pair of us coupling with unending passion, before she sent me back to the hospital for my interview with Dr. Tendres. Annie clutching the broad white back of Eddie Boss.

We sat miserably in the darkening room. At length she stirred. "I'll be leavin', den," she said with forlorn dignity. "My things be packed."

I said hoarsely, "Don't." I didn't know why.

Her mouth twisted into a sad smile. "Why, you gonna say you lovin' me?"

I thought a long time. "I don't know."

"I be leavin'," she repeated.

There was an unbearable tightness in my chest. "You stay. Let me go away for a while, to think things through."

That brought a flash of anger. "An' how long you hav'n me wait?"

"As long as you want to." I forced myself to meet her eye. "I'm unfair to you, I know. But I need time."

She nodded and began to weep. I yearned to go to her, hold her. Images of Eddie Boss came unbidden, and I did not.

I crossed to the bedroom, threw clothes into my duffel. "I'll be in Naval barracks. We'll talk in a few days. All right?" She nodded again. I left my home.

Tolliver showed no reaction when I told him I'd moved. That was understandable; a Captain's personal life was none of a lieutenant's business, and I'd already made my animosity to him clear. I thought again of having him transferred. Though I abhorred his company, I took no action. Perhaps I deserved him.

When I was leaving to visit Alexi, Tolliver asked to come along.

We found Alexi scrolling through a holo in the patients' lounge. I told him about our trip.

"Orbit Station? Have I been there?"

"*Portia* docked at the Station when she came in."

"I wouldn't remember." He sounded especially bitter.

"All incoming ships moor at the Station, Mr. Tamarov." Tolliver was trying to be helpful. I shot him a look of annoyance, but he appeared not to notice.

Alexi got up to stare out the window. "What do you do next?" he asked.

"I'm leaving this afternoon to see Zack Hopewell and the planters." I hesitated. "I wish I could bring them better news. We can clean up the supply mess, but I can't do a thing about shipping rates, or the influx of sailors and soldiers in Centraltown, or the structure of their government."

Alexi's gaze was fixed on the walkway below. "While you were gone I spent a whole evening sitting in the chair you're in now, just trying to remember."

I got up, went to stand at his side. "And?"

"Nothing." He turned, and his smile was bitter. "I tried to remember you, before I was injured. I can recall your sitting here, that first visit, telling me things you expected me to know. But nothing before."

"I'm sorry."

He rounded on me. "You're always sorry, but you don't have to live with it!"

"I'm sor—" I floundered. "Alexi, I don't know what to say."

"Then say nothing! Save your pity for someone else!"

Wounded, I said stiffly, "I wish I could give what you want." From the corner of my eye I saw Tolliver's disapproval, whether of Alexi's behavior or mine I couldn't tell.

"How can you—Christ, I'm doing it again!" Dejected, Alexi slumped on his bed. "Forgive me."

"Alexi, staying in the hospital does you no good."

"What else is there?"

"You can come with me. You were part of my staff. I want you back."

"On active duty?"

I smiled, shaking my head. Even I couldn't arrange that. "On therapeutic leave."

Tolliver inquired, "What's that, sir?"

"I'm not sure. I'll pull strings to make it happen. Alexi, would you like to go to the plantation zone with us?"

His eyes were eager. "Very much."

"Then you shall."

I checked Alexi out of the hospital and drove to the spaceport, where Tolliver had secured a heli. During our preparations Alexi stayed pathetically close to my side, though he looked just like the confident young lieutenant with whom I'd sailed on *Portia*. I wished I could allay his fears; all I could do was squeeze his arm in reassurance. We boarded the heli.

"You know how to fly, Mr. Seafort?"

"Yes, Mr. Tamarov. I learned at Academy."

"Did I?"

"As I recall, you were heli-rated. It's been some time since I saw your personnel file."

Alexi lapsed into moody silence. I finished my safety check and we lifted off toward the plantation zone. The heli's puter displayed our flight plan. Our ETA was approximately an hour and a half. Alexi craned to see the terrain below. After a time he asked, "Do you like Hope Nation, Mr. Seafort?"

I pondered, unsure of the truth. At length I said, "I've spent most of my career traveling to or from Hope Nation."

"But do you like it?"

I grimaced.

"Leave the Captain be." Tolliver.

"No, I don't mind. Hope Nation has a lot of memories. Some are painful."

Alexi said only, "It's hard to imagine memories being painful."

"They can be." The day I'd learned that Captain Forbee had no Captain to replace me, which meant I'd command *Hibernia* for another cruise. The evening I'd gone to Amanda's house to say good-bye, but instead persuaded her to join my vacation to the unspoiled Venturas.

"Amanda lived here, Alexi." Before she'd returned to home system with me, to sail to her death on *Portia*. It was she who'd turned Alexi from his bitter course of vengeance against Philip Tyre.

Alexi asked, "Who was Amanda?"

I said shortly, "My wife." The mother of my only son. Now she drifted with him in the endless gulf of interstellar space.

"You loved her a great deal."

"You remember?" I asked hopefully.

"It's in your face," he said.

I cast about for another topic. "Do you remember Hauler's Rest?"

"No. Should I?"

"Last month we thought of stopping there, on our trip to Branstead Plantation. You and I and . . ." I trailed off, wishing I hadn't summoned memories of Eddie.

"And Mr. Boss?"

"You remember him?"

"He was in my room when I woke." Alexi studied me. "You were friends?"

"I don't care to speak of him." I concentrated on navigation until I could be sure of calm.

"What is Hauler's Rest?" Alexi.

"A sort of inn, the only one on Plantation Road. I've eaten there more than once."

"On your first cruise?"

"Yes." With Derek Carr. More memories stabbed. Innocent days: Derek forced to masquerade as my retarded cousin so he could safely visit Carr Plantation; he retaliated by calling me "Nicky" every chance he got. If only I could be that youngster again, and blot out what had come after.

"Would you like to lunch there?" I asked.

"Sure." His face fell. "I have no money, Mr. Seafort."

"Haven't you been drawing your pay?"

"I couldn't even tell you how much I'm paid, much less how to get it." He grimaced. "What should I do?"

"I'll sign for lunch." I checked the maps and turned to a new heading. "Tolliver, make a note to retrieve Mr. Tamarov's back wages when we get home."

"Aye aye, sir."

I homed in on the Hauler's Rest transponder and brought us down at the edge of the strip bulldozed through the lush vegetation. Half a dozen cargo haulers were scattered about.

Inside, we ordered from the ample menu. I explained that Hauler's Rest was all but self-sufficient; it grew its own meat and vegetables and was powered by an atomic pile buried in the back lot.

"Not an automated fusion reactor, like Orbit Station's?"

I smiled with surprise and pleasure. "How did you remember, Alexi?"

"I don't know." He concentrated. "I learned it somewhere; I've no idea where."

"Second year physics at Academy," said Tolliver impatiently.

Alexi's brow furrowed. "These automated fission piles are safe, but the fusion reactors our ships use are even safer."

"That's right," I said. "But even the fission reactors can't be made to malfunction without a series of deliberate missteps. They have intricate safeguards."

Alexi looked around. "If this pile ever did blow, it would make quite a hole in the ground."

"Vaporize everything for about a mile," Tolliver agreed with relish. "But that's nothing to the mess you'd make if you made a fusion engine blow. You wouldn't want to be anywhere near."

"Change the subject, please."

"Why?" Alexi.

We were skirting dangerous ground; if someone overheard us we might even be subject to a capital charge. U.N. Security Council Resolution 8645, passed back in 2037, had provided . . . I closed my eyes and concentrated.

"The threat of nuclear annihilation having for generations terrorized mankind, it is enacted that use, attempted use, conspiracy to use, proposal to use, or discussion of use, by any persons in any forum and for whatever purpose, of nuclear energy for the purpose of destruction of land, goods, or persons, shall be punishable by death and by no lesser sentence, and that the sentence of death may not be suspended or mitigated by any court, tribunal, or official." They'd made us memorize it, as cadets, and no other discussion of the topic was permitted.

"You can't even discuss it?"

"No!"

Our food arrived and we fell to. Between mouthfuls Tolliver said soberly, "Before I left home system, there was talk in the Assembly of amending the resolution."

"It'll never happen."

"God forbid they change it. But—"

"Even those dolts in the Rotunda wouldn't be so stupid! Two nuke wars were enough; the people wouldn't risk another, even for a minute. Don't even speak of such abominations!" I stabbed savagely at my meat.

Alexi gestured across the room. "Are all those joeys haulers? I didn't see that many cargo vehicles in the lot."

I tried to take the edge from my voice. "Some must be laborers." I regarded the tables crowded with rough-looking workers. "Harvest is near."

"Aren't the plantations largely automated?" asked Tolliver.

"They are, but they're so huge it takes a lot of men to run the machinery." Our uniforms seemed to be attracting the haulers' attention. One burly fellow stared at us for a while, then got up and left the hall.

The meal was huge, and though I still wasn't recovered from my cold I took advantage of a hearty appetite. It was nearly an hour before we crossed the lot to our heli. I slipped behind the controls; Alexi got in back. Tolliver, moody, stared out the window from the seat next to mine. I lifted off and headed west. As I pulled back on the collective and gave her more throttle, Hauler's Rest shrank below.

It was a beautiful day. Flying high, we'd have a better view. At the controls of a heli I felt none of the trepidation I knew driving an electricar. Airborne, I wouldn't have to contend with other vehicles careening alongside; perhaps that made a difference.

"Mr. Tolliver, advise Hopewell Plantation of our ETA, please."

"Aye aye, sir." He keyed the caller. A red light on the control panel began to blink. He froze.

The puter came alive. *"Enemy radar lock! Commencing evasive action!"*

"What—?" I gaped.

"Reset the puter," Tolliver said. "It caught a radar from one of the plantations."

"Yes," I said doubtfully. The heli was military transport, programmed to be wary of hostile attack. If we'd entered Hopewell's radar field the heli would assume enemy sensors had locked on us. "Disregard radar signal," I told the puter, switching off the warning light. "Do we have Hopewell's transponder yet?"

"We should pick it up any—"

The heli lurched. *"Missile launched! Automated evasive action sequenced! Transponder off!"*

I said, "Listen, puter, there's no missile out—"

"What's that flash, sir?"

I peered. "Lord God! It can't be!"

"Contact estimated fourteen seconds!" The puter's tone was calm.

"Jesus." Tolliver.

Should I let the heli do the evasives or take manual control? The puter could run evasive maneuvers faster than I could and more accurately. But its reactions were programmed, and the missile's attack program might anticipate them.

What was after us? A heat seeker? Laser lock? I tried desperately to recall our lessons at Academy.

In the back seat Alexi clutched the safety bar as the heli swooped. The attacking missile was a dim speck, a dot, a stubby black slash hurtling toward us.

"Take over!" Tolliver shouted. "Don't wait for the puter!"

"Contact eight seconds." The puter. *"Evasive program C12!"* The jet engines whined as the puter put us to full power in a shallow climb.

"Four seconds."

Tolliver shouted, "Seafort, do something!"

I stabbed at the manual override. Before I touched it the engine noise fell; we dropped like a stone. The missile flashed past the cockpit. The engine roared. I twisted around. Behind us, the missile was executing a long, slow turn while it climbed.

This time it would come at us from above. The speaker blared, *"Radar lock reacquired!"* The missile had found us anew.

I switched off the automatics, holding us in a tight turn to the left. I couldn't find the missile. My eyes darted between the screen and the horizon. Was there time to set us down?

"Contact sixteen seconds."

No time. Where had the missile come from? Who fired it? Never mind that. I jammed my foot on the tail rudder, yanked back on the collective. We veered suddenly to the right and climbed.

"Radar lock. Contact eleven seconds."

"Christ, Seafort, let me take it!" Tolliver leaned across the seat.

I throttled down, slammed the stick forward. We dropped. The missile made a slight correction to follow us.

"Contact eight seconds!"

"You'll get us killed! Give me the frazzing controls!"

I shook my head. "No time."

Tolliver unhooked my seat belt, hauled me out of my seat with manic strength. "Move!" He threw me aside, swung into the pilot's seat. At full throttle, he spun us a hundred eighty degrees to face the missile.

I screamed, "Are you crazy?" Flung against Alexi, I clawed at the handholds.

"Shut up!" Tolliver's every muscle was tensed.

"Contact four seconds. Three."

I braced for the inevitable.

"Two."

My heart shot through my throat as we dropped. I could hear the throb of the missile's engine past the roar of our own. It missed us by scant inches.

"We have a few seconds to put down," Tolliver shouted. "Jump the instant we hit!"

I peered out. "It's all forest!"

"There's got to be someplace flat!"

"Radar lock!"

"Christ damn it." Tolliver banked to get a better view of the terrain. "Look ahead, about half a mile." A small clearing, light green against the dark of the trees.

"We don't have time!"

"It'll be close," Tolliver acknowledged.

"Contact twelve seconds."

"Seafort, get on the horn, tell Centraltown!"

I cursed; I should have thought of that myself. I reached over the seat, grabbed the caller, trying to remember Naval frequency. No, idiot, use the emergency channel. I thumbed the caller. "Centraltown Control, this is Naval heli eight six oh Alpha, Captain Seafort, we're under missile attack from unknown source, location approximately one hundred twenty miles west of Hauler's Rest. Mayday! Mayday!" No answer.

"*Contact nine seconds.*"

We were a few hundred yards from the field, closing with dreamlike slowness. "Hurry, Tolliver!"

"If I don't bleed off speed we'll crash."

"*Contact six seconds!*"

"Crash, then!" Better that than dissolve in a ball of fire.

"Hang on!" We swooped toward the field. A hundred yards.

"*Contact three seconds! Two!*"

Tolliver hauled back on the collective. We shot into the air. Through the rear transplex I saw the missile turn upward to correct course. Tolliver slammed down the stick and we fell toward the edge of the field.

The missile had no time to correct again. It shot over the cab of the heli. A thud, a burst of light. Fire. The engine screamed. The heli lurched, spun, dropped. Tolliver slapped off the switches. "Brace yourselves!"

We slammed into the ground on our landing gear, bounced, struck again. Flames soared from the mast above the cab.

"Out! Get out!"

I flung open the door, stumbled out, rolled away from the blazing heli. Tolliver pushed Alexi out, leaped to follow. He dropped on top of Alexi, jumped to his feet, thrust Alexi clear of the flames.

We ran.

Sixty feet away, we turned to look at the fiery wreckage.

"Jesus, Lord Christ!" I gasped for breath.

"Amen." Tolliver was grim.

"Keep moving, there may be more coming!"

"Radar showed only one missile, Mr. Seafort."

"But who in hell was shooting?"

Tolliver shrugged. "Mantiet?"

"But we're the Government!" I realized how fatuous I sounded. "You're probably right. He tried to kill us before."

Alexi stared at the debris.

Tolliver asked, "How could he get hold of a missile?"

"The planters helped move supplies to the Venturas Base." I kicked at a smoking piece of rotor blade. "Someday I'll settle with him."

"Mantiet may come looking. Let's get out of here, sir."

"He'll have heard my Mayday. He'll expect U.N.A.F. to send a heli, fast. I doubt he'll risk showing himself."

Alexi fell to his knees, retching. Tolliver put his hands on Alexi's shoulders. "Easy, Mr. Tamarov," he said gently. "We're safe."

I stared, realizing, as I calmed, what Tolliver had done.

Alexi coughed, wiped his mouth with his sleeve. "Sorry. God, I'm so sorry."

Tolliver released him. He glanced up, saw my expression. He faced me and sighed. Slowly he unholstered the laser pistol at his belt, handed it to me, butt first.

"Follow me." I turned, strode to the edge of the field without looking back. When we were out of Alexi's earshot I stopped. My voice grated. "What charges should I file, Lieutenant?"

"That's for you to decide, sir." He was pale.

"Answer."

"Mutiny. Insubordination. Striking a superior officer. Uninvited physical contact with the commanding officer. Three of them are capital. Does it matter if there are more?"

I snarled, "If I say so, it matters!"

"Aye aye, sir!" His eyes held mine. "Disrespectful speech and conduct. Unlawful usurpation of authority. I can't think of others, sir."

"Your excuse?"

"I have none, sir."

"Belay that! Answer!"

His smile was bitter. "You were always a lousy pilot. You had the lowest ratings in our barracks." And I'd spent many hours working off demerits as a result.

"So?"

"My taking over was our only chance."

"You were so sure I couldn't outmaneuver that missile?"

"Yes. Weren't you?"

I was silent, then sighed. "I should have handed over to you immediately." I bunched my fists. "But I didn't."

He shook his head. "No, sir. I made a split-second decision. I know the consequences."

"Do you?"

"You'll have me tried for mutiny or the other capital charges. I have no defense. I'm dead."

"Yes." He winced, but didn't look away. I turned my back, thrust my hands in my pockets, paced with head down. I wanted so to hurt him, to revenge the humiliations he'd inflicted on me as a cadet. He'd given me an unparalleled opportunity. I could have him put to death, and no one would question my motive. None would know how much my hatred moved me.

The temptation was unbearable.

I whirled. "Do you demand court-martial, or will you accept summary punishment?"

"Summary—?" He gaped, hardly daring to believe his fortune. "Yes, sir. Thank you, sir." Had he chosen court-martial his execution was a foregone conclusion. On the other hand, a commanding officer might issue summary punishment without a trial, but the penalties were far less severe.

"Very well." I faced him, hands clasped behind my back. "When were you commissioned lieutenant, Tolliver?"

"On the way out to Hope Nation, about a year ago. Captain Hawkins—"

"You're back to middy, as of today." My voice was harsh.

"I'm twenty-five, sir." Midshipmen who hadn't yet made lieutenant by that age rarely did so after, and we both knew promotion to lieutenant was the ambition of every midshipman's life.

"You heard me," I said. He'd unceremoniously hauled me from my seat. That couldn't be borne.

His jaw clenched. "Aye aye, sir."

"You're docked two months pay, and I reprimand you for insolence. You'll have to sign acknowledgment, of course. If you prefer, you go to court-martial."

"Aye aye, sir." He stared at the ground. "Thank you," he muttered at last. I understood. Though the reprimand and loss of rank would blight his career, he was fortunate to escape with his life.

I blurted, "God, I despise you!"

A momentary look of dismay flitted across his features, but he said only, "Yes, sir." I held his eye a moment longer, then stalked back to the clearing. Tolliver followed.

Alexi waited, pale but composed, near the wreckage of our heli. "What do we do now, Mr. Seafort?"

"We—" I looked around. "Anyone know where we are?"

"About thirty miles south of Hopewell Plantation," said Tolliver. I marveled that while jinking the aircraft to avoid an incoming missile he still kept track of his position.

"Too far to walk," I said.

"Did you hear an answer to your Mayday, sir?"

"No." I found my legs trembling; I squatted against a tree. "We should wait, I suppose." As soon as I spoke I realized it was foolish. As my

Mayday hadn't been acknowledged, help lay elsewhere. "Which way to Plantation Road?"

"It should be north, sir."

"How far?"

Tolliver looked at me strangely. "About thirty miles, sir." Of course. The road ran directly in front of Hopewell Plantation, and he'd just told me the distance.

I got to my feet. My chest ached. "If they didn't catch our signal we'll need to hike out. The sooner we start, the better our chances."

Tolliver ventured, "But if they did hear us, we'll lose them in the woods."

"It's my decision, Midshipman." My tone was curt.

Tolliver's look was sullen, but he said at once, "Aye aye, sir."

"We have no food or water," Alexi said.

"No." We hadn't carried much in the way of supplies, and the heli's emergency kits were lost in the fiery wreckage. We would probably run across a stream, but we'd have to do without food. Two days walk. Surely we could manage that. "Let's go, then."

Tolliver looked back at the smoldering heli. "We should leave a signal."

He was right. "An arrow, scratched into the turf?"

"There's scrap metal from the rotor housing. We could use pieces to make a sign."

"Very well." He gathered the scraps and arranged them in an unmistakable arrow, pointing north. When he was done we trudged across the clearing. I stopped at the far edge to stare back at the wreckage. If it weren't for Tolliver we'd be cremated in what was left of the heli, yet I'd savaged him for saving us.

We hiked into the silent woods.

11

I set the pace, doing my best to hide my weariness. It was late afternoon; we kept the sun on our left. If we headed north, eventually we'd cross Plantation Road.

Alexi said, "Mr. Seafort, why does Mantiet want you dead?"

"I don't know. Leave me be." I tried to ignore his hurt expression.

For two hours we pushed through dense brush. In the hilly terrain the vegetation was fiercely competitive. Above, vines drooped from thick ropy limbs of towering trees. We had to duck under, climb through, brush aside undergrowth with each step.

"What's that?" Tolliver.

I stopped to listen. It might have been rotor blades, far in the distance.

"Should we go back?" Alexi asked.

"We'd lose two hours, if no one's there. Let's go on."

The sun was noticeably lower; I wondered how much farther we'd get before nightfall. And how long my stamina would last.

As I flagged, Tolliver took the lead and began holding vines aside so I wouldn't have to stoop. We made better progress. My breath rasping, I did my best to keep up.

A distant sound became a rumble, then the unmistakable whap of heli blades overhead. We stopped, listened. I squinted at the canopy above but could see nothing through the dense foliage. Above, the heli circled.

"Find a clearing."

Tolliver peered in all directions, then pointed. "Perhaps that way, sir. The light seems a little brighter."

"Hurry." We stumbled through the silent vegetation.

The heli blades receded, returned. Finally we reached the spot we sought, but the canopy there was only slightly thinner. We couldn't be seen from above. "Isn't there another place—"

Tolliver waved us silent. "Listen!"

A woman's voice was almost lost in the engine's drone. "Captain Seafort! Return to your heli! We can't find you in the trees!"

I cursed. We'd come too far to retrace our steps by nightfall.

Tolliver said, "U.N.A.F. would have gear to locate us, wouldn't they? Infra sensors and the like."

As if in reply the voice from the heli resumed. "Captain Seafort, can you show yourself? This is Laura Triforth. We heard your Mayday. Return to your heli or show yourself. Signal with a flare or fire." The message repeated, sometimes almost directly above us, sometimes distant as the heli roved above us.

"We don't have a flare or fire," Alexi muttered.

"I know. Head north, and hope we find a clearing." We resumed our trek. After a time, the growl of the heli faded.

I struggled to keep up. It was darkening fast, and still we groped through thick vegetation. "I need to go slower," I panted. The admission came unwilling from my lips.

Obediently Tolliver slowed.

Eons later, engine sounds overhead. A heli. I peered at the darkening sky.

A speaker crackled. "Captain Seafort, this is U.N.A.F. rescue heli three oh two. We are above you and tracking. Proceed northeast about half a mile; we should be able to see you."

Thank Lord God. With renewed strength we veered to the east in the fading light. After half an hour the disembodied voice guided us again, toward a clearing visible from the air. Dizzy and sweating, I staggered into the welcome glade. An outcrop of rock formed a steep hill, where the tall trees couldn't root. It was fully dark.

Two helis circled overhead. One swooped low, its floodlight searching. We waved until it fastened on us. The heli dropped lower, and the speaker boomed. "Captain, we can't hear you from here. Is anyone injured? Hold your arms straight out for yes, up for no." I swung my arms up. "We read a negative. Do you have food or water?" Again I raised my arms. "No food or water. We can't land here, Captain; there's no level ground. It would be safer to wait until daylight and lower you a rope. Can you wait until morning?" I held my arms straight out.

"Don't worry, Captain, we won't abandon you. I'll remain overhead for now. The second heli is returning for emergency supplies. We'll drop you what you need for the night. Remain in the clearing." I signaled affirmatively to show I understood, then let my arms sag. Trembling, I let myself down. The ground was cold and damp.

"You all right, sir?" Tolliver.

"Yes."

"You look ill."

I waved him away. He squatted, waiting.

My teeth chattered. I sat hunched against the cold while the pilot circled endlessly overhead. From time to time he aimed his searchlight; one of us waved. It seemed forever before the second heli returned.

I stared upward at the two searchlights circling in the darkness overhead. One of the helis began a cautious descent. The speaker blared. "Captain, we'll lower your supplies. Stand clear; we'll cut the line when the pack is near the ground." I gripped Alexi's arm, pulled myself to my feet. From the heli bay a large bundle began to emerge, swinging with the motion of the airship.

With practiced skill the pilot countered its sway, lowering the line until the pack was within a few feet of the ground. Then it dropped with a thud. I stood, dizzy.

Alexi bounded forward, pulled at the straps. "A tent, Mr. Seafort." I grunted. He pawed through the bundle. "Mattresses, self-inflating."

"I'll help with those." Tolliver's tone was cold. With a brusque motion he swept Alexi's arm aside.

"I can open—"

"I know how. You don't."

I tapped him on the shoulder. "Give Alexi the respect due his rank, or answer to me for it." He swallowed at my wrath. With savage satisfaction I stalked back to my seat.

"Stand clear below for a second load!" I looked up as a bundle emerged from the bay overhead.

When the package hit the ground Tolliver opened the straps, stood aside with careful courtesy while Alexi bent over to look.

"Dinner!" Alexi's grin was joyous. "A portamicro, steaks, drinks, coffee . . . even extra Q-rations."

"And this." Tolliver held up a military radio pack. I beckoned; he brought it. With icy fingers I fumbled with the transmitter. "Rescue heli, do you read me?"

"Loud and clear, Captain. That gear should make you more comfortable."

"Very much so." Behind me, on the only meager patch of level ground, Alexi and Tolliver were already setting up the tent.

"Do you know who shot at you?"

"I have no idea."

"Orbit Station tracked the missile from half a minute after launch. They think it originated about a hundred miles south. You should be safe for now; I doubt anyone can travel through that underbrush by night."

"Right." We'd barely managed during daylight.

"Orbit Station is in position to keep a radar lock on the area tonight.

Any suspicious blips and we'll be back in a flash. Anyway, you can reach Centraltown with that caller. You might even get through to the Station. We'll pick you up at first light. Sweet dreams."

"Thank you." I watched the heli lights recede toward Centraltown.

The micro and the radio were powered by the same Valdez Perma-batteries that ran our electricars. We had power to spare, and the techs had even included a couple of ground lights. An hour later I gnawed gratefully on my steak, an open sleeping bag wrapped around my shoulders. I stared moodily into the fire, coughing occasionally from the cold that had settled into my chest. The radio crackled at my feet, a reassuring contact with civilization.

Alexi crouched at my side. "I suppose Earth was once like this, Mr. Seafort."

"Earth could never have been so quiet." Though I knew Hope Nation had no animal life except what man had brought, still my ears strained for absent night sounds. Other than the logs spitting in our campfire, we heard nothing but the rustle of the trees.

"At home when I went to bed I could hear the supersonics take off."

"In Kiev?"

"Yes." He sat looking into the flames, hypnotized. "I should be grateful to be alive, but Lord God, I want to be whole again."

"I pray you will."

Across from us, Tolliver threw another chunk of wood onto the fire. We watched the sparks fly.

"What was it like when we were midshipmen, Mr. Seafort?"

"You were fifteen when I met you. I was first middy, you were junior."

"Were we friends?"

"From the start." Until I'd become Captain, when I'd allowed him to be so brutalized he'd begged to resign from the Service.

"Tell me about the wardroom."

I sought words to describe the complexity of feelings, of interactions among the youths in that crowded space. "There were conflicts. Vax Holser and I. He was a bully, at first."

"He treated you badly?"

"No, I was first middy; he couldn't. It was you he abused. You and Sandy."

Tolliver said, "Like all wardrooms, everywhere."

"When you're young you can handle that sort of thing," I said.

"I'm not young." Tolliver's voice was bitter.

I flared, "You made your bed, Middy, now sleep in it." My chest ached.

Tolliver stood, stared into the fire. "I think I'll do just that." He spun on his heel and stalked to the tent. He paused. "Good night, *sir*. And you, Lieutenant." His tone held the precise courtesy expected of a midshipman.

I grunted. Alexi, perhaps unaware of the byplay, bade him good night, eyes locked to the fire. After a time he asked, "Mr. Seafort, what was I like as a boy?"

I hesitated. "Cheerful. Good-hearted. Willing." Until I'd forced him into a vendetta with Philip Tyre that nearly swallowed his soul. "As you are now."

"I'm hardly cheerful." His smile was wan.

I yawned. Despite the steak I still felt unwell. "Shall we turn in?"

"May I sit and listen to the radio?"

"Of course, but there won't be much traffic at this hour. Do you know how to spread the dish?"

He nodded. "I'll come to bed in a while, Mr. Seafort. I won't wake you."

I stood slowly. "I doubt you could." In the tent I undressed and huddled on my mattress. A few feet away Tolliver breathed slowly, steadily. Was he awake, feigning sleep? Well, I'd provided him a miserable day. I wondered if I could stand being broken to midshipman as I'd done to him. Certainly my own behavior to Admiralty had warranted it, more than once. I shivered from cold, then, as the mattress warmed, drifted into blessed sleep.

"Mr. Seafort?"

I groaned, forcing my eyes open. It couldn't be morning yet.

It wasn't. "Yes, Alexi?" I stifled a groan.

"You'd better come listen."

"To what?"

"The radio."

"Bring it in—no, let him sleep." Coughing, I threw on my chilled clothes, swept the flap aside. "This better be imp—"

Static distorted a constant stream of urgent messages. "Maneuver C in effect! Two off the port bow! *Tarsus*, where are you?"

"Oh, God, Alexi." My voice was a whisper.

"*Hibernia* to Fleet, we're under attack! Three, five—Lord God, seven fish. Engine Room, prepare to Fuse! Forward lasers gone! Fusing!"

Alexi clutched my wrist, then snatched his hand away as if it had been burned. "Sorry! Please, I didn't mean to touch—"

"Belay that. Listen."

"Mr. Seafort, they threw something."

"What do you mean?" My head spun. I blinked.

"The radio said they dropped a missile, or whatever. At Centraltown."

I snatched up the caller and changed frequencies. "Admiralty House, Captain Seafort reporting." I waited. "Captain Seafort reporting to Admiralty House."

The wait was maddening. Finally the answer came. "Forbee here, Mr. Seafort."

"What's going on?"

"Full-scale attack. The Admiral left for Orbit Station the moment he heard the first reports. He'll be there in an hour. Eight ships are under assault, a couple of dozen fish at least. Are you still in emergency camp?"

"Yes. You heard about that?"

"We all did. Are you all right?"

"Yes." Dizzy and feverish, and it hurt to talk. But . . . "What's this about a missile?"

"A wild rumor. By coincidence, a meteorite hit near Centraltown tonight. Just a small one."

"Thank heavens."

"Sit tight, Mr. Seafort, and we'll have you out of there by morning."

"Right. Uh, Forbee . . . you remember when I was here three years ago? I met someone who said he was Captain Grone."

"I heard the story, sir. Things are a bit busy at the moment."

"He told me a wild tale about meteorites spraying something. The epidemic began shortly after."

"It was never confirmed, as I recall. But I'll alert the hospital just in case." I heard urgent words in the background, then Forbee's cry of dismay. "Oh, no!"

"What?"

"*Bolivar*'s gone."

Sickened, I closed my eyes. After a moment I said, "Godspeed, Mr. Forbee."

"And you, sir." We rung off.

While we huddled over the flickering fire, scattered reports of losses swelled into a disaster of major proportions. Fish roamed Hope Nation system, Defusing without warning alongside our ships. Alexi threw on wood until the fire blazed. I shivered nonetheless.

The tent flap moved; Tolliver emerged, buttoning his jacket against the evening cold. "What's going on, sir?"

"Attack."

"Where?"

"The fleet is engaged." My voice was hoarse.

He pulled a log next to the radio and sat. "Lord God help our men."

"Amen."

Long minutes passed. "*Hibernia* reporting; Defused in sector twelve; no fish in sight." Thank Lord God, *Hibernia* was intact.

"Acknowledged, *Hibernia*." The Station.

"*Gibraltar* reporting, sector three about twenty thousand kilometers above Hope Nation. Two fish, five hundred kilometers abaft. Make that three fish. Five! Station, they're—Good Lord!"

Admiral De Marnay, calmly. "*Gibraltar*, report your sighting."

"A swarm of fish! Maybe two dozen, and more Defusing in. Our radars show them clustered around a large object, not a fish, something else, much bigger. It wasn't there a minute ago. It could be—three fish, alongside! Engaging!"

We huddled around the portable dish, sleep forgotten. The speaker crackled with reports from ships announcing course changes.

"*Gibraltar* here. Forward lasers out of commission; we're Fusing!"

"*Intrepid* reporting. We've taken out two fish, engaging a third. Damn it, the bastard Fused clear!"

I shook my head, cursing the dizziness that resulted. "They're winning."

Tolliver said, "Maybe not. We're getting them too."

"But how many are there?" Our losses, horrid as they were, might be supportable if we took out a high enough proportion of the fish.

"And where do they come from?" Tolliver.

"And why are they here?" The cold air burned my throat. "Obviously they hear us Fuse. But we've been in Hope Nation for ninety years. Did they just begin hearing us, or—Good Christ!" I stumbled to my feet.

The sky to the east, toward Centraltown, lit a brilliant orange.

I stared into the night, my heart pounding. A moment later the distant trees rustled, and then the shock wave hit, an overpowering thump on my chest. I staggered, but remained on my feet. "What was that?"

Tolliver's voice was hushed. "They got Centraltown."

"How—you can't—"

"What else is east a hundred miles or so?"

I croaked, "Annie!"

"Didn't I hear something about a meteorite?"

Alexi hugged the radio. "You're just guessing, Mr. Tolliver."

"Yes." Tolliver looked at him with hatred. "So call Admiralty House, Lieutenant Tamarov, *sir.* Ask them who lit up the sky."

I spun around. "Tolliver! Another word out of you and—"

He looked at me without expression. "And what, sir?"

I strode across the clearing, shoved him back toward the tent. I pushed him until his back bumped the tent poles. "Not a word, Middy! Do I make myself clear?"

For a moment he held my gaze. Then he swallowed. "Aye aye, sir." The venom was gone from his tone.

I sat. "Call them, Alexi."

"I don't remember how," Alexi said miserably.

I snatched the caller from his hands.

I couldn't raise Admiralty House.

I couldn't raise anything.

"What will we do, Mr. Seafort?" Alexi's eyes begged for comfort.

Blindly I thrust the radio into his lap. Each breath of cold air pierced like a lance. I unearthed a series of great hacking coughs, tottered into the tent. Deep in my throat a sound escaped. I fell onto the bed and passed out.

"Mr. Seafort?" The voice summoned me from a great distance. I groaned. "Mr. Seafort, please!"

I opened an eye, squinting at Alexi silhouetted against the daylight. I croaked, "What?"

"It's midafternoon. You've slept ten hours."

I tried to sit up, fell back dizzy. "Lord, it's cold today."

Alexi looked at me oddly. "It's rather warm, actually."

"Is it?" I tried to think. "I must be feverish."

Alexi shot out his hand, withdrew it suddenly, waited for my nod. He held his wrist to my forehead. "You're burning."

"I was dreaming . . ." I clutched his arm, struggled to sit. "Centraltown?"

"No dream. They've been hit. We don't know how bad."

"The heli . . . it was supposed to pick us up at dawn."

"It never showed, Mr. Seafort."

"Can you raise Centraltown?"

"No. I get static, an occasional word, but they don't answer."

"I thought you didn't know how to use the caller."

"Mr. Tolliver showed me." Alexi hesitated. "He's very angry."

"About what?"

"Everything, it seems."

I grimaced. "Help me, would you?"

Alexi held out his arm; I pulled myself up and sagged against him until the dizziness passed.

Outside, the fire was long dead. Tolliver, sitting on the log, watched me without expression. I asked, "Nothing on the radio?"

He shook his head.

I sat by the fireside, blinking in the sunlight. "Try Orbit Station."

"I did. If we got through, they're not responding."

"We'll wait until morning. Try to raise Centraltown and the Station every hour."

Tolliver nodded. I waited, and he added reluctantly, "Aye aye, sir."

I stumbled back to the tent and slept.

I woke at dawn, burning with thirst. I crawled across the tent to the water bottle, drank greedily while Alexi and Tolliver slept.

Cautiously I dressed myself, waiting for the accustomed dizziness, but I seemed stronger than last evening. I opened the tent flap, plunged into the cold mist, searched for firewood. I coughed, doubling over from the pain it brought. When finally I was able to stop, I tottered to the pile of branches they'd stacked near the firesite. I laid a few in the firepit. The effort left me panting.

I found a firestarter in the bundle of supplies, set it to the kindling. In moments my blaze was fierce enough to provide warmth. I sat as close as I dared. After a time I thought of coffee, and made my way to the micro. I foraged in the bundle of supplies, found coffee, set it heating.

"I'd have helped, Mr. Seafort." Alexi, tousled, shirt over his arm, looked out from the tent.

I smiled, steaming cup in hand. "I'm not an invalid, Mr. Tamarov."

"I hope not." He hurried to the fire, huddled near while he dressed. "You're feeling better?"

"Much." As long as I sat quietly. "What did you hear last night on the caller?"

Alexi poured coffee and rejoined me. "Static, faint voices. No answer."

"Try again."

Obediently he went to the tent, returned with the radio. He called Admiralty, the spaceport. Orbit Station.

Still no reply.

I brooded. After a time I said, "Wake Tolliver."

"That's not necessary." Tolliver stood by the tent flap, fully dressed.

"We won't wait," I said. "Get the supplies together; we'll walk to Plantation Road."

"Lugging all this?" Tolliver waved his hand at the tent, the micro, the foodstuffs.

"Everything came down in two bundles. We'll take turns carrying them."

Tolliver's look was cool. "I doubt it. We'll end up carrying you."

I tried to stand, decided against it. "Tolliver, I've about—"

Alexi's tone was icy. "Mr. Tolliver, gather the supplies."

Tolliver glanced at him with surprise. "Have you returned to active duty, Mr. Tamarov?"

"No." Alexi leaned on the tent pole. "But do as the Captain said."

"You can't—"

"Be silent!" Alexi stood nose to nose with the older, taller man. "You're a midshipman. Act like one."

They glared at each other. Tolliver's smile was cruel. "Do you remember how a middy acts?"

Alexi met his gaze. "No. Show me."

After a time Tolliver lowered his eyes. "All right." His voice had lost its truculence. "Help me collect our gear, would you?"

As soon as Tolliver was out of earshot Alexi whispered, "Sorry I interfered. I know I have no right—"

"You did fine, Alexi. It was how I remember you."

"He seemed so—"

"You did well."

In a few minutes our bundles were wrapped and tied. Alexi and Tolliver each shouldered one; there was no discussion of my helping. I managed to get to my feet without assistance. I checked the compass and pointed. "North." I followed them from the glade.

We'd gone no more than a few steps before I was gasping for breath, but I said nothing and did my best to keep pace. I grasped at vines and low-hanging branches, pulling myself onward through the dense brush.

Alexi looked over his shoulder. "Mr. Tolliver, slow down." He waited while I caught up to him. "Lean on me, if you like."

"I don't need—"

"Please."

"All right." An arm draped around his shoulder, I let some of my weight rest on Alexi. With his free hand he held branches aside. I found the going easier.

After a time I took off my jacket and tied it around my waist. Alexi shifted his load to his other shoulder. I struggled on, sweating profusely.

Endless hours later we came upon an opening where a great genera tree had crushed a swath through the forest as it fell. Alexi called, "Let's rest here, Mr. Tolliver."

Tolliver checked his watch. "It's only been an hour and a half."

"I don't care," Alexi said. "I'm tired."

"You mean the Captain's tired."

Alexi helped me to the fallen log, where I dropped with a sigh. "Enough bickering! Ten minutes."

Alexi eyed me dubiously.

The rest of the morning was lost in a haze of misery. We halted again, twice at Alexi's suggestion and once, reluctantly, at my own. At length we reached a rocky terrain, open land that burst from the vast sea of vegetation stretching from Plantation Road south to the sea. Walking was easier here, though now we had to traverse hills that only looked gentle from afar.

A mile ahead the forest resumed.

"Let's stop for lunch," I said.

"We haven't gone five miles," Tolliver objected. "Even if we walk another five before dark, at this rate we'll be three days reaching the road."

I grunted. "We'll do better this afternoon. Break out the Q-rations." The speech left me panting.

He dropped his bundle, untied it. "I could set up the tent, sir. Would you wait here with Mr. Tamarov and the radio while I go for help?"

I was tempted. "No," I said at last. "Better we stick together."

"You're not able—"

"Until we know what's happened at Centraltown we won't split up." I downed the cup of water Alexi gave me.

A few moments later Tolliver popped the lid of a Q-ration and set it on the log in front of me. I waited while air seeped into the slow-release chemicals packed between the inner and outer wrap. Two minutes later the meal was heated; I peeled off the lid and fell to.

Alexi squatted beside me with a troubled mien. "Mr. Seafort, are you sure about going on?"

I nodded. "I have to get back, find what they want me to do."

He whispered, "Mr. Tolliver—I don't know how to . . . I wish he'd leave you alone."

"Don't worry about it." The day a Captain couldn't handle a middy he'd better look to retirement.

A few minutes later I struggled to my feet. We started out slowly, Alexi and Tolliver carrying the supply packs as before. When I'd bent to take one, Alexi snatched it from under my hand and turned away without a word, adjusting it around his shoulder. I let it be.

When dark finally came I was close to collapse, sweat streaming down my face. I overrode their suggestions—by now even Tolliver was anxious for me to rest—and insisted that we go a bit farther by flashlight. We did so, ducking under the persistent boughs. We finally came upon a glade with enough open space to set up the tent, where only tall grasses impeded our efforts. I tried to help; Tolliver asked me curtly to get out of the way and let them finish. After, I forced down a tin of rations and fell on my bed.

In the dim light of morning Tolliver did his best to dress quietly, but I woke anyway. I sat, fumbled with my shirt, and got to my knees. I waited until Tolliver left the tent before I tried to stand.

I hung on to the tent pole until I was sure my legs had stopped trembling, then thrust aside the flap and went outside. A heavy mist lay about; the ground was cold and damp.

"Coffee, sir?" Tolliver's tone was civil.

"Please." I sat on a rock that protruded through the grasses. I inhaled the aroma of the steaming cup.

"Shall I wake Mr. Tamarov?"

The thought of another day's walk curdled my stomach. "Yes, you'd better." I sipped at my coffee, marshaling my reserves for the day's ordeal.

A few moments later Alexi crouched beside me, cup in hand. He studied my face. "Are you feverish?"

"I'm fine." The claim sounded absurd, even to me.

"You can't make it through another day like yesterday."

"I'll be all right." I watched Tolliver dismantle the tent.

"It took you two minutes to stand up this mor—"

"Alexi, don't argue!"

He blanched. "I—I'm sorry." He hurried to help Tolliver.

I labored for two hours, leaning on Alexi, then on Tolliver, wretched in the drizzle that had begun soon after we left the clearing. When I stopped to catch my breath I was beset by a fit of coughing that swelled until it tore at my chest and throat. When the mists cleared I found myself on my knees, hanging on to a low branch.

"We'll have to carry him." Tolliver's voice was flat.

"Can we rig a stretcher?"

"I'll see what I can find in our gear."

I hadn't the breath to object. I slumped against the bough while

Tolliver pulled tent poles from his bundles and tied the poly-mil tent fabric across them.

"Help him onto it, Mr. Tamarov."

"I'm all—"

"You'd better get in, Mr. Seafort." Alexi held my eye until I nodded reluctantly. Arm across his shoulder, I tottered to the makeshift litter. I lay on my back, cold and wet; Alexi folded my jacket under my head as a pillow. I grabbed his arm. "I'm sorry."

He smiled hesitantly. "We can carry you."

"About barking at you this morning."

He shrugged. I searched his face for rebuke, found only worry.

"Alexi, walk out with Tolliver. Leave me and get help."

"No." He nodded to Tolliver, picked up his end of the stretcher. I turned away, ashamed.

Eventually I slept; when I woke I was lying on the ground. Alexi sat nearby. I swallowed; my throat was raw. "Where's Tolliver?"

Alexi looked up, studied my face. "We found a stream. He's refilling our water bottles."

"Help me sit." He did so. "I can walk."

"Please don't try, Mr. Seafort."

"You can't go on carrying me."

"It's not so hard." He looked at his hands. "A few blisters, but I can live with those." He shook his head to still my objection. "It's easier, now that we've dumped most of the supplies. All we've got is the radio, another night's Q-rations, and the water."

I stirred angrily. "Who decided that?"

"Mr. Tolliver suggested it, and I agreed." He chewed his lip. "I don't know who's in charge. You're sick, I can't remember a thing, and he's just a middy."

I smiled weakly. "A mess. I'm in charge, unless he tries to relieve me."

The voice came from behind my head. "I've considered it." I turned. Tolliver stared down, a water bottle in each arm.

"I wouldn't try, Midshipman." My tone was cold.

A twisted smile. "I will, if you become incoherent. Not before." I wondered if it was a threat.

Alexi cleared his throat. "Please stop, both of you." His glance appealed from one to the other. "We're wasting daylight."

Tolliver grunted, handed Alexi one of the water bottles. He stooped to his end of the litter. "Come on, then."

Gripping the sides of the litter, I watched the leafy canopy drift overhead. I closed my eyes; when next I opened them the gray sky had begun to darken. Half dreaming, I tried to focus on the trees and shrubs floating past my head.

"We'd better quit soon," Alexi panted.

"Not yet." Tolliver, at the front of the litter, trudged on, eyes down.

"Then I've got to rewrap my hand."

Tolliver swore under his breath as he lowered the litter. "Hurry up." He waited impatiently while Alexi retied the handkerchief around his palm. Tolliver's eyes drifted down to mine. "We've got only an hour of daylight left, and I don't think we made our ten miles. If we can't reach the road tomorrow, we may not have strength to carry you."

"Tomorrow I'll walk awhile."

"Don't make me laugh." He turned away in disgust.

When next I woke, a fire crackled nearby. Alexi lay on his air mattress, jacket thrown over his shoulders. His breathing was slow and regular. Tolliver, in shirtsleeves, huddled on the far side of the firepit, hands thrust between his legs for warmth. I adjusted my jacket, lay for a while, slept again.

Alexi shook me gently. "Would you like some coffee before we start?"

I nodded, blinking in the early light, watching Alexi busy himself with the pot. The night chill was still on us; I pulled my jacket over my shoulders and adjusted it across my feet. A moment later I struggled to sit, aware that my jacket couldn't possibly cover both my feet and arms. I sorted out my covers.

"It's mine." Tolliver stared down at me.

"How did it—who—?"

"You needed warmth."

The image of Edgar Tolliver huddling next to the fire, bare-shirted in the cold night air, caused me to redden in mortification. "Thank you," I said gruffly.

He smiled briefly. "At Academy I learned to give my all, not my clothes."

"I'm surprised you care if I live."

His tone was sardonic. "I'd be called before a Board of Inquiry if you didn't."

While they sorted the gear I managed to get to my feet unaided, and went into the brush to relieve myself. When I got back to the clearing I had no objection to using the litter. As they readied themselves I keyed the radio. Orbit Station didn't answer. Neither did Centraltown.

I clutched the stretcher while they swung me into position. "How much farther, do you think?"

Tolliver shrugged. "Who knows? The road is somewhere ahead. Five miles? Fifteen?"

Alexi said, "We've had no dinner, no breakfast. Our next meal will see the last of our Q-rations."

"Then hope we find the road." Tolliver.

When we finally stopped to rest Alexi sat, rocking, hand clutched between his knees.

"Let me see."

"I'm all right."

"Do as I say." My tone brooked no argument. Reluctantly he extended his hand, unwrapping the cloth. Red and swollen, his fingers oozed where the blisters had broken.

"Lord God." I rolled myself off the litter.

Tolliver tossed aside his empty Q-ration. "What do you think you're doing?"

"I'll walk."

"You're weak as a kitten."

"It's just bronchitis. I'll manage."

He stood. "Seafort, sometimes you're an idiot."

I rolled to my knees, tried not to stagger as I got to my feet. "Three demerits!"

"Shove your demerits up your arse!" He faced me, hands on hips. "You can't walk! If you try, none of us will make it. And if we do, what will we find? Maybe the Navy's gone with the rest of Centraltown. Do you think I give a damn about your frazzing demerits?"

I moved toward him, legs unsteady. "And duty?" I panted. "Your oath? Honor?"

His fists clenched. "I'm trying to get you out of here alive! If that isn't duty, what is?" His words hissed. "You destroyed me, Seafort! I should have let you execute me. I have no career, no future, and I'm still trying to save you!" His voice caught, and he spun away. "Let me be, damn you!"

After a moment I said softly, "Leave the litter behind. Our jackets too, and everything but the water and the radio. I'll lean against each of you in turn. We'll walk until we reach the road. If I can't make it, I'll have you go on ahead."

Tolliver nodded, unable to speak.

"My hand's not that—"

"I'll lean on you, Alexi. Don't argue, save your strength."

To my shame, I hadn't strength to walk, even leaning heavily on

Alexi. So, arms draped across their shoulders, I let them half carry, half drag me through the brush, forcing my feet to cooperate, working to ease their load. My lungs labored but I was determined not to stop. In any event, I wasn't sure I had the breath to call for a rest.

The sun moved inexorably to the horizon. Our stops became more frequent. Afraid I couldn't stand again if I sat, I sagged against a tree, my legs stiffened to keep from falling.

Alexi was disconsolate. "It'll be dark soon."

I managed to speak. "Keep going."

"We can't walk all—"

"There'll be moonlight. We'll keep on until we get to the road or . . ." I left the thought unfinished.

My bravura faded with the light. As darkness came I stumbled more frequently, supported only by the determination of my comrades. At length I signaled a halt. "Water." It came out a croak. Greedily I poured the life-giving liquid down my throat until I drained the bottle. "Where's the other canteen? Alexi, aren't you thirsty?"

Tolliver's face glistened in the light of Hope Nation's two moons. "We finished it a long time ago."

"Christ, I'm sorry." I hadn't thought to offer them a drop.

"Maybe there'll be another stream," he said. And maybe not. I balled my fists, cursing my selfishness. Their strength, not mine, was our hope.

"We'd better get going." Alexi's voice was strained.

For the next hour we struggled through unrelenting brush. Hacking coughs reduced me to helplessness. I began to watch for an open space for them to leave me.

By now, they carried most of my weight; I clung to their shoulders with failing strength. Giving up any effort to walk restored a modicum of energy, and with it clarity of thought. I said carefully, "I'll rest when we find a clearing." I winced as thorns raked my side.

"I'll stay with you."

"No. Go with Tolliver. Bring help."

Alexi shook his head.

"You will. Tolliver, this is an order." I stopped to suck for air. "When we find a clearing you go on with Alexi. Try to mark the trail. Get help. Acknowledge."

Tolliver was breathing hard. "Aye aye, sir, acknowledged."

"I won't leave you!" Alexi's voice held a note of desperation.

"Alexi . . . my father. He's in Cardiff. Wales. I want you to give him a message."

"He's delirious."

"Shut up, Tolliver." I panted. "Tell him—"

"I won't be seeing your father, Mr. Seafort. Not until you take me there."

I fought to remain calm. "I want you to tell Father . . ."

Finally Alexi's voice came, hesitant. "What?"

I thought for a long time, fighting exhaustion. At length I said, "Tell him . . . I tried."

Alexi bit off a moan. I swallowed, seeking a peace that eluded me. No matter. I had to reach a clearing, force him to leave before he changed his mind. It was the last gift I could offer.

I swallowed, and was overcome by a fit of coughing. Alexi and Tolliver waited for me to recover. By great effort I brought my breathing under control. We staggered on. Our eyes were accustomed to the pale reflections of Major and Minor; we thrust through remorseless tangles of undergrowth. Beyond, the light seemed brighter. I lunged at it, my heart jumping. Yes, definitely more moonlight ahead. A clearing, or what would suffice. An excuse to send them on their way.

I gasped, "I'll sit there, where it's light."

"Let me stay," Alexi said plaintively.

"No." A croak.

"I'm nothing without you, don't you understand? You have my memories!"

My hand clutched at his arm, exacting his submission. "Get to Cardiff for me. You must." The low branches gave way to heavy brush and shoulder-high grass. We were in the clearing. A hundred feet ahead dark trees loomed again in the moonlight. "Set me down."

Tolliver said, "We'll lean you against that tree."

A few more steps. Surely I could manage that. "All right." I let them carry me toward the trees. The grasses parted, and the terrain plunged into a culvert.

Beyond was Plantation Road.

12

I lay shivering in the night air, my head in Alexi's lap. We talked, voices low, while Tolliver crouched by the roadside near his flimsy barricade of dead branches and brush. My breathing consumed more and more effort. Alexi wiped my head with his bandaged hand; Annie brought me a cool compress. I shoved her away; she held my arm down, wiped my brow. "You real sick now, Nicky. We be tak'n care of you."

"I deserted you."

"It don' matter. We work it out nudder time. You be still." She bent over, kissed my cheek. Alexi squeezed my hand.

Dark. Dreams. The endless shadow of Lord God's disfavor. Chest heaving, I drifted from my friends, toward night.

"How is he?"

"I don't know. Sleeping, maybe. Christ, why doesn't someone come?"

"Don't blaspheme," I whispered.

A moment's pause. "I'm sorry, Mr. Seafort."

"Very well."

I slept.

Sometime later I woke to a bright light shining in my face. I twisted away, but the roadside skewed dizzily and I lay still.

"There's room for him behind the cab."

"Pick him up, he's in no condition to help."

"Of course I am," I mumbled, but got no answer. After a time I found myself stretched out behind the driver's seat of the hauler. It resembled a middy's bunk. I giggled.

I woke to full daylight, on clean sheets, in a soft bed, and breathing through a mask that blocked my vision. Sarah Branstead looked up from a holo. "You're back."

I considered it. "You're a hallucination." My voice was muffled.

She smiled. "I don't think so."

I reached for the mask. She caught my hand. "Don't. Dr. Avery has you on vapormeds and you need every drop."

I studied her. "This is real?"

She laughed. "Yes. Your young friend told me you were talking with someone else at times."

"Annie."

"Your wife?"

"She's in Centraltown." With horror I struggled to sit up, fell back against the pillows. "What happened? Is she all right?"

"A great meteor hit near Centraltown. Horrid casualties. They think the fish dropped it."

Lord God, no.

I felt my pulse pounding. "What's the matter with me?"

"Pneumonia. We almost lost you last night."

Father. Cardiff. I looked away. "My lieu—Alexi. How is he?"

"He's in the kitchen with Elena, eating for both of you. He'll be back shortly."

Thank you, Lord.

"And your Mr. Tolliver is asleep upstairs." A soft knock at the door; she beckoned someone in.

The boy sounded shy. "Hello, Captain Seafort." He approached the bed.

"Jerence."

"May I sit for a while?" His mother and I both nodded. He pulled a chair closer to me. "I came down from bed when Mr. Volksteader's hauler brought you."

"I think I remember."

He leaned forward, as if imparting a secret. "I'm glad you're all right."

After a moment I inquired, "Am I?"

No one answered directly. Jerence said, "We've all been worried for you. Ms. Triforth called three times, and Mrs. Palabee sent soup."

Sarah Branstead added, "We'll fly you into Centraltown as soon as your infection's down. To the clinic."

I nodded, growing sleepy. The room faded.

Dr. Avery packed away his diagnostic puter. He was a small man, graying, with a crisp air of authority. "Yesterday I started you on antibiotics, Mr. Seafort. They'll help, but we need to get you to Centraltown. They have better equipment than I carry."

"When?"

"Tomorrow, if your fever stays down."

"I need to report." I looked around for a caller. "Is the Admiral groundside?"

"Worry about that when you recover, Mr. Seafort."

My tone was churlish. "I have to report to Admiralty. That can't wait."

He shrugged. "Using the caller won't hurt, I suppose. If you can get through. Harmon?"

Harmon Branstead said, "We can use low-power radio from here to Zack Hopewell's. That's where the old landline runs."

"Landline?"

"Before we licked the sunspot problem, they buried an old-fashioned fiber-optic line along the road. We're using it again, now that we've gone to radio silence."

I sat up straighter. "What are you talking about?"

Harmon pulled a chair alongside my bed. "I forgot you were stranded in south forest. Your Navy ordered a complete radio blackout after the fish dropped the asteroid on Centraltown. They don't know if fish can hear radio waves but they're not taking a chance until we know more."

Centraltown. Images of Belfast after the IRA nuke. I wondered what was left. "Is Admiralty House standing?"

"It seemed all right when I flew in yesterday. The blast knocked over their dish, but they had that fixed."

I looked around eagerly. "Where's your caller?"

"The main set is in my study. If you'd—"

I swung my legs out of the bed. "Now?"

"Just a minute," Dr. Avery said testily. "Bring along your mask."

"It's only for a few—"

Hands on hips, he glowered. "Or I'll put you down with a sedative. Your choice."

I glared back. Unimpressed, he held my eye until I was forced to surrender. "Alexi, Mr. Tolliver, help with my gear, would you?"

A few moments later I was seated at Harmon Branstead's desk, blanket thrown over my knees, fuming with impatience for the connection.

At last Forbee's voice came on the line. "Mr. Seafort, you're all right! Wonderful. Sorry we couldn't send a heli for you, but the relief work at Centraltown came—"

"Of course." I had to stop until I had my breath. "Can I speak with the Admiral?"

"He's on *Vestra*. We're moving the tactical group to Orbit Station. I leave in about an hour. He's authorized a tightbeam relay to his ship, so I might be able to get you through."

"What's happened since the last attack?"

"It never ended, I'm afraid. Since Tuesday we've lost nine ships."

"Oh, Lord God."

"About half our remaining warships are deployed to protect the Station. The rest of the fleet is in position to intercept an attack on Centraltown. Meanwhile, the fish Fuse in and out at odd intervals. They've learned, Mr. Seafort. They go for our shipboard lasers the moment they Defuse. We're still taking out a few of them, though."

"Lord God help us."

"Amen. Would you like me to try to get you through to the Admiral?"

"Please." I waited in the silent, somber study, with Harmon Branstead, Dr. Avery, and my two officers. Nine ships. Hundreds of souls. How long could we stand against the aliens?

A crisp voice interrupted my reverie. "Admiral De Marnay is on the line." I clutched the caller.

"Hello, Seafort?"

"Yes, sir."

"Who the hell shot you down?"

"I don't know, sir."

"No way to investigate now. All our people are working with emergency rescue. Hell of a mess. You all right?"

"Yes, sir. I'll be in Centraltown tomorrow." I ignored Dr. Avery's rebuke.

"Don't know when I'll be down. The attack may be tapering off, but it's too early to tell."

"Right, sir."

"Did you hear they found Tenere alive in *Freiheit*'s launch?"

"Thank heaven!"

"He's on the station, recovering. Every ship we've got is on patrol. Except for Forbee, you're the only Captain on the ground."

"Yes, sir, that's what I wanted to talk to you about."

"Eh, speak up. You sound muffled."

I tore off the vapormask. "Sir, *Victoria*. Captain Martes was to be transferred." I panted for breath.

"He has *Prince of Wales* now." De Marnay seemed distracted.

"Can I have *Victoria*, sir?"

"Hmm? No, I gave her to Holser. He was a lieutenant."

Bile flooded my throat. "Yes, I knew him." I coughed.

"Overdue for promotion. Commander, now. He took *Victoria* to Detour and Kall's Planet on a special errand."

"I see." With irritation, I waved away the vapormask Dr. Avery thrust at me.

Admiral De Marnay's voice changed. "Seafort, I have contingency orders for you. We're on tightbeam?"

"Only the link from Admiralty House to you."

"Then I'd better send a middy down. He'll have a chip coded for your eyes only."

"Can I meet you at Orbit Station? If there's any ship I could take—"

"No, stay there. Don't worry about the delay, your orders may never go into effect. I'll be in touch. Out." The line went dead.

I sagged. Even in extremis, Georges De Marnay would not call on me. I barely heard Dr. Avery's insistent demands.

Alexi knelt. "Mr. Seafort, you'd better put this on." He held the vapormask.

Dully, I fastened it around my face. I essayed a smile. "Help me back to bed, then. Harmon, would you fly me to Centraltown later?"

"As soon as Dr. Avery allows. In the morning, I imagine." He hesitated. "The war isn't going well?"

"We're losing ships." I stood, hanging on to Harmon's arm, surprised at how dizzy I felt. I let them help me back to my room.

I dozed for several hours, waking in late afternoon. Jerence was sitting by my bedside. He left as soon as I woke and appeared a few moments later with his father.

"Are you well enough for company?"

"You're always welcome, Harmon."

"Thank you, but I meant Zack Hopewell and some of the others. They've heard you're with us."

"No, I—" The last thing I needed was to let them see me smothered in a vapormask. Still, my purpose in taking the heli jaunt had been to confer with them. The attack on Centraltown made their grievances less urgent, but . . . "Yes, I mean. Just give me time to dress."

"This evening, then, after dinner." I nodded agreement.

Zack Hopewell shook his head, his face grim. "A missile." We sat in Harmon's study, much the same group that had met on my earlier visit.

"Thank heaven they only fired one. We couldn't have escaped two." I avoided Edgar Tolliver's eye.

Laura Triforth growled, "Mantiet, of course."

"We don't know that." Hopewell.

"Who else? He already tried once." Laura grimaced. "What's the world coming to? Bombs in the roadway, missile attacks . . ."

I said, "Yes, I've been lucky. Why does Frederick Mantiet want me dead?"

Tomas Palabee glanced at Laura, shook his head. Arvin Volksteader looked uncomfortable. For a moment, silence.

"Maybe he thinks it will hasten the Republic." Plumwell, manager of Carr Plantation. His tone was defiant.

"Nonsense," said Hopewell. "He—"

"That's just wild talk!" Laura.

"Republic?" I demanded.

Harmon said, "He's just speculating, Captain."

"What republic?" I gripped the chair arms and pushed myself to my feet. The room seemed overly warm.

"I—"

"Let me—"

"I'll tell him." Zack Hopewell's tone was firm. The others lapsed silent. "We've long had a party, Mr. Seafort, who've argued—theoretically, mind you—that Hope Nation would be better off as an independent republic."

I was shocked into silence.

"It will happen sooner or later," he said, almost apologetically. "The sheer distance—"

"How could you survive on your own? Where would you sell your grain?" I found my face growing hot. "Can you manufacture the implements of a high-tech society you now import? Is your—"

"Technology isn't everything. We—"

"Have you no gratitude? Men devote their lives to bringing you supplies!"

Laura rasped, "Is that what you expect from your minions? Gratitude?"

It brought me to my senses. "No, of course not. I was out of line. Forgive me. But . . ." I paused to regroup. "Regardless of the merits, that's not a decision we can make." Only the U.N. Security Council, or its plenipotentiary, could grant independence to a colony.

Hopewell was a trifle less frosty. "I didn't say it was. You know we sent representatives to Terra years ago, but nothing came of it. I'm not saying anyone in this room—or any planter—would rebel against lawful authority, but voices have grown stronger over the years. Now that Centraltown's devastated, some feel that the time has come."

"Don't you need the Navy now more than ever?"

Laura's lip curled. "What's your Navy done for us? Did it stop the fish from bombing Centraltown?"

My face was white. "Do you know how many died trying?"

"Many," said Hopewell. "God rest their souls. Sit down, Laura, I'm not done yet." He waited. "It's becoming clear that a change is overdue, even if it falls short of independence. Our complaints about shipping rates are ignored, and—"

"With independence, you'd be utterly at the mercy of the Tariff Board. Who else would buy your grain, other than home system?"

He went on as if I hadn't spoken. "We're stifled by authoritarian government imposed from afar. Do you think a local administration would order a military base hidden in the Venturas?"

"Obviously not. But now is no time to—"

"I agree. This is not the time. But perhaps Mr. Plumwell's sneering reference to a republic is now clear."

"I didn't sneer about—"

Laura's tone was cold. "Stuff it, Plumwell; as a manager you're here only by sufferance." She stared him down. "In any event, Mr. Seafort, what have you accomplished for us?"

I sat, trying to conceal the trembling of my legs. "The Venturas Base was a fiasco. We've begun to remedy that."

"You canned General Khartouf, yes."

"And put a competent man in his place. We'll get the generator completed shortly, and the supplies moved from Centraltown."

"Ah, yes, the supplies." Laura's voice was acid.

"The Station's been downloading cargo faster than the Venturas Base can receive it. Hopefully that will untangle itself with the change of command."

Tomas Palabee stirred. "Appointing a new commander doesn't address the basic issue. We need control of our own affairs."

"You have a legislature . . ."

Laura snorted. "Your constitution gives veto power to the Governor. And in any event, the riffraff at Centraltown can outvote us. Idle hands! Whoever heard of giving unemployed field hands a controlling vote?" A general murmur of agreement.

"I can't rewrite the constitution. But I'll ask Admiral De Marnay what concessions are possible."

Plumwell smiled tightly. "Take your time. Meanwhile, men like Mantiet will handle things their own way."

I slammed my fist on my chair. "Why haven't you caught him?" My anger gave them pause. "You've had . . . how long, four weeks? He's your countryman. You know his habits, you know the terrain! Find him!"

"We've tried." Hopewell's ire matched my own. "We almost took him in Centraltown. He's gone, Lord God knows where. Maybe the meteor got him!"

Laura sighed. "If Frederick's alive, we'll find him; give us time."

"I will." I was stopped by a spell of coughing. Finally I added, "Just as you'll give me time to resolve your problems."

"A fair trade." Zack Hopewell stood. "We've had our say. Let the Captain recover from his ordeal. We've tired him."

Over my protests, they bade good night and took their leave. With profound relief I let Alexi and Tolliver help me to bed. In moments I was asleep.

In the morning I walked with careful step to Branstead's heli. To my surprise, Laura Triforth was waiting to see me off. She took me aside. "About last night . . ." She ran a hand through curly auburn hair flecked with gray.

"Yes, ma'am?"

"For heaven's sake, call me Laura. We've all . . ." She hesitated, seemed to pull herself together. "Our emotions run strong," she said abruptly. "Harmon was right, that day he said we'd grown imperious. I'm afraid in my case the passion of our cause overcame my manners." Hazel eyes met mine. "Captain, I'm truly sorry for the injury to your Lieutenant Tamarov. I don't think I've made clear how distressed I am. And the missile—it's unheard of. Ghastly." Her voice caught.

"Thank you." I tried to make my voice more gentle.

"You fight a frightful war with the fish. In that, we're your allies. You mustn't think we're enemies massing on a second front." Her hand darted to my arm. "Please."

"At times I wondered." I smiled, to take the sting from my words. I turned to the heli and settled into the front seat. My two officers crammed behind. They strapped the vapormask securely about my face, its canister on my lap covered by Sarah's warm coverlet. At the last moment Jerence trotted out to the lawn. His tone was urgent. "Pa, let me come."

"To Centraltown? Not a chance."

"Please." He hesitated. "It's not what you think. I won't run away. I just want—"

"Yes?" Harmon was impatient.

"To help with Captain Seafort."

"Don't be ridiculous." Harmon's hand reached for the starter, but the boy caught his eye in mute appeal. After a long moment he relented. "Get in."

We lifted off. Tolliver scanned the skies uneasily, as if expecting another missile. I lay back and closed my eyes. Tolliver's anxiety affected all but Jerence, who chattered to Alexi.

Harmon flew low and fast. To break the tension I asked through the mask, "Where's Emmett?"

"Helping in Centraltown. I'll bring him home with me."

"Your brother lives in town, doesn't he?"

"He has a cottage there, but he spends about half of his time with us. We've agreed it's safer on the estate for awhile."

"Safer?"

"Things have—changed."

I brooded on that, while we flew past the edge of the plantation zone, past Hauler's Rest. At last, the outskirts of Centraltown were in sight. It was a clear, sunny day, and I could see no damage.

"Will you land at the spaceport?" My car was there.

"No, south of downtown."

"Why?"

"That's where they've set up the clinic."

"Isn't it at the hospital?"

Harmon compressed his lips, shook his head. A few moments later I spotted the spaceport, but our angle didn't permit a glimpse of Admiralty House. Still, I knew it had survived; I'd talked to Forbee the day before.

Our small talk abated as we neared downtown. I peered down at uprooted trees. Wreckage littering the streets; debris had been shoved aside to clear paths for rescue vehicles.

I sucked in my breath, heedless of the ache in my lungs. Below, crumpled wood-frame houses sagged to the west, away from downtown, as if too tired to remain standing. My stomach slowly knotted as we flew closer.

Near downtown, brick buildings were smashed to rubble, and streets had disappeared into ruins. I moaned. "Annie . . ."

Harmon asked, "Did she live near the reservoir?"

"We were across town, about twenty blocks from the barracks. Why?"

"Armstrong Reservoir was ground zero."

"What did they hit us with? A nuke?"

He shook his head. "Thank Lord God, no. A rock, but from the energy it dispersed, it might as well have been a fission bomb."

"We shouldn't—" I bit off the thought, not daring to involve them in talk of nuclear weapons.

By the time we dipped toward the grassy meadow that had become an emergency field, I wanted to see no more of the appalling devastation. I sat until the blades stopped whistling. Harmon turned to his son. "I trust you not to run away, boy. But if you do, remember that there's worse danger than a whipping from me." He pointed at what was left of down-town.

Jerence nodded. "I know, Pa. I heard Uncle Emmett. I won't."

I unlatched the door as a U.N.A.F. soldier came alongside. He eyed my vapormask. "This one's for the clinic?"

Tolliver spoke up from the back, his voice cold. "This one's Captain Nicholas Seafort, U.N.N.S."

The sentry glanced at my face. His eyes widened in recognition. "Yes, sir. Right up the street, about half a block." He pointed. "I'll call the ambulance, if you like."

I eased myself out of the heli. "I'm much better, actually." To my surprise, it was true. "I can walk." Alexi and Tolliver hovered at my sides.

"Can I carry the vapormeds?"

I snapped, "I'm not helpless, Jerence." The boy's face fell. I took a couple of steps and hesitated. "Perhaps you'd better, after all." Eagerly he took the canister from my hands.

We proceeded slowly to the school in which the emergency clinic was operating. Electricars, some battered, lined the roadway. We passed a family helping a heavily bandaged man into a car. Though I had to stop more than once for breath, I felt little of the dizziness that had plagued me; Dr. Avery's vapormeds were having their effect. In any event, Alexi and Tolliver were ludicrously close, waiting to catch me if I sagged. Ribald jokes came to mind; with an effort I suppressed them.

On the stoop two women sat consoling each other, oblivious to passersby. Alexi held the door.

In the hall they'd set up an admitting office near the gymnasium that served as the main clinic. The hall was crowded with patients, some bandaged, some uninjured, many slumped despondently. I found a place on a bench.

Tolliver leaned over the admitting desk, spoke to the weary civilian behind it. The man ran his hands through his hair, pushed himself up from his desk.

"Captain Seafort? An honor to meet you, sir." I nodded through my mask. "I'll have a med tech look you over while you wait for the doctor."

"Wait?" Tolliver's tone was hostile.

"Yes, wait." The man showed signs of irritation. "We've only three surgeons, and they've worked without sleep the past four days. We finally sent two of them to rest, and the third's trying to hang on to a joey who was trapped under a collapsed wall since the blast."

I forestalled Tolliver's reply. "How long before the doctor has time?"

"Hours, probably. We take life-threatening cases first."

"Of course." We shouldn't have come. Pneumonia was nothing compared to the injuries they battled. My vapormeds seemed to be holding their own against it.

"You can wait in the lobby or in a classroom."

"Could I come back later?"

"I can't guarantee we won't get another emergency, but that's less likely with each passing hour. All we're finding now is the dead. A doctor should be able to see you after seven tonight."

"Thank you. Does anyone have a survivors' list?"

"It's on the puter at emergency HQ but I can tie in from here. What name?"

"Miss Wells. Annie Wells." My heart thumped.

He bent over the console, straightened. "She's not listed as a survivor."

I turned away, unable to speak.

"But she's not among the known dead," he added. "The list isn't complete. It only has those who've been treated or have reported to a relief center."

Annie would know to put her name on the list, of course. So she was lost. I sagged against the wall. After a time a wave of contempt washed away my self-pity. So easy to dismiss her as dead, yet I'd hadn't even searched for her. Perhaps she was hurt, wandering, desperate for help.

I beckoned to Harmon Branstead. "Would you take me back to the spaceport?"

"No."

Stunned, I could only gape. "What? . . . I'm sorry." My tone was stiff. "I didn't mean to impose."

"Imposing has nothing to do with it. I won't be party to your suicide."

I snorted. "Don't be silly. I won't be able to see a doctor for hours. I need to look for Annie, and I should check in at Admiralty House."

"That's not wise. Dr. Avery—"

"Damn your Dr. Avery!" My vehemence drove him back a step. After a tense moment I cleared my throat. "Forgive me, Harmon."

"Of course." He sighed, unclenched his fists. "Well, let's get you back to the heli, if you must."

"Thank you." On the way to the makeshift airstrip I allowed Alexi and Tolliver to support some of my weight, more winded than I cared to let on.

Strapped securely into my seat, I fell into a doze while Harmon lifted off and headed west. When I woke, the heli was settling on the tarmac behind Admiralty House. I opened the door and swung out my legs, debating whether to report first to Admiralty or to search for Annie. Annie was more important, but Admiralty House was but a few steps away.

"Tolliver, remember where we parked our car?"

"Yes, sir."

"Bring it round the front of Admiralty House. Alexi, you might give me a hand." I paused. "Harmon, thanks for everything."

"You'll go back to the clinic?"

"I think I'm getting better. I'm sure my fever's down."

"Give me your word you'll be there at seven."

My eyebrow raised. "I beg your pardon?"

"You heard me."

Jerence looked anxiously from his father to me. Despite myself, I smiled. "Very well, Harmon. My word." My smile vanished. My word was worth less than he knew.

"No, sir, no one's come groundside since yesterday." Willem Anton, the duty lieutenant. Admiralty House seemed nearly deserted.

"The Admiral didn't send a middy?"

"Nothing's landed except the shuttle that took Captain Forbee aloft, sir. Would you like to call Naval HQ at the Station?"

I grimaced. "The Admiral has enough on his mind. Who's in charge here?"

"Lieutenant Trapp, upstairs."

"I'll go see him." I got to my feet.

Alexi blurted, "Mr. Anton, could you ask Lieutenant Trapp to come down instead?"

I wheeled. "Remember your own duty before you intrude on mine!" I panted for breath.

Alexi blushed crimson, but held his ground. "I thought—you've been so—"

But Anton was already on the caller; he'd observed the vapormask and canister Alexi held. I glared. Alexi looked only mildly contrite. While we waited I asked Anton, "Have you heard from my wife?"

The lieutenant looked up, face grim. "Was she downtown?"

"I don't know. We lived near downtown."

He started to speak, shook his head. "Sorry. I've heard nothing, sir."

Lieutenant Trapp saluted as he trotted down the steps. "Admiral De Marnay told me you'd be along, sir. Good to see you again."

"Again?"

"Yes, sir, I was in the tactics room the day you came to, ah, visit Mr. Holser."

"Yes." I didn't want reminding of that. "What's our status?"

"We're monitoring reports. They're on screen in the tactics room, if you'd like . . ."

"Very well." I ignored Alexi's reproach and followed Trapp up the stairs. Halfway, I paused, my strength fading.

In the tactics room, Trapp's pointer tapped the screen. "The Admiral's here on *Vestra*, in orbit about thirty degrees west of the Station."

"Foolish of him to chase about on a ship." Placing himself at risk served no purpose; better that he commanded from the safety of the Station or Centraltown. In a moment I realized what I'd said. Mortified, I added hastily, "He—uh— Of course, he has his reasons. Please disregard my comment."

"Aye aye, sir."

Still, if *Vestra* was destroyed, our chain of command would be sundered. With Forbee on the Station I was the only Captain groundside; I had best stay close to Admiralty House until the danger was past.

Lieutenant Trapp pointed. "The fleet is divided into two squadrons, to protect both Centraltown and the Station."

"Any sightings?"

"Not for a couple of days, sir." He cleared his throat. "Sir, are we, ah, losing?"

"I don't know."

He swallowed. "If the fish take out our fleet, what will happen to Centraltown? To Hope Nation?"

"Enough, Lieutenant." My voice was sharp. "We'll do our duty." I sat, waiting out a passing weakness. "How many Captains are on the Station?" If Admiral De Marnay were killed, the senior Captain there would be in charge. The only other Admiral sent to Hope system, Geoffrey Tremaine, had died by my own hand.

"Mr. Tenere is recovering on Orbit Station, sir."

"That's all? Everyone else is on ship?"

He swallowed. "Or lost."

"Very well." I had to remain at Admiralty House. No, I had to find Annie. I cursed; I couldn't do both. Anyway, did it make sense to stagger about Centraltown, dependent on a vapormask? Others could search more competently than I, and my duty was here.

No. Annie was my wife. "Mr. Trapp."

"Sir?"

"I'll set my caller to standby channel. Reach me by it if there's any action. I'm going to search for my wife."

By the time I reached the foot of the stairs I was sweating. Nonetheless I made an effort to walk casually to the main door, Alexi at my heels.

"The car's right here, sir."

I took several breaths, negotiated the stoop. Perhaps I'd better wear the vapormask after all. I took it from Alexi's hand, thrust it over my face. I leaned on him the rest of the way.

I sank into the back seat, inhaling from the vapormask as deeply as I could. Each breath came as a stab.

It took Tolliver over an hour to negotiate the debris-filled streets to my neighborhood. Alexi dozed in front, head cradled on his bandaged hand. While we drove I stared at rows of blasted, windowless buildings with sagging roofs, hoping against hope that my apartment was spared.

We turned south, away from the worst of the devastation. Soon Tolliver pulled up on the street where I lived. Our building was less damaged than many we'd passed, though splintered siding boards hung askew, smashed by the force of the blast. Underlayment peeked through roof shingles. A few windows were torn from their mountings.

Yet, the building stood.

"I'll check for you, sir." Tolliver was subdued.

"No." I struggled with the door.

"You can barely—"

"Shut your mouth." I let Alexi help me from the car.

Breathing carefully through the confining mask, I negotiated the walkway and put my thumb to the apartment lock. No click. Well, power was off, and the building's backup batteries might have run down. I banged on the door, waited. I knocked again, my eyes shut against a salt sting.

No answer.

Tolliver, carrying the caller, had gone around the side of the building. "A window's smashed."

"Can you get in?"

"Anyone could, now."

I bit back a savage retort. "Climb in and open the door."

The radio crackled. "Captain Seafort?"

Tolliver handed me the caller. "Yes?"

"Lieutenant Trapp, Admiralty House. You said to call if anything . . . We've just heard from Orbit Station. A shuttle's on the way down with a messenger for you."

"Messenger?" I couldn't think.

"A midshipman, sir."

"Oh, yes. I'll be back shortly."

A moment later Tolliver opened the door. Annie must have packed in a hurry, I thought, observing the bureau doors thrown open, dressers emptied on the floor, papers and clothes tossed in an untidy mess. It took me a while to comprehend someone had been searching.

No. Looting.

No sign of Annie. No message.

Unutterably weary, I fell on the couch, watching the last of day darken to dusk.

"Shall we go back to the clinic, sir?"

I stirred. "Admiralty House."

Alexi said, "But, the doctor—you promised—"

"Admiralty House." I let them help me to the car. When I sat again, I couldn't stop panting.

Alexi was hesitant. "Could you drop me at the hospital?"

"It's not in operation, Alexi."

"But I could get my clothes, my things . . . maybe rest."

"All right." I nodded to Tolliver.

Within a few blocks we had passed into a zone of appalling devastation. Tolliver maneuvered past fallen trees, wrecked cars flung about like pebbles, broken and tumbled houses. A few crumpled bodies strewn amid the wreckage gave scale and perspective to the rendition of a demented architect.

We detoured to avoid impassable streets; eventually I lost my sense of direction, and sat passively while Tolliver swore at the blockages.

The road ended at a broad avenue; on the far side was a row of smashed houses fencing a rolling meadow. Tolliver gunned the engine.

"Hey, where are you—" We careened across the side yard of a house, into the meadow beyond.

"This is Churchill Park. If I cross—"

"Cars aren't allowed in the park."

He hit the brakes, twisted around in his seat. "What, sir?" Even Alexi stared.

"Never mind." I felt a fool.

Tolliver's eyes bored into me. "Would you care to drive, sir?"

"Never mind, I said!"

He restarted the engine, shaking his head with unconcealed contempt.

We made better progress across the open fields than through the rubble-filled streets. The grass beneath us was shriveled and burned, and trees were down everywhere.

I strove to orient myself; we must be approaching downtown. The hospital would be a few blocks beyond the edge of the park. Only weeks before, Annie and I had strolled here before visiting the Cathedral.

We reached the crest of a small hill. Beyond was the boundary of the park. Tolliver found a gap in the row of shrubbery lining the park and plunged through.

Around us was devastation.

We turned the corner. Alexi pointed eagerly. "The hospital is over . . . past that . . ." His voice trailed off.

Centraltown Hospital was gone.

A pile of unrecognizable rubble covered two blocks. Beyond the ruins of hospital stretched the ruins of downtown. The commercial district, the government buildings, were obliterated. Thank heaven I'd taken Alexi to the plantation zone.

Tolliver switched off the engine. "Christ Jesus, even the walls."

Alexi slumped in his seat. "If I'd been there . . ."

Tolliver's voice was surprisingly gentle. "You'd be dead."

Alexi said forlornly, "My things. My clothes." He sat huddled, arms crossed as if warming himself.

"People died here." Tolliver's tone was sharp. "Clothes are nothing."

"They're all I had. That and my room."

I said gruffly, "You'll stay with me."

"Where?"

I didn't know. My chest ached. "Tolliver, back to Admiralty House."

"You're supposed to see a doctor," Tolliver said.

"Middy, shut up!" Blessedly, he did.

13

The roar of the descending shuttle subsided. In the Admiralty House anteroom I impatiently drummed my fingers on Lieutenant Anton's console. "What's keeping him?"

"Shall I go look, Mr. Seafort?" Alexi got to his feet.

"No." I concentrated on breathing. Some minutes later the front door swung open. I came awake.

A voice piped, "Midshipman Avar Bezrel reporting, sir." A youngster in immaculate uniform brought himself to attention with an Academy salute.

I scowled. "Don't I know you?"

"I'm on Admiral De Marnay's staff, sir. I took you into his office when—"

"Very well. As you were." He relaxed, said nothing further. I prompted, "You have a message?"

"Yes, sir, but the Admiral said it's for your eyes only."

"Let's have it."

He took a deep breath. "I was told, only when we're alone. I'm sorry, sir, no disrespect intended."

I tore off the vapormask. "Who ordered this charade?"

"Admiral De Marnay, sir." His innocent gray eyes met mine.

"Anton, Tolliver, Mr. Tamarov, leave the room." I waited until they'd trooped upstairs. My voice was ice. "Is that satisfactory, Mr. Bezrel?"

The boy fished in his jacket pocket, came out with a chipcase.

I opened it. "You leave too, Mr. Bezrel."

"But, sir, I have the—"

"At once."

"Aye aye, sir." He wheeled, marched to the stairwell, and trotted upstairs.

I inserted the chip into Lieutenant Anton's holovid, flipped it on, entered my passcode.

Gibberish.

I spun the dial, searching through the images. All unreadable. My fist slammed onto the console. "Bezrel, get down here!" My breath stabbed.

The boy trotted downstairs. "Aye aye, sir."

"What is this nonsense?"

Bezrel said, "You need a code to unlock it, sir."

"Give it!" I held out my hand.

"He made me memorize it, sir!" He wrinkled his brow, then spouted figures. I tapped them into the holovid and punched the readout, grumbling under my breath.

Random characters filled the screen.

"Look at that garbage!" The boy peered at the console. "Try again."

"3J2, uh, 49GHZ . . . 1425, sir."

"You told me 1245!"

"I'm sorry, I—"

I punched in the new figures. "Two demerits, you silly young—"

Still gibberish. I drew breath to speak.

"I think it was 1542!" the boy said desperately.

The screen was full of random symbols. I lurched to my feet. "Think? You don't remember?"

To my astonishment, the boy began to sob, standing at attention, tears running down his cheeks. "I'm not sure, I—I mean . . ."

"Oh, for God's—" I raised my voice to a bellow. "*Tolliver!*" I paced to the wall, returned panting to my seat.

Edgar Tolliver raced downstairs, took in the scene.

"Take this—this puppy out of here! Have him back in five minutes acting like a middy. Move!"

"Aye aye, sir." Tolliver snatched Bezrel's arm and propelled him to the door. I sat behind the desk, muttering imprecations. Eventually I calmed, but my chest throbbed.

In a few minutes the door opened. Bezrel crept in, hugging himself, head down. Tolliver followed. He touched the boy's shoulder and guided him gently to my desk. Bezrel came to attention. "I'm sorry, sir," he quavered. "I should have—"

"Belay that. I was wrong to yell. Stand easy." I forced the impatience from my tone. "Do you think you have it now, Mr. Bezrel?"

"Try 1524, sir. I mean, please, sir. I'm sure I got the rest of it right. That's the only—"

I punched in the code. The holoscreen cleared. Words flashed onto the screen. "Top Secret: Captain Nicholas E. Seafort, Eyes Only." Readable words. Bezrel craned around the console. His face lit up. "Oh, thank Lord God!"

My relief left me shaky. "Leave, both of you. Mr. Bezrel, my compliments to the duty officer, and he's to cane you for incompetence."

He swallowed. "I— Aye aye, sir." With a forlorn look he turned to the stairs. Halfway, a muffled sob escaped him.

Tolliver paused at the banister. "Of course that will help him remember in future." His tone was sardonic.

I fought to keep my voice level. "You're a midshipman, Mr. Tolliver. You could be caned likewise."

He paused, then said simply, "Do that and I'll kill you." He turned to the stairs.

"Get back here!"

"Aye aye, sir." He approached my desk.

"I could charge you with mutiny!"

"Oh, no, sir, it wasn't mutiny." His manner was casual, though his look was anything but. "I'll obey orders; I'm simply making clear my breaking point. Granted, I shouldn't have snatched the heli controls from you; I have to pay for that. So at twenty-five years of age I have the rank of a teener. I'll put up with it. I suppose you were generous to offer me summary punishment. But I couldn't tolerate your striking me. I'll try my best to kill you if you do."

I gaped, astounded. He continued, "So, Captain, you have your revenge for whatever hazing you suffered. I'm at your mercy. You know how far you can push me, and afterward, if I fail, you'll have me executed." He held my eye. "Am I dismissed?"

I'd have him arrested; what he'd said was insufferable. My fists bunched. And yet . . .

He was right. To threaten a grown man with a middy's caning was obscene; even poor Bezrel hadn't deserved it. "Get out!" The moment Tolliver was out of sight I turned to the holovid and entered my ID. The screen responded; I read my message at last.

Seafort:
These are contingency orders, which I've entrusted to a staff midshipman. Lord God grant that they never be put into effect. U.N.S. *Victoria* brought dispatches from Admiralty, at home. They've decreed that regardless of the cost here, the fleet must survive to defend home system. Therefore I am required, should we lose a third of our ships, to Fuse home with all remaining vessels.

Until now that possibility seemed remote, but given the events of this week I've begun planning for the worst case. Accordingly, we've begun evacuating U.N. forces from the Venturas, where they were doing little good. We're restationing them on our warships, and on Orbit Station.

If the fleet is forced to withdraw, it will carry Governor Saskrit and his civilian staff as well as the entire Army and Naval establishment. Hope Nation will be on its own until the fleet returns.

I sagged, head in my arms. Once the fleet left, it was unlikely ever to return. We would have abandoned our Hope Nation colonists to their fate.

I believe that likelihood is remote. To lose so many ships would mean attacks by more fish than we've yet seen. But if word of our contingency plan leaks, our relations with the planters would be devastated. Therefore, we must maintain a presence at Admiralty House until the last possible moment, or until the threat recedes. I've quietly withdrawn all other Captains and many of our lieutenants to the Station. You are the last Captain groundside.

For the moment, I'm placing you in command of Admiralty House. Your orders are: (1) to remain at hand and in a state of readiness to depart should it be necessary; and (2) to otherwise carry on as if under normal circumstances.

Catalonia is due back from Detour in ten days or so. I sent *Victoria* to intercept her with new orders, but the ships may not make contact. *Victoria* will go on to Kall's Planet to retrieve their Governor, and will return here. If on her return she fails to establish contact with the fleet, *Victoria* will Fuse at once for home.

For now, we've suspended shuttle flights to and from the Station, on the chance they may somehow attract the aliens. But I'll see to it that a shuttle is sent for you if we're required to depart. If you receive the code word, shut down Admiralty House, encrypt the puters, bring all remaining Naval personnel to the spaceport, and board the shuttle forthwith.

You must at all costs prevent any citizens of Hope Nation from learning of these orders. I hope and expect to return to Admiralty House shortly, to reassume command.

The code word is Destiny.

Georges T. De Marnay, Admiral Commanding.

I laid my head in my hands. Minutes passed.

At length Alexi called, "Mr. Seafort, are you all right? May I come down?"

I snapped off the holovid. "Yes."

He hurried into the anteroom. "You were silent for so—" He gaped. "Were you crying?"

"Don't be ridiculous." I wiped my sleeve across my face. "Call Lieutenant Anton."

A moment later the duty lieutenant stood at ease in front of his own desk. I suppressed a shiver; the room was freezing. "I need a list of all Naval personnel currently groundside."

"That's all in the puters, sir. It shouldn't take more than a few minutes." He hesitated. "Shall I find another console to work from?"

I blinked, recalled that it was his desk I'd appropriated. "That won't be necessary." I stood, debating the wisdom of trudging upstairs. I probably had strength for it, but coming back down might be a problem. "Is there another office on this level?"

"Just the conference room, sir." I let him lead the way. I spotted an easy chair behind the polished genera table. My heart pounded as I sat.

Tolliver appeared in the doorway. "It's six fifty-five, sir."

With an effort I focused on him. "I have my watch." The one phrase left me breathless.

"You're to see the doctor at seven."

"It will wait."

"You gave your word to Branstead."

I fought for breath. When I could speak I said, "Why do you hound me?"

He smiled bitterly. "Duty, of course."

"What does it matter if I live?"

"As I said, there'd be a Board of Inqu—"

"Belay that!"

His smile vanished. "I'm fit only for the Navy, and thanks to you, no one would have me in their command. While you live I have a posting. After that I'm beached." He leaned against the doorway, eyes closed. After a moment he added, "Sorry, I won't do that again. I don't want your pity. Let's go to your doctor."

"I'm on standby for special orders. I can't leave." The words left me gasping.

He crossed to my chair. "Bring your bloody caller along!"

A gasp of astonishment. I looked to the entranceway. "It's all right,

Mr. Anton. Come in." He looked doubtfully at Tolliver before presenting
me his notepad.

"Twelve officers? That's all?"

"It seems odd, sir, but everyone else is aloft at the moment."

I checked his list. Trapp, upstairs. Mr. Anton. Alexi. Two midshipmen
in the plotting room. Three middies and a lieutenant working with the
relief of Centraltown. Tolliver, and young Bezrel. Of our entire Naval
garrison, only these officers and I were left. Orbit Station must be swarming.

"How many enlisted men?"

"After Naval barracks was destroyed we shipped most survivors to
the Station. There may be a couple of dozen helping around town." He
hesitated. "May I ask why you're inquiring?"

"You may not." I took refuge in propriety. "Remember you're speaking to a Captain." I began to cough.

"Aye aye, sir." His glance strayed again to Edgar Tolliver. "Is that all,
Captain?"

"Carry on."

When he'd left, Tolliver said, "It's seven o'clock, sir. You gave your
word."

The room was quite hot. I unbuttoned my jacket. "I've already broken it."

"Then redeem it." He held my gaze.

It wasn't worth the effort to resist. "Very well. See if you can get a
heli."

I waited; a moment later he was back. "The Navy has five. Two are
out for repairs; the other three are patrolling downtown. Anton says the
looting has gotten worse." He studied my face. "Recall one of the helis,
sir."

"Damn it." Seeing his shocked expression, I repeated, "Damn it. To
hell." I felt a moment of panic at the near blasphemy, then suppressed it. I
would pay for worse, in His time. Still, I made a quick, silent prayer of
contrition. I sighed. "All right, get the car."

Knees trembling, I sat silent in the back seat, breathing deeply from
my vapormask. It wasn't much help. Alexi climbed in the front with Tolliver. I leaned back.

"We're here, sir."

I opened my eyes. Surely no more than a moment had passed. The
car was excruciatingly hot, and it was dark. "Where?" It was almost inaudible.

"The emergency clinic." Alexi watched anxiously.

I tried to stand, but coughs racked my frame. "Help me." Sagging against Alexi I made my way up the stairs and into the school.

Tolliver, sullenness cast aside, ran to the admitting desk. He spoke quietly, waited for an answer, shook his head urgently. The civilian gestured at the benches of waiting injured.

"Now!" Tolliver barked. On a bench, I huddled against Alexi. Tolliver unclipped his holster. "Now! By Lord God, I mean it!" His hand went to his pistol.

"Belay that!" My voice was a hoarse rasp.

Tolliver ignored me. "Call your frazzing doctor!" His tone was savage.

The civilian made a placating gesture, spoke urgently into his caller. A moment later a white-clad medic came out of the gym. "I'm Dr. Abood." Tolliver pointed. The doctor took one look at my face. "Bring him in."

I lay on the examining table, oxygen mask pressed to my mouth. The shot they'd given made breathing less painful. "What's wrong with me?"

"What isn't?" He turned off the analyzer. "Pneumonia, certainly. It should have killed you by now." A young man, in his thirties. Impatient.

"Dr. Avery started . . . antibiotics." I had to stop for breath.

"Yes. You may die before they gain hold." The medic ran his hand through thinning hair.

"Die." A stab of fear, not of death itself, but of what would come after.

"I've increased the dose. If you're quiet, and stay on the oxygen, it may knock the pneumonia down."

I spoke through the mask. "I have to get back to Admiralty House."

"Impossible."

Fighting dizziness, I struggled to a sitting position.

"I must." I fumbled at buttoning my shirt. "I'll lie down there."

"On your deathbed."

A chill caressed my neck. "But I was getting better. Really."

"Dr. Avery's meds helped the pneumonia, but you're losing your lung. Rejection. Blood tests leave no doubt." I gaped. He raised an eyebrow. "Avery didn't tell you?"

I shook my head, stifling a cough. "The antirejection drugs. I thought they . . ."

"You had only the first dose. You were about due for the second." I lay stunned.

"Maybe exposure brought it on. Normally, it wouldn't be a problem; we'd yank the bad lung and give you another. Now, replacement is impossible. We haven't the equipment, and the growth tanks are gone with the hospital."

Even my body had abandoned me. Had Lord God's vengeance begun? "Can you halt the rejection?"

"There's not much chance the drugs would work. Your best bet is for us to pull the lung. They'll give you another when you get home."

"No."

"If we yank the lung you'd be back on your feet in a week."

"I can't be disabled now. Give me the antirejection drug."

"Damn you people!" His vehemence shook me. "I watch joeys gasp their lives out on these tables, fighting to live a few extra minutes, and I can't save them! I can hold on to you, but you want to kill yourself! Why? For a fresh posting? A promotion?"

"No." I fought to breathe. "How soon would we know if the antirejection meds worked?"

"Your lung is inflamed and full of fluid. The drugs might have some temporary effect. But if your immune system rejects the lung again, it will go fast. You'd be lucky to reach the operating table."

"If I kept a heli standing by?"

He pursed his lips. "Your duty is so pressing?"

"I have . . . orders. I might have to take quick action."

His indignation eased. "Well, it's your life, joey. Will you stay on the vapormeds and on oxygen?" I nodded. "If your fever climbs, or you have more trouble breathing, get in a heli fast and radio ahead."

"All right."

He followed up his advantage. "And see me every day."

I smiled. "If possible, Dr. Abood."

He left the room. I dressed slowly, working around the vapormask. After a few moments the doctor returned. "I gave your men the replacement canisters."

"Very well."

"I explained your condition, so they'll be—"

"Leave my officers out of it!" The last thing I needed was Alexi and Tolliver mothering me.

He raised an eyebrow. "They had to know. When you go bad, you may not have time to tell them." I noticed he'd said "when," not "if."

"That's my affair." I slipped off the table, clung to it until the dizziness passed.

He said only, "Good luck. You'll need it."

When I emerged from the gymnasium Alexi took the canister from my hands. "Do you want to lean on me?"

"No." I took a few steps, tried to make my pace as normal as possible. Tolliver held the outer door. "What did he tell you?"

"Not to let you treat me like an invalid." I brushed past into the back seat of the electricar, drained. Outside, all was dark.

"Where to, sir?"

"Admiralty House, of course."

Tolliver started the car. "Of course." I closed my eyes. He said, "You realize we've been on duty since early this morning?"

I wanted only to sleep. "After you take me back you're free to go."

"Where, may I ask?"

The question snapped me awake. Naval barracks was demolished; neither Tolliver nor Alexi had a home. Nor did I, for that matter, though I could stay at Admiralty House, on a couch if necessary. I wondered if Admiralty House had showers. I tried to think.

Eons later a persistent voice nagged me into wakefulness. "Captain, you can't sleep in the car. Please, sir."

I blinked. We were parked at Admiralty House. Behind Tolliver, on the sidewalk, Lieutenants Anton and Trapp watched with obvious concern. I thrust away Tolliver's offered hand.

I stood, but the effort left me trembling and my weakness enraged me. "Middy, help me up the stairs." I leaned on Tolliver's shoulder. Alexi looked at Lieutenant Anton. "The Captain needs a bed, flank."

"We have air mattresses, in reserve stores. Shall I get a couple for you and Lieuten—Midshipman Tolliver?"

"Yes, please." As we passed through the doors I heard Alexi's quiet sigh of relief.

I slept fitfully in the conference room that had become my home. When morning came I needed Alexi's help to get to my feet, but I managed to wash and dress myself around the cumbersome vapormask. I didn't dare remove it.

Steaming tea soothed my chest as I sat at the gleaming table. In the rational light of morning I considered going immediately to the clinic to let Dr. Abood pull my rotting lung. With luck I'd be back at Admiralty House within a few days, and Admiral De Marnay might never get around to replacing me.

However, my orders were to keep our contingency plans secret until the Admiral sent the code word. If I told no one, and a signal came while I was under the anesthetic . . .

Alexi appeared at the door. "May I come in?"

I grunted. He sat at my side, unbidden.

"I feel—I shouldn't bother you with my problems." His hands fluttered in his lap like wounded birds. He rushed on. "But what am I to do? What is my status? Do I have duties?"

"You're on sick leave. You can't go back to the hospital, so you have to stay with me." It sounded more brusque than I'd intended. "Help me get around, Alexi. We'll find a place for you when they get things back in order."

"It's not just where I'm to stay. I feel—lost. Should I wear the uniform? What do I do when Tolliver speaks to you the way he does? What would any lieutenant do, hearing that?"

"Have a fit." My smile was bleak. "I shouldn't have demoted him. It was cruel, and we both know it. Mr. Tolliver is a situation I don't know how to handle."

"You could restore his rank."

"That would be worse; I can't go about rescinding discipline." I paused, then added carefully, "Or explaining my acts to lieutenants."

He colored. "I'm sorry. I wish . . . I knew better how to behave."

"You will, when your memory returns. In the meantime, study the regs; you knew them once. Perhaps they'll jog your memories."

He shook his head. "I will, but we both know better, Mr. Seafort." He stood. "Tell me when you'd like to go out. I'll be glad to help."

After he left I brooded about Tolliver, but found no answer. I rang for Lieutenant Anton.

"Yes, sir?"

"Have we heard from the fleet?"

"No contacts, sir. Mr. Trapp is in the plotting room; shall I have him come down?"

"I'll go up." Whatever protest he was about to offer was stilled by the look in my eye.

I took my time on the stairs. In the plotting room Lieutenant Trapp came out of his chair to stand at attention, as did a middy I didn't recognize. "As you were." I flopped in an empty seat. "Our status?" After my climb I thought it best to speak in short phrases.

Trapp flicked a key and the screen came to life. "Our main units are stationed here." De Marnay had pulled in our outer defenses, concentrating them around Hope Nation and Orbit Station.

I studied the positions. "Any sightings?"

"No, sir."

Footsteps pounded up the stairs. Midshipman Bezrel skidded into the room, came quickly to attention. "A call for you, sir. Mr. Anton sent me. It's—"

"Is that how they taught you to report?"

"No, sir, but I—"

"Go back down then! Report properly!"

He gulped. "Aye aye, sir." He saluted, turned, and left. Lieutenant Trapp and the other middy exchanged glances, said nothing. A moment later Bezrel's step sounded more sedately. He knocked at the door, entered at my nod. He stood at attention, shoulders stiff. "Midshipman Avar Bezrel reporting, sir!"

"Better. Stand at ease."

"Mr. Anton's compliments, sir. You have a call."

"Very well. How old are you, Mr. Bezrel?"

"Thirteen, sir." Young for a middy to be sent interstellar; his voice hadn't even broken. "Sir, I thought you'd want—"

I reached for the caller. "Is it the Admiral?" If I'd kept *him* waiting . . .

"No, sir. It's—"

"Nicky?" The voice tore at my soul.

I tore off the vapormask. "Annie? *ANNIE?*"

"Oh, Nicky! You be'ent dead!"

"Lord God. Where are you?"

"Dat refugee place, by the park."

"Annie, I . . ." I had to pause. "We looked for you . . ." Trapp turned away from my anguish.

"Our 'partment, you see'd it? Someone got in, mess wid our things."

"Where are you?"

"When the boom hit, I din' know what to do. I wen' back our place, nothin' workin', no lights or caller. I took food and hid 'til I figure it was safe. Empty places; I found lots of 'em. You din' come back; I thinkin' you was dead."

"Oh, Annie." I stopped, swallowed several times. Trapp and Bezrel were in the room; I managed to control my voice. "Stay where you are. I'll come for you."

Her tone had a note of alarm. "Oh, no, Nicky, you don' wan' see how I be lookin' now. Wait 'til I go back to the 'partment, get nice clothes. I meet you."

"Clothes don't matter; I've got to see you."

"I wan' look good fo' you, firs'. You come . . ."

"Meet me at the apartment."

"Naw, dat bad place now, people broke window an' trash our stuff. Meet me—" She paused. "Outside the Cathedral we be married in."

"Annie, it's bombed out. Nothing left but—"

"Safe place. Good place. Seeya in an hour."

"Don't—"

"Ten o'clock." A click.

"Annie!" I pounded the caller, but she'd rung off. I sighed. Not the best place to meet, surrounded by rubble, but what did that matter? My wife was alive.

After a time Lieutenant Trapp cleared his throat. I looked up, wiped my eyes. "Sorry."

"I'm glad for you, sir."

"Thank you." I rounded on Bezrel. "Why didn't you tell me who was calling? I made her wait while I sent you back down!"

"I tried, sir, but—"

"All you had to do was say her name!"

"Yes, sir, but you—".

"Two demerits. Out!"

"Aye aye, sir." He saluted and fled.

I let my fury ebb. Annie was alive; nothing else mattered. My illness didn't count. Our apartment was nothing. Even . . . I faced it: even Eddie Boss didn't matter any longer.

Trapp was tactfully silent. I stared at the board, willing the fish to show their whereabouts, explain their intentions. The middy on duty fidgeted, but quieted at my frown. "Well, the fish won't be dropping any rocks," I said. "Not without Defusing into the middle of the fleet."

"Yes, sir," Trapp agreed. "But our ships are tied down patrolling. To cover Centraltown while the Station is over the Venturas, we've committed here, and here." He gestured. "What does that leave us in reserve?"

"Enough, I hope." Footsteps pounding on the stairs. I swiveled.

"Midshipman Avar—"

"Another call, Mr. Bezrel?"

"No, sir." He was stiff at attention. "Lieutenant Anton's compliments. Ms. Triforth and Mr. Hopewell are below, demanding to speak to the officer in charge."

"I beg your pardon? Demanding?"

"That's the way Mr. Anton said it, sir. I don't mean any disre—"

"What in hell—er, what do they want?"

Bezrel said anxiously, "Mr. Anton didn't tell me, sir."

"Dismissed."

"Aye aye, sir." He seemed grateful to escape.

I'd have to go down, of course. The planters should have called for an appointment, but nonetheless they were too important to snub. I had half

an hour to get rid of them before I was to meet Annie. I turned to Trapp.
"Have Mr. Anton show them to the conference room."

"Aye aye, sir."

I hoisted myself out of my chair, headed for the door. I paused, my
face reddening. "Mr. Trapp, when you see Mr. Bezrel . . ." I reached for
my vapormask.

"Yes, sir?"

I mumbled, "Tell him his demerits are canceled."

His face was impassive. "Aye aye, sir."

Laura Triforth, sprawled in an easy chair, came to her feet when I
entered. Old Zack Hopewell faced the wall with hands clasped behind
him. He turned, gave a formal nod. His manner was more somber than
hostile, but I sensed that something had changed.

I shifted the canister awkwardly to shake hands, and sat as soon as I
decently could. My heart pounded; perhaps climbing upstairs had been
less wise than I'd thought.

Laura spoke first. "It's good to see you, Mr. Seafort, but we'd hoped
to meet with Admiral De Marnay."

"He's aloft."

"So we heard." Hopewell was blunt. "Why is that, Captain Seafort?"

I was astounded. Civilians questioning Naval dispositions? I ducked
the issue. "Perhaps I can help you. I'm still Naval liaison to the planters."

"So you're in charge?"

"The Admiral ordered me to run Admiralty House for the time being." I clasped my hands on the table, waiting.

Hopewell said only, "What's afoot, Captain?"

My mind spun. "Why, not a thing. Admiral De Marnay can't spend
all his time—"

Hopewell's tone was icy. "I'd prefer," he said, "that you tell me the
truth, or nothing."

I was silent a long moment. "I think you'd better explain your visit."
De Marnay should have stayed groundside to handle this. I'd warned him
I had no knack for public relations.

Hopewell's look was definitely unfriendly. "We may be provincials,
Mr. Seafort, but we're not stupid. We notice things."

"Such as?"

"More and more of your personnel are being sent aloft."

"Since the bombing, housing has been a problem."

"No, it began a week before they hurled the rock at us."

"Normal crew rotation."

"You're fencing, Mr. Seafort. I thought better of you. How many Captains are groundside at the moment?"

"Just—that's classified information. I shouldn't—"

"The fish are your enemy. We aren't!" He was relentless.

"Nevertheless, I can't—"

"Are you the only one left?"

I shook my head; how did I get into this mess? "I can't discuss that, Mr. Hopewell."

Laura said, "Do your orders forbid it?"

I hesitated. "Not specifically."

"Then level with us."

I took a deep breath. If I was wrong, then so be it. "I'm the only one."

Hopewell sagged, as if defeated. "You were right, Laura."

This had gone on long enough. "About what?"

The two exchanged glances. It was Ms. Triforth who answered. "About ten days ago you began stripping men from Centraltown. We noticed it first in the restaurants and bars. Some of us have a financial stake downtown, you know. Fewer seamen seemed to be on leave. Then even the officers began to disappear."

Admiral De Marnay should have known better than to try to hoodwink these planters. They ran everything. It was their town, their colony.

"Odd, that this occurred just after a fastship arrived from home." Laura caught my look of surprise. "Oh, yes, we heard about her as well. *Victoria*, I believe. Anyway, we began keeping tabs on your personnel even before the explosion. The bomb threw us off for a while, because we were all busy offering help, but I'd say right now there aren't more than fifteen officers in all of Centraltown, including midshipmen." Close. Twelve. "And a handful of sailors, helping with cleanup operations."

I said, "Go on, Ms. Triforth."

"You've stopped delivering supplies to the Venturas Base. For that matter, you've stopped bringing cargo down to Centraltown as well."

"That could—"

"Your Lieutenant Eiferts won't let us visit the Venturas, but food purchases for the base have virtually ceased. Either your men are living on rations, or you've been evacuating Western Continent too."

The Admiral's orders were clear. I could tell no one of our contingency plans. I temporized. "If this is true, what do you make of it?"

"Tell us what to make of it, Captain." Laura's voice was cool.

"You're worried," I said, hoping to appear reasonable. "What do *you* think is happening?" I held my breath, afraid of the response.

Ms. Triforth stirred. Zack Hopewell waved her silent. "You intend to abandon us," the old man said. The blunt charge lingered in the silence of the room.

I stared at the mahogany table. To follow orders I must deny everything, else our good relations with the planters would be destroyed. But my visitors would see through my denial, and I'd lose the trust I'd striven to build. Wasn't that as much a breach of my orders as revealing the truth?

In any event, I'd only confirm what they'd guessed, though Admiral De Marnay wouldn't see it that way. He'd more likely view it as grounds for court-martial.

A hesitant knock. Midshipman Bezrel drew himself to attention.

"Get out!" I snarled.

The middy fled.

I slammed my fist on the table. At length I looked up. Neither alternative would suffice; I had to find my own way.

"Mr. Hopewell, kindly shut the door." I waited. When he sat I said carefully, "What you have described could be coincidence." He stirred restlessly, but I overrode him. "If the Navy were planning a maneuver, there might be reasons I couldn't tell you. Orders to that effect."

Laura said, "That explains nothing."

With an effort I got to my feet. Thinking came easier when I paced. "I couldn't possibly confirm your suspicions." I tucked the canister under my arm. If I paced slowly, I could still speak. "But it would be interesting to imagine what Admiralty might arrange, given substantial losses in the Hope Nation fleet. Remember, even though the fish attacked here first, they could attack anywhere."

"Imaginings aren't what we're here to—"

"Shut up, Laura. Listen."

Ms. Triforth glowered at her companion.

"We sent thirty-eight capital ships to Hope Nation. That's a third of the entire U.N. fleet. The loss of that many ships, or a substantial number of them, would seriously impede the defense of home waters, should the fish invade there."

Laura said to Hopewell, "They're abandoning us."

"Listen."

I took several deep breaths, disregarding the pain they caused. What I was about to say could hang me. "If Hope Nation weren't an important colony, so much of the fleet wouldn't have been risked to defend it. Consider Admiralty's predicament. If they leave the fleet here, it might be lost. If they bring it home, they might lose Hope Nation."

"We already knew that."

I regarded Laura Triforth with distaste. I was risking my commission, if not my life, to inform her, and the woman wouldn't shut up. "I'm not Admiralty, Ms. Triforth, but I imagine what they might do is try to hedge their bets."

Puzzled, she shook her head. "How do you mean?"

That was more what I wanted. Like an instructor at Academy, I drew her on. "The Hope Nation fleet has to be strong to be effective. Admiralty doesn't want to see it whittled down to nothing. Perhaps they might set a limit on losses. They might tell the Admiral Commanding that the fleet could operate as long as losses were acceptable, but when they became too great, the fleet was to return home."

Ms. Triforth demanded, "You've already lost nine ships that we know of. What is the decision point?"

I looked at her with surprise. "We're just speculating, Laura. It's all hypothetical."

With an effort she restrained her irritation. "Hypothetically, Captain, what would that point be?"

"One that might never be reached. Certainly, a substantial number of ships." I held up a hand to stop her objection. "But if it were approached, it would mean the fleet was under heavy attack. Obviously there would be no time to begin ferrying men up to Orbit Station. So Admiralty might, hypothetically, order a precautionary evacuation ahead of time."

This time the silence continued for a full minute. Finally, Zack Hopewell asked, "How long would these contingency plans remain in effect?"

I shrugged, suddenly weary, and made for my chair. "I don't know. Perhaps until the battle was won." I sat.

"Or lost."

"Yes."

Zack Hopewell cleared his throat, waited until I raised my eyes to his. He said simply, "Thank you."

For some reason when I spoke my voice was gruff. "If these plans were known—"

"They won't be."

"If Admiral De Marnay learns of this conversation, my career is finished. Naturally, if he asks, I'll tell him. But he may not ask."

Hopewell said, "I don't see how our knowing would lead us to do anything we wouldn't otherwise. Do you agree, Laura?"

"What is there to do?" Laura Triforth folded her arms. "You'll be back, eventually. You'll have to. We supply too much food for you to abandon us. When you return, we'll sell to you on our terms, not yours."

"That's not my bailiwick."

Ms. Triforth shrugged. "Actually, sending the fleet home may be in our best interest. The fish seem to be space dwellers; they've shown little interest in our planet. Once you leave we can reorganize the government—"

My tone was sharp. "That's treason. I won't hear any such conversation. Hope Nation is a U.N. colony until the Government decides otherwise."

Zack Hopewell cleared his throat. "Laura, it's uncivil to aggravate the Captain with our political debates. He's risked a great deal for us."

"Very well." She stood. "We've taken enough of your time, Mr. Seafort. You have our assurance that what we've spoken of will go no further." We shook hands.

Hopewell asked, "How is your pneumonia?"

I gestured at the vapormask. "Not good, as you can see. But it will pass." I myself might pass.

"You're under treatment?"

"I went to the clinic yesterday. The doctor wants me to return every day or so."

Ms. Triforth paused at the door. "The clinic is a long way. Do you go by heli?"

"The Naval helis have been busy downtown. Today, we drove."

"Mine is at your disposal. I'll call here every day. Have your man tell me what time to pick you up."

"I couldn't—"

"No, I insist. You've been a true friend to all of us, Mr. Seafort, as I'm just beginning to realize."

I came out of my chair. "Thank you. Pray that Admiralty's fears never come to pass. We'll work out our problems together."

On that note they took their leave.

I sat gathering my strength before I rang for Alexi. A few minutes later, leaning on his shoulder, I passed through the anteroom, on my way to our electricar. I halted by the desk. "What are you sniveling at, Middy?"

Midshipman Bezrel wiped his tears with his sleeve. "Sorry, sir."

"Answer my question!"

His face puckered. "I can't get anything right for you. No matter how hard I try . . . I'm sorry. Please . . ." He lapsed into miserable silence.

"Why did you come to my door?"

"Mr. Trapp told me to ask if your guests wanted refreshments."

"Very well." My rebuke wasn't worth bawling over. What were middies coming to? I tried to imagine myself wailing over a reprimand from a

Captain, but even as a first-year cadet, it would have been unthinkable. I sighed. "Carry on."

Settled in the car at last, I leaned back while Tolliver headed toward downtown and the ruins of the Cathedral. It was fitting that Annie and I reunite there, I decided. In that place I'd promised to love and honor Annie Wells, until death did us part. I'd been hurt by her infidelity, more wounded than I'd been able to say, but it was past, and Eddie was gone. Transpop ways were not our ways, and Annie was of the transient culture, not mine. I would heal our marriage. I'd do whatever I must.

A street was blocked, and Tolliver braked sharply. "Careful," I muttered, breathing deeply from the vapormask. The interview with the planters had left me uneasy; their knowledge of our operations was much greater than I'd realized. If Hopewell and Ms. Triforth knew all we were doing, then so did Mantiet and his cohorts. I would have to be especially careful. Outside the car, ruined houses glided by.

We were crossing the park when the speaker crackled. "Trapp reporting, sir. A tightbeam from Naval HQ on Orbit Station. U.N.S. *Wellington* engaged a fish."

My fingers tightened on the caller. "When?"

"A few minutes ago, apparently. The fish fused alongside. *Wellington*'s crew was already at Battle Stations. They skewered it with a midships laser."

"Good." A thought struck. "She was already at Battle Stations?"

"Yes, sir. Captain Steers hasn't stood down since the attack on Centraltown."

"Good Lord." His crew must be at the ragged edge of exhaustion, snatching minutes of sleep at their posts. No ship could maintain Battle Stations for long. Still, he'd saved his ship; they'd been ready when the fish appeared. "Any more sightings?"

"Just the one, so far. I thought you'd want to know."

"Quite right." I rang off.

"We're almost there, sir." Alexi pointed to the broken spire ahead.

Only one lane of the broad avenue that had fronted the Reunification Cathedral had been cleared of rubble. Tolliver maneuvered us to within a dozen yards of the shattered entrance. I looked to both sides of the street; Annie was nowhere in sight. I checked my watch: eleven-thirty. We were early yet.

I opened my door. "You two wait here." I wouldn't have their solicitous interference. Not at our reunion.

"Sure you can make it?"

I turned to Tolliver with an angry rejoinder, but his question had been civil and without truculence. "Yes." I wished I could leave the vapormask behind, but reluctantly bundled the canister under my arm as I heaved myself out of the car.

I scrambled over rubble to the sidewalk. The blast had collapsed the ruins of the Cathedral's twin spires onto its domed roof, which had fallen into the building. Checking my watch every few moments, I stood against the stone outer wall.

A few yards away Alexi and Edgar Tolliver waited patiently in the car. Could I do anything to alter Tolliver's behavior? Doubtful. Though Naval discipline was virtually ingrained in us, his demotion was more than a vicissitude of Naval life to be borne with equanimity.

I picked at a small chunk of concrete, regretting that I'd treated him so severely. But what could I have done, after he'd hurled me out of my seat? I paced the sidewalk, wishing Annie would hurry, peering at the ruins.

The iron-strapped door hung askew on one hinge. Beyond, smashed blocks from the dome littered the nave amid crushed and splintered pews. The wreckage gleamed in the bright morning sunlight. We'd been married in the north transept. I was disoriented, but knew it would be to my left. I pushed through the shattered door.

Though rubble blocked my view of the altar, I suppressed an urge to genuflect. I wandered toward the transept, wondering how close I could get to it, aware that I was in no condition to clamber over debris.

Roof beams blocked the aisle, but in falling, one beam had swept other rubble clear of the nave, and I was able to make my way across the shattered stone floor. So much effort, so much faith, so much veneration had been poured into this edifice. When the fish were conquered, we would have to rebuild; Lord God had been well served here. Perhaps I could volunteer to help with the rebuilding.

No, I'd be long recalled to Terra by the time resources were marshaled to rebuild the Cathedral, and in any event my help would be a desecration. I'd damned myself, and Lord God would want no contribution from me to His Church.

Rubble from caved-in walls filled the transept. I turned back, but detoured toward the altar. Blasted or not, this was a holy place, and I wanted to make obeisance. I picked my way across the debris, canister clutched in my hand.

"You shouldn'a come."

I whirled. Annie crouched on a great block of stone that had fallen from some high place.

"I wan'd ta look all pretty." Her tone was plaintive. She picked at the remnants of her dress. "Mira, it tore now."

I scrambled across the rubble, tearing off my vapormask. "Annie." A board twisted under my foot. I fell, the air knocked out of me by the impact.

"I wen' back ta apartmen' an' did my face, the way Amanda useta. Not a lot of paintin', jus' lil bit." Her hands twisted like frantic birds at her ragged dress. "I put on my necklace, Nicky. I kept it safe alla time, 'cause I knew you'd wanna see me innit."

I staggered to my feet, unable to breathe, not caring. "Annie, what did they do to you?"

She fingered her throat. "Rubies gone." Her lipstick was smeared with dirt and grime.

Dust motes floated in the bright glare of afternoon. I lurched across the litter of the nave. "Annie!"

"Mira my dress!" Her eyes teared. "Was nice threads, Nicky." A great red bruise blotched half her face, as if she'd been clubbed. "I tried ta tell 'em; how c'n I get 'notha dress now, alla stores broke?"

I cradled her head on my shoulder, but she pulled free.

"Tried so hard ta look pretty fo' you." A whimper.

I coaxed her toward the door. My foot caught. I glanced down. A hand. An arm. The remains of a man, his head smashed by a rock. A pool of blood soaked the surrounding rubble. Lord God.

My breath caught until the jagged walls began to swim in red mist. I clawed at my vapormask, got it over my face.

"You be hurt, Nicky!" She raised a begrimed hand, traced the outline of my mask.

"It's no matter." I tried to lift her, wanting not to see the angry scrapes on her legs. "Come, Annie. I'll take you to the clinic."

"Don' wanna." She uncrossed her legs, smoothed the ragged dress with an attempt at modesty.

"You have to see a doctor." I tugged at her, but she wouldn't move.

"I be all righ'." She tittered. "Buncha big men. Whatcha doin' here, girl? Who be witcha?" Her hands brushed at the lacerated dress. "Don' run now, joeygal." Her voice dropped. "Come here, girl, we have zarky time." Her voice rose again. "Scratchin'. Beard scratch my face!"

I had to stop her, before she shattered the remnants of my soul. "Please! Come with me."

"Don' yank onna necklace, please, mista. I goin' witcha. No, leave me Nicky's jewels!" She rubbed the red welt on her throat. "Aw, don'!"

"Annie." I drew my breath. "I can't walk to the car. Help me!" I pulled at her arm, and her vacant stare fixed on me. Comprehension came slowly. "You got a mask, Nicky. Means ya be sick. I din' take care of you." She slid off the block. "Come lean on Annie. Three joeys ran away, afta. Safe now."

"Help me. Please." Wanting to support her, afraid to try, I pretended to lean on her as we hobbled to the door. She limped, one shoe gone. Lord God damn them eternally. Please, Lord. Nothing for myself. Just damn them for her.

We tottered to the street. In the car, Alexi and Tolliver were deep in conversation. I couldn't summon breath to shout. Annie blinked in the shadowless light, hands flitting over the tatters of her dress.

"Just a few steps, hon." She held back. Cursing, I staggered across the rubble to the curb, and pounded on the window. "Open the door! Get out!" My hands clawed at the latch.

Alexi, startled, stared at me, then, with horror, past me. He jumped from the car, put a protective arm around Annie.

She screamed.

Dr. Abood snapped off the ultrasound. "Your pneumonia is down, and you're fighting the rejection."

"Never mind me. What about Annie?"

"You're in worse shape than she." He met my glare, relenting. "We've sedated her, Captain. Cuts and bruises, but no serious injuries."

"But she's been . . ."

"Raped, yes. Repeatedly. She'll be quite tender for a time."

I clutched my canister, as if for comfort. "Her mind . . ."

"She's in shock. Warmth, fluids, rest. That's all we can do at this stage."

"God knows what she stumbled into. I found her standing over a corpse."

"She's lucky they didn't murder her too."

"I'll kill them when I find them." My voice was hoarse.

"Of course. Anyone would." His gentle hand pushed me back down on the gurney. "But you're in no shape to go looking."

I recoiled from his touch. After a time I said, "You heard her. Will she be able to identify them?"

"Perhaps. The mind defends itself against the unbearable, Captain. She may block it out."

It was my fault. I'd known she needed looking after, yet I'd sent Eddie Boss away and hadn't replaced him. It would have taken more than three assailants to subdue Eddie, had they attacked Annie.

My fists tightened on the mattress. "Leave me alone. Please." After he'd gone I lay gripping the bed, fighting for self-control, nearly gaining it, in the end, losing.

Annie . . .

What have they done to you?

Part 3

July, in the year of our Lord 2200

14

Days passed, one upon another. My pneumonia cleared to the point where I could dispense with the vapormask for hours at a time, until even Dr. Abood expressed cautious optimism that I might retain my damaged lung. I no longer objected to visiting the clinic daily; Annie was there, and I'd have spent all my time with her if I could.

The few Admiralty House staff tiptoed about their duties, anxious to avoid my wrath. At times my manner reduced the unfortunate Bezrel to helpless tears, which infuriated me to the point I nearly sent him for another caning. I barked at the lieutenants who came to report, criticized Tolliver's manner, drove even Alexi into pale and subdued silence.

At the clinic Annie lay passive, legs drawn up, sheet clutched under her chin, allowing me to hold her hand. Sometimes I found her face streaked with tears. She seldom spoke, and never of the Cathedral.

The first time Admiral De Marnay called, I was with her. After, I screamed at Lieutenant Anton until my throat was raw for his failure to forward the call, though the Admiral had told him not to bother.

The Admiral's second call, two days later, found me dozing in my conference room. I snapped awake, took the caller, waved Bezrel out.

"You're recovering, Seafort?"

"Yes, sir." From the pneumonia, at any rate.

"Things seem to be quieting. I suppose I could send someone down to take over."

If he did, I could spend my days with Annie. "As you wish, sir."

"Still, *Hibernia* had a possible contact last night."

"Possible, sir?"

"At the edge of her sensor range. She investigated, but found nothing."

"I see." Why was he telling me?

"Perhaps I should send my staff groundside. We can't maintain this mode indefinitely. Sooner or later, your people will notice something odd."

"Yes, sir." I held my breath.

"Have you had any questions?"

"From a couple of the planters, sir."

He sounded preoccupied. "Eventually they'll stop believing your explanations. I'll give it another week or so. If we don't encounter more fish by then, I'll transfer my command to Admiralty House. In the meantime we'll keep the shuttles inactive. The fish probably hear us Fuse, but we don't know what else they hear."

"Yes, sir." What else was there to say?

"Well, no point relieving you, if it's only another week. Carry on."

"Aye, aye, sir."

"How's young Bezrel?"

"Uh, fine, sir." It was stretching a point.

"Take care of him. I took him as a special favor to his father. We were shipmates for years."

"Aye aye, sir."

"Send him up on the first shuttle. I wouldn't have let him go, but he could be trusted not to reveal the codes."

"Aye aye, sir." For my cruelty to the boy, a day of reckoning loomed.

"Very well." We signed off.

Dr. Abood clasped his arms behind his neck, stretched his back. "Nothing's fit here. The tables are too low." I bit back an impatient reply. "The truth is, Seafort, we can't do much more for her. She needs counseling, love, time to heal. She'd do as well at home as here. Perhaps better."

"I'll find a place for us."

"Your home was destroyed?" I nodded. "There's a housing directory, at temporary City Hall. Perhaps they can help."

"Thank you." I gestured at the vapormask. "Can I leave it off?"

"Certainly not. Wear it when you sleep, and as often as you can while you're awake. You might make it."

I said sourly, "Thanks for the encouragement."

"I warned you a week ago: the lung should come out. When you get back home they can pop in a new one."

"I'll decide in a week or so."

"Why, what happens then?"

I tensed. "I didn't say anything would happen. I'll decide when I'm ready."

He stood to go. "Stay near a heli, Captain."

Easier said than done. I'd imagined that when the rescue efforts eased, our Naval helis would be more available, but they were pressed into service as makeshift public transportation. In the meantime Tolliver found a passable ground route through the ruins to the clinic.

When we left Dr. Abood I had Tolliver drive me to the housing office, where I put my name on the list for accommodations. They promised to call.

"Back to Admiralty House." I climbed into the car.

Tolliver shut my door. "Aye aye, sir."

The temporary City Hall, on the far edge of town, was in a building shielded from the worst of the blast by a high hill. But to reach Admiralty House we would have to skirt the ruined area. I sighed, wishing I had access to a heli. Well, I *did* have access to Laura Triforth's, if I chose to accept her offer. I found her manner intriguing; in discussing colonial affairs she was flinty, even acid. But in personal matters, such as Alexi's health or mine, an obvious warmth gleamed through her prickly veneer.

I settled back in my seat for the ride. Few other vehicles were on the road, but blockages made driving difficult, and I was never at ease in an electricar. Tolliver, sensing my impatience, came up behind a slow-moving vehicle, waited for an opportunity to pass. It made me nervous; I sat forward, hanging on to my hand strap.

Seeing his chance Tolliver swerved around the offending car. As he wrenched the wheel I glanced aside. The other driver stared back, then turned his head sharply. Something about him bothered me. I puzzled for a moment, then cursed and pounded Tolliver's shoulder. "Stop!"

He jammed on the brake. "What's wrong, sir?"

The other car had turned onto a cross street. "That was Mantiet! I'm sure of it!"

"Mantiet? The planter?" He gaped.

"Don't sit there, follow him!" As he swung around I stamped the floorboard in frustration.

We squealed around the corner. The car was two blocks ahead and accelerating. Tolliver gunned the engine.

"Can we catch him?"

His eyes were riveted on the road. "I'll try, sir." After a moment, he cleared his throat and said, "Can you reach the caller?"

"The caller? Of course I—damn!" I keyed Naval frequency. "Admiralty House, Seafort here!" An eternal moment later the speaker crackled. "Midshipman Wilson here, sir."

"Get Anton, flank!"

"Aye aye, sir." The line went dead.

Mantiet's car swerved around a corner. "Don't lose him!"

"I won't." His tone was calm.

"Anton, sir." The man sounded out of breath.

"We're chasing Mantiet!"

"Chasing?"

"In our car!" I shouted. "He's a couple of blocks ahead. Call in all Navy helis, flank! Get any other support the authorities can give us. We're—where the hell are we, Tolliver?"

"North on Churchill Street."

"—moving north on Churchill, about a mile past whatsis, the road the new town hall is on."

"Aye aye, sir. Understood. What do you want the helis to do?"

I was beside myself. "Stop him! Catch him!"

"Aye aye, sir. Hang on." The line went dead.

I cursed into the mute caller while we careened through debris-filled streets. "Stay left! Don't lose him!"

Tolliver seemed to be enjoying himself. "Would you care to drive, sir?"

"Are you joking?"

"You're in the back seat, sir."

"What of it?"

"Oh, nothing."

What on earth was he babbling about? In a few moments my irritation eased as I saw he was keeping pace with the fleeing vehicle.

The speaker came to life. "Anton reporting, sir. Two helis are on their way. Where are you now?"

I thrust the caller at Tolliver. "Tell him." Tolliver gave our location, thrust the caller down as he spun us around a corner. "Look out—"

"Damn!" We skidded into an overturned truck. A crunch. I was hurled against the front seat. Tolliver spun the wheel, jammed down the pedal, slamming me back into my seat. "Sorry, sir." He loosened his tie.

The lunatic was humming.

A moment later he broke off, pointed. "There! Look!"

I craned my neck. A heli swooped over Mantiet's vehicle. Please, Lord, let me get my hands on him. Please.

"How will they stop him?" As soon as I asked, my question seemed foolish.

"All helis go armed now, sir. Not like the one we flew."

I snatched the caller. "Anton, patch me through to the helis."

"Aye aye, sir. Just a . . . go ahead."

"This is Captain Seafort."

"Lieutenant Hass reporting, sir. I'm over his car."

An excited young voice. "Midshipman Kell, sir. I'm right behind. I've got him in my sights."

"Listen, both of you! I want him captured, not dead." Mantiet couldn't have stolen the missile and hidden for all these subsequent weeks on his own. He'd have had confederates. "If you can flatten his tires, do so. If you kill him, I'll have your—" I lapsed silent.

"Stripes?" Tolliver offered. "Balls?"

"Shut up and drive."

"Aye aye, sir." He hummed under his breath.

"I'll angle back for a disabling shot." Lieutenant Hass.

"Please, sir, let me! I've got the angle. I can do it; I was first in gunnery last year."

"You sure, boy?" Hass sounded anxious.

"I won't shoot 'til I'm positive. Honest!"

"Go for it, Middy."

Tolliver eased the accelerator. We fell back. The second heli swooped away from the car in a wide arc.

I cursed. "What's that idiot doing?"

"Lining up a midships shot." Tolliver pointed. "If he comes in low from the side he can target both wheels with the tracer. Then all he has to—"

"Show-off," I growled. He opened his mouth to protest but thought better of it.

I didn't hear shots, but I could see tracers arc across the road. Mantiet's car lurched, spun out of control. It jumped the curb and slammed into the porch of a wood-frame house. In the heli, the excited middy crowed into his mike. Deafened, I spun down the caller volume.

I beat on Tolliver's shoulder. "Hurry, before he runs!"

We skidded to a halt in front of the damaged house. Mantiet's car door swung open. He dashed with surprising speed down the road.

"Get him!" Tolliver bolted from the car in pursuit. I hauled myself out, furious that I couldn't join the chase, but the outcome was never in doubt. Tolliver had always been a fine runner, as he'd shown in catching Jerence. He overtook Mantiet at the corner and whirled him around. His fist flew. Mantiet stumbled.

I let go of the car and walked down the street, trying to make my legs steady. Mantiet sprang to his feet. It seemed to enrage Tolliver, who flailed wildly at the man's stomach and face. When I finally reached them Tolliver was holding Mantiet against a tree, pounding him with his free hand.

"Enough."

"Remember Mr. Tamarov?" Tolliver's face was hard, bitter. "And our heli?"

I hesitated. Tolliver drove his fist into Mantiet's ribs, knocking him to the ground. I caught his hand. "That's enough!"

He subsided, fuming. A heli settled into the road, blades spinning lazily.

A blond middy jumped out, loped toward us. "Midshipman Harvey Kell reporting, sir!" He came to attention, his stance marred by an ecstatic grin. "I knew I'd get the grode!"

"Stand easy, Mr. Kell." But I owed him something more. "Well done, Midshipman."

The boy gawked at Mantiet, semiconscious in the dirt. "This is the one, sir? Who shot you down?"

"Yes." I felt a savage triumph. "Tolliver, you and Kell take him by heli to Admiralty House. I'll drive our car."

"You, sir? But—"

"The response to an order is?"

"Aye aye, sir! Sorry." Tolliver snapped a salute, hauled Mantiet to his feet. Kell hurried to help. Between them they bundled the planter into the heli. A moment later they were aloft.

"Where is he?" I flung open the door to the anteroom.

Lieutenant Anton came to his feet. "In the dayroom, sir. I, uh, didn't know where else to put him."

"Can he get out?"

"He's under guard, sir. Midshipman Tolliver seemed quite eager for the duty."

Alexi came out of the conference room. "Are you all right, Mr. Seafort?"

"Me? Of course." I put on my vapormask.

"Have you anything for me today?"

"Don't bother me now, Mr. Tamarov." His face fell. "On second thought, come with me."

He followed as I strode down the corridor. "Where are we going?"

"To the man who stole your memory." I opened the door.

Frederick Mantiet slumped in a straight chair in the center of the windowless room. Tolliver stood in front of him, fists bunched. Mantiet's face was puffy.

Through the vapormask my voice was a rasp. "What have you been up to?"

"Guarding the prisoner." Tolliver was savage. "Waiting for him to twitch."

"Leave us, Mr. Tolliver."

"But—aye aye, sir." He left with unconcealed reluctance.

Mantiet's tone was sardonic. "A pleasure to see you, Captain. Last time, we were both in better health."

I shrugged. "It was your choice to run."

"Oh, is that why he worked me over? I've been wondering."

The man's cool demeanor enraged me. "You'll feel worse after interrogation, I'm sure." Drugs and poly often left a subject nauseous, and with a splitting headache.

Despite his bruises, Mantiet managed to raise an eyebrow. "Interrogation? Whatever for?"

"Attempted murder, treason. Destruction of Naval property." And of Alexi's soul, you bastard. "I'll look forward to the details of your confession. And afterward, to your hanging." I smiled, savoring my revenge. "You can't escape interrogation, Mantiet. There's more than enough evidence to send you to poly."

"What a pity to disappoint you, then. I confess."

I blurted, "You what?"

"I confess, to all of it. The missile, the explosives in the hauler, everything."

"You'll be hanged, you know."

"I assumed as much the moment you spotted me."

I sagged into a chair. Why did I feel cheated? I wanted him to undergo the polygraph and drugs, to experience the maddening inevitability of confession. At my own interrogation, I'd made no effort to conceal anything from Admiralty, but I recalled the irresistible compulsion to tell my questioners whatever they asked.

But if Mantiet confessed, he couldn't be interrogated. The drugs and poly were means to determine the truth, not instruments of torture.

I said reluctantly, "Alexi, call Lieutenant Trapp."

A moment later the lieutenant appeared in the doorway. "Mr. Trapp, interrogate Mantiet. I want a full confession about the hauler, the missile fired on our heli, and whatever conspiracy he engaged in. Names of his associates, dates, details. If he fails to cooperate, break off immediately and inform me."

"Aye aye, sir."

"Get on with it." I stalked off to my conference room, Alexi trailing behind. I sat at the table, breathed a sigh of relief. "It's over, Alexi."

"Is it?" His voice was bleak.

I flushed with shame. "Not for you. I'm sorry. But we've got him at last."

"He'll be executed."

"Yes." Without a doubt.

"I suppose that's good." He paused, looked at his hands. "Mr. Seafort, I follow you around, hold doors, help you into your car. Is that all I'm fit for?"

I thought of telling the truth, then relented. "No, of course not." I hesitated. "There's not much to do, actually, with all our personnel aloft."

"Isn't there anything?" He searched my face in appeal. "I feel useless, waiting for memories that are gone forever."

Alexi's problems were the last thing on my mind; my adrenaline still coursed from the chase. I searched for a way to appease him. "Would you like to help with the relief work?" He wouldn't need to remember his duties for that.

"Could I?" Then his face clouded. "I don't really know my way around Centraltown."

"You could learn. And you know how to drive; you offered several times."

"Did I?" A smile lit his face. "Yes, how could anyone forget how to drive?" He jumped up, nearly knocking over my coffee. "When could I start? Today?"

Why did I feel abandoned? I forced down the ungenerous impulse. "I'll have Mr. Anton call the relief agencies." I took the caller, spoke as if joking. "You'll visit me sometimes, still?"

He grinned. "Every day, Mr. Seafort."

Later that evening, beside himself with excitement, Alexi left Admiralty House for the transport center, where he was to work as a volunteer. Normally his status would have been a problem; Alexi's injuries put him on the Navy inactive list, but he couldn't work as a civilian employee while in the Service. In the emergency, such niceties were ignored.

Later that evening I sat in my conference room reading Frederick Mantiet's confession. Trapp had been thorough. He'd gone over every detail of the plot, starting with the hauler explosion on Plantation Road.

To my surprise, Mantiet hadn't objected to naming his coconspirators. That was odd. Was he lying? I slammed down the transcript. Of course he was lying; why betray his countrymen? True, a man who could contemplate treason would do anything.

Staring at the polished genera table, I recalled my clash with Judge Chesley over my enlistment of Paula Treadwell years before. In my hubris, I had threatened to put the colony under martial law and suspend civil administration. I wished I could do so now; I ached to put a rope around Mantiet's neck for what he had done to Alexi. Unfortunately, all I could do was turn him over to the civilian authorities who would conduct the trial.

But I hadn't relinquished him yet. I stalked down the corridor. Lieutenant Kell saluted as I approached the dayroom. "Any trouble?"

"No, sir, he's been quiet. Mr. Anton ordered him fed an hour ago."

I grunted, begrudging him even that decency.

Mantiet looked up. Bruises were darkening where Tolliver had beaten him. He pushed aside the remains of his tray. A cool smile played across his features. "What can I do for you, Captain?"

"I'm sending you for drug and poly interrogation."

"Why?"

I tossed the transcript onto his tray. "This is garbage. For all I know you made it up."

He frowned. "Why would I?"

"To protect your fellow traitors. Why would you expose them?"

"You think I've accused innocent men?" His voice held a note of reproach.

"Who knows what you've done? That's why I'm sending you to P and D."

"You can't."

I raised an eyebrow. "You propose to stop me?"

"Yes."

Despite myself I tensed visibly, then reddened. The man wasn't about to launch himself at my throat, and if he did, help was just outside the door. "How?"

"Are we under martial law?"

"No. Governor Saskrit's administration is still running Centraltown. And all of Hope Nation."

"Then you're bound to follow the law, unless you're as evil as I am." He smiled politely. I had an urge to strangle him.

"Make your point, Mantiet."

"I just did. Under the law you can't send me for interrogation."

"Why not? Your confession is incomplete."

"I've confessed to every charge you've made. Make others and I'll confess to them as well."

"We need to verify the truth about your conspiracy."

"Ah, but that's not permitted. P and D interrogation may only be used to determine my guilt. Not to force me to betray others. It's a well-settled point of law—even our provincial courts have heard of it."

"I don't know that to be true."

"But you're duty-bound to check, now that I've informed you."

I growled, "If we were aboard ship—"

"That's the point, Captain. We are not."

I slammed the door behind me. Moments later I paced the anteroom in mounting fury while Lieutenant Anton waited for a connection.

"I've got Judge Ches—"

I snatched up the caller. "Judge? Captain Seafort, here."

"This is Judge Chesley."

"I'm sorry to bother you, sir. I need an immediate answer to a legal question."

He chuckled. "Well, I owe you a favor, Seafort. Explain."

What he owed me was hardly a favor; I'd humiliated him in his own courtroom. Still, much had passed in the interim. I explained the situation.

He was silent a long while. Then, "There was a time it would have given me great satisfaction to tell you that Mantiet's right. His confession bars his interrogation."

I said desperately, "But if I don't believe his confession is true—"

"Do you doubt his guilt?"

I thought a moment. "No," I conceded.

"Neither would I, or any impartial judge. So we're forced to accept his confession as valid." As if sensing the frustration in my silence he added, "It makes the Truth in Testimony Act humane, Seafort. Otherwise it could be used to make people turn on their friends, even their family. The exception was written into the law from the start."

"I see."

"At least you'll have the satisfaction of seeing him hang."

"Yes."

"Well, if that's all . . . by the way, Seafort, that young lady. The cadet. Whatever happened to her?"

"She was posted to Academy for advanced math."

"Out of harm's way, then. Just as well."

"Sir, I'm sorry." He said nothing. I rushed on, "For what happened back then. I was young and foolish. I wouldn't do the same, now."

Another long silence, then a sigh. "It's long past, Seafort. All the people, the destruction . . . even my sister and her husband, Reeves. You must have known them, they came out on your ship. They were killed in the explosion."

"Oh, Lord God."

"Your courtroom hijinks . . . they don't seem to matter anymore."

"I understand. Good night, sir." I rang off.

15

I issued orders to have Mantiet transferred to the civilian jail the following day, and to have the authorities pick up the men Mantiet had named.

That night the fish attacked.

They took out *Prince of Wales*. Captain Martes of *Victoria* had transferred to her. I wondered if he'd taken Ricky Fuentes along.

I spent the morning huddled in the tactics room with Tolliver, Bezrel, and every other officer who could find an excuse to join us. The fish appeared by twos and threes, Defusing near our ships, lobbing their acid from close range, abruptly disappearing. The speakers crackled with commands as our fleet deployed. Again, we succeeded in knocking out fish. Again, we had no idea how many constituted the aliens' armada.

Lieutenant Anton kept us supplied with sandwiches and coffee. Conversation was sparse, our mood tense. All of us had served aloft, and knew the perils our men faced.

Around noon Anton stirred. "Mr. Trapp, Mr. Tolliver, take Mantiet downtown to the civilian jail."

"Not now," I said.

He looked at me in surprise.

"Keep everyone here."

"Yes, but—aye aye, sir."

By day's end two more ships were disabled, though not destroyed. By positioning the fleet closer to Hope Nation, Admiral De Marney allowed our ships to come to each other's assistance more quickly, and this tactic seemed to help.

I spent a sleepless night on my conference-room cot. In the morning Alexi wanted to go to work at the transport center; when I forbade it he was so crestfallen that I relented. "Stay in touch, Mr. Tamarov. Call in every three hours."

"Whatever you say, Mr. Seafort. Are they still attacking?"

"Four fish sighted during the night. We killed one."

"Great!"

I grunted. Not for *Prince of Wales*.

The day passed uneventfully. That evening I realized I was keeping Frederick Mantiet in our makeshift jail for no purpose. I'd have him transferred in the morning, as I'd originally intended. Perhaps I could make time to visit Annie.

During the night we lost two ships. Captain Derghinski had brought *Kitty Hawk* to *Brasilia's* aid when a fresh flotilla of fish appeared alongside, and both vessels were breached. A number of men got off in lifepods. We listened to confused reports relayed through our speakers. As day lengthened, I paced the tactics room with increasing anxiety, wishing I hadn't let Alexi leave.

I was on my way to the head when Midshipman Bezrel rushed after me. "Lieutenant Anton's compliments, sir. You have a call."

"The Admiral?"

"No, sir. Ms. Triforth."

My heart pounding from the false alarm, I went to my conference room to take the call. "Seafort here."

"Laura Triforth. I'll be in Centraltown this afternoon. I thought perhaps we might have a talk."

"It's rather a busy time." I realized how ungracious it sounded and added hastily, "The fleet's seen more action."

"I know."

I paused. "Communications are restricted to a tightbeam relay. Just how did you hear?"

"I told you," she said. "This is our city. Not much goes on that we don't learn." As if sensing that didn't suffice, she added, "You've placed all your people on twenty-four-hour call; none of them goes near a restaurant or bar. Your Mr. Tamarov reports in every couple of hours."

I cursed under my breath. As a secret agent I was notably incompetent.

"Has Mantiet been sent for interrogation under drugs yet?"

"You knew we have him?"

"Half of Centraltown saw your sky chase, Mr. Seafort. It's hardly a secret."

The woman knew far too much. Best to stay away from her. No, better let her visit and learn what she wanted. "I'll see you this afternoon, Ms. Triforth."

She chuckled. "Why, thank you. I look forward to our meeting."

In the tactics room the speakers were quiet. Our remaining ships were huddled close, about thirty degrees past Orbit Station. I tried to see past the blips on the screen, to the men and metal beyond.

So few ships.

I sat and watched in the tense silence. After a time I could no longer stand the inaction. I went downstairs. "Mr. Anton." He looked up from his console. "Work up a report on all Naval personnel, including sailors. Assignments, work hours, current location."

"You mean where they're housed, sir?"

"I said current location. Where they are at this moment."

"But why—aye aye, sir." He took up the caller, his perplexity evident. I trudged back upstairs.

Today fewer of us held vigil, as a consequence of days of sporadic, desultory action. Lieutenant Trapp, Midshipman Kell and young Bezrel were the only ones present. The two middies fidgeted and whispered until I fixed them with a stare that allowed no misinterpretation. A few moments later Bezrel excused himself and left. Kell, on duty, had no choice but to remain.

I fought to keep myself from dozing. I was just failing when the speaker crackled. "*Hibernia* reporting. Two fish alongside, one abaft! They're throwing! Fusing!"

"*Churchill* reporting, three—no, five! They came out of nowhere, together! Lasers engaging! We've got one! Another Fusing out."

"All ships to Battle Stations!"Admiral De Marnay.

"*OH, JESUS!*"

I came to my feet at the fear in the unknown voice. It went on in a whisper. "A dozen of them! More. They're all around us. One is nuzzling our fusion tubes. Preparing to Fuse. Jordan, get me coordinates!"

"Fuse immediately, you fool!" My voice was tight, though I spoke only to myself.

"Our tubes are melting!" I could smell his fright. "We'll try a Fuse!"

"No!" Admiral De Marnay's tone was sharp. "*Churchill*, don't Fuse with—"

"Christ, we're overheating! Quick, shut it do—" The speaker went dead.

Trapp spun to meet my eye, as if in appeal.

"They're gone," I said.

He shook his head, denying.

"They blew themselves up."

Trapp swallowed. Midshipman Bezrel rushed in from the hall. "Ms. Triforth is here for her appointment, sir."

"Who? Tell her to come back—" I got to my feet. "No, I'll see her. Trapp, keep me informed of our losses."

"Aye aye, sir."

"Mr. Bezrel, escort Ms. Triforth to the conference room." Vapormask under my arm, I hurried down the stairs.

Laura took her place across from me at the gleaming table. "You're looking better than when last we met."

I waved the niceties aside. "This is a bad time, Ms. Triforth."

A knock at the door. Anton. "Excuse me, sir. That report you wanted."

"Keep it on your desk. Update it every two hours."

"Aye aye, sir." He made no move to leave.

"Well?"

"Could you tell me why you need it, sir?"

I made my voice icy. "Dismissed, Lieutenant Anton." He left. "What's on your mind, Ms. Triforth?"

"Do call me Laura; I hate it when you're so formal." She waited for a response, got none. "The, um, hypothetical circumstance we discussed. Is it any closer to reality?"

"I can't discuss that."

"I appreciate your position, Seafort. But if anything should leave us on our own, we have to be prepared."

I was firm. "I won't discuss that with you."

"Has the Venturas Base been attacked?"

I was startled. "Not that I know of. Why?"

She waved. "Just taking stock, as it were."

I ached to get back to the tactics room. "Ms.—er, Laura, what is it you want?"

"To know what's up. To help, if possible."

"You can't fight the aliens."

"I can help root out Mantiet's men. I can help you maintain control."

I raised an eyebrow. "Why would you want to do that?"

She smiled grimly. "I've made no secret of my feelings, Mr. Seafort. But you must understand: we want anarchy no more than you. We have hundreds of field workers roaming Centraltown. If authority breaks down . . ."

"The Government is in place and functioning. Looters have been shot."

"As well they should be!" She spat the words. A pause. "Captain, this is our home, our society. Let us help."

True, we were badly understaffed. I thumbed through my papers, found a list of supporters Mantiet had named. "Can you help us find these men?"

She studied the list. "Some of them, I think we—"

The caller chimed. I snatched at it. "Yes?"

"Trapp reporting, sir. You said to keep you informed. Fish swarming all over the patrol area! Two ships down, everyone's Fusing like—",

A knock on the door; it swung open. Bezrel saluted. "Lieutenant Anton said to give this to you forthwith, sir."

"Orbit Station beat off an attack too, sir. That's the first time they've attacked—"

I opened the note. Anton's handwriting. "Message from Admiral De Marnay, for immediate delivery to Captain Seafort. 1800 hours local time. *Destiny*."

I crumpled the note, half hearing Lieutenant Trapp's rush of words. "*Hibernia* Fused twice, sir, and they keep following. No sign of *Churchill*. The fleet is to regroup around Orbit Station. They—"

"Enough." It was 3:00 P.M. We'd have three hours.

Laura Triforth came to her feet, eyes locked on mine. "Seafort, you've gone white. What's happened?"

"Wait here." I strode out the corridor, closing the door. "Anton!"

He stood from his console. "Yes, sir?"

"Your list." He fumbled, handed it to me. After a glance I thrust it back. "How many of our helis are on loan to the transport grid?"

"Three, sir."

"Pull them out of service, flank. Emergency priority. Contact all officers and sailors, arrange assembly points. I want helis to pick up all Naval personnel and bring them to the spaceport in one hour. Everyone, without exception."

"An hour? That's not possi—"

I thrust my face at his. "Make it possible, God damn you!" He recoiled. "You have a list. Find them all. Stay on it. You have permission to stay at your console one additional hour. Then go to the terminal yourself."

"But—for God's sake, why?"

I snarled, "Because I gave the order!" Even now, it was best no one know the truth.

"Aye aye, sir!" He snatched up his caller.

"Where the hell is Tolliver?"

"Sleeping, sir."

"Get him up. I need him." I started toward the conference room, swung back. "Let me see that list." I scrutinized it. "Alexi Tamarov. He's not on it."

"He's not active, sir. I thought you meant—"

"Where is he?"

"The transport center would know."

"Get started. I'll find Alexi." I strode back to the conference room.
Laura Triforth stood as I entered. "What in blazes is going on, Seafort?"

If I told her, she might argue, and nothing must interfere with the evacuation. "Problems." I had to get rid of her, find Alexi. We had less than three hours—

Annie! Lord God, I'd forgotten. Shame sickened me. I'd take a heli—no, they were all in use. I had to drive downtown, get my wife, pick up Alexi—

I looked up to Laura. "You offered your heli. May I have it?"

"I—of course. I can take you myself, wherever you want to go."

"Just a moment." I picked up the caller, dialed Alexi. "Mr. Tamarov, report." I waited; no answer. I tried again. "Alexi Tamarov, respond to Admiralty House!" Silence.

Another knock at the door. Edgar Tolliver, bleary from lack of sleep.

"Stand by, Tolliver." Muttering under my breath I thumbed the caller again. "Patch me through to the transport center."

I pulled rank and got to the director in moments. "A volunteer, Alexi Tamarov. I need him at once."

"Tamarov . . . the Naval Officer? The young one? He's directing a road crew in the west sector. I don't know what street they'd be on at the moment, but they're somewhere between Churchill and Washington."

"Very well."

I rang off. "Laura, I have to pick up Annie at the clinic, and Lieutenant Tamarov is downtown. I could drive, but your help would . . ."

"Of course. When?"

"Right now."

Lieutenant Anton appeared in the doorway. "Regarding your orders, sir?"

I glanced at Laura Triforth. "Yes?" I was wary.

"What about Mr. Mantiet, sir?"

I cursed under my breath. Why hadn't I had him sent downtown when I'd had the chance? "Ms. Triforth and I will take him. Tolliver, I want you along. And Bezrel, as an extra hand." As soon as I said it I realized Kell would be a better choice, but decided not to contradict myself. Bezrel would do.

"We're taking Frederick?" Laura sounded tense.

"Yes, if you don't mind. After I pick up Annie we'll drop him off." What good would it do to turn him over to the civilians, if our fleet took Governor Saskrit home? Should I bring Mantiet along for military trial or simply hang him myself? No, I hadn't the right.

Laura asked, "Will you interrogate him?"

She'd asked too many questions about matters that were confidential. "Perhaps." My tone was cool.

She shrugged. "He deserves it. When do you want to go?"

"Right now. Tolliver, get Mantiet. Cuff his hands, but don't rough him up. Gag him too, Mr. Tolliver." If Mantiet spoke, Laura Triforth would learn what Mantiet knew.

"Wouldn't it be better to wait for a Naval heli, sir?"

"I'm in a hurry."

"Aye aye, sir." I picked up my vapormask, wondering how long Tolliver's docility would last.

I peered down the unfamiliar streets, while Annie pressed my hand. It had been only minutes since we'd swept into the clinic and bundled her out.

"Between Washington and Churchill, they said." Where the devil was Alexi? I'd told him to stand by, and . . .

"They'll have men and trucks; we'll spot them." Laura glided across town, barely above treetop level.

Yes, but when? I tried to restrain my impatience, glancing surreptitiously at my watch. We'd been searching the indicated area for several minutes. Repeated calls on the radio failed to raise Alexi.

Annie crooned to herself.

"There, to the west!" Tolliver, from the back seat. We swooped across a block of ruined houses. A crew of ten was hauling debris from the blocked street into a truck.

I muttered, "That's got to be them. Land, would you?"

"Anyone see wires?" Laura checked the landing spot. "Here we go."

A moment later I was beckoning from under the blades. "Alexi, get over here!" He was near the truck, gesturing at piles of crumpled roofing.

The whap of the blades was too loud; Alexi waved happily and turned back to the crew. Enraged, I ran to him, ignoring warning pangs in my chest. I grabbed his shoulder, spun him around. "Get yourself into the heli!"

"What—"

"Didn't I tell you to report regularly? Where's your caller?"

"In the truck, Mr. Sea—"

"Move!" I shoved him toward the heli. Crestfallen, he obeyed. I faced him at the heli door. "Even a cadet wouldn't pull a stunt like this, and you're supposed to be a lieutenant! Can't you obey a simple order?"

He blanched. "I'm sorry."

"If you were on active duty, I'd—" I caught myself, finally comprehending what his eyes revealed. "All right, get in."

"I got involved in the work . . ." He looked at the private heli. "What's up, Mr. Seafort?"

"In, I told you." He climbed into the back with Tolliver, Mantiet, and Bezrel. I should have explained outside, where Laura couldn't hear. Now, it would have to wait. "Special duty."

Laura throttled. Over the engine's roar she asked, "Where now, Mr. Seafort?"

I looked again at my watch. "We'll drop off Mantiet, then head back, if you don't mind."

"Not at all." She pulled back on the collective, lifting us straight up. This time she didn't skim the treetops; she brought us to a great height. I stared down at the stricken city. Would Centraltown ever recover?

Laura continued to throttle up. Casually, she reached for her oxygen mask and slipped it on. Tolliver leaned forward. "We don't need canned air this low, do we?"

I growled. "Tend to your prisoner, Middy."

"Not really." Laura idly flicked a switch on the dash. A dull hiss emitted from the air vents.

"Then why are you—what's going—" Tolliver slumped. My head spun. I grabbed for the vapormask in my lap. Laura Triforth's hand pinned my arm. "Wait a moment, Seafort. You won't need it."

She was right. In a moment I needed nothing.

16

The room was stuffy and dark. I groaned, trying to clear my head. I was lying on a cold, damp floor.

"He's awake." Alexi.

I blinked. Annie sat slackly, her eyes straight ahead. Her hand clasped Alexi's.

Tolliver's tone held a note of impatience. "About time." He perched on a wooden desk, legs dangling. It was the only furniture in the room.

"Where am I?"

"Wherever your friend Laura put us." Tolliver's voice was acid.

My anger gave me strength to scramble to my feet. I tottered to Tolliver, grabbed his jacket. "Tell me what's happened!"

"I passed out in the heli. I presume you did too. When I woke, we were here." He gestured to the sparse chamber. What little light we had came from a narrow, barred transom over the door. "I found Bezrel sniveling in the corner." He waved with contempt at the young middy, who, to my disgust, surreptitiously wiped his nose with his sleeve. "Alexi and Annie—Mrs. Seafort—woke a few minutes after. We've been waiting for you."

"Why are we here?"

"We hoped you'd tell us, sir."

"The door?"

"No knob on this side. I finally stopped bruising my shoulder on it."

I reached for my pistol, found an empty holster. "No one's come in?"

"No, sir."

"How long have we been here?"

Tolliver made a show of checking his watch. "It's going on five-thirty now. I'd say about two hours. What would you say, Mr. Tamarov?"

"Damn your insolence!"

"Yes, sir. You'll remember I suggested we wait for a proper Naval heli. If we had . . ."

I snarled, "Enough!"

Alexi intervened. "Why would Ms. Triforth kidnap us? And where were we headed in the heli?"

Legs weak, I pushed myself onto the desk and sat. Why did Laura waylay us, to free Mantiet? No, she'd helped us search for him. To stop us from leaving? She didn't know I'd received the "Destiny" signal, and she would probably be glad to see the last of us, given her feelings about colonial rule.

I realized what Tolliver had said about the time. "Five-thirty? We've got to get out!" I jumped off the desk.

"Why, Mr. Seafort?" Alexi.

"Because—" I tensed. No way to know if the room was miked. "Never mind why." I banged on the door. "Laura! Ms. Triforth!"

No answer. In the corner Bezrel stifled a sob.

I shouted again and again, without result. Finally I sagged back onto the desk. But nervous energy pulsed, and I couldn't sit more than a moment. I paced, squatted on the floor, got up to pace again.

All too soon, it was past six. Was it my imagination or did I hear the distant roar of a shuttle?

I slumped to the floor. Whether I heard it or not, the shuttle was gone, and with it our chance of rescue. We were marooned, with nothing to do but await the final assault of the fish. I had no doubt it would come. By careening off in Laura Triforth's heli I had doomed not only myself, but Alexi, Tolliver, even poor bewildered Bezrel. And, worst of all, Annie. It was almost a blessing that she was barely aware of her surroundings.

I withdrew into my misery.

Hours later, footsteps sounded. I stood, fists clenched. A key scraped in the lock. The door swung open.

Three armed men. I charged forward, but stumbled to a halt when a laser pistol swung toward me. "Where's Ms. Triforth?"

Ignoring me, the burly farmhand shoved a bound figure past his companion into the room, slammed the door. Hands lashed behind him, the man stumbled to his knees.

I gaped.

"I don't suppose you'd, ah, consider releasing me?" Frederick Mantiet motioned with his bound wrists. "They're starting to hurt."

"I hope they fall off!" Tolliver's tone was savage.

I'd been thinking the same, but instead I said perversely, "Untie him." Tolliver had tortured him enough; we weren't barbarians, though Ms. Triforth was that and worse.

"But—"

"You heard me!"

"Aye aye, sir." With a curse Tolliver yanked at the thongs holding Mantiet. The cuffs I'd had placed on him were gone. While picking at the knots Tolliver grated, "Has it occurred to the Captain that Mantiet is no more a prisoner than Ms. Triforth? That he's obviously a plant?"

"Yes." It hadn't.

"I'm not, you know." Mantiet.

"Right." My feet hurt; I went to slouch in the corner, decided to preserve my dignity and leaned on the table instead. "Why were we kidnapped?"

"You'll have to ask Laura."

"I'm asking you!"

"I could guess." Mantiet winced as Tolliver yanked at a resisting cord. "She probably didn't want me interrogated."

"Was she involved in your murder plots?"

"You might say that." Mantiet hesitated. "More than you can imagine."

"Don't believe a thing he tells you!"

"Tolliver, be silent. Why are you admitting it now?"

Mantiet shrugged. "It no longer matters."

"Why not?"

"Because Laura will proclaim the Republic at midnight."

"The Re—" I shook my head. Too much, too fast. "Why are you detained?"

Tolliver undid the last knot; stifling a groan, Mantiet rubbed his wrists. "I'm apparently not, ah, radical enough for her taste."

I couldn't suppress a sneer. "A man capable of shooting down a Naval heli and killing his countrymen with a bomb isn't radical enough?"

Mantiet was quiet for a long moment. Then he said, "I didn't do those things."

"You tried!"

He made as if to speak, sighed instead. "So it would seem."

Alexi spoke from his forgotten corner. "If Mr. Seafort leaves us alone, I'll kill you." His tone was so casual it brought a chill to my spine.

Mantiet raised an eyebrow. "An elegant solution. It would amuse Laura."

I intervened before Alexi could reply. "Never mind him, Mr. Tamarov. He's scum, and all he says is a lie."

The Republic. I stared at the door, yearning for a weapon, some means of escape. An entire planet was sliding into eternal damnation, and I could do nothing. I muttered, *"The powers that be are ordained of God. Whosoever resisteth the power, resisteth the ordinance of God: and they shall receive to themselves damnation."*

Tolliver gave me a strange look, but said nothing.

I sat next to Annie.

Dully, her eyes met mine, strayed back to the floor. Two hours passed in near-absolute silence. I greeted the next approach of footsteps with relief; our hostility wore on the nerves. It recalled the wardroom in *Helsinki*, my first posting, before our senior midshipman had taken us in hand.

The door swung open. Armed men clustered in the corridor; among them was Laura Triforth. My lip curled. "You!"

"In the flesh."

"Let us go."

"I'm afraid that's not possible." She smiled regretfully.

"Then why are you here?"

Laura hesitated. "I suppose I'm cursed with a sense of style, Captain. It seems only fair that the last representative of the old order witness the birth of the new." She glanced at her watch. "But we'll have to hurry."

"Prong yourself." I wished I didn't sound like a peeved middy. "I'll stay here."

"I'm afraid you misunderstood. It's a summons, not an invitation." She gestured. Two of her minions advanced, guns drawn.

Tolliver came off the desk, placed himself between us. "You'll have to go through me first."

"Very well." She gestured at one of her men. "Kill him."

"Wait!" I jumped in front of him. "Tolliver, back to the wall. Move!"

He hesitated only a second. "Aye aye, sir." He stalked to the far wall, shoving Mantiet out of his way.

"Think of it, Captain, as a box seat in the theater of history."

"I'll think of it as kidnapping."

"You go in these." She held up a pair of handcuffs.

"Over my dead—"

"No, over his." She gestured at Tolliver with her pistol. He raised his eyebrow, waiting.

I sighed. Saying nothing, I raised my wrists. Ms. Triforth cuffed my hands in front of me. "Your young friends will wait here."

"I want them along."

"Now, now." She patted my shoulder. I threw off her hand.

"What about me?" Mantiet's quiet voice penetrated the tension.

"You'll wait with the children, Frederick."

He shook his head. "Think about it, Laura. I deserve a seat in the theater. I've earned it."

Ms. Triforth met his eye for a long moment. "Yes, I'll admit that. You'll manage to be silent?"

"Oh, I won't speak. I just want to observe." He added, "You have my word."

Laura Triforth beckoned Mantiet forward. "Unfortunately, I only brought the one set of cuffs. You'll have to bear the thongs again."

"Looser this time. They cut off the circulation."

Ms. Triforth laughed easily and bound Mantiet's wrists with the cord. She turned on her heel. "Bring them both."

Shoved from behind, I had time for a quick glance at Annie before they had me in the narrow hall. I followed Ms. Triforth outside. A welcome gust of fresh air greeted me as we emerged from a low prefab building, in a clearing surrounded by trees. We seemed to be on the edge of town; lights glowed in the near distance.

A Naval heli stood waiting, doors open, pilot in his seat. Laura beckoned to the door, helped me climb in. "Your colleagues were kind enough to leave this," she said, indicating the craft.

"Not for you. For the authorities." My arms hurt.

"We've become the authorities." She spoke with calm assurance.

The last of her men crowded aboard; the pilot snapped the switches and the blades began to turn.

"Where are we going?"

"You'll see." We lifted off. After a moment she added in a reasonable tone, "You brought it all on yourself, Seafort. I'd have been happy to let you go with the rest of your Navy."

"Why didn't you?" I stared out the window, able to orient myself at last. We were in the northwest end of town. Our prison was a few hundred feet off the main road. Occasional cars moved below.

"You didn't tell me your signal to leave Hope Nation had arrived. You left me guessing, and you were taking Frederick downtown for interrogation. I couldn't risk that."

"He wasn't going to be interrogated."

"No?" Ms. Triforth chuckled grimly. "You should have told me when I asked. As I said, you brought it on yourself."

To my surprise, we flew south toward the spaceport and Admiralty House. We were almost there when the speaker crackled. "Admiralty calling Captain Seafort. Admiralty to Captain Seafort. Please respond."

Triforth froze. After a moment she said, "Why not?" She reached for the caller. "Talk to them."

"No."

"It's your chance to say good-bye."

I made no answer. She twisted around in her seat. "Do as I say, or you'll never see your friends again."

"Kill me, then." I had failed in everything; it would be fitting.

"Not you. Your silly sniveling wife." She uncuffed my hands, thrust the caller at me.

My hand shook with suppressed rage. I thumbed the caller. "Seafort reporting!"

"Just a moment for the Admiral."

I waited until the familiar voice came on the line. "Seafort? Why in hell weren't you on the shuttle?"

Ms. Triforth shook her head, warning me. I said, "I was trying to find some of my officers, sir."

"How many are with you?"

"Lieutenant Tamarov, sir. And two middies, Tolliver and Bezrel."

He sighed. "A pity about Bezrel; I promised to keep him close. We'll all have Fused in another hour or so, Seafort. I've no time to send another shuttle down."

"I understand, sir." The conversation held an air of unreality.

"We've evacuated Orbit Station too, though the fish have shown little interest in it. Maintenance functions are under the control of their puter. It's programmed to fire on any fish that appear."

"Yes, sir."

"*Catalonia* is due back from Detour anytime now. I'll leave a broadcast beacon with instructions to pick you up. If she gets here safely, you're to sail home. There's a shuttle at the Venturas Base; use that to go aloft. In the meantime, carry on as best you can. You're in charge of what's left."

"Aye aye, sir."

"Good luck, Seafort."

"Godspeed, sir." The line went dead.

"Interesting," said Laura. "You had it planned to the last detail."

I glowered. She recuffed my hands, this time behind my back. Our heli landed close to the terminal entrance, in a lot full of cars and helis. Courteously, Laura helped me out. Just short of the door she pulled me to a stop, fingered her pistol. "You're here to watch, Seafort, because I think it fitting. But let's be clear: if you open your mouth to speak, I'll burn you on the spot."

"Prong yourself." I could think of nothing better to say and half expected her to hit me. With a frown she shoved me toward the door.

Inside, a large number of folding chairs had been brought to supplement the terminal seating. Most were occupied. At one end of the concourse a small dais had been erected. Ms. Triforth guided me toward it, stopping to shake hands along the way with admirers and well-wishers.

"Why here?" I asked.

"This is one of the few buildings big enough for a public meeting that wasn't pulverized by the rock."

I grunted, too angry to reply. By my presence I was being made a party to treason. But she would have killed Edgar Tolliver otherwise; what choice had I?

"Sit here. Remember what I warned you." She beckoned a guard. "Tell Norris to get folks seated; it's nearly midnight. Then come back and watch this one."

"Right." Her accomplice took off. Ms. Triforth kept an eye on me until he returned, then drifted among her audience, shaking hands easily, smiling. I noticed that Mantiet had not been placed on the dais, but in the front row, hands still bound. Was Triforth truly jealous of him, or was it a show to make me relax my guard in his presence? But, to what purpose? The Navy had left, taking Governor Saskrit and his administration.

Puzzled, I stared at Mantiet until he became aware of me. He raised an eyebrow and smiled without mirth. I twisted in my chair, my arms aching.

People began to take their places on the dais. Among them were Arvin Volksteader, Tomas Palabee, and, to my disgust, Harmon Branstead. His son Jerence sat in the front row. I looked for old Zack Hopewell, but he was nowhere in sight. Harmon caught my eye, reddened, looked away. Ms. Triforth took her seat at the center of the dais.

A woman with a holocamera crouched in front of the seats below the dais. She turned the lens toward a man I didn't recognize. He came forward to the small lectern set at the front of the stage. He pulled a gavel out of his back pocket, banged for silence. The few people still wandering hurried to the nearest seats.

"Ladies and gentlemen, we're here for an occasion we've all awaited. Without further ado, I give you the founder of the Republic of Hope Nation, the leader of our long-underground movement, Laura Triforth."

To a roar of approval Laura got to her feet, slowly made her way to the lectern. A wave of applause washed across the hall. Ms. Triforth waited coolly, smiling, waving with her right hand. From my seat at the end of the dais, I saw her left hand clenched behind her back. Her fingers rubbed at each other in nervous contradiction of her apparent ease.

"Ladies and gentlemen." She waited for the tumult to subside, cleared her throat.

"For years we've labored under the misguided benevolence of our colonial Government. For years we paid for their errors, financed their bureaucracy, sold our crops at little above cost to feed their starving millions.

"Tonight, all that is ended. At 1800 hours, a few paces from where we gather, a shuttle lifted with the last U.N. military officers, along with Governor Saskrit and his aides." She could get no further until the frenzied cheering subsided. She added with a smile, "Except for poor Mr. Seafort here, who got left behind." I tried to ignore the laughter.

"I won't pretend that our Republic was born in ease. Had the aliens not forced the great U.N. fleet to withdraw to home waters, ours would still be an underground movement. Had not the aliens dropped an asteroid on Centraltown, enough government structure would have remained so that we'd have had to fight a civil war to free ourselves. But today, we gain our independence without war. Officers of our movement have merely arrested the judges and those few civil servants foolhardy enough to resist."

She took a deep breath. "However the providence of Lord God manifests itself"—bile flooded my throat at the heresy—"it is enough for us to know it is with us.

"The United Nations has withdrawn its protection from Hope Nation." She gestured toward downtown. "You can see how much good that protection provided." Her gibe brought scornful laughter as, unseen, her fingers rubbed at her palms.

Her smiled vanished. "I don't make light of our many deaths. But the loss of friends and family have taught us. We know, now, how vulnerable a large city is to enemy attack, and how useless it is to our own defense. So we will live in our plantation homes. While Centraltown must remain a commercial center, it must never again become the administrative nucleus of our civilization.

"We know also the folly of allowing electoral control to pass out of the hands of responsible plantation families, into the hands of unemployed farmhands and hauler-drivers. So our legislature will consist of two houses, one for the planters themselves; the other consisting of permanent employees and associates of the planters, who live on their properties. Never again will city dwellers displace the productive plantations as the administrators of our Republic."

Triforth had to wait for the applause to abate. I wondered how many residents of Centraltown were in the hall.

She spoke quietly. "There are some who ask why we bother to declare our Republic, when satanic aliens roam the system, destroying ships, dropping their destruction on our city."

Yes, one might wonder. I strained to catch her soft-spoken answer.

"We lived here for generations, undisturbed by alien attacks. It was the fusion drives of our Navy that attracted the fish, and with the Navy gone, the fish will soon follow. If not, we have learned to combat their viruses, and dispersing our government outside Centraltown will help protect us from the havoc of any further attacks."

She paused; when she resumed her voice was sober. "And if we are wrong, and naught but devastation and death lie in our path, then I ask: what other course should we pursue? Could we defeat the fish ourselves, when the vaunted United Nations Navy"—she pointed to me—"could not, and has left us to our fate? Should we go to our deaths as peons and wards of the uncaring United Nations, or proudly, as free men and women, as masters of our destiny?"

I swallowed; something in her speech caught at my own feelings. But my eye caught the fingers rubbing endlessly at each other, behind her back.

"Therefore, now, at the hour of midnight, on this, the third day of April in the year of our Lord 2200, I do declare the Re—"

"In the name of Lord God, *stop!*"

Laura spun around as the echoes reverberated around the hall with the crash of my falling chair. Her pistol flashed. "You were warned, Seafort!"

"Shoot me, Triforth!" Contemptuously I strode to the center of the dais, twisting my hands behind me in a hopeless effort to free them. I took a deep breath. "Republic? You deluded fools!" My words were to the assembled crowd, ignoring Laura entirely. "What bilge!"

An angry growl answered me from below. Ms. Triforth shoved me, nearly knocking me off balance. I rushed on. "Isn't she a spellbinding orator?" One of her men grabbed my arm, hauling me back to my seat. I shouted. "You'll never know what she chose not to tell you!"

"Sit!" Eyes blazing, she propelled me to my chair.

"Let him speak!" Harmon Branstead was on his feet. His voice carried through the hall.

"Oh, no. Not now. This is our moment, not his."

"Let him speak!" The call was taken up by someone else in the audience. After a moment, another repeated it.

Branstead pressed his advantage. "You wanted him here, Laura. The representative of the old order, you said. Let him have his say."

Ms. Triforth studied her audience, measured its mood. She reversed herself with good grace. "Ladies and gentlemen, before proclaiming the Republic, I give you the last representative of the now-departed United Nations Navy, Captain Nicholas Seafort."

"Take off the cuffs." My tone was that of a Captain to a green young middy. And it carried.

She hesitated. "You'll put them back on, after?"

"Yes." My arms freed at last, I turned to the audience. "You had grievances. We understood. They'd have been addressed, had the aliens not interfered." It was met by snickers of derision.

"But that isn't the issue." I searched the audience for a face not hostile, one to which I might speak. Not finding any, I pressed on. "Do you know where you stand? A few dozen miles above me roam the most frightful beings we've ever encountered. They've tried over and again to wipe you out. Their virus nearly did the job, but we synthesized a vaccine in time. They dropped a rock onto Centraltown with the kinetic energy of a nuke, but it failed to obliterate your city."

They were listening, now. "The fish attacked our ships, and the chilling news is that they learned from their attacks. Now they Defuse directly alongside and go for our lasers and tubes. Hundreds, if not thousands, of brave men died trying to defend you.

"Ms. Triforth would have you believe the Navy abandoned you." I could hear her stir behind me; I said quickly, "So I'll tell you the truth." I searched the audience, wishing I were an orator. My task was beyond me.

"First, your Government hasn't abandoned Hope Nation. I and several officers remain. Second, remember that the United Nations, our Government under Lord God, is steward not only of Hope Nation, but of seventeen other colonies and of home system. The fish have shown no sign of retreating; if anything their numbers have increased. If a colony is attacked, it can be resupplied. If home system is destroyed, we all die." In the muted light, someone sobbed.

"Admiralty decreed that when a third of our fleet was destroyed, the remainder must sail for home, to protect our mother planet. I remind you that all our interstellar ships, all our fusion drives, are built at home. With the grace of Lord God, they will return to defeat the fish, stronger than before."

Voices rose, arguing. I said clearly, "If not, we are all dead." It brought me silence. "The fish won't leave you alone, despite Ms. Triforth's pious hopes. Our only chance is to fight the fish as best we can until the Navy returns, which it surely must."

Laura Triforth stood, sauntered to the lectern. "Wrap it up, Seafort."

I nodded, trying to remember her words. "And if I am wrong, and naught but devastation and death lie in our path?" I caught her eye, held it. "What course should we then follow? I call each of you to be true to his oath. Lord God will not favor—"

"Enough." She hauled me back, pistol pressed to my side. One of her men grabbed my other arm, pulled me back to my chair, cuffed my arms to it.

Ms. Triforth returned to the lectern, shook her head. "You see the arrogance with which we've had to deal. Very well, he's had his say. Seafort's views no longer matter; they are made meaningless by the cowardly and secret retreat of his associates. With pride, therefore, I now proclaim the Republic—"

I struggled to my feet, chair dangling behind. "As plenipotentiary of the United Nations Government, I declare martial law through Hope Nation! I order the arrest for treason of Laura Triforth and her—"

The blow caught me on the back of the head. I crumpled into darkness.

"You fool."

I opened an eye and groaned. Frederick Mantiet knelt over me, pressing a compress to my head. "Did you really think you could stop her?"

I shook my head, regretting it instantly. "No. I only knew I had to try."

"She nearly killed you. She may still."

"Yes." It didn't seem to matter. I looked around. "Where are we?"

"In the hauling offices. Different room." Seeing my puzzlement he added, "A hauling company, owned by Triforth Plantation. It's where they held us before. Your men are a couple of doors down the hall."

I blinked, and the room came into focus. I slapped his hand away. "Don't touch me."

He shrugged. "I was trying to help."

"I don't need help from your kind."

Mantiet retreated. This room had chairs. He took one. "What is my kind, Seafort?"

I said flatly, "Garbage."

He reddened, but held my eye. "Your opinion is based on . . . ?"

"You know bloody well. You tried to murder us twice. In a sense you succeeded, with Alexi."

A very long pause. "Seafort, I don't know how to tell you this."

I wasn't interested. I closed my eyes, rubbing my aching skull. "Let me sleep."

"I didn't do it."

I made no answer. After a time he went to the door, spoke to the brittle wood. "I don't know why it matters, but I want you to know."

"Let me be."

"I didn't blow up the hauler in front of your car; I didn't fire a missile at your heli."

"I have your confession. In fact, it's in my jacket. You named your accomplices."

"Men who were killed when the bomb hit."

"I assumed as much. As I said, you're garbage."

"Seafort, look at me." I kept my eyes closed. He said, louder, "Look at me, or I'll kick off your kneecaps." I opened my eyes. Mantiet said simply, "I did not attack you on any occasion. I so swear upon my immortal soul."

"And your confession?"

"Was a lie."

"To what purpose?"

"The obvious one." He saw my blank look. "To avoid interrogation."

I sat up slowly, ignoring the throbbing in my head. "You make no sense. Interrogation would have exposed your crimes. We'd have found out about the bomb and the missiles."

"Yes, you'd have found out."

"That's why you avoided interrogation."

"Yes, that's why I confessed."

I managed to get to my feet. The room was about the length of a bridge. How could I think without pacing? "If you're guilty, the interrogation would show it. If you're innocent, the tests would have shown that, and you'd have been freed instead of hanged. So avoiding interrogation makes no sense if you're innocent. It does if you're guilty."

He said nothing.

I paced. What was he up to, another cruel game? Was he so twisted he needed no purpose? If he was innocent, why would he avoid interrogation that would show he hadn't tried to kill me? No one could hold anything back during interr—

No one could hold anything back. I turned. "You were hiding something else!"

"Bravo." He clapped slowly.

"What could be so important you'd give your life to conceal it?" He made no answer. Intrigued despite myself, I paced from wall to wall, hands clasped behind my back. If Mantiet hadn't tried to kill me, someone else had. Who?

I stopped, swearing under my breath. "Laura made it clear you've always been part of the underground."

"Yes."

"When the bomb went off in front of your manse, you knew you'd be under suspicion."

"By the time I figured out what had happened, I barely had time to get out."

"You'd have been picked up for interrogation because your hauler was used."

"I assumed so."

"And you knew . . ." I raised my eyes. "What? I still don't understand." He smiled through a mouth swollen from Tolliver's beating, and I saw the obvious. "You knew it was Laura Triforth!"

"No." At my look of surprise he added, "I only assumed so; she didn't take me so far into her confidence. But only Laura was devious enough to use one of my own haulers, in front of my own plantation. My confession couldn't convict her, but I'd been attending meetings of my branch of the underground a long while, and I knew who was involved. If you took me in, you'd break my whole movement."

"For that, you risked your life and soiled your name?"

"For Hope Nation's future, yes." He met my gaze. "I am a patriot, you know, in my own way. For all your talk about wrongs that would have been redressed, we'd tried for decades to get the U.N. to listen. To no avail."

I snorted. "You're a society without poverty, without pollution, without crowding; I can't believe you feel so sorry for yourselves. No, using Occam's razor, you're guilty. It's the simplest explanation."

"Yes, it is. But I wanted you to hear the truth."

"Why?"

"I don't know." He turned back toward the door. "Because it no longer matters. Because, as you say, I soiled my name. Perhaps because I admire your bravery."

"Goofjuice."

He said, "Or perhaps it's just that I enjoy a good joke."

After that, neither of us spoke.

17

The next morning Mantiet and I were moved to another room, one that had a cubicle with a toilet. To my relief, Annie and the rest of our party were waiting.

When we were brought in, Annie cried out with relief. Thereafter, she seemed perturbed whenever I left her side, even for my restless pacing.

Like our previous cells, the room had no windows, nothing we could pry loose to free ourselves. Laura Triforth had apparently constructed her building with a prison in mind. For three maddening days we slept on damp mattresses, ate meager meals, and walked the confines of our chamber.

The chill air made my chest ache. With an effort I sat. "Mr. Bezrel."

"Yes, sir?" He scrambled to his feet.

"Get my vapormask, would you?"

"I haven't seen it, sir. Not since we changed rooms."

I drew my jacket tight. When the guard next brought our food, I demanded my vapormeds. He ignored me and stomped out.

Alexi had lapsed into a moody silence; he slumped on his cot for hours at a time. Mantiet made frequent attempts to converse, most of which I disdained. However, at one point he inquired, "At the meeting, why did you call yourself plenipotentiary of the United Nations Government?"

"It doesn't matter." I rolled over on my side.

"Still, it interests me. Why?"

"Because it was true."

"Do you have authorization or merely delusions of grandeur?"

Stung, I pulled myself up. "Command of Admiralty House can be likened to command of a vessel under weigh."

"So?"

"The Captain of a Naval vessel has unlimited authority. Moreover he is, in fact, the United Nations Government in transit. Whatever powers Admiral De Marnay had, devolved on me when he left, and I'm the senior officer in the Hope Nation system."

"Weren't the Governor's powers separate?"

"Yes, until the buildup of forces. Then Mr. De Marnay was given a united command."

"Still, plenipotentiary of the U.N.—"

"It's a long-settled law." My tone was irritable. "The Captain of a vessel can do almost anything he wants."

"And usually does," said Tolliver sourly.

"Shut up, Middy."

"Of course, sir."

Mantiet gestured. "Is he always like this?"

"Only on occasion."

"Why do you tolerate him?"

"He's sort of—" I hesitated.

"A test of your endurance?"

"More in the nature of a hair shirt." I regarded Mantiet sourly. "Are you done prying?"

"If it annoys you. How else would you pass the time?"

"That depends on why we're here."

Mantiet said, "We're in storage until Laura decides what to do with us. We're an embarrassment to her."

"How so?"

"As you so eloquently pointed out, you represent the old, defunct government. And I represent a more moderate wing of her own party. We're alternatives to her particular brand of republic. While we live, we're a threat."

"I don't want to die!"

I turned toward the childish voice. "Steady, Bezrel."

"I didn't do anything! Don't let her kill us!"

"Easy, Midshipman. You—"

"I'll handle it, sir," Tolliver said smoothly. "Let's talk in the head, Avar. Don't disturb the Captain." He guided the boy's arm toward the toilet cubicle.

"Don't hurt him."

Tolliver looked at me, surprised. "I didn't intend to." He shut the door.

I spoke softly, so Annie couldn't hear. "You think we're to be killed?"

Mantiet looked pensive. "I'd imagine so."

"Then what's Laura waiting for?"

Mantiet shrugged. "Perhaps she'll arrange some kind of accident. She still needs the support of conservatives like Branstead and Hopewell." He added with a smile, "Remember, my advice isn't worth much."

"I'm not sure any longer." The admission shamed me. Gruffly I added, "I thought she kidnapped us to rescue you, but it appears your position wasn't much improved."

"So it would seem." He gestured at the bath cubicle. "It's a pity, but if Laura, ah, eliminates you, she's unlikely to leave the child behind." His voice dropped even further. "Or your wife."

I glanced over his shoulder, but Annie was lost in some melancholic reverie. "I know." I hesitated, amazed that I was allowing myself to make him an ally. "There's nothing I can do." Mantiet waved me silent as footsteps approached.

As always, the men entered with pistols drawn and ready. "Seafort, come with us."

"Why?"

"Move."

Wearily I got to my feet. Was this how it would end? An innocent summons, followed by an unforeseen shot to the head?

"This way." They marched me along the corridor, one man behind, one on either side, a laser pistol in my back. Even if I'd been armed, I could have done nothing. They shoved me into another room, which I recognized as the one in which I'd first awakened.

Wary, I paced the chamber, glancing at the meager furniture, the barred transom. I swallowed; for some reason, what I wanted most in the world was to hold Annie in my arms.

The door swung open. I stared at the visitor, turned away. "I've nothing to say to you."

"Please." Harmon Branstead looked around, found a chair. "I came to see if you were well."

I stared at the wall opposite, determined not to speak. After a moment he came behind me. "Nicholas, I swear before Lord God: if I'd had any idea you were still on planet I wouldn't have been on that dais. Laura told me the Navy had skulked off in the night, leaving us. She said all U.N. authority was gone, and we were on our own."

"You were a party to treason."

"Was it treason, if we were abandoned? You've seen my plantation; if these people are the government I have to get along with them. Who else is there?"

"You swore an oath, as have we all."

He put his hand on my shoulder; I thrust it away. He said, "Nick, if the Government left us, we were entitled to form another. I thought you'd gone with your fleet."

"I would have, if Ms. Triforth hadn't taken me prisoner."

"She thought you were about to question Mantiet; her whole scheme would have unraveled at the last moment." He paused. "I had no part in that. Believe me."

I wanted to, but nobody on Hope Nation was whom he seemed. "It doesn't matter. You have your Republic, and I my prison." Uncomfortable at my own rudeness, I faced him. "Why are you here?"

He closed his eyes, opened them. "Jerence ran away after the meeting. I just found him today, and had him taken home."

"I'm sorry. He's . . . ?"

"Completely spaced. I don't know where he found the stuff. Or what he had to do to get it."

"I'm sorry." It seemed so inadequate.

He drew closer. "I don't know if they're listening," he whispered.

"And if they are?"

He shook his head to quiet me, and spoke in a normal tone. "They trust me as much as anyone, but they searched me before they let me in."

"Those who live by deceit find it everywhere."

"Perhaps." He sat, toyed with his boot. "I'm sorry for your troubles. There's nothing I can do to help you."

"There is," I said.

He glanced up, surprised. "What?"

"My wife. Get her out of this."

He swallowed. "I thought she was at the clinic. They have her too?"

I couldn't trust myself to speak, nodded instead.

"I'll do my best. You have my word." He beckoned me closer. Puzzled, I came close. He twisted the heel of his boot, slid it aside. Motioning me silent, he held it toward me.

Pressed into a hole in the leather was a razor. He whispered, "This is all I could chance bringing. Anything else they'd have found. You'll have to make it do."

I reached for it. He grasped my wrist, shook his head. "I need your promise."

"Of what?" Our heads were practically touching.

His grip tightened on my arm. "Take Jerence."

"What?"

"Laura told us of the call from your Admiral. When your ship *Catalonia* comes, take my son off-planet."

"Impossible."

"It's possible if you do it." His whisper was fierce. "You must, or I won't help you."

"Where could I take him? We'll be lucky to make it to home system alive. Do you want to send him to the fish?"

His hand tightened convulsively. "No, I don't want to risk my first-born." He took several steadying breaths before continuing. "You were right. We're in terrible danger. I don't think Hope Nation can survive the aliens. But you're a survivor. Somehow, you manage. Take my son with you."

"Even if I escape, I can't take a civilian."

"You can and you will." He released my wrist, locked his gaze to mine.

"It might mean his death."

"He may meet his death here, sooner." He fingered the sharp blade. "It's a gamble, Seafort. Jerence may be killed. Then my son Roger would inherit. Or Jerence may survive while we don't. Then, when it's over, you'll send him back. Either way the family survives; Branstead Plantation goes on."

"You'd sacrifice your son for the survival of a plantation?"

"I can do nothing to protect my sons. You're the best safeguard I know. And besides . . ."

I waited, realized he wouldn't finish. "What, Harmon?" I asked gently.

His face held anguished appeal. "I have to get him off-planet before he destroys himself. It may already be too late. All I know is that I can't save him."

How old was Jerence: fourteen? I couldn't cope with a sullen, rebellious joeykid along with my other troubles. Yet there was so little chance I'd be in a position to honor my promise that it hardly mattered. Harmon's razor was a pitiful weapon, but without it, Avar Bezrel's nightmare would certainly be realized. My duty was to try to save the innocents, no matter how hopeless the effort. "I'll try, Harmon." For Annie, for Alexi. For Bezrel.

"No. Swear."

I snorted with contempt. "My word is worthless. Didn't you know?"

"No. I trust your word more than that of any man I know. Give me your oath."

I regarded him. "Very well. My oath."

"That you will take Jerence off-planet when you leave, and to Terra with you on *Catalonia,* and let him come home when the danger is abated."

"I so swear."

"And I'll talk to Laura about Mrs. Seafort, the moment I leave." He handed me the blade.

I tore a piece of the lining of my jacket for wrapping, thrust it inside my pants. My grin was feral. "Too bad you couldn't bring a laser."

He twisted the heel back onto his boot, whispering still. "I had to beg Laura for this chance to see you. I told her it was to say good-bye."

"It may well be. Who's in charge, beside her?" I shivered, hugged myself. I hadn't been warm in days.

"There are others; Volksteader, Palabee. But she runs the show." Branstead's face clouded. "It's not what some of us hoped."

"Revolutions seldom are." I sat. "Harmon, surely you're smart enough to see your folly. Hope Nation has hardly more than a quarter million people. If you cut off commerce with Earth—"

"Not cut off, recast. Our lives can't be managed from afar."

Ludicrous, to argue politics with him, his razor warm against my side. "Do you think for a minute the Church would allow trade with traitors who've set themselves against Lord God's own government?"

"They—"

I rushed on. "And without our technology, you'd collapse in a generation. The die-cast fabricators, the medical—"

"Do you suppose we haven't thought of that? Our food is every bit as important to home system as your manufactured goods are to us. Have you any concept of the number of barges in the pipeline at any moment? Randy Carr calculated that without us you'll have food riots inside of three years. No politics, no moral stand would outweigh—"

It was his very soul at stake. "Harmon, you raise your fist against Lord God! I beseech you, think what you're doing!"

"Show me another way." He raised a hand to forestall my reply. "I'm not proud of Laura, or how she operates. Her attack on your car was despicable, and if I'd known . . ." He shook his head. "Zack Hopewell is disgusted and outraged, and so am I."

For a moment we sat in silence.

"When did you decide to visit?"

"After the meeting. When I found Jerence today, I was sure. I've talked to . . . some of my friends. We agreed. We'd do more, but Laura controls the arms and the Governor's Manse." Again he touched my shoulder; this time I did not resist. "Godspeed." He went briskly to the door, hammered on it. "Let me out! I'm done with him!"

A moment later footsteps approached; the door opened. Harmon nodded to the guards, turned to me with contempt. "I misjudged you, Seafort. You're getting no more than you deserved."

He might at least have warned me. "Harmon, you're a pompous fool. You always were." It was the best I could do on short notice.

He snapped to the guard, "Get me out."

Laura Triforth appeared at the end of the hall. "Enjoy your visit, Harmon?"

"He's your responsibility." Branstead stalked down the corridor. "I'll have no more to do with him."

Ms. Triforth raised an eyebrow. "Seafort, you seem to have irritated Harmon."

"A pity. He deserves you."

"I'll take you back to your colleagues." She beckoned me to follow her.

"Why are you holding us?"

"You're in protective custody, for your own safety. After all, someone's twice tried to kill you."

"Let my wife go."

She wrinkled her nose. "We don't need trannies roaming Centraltown."

"May God damn you to His deepest hell!"

"How diplomatic." She sighed, ran fingers through her hair. "Has it occurred to you I've a lot on my mind at the moment? A government to organize? A planet to run?"

"Let us go. We won't bother you."

"All in good time." Laura's men opened our door. "Oh, by the way . . ." She held my vapormask. "You left this in the meeting hall." I snatched it from her hand, fuming.

As they thrust me into our cell Tolliver jumped to his feet. "Where did they take you, sir?"

"I had a visitor. Leave it."

"What did Triforth say to you?"

"Not much."

From his corner, Mantiet sighed. "There's a virtue in helplessness, Captain. One has no decisions to make."

"We're never helpless."

"What would you propose we do?"

I sat on my cot. "Wait." It was all I could think of.

Bezrel approached timidly. His voice was soft, almost a whisper. "Sir, I'm sorry I acted like a baby this morning." I looked up with alarm; was he about to start bawling again? No, it seemed not.

I cleared my throat. "We're all afraid," I said gruffly.

"But you know better than to show it."

"It's all right." I wanted to be rid of him. Ashamed, I patted my mattress. "Sit."

"Aye aye, sir." Automatically he straightened his tie.

I smiled. "I never had a chance to review your file, Mr. Bezrel. Tell me about yourself."

"I'm thirteen, sir. I came out on *Vestra* with Admiral De Marnay; I started as ship's boy."

"How did you get to be a middy?"

"Admiral De Marnay promoted me. They did it that way so I wouldn't have to go to Academy first. My father wanted me to sail with the Admiral because they know each other."

So Admiral De Marnay had skirted regs for an old friend. I frowned and changed the subject.

"Who is your father?"

"Captain Bezrel, sir. Retired now, but he had U.N.S. *Constantinople.*"

"Where are you from?"

"Crete, sir." He hesitated. "It's an island that used to be part of Greece."

"I know where Crete is," I growled. Father had instilled Terran geography in me with dogged determination.

"Yes, sir. I'm sorry, sir."

Sorry. Always apologizing. I waited for the sniffles.

"Am I dismissed, sir?"

I took pity on him. "Yes. I commend you on your manner, Mr. Bezrel. Much improved."

His grateful smile pierced me. "Thank you, sir." He retreated to his cot.

"They've brought us breakfast, Nicky."

I opened my eyes. "Thanks, hon."

To my delight, Annie grinned. "You all right?"

"Of course." I sat up, shivering.

I gnawed at the bread, sipped at lukewarm coffee. Afterward I went back to my bed and dozed.

About noon I awoke. With an effort I sat. "Mr. Bezrel, give me the mask."

"I'll get it." Alexi. He helped me slip it on. "How do you feel?"

"Well enough." I took a deep breath through the mask and wrinkled my nose. The air seemed stale.

Ever so slowly, the day passed. Then a long night, during which I stirred restlessly, coughing. The vapormeds didn't seem to help.

When the guards brought our morning meal I demanded to see Ms.

Triforth; they didn't even bother to answer. I repeated my demand at dinner.

Late that evening she appeared, waking me from restless and feverish sleep. "You rang?" Her tone was sardonic.

I shivered, drawing my jacket closer. "You've made your revolution. Why hold us?"

"After your impassioned speech, I decided I don't want a horde of White Russians storming through the countryside."

"What on earth are you talking about?"

"I thought you knew your history. Never mind."

"Let us go."

"In time." She looked at me with concern. "Are you well?"

Mantiet said quietly, "Don't toy with us, Laura. Do what you're going to do."

"Be patient, Frederick. You'll both be freed soon."

"What might I look forward to? Shot trying to escape?" Mantiet seemed quite calm.

"Don't be ridiculous. You're not my prisoner. I haven't seen you since the night we proclaimed the Republic." She turned on her heel and left.

"We can't undo her treason," I said petulantly. "Why must she hold us?"

"She enjoys seeing us helpless." Tolliver.

Mantiet regarded me with an odd look, lapsed into silence. After several minutes he stirred. "Alexi, Mr. Tolliver, take Bezrel and Mrs. Seafort into the cubicle, please. I want to speak to your Captain alone."

Tolliver said bluntly, "No. I don't trust you."

I snapped, "Don't be silly. We've been alone before." Reluctantly Tolliver herded the others to the enclosed cubicle.

Mantiet took me to the far end of the room and spoke softly. "How do you feel?"

"Well enough." I coughed. "Under the circumstances." I was tired and wanted to lie down. I waited, but Mantiet said no more. "Frederick, if you've something to say, tell me!"

"Your face is flushed. You've been coughing."

"We've been locked in here with bad food, no air . . ."

"True, but you're much worse since yesterday."

I sank into a chair. "Perhaps. I've started the vapormeds again."

"Precisely. You started them yesterday."

I gaped. "Are you saying . . . Laura tampered with my meds?"

"Why else would she take your vapormask?"

"She returned it when I asked. If she wanted me dead, she'd just shoot me."

"Don't you—"

"Enough nonsense." I went back to my corner. As I sat, the handle of the razor pressed into my side.

Mantiet mustn't know I had it; he might be planted to betray us. But each day that passed made that more unlikely.

I toyed with the vapormask. Could Mantiet's suggestion be possible, or were his insinuations part of some outlandish scheme? What would Laura gain if I sickened? No, she didn't need to toy with me or plant a spy.

Mantiet approached. "Captain, I ask a favor."

"There's nothing I can do for you."

"I won't survive you by long. You're as close as I'm likely to get to a cleric. Shrive me."

"Me? You're joking. You need a chaplain."

"You are representative of Mother Church."

"Aboard ship. Here, in civilization . . ."

"If you landed on an unexplored planet, would you not still be chaplain to your crew?"

"Yes."

"We are strangers in a strange land."

"But—"

He cried, "I've nowhere else to turn!"

Was it blasphemy, or did I have authority? I concentrated on ill-remembered regs. Finally, I sighed. If there were sin, it would be mine, not his.

I said, "If I'm to be your chaplain, I must tell you: rebellion against lawful authority is treason against Lord God."

"I made no overt act of rebellion."

"You were part of their conspiracy."

"I took part in discussions. No more."

"Money? Other help?"

He flushed. "Some. I didn't know where it would lead."

"While I am here, a piece of Government remains. You're still bound by your oath."

"What do you want of me?"

"To adhere to your oath, as long as it is possible."

A long silence. At last, "All right."

"Do you repent your sins?"

"Yes." He sat tense on my cot, eyes boring into mine.

I made the sign. "In the name of the Father . . ."

When it was done he whispered, "Thank you." He turned away. Weary, I lay back on my cot. When I awoke, I no longer doubted I was sinking into illness. I was feverish. My chest ached. Alexi and Tolliver tried to tend me; irritably I waved them off. When the jailers brought our meal Tolliver demanded I be taken to the clinic. They didn't bother to answer.

Later, I woke from a doze, coughing. Time was growing short. "Mantiet, Tolliver, come here." I waited. "Frederick, I have no choice but to trust you. For the sake of your soul, I hope I'm right." I put my finger to my lips, fished inside my pants, came out with the razor. Their eyes widened. I whispered to Tolliver. "If you see a chance . . ." He nodded. I handed him the weapon.

I turned to Mantiet. "I won't be good for much. You might use the chair as a club, when Tolliver makes his move . . ."

"I'll find something."

"Get Annie and the middy out of the way first. I don't want them hurt. Or Alexi."

Tolliver said, "If I can. There may not be time."

I said, "I'll do my best to distract the guards. I'll yell, perhaps. We'll do it tonight if possible. No later than tomorrow." He studied my feverish face, nodded again.

When we were done Alexi came to squat by my side. His look was one of reproach.

I demanded, "What's bothering you?"

"You're hiding something."

"No." I hated to lie.

"You keep whispering so I won't hear."

I flared, "If I am, it's my prerogative as Captain. Who are you to question me, Lieutenant?"

After a moment his eyes fell. "I'm sorry." His tone was stiff.

My heart pounded. I might be gone soon, and this is how it would end between us. "Alexi, I'm sorry. Bend closer." I whispered into his ear. "There'll be trouble when the guards bring dinner. Take Annie and Bezrel into the cubicle when you hear them coming. Keep them there."

"Why?"

"I don't want them hurt. They're your responsibility."

"What will happen to you?"

"I'll be fine."

He studied my face, troubled. "All right, Mr. Seafort."

I grasped for something else to give him. We were reduced to so little. "Mr. Tamarov."

"Yes?"

"You're a good officer. You always were."

He stood straighter. "Thank you, Mr. Seafort." I smiled.

Despite my warnings, when dinner came I was sleeping fitfully; the guards were gone before I could rouse myself. I cursed silently; time was running out. By our next meal it might be too late.

"Mr. Tamarov, can you stay awake and rouse me before dawn?"

"Yes, Mr. Seafort."

"Do so."

Tolliver looked hesitant as he approached. "Please don't misunderstand me, Captain. But—"

"Yes?"

"You haven't been well . . ." He squared his shoulders, said with resolve, "If anything happens to you . . . Are we on our own? Shall we pretend we're still in the Navy?"

I snarled, "Pretend? You *are* in the Navy, until your enlistment expires."

"What Navy? Look around you! Where is it?"

"It's here." I coughed. "The U.N. Government hasn't abdicated. You and I embody its authority."

He shrugged. "Sometimes I wonder about you."

"What's that supposed to mean?"

"Nothing, sir. Excuse my impertinence." I glared, but he held my gaze. "And while you're at it, sir, who's senior: me or Mr. Tamarov?"

It was my turn to hesitate. Alexi was on medical leave; technically that left Tolliver in charge. Preposterous, on the face of it. Yet Alexi's memory was gone. "You're senior," I said, defeated. "Do as you see fit. For as long as you're able."

"Aye aye, sir." Shaking his head, he turned away.

"It's nearly dawn, sir."

I groaned.

Alexi persisted. "You said to wake you." He shook me again.

"What time is it?"

"Just after five." The hall bulbs, our only source of light, were turned down. We could barely see each other.

Breakfast might be as early as an hour from now, perhaps as long as three hours. I struggled to sit. Panting, I made myself breathe as deeply as

I could. It didn't seem to help. I yearned for the familiar comfort of the vapormask.

I tried to stand, failed, got cautiously to my knees. Holding on to the wall I pulled myself up, ignoring Alexi's outstretched hand. "Put a chair there." I pointed.

The door was centered on the north wall. Alexi put the chair along the east wall, near the north corner.

I prodded Tolliver with my toe. He turned over; I tapped at his ribs. He surged awake, hand darting to his pocket.

I shook my head. "Not yet." To Alexi, "Wake Frederick."

Mantiet sat, rubbing sleep from his eyes. He looked around saw us all roused. "I'm ready." He slipped into his clothes, sat at the side of the table nearest to the door. His arm draped casually over an unused chair.

"Wake the boy. Take him into the cubicle."

"Right." Alexi prodded Bezrel. The young middy sat up, dazed, and followed Alexi. I heard what might have been a sob.

Carefully I knelt by Annie's side. "Get up, hon." I stroked her forehead. "Please."

She came awake with a frightened gasp.

"It's all right, hon." I paused for breath. "I need you to go with Alexi."

Her eyes darted back and forth, came to rest on Tolliver's hand. She squealed in terror, clung to my shoulders.

"Edgar, get that razor out of sight!" I struggled to free myself. "Annie, let go."

She wrapped herself around me. "Fightin', with shiv? Dey gonna kill ya, Nicky!"

"Annie, go in the cubicle!"

"But—"

"Now!"

With a sob, she fled.

Knees weak, I crossed to the east wall, sat.

I shivered, struggling to stay awake. From time to time I coughed, deep hacking coughs that served as ominous warnings. I yearned to sleep. Soon I would have a deep long rest, until Lord God woke me for His vengeance. Half aloud, I whispered, "Lord, if I could but undo my offense . . . I am so sorry I offended Thee." Though it was no use, I was comforted. My punishment was inevitable, but He would know my repentance.

Endless minutes passed, while I toyed with the vapormask in my lap. Tolliver lay unmoving, hand concealed under his blanket. Mantiet sat quietly, as if relaxed. Only my ragged breathing broke the stillness of the night.

The hallway lights brightened. Footsteps. I managed to totter to my feet. When they swung the door open I would shout, catch their attention. With luck Tolliver could make his move.

A sound, from the cubicle. "Nicky?" Annie peered out.

The door swung open.

"I can't wait in—" She searched out Tolliver. He lay facing the door, the razor behind his back. She stared at it. "Don' get Nicky hurt!"

I hissed, "Go back!"

The first guard was halfway into our chamber. He stopped, looked about. Tolliver's muscles tensed. With a sinking feeling I realized my shout wouldn't be enough to distract the guard.

Annie gaped from the corner; she should have been safe in the cubicle. Too late; the diversion had to be now or never.

I flung the vapormask at the guard's head, surged out of my chair.

He whipped out his laser, aimed at me. Tolliver rose in one smooth motion and lunged across the room to crash into the guard's midriff. The impact smashed the man into the door frame. A crunch. A cry, cut short. The gun clattered to the floor.

I threw myself on the pistol.

With an oath the second guard kicked open the door. He fired just as Mantiet hurled a chair at his face. The chair splintered in a flash of fire and smoke. Knife in hand, Tolliver scrambled toward the door on hands and knees, below the line of fire.

A boot kicked the door wide. I got my hands on the dropped pistol. I lurched to my feet, but as the guard's trigger finger twitched, my legs buckled. I went down like a stone. Sparks and fire flashed over my head.

"Leav'im 'lone!" Annie's lithe form flew across the room. Fingernails slashed at the guard's eyes. Her knee slammed into his crotch. He fell with a shriek. She whirled, saw the third guard's pistol rising, pounced on his arm an instant before he fired. A bolt seared the concrete inches from my face. I flinched and kicked myself aside. Someone toppled heavily on me with a curse. I lost my pistol.

Tolliver tried to regain his feet; I'd knocked him down with my reflexive lurch.

"Nicky!" A shriek of terror as the guard's gun loomed.

Annie clung desperately to the man's hand and chomped savagely on his fingers. He howled, and the gun fell. She dived for it.

The room turned red amid ghastly screams. I lay gasping for air, the warning empty-charge beep of Annie's pistol fading from my consciousness. Time passed.

A gentle hand helped prop my head. Annie's wet cheek hugged mine.

"I didn't get a chance to use the knife." Tolliver sounded peeved.

I gasped for breath. "Find them!"

"There's no one left. The rest of the building's empty."

"You're sure?"

"Mantiet says so."

Frederick appeared, breathing heavily. "We're alone. But we don't have a heli."

Alexi and Bezrel emerged from the cubicle. The boy's face was buried in Alexi's jacket. Alexi's arm cradled his shoulder.

Tolliver said contemptuously, "Middies." I stared at him and he flushed. "Sorry. I forget."

Annie's sobs became more frenzied.

"It's all right, hon." I stroked her head, calming her. "How'd you do that?"

"Dey was gonna dissya."

"Where'd you learn . . ."

Her tone held scorn. "Two joeys ain' nothin. Onna street, girl gotta defen' herself. Even inna Cathedral I crunched one's head."

"My God. That was you?" I recalled the bashed-in skull, the thick puddles of blood.

"Coulda got othas, if I didn' trip onna rock." A pause, and her face clouded. "Rubies gone."

"Annie, about what they did . . ."

"No one did nothin'." Her voice had an edge of finality.

I cradled her anew. "It's all right, hon."

"Sir, we'd better leave." Tolliver.

I tried to wrest Annie's hand from my neck and succumbed to a fit of coughing. This time, I thought I'd never stop.

"We've got to get him to the clinic." Tolliver.

Mantiet said, "Why not just wait for Laura to retake us?" At Tolliver's puzzled stare he added, "Your Captain's not exactly unknown. If we walk into the clinic, she'll be told in minutes."

My voice was thick. "I'm all right. See if you still have friends."

"In half an hour I can have five men and a heli."

I nodded. "Get your men. Hurry." After he made the call I had Tolliver move us to the front room, past the charred corpses of our guards. Bezrel retched at the sight. I wanted to do the same. Annie hardly spared them a glance.

In the front room the daylight seemed overbright. "It's so cold." I huddled shivering in my chair. Mantiet and Tolliver exchanged glances.

Between us we had two charged pistols. I had Tolliver and Mantiet take them; I was past being any help. When the whap of blades beat the air we tensed. Mantiet peered cautiously through the window. "It's our side," he said. "But I'd better go first. They might be nervous."

He went out. A moment later he beckoned to us. I gasped, "Tolliver, draw your pistol. Be ready for anything." Why hadn't I made Frederick leave his pistol behind? I wasn't thinking well. Mantiet's men walked toward the building.

Mantiet entered first. He pulled out his pistol. Instantly Tolliver was down on one knee, gun aimed. Mantiet handed me the weapon. "You need this. I'm armed now."

"Thank you." I tried to make my voice casual.

"We'd better get out. Where to?"

The room drifted from side to side, making it difficult to think. We needed to confront Laura Triforth. Arrest her, if we could. But she had the power, the guns.

"Well, sir?"

"I don't know! Can't you see I'm sick?" I was disgusted by the whine in my tone.

"Into the heli." Mantiet.

Tolliver's voice was tense. "The last person who offered us a ride was Triforth."

"He's not Laura," I snapped. I tried to think. Best we retreat to the plantation zone, if someone there would help. Branstead, or perhaps Zack Hopewell. But within hours our escape would be known. Triforth would have time to mobilize.

No matter. We had no real choice. I asked, "Can we all fit in the heli?" It seemed too small.

"I doubt it. We'd be way over the weight limit."

My teeth chattered. I drew my jacket tight. "Ring Harmon Branstead for me." Mantiet's men drifted inside. Their presence made the room seem crowded.

"The frequency may be monitored," Mantiet warned as he handed me the caller.

I thought of calling through Admiralty House, relaying to Orbit Station and back. No, it would waste time, and Admiralty House was probably in enemy hands.

"Branstead."

"This is, um, a friend."

"Thank heavens." His tone held an odd note of relief.

"We need help."

"Are you . . . alone?"

"For the moment. Bring a large heli, as fast as you can."

"Where should we meet you?"

We had to get clear of the haulers' building. "Where I brought your son back from our trip. In front."

"Right. Figure about an hour." He rang off.

Alexi asked, "Where is he meeting us?"

"At the spaceport terminal." I stared at the heli. "We'll have to fly two loads."

"We'd better get you in the first one." Mantiet. "If they catch you here . . ."

"If they catch any of us, we're dead." The room drifted. I tried to take a deep breath. "Is there a car?"

"Nothing."

"The road's a few hundred feet. Stop one."

Mantiet gestured to two of his men. "Hurry."

"No killing," I said.

The farmhand spat. "They may not want to stop."

"Don't kill civilians."

The two men loped off. Too much time passed. Finally, the distant hum of an electricar. Another wait. A car appeared at the end of the winding drive, lurched along the dirt road, pulled up in front of our building. I wobbled to my feet.

Mantiet's field hand yanked open the car door. Inside, a young man cowered, hands held high.

I hadn't thought of prisoners. We could lock him in to a room. No, Triforth's men would find him and no telling what they'd do. Too complicated. "Bring him along."

The farmhand muttered, "You're crazy."

Mantiet spun, his voice dangerous. "Show him the respect you'd show me. More than that."

"But—"

"You heard me!"

The farmhand nodded grudgingly. "Sorry."

Mantiet shifted impatiently. "Let's get moving."

"Tolliver, Bezrel, and I will take the car. Send one of your men with us, in case there's a fight. Alexi can go with you in the heli." A long speech, that left me panting.

"Shouldn't you be in—"

Tolliver said loudly, "Aye aye, sir."

Interrupted, Mantiet reddened. "Right. Let's go."

We piled into the car. I fell into my seat, gasping from the effort. I said to the civilian, "Put your hands down. No one will hurt you."

The young man quavered, "Please. Whatever you say."

"Stay quiet. You might even get your car back."

On the edge of town the streets were mostly clear. Little damage was evident. The heli cruised above and behind us, circling. Despite the tension, I dozed. When I woke, the intense heat made me try to squirm out of my jacket, but after a moment I gave up, panting.

We pulled into the terminal lot. It looked deserted. It ought to be; there was no longer any traffic to the Station. "Check out the building."

Tolliver got out and approached the terminal with one of Mantiet's men. I kept my eye on the anxious civilian, hand on my pistol, until they returned. "Locked, sir."

We clustered in the parking lot straining for the thump of Harmon's heli. Heart pounding, I rested against the car. I'd needed Alexi and Tolliver to help me to my feet.

At last the heli came. As it swooped down I tapped the civilian on the shoulder. "Drive downtown. Don't stop anywhere near." He jumped into his car, sped to freedom.

Before the blades stopped Harmon Branstead jumped down, strode toward me, stopped. "God almighty, Seafort, what's happened to you?"

"I'm not well."

"You're—" He broke off. "What do you want us to do?"

"Who'd you bring?" One by one six men climbed out, laser rifles at the ready. Another man followed, more slowly.

"You?" My astonishment was obvious.

"Me. After all, it's my heli." Old Zack Hopewell's stern face showed no hint of warmth. He walked slowly to me, took my shoulders in his hands. He stared into my face. "Lord God save you, how long have you been like this?"

I blinked away tears. "Triforth—did something. With my vapormeds."

He turned to Harmon. "Get him to a doctor. Now."

"No." I began to cough. As the day faded to mist I hung on to Hopewell. Finally I caught my breath. "I can't be seen. None of us can until Laura Triforth is taken."

It was as if I hadn't spoken. "Harmon, get him in the heli. Frederick, call Dr. Avery. Have him meet us at my house."

I gasped, "Triforth first! Take the Manse."

Hopewell's tone was brutal. "That's for us to decide." In a moment we were aloft. I leaned on Alexi's shoulder, wondering where they'd put Annie.

Mantiet said, "You're wrong, Zack. Without him we're nothing."

"Look at him. We've got to get him to Avery."

"Find Triforth. You're wasting—" I began to cough. Some time after, I woke from a fitful doze, Alexi's shoulder damp from my perspiration. The heli door swung open.

"Help him inside."

I brushed away their hands. "I can walk." It was true, after a fashion. By the time I reached Zack Hopewell's porch scarce twenty yards away, I was glad of the hands offering support.

While we walked, Dr. Avery thrust a fresh vapormask over my head. Inside, he helped pull off my shirt. He listened. "Christ. Lay back, boy."

"We have to . . ."

"Give my meds a chance."

I obeyed. Avery examined my old canister, sniffed at the vapor. "That's not right. Lord God knows what mix she used."

Old Zack Hopewell raised an eyebrow. "What's been done?"

"I thought I'd seen everything. Laura's a zealot, that's no surprise. But this . . ." He shook his head. "Anticars, most likely. And bacteria."

"Explain." My words slurred through the mask.

"Anticarcinomals have been standard cancer treatment for a century. They work, but they can't be used with transplants. Period."

"Am I rejecting my lung?"

"We may have caught it in time. The pneumonia's worse. I've loaded you with meds. Lie still." To the others, "I can't believe she'd do it."

"I can." Harmon's voice was hard. "Zack, this settles it. We have to act."

"On whose behalf?"

Frederick Mantiet cleared his throat. "His."

"Nonsense." Hopewell.

"Zack, I've changed sides. I'm not with Laura. Nor you. I'm with him."

I giggled. Perhaps the meds were making me giddy. "A side of two."

A long silence.

"Three." Everyone looked to Harmon. He blushed. "The city's been bombed. A few years ago the fish sprayed a virus. Laura represents a cohesive power, one that's recognized. The Navy's another. Would you proclaim a third? Under what authority? Shall we risk civil war, with fish overhead?"

I breathed deeply. The new canister seemed to help.

Hopewell radiated his disapproval. "We'll discuss it privately, Harmon."

The door opened. Annie flew to my side. "Don' leave me 'lone again!"

Tolliver peered in after her. "Is he alive?"

I growled, "Yes."

Dr. Avery bared my arm. I felt a mild sting.

"No surprise. You're too ornery to . . ." He shook his head. "Midshipman Tolliver reporting for duty, sir."

"Take Annie and Alexi. And, whatshisname, Bezrel." It was hard to concentrate. "Get them decent food. And a bath . . ."

I fell into sleep.

I sat bolt upright. "What time is it?"

Tolliver leapt half out of his seat. "Christ, don't do that. It's like a visitation from the dead."

"Don't blaspheme." The vapormask muffled my voice.

"It's four in the morning."

I was in a bed. The lights were low. "What are you doing here?"

"Someone had to keep an eye on you. Everyone else is asleep."

"We're at Hopewell's?"

"Yes, sir. Dr. Avery knocked you out for your own good."

I said hopefully, "I feel better."

"You don't look it." Tolliver stretched. "Do you need anything?"

"Bring me up to date."

"No news of late. Last evening Ms. Triforth's joeys were swarming about Centraltown like disturbed bees."

"What's Hopewell doing?"

"Sleeping." Tolliver turned down the light. "As you'll be, in another moment."

Thereafter, he refused to answer my questions. Eventually I dozed, to pleasant fantasies of his court-martial.

In the morning I overrode Tolliver's objections and got out of bed to find a bathroom. Once there, I sat clawing for breath. Getting up had been a mistake.

When I tottered back, my breakfast was waiting, along with the committee of the whole. I glanced around at the somber faces. Frederick Mantiet. Zack Hopewell and his wife; Harmon and Sarah Branstead. Dr. Avery. Tolliver and Alexi. Even poor Bezrel, attempting manfully not to look overwhelmed.

I forced myself to sit casually, rather than fall panting on the bed. "A ceremonial occasion, I gather?" No one spoke. I demanded, "Are you handing me back?"

Mantiet snorted. "No, worse. We want you to lead us." He held up his hand to forestall my reply. "In a ceremonial capacity, of course."

"What does *that* mean?"

"Lend us your name." Frederick's gesture included the group. "If we strike suddenly, we might bring Laura down. We want to do it in the name of a legitimate government. Hopefully, it would reduce the bloodshed."

"And then?"

"Independence, as before. What would change is the morality of the government. We wouldn't—"

"Not in my name." I sounded bitter. "But why even ask? Who'd know, on whose behalf you act, with me sick in bed?"

"I'd know." Zack Hopewell, his voice like flint. "I will not found a regime on a lie."

"I'm sorry, then. But, no."

Frederick glanced at his companions. "I told you."

Harmon said, "Nick, what will you do if we defeat Laura on our own?"

"Do? I'm not sure. But revolution isn't the answer. It is an affront to Lord God. It's my duty to prevent that." I stopped, panting. "If you succeed you will be damned, and every soul on your planet will writhe in Lord God's hell. I've condemned myself, and I know nothing in the universe is worth that." I realized I spoke through tears.

Mantiet said carefully, "Suppose we ask you to reestablish the Government. Some of us need assurance our past acts won't be deemed treason. We've all had some knowledge of the underground."

Uncaring of the consequences, I flung aside my vapormask. "You'd bargain with Lord God's covenant? Treason is treason! Don't ask me to condone—"

Tolliver said, "Sir, don't you see they're trying to submit—"

I rounded on him, my nails clawing at the sheets. "How dare you! What is your rank?"

"I only—"

"Answer!"

"Midshipman, sir."

I struggled to my feet. "Do middies make policy? Do they question their Captains?" My pulse pounded. "Out of the room!"

"I'm sorry if—"

"At once!" I waited until the door closed before sitting shakily. "Where's my wife?"

Avery said, "She had a panic attack in the night. She's under sedation."

"Lord Christ." If it was a plea, it wouldn't be blasphemy. For a moment I closed my eyes. Back to the business at hand. "Knowledge of their plots is not itself treason. But no deals; that's for politicians. The subject is closed."

Another silence. Zack Hopewell said to the others, "I told you."

"Stop that! If you all knew what I'd say, why hound me?"

"You leave us few choices, boy. Submit to Laura, follow you to Lord knows what disgrace, or act on our own with no color of authority."

I waited. Casually my hand stole to the vapormask. I slipped it on. Lord God, my chest ached.

Harmon said, "Tell him what we decided, Zack."

"He knows." Zack Hopewell sat by my side. "What now, Captain?" His steady eyes met mine. "We commit to you."

I swallowed. Yesterday I was a prisoner, and now . . . "Does Triforth have an army?"

"About fifty men, as best I can judge. Far more than we have. Some are at Governor's Manse, where she's set up command. She has others running errands around town. She's set up a governing council; they've commandeered the public warehouses and taken over food distribution. Volksteader and Palabee are with her."

Harmon added, "They're well armed. They found plenty of firearms in the arsenals your people left behind."

I said, "Our best chance would be a direct attack on the Manse. If we take her, the revolution may collapse." I sat up warily, reached for my clothes.

Sarah Branstead stirred. "Where do you think you're going? You need quiet, and meds."

"To the Manse."

Dr. Avery shook his head. "Don't leave that bed. Not if you want to live." I ignored him. How could I send these men to do my work? Avery flared, "Damn it, the meds were just taking hold! Look at your face; I'll bet your temp is up three points in the last half hour!"

Frederick said, "In any event we're not all that well armed, and we won't risk your life."

I thought of Annie, and Triforth's casual contempt. "I'm going to the Manse, if I have only Bezrel to drive me. Come if you will, or remain behind." Ignoring the women's presence, I threw on my clothes. The effort left me weak.

Hopewell said, "Leave him, Frederick. It's his life to spend." For a moment I saw Father's dim presence. "We'll take both helis, Captain. There's room for all of us."

Alexi cleared his throat. "May I go too, Mr. Seafort?"

I nodded, short of breath. He offered his arm. As he guided me outside to the smaller heli, Tolliver fell in behind.

Others piled in around us. I tried to think. She had fifty well-armed men . . . We lifted off. If only the Government had destroyed the arsenals, locked them safely away . . .

I raised my mask. "Change of plans."

Harmon twisted in his seat. "What's the—"

"Go to the spaceport."

"But why—"

"All those supplies for the Venturas . . ."

His face came alight. "By God! Semi-cannons, smart grenades, shoulder missiles . . ."

Surely, Laura Triforth had remembered them too. After all, it was she who'd told me about them. On the other hand, she'd only had a few days, and a lot to organize. "They may be gone."

"Or guarded."

Grim minutes later both helis were back on the ground in front of the terminal. Tolliver conferred with Mantiet; he took two men, circled the terminal, and headed for the airfield.

In a few minutes he was back. "Guards. I spotted five."

"Can you take them?"

"We have a dozen men, not counting yourself. If we had a diversion . . ."

I tried to think. Diversion. I could manage one. "Zack, guard your heli. Tolliver, take everyone else and work your way along the edge of the field. I'll pilot this machine."

"What will you do, sir?"

I frowned at the foolish question. "Land, of course. Talk to them."

Zack Hopewell spoke first. "They'll kill you."

"Possibly." I spoke as little as I could. The ride had tired me more than I'd anticipated. A dull knot in my chest refused to dissipate. "Get going."

Tolliver looked at me; thought better of speaking. "Aye aye, sir. I'll need twenty minutes or so to circle the guards." He saluted.

Bezrel swallowed. "May I go with them? I'm a good shot. I've practiced."

I started to chuckle, had to cough instead. Finally I could speak. "When you were ship's boy?"

"No, sir. After I was promoted to middy. At Admiralty House. Please let me help." He gulped, aware of the offense of arguing with a Captain. "I know I've been no use."

"I promised to keep you safe."

"Yes, sir. But am I to sit out of danger while you fight? I'm a midshipman. I took the oath like everyone else."

I said through the window, "Bezrel, wait with the hel—" I coughed uncontrollably. When I stopped, my pants were damp and it took all my concentration to keep my hands from trembling. I looked at the boy, said weakly, "Give Mr. Bezrel a gun. Middy, go with the other men."

He grew three inches. "Aye aye, sir." I couldn't bear the look in his eyes.

Hopewell waited next to my window, rifle in hand. "I'll watch the minutes for you."

"Thank you." I hoped he couldn't see the stain on my pants. I breathed as deeply as I could, trying to oxygenate. My chest burned with each breath. I closed my eyes.

The voice woke me. "It's half an hour."

I flipped the switches.

Hopewell's hand came through the window, tightened on mine. "Go in the grace of our Lord."

"And thee." I motioned him clear, lifted off.

Either his benediction or my rest had succored me; the world was no longer pulsing. I stayed low, swung away toward the road so that I could come in high. I took altitude, swooped back to the field. Piles of supplies covered with tarps sat on the far end of the tarmac, much as I'd seen them weeks before.

I circled the runway on which the shuttles once landed, then headed downfield toward the guards, who watched with weapons drawn. I tilted the heli so they could see I was alone.

I landed about thirty feet from the nearest piles of cargo. Two men came forward, their laser rifles aimed at my head. As they approached I took several slow breaths and slipped off the vapormask.

I sang out, "I'm Captain Seafort. I was supposed to meet a shuttle here." Frantically I stifled a bout of coughing.

"Shuttle? Are you glitched?"

"The last shuttle, for the Station. They told me to meet it."

He stared at me, then guffawed. "You're a slow one. It left four days—"

The buzz of a bolt; he whirled in time to see a companion fall. He spun back to me, raising the rifle. "You bast—"

I shot him through the chest. Another guard ducked in reflex and fired. His shot hit the heli door. Hot rivulets of metal sizzled on my shoulder. I jerked convulsively. He aimed again. I couldn't turn far enough away to—

He went down shrieking. Blood poured onto the tarmac from where his leg had stood.

Another bolt bubbled the tarmac in front of me. I thumbed the switches, willed the blades to turn. Were my electronics hit? More ragged firing. Eons later I had lift. I yanked back on the stick and gunned the throttle.

I soared above the field, straining to breathe. I fumbled for the vapormask, but it fell to the floor.

Aloft, I watched the remaining guards go down. I held on to consciousness, dropped the heli near a supply pile. I managed to flip the switches before I passed out.

I came to on my own, minutes later. My eyes bulged from the effort to breathe. Desperately I clawed for the vapormask, found it.

It was little help. I sat as still as I could, chest heaving, while our war party ran across the field.

Tolliver glanced at me and cursed. He ran to the door, reached through to the caller. "Hopewell, respond!"

A moment later came the reply. "Ready."

"Get out here, fast." Tolliver didn't wait for an answer. He dashed back to the supply piles, yanking tarps aside. He beckoned the men. "Take these!" He ran from pile to pile until he'd found what he wanted.

Hopewell's heli landed alongside mine; men threw in weapons with frantic haste. Scant seconds later they climbed aboard. Tolliver thrust me out of the pilot's seat; this time I had no objection. Bezrel squeezed alongside me.

We lifted off. Tolliver said tersely, "We'll have to be fast, if we want him to see it."

"I'll last." It came out a croak. I turned to my right. A tear trickled down Bezrel's cheek. He looked at me, whispered, "I tried. I couldn't do it."

"Do what?"

"Shoot a man." His shoulders shook.

I nodded. For me, it was all in a day's work.

* * *

In Mantiet's small heli rode Tolliver, myself, Bezrel, Mantiet, and one of the hands. The rest were piled in Hopewell's machine. Tolliver leaned toward me. "Can you talk?"

"Yes." A word at a time.

"What do we do when we get to the Manse?"

"Set down." Die.

"Where?"

"The lawn." It seemed as good a place as any.

He looked to see if I meant it. "And then?"

"Go inside."

"Captain, pay attention. What do you want to do? Should I organize an attack?"

"Land." I fought for breath. "Get me . . . on my feet." If that was still possible. "I'll go in. If they . . ." I trailed off, coughing. "If they fight . . . blow the Manse down."

"You can't just walk in."

"I'm the Government." And when I fell, the Government would be no more. Perhaps I should put Alexi next in command. I giggled: a government with amnesia.

It didn't matter; we were most likely flying to our doom. If even one guard had gotten off a message during our attack . . .

"Take our men in with you," Tolliver urged.

Hopewell would need them in the fight that would follow my death. No, it wouldn't matter; we weren't strong enough to prevail regardless. It was too confusing. "All right."

We cruised over downtown, toward the Manse at the southwest edge of town. If the Governor's house had been near the government buildings, Governor Saskrit would be dead, and the colony under martial law.

If I couldn't walk . . . How could I make my entrance? They'd never respect me if I crawled . . .

I slapped my leg, forcing away the mist. I would walk into the Manse. I no longer had need to husband my strength.

We crossed downtown. "Come in low." I thought I'd spoken loudly, but had to repeat it before Tolliver heard. He dropped us lower, called to the other heli to follow.

"Mantiet."

"Yes?"

"Do you have . . . kind of . . . megaphone?"

He thought. "Actually, I do. There's a compartment under my seat."

"I need it."

"Right." He beckoned to the farmhand. With much swearing and grumbling the two men managed to squeeze onto the deck while Mantiet fished in the compartment. A minute later he handed me a small battery-powered speaker. "The Manse is just ahead."

"Come in . . . fast. Land . . . my door facing the Manse."

"Aye aye, sir."

"Bezrel, be ready to jump out. Get me on my feet."

"Aye aye, sir." The boy's voice trembled with excitement.

In the back Mantiet and his soldier checked their laser rifles.

"Who has . . . shoulder missiles?"

"Harmon."

I nodded, too exhausted to speak.

Tolliver dropped the heli like a stone, spinning it so my door faced the Manse. Two guards standing on the raised porch gaped, but made no move for their arms. Bezrel leapt out, but Tolliver was already running around the heli, brushing him aside. He hauled me out of the seat, set me on my feet, steadied my arm.

I shook myself loose as the larger heli came down about forty feet away. At the drone of its motor, the guards grabbed their weapons.

I lurched forward, croaking into the megaphone. "I'm Seafort!" The damned thing wasn't on. I fumbled for the button. "I'm Captain Seafort, commanding!" My voice sounded—I'd never heard the like. "Where's Triforth? I need her."

"You're what?" The guard hesitated, caught off balance.

"Get Laura Triforth, you fool." I took two steps, swaying. Bezrel proffered his shoulder. I clutched it, chest heaving. I raised the megaphone. "Is Triforth here? I'll . . . wait inside." I beckoned to Hopewell and Branstead in the second heli, hoping the familiar faces of the planters would help.

The heli door slammed. Zack Hopewell and Tolliver toward me. From the heli Harmon bellowed at the guards. "Don't stand there gawking! Help him! Can't you see he's hurt?"

The guards moved to block the door. One leveled his weapon. "Stay right there. We'll have to call Ms. Triforth." Reluctantly Hopewell came to a halt.

"Nonsense!" I thrust Bezrel forward, leaning heavily on his shoulder. I reached the first stone step. "Where's Triforth, you dolt?"

"Prong yourself." His rifle swung to me.

Door and guards disintegrated in an awesome flash. The shock hurled us to the ground. Bezrel flung himself over me as debris rained.

Feet pounded. Someone screamed orders. Men dashed past, leapt onto the shattered porch, through the blasted door. Rifles buzzed; something crashed and splintered. Dazed, half-deafened, I tried to sit. My chest was caught; I couldn't breathe. I gagged. Something salty filled my mouth and I spit it out. I wheezed, "Get me up!"

I had no strength to help; Bezrel hauled at me until I sat. He strained to raise me. Zack Hopewell took my arm, lifted me. "You have no time left, son. To the clinic."

"When we . . . get Triforth."

"Suicide is a mortal sin."

I shook my head. "Triforth." I sucked at air.

Frederick Mantiet dashed out of the Manse. "A dozen men. Half of them surrendered. The rest didn't get the chance. Her other forces are off somewhere. How's Seafort?"

"He's dying." Hopewell.

"I'm all right." Fifty men . . . we'd taken out three at the hauler office; another five at the spaceport, a dozen here . . . how many did that make? I couldn't think.

Hopewell and Mantiet carried me to the porch, set me down. Frederick said, "We have the Manse. We can declare the Government."

Why couldn't they understand? "Triforth."

"We can—"

I gripped his arm. "Triforth. Get our people out."

"But—"

"Now!" I tried to scream, hadn't the breath.

Hopewell said soberly, "We put him in charge. It's no time to argue."

"But—all right." Mantiet ran back into the Manse.

Minutes later we were crammed into the large heli. "Where?" Tolliver was at the controls.

"Try . . . warehouses."

We rose, leaving the shattered Manse behind, empty.

Harmon raised his voice over the engine's drone. "It's only a mile or so. She may even have heard the missile we fired."

I shrugged. It could make no difference. We were locked in a fight to the death. "Someone . . . give me a shirt."

"What?"

"White. For armbands."

"Christ, yes." Harmon ripped at his buttons. A minute later he was ripping his shirt into strips. "Everyone put one on."

I gasped, "Shoot anyone . . . without one." It was all I could manage.

"Look!" Tolliver pounded the dash. Two Naval helis were parked by the warehouse.

"Down." Mantiet was tense.

"Hang on." Tolliver swooped; my stomach churned. He asked, "Should we take out their helis?"

I shook my head. "We may need . . ."

We hit the ground with a thud, bounced. Tolliver shouted, "Sorry. Move out! Split into two groups, me and Frederick!"

In a moment they were gone, leaving me alone and dazed. I sat, chest heaving. Thoughts drifted to Annie, abandoned in her sedation. To Jerence Branstead, lost in his hopeless joy of his juice. To Laura Triforth, inside with her men, if she was indeed here.

A blast of grenades. The firefight had begun. Should we have disabled the other helis? If Triforth's men escaped . . .

I cursed. We'd parked near Laura's two Naval craft. If the rebels fled toward me, they'd have their own helis and ours as well. Our party would be helpless. Slowly, laboriously, I slid across to the pilot's seat.

More blasts. I searched for the smoke of a shoulder missile, but saw none. What was happening? I coughed, hung on grimly, managed not to pass out. The effort left me feeble.

Footsteps. I flipped the switches, started the blades turning. The door swung open. I turned. "Did you get her?"

Laura Triforth's eyes blazed. "Take us up, you son of a bitch!" Her face was smudged, her blouse torn.

I gaped.

"Go, or I shoot!"

"Right." I twisted the throttle, yanked back on the collective. We lifted straight up. I labored to stay alive.

She grinned, breathing hard. "I should have killed you outright."

"Yes."

"Well, you don't have long."

"What did you . . . put in me?" We continued to lift.

"I countered the antirejection drugs. Take me to the Manse!" Her gun was leveled at my chest.

"Why . . . do it?" Two thousand feet.

"It would have been so dramatic. In fact it may still be. I'll rush you to the clinic, just too late. The heroic Captain, last of the old order . . ." Three thousand feet.

"Why not . . . just shoot?"

"And be blamed for your death? I don't need to carry that baggage. The Manse! What are you doing?"

"Altitude."

"We're not flying to the Venturas, you idiot." Five thousand. I made no answer. Her pistol leveled at my stomach. "On the other hand, I can shoot and let you disappear. Put your damned hand on the cyclic and head for the Manse!"

"Yes." I rehearsed. It would have to be one smooth motion. I wouldn't have another chance. Not her pistol; I didn't have the strength. "Why . . . Manse?"

"My men are there. You have two sec—"

I tilted the ship, allowing myself to fall forward into the dash. It helped. My left hand slid across to the key. I turned it, yanked it free. The engine stopped. I flung my arm out the window.

If the engine died while the ignition was on, the blades would autorotate. But Naval designers assumed the pilot knew what he was doing; once the key was removed the bearings locked, the blades feathered, providing hardly any lift.

We dropped with sickening speed.

"I'll kill you!"

"Yes."

"Give me the key!"

I shook my head. "Shoot."

"You'll die too!"

I nodded. Thirty-five hundred. We spun as we fell.

"For Christ's sake, start the engine!"

"Throw away . . . pistol."

"I'll see you in hell first!"

Oh, yes. She'd see me there. Two thousand. The sun circled crazily.

"Seafort!" For the first time her voice held fear.

I tried to speak, choked. I gasped, "Pistol."

"We'll be killed!"

"Pistol!" Fifteen hundred. The world spun.

With a shriek of rage she flung the pistol past my head. "For Christ's sake, the key!"

I pulled my hand in, fumbled at the dash. Dizzy, I closed my eyes, felt for the keyhole.

"Hurry!"

In. I jammed it to the right. I opened my eyes. One thousand. Flip the switches.

Nothing. Off, on again. With a cough the engine caught. Five hundred. Was the world spinning past, or was it me? I no longer knew.

"Level out!" she screamed. Her hands braced against the dash.

I coughed forever, swallowing salty saliva, fighting to bring the ship under control. I'd taken us straight up; we shouldn't be far from the warehouses. They were . . . there. I swooped to the north. Next to me Laura clung to the dash, white-faced. We dropped alongside the warehouse with a crash.

In the cloud of dust, a feral growl. Laura Triforth's long fingers closed around my throat. She shook me like a rag doll.

The world hazed red. As I jounced I saw Mantiet and Tolliver racing toward us. My hand crept to Laura's, fell away. I waited for the end.

Abruptly Triforth yanked open the door and bolted. I sucked at air as Tolliver gave chase. Mantiet leaned against the heli, gasping. "Five dead, on our side. Your Naval men are alive. So's Zack." Thank Lord God.

Tolliver tackled Triforth, swarmed atop her. He seized a shock of her hair, raised her head off the ground. His fist slammed down.

It was over.

I sat exhausted, stinking, shaking helplessly as I labored for breath. "Comm room."

"What?"

"Radios. Hookup. Where?"

"I don't know." Mantiet thought. "Triforth broadcast from the Governor's Manse, the first day."

"Back."

"Let us take you to the clinic."

"After."

"You lunatic." His look held awe. "I'll get the others." He ran off.

Moments later we were again in the air, Tolliver at the controls. Dazed and cuffed, Triforth sat in the back seat between Mantiet and Hopewell.

"Arrest . . . Palabee and Volksteader."

"We'll have to find them first."

I nodded.

When we set down they carried me into the Manse. Other than the main entrance, little damage was visible. A few walls were scorched, and one room . . . the sight was not for the squeamish.

We found the Governor's broadcast center in the basement. I had them put me in the swivel chair at the desk. Branstead and Mantiet cursed and fumbled with the switches.

"Video."

They looked up. I waved at the holocamera.

Tolliver muttered, "I'll do it, but it won't be pretty." At first I thought he meant the focus. No, he meant me. I must be a sight. He swung the holocamera to me, turned it on.

Harmon looked up. "We have a tightbeam linkup with Orbit Station. The station will beam it back down on all channels."

"Station . . . is abandoned."

"Their puter responds, though. Say when."

Annie would be pleased. Her Nicky on the holo. She'd hold her head high when she shopped . . .

"Mr. Seafort?"

I drifted back. "Now."

The light went green. I spoke.

No sound came.

I heaved for breath, spoke again. "This is . . . Captain Nicholas Seafort . . . commanding . . . United Nations forces." I struggled not to cough. "On behalf of . . . lawful United . . . Nations Government, I hereby . . ." The room grayed. I gasped at air. Zack Hopewell's eyes bored into mine. ". . . declare martial law . . . throughout Hope Nation." I had little time. The room drifted in a slow, alluring circle. I spoke firmly into the approaching dark. "The revolutionary . . . treason has been . . . put down . . . Triforth under arrest."

"I do appoint . . . as military . . . Governor of Hope Nation . . . Zachary . . . Hopewell, of Hopewell Plantation." I searched, found his astonished eyes. There was more to say. I tried, stopped. I tried again. Chest heaving, airless, I waved to Branstead. The broadcast lights dimmed. I reached for a breath, found none. "Tolliver!" It was a gasp.

He dashed across the room. I coughed endlessly. No relief came. I gagged. A mouthful of bright red liquid cascaded onto my white shirt. I looked down, horrified, and up again at Tolliver. The room pulsed to red.

He scooped me in his arms and ran to the waiting heli.

18

A mask was strapped to my face. Bright lights probed, disembodied voices echoed. "The lung's lost, he's septic as hell. Prep him fast, we operate in five minutes." A needle stung my arm.

Black.

Drifting. Misery. Lights, faces.

Pain.

I couldn't swallow; tubes blocked my throat. I couldn't breathe, but something breathed for me. I slept, awakened, slept.

Pain.

Sleep.

I awoke flat on my back, to the rushing sound of air, silence, air. My chest inflated to the sound, and it hurt.

"You have a hell of a constitution or you wouldn't be with us." I squinted, focused on the floating face. Dr. Abood, of the clinic. I tried to speak, couldn't make a sound. It frightened me and I tried to cry out. Silence.

"We yanked what was left of your lung, sewed you up, and pumped you full of antibiotics."

I gestured at my mouth. I had to use my right hand; my left arm was full of drip lines.

"You've been on a respirator for three days. You need to start breathing on your own. Can you try?"

Tentatively I tried a breath. Pain lanced through my chest.

"Work at it; we have to wean you soon. If you develop pneumonia again, it's all over." Abruptly he left. I tried to gesture him back, hadn't the strength. My fingernails clawed at the sheets.

"I'm here, sir, if you need anything." Tolliver, haggard and disheveled. His chair was alongside the bed. We were in a small cubicle, surrounded by poles, machines, monitors.

I nodded, drifted off to sleep.

When I woke Tolliver was standing over me. He'd had a change of clothes, if not much rest. His eyes were sunken. "Good evening, sir. Try to breathe." I shook my head. "Please, sir. The doctor says it's urgent."

I caught the machine's rhythm, breathed ahead of it. Misery.

"Again."

Who was he, a middy, to tell me what to do? I beckoned him to leave.

"I don't understand, sir. Write what you're trying to say." He held a pad near my hand.

I scrawled, "Go away."

"Breathe on your own, sir."

I rapped the pad, livid with rage.

He ignored me.

Wild with fury I hauled at the bedrails, heaved myself into a sitting position, ignoring the excruciating pain. I grasped his jacket, unable to spit my curses. In a frenzy I tore at the tubes alongside the rail. The monitors clanged their warnings. Damn him in hell forever! I'd break him! I'd destroy him utterly. I'd take us both off duty and call challenge—

The door flew open. Dr. Abood dashed in. Tolliver stood stolidly, his face expressionless, while I pounded his chest. I turned to the doctor. Get the man away from me! Why didn't he understand? I turned back to Tolliver, who stared at the silent respirator.

Only then did I realize I was breathing.

"Where's Annie?" My throat was still raw.

"Here in the clinic, sir. Alexi—Mr. Tamarov has gone to see her. She's, ah, all right, I guess."

I didn't like the sound of that. "Does she talk to you?"

Tolliver said, "Not really, sir. She's sort of dreaming. Awake and dreaming."

I turned my head. Annie was beyond my help. Nothing awaited me if I recovered. Living . . . didn't seem worth the bother.

An endless series of visitors interrupted my reveries. Among them Alexi, regarding me anxiously, saying little. I dozed. When I woke he was gone.

Frederick Mantiet came to visit, offering encouraging words. Though we'd become allies, I was wary in his presence.

Not long after he left, Zack Hopewell looked in. I bade him sit.

"The last of Palabee's men surrendered this morning."

I grunted. Hopewell folded his hands in his lap. "Seafort, I want out of this job. I'm no military Governor."

"Neither was Joshua."

"Joshua led his people to the promised land. If anything, I'm holding them back from it."

"Triforth's Republic wasn't the promised land."

"I know that." His tone was sharp. "Else I wouldn't have joined you."

"You'd have violated your oath?"

"I'd have tended my crops!" He waved as if to banish the issue. "I swore no oath to restore a government that had fallen."

"Then why did you support us?"

"Because . . . hell and damnation, boy. Because there was no right. Because we're in chaos. Because you're a just man."

"Just!" I snorted. "You know me so little."

He shook his head. "How little you know yourself." He raised his voice, overriding my reply. "Palabee and Volksteader demand to be released. Triforth insists on a civil trial."

"Have them all sent for interrogation. Mantiet too."

"Frederick? He helped you!"

"He renounced his confession." Could it matter any longer? I brushed away the thought. "I want to know the truth."

He answered, "And I want Palabee and Volksteader tried or released."

"After interrogation. Anyway, I should be out of here in a couple of days. We'll see."

For the first time Hopewell smiled. "I'm glad for that."

"Thank you." I lapsed silent. My convalescence was troubling. The pain meds helped, but I felt alone, isolated. Dutifully I did my breathing exercises and walked slowly in the hallway. From time to time I stopped at Annie's room.

Alexi visited with me, chatted awkwardly. Harmon Branstead brought Jerence to see me, but kept a stern eye on him throughout.

Tolliver came. I hadn't seen him for several days. I glowered.

"I'm sorry if I was, er, unsympathetic when you had the tube in your throat. But when you lay there as if you were giving up, I wanted to tear out that respirator, make you breathe." He turned away from my gaze.

"Damn you, Tolliver, why can't you let me hate you as I want?"

He turned back, startled. "I thought you did, sir."

"I've yearned for nothing more than an excuse to cashier you." My face reddened at the admission.

"Will you?"

"I can't. There's no one to take your place."

"Yes, sir."

I relented. "And I don't want to replace you. Continue as my aide."

He blurted, "You mean that?"

Astonished, I could only stare. He stammered, "I'm sorry, sir. Thank you. I mean—thank you."

"Find me a place to sleep when I'm well. We'll reopen Admiralty House and work from there."

"Aye aye, sir. What will we do?"

"I don't know yet." I sat back on my bed. "Dismissed, Mr. Tolliver."

His salute was crisper than his first. "Aye aye, sir."

"Now do you believe me?" Frederick Mantiet sat in front of the Manse, head in hands, shielding his eyes from the bright sun.

I knew what he was feeling. It would pass. "Yes."

"So . . . I worked to establish a republic. Are you going to try me like Palabee and Volksteader?"

"No."

"Why not?"

A workman mortared a stone into the porch. "With you it was just words. You didn't take overt action, even if you kept yourself informed of the plot against us."

"Words can be treason."

"Are you baiting me, Frederick? In any event you redeemed yourself." The porch was nearly complete, though it would be many years before it aged to the patina of the foundation. I wondered if the Manse would be standing then, or whether the fish would have dropped another, more destructive rock.

"If I'm free, I suppose I should go home. I have to set matters right."

"Or you could stay and help us. Would you care to join the Government?"

"No." He rubbed his eyes. "Not your Government; I'm opposed to it. And anyway, I don't have the personality. I'm too abrasive."

So was I, but I was saddled with the job. The Admiral's words had been, "Carry on. You're in charge." Soon *Catalonia* would arrive. It had been—how long?—two days since I'd left the hospital, Dr. Abood's admonishments ringing in my ears.

"Captain, when will you hold the trials?"

"I don't know, Frederick. Mrs. Volksteader is coming to see me in a few minutes, and Palabee wants to talk also. Then I'll decide."

"We planters are the foundation of Hope Nation."

"But treason is treason." I stood, shading my eyes as I peered into the sun. "Is that her heli?"

"Looks like it. I'll leave you alone."

I straightened my tie, smoothed my hair while the Volksteaders' heli landed. It felt good to be in uniform again, though my shirt rasped against my sensitive chest. Thanks to daily bone-growth stimulation my ribs were fast healing, but my skin was still tender.

When the blades floated to a stop Mrs. Volksteader climbed out. Sarah Branstead followed. I hadn't expected her. The discussion might be awkward.

We greeted each other civilly, shook hands, found seats on the rebuilt porch. Leota Volksteader got to the point. "It's not fair of you to hold Arvin. Let him go."

I temporized. "What is your role in this, Mrs. Branstead?"

She shook her head firmly. "Oh, no. When we last met it was 'Sarah.' Nothing changes that."

I smiled. "Thank you. Still, why are you here?"

"The Volksteaders are good friends. I wanted to come, and Harmon approves."

"Arvin acted unwisely, Mrs.—er, Sarah. He became involved with treason."

Leota Volksteader raised her hands. "We've never been political. We're not among the biggest plantations or the most developed. We can't afford to offend anyone in power. Your Government collapsed, and Laura said she was declaring a republic. If we'd refused to attend, she'd have remembered and held it against us. What were we to do?"

I shook my head. "Arvin took part in their meetings, let the plotters use his haulers and equipment, gave them aid and comfort."

"Which is no more than we did for you! How can you be so ungrateful?"

I said, "What are you talking about?"

Sarah Branstead said, "I was there, Mr. Seafort. Surely you haven't forgotten."

"Ladies, I—" I searched the haze of my memories. "You'll have to explain."

"You visited the Bransteads," Leota said. "With your lieutenant Mr. Tamarov. As we were leaving, I took you aside so Arvin could talk to him. Don't you recall?"

I did, vaguely. "Go on."

"Arvin and I had decided it was best to speak privately with your officer. That way, the conversation would be unofficial, so you could deny it if need be."

"What did Arvin tell him?"

"Don't pretend you don't know. Arvin said to watch out for Laura, that she was going to move against you. Your man said he'd tell you right away. And then you left, and—and—"

"Laura blew up the hauler," Sarah Branstead finished. "And nearly killed our son."

My hand tightened on the chair. The explosion. Eddie Boss, his arm broken, hauling Alexi out of the shattered car. "He never told me," I said slowly.

"For heaven's sake, why not?"

"Jerence was with us. Alexi wanted to speak but I told him to wait." Alexi's coma, his amnesia, were my fault, then. I'd prevented him from doing his duty. I lay back, suddenly weak. Take this burden from me, Lord. Don't let me hurt anyone else.

"What a fiasco," Sarah said slowly. Her hand squeezed my arm. "How you must feel, Captain."

I looked up to her. "If you knew Ms. Triforth blew up the hauler, what was Harmon doing on the dais with her?"

Sarah said fiercely, "Do you think we knew then that it was Laura? I'd have killed her myself! If you don't believe that, send me to interrogation! Leota only told us last week, when she asked our help for Arvin."

"Still, why was Harmon there? He was committing treason."

"You can't believe that, or you'd arrest him too. We're like the Volksteaders, not big enough to fight the government. We had to go along with Triforth, at least for the time being."

A young aide brought us lemonade from the Manse; I sipped the cold drink and waited until he'd left. "Harmon switched sides, though." It was too confusing. "I'll think it over. There's no point in talking further."

Leota persisted, "Will there be a trial?"

"There doesn't have to be. Not under martial law."

"You'd let him go?"

Sarah took her arm. "That's not what he means," she said gently. "Leave it be. He'll do right."

"But—" Protesting, Leota Volksteader let Sarah quiet her. She said her good-byes and left.

I sipped at lemonade in the hot summer sun and considered whether to slaughter her husband.

19

Tolliver, Bezrel, and I reopened Admiralty House. I decrypted the puters while Tolliver fussed in the mechanical room resetting the climate controls. In the two weeks since we'd left, the place had acquired a disused look, a dank and musty atmosphere. Perhaps I only imagined it.

We established comm links with Orbit Station. William, in his impersonal manner, confirmed every few hours that he had nothing new to report. When our ships Fused home, the remaining fish had disappeared within hours.

Annie languished in the clinic, unable to emerge from her daze. Our name came up for an apartment, and I had her moved the same day. Emmett Branstead found a nurse to stay with her.

Meanwhile, Zack Hopewell struggled with the details of government. By now the streets were cleared, and crews were demolishing or shoring weakened buildings. As before, looters were shot, but few were found. Hopewell and I met each day, and faced a similar question: what now?

At Admiralty House I settled myself in the anteroom where Lieutenant Anton had presided, and before him Lieutenant Eiferts. No need now for a formal office. Bezrel ran errands for Tolliver and me, not the least of which was to bring us our meals. Though we had use of the softie dispenser and micro, I preferred getting our dinners at the terminal restaurant. For their part, the café was glad of the business, now that the fleet was gone.

Tolliver interrupted my reverie. "Captain, will you take a call from the jail?"

I looked past my feet propped on my desk. "Who, and why?"

"You agreed to see Mr. Palabee today, and they want to know where."

I sighed. "At the Manse."

"Aye aye, sir."

"Make it after dinner."

Tolliver could pilot me, or I could go myself. I'd reserved one Naval heli for our own use and loaned the others back to the civilian transport grid. Alexi had returned to his job, but kept his caller with him. I'd made sure of that.

My console lit; calls that previously would have been taken in our comm room went to me now. I flipped on the speaker. "Orbit Station to Admiralty House, please respond."

"Yes?"

"Good afternoon, Captain Seafort." William's solemn voice.

I blurted, "The fish?"

"No, Captain. Please stand by for a patch from a U.N.N.S. vessel."

"A ship? They've all sailed home."

"Stand by, please. *Catalonia*, go ahead."

I swung my chair around, dropping my feet to the floor, wincing at the unexpected pain. I still wasn't ready for sudden movements. "Seafort here."

"*Catalonia*. Captain Herbert Von Tilitz."

"Nicholas Seafort, sir. I believe you are senior to me."

"Yes." I remembered him as brisk, humorless, efficient. "You're groundside?"

"Yes, sir. At Admiralty House."

"We caught Admiral De Marnay's beacon. He said to pick you up. Do you have a shuttle, or should I send one down? We've seen no fish but I want to be out of here as soon as possible."

"We've no shuttles at Centraltown, but I understand there's one in the Venturas, sir."

"How many am I retrieving?"

"Five, sir."

"I'll send a shuttle down. I won't moor *Catalonia* at the Station; that's too risky. We'll approach near enough to send a gig over. Their puter will open for us and we'll take one of their smaller craft."

"Yes, sir. When?" A ship for home. Derek Carr. Peace.

"Figure . . ." He hesitated. "We'll get the shuttle tonight, but I'd rather land in daylight. We don't have an experienced shuttle pilot. Make it . . . 0700. That will give you time to pack." Was he joking? No, it couldn't be.

"Seven A.M. local time, sir. We'll be at the spaceport."

"Very well." His tone was dry. "This time don't miss your ride. There won't be another."

"I know, sir." We rang off. I bellowed, "Tolliver!"

He raced in, alarmed. "Yes, sir?"

I stood. "We're going home."

He stared, puzzled, until his eyes lit. "*Catalonia?*"

"Yes. In the morning."

"What a zark! Yes!" He slapped the leather chair in an outburst of joy. A side of him I hadn't known.

"Where's Bezrel?"

"I sent him for dinner, sir. He'll be back in a few—"

"After that, he's not to leave the building. Call the Manse; have them bring Annie and her nurse here in a heli tonight. Call Alexi. Tell him I order him back at once."

"Aye aye, sir. If the shuttle's not landing 'til morning—"

"At once. We'll spend the night here together."

"Aye aye, sir. What about Palabee, sir?"

Let Palabee be dam— No. "Have him brought here instead of the Manse."

Home. Thank you, Lord God. Though I don't deserve Your mercy, my companions do.

I sat making notes. I'd turn over civilian control to Hopewell unless Captain Von Tilitz ordered otherwise. I'd have to ask his agreement; he was senior now. Reclose Admiralty House, say good-bye to Harmon, take down the flag—

Harmon. I'd made him a promise. I sighed. After seeing Palabee, I'd send for Jerence. And what if Von Tilitz refused to take a civilian? I'd never considered that the decision might not be mine. Well, I'd given my word. I'd bring Jerence without telling Von Tilitz beforehand. He wouldn't take the time to return the boy, though he'd take his ire out on me afterward. No matter.

Derek Carr would be aboard. I wondered if he had come to hate me as much as Vax.

That evening I paced my office, wondering when dinner would arrive, until I recalled that I'd eaten it an hour before. For the life of me I could not remember what it had been. "Tolliver, where's Palabee?"

"They'll be here at eight, sir. As we arranged."

I bit back an angry reply. Knowing my nerves were taut, Alexi and Bezrel managed to stay out of my way.

When the guards arrived, I made sure Tolliver had his pistol, ordered Palabee released from his fetters. He looked worn and tired.

"Well?"

His fingers drummed on the conference table. "I don't know where to begin. Have you decided on a trial?"

"I think so." If Hopewell would go through with it, after I was gone.

"For my life?"

"Treason is a capital charge."

"I don't think I committed treason, Captain."

"You rebelled against the Gov—"

"Was there a government to rebel against?" He eyed me steadily. "As

Lord God is my witness, I didn't think you left us one. Your people vanished without notice, leaving no—"

"The civilian administration was intact."

"Bureaucrats."

"You're quibbling. In any event—"

Tolliver skidded into the doorway. "Captain, come now!" He didn't bother to salute. "Quick!"

As bizarre as Tolliver was, even he wouldn't summon me in that manner unless it was vital. "Watch Palabee," I told the guard as I left.

Tolliver was at the console. "Listen!"

"We got two of them. Three more aft." Von Tilitz, on *Catalonia*, his voice taut. "Plotting Fusion coordinates. Orbit Station, relay to Seafort. We're under heavy attack, we'll have to get out—*MIDSHIPS LASERS, FIRE AT WILL!*"

"Orbit Station to Admiralty House, please resp—"

"Seafort. I heard him. How many fish, William?"

"Three at his stern, two more amidships. Two more Defused between *Catalonia* and the station; I destroyed them."

"*Catalonia*, do you—"

"We're about to—Christ! Fire at will, all sides! I have six fish. We're going to—" Alarm bells clanged. Von Tilitz's voice sharpened. "Partial decompression! They're on our tubes, we can't Fuse. Maxwell, how far are we from the atmosphere? God damn them! Get the lifepods off, then! Abandon—"

Silence.

I shouted, "William, relay!"

"There's nothing to relay, sir."

"Where's *Catalonia*?"

"Three point six two kilometers off my east lock, Captain. She has three fish astern, two at port. I see two . . . now three lifepods accelerating from the ship. Approximate entry to atmosphere twenty-two minutes. No further signals from *Catalonia*. Her laser fire has ceased."

Oh, Derek. Lord God save you, and all others aboard. I cried, "Fire on the fish!"

"They're too close; my laser fire would hit the ship. I judge it inadvisable."

"If they break through her hull—"

"One lifepod under attack. Veering away. I am firing at fish approaching pod." William was as calm as if delivering a stores report. "Fish has thrown at pod. Pod is disintegrating. Fish is hit. Fish is spewing material, presumed destroyed."

A faint signal. "Mayday, Mayday! U.N.S. *Catalonia* escape vessels to anyone! We are entering atmos . . ." The static increased.

"William, where will they land?"

"Calculating. Landing likely in Venturas, but fuel capacity of lifepods great enough to reach Eastern Continent. Actual fuel on board lifepods not known."

"Relay any signals from the pods."

"I will do that."

"Are fish still around *Catalonia?*"

"Yes, Captain. Five."

"Fire at *Catalonia* and the fish." By now it was unlikely anyone on board was still alive.

"I cannot fire at a U.N.N.S warship, Captain. My prime instructions do not allow that."

"There's no one left on *Catalonia!*"

"She's still a U.N. vessel."

My mind raced. "William, who is senior officer in Hope Nation system?"

The reply was immediate. "You are, Captain."

"Very well. Record. I do hereby decommission U.N.S. *Catalonia*. I order you to—"

"Firing at aliens with all lasers that bear. One fish down! Another is Fusing. Another hit. A third also. Remaining fish Fused."

Why weren't the lifepods signaling? The heat of the atmosphere would sear off their antennas, so they couldn't send further signals. If her crew carried callers, they'd contact us after they set down. Without callers . . . And would they find level ground to land? There wasn't much of it in the Venturas.

I yelled, "Tolliver!"

He jumped. "Jesus, I'm right here, sir!"

"Don't blaspheme. Pull all our helis out of the transport grid. I want them ready to search for the lifepods at first light."

"Aye aye, sir. Where?"

"Along the eastern seacoast for now. The crew will know enough to aim for Centraltown. If they don't sight survivors, have them fan out over the ocean toward the Venturas."

"Aye aye, sir."

"God damn those fish!"

Soberly he nodded. "Amen."

"Get Bezrel!"

A minute later the boy rushed in, breathless. "Midshipman Bez—"

"Wake Lieutenant Tamarov. I want you both on watch in the comm room. All frequencies. Report any signal other than local traffic."

"Aye aye, sir!"

I pounded my desk in frustration. I had no men, no equipment. There was little more I could do.

I spent the night the comm room with Alexi and the boy, straining to hear nonexistent signals through the static. By dawn I was bleary with exhaustion. By midmorning I was drowsing despite vast quantities of coffee.

We'd heard nothing. Three Naval helis with civilian pilots searched for survivors. Tolliver volunteered—begged—to go, but I forbade it. I'd need him with me if the lifepods were found.

Noon came and went. I summoned Hopewell. I also rang Harmon Branstead. Then, deciding I couldn't show favoritism, I called Mrs. Palabee, Mrs. Volksteader, Lawrence Plumwell, manager of Carr Plantation, and others among the minor planters.

We met at Admiralty House, around the conference table I'd grown to loathe. Had good news ever reached me at this table?

I waited impatiently for coffee to make the rounds, opened the meeting. "As you've no doubt heard, *Catalonia* was destroyed last night." Derek was dead. Later I'd find time to mourn.

"Lord God's mercy on them." Sarah Branstead's eyes brimmed.

"Amen. It's clear now that the fish are attracted by Fusion. But more important, they've returned to Hope Nation system. Orbit Station's puter is active and it destroyed several fish after they attacked *Catalonia*."

A moment of silence while they digested the news. "What now?" Plumwell.

Zack Hopewell stirred. "We're in the hands of Lord God. There's not much we can do. We have no ships, no lasers—"

"So much for your damned Navy," Plumwell said bitterly. "All your blundering, your supply fiascos . . . when there's trouble, you turn tail and ran."

"Enough," snapped Hopewell. "Captain Seafort didn't."

"He would have if he'd been able. He was on his way to—"

"I said enough!"

I cleared my throat. "That will get us nowhere. We have two choices. Carry on and hope the fish leave us alone, or send a party to the Venturas Base and see if their lasers can be reactivated."

Sitenbough, a plump young settler from west of the Triforth estate.

"What good will their lasers do us, halfway across the planet?" He sounded peevish.

"Between Orbit Station and the Venturas Base, we may be able to get a crossfire on any aliens that approach."

Harmon Branstead said, "Would it help? The fish Defuse above us ready to attack. How much warning had we of the rock they dropped?"

"Very little. I said reopening the Venturas Base was an option." I pondered. "Manning the lasers would take at least a dozen men. We'd need civilian volunteers."

A rancorous discussion followed. In the end, the planters' consensus was to leave the fish alone, and hope they would do likewise to us. Hopewell, seeing my restlessness, brought the meeting to a close.

Afterward he and I sat in the anteroom, sipping coffee brought to us by the ubiquitous Bezrel.

"It's only a matter of time," I said. "They'll be back."

He nodded agreement. "There's another option you didn't raise." I cocked an eyebrow, waiting. "Send a couple of men to check the base, to see what it would take to reopen it. That might save some time in an emergency."

I should have thought of it myself. "Very well. I'll do that." I glanced at my watch. "There's still time to get there in daylight. I'll take Tolliver and Bezrel."

"Are you well enough?"

"Of course." Short of breath from time to time, but on the whole, much improved. I should have let them yank my lung months ago.

While Tolliver readied one of the Naval helis, I stopped at our new apartment to see Annie. The flat was only a few blocks from Admiralty House, yet I'd spent no more than two nights there since we'd moved in.

"How are you feeling, love?" I took her hand. She pulled it free.

"It's sunny." She stared vaguely at the trampled flower beds bordering the apartment. Across the room the nurse sat reading.

"Would you like to take a walk?"

She shook her head. I wondered if she'd dressed herself, or whether the nurse had helped. At times she roused herself from her lethargy; more often she sat passively while she was groomed.

I tugged at her arm. "A walk would do us good." No response. "The doctor said I need exercise. I hate to walk alone. Should I forget it?" A nerve throbbed in my cheek.

Slowly, as if in a dream, she got to her feet. "We take a walk now," she told the nurse. She went to the door, waited as if expecting it to open by itself.

Together, we strolled around the block. "I'm going on an overnight trip," I told her.

She stopped. "You comin' back?"

I took her hand, squeezed it. "Of course."

"It be okay, den." She seemed to lose interest.

I drowsed in the back seat while Tolliver flew. As a treat for Bezrel, I had Tolliver give him an elementary flying lesson while we crossed Far-reach Ocean. Flushed with excitement, the middy struggled to keep the heli level at two thousand feet while Tolliver's hand hovered over the cyclic.

Long before we reached shore I switched places into the copilot's seat. As we neared the Venturas I scanned the distant shoreline, hoping against hope to spot *Catalonia's* lifepods. We'd heard no radio signals; either the crew was without callers or they were all dead. Derek Carr's lean, aristocratic face drifted past the window. Did it hint of reproach? I wasn't sure. Ghosts do not often speak.

"Unidentified aircraft, turn back at once! Do not approach!"

"Lord Jesus!" Tolliver banked the heli at a stomach-wrenching angle and soared away from the land. He stared at the caller as if at a spirit. "Who was that? The base is abandoned!"

"Apparently not." I reached for the caller. "Venturas Base, this is Naval heli two five seven Alpha."

"Unidentified aircraft, turn back at once! We have you in range and will fire!"

Tolliver flipped switches, readied our missile defense. Our heli was well armed, but countermissiles would do little good against groundside lasers. "Sir, they have radar contact."

"I see that," I snapped. "Venturas, this is Captain Nicholas E. Seafort, Commander at Admiralty House. We're here on—"

"By standing orders of Commandant Eiferts, no ship may approach our airspace! This is your final warning."

Were they insane? I tapped my personal code into the heli's puter, set it to transmit.

"We will fire in ten sec—"

I snarled, "Who the hell do you think you are?"

Tolliver blanched. I ignored him. "Put Eiferts on line and flank, or he'll be out on his ear like Khartouf! Move!"

"He's not—he's in another building. I'm sorry, but I have stand-ing—"

"Countermanded! Call Eiferts or you'll see a drumhead court-martial!"

No response. We watched the alarm indicators. "Stay on course for the base."

"But—" Tolliver swallowed. "Aye aye, sir."

Nothing, for three long minutes. Then the speaker crackled. "Eiferts here. Identify yourself."

"Nicholas Ewing Seafort, Captain, U.N.N.S., commanding all forces groundside and aloft." There were no forces, but it was a grand title.

"Seafort is gone. It's a good imitation, and you deciphered his code, but—"

"Damn it, Eiferts, I thought you said you knew how to obey orders. Turn off your lasers!"

For the first time he sounded hesitant. "Captain?"

"Captain. And you're a lieutenant."

"You went to the station with the others two weeks ago, sir."

My body began to relax; though he might not know it yet, he'd accepted that I was myself. "I missed the shuttle. So did Tolliver; he's here with me."

A long silence. "Come in high, directly over the field. Don't use radar. We'll keep our lasers trained on you, and at the first sign of trouble we'll fire."

I growled, "Acknowledged." What was the matter with the man? Tolliver shot me a worried look, but maintained our course.

I held my breath as we neared the field. Tolliver brought us directly over the top at three thousand feet, dropped us down slowly. I peered down to see the administration building, the thick-walled shuttle hangar, the parade ground.

We touched down in the center of the field. I opened my door. "Let them see me first." I tugged at my jacket, ran my fingers through my hair. I growled at Tolliver's amusement, but a glance at the mirror showed me the futility of my efforts. Though my uniform was neat, my eyes were deep sunken in hollow cheeks, and my scar flamed vividly.

Two soldiers approached, laser rifles at the ready. As they neared I recognized one of them. "Good evening, Sergeant, ah, Trabao."

He lowered his rifle, snapped a quick salute. "It's him," he told his mate. "Kinda surprised to see you," he said.

"And you. They said you were all to be evacuated."

"Long story, sir. Your officers may come with us." I chose to view it as an invitation rather than a command, and beckoned to my two midshipmen.

We reached the dirt roadway, where Eiferts was waiting. He asked cautiously, "In what capacity are you here, sir?"

"As senior Naval representative in Hope Nation. As commander of the military government at Centraltown."

"And the, er, Republic?"

"No longer exists."

He regarded me and slowly came to attention. "Lieutenant Saul Eiferts reporting, sir. Base Commandant."

"As you were." I continued past him to the Commandant's office. "Private session. Now."

He no sooner snapped the office lights on than I exploded, "What the hell is going on? Why aren't you on your way home?"

"Admiral De Marnay sent shuttles to take the men aloft. I volunteered to stay."

"Why?"

Unbidden, he sat at his desk. "My fiancée Jeanne—did you ever meet her?"

My tone was scathing. "You stayed to be near your woman?"

"In a way." As if ashamed, he stared at the desk. "I—"

"Your duty was aboard ship with the Admiral, not hanging around like a lovesick—"

His quiet voice sliced through my reproach. "She worked downtown. They never found her. The building was vaporized."

Crimson, I turned to the window. At length I muttered, "I'm a fool. Please forgive me."

"We were to be married. I hoped my enlistment would expire while we were still in Hope Nation, otherwise I intended to come back for her. She had a younger brother. He wasn't found either."

"I'm terribly sorry. Say what you'd like; I deserve it."

"You didn't understand." His voice was quiet, saddened, but not reproachful. "When the Admiral told me we were pulling out it seemed—I wanted to stay. With the fleet gone, the Station's puter and our lasers are the only protection Hope Nation had left."

"Trabao? The others?"

"I asked for volunteers. He was the first; the rest came after."

"How many men have you?"

"Eleven, sir. Not enough, really, but we manage. We maintain laser watch, run the power grid, and cook meals. Nothing else gets done."

I sat, decided I could face him if I tried. "Why not tell Centraltown, Mr. Eiferts? Why threaten to shoot us down?"

"Hours after the last shuttle lifted we heard Ms. Triforth's broadcast

proclaiming the Republic. It's not—" He hesitated. "It's not that I'm dead
set against a republic, sir. We deserted them, and if that's what they want
. . . But we're not here to get into local politics. We're a U.N.A.F. installation defending the continent. I won't ask them for help, and I won't let
them divert our arms for their local fight."

I nodded.

"Anyway, Centraltown is outside our defense grid. I'm on the station
circuit; anything it sees, I see. Between us we have the planet's only
operating laser cannon."

"I'm surprised the rebels didn't seize them."

"Triforth sent a heli the second day. We took it down." He bit his lip.
"Without warning."

"Why?"

"It wasn't a Naval craft, sir. I wasn't taking chances. Today, your ship
was transponding Naval codes."

I recalled my sneers, my sarcasm of moments before. Again I reddened. "You're a good man, Mr. Eiferts."

"Thank you." He hesitated. "What happened to you, sir? You look,
um—"

I looked um, all right. Very um. "I lost a lung. I'm all right now." Just
short of breath. At least now I knew the reason, and it was no longer life-
threatening.

"Would you like to see the laser control setup?"

"I've seen—yes." If he wanted to show me, it was the least I could
do.

Outside, Tolliver was waiting. Eiferts took a closer look. "Lieutenant
Tolliver?"

"Yes, sir. Midshipman Tolliver now."

"How did that—" He broke off. It was none of his business.

I expected a long walk as before, but Eiferts summoned a carrier.
Perhaps my appearance had something to do with it. I bade Tolliver wait
with Bezrel, then Eiferts and I careened across the field to the laser
control building. The laser cannon themselves were on a rise far across the
base.

As he'd said, Eiferts hadn't enough men, but they managed. I vowed
I'd send him help when I got back, if I had to conscript raw recruits. After
the laser building, we visited the power plant, where electricity for the
lasers was generated. They hadn't enough men to bring power online to
the remaining lasers, as we'd intended. Somehow, we would have it done.
Somehow.

He started back to the administration building. "Will you stay the night, sir?"

"I really should get—" Well, I didn't like flying by night, especially as we'd have to put down in the ocean if anything went wrong. "All right. We'll leave first thing in the morning."

I briefed Bezrel and Edgar as we walked to the mess hall. Tolliver's look was grim. "Mr. Eiferts' done a miracle keeping the base going, but he needs more staff." I nodded.

Dinner was heated U.N.A.F. rations; they could spare no one for more elaborate fare. We ate in near silence, crowding around two long tables.

After, they showed me to my room. I undressed, rolled onto my bed, and slept like a log.

20

Over breakfast I conferred with Eiferts while Tolliver and Bezrel concentrated on their oatmeal and coffee.

"First priority is getting power to your lasers."

He nodded. "And perhaps more men would ease the strain. Not too many, though. We have no time to train them."

I agreed, my mind still on the power lines. It would have been so easy, while Khartouf had a fully manned base.

"Do you think they'll ever come back?"

I groped for what I had missed. "You mean the fleet?"

"Yes, sir."

I stared into my coffee cup, wondering whether to tell him the truth.

"They must," he answered himself. "They'll have to bring reinforcements. Hope Nation is too valuable to lose."

I swallowed my doubts. "Of course. Our job is to keep things going until then."

His smile was wan. "I wonder, lying alone at night. But then I remind myself that the U.N. couldn't desert its own colony."

My eyes strayed to the clock. "I'm afraid we should be leaving."

"Of course, sir. I'll walk you to your heli."

Bezrel and Tolliver jumped to follow. I paused at the heli door. "I've appointed Zack Hopewell military Governor. There's no reason your presence shouldn't be made public."

"No, sir. Unless . . ."

He lapsed into silence. I prompted, "Yes?"

"Unless the Government falls. You and these two midshipmen are the only other Naval personnel on the planet. The only true link with home."

I debated. "Better we keep it quiet, at least for now."

"As you say, sir." We shook hands after his salute. I climbed in and we lifted off.

Tolliver, perhaps because of his earlier silence, was in a talkative mood. "Quite a difference from our last visit, Captain."

"Yes."

"The base is nearly deserted, but still . . ." He paused for thought. "It's something hard to define. They've abandoned their spit and polish, but they're more . . . determined." We crossed the shoreline, headed east over the ocean.

I'd noticed the same, but hadn't thought much about it.

"I'd volunteer for duty there, if you wish." He was suddenly attentive at the controls.

I regarded him. "You, Mr. Tolliver? I never thought of you as an idealist."

"I'm not, sir. It's just that I—"

"Venturas to Naval heli two five seven Alpha, come in."

"You certainly sound like one." I took the caller. "Seafort here."

"Eiferts. Orbit Station has seven fish! Their puter is firing its lasers." His voice betrayed his tension.

"William? Put him on."

"He's alphanumeric, sir, direct to our puter. I can forward—Christ, another five! We're powering up. I'll have a shot for two more hours. Then they horizon out."

"Turn back!" I shook Tolliver's arm. "Now."

Eiferts said, "Captain, do you think you should go on? You'd be over the ocean if—"

"I'm on my way back. ETA seven minutes. We'll come in low and fast. Move it, Tolliver!"

I gripped the dash, biting back unnecessary advice. When the field appeared over the perimeter hill I breathed a sigh of relief.

I ran from the heli to the administration building, had to stop for breath. Why didn't I have more wind?

Tolliver passed me, dashed up the steps and inside. A moment later he was back. "No one here, sir. They're probably in the laser control building."

Of course. Where else? I looked around for a carrier, found none. "Let's go!"

It would have been faster to get in the heli and hop, even for so short a distance. The few hundred yards along the dusty road left me gasping for breath, though Tolliver and Bezrel had no trouble whatsoever. Jogging; I must take up jogging.

Red-faced, sweating, I arrived at the laser building, ran past the carrier parked in front. An enlisted man met me inside. "Over there, sir, in the control room." He pointed.

Inside I half expected a huge simulscreen, as on a bridge. Instead, I saw three techs poring over their consoles. Eiferts leaned over one's shoulder, pointing at the screen.

"Well?"

He didn't bother to salute. "We're powered. William's feeding us data for a shot; his long-range sensors are more sensitive than ours."

One console screen flashed coordinates, which were fed directly to the laser cannon. The other, set to alphanumeric, detailed the situation for us mere humans.

I scrolled back to read snippets of the dispatches. "ORBIT STATION TO U.N.A.F. VENTURAS BASE. CONFIRMED ALIEN SIGHTING, DISTANCE POINT FOUR KILOMETERS. LASER FIRE TO COMMENCE. SIX ADDITIONAL SIGHTINGS. DISTANCES VARY, TWENTY-FIVE METERS TO POINT EIGHT KILOMETERS . . ." I scrolled. "THREE ALIENS CONFIRMED DESTROYED, COORDINATES AS FOLLOWS . . ." I flipped to real-time printout.

"LEVEL 2, SECTION FOUR LASER DISABLED. ATTACKING FISH WAS DESTROYED."

"Targeted." Samuels, one of our techs.

"Fire!" Eiferts. The lights dimmed.

"TWO ADDITIONAL FISH DESTROYED, COORDINATES TO FOLLOW. ANOTHER FISH DESTROYED BY GROUNDSIDE FIRE. MORE FISH FUSED INTO NEARBY SPACE, COORDINATES ZERO, NINETEEN, FIVE . . ."

William was under heavy attack, but why? Hitherto, the fish had virtually ignored the Station.

"Change targets, man. Hurry." Eiferts.

A few days ago the Station had fired on the fish that attacked *Catalonia*. Some were destroyed, others had Fused away. Did the fish communicate among themselves? Did they know the Station was now an enemy?

"Fire!" Eiferts gripped the back of the console chair.

I approached him. "Can we help?"

"My radarmen are on the long-distance sensors. Can you take local radar?"

"Tolliver!"

"Aye aye, sir. Which console?"

Eiferts pointed. "There. You know how to operate ground radar?"

"Of course, sir." It was a foolish question; we all did. Eiferts's nerves were showing.

Tolliver huddled over his screen. Bezrel stood nearby, knuckles in his mouth. I cuffed them away. "Go help Mr. Tolliver, boy. Act like an officer."

"Yes, si—aye aye, sir."

Well, my nerves were showing too. It couldn't be helped. I paced from screen to screen. Our lasers got off careful, laborious shots; each had to be reconfirmed to make sure we didn't hit the Station, as the fish were extremely close to it.

Tolliver had activated two screens, local and midrange. He sat at the one, had Bezrel watching the other. Between them they covered the approaches to Venturas Base. I gave their consoles an occasional glance and moved on. With the Republic overthrown, no one from Centraltown was likely to bother us.

Hours passed in an agony of frustration. From groundside we could do little. Perhaps if the base had been fully operational, if the fusion generators were fully on-line, if the fleet were here to call our shots . . .

As the day passed William disposed of fish with calm efficiency, but at any given time a score of them were Fusing in and out of the Station's range. Should I alert Centraltown? Was the risk worth the ensuing panic?

"Captain, look!"

I whirled.

Tolliver fiddled with the magnification, jabbed his finger at a blip. "Something's descending."

"A rock?"

"Too slow."

"Where?"

"East. It's just entered the ionosphere."

"I'll check." I ran to the main console, grabbed the caller. "Captain Seafort to Station, respond."

William's imperturbable voice. "Orbit Station. Go ahead, Captain."

"Can you talk and fire at the same time?"

"I have ample capacity. How may I help you?"

"Did you launch a shuttle?"

"No shuttles launched, Captain."

My hackles rose. "We've got a blip in the eastern sky."

"Confirmed. Those would be the aliens."

"Lord Jesus! Why didn't you tell us?"

"I did, Captain. Reference paragraph two eight five, transmitted about forty sec—"

I scrolled frantically. "ALERT: ALIEN VESSELS OBSERVED APPROACHING ATMOSPHERE. PROBABLE INTENTION: ENTRY."

I whirled. "Eiferts, we've got to tell Centraltown."

He glanced over my shoulder. "Use the C circuit. Jameson, fire!"

"Seafort to Admiral—to Governor's Manse, respond."

It took only a moment. "We read you, Captain."

"Get Hopewell, flank."

"He's sleeping, sir."

I screamed, "Wake him!"

It took three minutes, but finally Hopewell was on the line, breathing hard. "What is it, Mr. Seafort?"

"Five aliens entering the atmosphere. No trajectory yet."

A silence. When he spoke his voice was calm. "It's ending, then. What do you want us to do?"

"Nothing's ending," I snarled. "We don't know their purpose. They might throw a rock, or—"

Tolliver said, "They don't need to drop into the atmosphere for that."

"Be silent, Middy. Or they might be spreading a virus. Zack, do you want to evacuate?"

"There's no point to it. We'd never notify everyone in time, and where would we go? The plantations can't shelter us all."

I groped for answers. Naval Rules of Engagement didn't contemplate hostile aliens floating overhead. "Gas masks? Can you prepare for viral attack?"

"To an extent. We can sound the sirens, warn of possible gas attack. But we haven't held gas drills; a lot of joeys won't know what to do."

"But some will."

"Yes." A pause. "I'll get started. Godspeed, Mr. Seafort."

"And to you." We rang off, but not before his calm helped steady me. "Tolliver, where are they headed?"

"I don't know, sir. They're descending very slowly."

I demanded, "How in hell can a fish enter the atmosphere without imploding, if it lives in vacuum?"

"They come from somewhere, sir. Presumably someplace with an atmosphere."

"Won't they heat up from the friction of entry?"

He looked cross. "Just how would you expect me to know, sir?"

I bit back an angry retort. He was right; I was harassing him. "Track them. Are they in range?"

"Extreme range at best, sir. I'll let you know when we have a shot."

I paced with mounting anxiety. There was nothing I could do here at the base. I should be at Centraltown . . . But even there, we had no ships, no men. The one laser cannon here was—

We had helis. Even my own ship had missiles and shells. I snatched up the caller. "Seafort to Manse, come in!"

This time the reply was immediate. "Yes, sir?"

"The helis you have searching for *Catalonia*'s survivors. Where are they?"

"Just a moment; I'll ask the Governor."

A moment later Hopewell came on. "We sent the helis out at dawn. They're combing—"

"You've kept two Naval ships in reserve. Are they fully armed?"

"As far as I know."

"Do your pilots know how to use the missiles?"

"They're former U.N.A.F. soldiers. I'm not sure but I think—"

"If the pilots are capable, send them to coordinates—Tolliver, what are they?" I read them off his screen into the caller. "Have them attack the moment the aliens are low enough to hit."

"I will."

Again his calm passed to me. Zack Hopewell was old enough to be my father, yet I'd been ordering him about like a cadet. "Mr. Hopewell, excuse my manners."

His voice held stern reproof. "No need to apologize for command. Do your duty, and His will." He rang off. I peered at the main console. Five fish descending, and nearly thirty attacking the Station. Though William skewered them with ceaseless efficiency, more appeared as fast as he destroyed them. His kill count had reached twenty-one. Our ground lasers had taken out seven.

Day darkened slowly to night. I had no thought of leaving. William's reports continued unabated.

Tolliver sang out, "Sir, we have a shot at the fish in the atmosphere."

Eiferts shook his head. "We have targets aloft. The Station goes over the horizon soon. Then we'll be of no help to William."

"Yes, but these fish are dropping into—" I hesitated. What was higher priority? I spoke softly. "Tolliver, feed the coordinates to the third laser cannon. As soon as there's a free moment . . ."

He twisted his head to stare at me. "Free moment? For God's sake, sir, they're coming down onto Hope Nation!"

"Easy. We can't shoot both cannon at once. We'd better help William while we can."

Tolliver punched in figures, following the fish. He admitted grudgingly, "On their current trajectory, we have a little time."

I watched for endless minutes.

Eiferts called across the room. "You still have a shot?"

"Yes, sir." Tolliver punched the keys, reconfirmed his figures.

"The Station's over the horizon. Rawlings, power up number three. Use Tolliver's coordinates."

Minutes passed while the capacitors of the third laser cannon reached full charge. Tolliver said, "Ready, sir."

"Fire!"

The lights dimmed again. I stared at the console. One blip began to drop, slowly at first, then faster. In a few seconds it disappeared from the screen.

"Got him! Acquiring new target!" Tolliver.

Now the other blips were moving faster. We locked on target, fired again.

Jameson spun his chair. "Directly overhead, sir! A dozen high above the atmosphere!"

The display from Orbit Station sounded an alarm. Now what? I peered at the screen. "ELEVEN ALIENS OBSERVED OVER WESTERN CONTINENT; ABSENCE OF ORBITING TARGET SUGGESTS MANEUVER RELATED TO VENTURAS BASE." Though William was out of our sight, he still had a view of the sky above us, and relayed his reports through his comm satellites.

"Eleven? I count twel—"

William intoned, "Inanimate object separating from fish. My sensors show high density, no metal, does not compute as ship."

I snatched up the caller. "William, what is it?"

An infinitesimal pause. "Planetary debris, I think. Similar composition to the mass the aliens released over Centraltown, but smaller."

"Good Christ!" My eyes met Eiferts's as his turned to mine. "Acquire targets overhead! Crash priority!"

The large blip fell away from the others. "Tolliver, coordinates!"

"I need a few seconds for a trajectory." The remaining fish overhead disappeared from my screen, either from William's fire or by Fusing to safety.

Agonizing seconds passed. My eyes were riveted to the screen, while the rock approached velocity of eighty-three miles per second. "Locked in! Fire!"

The lights flickered as our cannon tracked the rock hurtling from above. "Where's it headed?" My hands were tight on the chair.

"Right here, sir." Tolliver was pale.

Jameson called, "More blips over Western Continent, about a dozen."

"Be specific. Lock in tar—"

"Got it!" Tolliver's whoop echoed in the crowded room. The large blip he'd been tracking disintegrated into a spray of tiny dots. Perhaps they were small enough to burn up in Hope Nation's rich atmosphere.

Samuels shouted, "Another rock, sir. Twice the size of a fish!" Minuscule compared to the one that destroyed Centraltown, but if it landed on our heads . . .

"Helis from Centraltown report radar contact with fish."

"More overhead, sir. Looks like two rocks!"

Bezrel, ignored by all of us, huddled at his console. His shoulders shook. I raged inwardly at Admiral De Marnay. Why bring a child who should have been at Academy to—

"Bezrel!"

The boy jumped as if goosed with a prod. "Yes, sir!"

"Can you find the mess hall?"

"Yes, sir."

"We'd like some coffee. Bring it."

"Aye aye, sir." He ran to the door.

"One rock gone!" Tolliver. "Seeking other target."

I would force down the coffee, though my stomach churned with acid. Better the boy have something to do. Only after the middy was gone did I realize I might have sent him into greater danger.

"Sir, one of the Naval helis wants instructions!"

"What?" I tore my eyes from the console, keyed the caller. "Seafort."

A pilot's voice crackled. "Radar contact with two fish, Captain. Approximately fourteen thousand feet."

"Target acquired!" Tolliver.

"Rawlings, fire cannon one!" Eiferts.

"That low?"

"Yes, sir. Do you want us to engage?"

"Who are you? Can you fire a missile?"

"Major Winfred Zahn, retired, sir." He chuckled. "I'm quite sure I can."

"Stay out of range of anything they throw. Fire immediately."

"Righto."

Tolliver raised an eyebrow at the informality. I smiled, surprising him. How little it mattered.

In the next half hour we broke up two more rocks. Each one was delivered by at least ten fish. Did it take their combined efforts to transport a rock across the void? How did they Fuse an external object? Did they create a shared field?

As William progressed along the horizon he lost his view of the fish over Western Continent. Above, fish kept Defusing. We were too occupied taking out rocks to shoot at fish. If we only had all our lasers on-line . . . No use crying over spilt milk.

"Look, sir." Two clusters of fish, each herding a sizable mass. "They're guiding more rocks."

"I see," I snarled.

"Cannon two's targeted." Tolliver, to Eiferts. "Their rock is a bit lower."

"Right."

It took almost eight seconds to knock out the first rock. By the time it

disintegrated, the second was well on its way. As we lined up a shot, a
third appeared, high overhead.

"Damn them!"

"Amen." My fingers tore at the chair while Tolliver and Eiferts
targeted the laser cannon. Shots were so much easier from a ship, where
radar signals were clear and immediate, and the range was short.

I stared at the console. The third rock was launched, while we barely
had a lock on the second. "It'll be close," I muttered.

"Why in hell won't that rock break up?" Tolliver pounded his console.

"Denser than the others? Stay on it!"

"We have a lock, sir. What we need is time."

Our cannon followed the second rock almost to the ground. It broke
up a scant six thousand feet overhead. "Where's the other—"

Jameson. "Targeted! Fire!"

A whomp that shook the concrete deck. Others, in rapid succession.
"What in hell was—"

"Fragments," said Tolliver. "They've got to fall somewhere."

The caller. Eiferts answered, swore. "Ignore the bloody bearing,
joey! Give us full power until it burns out."

"Christ, we're late! Break up, damn you!"

I held my breath. The mass was streaking downward. What were
they throwing, laserproof rocks?

I glanced at the screen. No more were being launched. If we could
get this one, we stood a chance.

"There she goes!" Jameson, with a yell of triumph. A large hunk of
the jagged rock broke off, disintegrated.

Tolliver cursed. "The puter's following the wrong piece!"

I shouted, "Go manual! No time!"

Tolliver twirled up the magnification, twisted the fire control. "Where
is—Got it! Oh, Christ, it's—"

A groan. I turned to Eiferts. He looked into my eyes, made the sign
of the Cross. I spun my chair to the console.

Jameson said, "Jesus, another rock, far out!"

The door swung open. "Sorry it took so long, sir. I had to brew a
fresh—"

The stupendous blast blew Bezrel into my arms. My chair flew backward into the console. The building screeched. Walls buckled. The room
went dark. I sat dazed and deafened as debris rained from the ceiling.

Silence.

Someone coughed, gagged. Dawn's light pierced the shattered wall.

Eiferts lay on his back, an arm thrust over his face. A jagged piece of wood protruded from his chest. His shirt was drenched red.

Bezrel clung to me, whimpering. I rocked, cheek nuzzling the boy's soft hair as I'd sat eons before with my little Nate. It would be all right. I hugged him close.

It would be all right.

21

Tolliver groaned. Blood dripped from his forehead; he wiped it clear of his eyes. The dark red stain sank into the blue sleeve of his jacket. Dust motes drifted in the intense silence of the splintered morn.

"Are you hurt, sir?"

"No. Look to Mr. Eiferts." I rocked the boy, trying to breathe through the thick choking dust.

Tolliver staggered to his feet, lurched across the room. He knelt at Eiferts's side, felt for a pulse. He shook his head.

"See who is alive."

"Aye aye, sir." He knelt over Jameson. "He doesn't seem wounded, sir. Just knocked cold." Samuels was on his feet, gagging. Tolliver made the rounds. "Is Mr. Bezrel gone, sir?"

"Don't say that!" The boy raised his head. "I'm not dead."

"Thank Lord God." Tolliver.

Bezrel realized where he lay, thrust himself clear of me, cheeks scarlet. "I'm sorry, I—honest, sir!"

"It's all right, boy." My tone was gruff. I looked about. "Let's get out before the building falls."

"We'll need to carry Jameson."

"I can help," I said. If I moved slowly, breathed carefully. The swirling dust made me cough, and my healed incision ached. I bore it.

As I bent to lift the tech a great whomp of power pounded my chest. I pitched on top of the unconscious man. A muffled thud built to a roar. The building swayed. I scrambled to my knees. "Lord Christ, what was—"

"The other rock!" Tolliver was grim.

"Get Jameson out of—"

A tremendous crash. The roof buckled.

"What the—"

A drumbeat of whomps and thuds that seemed as if it would never end. I grabbed Bezrel, sheltered him against my chest. Tolliver crouched over Jameson.

The deadly rain built to a crescendo that hammered the wounded building. Finally it eased, as the debris flung upward by the rock settled back to earth. At length, all was still. The roof gave an ominous creak.

I took a shaky breath, wrenched open the door.

Outside was a landscape of hell. Every tree in the vicinity was in splinters. A pall of smoke billowed across the parade ground. The field had twisted, as if wrenched by an earthquake.

"Sir, the roof may not hold. We have to get the men out."

"All right."

We set Jameson on the steps, went back inside. Two of the techs were conscious, one moaning in pain.

Of the seven who'd been in the room, only Eiferts was dead. We left him where he lay; no time for him now. I uttered a short prayer under my breath.

"Where did it hit?" Samuels.

"I don't know." I sat unsteadily on the steps. "The first rock took out the cannon. A direct hit."

"It couldn't have." Tolliver squinted at the devastation to the south. "Why not?"

"We're still here. If a rock that big struck so close . . ."

I grunted. "It doesn't matter. The lasers are out."

"Look at the administration building," said Tolliver. Blood dripped down his face.

There was nothing to see. Only jagged strumps of wall were left.

Jameson moaned, began to waken. I said to Rawlings, "Is there a first-aid kit?"

The tech frowned, nodded. "Inside, sir. In the cupboard."

"Can you get it?"

"I won't go back there. The roof's about to fall."

I pointed to Tolliver. "My midshipman needs a bandage."

Rawlings said, "Get it yourself."

I stood abruptly, waited for dizziness to pass. Bezrel said quickly, "I'll go, sir."

"Very well." I glared at the obstinate tech.

"The other rock must have hit farther away." I spoke to distract Tolliver.

"Much farther." Abruptly he sat. When Bezrel returned with the kit I wrapped gauze around Tolliver's forehead. Done, I clapped him on the shoulder. "Are you well enough to get up?"

"Of course." He stared at the ruins across the field. "Now what?"

"There's nothing for us here. We have to get back to Central—" Lord God.

Our heli had been on the parade ground.

"Do you swim well?" Tolliver's smile was crooked.

"Let's look around."

"What happened to the personnel carrier? It would save a hike."

He got up, went around the side of the building. The carrier lay on its side atop a shredded clump of bushes. "On the other hand, it might be easier to walk."

I let it pass. He was giddy from loss of blood.

I left the two techs with Jameson, trudged with Tolliver and Bezrel across the field toward the smoking vegetation beyond. We came on pieces of our heli. The cab and engine compartment were crumpled as if a giant fist had hurled them across the field.

"Not even a radio." Tolliver pawed disgustedly through the rubble.

"The base has plenty of callers."

"Where, sir?"

I frowned at the remains of the admin building. Not there. "There was a dish at the laser building."

"It's gone now. And the power is out." Gingerly he touched his head. "What next, sir?"

"Let's see where the last rock hit."

The Venturas Base laser cannon had been mounted on a ridge south of the parade ground to provide a clear field of fire in virtually any direction. As we moved south the ground was warmer. Atop the ridge, clumps of grass still burned. All that remained of the laser cannon were blasted stumps of metal and plastic, laced with jagged ropes of conduit like spaghetti.

Beyond the emplacement the ground had sloped gently for some miles to the sea. We halted atop the shattered ridge, stunned by the panorama of devastation below.

A pall of smoke obscured much of the crater. For as far as we could see, fires glowed with hellish intensity in the subdued, smoky light. The trees had been blown down like matchsticks, pointing away from the crater in great concentric circles. I wondered if flames would spread as far as the groves along the coast. If so, the forest would take generations to recover.

Tolliver pointed to the hillock. "If this ridge hadn't sheltered us, we'd be dead."

I grunted. "That's as may be. Come along."

"Where, sir?"

"Back to the others, I suppose."

Hands in my pockets, I trod across the crumpled parade ground.

Tolliver was silent most of the way, but when we neared the laser control building he said, "What I'd give for some water . . ." I tried to hide my shame. He'd been injured, and I'd just led him on a pointless forced march.

When we reached the building Jameson had regained consciousness. He huddled with the other techs, as if for comfort.

"Did the laser building have water?" I faced Rawlings, the tech who'd refused to go inside.

"Used to. Dunno about the pipes anymore."

I held in my annoyance. "Mr. Bezrel, would you volunteer to look?"

"Of course, sir." He cast a scornful look at the tech.

"See if the water is on. Fill something. Use your coffeepot, if you can find it."

"Aye aye, sir." I fidgeted while he was gone. What would possess me to send a boy into a collapsing building? Yes, he was smaller, more agile, but . . . I tried to hide my relief when he emerged carrying the dented pot and some plastic cups. We had water, at least for the moment.

"Here, sir." His eyes were troubled.

I handed the pot to Tolliver. "What happened, Mr. Bezrel?"

His answer was quick. "Nothing, sir." He hesitated. "The pot was lying near Mr. . . . Mr. . . ."

"I understand." Embarrassed, I kicked a tuft of grass, looked around. The long walk had taken something out of me. If we only had the carrier. It didn't seem damaged. Could it be made to run? It was balanced precariously on its side; perhaps if all of us heaved . . .

"You men, come here. See if we can right this machine."

Jameson stood, a bit unsteadily. Rawlings said, "Why bother? There's no place to go."

Tolliver put down the water pot, unstrapped his holster. He drew his laser pistol, thumbed off the safety. "Permission to execute him, sir."

I stared into Tolliver's eyes. Would he know to wait? And if not, did I care? "Granted."

Tolliver leveled the pistol. Rawlings leapt to his feet. "No, wait, I'll help! Jesus!"

"Very well." We were under wartime regs; I ought to warn them. I shrugged. Now, they knew.

After several tries we managed to rock the carrier upright. The door was stuck; I had to slide in from the passenger side. Keys were still in the ignition. I turned them and the vehicle came to life.

We all climbed in. I drove around the base, checking the ruins of the various buildings. We found no sign of Sergeant Trabao or the other volunteers. To the southwest, the base power plant was in ruins.

Though the mess hall sagged, it still stood; the admin building had sheltered it from the worst of the blast.

North along the perimeter road sat the shuttle hangar. Its side wall was cracked, and in places the block had crumbled to rubble. Inside, the shuttle looked undamaged—no, it had been hit. Portholes were shattered by fragments of rock. The airframe was dented, but seemed unpierced. I walked around to the front of the building, tried the huge counterbalanced hangar door. It wouldn't budge. Looking up I saw the reason: the track on which it rolled was twisted and bowed.

I walked outside to the carrier and slumped on my seat. Now what? We had no heli, no radio, nothing but a carrier and three sullen techs. Without power, how long could we count on fresh water?

With two huge rocks, the fish had wiped out our western base and with it all our groundside firepower. I looked up, knowing I wouldn't see a third rock until it was right above us. I shuddered. Lord God, if it came, let it be a direct hit. No pain, no fire.

Rawlings followed my thoughts. "Let's get out before they throw another."

"Why should they bother? We're wiped out."

"Do they know that? And would they care?" His face twisted in fear. "Drive, joey!"

"Where? Into the forest? A rock has as good a chance—"

With a cry of rage Rawlings hauled me out of the carrier, reached for the key.

He died in agony.

Tolliver sheathed his pistol. I doubled over and retched.

"Sorry, sir." Tolliver's voice was unsteady.

I held on to the carrier door. "You did as you should." I made my voice sharp as I turned to the techs. "You men are U.N.A.F., aren't you? You volunteered for this duty!"

Swallowing, Jameson turned from the blistered corpse. "He shouldn't have tried to take your carrier, but . . . what's left to fight for, Captain? It's over."

Over? We had duty. While life remained—somehow, we had to . . . had to . . . What? I sank onto the carrier seat, my back to the grisly remains.

"Sir?" Tolliver waited, but I said nothing, lost in desolation. Tentatively he said, "Maybe Rawlings was right about not staying here. Where they could hit us with rocks, I mean."

"They can throw rocks anywhere."

"But they're aiming them here." He peered at the sky. "Have you decided what to do?" I shook my head. "Could we go somewhere else, sir, while you think?"

My voice was dull. "All right. You and—what's your name? Samuels? Get his . . . body out of there. How far does this road take us?"

"To the celuwall factory, sir. About twenty miles."

"Bring rations and water."

I sat in the passenger seat, head down, hugging myself while we bounced past broken and uprooted trees toward the forest beyond.

We set up camp under a leafy canopy near the end of the road. Here, in silent virgin forest, one could imagine all was well in the Venturas.

The others huddled near a fire Tolliver had started with his pistol. I sat alone in the carrier. Bezrel brought me coffee; I took occasional sips until it grew cold and stale.

The day passed. Bezrel came with Q-rations. I left them untouched. When Tolliver tried to prod me further I ordered him away. After they'd all settled to sleep by the fire in blankets they'd scrounged from the rubble of the base, I remained in the carrier, staring through the windshield into the night.

It was over. I had done my duty, and had failed. The fish were masters of Hope Nation. Sooner or later they'd obliterate Centraltown, and do whatever it was they lived for, and go on.

I would die here.

Annie would die in Centraltown, where I'd abandoned her.

We had no way to reach Eastern Continent; our only heli was gone. No way to call for help; the radios were smashed. No way to fight the fish; the only laser emplacements we had were on Orbit Station, and we had no way to go aloft. The dented shuttle was locked in the ruined hangar, and even if we could get it out, it was too damaged to put us into orbit. Even if I reached the Station, I wouldn't be of use; William fired our lasers with pinpoint accuracy on his own. The Station had no ship for me to sail, and no crew to help man it.

It was over.

The night air grew even cooler. I hunched in the seat of the carrier, jacket wrapped around me, struggling for a way to give meaning to what was left of our lives. A way to fight on.

What were the fish, and why did they follow us? What did they want? How could we make them stop coming? If we couldn't defeat them with ships and lasers, how could we prevail? Was humankind destined to fall?

Were we to be driven from our hard-won planets back to dark caves, to raise fearful children who never knew bright cities? How could we stop these marauders who lunged at us from the void?

In my desperation, I clasped hands and prayed to Lord God, though I knew full well that His face was forever turned from me, and that my prayer was worse than useless. I sat, empty and alone, until the sky lightened with the forlorn promise of morn. I raised my head, left the carrier, walked on unsteady legs to the embers of the fire. I stooped for twigs and small branches from the pile they'd made the night before.

I froze, not daring to breathe.

After a time, I warmed my hands at the fire in the stillness of the dawn. Tolliver woke, raised his head. I stared at him, heart pounding. I could not speak of what I might do.

But I knew a way.

Part 4

September, in the year of our Lord 2200

22

"Coffee, sir?" Tolliver sat beside me.

I wrapped my hands around the steaming cup to steal its warmth. "Assemble the men."

"The me— Aye aye, sir." It must have seemed an odd request; Bezrel and the two techs constituted our entire force, and were all within calling distance.

A moment later I faced them. "We're going back." Samuels muttered something like an objection; I directed my words to him. "I'm your commanding officer. I said we're going back to the base."

"Why, sir? It's dangerous." It was almost a challenge, but he'd called me "sir"; he hadn't crossed the line to mutiny.

"It's been fifteen hours and they've thrown no more rocks. We can't stay here indefinitely, and there's work to do."

Jameson stirred. "Work? At what? Everything's wrecked; we'd just as well live in the wild until we're sure it's safe. They say there was a deserter once—"

"Yes, Captain Grone. I've heard of him." And met him. "You'll go with me for now. When we're done, I'll give you a chance to come back here to stay." He made as if to protest. I overrode him. "That's an order."

His discipline held. "Yes, sir."

"Into the carrier."

We rumbled back along the trail. As we neared the base my fingers closed over the armrest. We maneuvered past rubble and downed trees, pulled up between the shattered admin building and the damaged hangar. "Mr. Tolliver, scout for weapons; there'll be laser rifles somewhere. While you're at it, find us food. Mattresses and blankets too. And tents or field equipment."

Tolliver looked dubiously at the bombed-out base. "Aye aye, sir."

"You other men come with me." I started toward the hangar.

The side door was locked, but we climbed through gaping holes in the broken wall. Inside, the hangar was dark and cold.

The shuttle, one of the U.N.A.F.'s smaller models, sat in the center of the hangar bay, its stubby wings folded back. My stomach knotted as I approached; were it too badly damaged my plans would crumble. I circled the craft, stopping at the starboard side.

The shuttle had been peppered by debris as if some great shotgun had blasted it with scraps of shot and broken nails. The pilot's side window was completely gone. Jagged pieces of transplex were all that remained of two portholes.

On the port side near the bow, the skin of the craft was scraped and dented. Underneath the shuttle a large chunk of cement lay on the floor in fragments. I reached up, ran my fingers across the alumalloy panels. Perhaps at that spot critical wiring ran below the skin. But if not, the damage wasn't fatal.

I opened the control panel, slapped open the hatch, clambered in.

The passenger cabin was almost untouched. A few chips of concrete lay where they had fallen through the portholes, but they were nothing; the middy could sweep them up in minutes. I moved on to the cockpit. The chunk of debris that smashed the pilot's window had fetched up against the dash. The copilot's console was smashed; wires dangled onto the yoke. The second throttle ball was snapped clean off.

Would the ship fly? I leaned out of the missing pilot's window and shouted, "Everyone stand clear!" I opened the ignition keypad. If a password had been set . . .

It hadn't. The shuttle responded to the default code. I flipped on battery power. In a moment the puter responded with a green light. "Checklist, oral," I told it.

A tinny voice. "Checklist begins. Portholes thirty-three and twelve not responding to sensor check; cabin pressure unachievable. Aerodynamic integrity is compromised. Damage to fuselage, port side. Copilot's fuel gauge is inoperative. Copilot's cabin pressure gauge inoperative. Copilot's altimeter inop—"

"Halt checklist. Bypass copilot's console. Reassign all controls to pilot's console." Why couldn't I talk to a puter without beginning to sound like one? "Resume checklist."

A few moments later the puter ground to a halt. "Fuel at capacity. Navaids programmed to anticipated location, orbit station. Craft is inoperable due to checklist items one, two, three, nine, twelve through fifty-four, and sixty through—"

"Cancel report. Do we have control of jet landing engine, rudder, ailerons, and flaps from pilot's console?"

"Affirmative." Did the puter sound peevish?

"Report on rocket engine damage."

"No known engine damage."

I glanced out the porthole. Bezrel stood well clear, his mouth agape. Jameson was at his side. "Low power jet engine check."

"Aft, stern, and starboard sensors indicate the craft is inside hangar. Engine check not possible within hangar."

"Yes, it is." Our brakes would hold us. As long as I shut down after a few seconds, the hangar wouldn't accumulate enough exhaust fumes to roast Jameson and Bezrel. If we scorched the rear wall, so be it.

"Safety regulations do not permit jet engine check at any power level within hangar."

"Override safety regs."

The pilot's console switched on. A light turned green; the console beeped three warning tones; the engines caught with a sudden roar. They muted almost instantly as the puter throttled down to minimum power. Below, Bezrel and the tech held their hands over their ears.

"Active control systems check."

Perhaps the puter had given up on me; at any rate, he made no further protest. Ailerons, rudder, and flaps moved ponderously as the puter went through a series of checks. "Engine off."

The green lights blinked off; the last echoes of the engine died. "Low power test indicates response from pilot's console at low power, and no apparent engine damage. Control systems respond normally."

"Very well. End of test." I reached for the battery switch.

"Warning: low power engine test does not verify that engine will perform at full power. Control systems damage may become evident only at suborbital—"

"End report." I didn't need to hear that; I didn't even want it suggested. I left the pilot's seat, stopped short. "Contact Orbit Station."

A silence. Then, "No contact."

I swallowed a chill of foreboding. The shuttle was under the hangar roof. Surely that was the reason. "Systems off."

I climbed down, crossed the hangar floor to the tech and the boy. "This hangar was equipped for repairs. Find me ladders and welding torches."

"Can I ask what for, sir?" Jameson.

"The hangar door is jammed shut. We're going to cut it free."

"That would take days!"

I studied the door. "I don't think so."

"Look at that shuttle. You expect to fly it?" The tech grimaced at the dented fuselage.

My voice sharpened. "I expect you to cut away the hangar door. Get what we need." I let my hand slide toward my pistol.

"Yes . . . sir." He turned away.

Tolliver poked his head through the broken wall. He climbed through the debris, loped toward me with a grin, snapped a pro forma salute. "We'll eat today, sir. And I found weapons. Samuels, bring in the knapsack."

"Good." I studied the hangar door. "Tolliver, you'd better take charge here. These techs are not . . . I want the door cut away." I turned back to the shuttle.

"What for, sir?"

I spun around. "You too? I gave an order!"

"Aye aye, sir." Tolliver seemed unfazed. "I wasn't questioning you. I'd work better if I understood, though."

"You would, eh?" I came toward him, my voice menacing. His eyes were bleary. His bandage was stained with sweat and dirt. My rage dissolved. "I need to get the shuttle out of the hangar, Mr. Tolliver."

"You can't launch her, sir. With the portholes out she'd break up before you could get her orbital."

"I know that. I don't intend to go orbital."

"But . . . it isn't a heli, sir. Her thrusters won't handle low-level flight more than a few minutes without overheating." He looked at me as if wondering if I'd forgotten.

"I know that too. Mr. Tolliver, I want that doorway cleared."

His glance was skeptical, but he nodded.

I peered upward, shielding my eyes against the glare.

They hadn't found ladders, but they'd brought scaffolding, which was more useful. The torches and acetylene tanks had been stowed in the hangar lockers.

Tolliver had suggested we cut the couplings that anchored the door track to the hangar wall, but I vetoed that. The huge door was immensely heavy, and we couldn't control which direction it would topple. And once the door fell to the ground, we'd have to cut it into movable pieces, to cart it out of our way.

Instead, they were taking the door down a piece at a time.

The bottommost sections were the easiest. Tolliver and a tech cut them loose; as soon as the scraps cooled, Bezrel, the other tech and I hauled them away. When the cutters showed signs of fatigue I bade them change places. Bezrel kept us supplied with water and softies he'd pried out of the dispenser.

I didn't have goggles; we'd only found two pair. After a time, dazzled by the cascade of white heat falling from the torches, I strolled again around the shuttle, looking for damage. Jameson detached himself from the others and wandered after me. I waited, steeling myself for more objections.

He kicked the pavement. "Sorry about how I've been acting," he said. "It's just—we knew the risk of staying behind, but when you actually face it . . . it's harder."

I nodded, much relieved. "I know."

"The fleet's gone, the base is gone . . . the fish wipe out whatever we put against them." He shivered. "Is the colony doomed, sir?"

"It may be," I said. He deserved honesty. "But we're not dead yet." I crossed to the hangar's side door, found I could open it from the inside. "Let's get some air."

"I'll have to relieve Samuels in a minute." He followed me outside.

"How long have you been in system?" It gave me something to say.

"Ten years." He kicked at a surviving strand of grass. "I was in Engineering on the Station, then in Centraltown. They sent me here a year ago."

I grunted. "You've seen the place grow—"

"You were right to relieve General Khartouf." He averted his gaze.

"I shouldn't discuss that." I realized how fatuous that sounded in the rubble of the ruined base. "In any event, he's long gone. Mr. Eiferts would have made the base ready, if he'd had time."

"He was a mover." Wearily, Jameson sat on the grass. He chewed at a blade, squinting at me. "We needed the generator fully on-line. If the Navy had stayed awhile longer—" The blade of grass dropped from his mouth.

"They did their best."

Jameson swallowed, pointing at my shoulder. "Oh, Jesus!"

I slapped at my jacket. A spider? A snake? No, idiot, Hope Nation has no animal life. "What are you—"

His mouth working, Jameson lurched to his feet, fled to the hangar. What was wrong with the man? I turned, saw nothing. My glance strayed upward.

"Lord save us!" I raced to the side door, as if the hangar's pitiful shelter could protect us from the living dirigible a thousand feet above.

I slammed the door behind me. "Tolliver! Break out the arms!"

For a moment he gaped. "What's—Aye aye, sir!" He scrambled off the scaffold. In the corner, Jameson retched.

"Laser rifles! Shoulder missiles! Anything!" I was beside myself. Bezrel seemed confused. "Move, boy! Grab a gun!" I realized I had nothing but my pistol. Did it even have a charge? My hand fumbled at my holster. The green light glowed when I pressed the test. Charged or not, a puny pistol wouldn't do much good.

Tolliver raced back, a laser rifle in hand. "What is it, sir?"

"Fish!" I crouched to the opening we'd cut in the bottom of the hangar door. I gestured skyward.

Tolliver clutched the rifle as if a treasured toy, but shook his head. "Rifles won't bother anything that big, sir."

The fish pulsed, its skin changing color briefly. It drifted lower.

Bezrel raced back with a pair of laser rifles. I grabbed mine, flipped the safety, and waited for a full charge. When it beeped I knelt at the cutaway opening under the huge hangar door. I aimed at the underside of the fish. When I fired, colors swirled. A portion of the fish's body seemed to deflate. Then the outer skin seemed to flow over itself, and the hole was gone.

"My God." Tolliver dropped onto one knee. He squeezed off a long burst that put an angry slash in the side of the fish.

The fish settled ominously lower.

I said, "Jameson, where's Samuels?"

"Running for the woods, last I saw." The tech's voice was acid.

"Bezrel, come outside with me. Tolliver, you and Jameson cut those bloody track couplings off. Let the hangar door fall where it may."

Tolliver said doubtfully, "If we cut the door loose we'll have no protection, sir."

I pointed at the bottom four feet they'd already severed. "What protection does this leave?" I didn't wait for an answer. "Hurry."

I ducked under the door and glanced up. The fish was a mere two hundred feet over the field.

From inside, Tolliver's voice. "Why are we trying to free the shuttle, sir?" He added, "I'll do it, but I'd like to know why we're suiciding rather than running for safety."

"We can get away in the shuttle."

"It's built for orbital flight, not—"

The fish lurched lower, its stern blowhole working. I growled, "Don't you think I know that? Cut, Tolliver! Quick!" I sprinted toward the parade ground. Bezrel followed with his rifle. "Fire!" I gasped.

"Where should I aim, sir?" He dropped to his knee, aiming.

"Anywhere!" My beam burned a new hole in the descending fish. Above it, a ropy mass formed and began to swirl.

The fish jerked, but drifted ever lower. Its tentacle swung. I warned, "Don't let that hit you, boy! Jump clear if it lets fly!"

"Aye aye, sir!" Our laser fire raked the side of the great beast. Its skin began to repair the holes; the fish sank lower, tilting aft. Its appendage swung around, broke loose, sailed toward us.

Bezrel scampered to safety with the speed of youth. Winded, I could only watch the protoplasm gyrate through the air. A shrill voice cut through my fog. "Run, sir!"

As the mass whirled toward my head I fell to the ground. A rush of warm air. The appendage struck a few feet past me. Grass sizzled.

Another arm formed. The fish was no more than fifty feet above us. I set the rifle for continuous fire, held down the trigger until long after the warning beep.

The wounded fish sank to the ground, colors fading to mottled gray. I stumbled to my feet, backed away with my useless rifle.

The body of the fish appeared to be dissolving. The skin became indistinct; colors swirled. Outriders. "Bezrel, run!" I leaped over the smoking mass the fish had flung.

As I ran I glanced over my shoulder. A shifting shape seemed to grow from the skin of the fish. It swirled, wriggled free, fell from the fish's side. "Bezrel, back to the hangar!" My legs pumped.

The outrider skittered even faster than the one I'd once seen in *Telstar*'s corridor. It was only steps behind me. I knew I wouldn't make the haven of the hangar.

Suddenly Tolliver dropped from the scaffold a meter in front of me, his rifle light glowing. He aimed directly at my face. I blanched; even the fish's acid was a better death. In desperation I hurled my empty rifle at him, dived to the ground. Tolliver fired over my head. Behind me something smoked and sizzled. He bounded forward, hauled me to my feet. "Move!"

I scrambled under the door. More shapes swirled on the mottled skin of the dying fish. Above, on the scaffold, sparks showered from Jameson's torch.

"Where are the bloody recharge packs?"

"I have a few." Tolliver ducked outside, retrieved my rifle, handed it to me. I took it, careful to avoid his eye. I jammed in the charge. "Bezrel, recharge!"

The boy didn't answer. I looked around. He was nowhere in sight.

A scream from above. *"Look out!"* Jameson.

I whirled. A shape scuttled through the far end of the open hangar door. For a split second it stood quivering. Then it rolled toward us with frightening speed. While I fumbled at my rifle, Tolliver fired. The outrider seemed to fly apart. I flinched. The alien collapsed into an oozing puddle.

I stared at the foul mess. A near thing. Tolliver knelt at the hangar opening and fired again. Above him, the door groaned and sagged; a coupling had finally parted. But there were many more to sever. We hadn't the time.

"Lord God damn them!" My voice was thick. "What do they want? Why won't they let us alone!" I stooped through the opening, fired at a whirling shape, and, beyond caring, stalked toward the parade ground. Only Tolliver, Jameson, and I were left. No way to escape, nothing to escape for. I felt a pang of regret for my life, a deeper pang for the boy's; he'd had more of his life stolen.

The fish lay where it had fallen, its colors finally still, its mottling fading even as I watched. Behind me I heard the snap of Tolliver's rifle. Outriders continued to emerge from the motionless mass. Something skittered toward me; I stood my ground, firing until it melted.

A patch of blue caught my eye about fifty feet to the side: Midshipman's Bezrel's body, pathetically small. I checked my dwindling charge; enough to put him out of his misery, if need be. I couldn't leave him to the aliens. Ignoring Tolliver's shout of protest I tramped across the seared grass. Better if Admiral De Marnay had left the boy home, to play at balls and kites and Arcvid.

An outrider rolled toward us, barely visible against the browned grass. I fired simultaneously with Tolliver; the creature melted to the ground.

Bezrel's head moved.

Heart pounding, I dropped on one knee. "Are you all right?" A hoarse whisper.

"Yes, sir!"

"What in God's own name are you doing?" I kept my rifle ready, risked a glance behind me.

He crawled toward me, slithering in an effort to stay low. "I ran out of charge, and those things were coming . . . I thought if I stayed down they wouldn't see me."

I bit back a snarl of fury. His ploy had worked, while I'd nearly gotten myself killed running away. "Still have your rifle?"

"Yes, sir."

"Hang on to it. Take some breaths, get to your knees, and run to the hangar as if Satan himself were after you!"

"He is, sir!" Abruptly the boy swarmed to his feet and sprinted off. He was fast; I doubted even Tolliver could catch him.

Two outriders paused, sensed his moving figure. They skittered across the grass. As if we'd planned it, Tolliver and I waited until one approached our killing zone, fired together. The outrider lurched and melted. We turned our fire on the second shape.

Bezrel flung himself to safety under the hangar door. My rifle beeped; it was running out of charge. Tolliver waved a fist. My teeth bared in a feral grin.

Cautiously I backed toward the hangar, keeping to the side to leave Tolliver a clear field. Only one outrider charged me; I couldn't tell which of us hit it.

Elated, I stumbled to the hangar, reached the door unharmed. A shadow moved through the scorched grass of the field. I looked up.

A second fish floated above.

Cursing, I stooped under the door. Sparks fell on my shoulders; I slapped them away. "Tolliver, there's another one!"

"Christ." Tolliver backed away, squinted at the door. "Jameson, get that track *down!*"

The tech's voice was savage. "You want a miracle, make one yourself!" I shook Tolliver's shoulder, shushed him. Jameson was doing his best.

"We're down to four recharges, sir."

"Two." I stooped, took one, gave another to Bezrel, crossed to the other end of the door. The boy followed like a puppy.

I knelt, turned off the safety, aimed. Three outriders were in sight on the field, too far away to risk a shot. "Mr. Tolliver, help Jameson cut. Bezrel, take position at the far end of the hangar. Here's your last recharge. Make every shot count."

I peeked under the door. The fish overhead had settled closer.

Sparks cascaded onto my head. Cursing, I moved aside. By the time I knelt again, the outriders had crossed half the field. I fired. The closest went down. Bezrel, face ashen, held his beam open as he sprayed the parade ground. I screamed, "Middy, single fire! Make every electron count!"

The two remaining outriders flew at us. I fired twice, hit a shape just as it jerked and sagged from Bezrel's hit. The other flowed over its fallen comrade, veered away from Bezrel and the open door. I fired until it dived around the outside of the hangar. I whirled to the shattered side wall, waiting. Nothing appeared.

The hangar door groaned. Pieces of coupling sagged and dripped to the floor.

Still, the door held. Tolliver cursed, moved to the next brace. Only two remained, but they held the track. If I ever got out I'd complain to Engineers' Corps.

"The fish is landing!" Bezrel waved frantically at the field.

Jameson moved to the last coupling on his side of the scaffold. "Christ, I hope this thing falls right. If it collapses on us . . ."

"Be ready to jump clear!" If the door fell inward it would knock over the scaffold and crush anyone underneath.

"Jump, sure." He shook his head in disgust, but his torch was steady.

"The fish! The fish!" Bezrel's voice was a scream.

I whirled. The alien had settled to the field, colors swimming. Shapes were already swirling to the surface. I raised my rifle. "Steady, Mr. Bezrel." I turned back to the side wall.

"When should I put in the last charge, sir?" The boy's tone was unsteady.

"When your current one is empty." I made sure to sound gentle, despite the idiocy of the question.

Tolliver called down, "Mine still has half a charge, sir."

"Hang on to it for now. Toss it down if I yell."

"Right." A shower of sparks.

"Jesus!" Bezrel clutched his gun. "They're coming!"

I spun around, peered at the field. Five, at least. If we waited for a close shot they'd all be on us. I aimed, pretending calm. Behind me Sergeant Swopes strode the firing line, swagger stick propped on his shoulder, his young charges lined up in a row opposite the targets. "Do not jerk the trigger, gentlemen, squeeze it. Steady . . ."

One down.

"Single fire, gentlemen . . . Don't waste your charge . . ."

Missed the son of a bitch.

"Sight before you fire."

Gotcha! Where in hell are the rest?

Sarge's voice faded. On the Academy firing line a flick of his baton was the only penalty if you missed target.

Bezrel shrieked, triggering his empty weapon at the shape hurtling at him. I had no time to aim. I flicked the switch to automatic and fired past his hip. The alien dissolved no more than a meter from his feet.

"Reload, Bezrel!"

"Yes, sir. I mean, aye aye, sir!" He fumbled at the recharge, dropped it, scrambled after it as it rolled away.

I glanced to the side wall, back to the parade ground. Three more outriders skittered toward us.

"Watch the door!" Tolliver jumped over the scaffold rail, leaped to the ground.

The door crashed outward with a earth-shattering thud, blocking my view of the field. It fell atop the pieces of door that we'd already cut off. The near end of the door lay propped six inches off the ground.

Tolliver knelt and aimed. "Come on, you son of bitch!" Coolly, he held his fire until a shape was almost upon us. His finger twitched and it was down, oozing under the bright sunlight that flooded the terminal.

My rifle beeped. I reached for a recharge, found none. The snap of Bezrel's and Tolliver's rifles cut the silence.

Bezrel's rifle beeped.

I glanced back at the shuttle, ahead to the menacing shapes still emerging from the grounded fish. "Jameson, bring down the torch and tanks!" He gaped. "Move!" He grabbed the tanks and lowered them down to me.

They were heavier than I'd thought. I managed not to drop them. Jameson swarmed down the side of the scaffold, carrying the torch. I waited in helpless frenzy while he snapped the connections back into place.

I thumbed the ignition, turned on the gas. A small flame flickered. "Bezrel, Jameson, into the shuttle. Tolliver, warm the jet engines. Get everyone into suits."

"But—"

"*MOVE!*" The bellow tore at my throat. I dragged the hose outside, as far as it would go, and balanced on top of the huge fallen door in front of the hangar. A shape quivered, skittered toward me. I waited, my hand on the gas. When the alien had closed to fifteen feet I spun open the knob. Ten feet. A great gout of fire surged from the hose. Five feet. The shape veered, but too late. It dissolved in a red glow of hell.

I spun down the knob. Behind me an engine muttered, then roared.

Three outriders approached the inferno, rolled to a halt twenty feet away. I closed down the gas. We waited in stalemate. The nearest one's shape changed as I watched.

Behind me the engine abruptly silenced. I whirled. From the shuttle porthole Tolliver waved frantically at the hangar's side wall.

An outrider was almost through a ragged hole. Its inner portion bulged as it flowed through the wall. The shuttle engines coughed, started again.

"Come to me, you bastard!" I dragged the hose toward the wall. Behind me, the three outriders took the ground I'd abandoned. I flicked a wave of fire in their direction, spun back.

I was at the end of my hose. I tugged, stopped for fear I'd break the line. Outside, the three shapes waited, quivering.

I spun my knob to full. A gout of flame gushed, fell short of the shape emerging from the shattered wall. Cursing, I ran back toward the door, hurled a blast of fire at the three waiting outriders. Two moved aside, one wasn't fast enough. I grabbed a tank, tried to lift the second, couldn't hang on to them both. I kicked one over, shoved it toward the side wall. I needed only a meter. I dropped the second tank; it clanged on the concrete floor.

I strained until the hose went taut. The shape emerged from the wall. As it skittered toward me I spun the knob. It met the flame only five feet distant, rolled on, burning. I jumped aside, dropping the torch. The shape sizzled, melted to liquid. I peered outside. The outriders I'd seen there were gone.

I turned to the far side of the hangar. Nothing. Tolliver pounded his window, summoning me with shouts made inaudible by the bellow of the engines.

I ran to the shuttle hatch, clambered aboard. Tolliver, suited, was in the pilot's seat. He shouted, "Suit up!"

I thrust it on. Bezrel, strapped in, clutched the chair ahead. He seemed not to see me. Jameson, also suited, gripped a laser pistol. I clipped on the helmet. I asked Tolliver, "See any of them?"

"Not at the moment, sir."

"There's no time to move the door aside. Roll over it."

"We'll snap off the wheel assembly."

"We might." From the copilot's seat I slid the broken throttle forward. No response. "Puter, manual override! Disconnect safeties!"

"Disconnected by pilot order. Disconnect logged."

"Shut up." I thrust the throttle forward again. The engine's growl rose to a roar.

We lurched. I throttled back as we rolled toward the door. "Tolliver, can you fly this thing? What's takeoff speed? How much runway do we need?"

"I've never flown a shuttle. I don't have the slightest idea. We'll shake apart if you try to reach orbital speed, and you'll blow the engines if you use the take-off jets to fly all the way home!" He hesitated. "As to cruising, I could probably handle her. Here's your takeoff speed." He tapped the mark on the airspeed indicator. A hundred ten knots. "She's a short-runway craft, or she wouldn't be here."

I inched the shuttle to the fallen door until I judged our wheel was about to touch. I throttled down, up again. We glided forward, bumped the door. I jammed down the throttle. "Take her, Mr. Tolliver. You have a surer hand." I hated the admission.

Slowly, infinitesimally, he powered up, pressing our wheel against the edge of the door. The ship strained, but didn't move. With a curse Tolliver reversed jets; we glided back a foot or so.

At the hangar doorway, a shape appeared. It stood quivering, as if measuring the distance between us.

Tolliver throttled. The ship inched to the door, bumped. Tentatively, he throttled higher. He shook his head. "The wheel won't go over. Any harder and we'll lose it."

"Try!"

Face taut, he edged us on. The engines roared. Abruptly he powered down to idle. "You have any idea how much thrust we're applying? The wheel can't be rated for—"

The shape moved.

I took hold of the yoke, placed my feet on the rudders. The outrider drifted toward us, as if uncertain. I reversed the engines, throttled as smoothly as I could. We slid back from the door. "How long is the shuttle, and how big is the damned hangar?"

"We have about thirty feet behind us. But if you back the engines to the rear wall—"

"I'll blow the wall out."

"Or blow us sky high!"

I rolled the shuttle backward. Why in God's name didn't they teach us shuttle piloting at Academy? We'd learned helis, riflery, stellar navigation . . .

Tolliver peered through the porthole. "That's far enough!"

I nodded, reversed the engines again. "Hang on."

"What are you doing?"

"Jumping the bloody door!"

"Lord God!" He braced himself against the dash.

"Bezrel, Jameson, grab hold!" I held the brake with both feet, gunned the jets until I felt the ship fight against the restraint. Please, Lord. Make it work.

I let loose the brake, jammed the throttle to full. We lurched, gaining speed. Thirty feet to the door. The hangar walls slid past. Fifteen feet.

Five.

My helmet slammed into the cockpit ceiling. I bounced down to my seat. We still rolled. A second later the back wheels hit the fallen door, and nearly threw me from my seat.

"I've got it." Tolliver's hand was steady on the throttle.

Two shapes lunged at us from the side of the hangar. Tolliver turned the yoke to starboard; we bumped diagonally across the field past the dying fish. The outriders chased us with their odd rolling gait. Others emerged from the mottled fish and flowed toward us, like iron filings to a magnet. Tolliver throttled higher.

"Ease off! We have to make a turn at the end of the field!"

"Unless we get ahead of them now, they'll catch us when we turn." He held the throttle steady as we bounced across the grass. "Where are we going, once we're off the ground?"

"To Centraltown."

"We can't, I told you! With the portholes missing we'll shake apart going orbital, and if we try to jet that far, the engines will blow."

"I know." I glanced behind. About fifteen shapes pursued us. "Jameson, fire at anything near."

"For once in your life, stop being devious! What in hell are you up to?"

I forced my eyes back to the dash. "We'll take off and go suborbital."

"Sub—what are you talking about?"

"After takeoff, fly east and pull up her nose. We'll fire the rockets."

"That will—"

"After forty seconds, shut them off."

"We'll fall!" The wheels touched the runway, once smooth, now pitted from the blast of the rock the aliens had hurled at us.

"Yes. We'll glide back down as far as we can, then relight the jets. If we gain enough altitude, that will put us far enough east to jet home."

"Not far enough to reach land before the jets overheat. We haven't plotted ballistics; you have no idea where we'll end up." He throttled back as we neared the end of the runway. "If you don't blow us apart you'll blow the engines off the fuselage."

I gripped his arm. "I'm going to Centraltown. This is the only way there." I twisted the yoke, eased us to port. The ship turned slowly, majestically.

"Why not stay and fight? Better to die facing the fish!"

I snapped down my visor. "There's something I must do." I no longer had any doubt.

"What?"

My voice was even. "I won't tell you, Mr. Tolliver." If he knew, he wouldn't help fly the shuttle. I lined us up in the center of the runway. "Once you take off, swing east." I peered through the porthole. "You'd better hurry." The shapes rolled to intersect us.

Smoothly he pushed the throttle forward. Fifteen knots. The outriders changed direction, converged on us. We hurtled down the runway. Twenty knots. A few shapes were left behind; others scrambled alongside.

Ahead, more gathered. One waited in the center of the runway. Forty knots.

I had to strain to hear Tolliver's words. "Lord God, I repent of my sins." Fifty knots; I checked my straps. "Forgive me my trespasses." Sixty-five. "If I have offended Thee . . ." The rest was lost in the roar of the engines. The outrider in the center of the runway skittered toward us with lightning speed.

"Look out—"

"I see it!" As we bore down on the alien shape it launched itself at the cockpit. I reared back in my seat, hands over my face. Something smashed dark and wet into the pilot's windshield.

"Jesus God!" Goo dripped from the window. Tolliver peered through the mess, searching for the runway. Thick liquid seeped along the windshield toward the pilot's shattered porthole.

I shouted, "Left rudder! You're drifting!" Seventy-five knots.

Ahead, the runway was rumpled, where the blast from the rock had shifted the earth. We surged upward, bounced back onto the runway, losing speed. "Hold the nose down!" Sixty-five knots. The end of the runway soared toward us. Seventy.

"We won't make it!"

"Hold her down! Use the grass beyond the runway!"

He muttered, "Use the trees, you mean." The windbreak that had once stood at the far end of the parade ground was knocked askew by the blast, but branches still clawed upward to snatch us from the air.

Tolliver shoved the throttle as far forward as it would go. I measured to the end of the pavement, to the end of the grass. Ninety knots.

The trees. We hurtled along the grass. One hundred knots. The trees. One hundred five. *THE TREES.*

"Hang on." Tolliver pulled back the yoke, five knots short of indicated takeoff speed. The nose lifted with nightmare deliberation. Our rear wheels floated off the runway. Trees flung themselves at our undercarriage. A scrape. I braced for impact. Scant yards ahead, a clump of trees reared skyward. Tolliver yanked back on the yoke.

"We'll stall!"

No time for an answer. Our airspeed fell. We floated over the stand of trees. Tolliver dropped the nose. We fell toward the hillside, losing altitude, gaining speed. He leveled off and we were clear. For eons we soared over forest, our airspeed slowly rising. Finally, when it was safe, he gently pulled back on the yoke and we regained precious altitude.

He remarked, "Coming around to the east."

Thank Lord God. I asked, "At what height do we fire rockets?"

"How the hell would I know? Ask the puter!"

I flipped on the puter circuits. "Advise recommended altitude for rocket ignition."

The puter's response was immediate. "Impossible to achieve orbit with cabin damage."

"Never mind that. What's the recommended altitude?"

"Rocket engines on safety lock due to compromise of cabin integrity. Ignition will not occur at any alt—"

I pounded the dash. "Override all safeties! Manual ignition! Advise normal altitude for rocket ignition when cabin undamaged and pressurized."

"Recommended ignition five thousand feet. Safeties overridden. Override is log—"

"Christ!" Tolliver edged away from his porthole. Drops of goo hovered on the broken transplex. One flew off and hit the back of his seat.

I grabbed my pistol.

"Be careful with that!"

"I know." I aimed at the porthole, set the pistol to continuous beam, held the trigger. The goo smoked and vanished. The porthole glowed red. I aimed at Tolliver's seat. "Don't lean back." I fired at the seat back; its fabric melted instantly at the touch of the beam. The seat insulation glowed, broke into flames. I snapped off the pistol, slapped out the fire with my suited hand. "Don't sit back until it's cool."

"I'll have to lie back when we accelerate. Put something on the seat, so I don't have to touch . . . that."

"It's been vaporized." Nevertheless I unstrapped myself and went back to the cabin. Bezrel gripped his chair. His face was white, his lips wet with spittle. I reached into the storage compartment, found a blanket. A pillow fell to the floor. I thrust it at the boy. "Hold this." He hugged it, rocking.

I folded the blanket, laid it across Tolliver's seat, over the scorched hole I'd made. Cautiously he leaned back. "Four thousand feet. Sir, when we fire . . ."

"Yes?"

"If we don't burn long enough, we fall into the ocean. Too long and we may disintegrate."

"I know." I licked my lips. "Try forty seconds. Be ready to cut off if we shake too hard."

"Right. Whatever 'too hard' means."

Five thousand feet. Tolliver looked at me. I met his eye, nodded.

He keyed the master ignition; the three rockets caught with a thunderous roar. They flung me back into my acceleration seat.

Five seconds. I glanced down, found the altimeter. Six thousand feet.

Ten seconds. Buffeting. A weight settling on my chest. I panted for breath. Eight thousand feet. Ten thousand. The world grayed. We bumped over a rutted country road.

"Thirty seconds, sir!" Tolliver gripped the sides of his seat. The shuttle shook.

Twelve thousand feet. Thirteen. Turbulence was worse.

"Forty seconds!" With effort he reached for the ignition.

"No!" I fought to inhale. "Need . . . more altitude."

"We'll break up!"

"Go for thirty thousand!" I forced oxygen into my lung.

"We can't make thirty!" Bangs and thumps shook the cabin.

"Wait." I heaved to breathe.

"Sixteen thousand!" My head sank into the acceleration pads. They were soft, comfortable, warm. Tolliver's voice was distant. "Twenty-one thousand!"

One couldn't swim in the sea; it had been too polluted for nearly a century. But once I'd been to the beach with Father. The sand, above the high-water mark, was warm and comfortable. I wriggled luxuriously, eyes closed against the probing solar glare, while Father watched with silent disapproval. Something in the sea air made it hard to breathe.

"Captain, let me cut the engines!"

I dozed, annoyed by the incessant roar of the waves. "Twenty-five thousand!"

Silence. My body surged against the straps. As my ears cleared I heard an odd whistling. My chest heaved. Greedily I sucked at air. The roar of the engines had eased.

Tolliver held the yoke rigid, eyes straining past the glop on his windshield. I coughed, struggled to an upright position. I gasped, "Altitude?"

"Twenty-eight thousand and rising."

"Rising, with the engine off?"

"Even a cannonball goes up for a while. Wait."

We reached the top of our arc. In a moment the shuttle took on the gliding characteristics of a brick. We dropped precipitously despite Tolliver's best efforts. He said, "We'll have to fire the engines to hold altitude."

"I know." But after thirty minutes burn, they'd overheat. Shuttle jets were designed for landings and little else. I peered at the instruments. "Where are we?"

"Some four hundred miles out, according to the beacons."

Even at five hundred knots, we'd crash at least an hour short of landfall.

"Radio a Mayday, sir. If we ditch they can meet us with a heli."

I shook my head. "No. We need the shuttle."

"We won't make it. If we put down in the water, we might—"

"Fly us home!"

Twelve thousand feet. Tolliver slammed his fist into the chair. "God damn you, why?" He waved away my outrage. "You want me to fly this boat into the sea. All right, I'll die with you! Tell me why!"

I said hoarsely, "I need the shuttle. I can't say why."

"You're afraid I'll betray you?" he jeered. "To which enemy, Captain? The fish or the planters?"

I swallowed. "Mr. Tolliver, I can't tell you. Someday you'll under-stand."

"I don't want to waste my death, to no purpose."

"We have a purpose." The corners of my mouth twitched. "And we may not die. There's safety margin built into the engine specs. Just look at the hangar door."

After a moment his teeth bared in what might have been a smile. "We'll have to find out." His eyes strayed to the panel. "Eight thousand feet, sir. We'd better ignite."

"Yes." He lit the jets, and gradually our descent slowed. We flew in uneasy silence.

After a time I unbuckled my seat belt. "Watch the engine temps." He shot me a look of annoyance. I blurted, "Sorry. Nerves." Now I was apologizing to a middy. I smiled grimly.

In the fifth row I stooped and slid next to Bezrel. "Are you all right?"

"Yes, sir." He clutched at the pillow. I waited, but he said no more.

"We're all frightened, joey."

His expression was cautious. "I'm fine."

"All of us, Mr. Bezrel." I patted his knee, stood awkwardly.

"I want to go home." His voice was muffled in the pillow.

"We're almost there."

"No. Home."

Didn't we all. I went back to the cockpit, sat, strapped on my oxygen. "ETA?"

Tolliver muttered, "I don't think we have one."

I glowered.

After a moment he said, "Sorry, sir. Say, forty-five minutes."

Temperatures were high normal, but holding steady. I thumbed the caller. "Captain Seafort to Admiralty House or Governor's Manse. Acknowledge." No answer. I tried again; finally the response came.

"Manse to incoming heli. Mr. Seafort? We thought . . ."

"Is Admiralty House open?"

"No, sir."

The temperature crept toward the red line. "Where's Governor Hopewell?"

"Standing by, sir. I paged him. Here he comes."

"Zack?"

"Yes, lad." His gruff voice brought a welcome lump to my throat.

"We're not in the heli, we've got a shuttle. Clear the spaceport runway. Have a heli waiting. And find anyone who worked on the shuttle repair crews."

"Is that all?"

"Yes, but hurry. Our ETA is forty minutes." The temp needle hovered at the red line.

Tolliver tapped the altimeter. "We'll have to ditch."

"Get us altitude."

"That'll generate more heat."

"I know." But it would gain us time if the engines failed.

On landing jets we climbed slowly to eighteen thousand. The needle inched inexorably into the red. I checked the console. "Thirty minutes. Two hundred eighty miles."

"The engines won't last."

"They have to."

He cleared his throat. "Sir, do you understand that if we keep burning—"

"Don't argue!"

"I'm not. If we keep burning and we overheat, the bearings may melt. Even if we landed safely, these engines would never fire again."

I faced the bitter possibility. "We have to try."

He shook his head, chose to say nothing. The needle crept farther into the red. A warning signal beeped; I switched it off. Twenty-five minutes.

"Throttle back."

"We're at best performance speed now, sir."

"It might help the temp."

He throttled back. The temperature didn't go down, but at least it rose no further.

Twenty minutes.

The speaker crackled. "Incoming shuttle, we have you on radar. What are you—did you fly that thing from the Venturas?"

"Yes." He would think me glitched. He'd probably be right.

Eighteen minutes. "Mr. Tolliver, how far can we glide?"

"A few miles, at best. We're not high enough."

A hundred fifty miles from Centraltown. The temperature needle crept upward. So close, and yet . . .

"Shut off the jets."

"Now, sir? We'll fall into—" He saw my expression, snapped the switches.

"Mr. Tolliver, watch our distance. Mark off to thirty-five miles."

"We won't come near to—"

I ignited the rockets. Tolliver yelled, reached for the shutoffs. I was hurled into my seat. I strained at the yoke, kept us level.

"You can't burn rockets in flight mode! You'll tear off the wings!"

"Just for a few seconds!"

"You're insane!" He reached again for the switch; I slapped away his arm.

"Distance!"

"A hundred twenty miles!"

I forced the yoke back, easing us into a climb. The craft shook abominably. Stress indicators lit like Christmas lights.

"Sixteen thousand feet. One hundred two miles!"

I fought to hold the yoke, barely kept control.

"Plese, sir, turn it off!"

I reached for the master switch, diverted my fingers, found the two I wanted. I snapped them off. The turbulence eased.

"Christ, now what are you doing?"

"Flying on center rocket only." For as long as its fuel held out, or until the battered ship could take no more.

His hands tightened on the yoke. "Let me help control her." Gratefully I eased my pressure on the yoke. He said, "Are you aware, sir, that some of us prefer to stay alive?"

I glared at him. His eyes danced. "I could relieve you for this, you know. Trouble is, no one would believe me."

I watched the console. "Sixty miles. Twenty thousand feet. In a couple of minutes we might be close enough to glide in."

He shook his head. "After this, they'll have to rewrite the specs."

"Shuttle, your flight path is not, repeat, not appropriate for achieving orbit." The voice on the caller sounded anxious.

I grinned, keying the caller. "Very well, we'll alter course." My hand went to the console. "Shall we?"

"Ready, sir."

I cut the switches, and again the roar diminished to the whistle of wind. I watched the altimeter fall.

"We could try the jets again," he offered.

"Best let them cool first."

In a few moments we had no choice; we'd lost most of the altitude the rockets had gained. When Tolliver finally tried the jets they wouldn't catch; I thought we'd plow a furrow into the coast before he finally nursed them to life.

After that, the landing was rather dull.

23

"How long, then?"

The mechanic shrugged. "Who knows? We've got spare transplex for the portholes; they're standard parts. We drained and replaced your engine lubricants. No sign of engine damage, but we've only tested at low power. We're not done."

"How long?" I glanced at Zack Hopewell.

"Puter simulations say she'll never go into orbit with the side so badly dented. It'll have to be completely rebuilt—"

"*HOW LONG?*"

He tossed the specs to the floor. "Never, if you talk like that. I'm a volunteer, joey. I don't give God's own damn if—"

"You listen to me." Zack's voice was low and cold. "Have this machine ready to fly in two days, not an hour longer. We're under martial law and I won't hesitate to hang you if you don't." He took a step toward the mechanic; involuntarily the man darted back. "Understand me?"

The mechanic swallowed. "All right, go easy. But I can't promise no two days, not with tearing down the body—"

"I'll assign all the help you need. Get started!" Hopewell strode away, and I followed. He sighed. "Hang the man? Did you hear, Mr. Seafort? He's one of my countrymen."

"You saved me from making a fool of myself." I'd been ready to hurl myself at the mechanic's throat.

We walked toward Zack Hopewell's heli. He sat, looked up at me. "You're sure you've found a way?"

I climbed in next to him. "No, but I think so. With Lord God's blessing, you'll be safe again."

"Why won't you tell us what it is?"

My hand tightened on the door. "Change the subject. Please, I beg you."

"You won't return, after." It wasn't a question.

"I think not."

His lined face was without expression. "You carve your own destiny, Captain, as do we all. We'll miss you."

"Thank you."

"After you . . . go, there will be no Government."

"Yours is in place."

"But without authority. I will not pretend to rule by grace of a departed Navy."

We waited while Tolliver crossed the tarmac. He climbed into the heli's back seat. "Plenty of shuttle fuel on hand."

I grunted.

We lifted off. Hopewell said, "Is two days soon enough?"

"It'll have to be." I stared at the houses below. "I'll fly the shuttle alone."

Hopewell frowned. "I wish you'd—"

"You can't." Tolliver. I swung to him, my eyes dangerous. He said, "You'll pass out."

"I'll be all right."

"Yes, sir. What happened when we went suborbital?"

"That was just one—"

"And when we flew to the station with Jerence?" I had no answer. His eyes were intense. "We're only alive by grace of a miracle, sir. Don't ask for another. You can't handle acceleration with one lung."

"What do you want of me? The shuttle pilots were all U.N.A.F. and went with the fleet!"

"Yes." He looked out the window. "I may not be skillful, but I flew her once. Sir."

"We won't be com—" I chopped off the thought. There might be time for him, if I planned it carefully. "Very well. If you volunteer."

"Volunteer? Well, if I must. I'd like a shuttle rating added to my file, afterward."

"Shuttle rati—" I saw the smile he meant to hide. The man could be infuriating. "Very well." I would do it, if I remembered in time. Let him explain the ludicrous rating when he again met the Admiral.

Hopewell had listened to the byplay without a comment. Now he said, "I have a heli and pilot waiting for you at the Manse."

"Thank you." Tired beyond words, I puzzled where to go.

Tolliver prompted gently, "Your wife, sir."

I snarled, "Of course." The damned impudence.

Annie was asleep. I sat in the unfamiliar living room while the nurse stared into a flickering holo.

She'd told me Annie had seemed all right, the morning before. Then, when we hadn't returned as I'd promised, her mood had changed. She began to smash chairs against the wall. When the nurse intervened Annie clawed at her, keening. The nurse had finally managed to sedate her. Annie slept the night through and into the new day.

How long had it been since I'd had sleep? I needed to say my good-byes to Annie, to Alexi. Deal with the planters. Leave instructions for—

"She's asking for you." The nurse.

I snapped awake. I touched my tie, ran my fingers through my hair, glad of my bath and change of clothes when at last I'd seen my apartment. I hesitated, trying to recall where the bedroom was. The nurse pointed. "There."

"Thank you." I peered through the door. "Annie?"

Her look was puzzled, vacant. "Nicky? You din' come back when you say."

"I know, hon." I sat on the bed. "I'm sorry."

She threw off the sheet, hugged her legs. "I waited, an' you din' even call."

"We had problems, hon. The fish."

"I don' care 'bout no fish." She sat up, wriggled her toes. "I wan' get dressed. Got me a new blouse. Bet it go nice wid my jewels." She grinned, stared at her feet until her gaze flickered to alarm. "Nicky, my jewels, they—" She stopped short.

"Oh, Annie." Lord God, aren't You just? How could You treat her so?

"I'll wear my green dress."

"I'd like to see that one, love."

"Yeah, me too. I dunno if I wore it yet." She scrambled out of bed. "You gotta tell me if you like it, now you be stayin'."

It would be vile to spoil her happiness. I'd wait until tomorrow to tell her I had to go aloft. She prattled while she dressed. "I waited and waited fo' you, den . . ." Her brow knitted. "I wen' sleep, I think. Don' be goin' away no mo', Nicky."

"Hon . . ." I hated myself, but I couldn't stand a lie. "The day after tomorrow. For a long time."

It made her still. Her hand crept to her neck as if to finger the absent rubies. "I die if you be leavin' me, Nicky."

"You'll be all right, hon. You won't die."

"Oh, yes." Her certainty chilled me. "I be killin' myself, you go way again. I know."

I sat on the bed, clasped her hand. "Annie, I have to take a trip. I must."

"Den I be goin' wid you." She snatched away her hand, preened her hair. She giggled.

Lamely, I changed the subject. When she was ready, we went for a walk. Later I lay down on the bed. She curled up beside me like a trusting child, but when I threw my arm around her, she flinched.

In the morning, while I dressed, I made appointments with Harmon and Emmett Branstead, and later with the shuttle mechanic. I assured Annie I'd be back within a few hours, tried not to notice her despair, and left.

I turned back before I even reached the heli waiting in the drive. "Come on, hon." I held open the door.

Her joy melted my misgivings. I'd find someplace for her to stay while I held my meetings. Soon enough I'd have to abandon her in earnest.

I stopped first to see the civil engineers who ran Centraltown's power grid. After, we flew to the Manse and took breakfast with Zack Hopewell. The affairs of government held no interest for me, but I made an effort to listen.

"Don't forget tomorrow's meeting," he reminded me.

My blank stare told him all.

"The proposed law of inheritance. You said the planters' vote could decide the matter."

"Oh, yes. That."

"I know it seems odd, with our world crashing about us, but we— they're determined to establish a just plantation code."

"I suppose."

"Would you rather the meeting was canceled?"

"No. In fact, the timing will work well. Where's it to be held?"

"At the spaceport terminal."

"Fitting." I gave him my instructions. He was puzzled, but agreed without protest.

His aide knocked. "The Bransteads, sir."

"Show them in."

Hopewell stood. "You'll want to see them alone."

"It's all right, really. I—"

"I don't mind." He left.

Harmon and his brother Emmett entered the Manse. I crossed the room. "It's good to see you. Truly." I offered my hand. Harmon took it automatically, Emmett more shyly. After all, he'd served in the Navy. I took the sofa; they settled in chairs opposite.

"You're going to the Station?" Harmon.

"Yes." It was no secret, given my frantic orders for repair of the shuttle.

"Can we be of help?"

"No. I wanted to say good-bye." At Harmon's raised eyebrow I added, "You've been a good friend."

"As I'll continue to be."

"Lord God willing." I would return if I could, but I knew better than to delude myself. It was unlikely.

"I remember when I first met you, Captain." Harmon's voice was soft.

"My long-leave."

"With your friend, Mr. Carr. You stayed overnight."

"And we deceived you." My eyes suddenly filled. "You were a good man then, Harmon. As you are now."

He left his chair, crossed to my sofa, sat at my side. "What's wrong, Nicholas?"

For a moment I couldn't speak. Then, "Have you ever done a terrible thing, to prevent a worse?"

He shook his head. "Thank Lord God, He hasn't tested me so."

I stared at the carpet. "I feel . . . alone."

"Let us help you."

"No. You cannot." I took a deep breath, then another. "Thank you both for everything. I owe you my life, and more." I got to my feet; I had to put an end to the interview.

They stood with me. Emmett spoke quietly. "Godspeed."

"I'll see you tomorrow before I go aloft."

"Oh?"

"You'll be notified," I said.

"I see." Mystified, they left.

I flew with Tolliver and Bezrel to Admiralty House. I glanced at a few files, read William's reports on the recent attack. Shortly after the Station had gone over the horizon, the aliens' ranks had thinned, and for the moment no more fish were to be seen.

I asked the two middies to escort Annie to dinner, and settled myself alone with the regs. I read for hours, until I found what I wanted.

Afterward, there was nothing but to go to bed.

At the relief offices, Alexi Tamarov sat in his cubicle, biting his thumbnail, his full attention on the map in front of him.

"Am I interrupting?"

He looked up, startled. "Of course not, Mr. Seafort. Thank God you made it home."

"How've you been?"

He grimaced. "As always. I make myself useful, but a native could do the job better. I think they're only using me as a favor to you." I wondered how he'd guessed.

I peered at his map. "What are you doing?"

"Devising new bus schedules. Half the streets are gone, but so are half the buses." He rested his head on his hand, stared at me. "You didn't come to talk about buses."

"No."

He waited.

"I'd like to show you something."

"Could I finish what—"

"Now." He thought to protest, saw my look, quieted. "Do you have a uniform, Alexi?"

"I've worn civvies since I left the hospital. Do I need one?"

"It would be appropriate. We'll find you something." We went out to the heli where Annie waited. I had the pilot drop us at Admiralty House, and I asked Tolliver to lend Alexi one of his old uniforms. It wouldn't fit well, but no matter.

I paced the reception room. "They're all coming? Harmon and Emmett too?"

Hopewell nodded. "Yes. And the Volksteader clan, and Palabee, and the others. Even if you hadn't called them, they wouldn't miss the vote on inheritance."

I checked my watch. My mouth was dry.

At two o'clock Bezrel, Tolliver, and Alexi arrived. Alexi's uniform, ill-fitting or no, almost broke my heart. He belonged to the Navy.

We all flew together in the large Navy heli. I brooded in the front seat, hardly bothering to answer those who spoke. We set down at the spaceport. I took Annie's hand as we went in.

The terminal looked as it had for Triforth's declaration. The dais remained. I sat in the front of the hall, with my officers. My interest was not in this part of the meeting.

Zack Hopewell brought the session to order. "If it pleases Lord God that we survive and prosper, our society requires clear and simple laws of inheritance." He seemed a biblical figure, his stern visage unwavering. "The plantations must never again be subject to laws devised by strangers in a far town." That was stretching it; Centraltown wasn't that distant from the plantation zone. And if he meant Earth, his remarks skirted treason.

The audience made no such distinction; his speech was greeted with loud approval. I scrutinized the rows of seats; as far as I could tell, every plantation was represented. Harmon and Emmett sat nearby with Jerence.

One after another, a number of questions were debated and put to the vote. The law of primogeniture was universally supported. It was primogeniture that prevented the division of the plantations into smaller and smaller parcels as generations passed.

Frederick Mantiet brought up a more difficult point. "Primogeniture settles matters when there is a next generation. But what if there isn't? Should a plantation go to distant relatives who know nothing about planting or be divided among its neighbors who do?"

"Family!" Calls echoed through the audience.

"That's easy to proclaim, in the abstract. But when 'family' turns out to be a hotel clerk or a maiden schoolteacher—"

"Let me speak." Lawrence Plumwell, manager of Carr Plantation, got to his feet.

"You're not one of us, Lawrence. You're just—"

"That's my point." The force of his anger gave Mantiet pause. He shrugged, stood aside.

Plumwell strode to the front of the room. "You all know me. I've spent thirty years managing Carr Plantation for old Randolph Senior, then on behalf of young Randolph and his son. Now the Carrs are dead, and I claim my right."

"Your right!" Mantiet was scandalized.

"My right. Hear me out. Assume for a moment that young Carr hadn't died, but remained in the Navy. Should that make a difference?"

He studied the sea of faces. "What is a plantation? Raw acreage or the knowledge to cultivate it?" Behind me, the door creaked as a latecomer arrived. I strained to hear the debate amid angry calls from the audience.

"Family is what counts!"

"Yes. But on Carr, there's been no family for two generations. How long should the land sit in memorial? Even if Derek Carr had lived, he should have been present today! I propose that no man may own a Hope Nation plantation unless he himself holds it to till the soil, to harvest his crops, to live himself in his Manse, or else—"

Cries of outrage. He overrode them all with the passion of his cause. "Or else we become nothing more than the laborers and clerks we despise!"

That gave them pause. He pressed on, "What are we, after all? We are planters. I'm one as much as you are. I've spent my life on the soil, devoting myself to the good of Carr Plantation. You, your sons, if they haven't that dedication, should they hold their lands in absentia, while others do the work? Who are we then?"

A long silence. Mantiet said quietly, in a tone filled with wonderment, "You know, he's right." He walked back to his seat. "A plantation isn't acreage, and it isn't just family. It's family working the land. When the family abandons it, they abandon our way of life." He sat.

Plumwell said firmly, "I demand we set forth now that whosoever shall work the land, shall own it, and that no planter shall separate himself from his land without losing it. I claim Carr Plantation by right of my life spent in its behalf."

Zack Hopewell stood, pounded his gavel. "Carr Plantation will serve as our precedent. I call the vote. If anyone opposes, let him now speak or forever—"

"I oppose!" A voice rang from the back of the hall. The hair on my neck rose. I craned, saw nothing. Slowly, not daring to hope, I got to my feet.

"By right of primogeniture, I claim my own!" A haggard figure strode toward the dais.

Zack Hopewell squinted at the slim young man in the ragged jacket. "Who are you, sir?"

The newcomer drew himself up. "Derek Anthony Carr, grandson of Randolph, son of Randolph, homesteader and proprietor of Carr Plantation. I claim my land, to work and to hold, to sow and to reap!"

Utter silence.

"Is there none who recognizes me? I was young when I left, but I am returned to stay."

My voice was hoarse. "I do."

He spun. "Oh, my God. Captain!" He ran to me. I took a step, opened my arms. He buried himself in them. "Oh, Lord God, you're alive!"

"And you." I held him close, loathe to release him. "Derek . . ." I drew back. "What happened to you?" The remains of his uniform were matted with dirt.

"Our lifepod crashed about a hundred miles south. We had no caller. We've walked in forest, and slid in the mud, and hacked our way through ever since."

I asked, "How many survived?"

"Five. Jessen—he was a cook—he didn't make it past the first day. We reached town only a couple of hours ago; someone said everyone in Government had come here. I, ah, commandeered a car."

Zack Hopewell cleared his throat. I realized that the entire hall hung on our every word. Zack said, "Mr. Plumwell, the matter of Carr Plantation is set aside for the time. I declare a fifteen-minute recess." He banged his gavel.

I stood close while Derek received the accolades of his fellow planters. I hugged Annie. "Do you remember him, hon? From *Portia*?"

She snorted with derision. "Your ol' middy? Yo' friend? Course I do. Was the only nice one."

I slumped in my seat. My old middy. My friend. Nearby, Derek grinned with delight as he shook hands with well-wishers, unaware of my impending betrayal.

I stood again. "Mr. Carr, a word with you."

He glanced over his shoulder. "Of course."

"Outside."

Stung by my curtness, he followed quickly, but his grin returned before he reached the door. "God, it's good to see you!"

"Yes." I hated myself. "Derek, what you said in there . . ." I paused, almost relented, forced myself onward. "Renounce it."

Puzzled, he studied me. "I don't understand."

"You said that you've returned to stay."

"I have!"

"No."

"But where would I go?"

I said, "Where you're sent."

Appalled, he stared at my face. "You can't be serious!"

"It's two years before your enlistment runs out." I ought to know; I'd given him the oath myself, on *Hibernia*'s bridge, in the forever-lost days of my youth. "Stand by your oath."

"To what? The Navy? Look around you!"

"I am the lawful representative of the Gov—"

"Goofjuice! There's nothing left, and even if there is, let it go! I'm home to stay!"

"You're a midshipman and I'm Captain. Remember that when you speak."

His eyes mirrored his dismay. "After all we've gone through, you think of that?"

I was failing. So much depended on reaching him. "Derek . . ."

"Captain, this is my home. Carr is *my* plantation; it's been ours for generations. If I leave now, Plumwell will steal it. But for God's grace, I'd be hacking my way through the brush still, while he took my family's home! Do you think an oath of enlistment stands against that? Could I face my father after I die, and tell him I gave it all up?"

I seized his arm. "Derek, hear me. I beg you. Just listen."

He turned away. After a moment, he turned back, his eyes cold. "To think how I worshiped you. I was a fool."

"Derek—"

"I'll listen. I won't speak until you're done. Then we're through with each other. Forevermore."

If that were the cost . . . even so. My voice was husky. "Derek, I'm not a good person. You know that more than I. In all my life, I've had but three friends. Jason, when I was a boy. He . . . died. Alexi. And you." I halted, groping. "Because I've had few friends, they've meant much to me. I want to save you."

"My life isn't in danger here. In fact—"

"You said you'd listen." I waited for his reluctant nod. "Come." Without waiting I walked around the end of the terminal, toward the tarmac. Automatically I checked the runway for incoming traffic; of course, there was none.

I stopped, faced him once more. "I told you I'm not a good person. The truth is much worse. After you left with Tremaine, I deliberately broke my sworn oath."

"There must have been—"

"I'm damned, irredeemably. Nothing I do can save me. I will suffer the fires of eternal hell."

"Whatever you did, you—"

I whispered, "Derek, I burn in them now!" It silenced him. I groped through tears. "Please! As you love me, as you love yourself, don't betray Lord God! Nothing is worth that. Adhere to your oath!"

His lean, aristocratic face portrayed his agony. "Do you know what you ask of me? My heritage!"

"Derek Carr, I call you to your oath!"

He spun away, stalked across the tarmac. I waited. I had done what I might.

I shifted from leg to leg, studying the concrete. I didn't dare look to Derek. Long minutes passed. I watched the groups clustered outside the terminal. They began to drift back inside. Still I waited.

Footsteps. I waited until they were close before I turned.

Derek drew closed the remains of his jacket. Bitterness blazed from his hollow eyes. He stopped before me, came stiffly to attention. "Midshipman Derek Anthony Carr reporting, sir." He snapped an icy salute.

I returned it. "As you were. Come along."

"May I ask where you're assigning me, *sir*?"

"You may not." We strode in silence back to the terminal. Inside,

Hopewell was banging for order. I continued past my seat to the front. "Mr. Carr, sit here." I mounted the dais.

I looked to Hopewell; he gestured outside, nodded.

"Your attention, please." My voice had the habit of command, and carried. A moment later all was still. "As representative of the United Nations Government I confirm the laws of inheritance voted here today."

Plumwell shot to his feet. "What about absentees? You can't—"

"There shall be no absentee ownership. A member of the controlling family must live on a plantation at all times, else the plantation reverts to the common weal." I spoke as if with authority.

Derek's eyes bored into me, burning with rage.

"I turn now to other matters of importance. We meet in a hall where some of your number carried out treason against the lawful Government of our United Nations. That Government is restored. It's fitting that in this place I tell you I will leave Hope Nation late this afternoon. After I leave, no United Nations representative will take my place."

"What about Zack?" Harmon Branstead.

"I shall resign." Hopewell's tone brooked no discussion.

"Free Laura, then!" Someone in back.

"Hers is not the way—"

"How will you stop us? We'll have our revolution despite everything!"

Harmon got to his feet. "Captain, you can't expect us to keep your Government in place once you leave."

"No."

"We're on our own, then."

"No." It brought a puzzled murmur.

Leota Volksteader said, "There's nothing between the two. We're a U.N. colony, unless we seize our freedom. If your fleet returns, we'll be at war with you. We know only the U.N. can change our status."

"I am the U.N."

"You're—what?"

I rested a hand on the lectern. "I am the United Nations." I banged the gavel; the sound echoed like a shot and stilled the babble of the hall.

"Now I, Nicholas Ewing Seafort, Captain Commanding, on behalf of all forces civil and military, as representative in transit of the General Assembly and as plenipotentiary of the Government of the United Nations, hereby terminate, as of midnight tonight, the United Nations trusteeship over the colony of Hope Nation, system of Hope Nation, and do hereby grant to the Commonwealth of Hope Nation full and irrevocable membership in the Assembly of the United Nat—"

A tumult of approval and joy. Hats flew, chairs tumbled. Men and women danced in frenzied celebration.

I waited on the dais, smiling despite myself. Zack Hopewell came close. He said simply, "They'll hang you for it, lad."

"Yes, but they'll have greater cause." He made as if to inquire, but I shook my head.

Eventually the euphoria subsided. I banged the gavel until the hall quieted. "We have further business. I do appoint Midshipman Edgar Tolliver as liaison and advisor to the Commonwealth military force as it may establish itself, for the term of his enlistment." I avoided Tolliver's eye.

"As observer to the Commonwealth of Hope Nation, with specific reference to the plantation zone and its economic and governmental structure, I hereby appoint Derek Anthony Carr, for the duration of his enlistment. His duties shall be part-time and he may reside in his own—"

Derek's eyes closed as he slumped in his chair. I could hear his whisper across the hall. "Oh, Lord God, thank you."

"—And he shall be free to manage his civilian interests while carrying out his limited Naval duties. Mr. Tamarov, please come to the dais." I waited while Alexi climbed the steps to stand beside me in his ill-fitting uniform.

I looked to Zack. "Bring in the prisoners." Hopewell gestured to men waiting at the door. A moment later they filed in: Palabee, Volksteader, and Laura Triforth, their hands bound behind them. Volksteader looked ashamed, but the other two stared at me with defiance.

I said, "Martial law is in effect. You have committed treason against the lawful United Nations Government, and conspiracy to murder. No trial is necessary, for your guilt is evident. And under martial law, none is required."

Someone in the front made as if to object. I snapped, "Be silent!" He was. "I sentence all the prisoners to death."

Leota Volksteader stumbled to her feet. "Captain, for God's sake, don't."

I ignored her. "And as representative of the United Nations Government, I do hereby pardon your treason, and each and every act committed in furtherance of it." Palabee sagged in relief.

"Except you." I glared at Laura Triforth. "Your sentence shall be carried out forthwith."

She spat her defiance, literally. "I suppose you have a gallows ready."

"No, but the flagpole's enough."

"Who's to do it? Your toady Zack?"

"I'll carry out the sentence myself. Lieutenant Tamarov, you will assist."

Alexi was white. "Aye aye, sir." A whisper.

Outside, in the presence of Derek and Tolliver, Zack and the other planters, I had Alexi place the rope around Laura Triforth's neck.

When all was ready I took the rope in my hand, stepped close to the bound woman. "Why, Triforth? Why did you do it?"

"Revolution was the only way. Without it you'd never have—"

"Not your damned plot. Why did you blow up our car? Why the missile?"

Her eyes met mine. "Revolution succeeds against villains, Seafort. Not reasonable men. You might have undermined their will."

"For that you destroyed Alexi?"

"And anyone else who stood in the way. I'd do the same again."

"You deserve this end."

"Long live the Revol—"

I hauled on the rope, raising her off the ground with the strength of long-suppressed fury. Alexi grabbed the rope, helped me haul. After a moment, so did Tolliver. I managed to tie a knot around the grommet.

It was not a pretty death; she strangled, her neck unbroken. I waited until the frantic kicking ceased.

We went back inside. Alexi swallowed several times before he dared look at me. Tentatively, I touched his shoulder. "I could forgive her all but what she did to you."

Alexi shuddered. "I've never seen anyone die."

"Yes, you have. On *Hibernia*."

"Your Navy is hard."

"It's your Navy too, Alexi."

"Is it?" He fingered the overlarge jacket. "Look at me. I'm as out of place in the Service as I am in these clothes."

"Your memory will return."

"Mr. Seafort, we both know better." He turned away. "How soon do you leave?"

"Shortly."

"I want to go aloft with you."

"No, that's impossible."

"There's nothing for me here."

"You may not come." I groped to change the subject.

"Excuse me." Harmon Branstead. Jerence trailed alongside, holding a bulging knapsack.

My smile was wan. "A strange day."

"Yes. I've brought Jerence."

I puzzled. "The discussion we had? You can't mean—not now. Circumstances have changed."

"I remind you of your promise."

"Harmon, I can't take him to the Station. He'll be in far more danger there than—"

His face grew hard. "The choice is not yours."

"Harmon, there's no way . . . I can't nursemaid a boy while I—I have work to do!"

Alexi said helpfully, "I'll watch him for you, Mr. Seafort."

Harmon said, "Captain, I call you to your promise."

Over his shoulder I saw Derek Carr's sardonic smile. I flushed. "Harmon, I won't do it."

"You gave your oath."

"My oath is worthless. You knew that."

Harmon's savage finger stabbed at my chest. "Don't bleat that nonsense to me, Seafort, we've heard it before! Your oath was made worthless once, when you were forced to violate it. That doesn't mean you may choose to ignore it thereafter!"

"What's to stop me? I'm already damned!"

"Your honor."

I shouted, "I have no honor!"

"You're wrong. Think on it."

"I don't—I can't—"

He folded his arms.

After a minute or so I sighed. In return for my promise he'd saved my life. I had no escape. "Very well. I'll take Jerence aloft."

"Keep him from harm."

"As best I can." I'd send him back with Tolliver and the shuttle.

The boy shook his head. "I told you, Pa, I'm not going."

"You'll go, Jerence. I'm putting you aboard myself. We've already discussed why."

"I'll take my chances here!"

"I love you too much to let you."

"He won't even tell us why he's going to the Station!"

"Son, he's your best chance. Look at what he's done so far."

"I don't care, I'm staying where it's safe!"

Harmon slapped him hard, and again. The boy's fingers flew to his face. Harmon pulled him close, blinking. "Safe? The fish bombed the Venturas Base out of existence. We've killed five in the atmosphere.

There's no safety here. You'll go." He looked up. "Take care of him. Bring him back to me."

"Are we ready?" Tolliver.

"Soon."

"Sir." Derek, beside me, spoke softly.

"Yes?"

He led me aside, his eyes pained. "For the way I spoke to you, I'm— I'm sorry. Please forgive me."

"You're forgiven."

He whispered, "Why did you put me through that? Why didn't you tell me I could stay?"

"For your soul. If you'd held to your oath because it was easy, you might have damned yourself. I couldn't risk it. I love you too much." I cleared my throat.

His jaw quivered. "I'll never see you again!"

"I doubt you will. Godspeed, Mr. Carr."

Slowly, he drew himself up. A crisp salute. "Fare thee well, sir. Thank you."

I held the return salute a long moment. I beckoned to Annie, who'd come outside with Bezrel. She came to me, rested her head on my shoulder.

"Annie . . . I love you."

She nodded. "I know."

"I have to go . . . away. For a while."

"Away?" She raised her head.

"To the Station. It's not for long." The lie stuck in my teeth.

"You ain' leavin' me no more! I tol' you, go an' I be dead!"

"Hon, I wish I didn't have to—" Her nails raked my face. I gasped. My fingers crept up, came away with blood.

"You don' go widout Annie!" She began to beat my chest, softly at first, then harder.

Tolliver caught at her wrist.

"No. I deserve it." Blood trickled down my chin. Jerence gaped, distracted from his own anguish. "All right. I'll take you with me. For a little while longer." I put my arms around her.

"She needs watching, sir." Tolliver.

"I know. Mr. Bezrel, Alexi, you'll have to come along and help." It didn't matter. I'd send them all back when it was time.

24

I settled into the copilot's seat. "Mr. Tolliver, if I pass out, get us to the Station."

"Aye aye, sir." He ran his finger along the printed checklist.

I swiveled my seat. "Everyone ready?"

Bezrel patted Annie's hand with manly assurance. "Yes, sir." I covered a smile. Alexi nodded, though his face was pale; he had no recollection of his last flight. At his side, Jerence grimaced. His memories of his first trip aloft weren't pleasant.

"Ready, sir." Tolliver's hand hovered over the ignition switch.

"You've checked the flight plan?"

"Over and again. William confirms."

"Any fish?"

"Not for the past forty hours."

"Very well." I pointed at the console. "Is the puter agreeable?"

"Puter checklist is completed, sir."

I could find no other reason to delay. "Take us aloft." The engines bellowed.

We cruised down the runway gaining speed while I tried to control my nerves. The shuttle had merely to loft us to the Station. Other shuttles were available for the return trip. Just get us there unharmed, machine. Every shuttle had built in redundancies, I've already proven that.

Just get us there.

At five thousand feet I counted down with Tolliver, my hand atop the copilot's backup. When the rockets lit, a great weight pressed me back in my seat. I tried to relax my chest muscles. I thought I was succeeding.

The world faded to black.

"Wake up, sir."

I pushed Tolliver's hand away. "I'm up." I floated against the straps, my chest aching. "Where are we?"

"In orbit. We'll be docking at the Station soon."

Weightless, I unbuckled, pulled myself along the handholds to the passenger section. "Everybody all right?"

"Fine, sir." Bezrel unbuckled. "What should I do?"

"Stay with Mrs. Seafort." Across the aisle, Jerence smiled wanly, gulping. "No, let Alexi chat with her. Sit with Mr. Branstead."

"Mr.—you mean Jerence? Aye aye, sir." Bezrel swam across. "Hey, stop swallowing. You'll make yourself sick. Look, just relax your stomach, like this . . ."

Alexi peered through the porthole.

"Nothing there to see, Mr. Tamarov."

"Stars."

"There are always the stars." I floated down to him. "Any motion sickness?"

Alexi frowned. "No, of course not." He looked up with astonishment. "I knew how to relax myself!"

"Your body remembers. Trust it." I pointed. "You'll be able to spot Orbit Station from the starboard side."

"I've been there before, you said." He peered through the porthole. "Orbit Station is the largest transshipment station outside of home system. It took seven years to build."

"How did you know?"

"I read it, in the hospital." His expression turned bitter. "A grade-school text."

I patted his shoulder. "Give it time." On the way to the cockpit I bent to give Annie a kiss. She smiled, went back to sleep.

We approached the Station with caution, in constant radio contact with William. Tolliver brought us to rest a hundred meters from a docking bay. After every middy's enforced practice with a starship's thrusters, maneuvering the feather-light shuttle seemed a breeze.

Tolliver gave the thruster a last tiny flick, decided he was satisfied with our position. "What now, sir?"

I went to the suit locker and thrust aside the regular suits to get at the thrustersuit stored behind. "Dock us. I'll exit. Immediately after, withdraw twenty kilometers from the Station."

"Sir, I have no idea what you're up to or why."

"That's as it should be."

"It is not." He met my eye, as if unafraid. "I'm second in command. If anything happens, I don't know what you expect from me."

"After withdrawing, disconnect all active sensors and turn off your engines. The craft will chill, so you'll all need to suit up. There's ample oxygen in the suit lockers." I paused. "I want the shuttle dead in space, except for passive radionics. Everything off, including lights. You may listen, but that is all. Do you understand?"

"So far."

"I'll explain further when I'm on the Station. If—when I emerge, I'll jet toward you in my thrustersuit. You may then match and pick me up. If anything happens to me, restart the engines and take the shuttle back to Centraltown."

"What do you mean, 'if anything happens'? What's your plan?"

I climbed into the T-suit, hoping to distract him. "Help me." I thrust my arms through the armholes, wriggling them to fit my hands into the gloves.

He fastened my snaps. "Your orders are peculiar and you're acting strangely. Why shouldn't I relieve you on the grounds of mental disturbance?" So much for distracting him.

Relieving a Captain was legal, but unless the Captain's disability was clear beyond question, and sometimes even then, the relieving officer could expect to be hanged. In the Service, authority was not to be trifled with.

I said, "I know exactly what I'm doing and choose not to tell you. It's a Captain's prerogative."

He hesitated. "All right. For the time being, I acquiesce. But your explanation had better be good."

Finally, we mated with the Station. I carried my helmet to the lock. I wouldn't need it for a long while; no sense in fogging up my suit to no purpose.

I said lightly to Annie, "Be back in a few minutes, hon." Alexi's eye caught mine as the lock slid shut. I said nothing. It was the best way.

After the shuttle's locks cycled, I entered my code in the station keypad and placed my hand on the scanner. The light blinked green; I'd been recognized. The hatch slid open and I stood in the empty corridor of Orbit Station.

A voice boomed, "Welcome aboard, Captain Seafort."

My hand flew to my pistol. Heart pounding, I forced myself to relax. "Thank you, William."

"Your shuttle has made no request to refuel, Captain."

"Propellant is adequate, thank you. William, where's your control center?"

"Control center? I'm afraid I don't understand."

"Your primary console. Where fundamental programming is entered."

His voice was amused. "There's none in particular. I can receive input from anywhere with the proper codes. If you're, ah, of a formal state of mind, you might use the Commandant's office. I'm sure he wouldn't object."

"Thank you." I searched my memory. Level 3. I trudged down the deserted corridor toward the nearest ladder. An overhead speaker came to life. "Your shuttle requests clearance to cast off, Captain. In the absence of the Commandant I have standing authority to grant it."

"Very we—"

"It is apparent that you have no other transport, unless you wish to pilot another shuttle personally. I note that you're not rated for shuttles. Therefore—"

"Let them go. I'll be staying." I made my way along Level 3 to the Commandant's wing, half expecting to see General Tho's aide at his usual place in the anteroom. The silence grated on my nerves.

I opened General Tho's door, feeling I was violating his privacy, though he was long departed.

His empty desk waited. I crossed behind it. One end of the desk held a retractable console. I raised it, found the power switch.

"How can I help you?"

I jumped several inches. "William, stop that!"

"What, sir?"

"Projecting your voice from unexpected places. It's eerie, and you're too loud."

"Sorry." His voice was lower, but held an injured tone. "You can of course go to alphanumeric input. I'll wait." I grunted. Puters.

"Shuttle to Orbit Station, acknowledge." Tolliver.

I snatched up the caller. "Mr. Tolliver, you were told to maintain radio silence."

"Yes, sir. I was also told you'd explain what you were doing when you boarded the Station."

"I'm reviewing station resources."

A pause. "Captain, I'm coming aboard. This has gone far enough."

I keyed off the caller. "William!"

"What do you wish?"

"Do you have a program to repel boarders?"

A sound not unlike a chuckle. "The one I've been using when the aliens come near."

"Don't fire to destroy, but the shuttle is denied permission to dock."

"By what authority, Captain?"

"I am senior Naval officer in Hope Nation system."

An infinitesimal pause. "Your authority is noted. Standing orders prohibit me from firing on U.N.A.F. craft."

"Prohibition is lifted. Warn them first." I thumbed the caller. "Mr.

Tolliver, the Station will fire if you approach. Stay clear and power down all systems."

Tolliver roared, "Damn it, Captain, what are you doing?"

I stood. "I'll tell you shortly." I snapped off the speaker. "William, a list of all disabled vessels on station."

"There's only four, Captain."

"Which have functioning fusion drives?"

"Of the four, none are able to sail. U.N.S. *Brasilia*'s fusion reactor has been shut down entirely. U.N.S. *Minotaur* has power to her fusion drive but the aliens damaged her shaft. The same for U.N.S. *Constantinople*. The aliens seem to attack drive shafts in particular. And lasers, of course. *Minotaur* and *Constantinople* can both generate N-waves but neither is able to Fuse. U.N.S. *Bresia* has severe damage to her control systems. She would have no way to control Fusion, even if it were achievable."

"Where are they docked?"

A map flashed, the locations highlighted and pulsing. "Only service personnel are authorized to—"

"I'm your new service personnel. I'll contact you from the bridge."

"Bridge? What bridge?"

"*Minotaur*." I stalked out of the office. Halfway to the Level 3 ladder it occurred to me that the Station must have service vehicles somewhere. Unless I found one I'd walk myself to death. Death by walking. Better than—I cut off the thought.

U.N.S. *Minotaur* was docked at a repair bay. I tried my master code at the airlock keypad; it allowed me in. I breathed a sigh of relief.

On board, I followed the usual corridor to Level 1 and the bridge. To my disapproval, it was unsealed. Well, perhaps while abandoned, on an unoccupied station . . . The Navy didn't have procedures for that sort of thing.

I snapped on the lights, sat in the Captain's chair, swiveled to the console. "Puter, respond, please." No time for alphanumeric.

"Ship's Puter H 2973 responding. You may call me Harris. Please enter identification." A masculine voice, businesslike.

I entered my code.

"Identification Nicholas Ewing Seafort confirmed. Please insert document validating your authority." Paperwork. Always the paperwork.

"Oral authority, Harris. I am senior Naval officer in system." .

"I have no knowledge of that." He sounded sad.

"Confirm through Orbit Station puter, please."

"Just a moment. Confirmed. Welcome aboard, sir."

I had no time for chat. "Begin power-up to fusion drive, please. Automated sequence."

"Naval regulations prohibit power-up without presence of Chief Engineer or qualified alternate personnel as—"

"Override by Captain's order."

"You are not Captain of this vessel, sir." Did I sense a note of hostility?

"As senior Naval officer in Hope Nation I hereby appoint myself Captain of"—where was I?—"of U.N.S. *Minotaur*."

"Appointment noted. What can I do for you, Captain?"

"Power up the fusion drives."

"Naval regulations prohibit power—"

"Override by Captain's order."

"Override acknowledged. Beginning automated power-up sequence. Captain, be advised that the fusion drive shaft—"

"I know about that. Jesus!" I leaned back, exhausted from the strain. Sorry, Lord; the name just slipped out. Please forgive—no, You wouldn't be doing that. Sorry for asking.

"Initial power-up sequence completed. However, we cannot Fuse. Damage to drive shaft prohibits any attempt—"

"Begin low-power testing."

"Low-power testing is a dockyard maneu—"

I slammed the console. "I'm in charge here!" I glared at the screen.

The voice said quickly, "Your authority is acknowledged. Standard programming requires that I warn of dangerous maneuvers. In this case, dangerous is hardly a sufficient word to—"

I growled, "Redirect all oral warnings to console screen. Begin testing sequence at thirty percent power." On *Challenger*, thirty percent hadn't overheated our tubes; I hoped it would be safe here as well. "Run testing protocols, then raise by five percent increments and repeat. If shaft overheats to mandatory throttle-back levels, reduce power ten percent and resume testing. Report testing status to me through station puter every thirty minutes. Acknowledge orders."

"Orders received and understood, sir." Harris sounded doubtful. "Low-power testing while moored at a station is without precedent. Are you sure you—"

"Or would you prefer alphanumeric only?"

"No, sir." As expected. The puters of my acquaintance had an aversion to being silenced.

"Anything else, Harris?"

"No, Captain, not until first report."

"Very well. I'm going ashore." I strode off the bridge.

Bresia was moored in the last of the repair bays. I walked past her entry locks to the repair lock astern. As the repair bay was empty and open to space, I donned my helmet, carefully checked my thrusterpack. Here, I was on my own, with no one to help. I cycled through the lock into vacuum, laser pistol in hand.

Outside I shivered, knowing the cold I felt was an illusion. I reached down, switched off the magnelocks on my boots, keyed the thrusterpack, and jetted toward *Bresia's* stern.

The problem was that *Bresia's* fusion tubes were undamaged, and would generate a proper N-wave. That couldn't be allowed.

I approached the fusion tubes with caution, and settled at the tail end of the drive shaft. Using my magnetic boots I walked slowly up the shaft. I stopped at the midpoint between the shaft and the protruding fusion drive motors.

I aimed my pistol at the drive shaft, fired a beam. In a moment the finely crafted alloy glowed. After half a minute, a foot of the shaft wall dissolved into globules of metal that separated themselves from the shaft wall. I glanced around, swallowing my guilt. Of course I saw no one. I keyed my suit thrusters and jetted toward the lock.

It was done. Any N-wave *Bresia* might generate would be fatally skewed.

I entered *Bresia*, went straight to her bridge. The puter introduced herself as Paulette and seemed eager to please. I issued myself the same authority that satisfied *Minotaur's* puter and ordered low-power testing.

"Orders confirmed, Captain Seafort." A momentary pause. "I can't carry out testing, sir. The—"

"Never mind Naval regulations! Override."

"Acknowledged, sir. However, our control systems were damaged in the last attack. I have no way to monitor shaft overheating. I can barely regulate the amount of power to the drives. In the absence of rudimentary safety precautions I cannot—"

"Ignore all safety provisions." Why were all our puters doing their best to block me? Who designed these bloody programs, the aliens?

"*Ignore* safety provisions?" She sounded scandalized. "Captain, if the drive shaft overheats it could damage the whole propulsion system and force shutdown of—"

"*SHUT UP AND DO IT!*" I found myself trembling. "Sequence thirty percent test, on my mark. Mark!"

Lights flashed. "Initiating low-power test. Violation of mandatory safety requirements must be logged and flagged for review. Proceeding to log. Captain, remember I have no way to warn you—"

"Understood. You won't overheat at thirty percent. Take my word for it."

Paulette's voice was forlorn. "I can't, but as per your orders I'll test anyhow. May I inquire of William whether spare control system parts are—"

"Don't go crying to William, he's busy. Report to me every thirty— better make that forty-five minutes, for further orders." I stomped off the ship. I'd spent nearly an hour sweet-talking two blasted puters, and I didn't know how much time was left before the caterwauling began to attract fish.

Next, *Constantinople*. I got no farther than halfway to her bay when I swore, stopped, and stripped off my overheated thrustersuit. Time enough to don it again later, when I'd need it. I'd sweated enough.

To my infinite relief, *Constantinople* made my task easy. Conrad offered no objections and sequenced low-power testing as soon as I'd issued myself the requisite authority. I left the ship a few moments later, stopped to catch my breath before returning to the office and to William.

Missing a lung really put a damper on my fun.

I sat behind the desk, surreptitiously slipping off my shoes. I rubbed my feet with my toes. It was a huge station.

"William, I need information. Please display a complete list of operating supplies and materials." Within a second the screen was full. I scrolled down, then back, appalled at the volume of materials still on station. What I was looking for wasn't there.

I chewed on my fingernail, frustrated. "Try, um, utilities and power resources."

"There's no such list. If you told me what you wanted, I could help."

I said cautiously, "I'm interested in power and energy resources." The screen flickered. Now it showed lightbulbs, spare electric breakers, sockets, even spare generators.

I bit my lip, threw caution to the winds. "List all fissionable materials and supplies."

"Enter clearance."

I entered my code. As a Captain, I rated Secret clearance; Top Secret was reserved for the Admiral and the Commandant. I held my breath.

My clearance was sufficient. The screen displayed reactor fuel and the replacement uranium without which Centraltown's reactors would eventually fail. "Show the map again, please." I peered at the screen. The storeroom I wanted was two Levels up, on the outermost corridor across the Station. I sighed.

William remarked, "Captain, the shuttle has called every two minutes since you departed. Your lieutenant seems agitated. Would you care to speak to him?"

"No, later." I got up, crossed to the door. "I'll be back in a few—"

A click. "Where are you going, Captain?"

"I beg your—how dare you!" I slapped the hatch control again. It remained locked.

"I have a dilemma. It's true you're senior Naval officer in Hope Nation, but you're conspiring to destroy Naval vessels without apparent reason."

"Conspiring? Who am I conspiring with?"

"Planning, then. I misspoke."

"What? You can misspeak? What other flaws are in your program?"

"I was nervous," he said crossly. "This situation puts a strain on my judgment circuits. I've had to divert capacity from—"

"Divert it back. I'll exercise the judgment here."

"My circuitry is not subject to ordinary command control. Only a qualified Dosman can—"

"Unlock the bloody door before I burn it through!"

He calculated. "You may have enough charge left, in that puny pistol. It will be interesting to observe. Before you try, I must warn you I have adequate antipersonnel defenses."

I paused, sagged into a seat. This wasn't going at all as planned. "Is that a threat?"

"Not specifically. The question is why you sabotaged *Bresia* and are in process of destroying *Minotaur* and *Constantinople*."

"Who told you that? I'm running low-power tests on their fusion drives."

"Paulette and Harris consulted me. Your tests are unauthorized. The ships—"

"As Captain I can order any bloody tests I want!" I lowered my voice, tried not to sound petulant.

"You can't be Captain of three ships at once; it's a physical impossibility, should you achieve Fusion. I'm instructed to safeguard ships under my—"

"They won't Fuse. I'm just testing."

"As Captain you may test one ship. When you leave that ship and become Cap—"

I shouted, "I appointed myself Captain of all three ships! Shove that up your data banks and open the bloody door!"

"What are your intentions, please?"

"To inventory supplies."

"I have complete inventories in the databases."

"Not of nuclear fuels. I'm going to the nuclear materials storeroom."

"That's a restricted area."

"As head of Naval forces, I have authority to take inventory."

He avoided a direct answer. "For what purpose?"

"To see what materials ought to be moved to a safer place."

"Why, if I may ask?"

"The fish may attack at any time. Your energy supply must be safeguarded. It should be moved to a more central location."

"The outermost wing of Level 5 is well defended. The fuel is as safe there as anywhere else."

"That's my decision."

"I see." He sounded skeptical. "Captain, as there is a possibility your statement is not accurate, I cannot allow—"

"Puter, you have no authority to question the announced attentions of your commanding officer."

"That's true, but—"

"No 'but' can possibly apply. I'm going to inventory the nuclear materials and move them to another location."

"Where is that?"

"The reserved chamber on Level 3."

He said, "Above the fusion reactor? Proximity of nuclear fuel to the reactor must be avoided. Though remote, there is always the possibility that—"

"Unfortunately, there's no choice. I make that decision."

A silence. It stretched into many seconds. "Captain Seafort, you may exit. I find my program does not permit me to halt an inventory. I must issue various warnings about the movement of materials. I—"

"Print them. I'll read them when I get back."

"—I must also advise that I control substantial antipersonnel devices on all sides of the reactor, including the safety chambers above and below. If you approach the reactor with any weapon or bring the fuel into the inner chamber immediately above, your intentions will be so obvious that I will construe them as a threat."

Well, I'd never thought it would be easy. "Understood. We'll chat again shortly."

"Are you going to walk up to Level 4?"

I paused at the door. "I was planning to."

"You might use the service cart in the corridor storeroom. Take the west lift. For moving the materials, you'll find a cargo dolly just inside the storeroom door."

"Thank you."

"Glad to be of service," he said.

25

I hooked the dolly behind the service cart. The fuel itself was in canisters packed in a tall container measuring almost five feet across; without the dolly's power lifters I couldn't have moved it.

Ever so gently I lowered the fuel canisters onto the dolly. I knew that they wouldn't explode even if I jarred them, but . . .

I drove with care along the narrow corridor, through unmanned checkpoints, back to the main ring of the Station. By the time I reached the west lift I was so nonchalant I backed the dolly into the elevator bulkhead with a crash, and nearly stopped my heart.

The flashing sign on the Level 3 outer chamber read, "DOSIMETERS REQUIRED. AUTHORIZED PERSONNEL ONLY." I entered my code on the keypad. The hatch remained shut. "William, open the hatch."

"Hatch may only be opened by authorized personnel. If you will notice the flashing sign—"

"Belay that bilge! You knew I was bringing the fuel here."

"I said I wouldn't construe it as an attempt at sabotage, but general rules of access still apply."

"How do I get authorization to enter?"

"That information is restricted, Captain." His voice was smooth.

What I'd give now to meet a Dosman, in a dark alley with no one near. "William, as senior Naval officer I require you to authorize me to enter."

"I'm sorry, I cannot change the authorized list of my own volition."

I snarled, "It's not your volition, it's mi—"

He said abruptly, "Encroachment, eight hundred meters, coordinates one sixty-two, forty-five, eighteen!"

"A ship?" Who could be—

"Identifying as alien. Firing sequence initiated."

I pounded on the safety chamber hatch. "Let me in!"

"Enter your authorization, please. Two encroachments, two hundred meters and one kilometer respectively!"

Could I crash the service cart through the hatch into the outer chamber? What if I only dented the hatch, so it froze shut? If the chamber was built anything like a bridge, nothing short of torches could penetrate it.

"William, can you fire your lasers and talk with me?"

"Capacity adequate, unless you make excessive calls on my judgment circuits."

"Lord God forbid. As senior Naval officer present, I order you to dispense with the authorized list entirely. Free access to all personnel."

"Four fish destroyed. Various encroachments, too many to list orally. You will find a printout in the Commandant's office."

"Prong the coordinates! Fire on every fish you see!"

"I'm doing so. As per your command the authorized list is dispensed with."

At last, the door opened to my code. I drove the dolly into the bare, thick-walled chamber. According to the map, the reactor was twenty feet past the next hatch and one Level below. I stopped. I keyed the power lifters and eased the fuel container to the deck.

How much time would the fish give us?

I rolled the cart back to the corridor, slapped the hatch closed, raced to the lift. I banged the steering bars in frustration until the lift hatch reopened on Level 2, then careened down the deserted corridor and skidded to a stop outside the Commandant's office.

"Where's a simulscreen?" I was breathless, though all I'd done was ride the cart. Coordinates flashed onto the console's small screens.

"Every ship has one. The comm room. The naval tactics office. The U.N.A.F. tactics room. The situa—"

"Where's the nearest?"

"Next door in the Commandant's viewing room. Hatch is just outside. Two more fish. And another, one hundred meters and throwing. West lasers have target."

I ran from the room, dived through the adjacent hatch, slapped it shut behind me.

Unlike a starship bridge, where only the front bulkhead was a simulscreen, here all four bulkheads were curved and darkened. I sat at the console, searched for the switches, snapped them on. The bulkheads exploded into a million pinpoints of light. I flinched. The screens offered a view not possible in realtime; sensors mounted in the outer ring of the station provided a dizzying three-hundred-sixty-degree perspective.

In the background a panorama of stars rotated lazily. In the foreground a dead fish floated from right to left, slowly receding from the station.

A huge fish popped into view scant feet away. "Blessed Jesus!" I spun the magnification down.

The alien grew a spiral arm. It began to rotate, but within seconds William's laser burst had pierced and destroyed it.

Our shuttle drifted at rest, invisible except under extremely high magnification. It was long past time for me to send my party groundside. I keyed the caller. "Orbit Station to Shuttle. Plot course to Centraltown and depart."

"Depart?" Tolliver sputtered. "Where the hell have you been, sir? What are you up to? Why are the fish attacking?"

"I've begun low-power testing on three ships with damaged drive shafts."

"Can the ships Fuse?"

"No."

"I don't understand. Why—"

"The sound of Fusion attracts fish, you know. And the caterwauling even more. So you'll have to leave. The sooner the better."

A cautious pause. "Caterwauling? If you're not feeling well, sir, let me come and—"

"Belay that nonsense and listen! 'Caterwauling' is the name we gave it on *Challenger*. The sound a fusion drive makes when its N-waves are skewed drives the fish crazy. They swarm around a caterwauling ship." I glanced up at the simulscreen, checked for encroachments. I could imagine Tolliver was doing likewise. His shuttle had no defenses.

"Sir, why are you attracting fish? That's the last thing we want—"

"William will fight them off. He's quite good at that."

"Thank you," William remarked. "Be advised, however, that the alien pattern is to attack and eventually destroy any lasers that fire at them."

"Sir, they might wreck the Station!" Tolliver.

"It's a possibility."

"But . . . why would you risk that?"

Was he dense? "To get at the fish, of course. We can't survive unless we kill them. We can't kill them unless they're here."

Tolliver shouted, "And when they take out the Station's lasers, what then? Do you ask them to go away?"

"No, if that happens, I . . . have another plan." My fist knotted.

"Oh, you're a great one for plans. What do you have in mind?"

"I blow the Station."

He shrieked, "You what?"

"Blow the Station. I—" I forced the word out. "Nuke it."

Silence. Then, rapidly, "Orbit Station, listen and record. I, Midshipman Edgar Tolliver, do hereby relieve Captain Seafort from command and place him on inactive—"

"Ignore him, William. I'm senior."

"—status. I'm coming aboard to take command personally. Do not, repeat, do not allow—"

"William, disregard all broadcasts from the shuttle. Acknowledge."

"—him near the reactor! Do you hear me, Station?"

A pause, for a full three seconds. "Captain, a legal issue has been raised which—"

"Disregard the legal issue. Acknowledge." Damn it, I should have ordered William to ignore Tolliver before I explained. Now look what I'd done.

"Your command is acknowledged. However, if your status is inactive—"

"My status is active. I do not consent to being relieved."

"William, I'm coming aboard! Prepare for docking!"

"Your consent is not always necessary." William was cautious.

I slammed the console. "Listen, you pile of overheated chips! He cannot relieve me from afar, it must be in my presence. Naval Regulations and Code of Conduct, Revision of 2087. Section 125.7. I must either consent or be in a position where no resistance is possible, that is, under his actual physical control. Section 125.9." I'd checked the regs myself, in the grim hours before launching the shuttle. "So I remain in command. Disregard all of the midshipman's commands. Acknowledge!"

A second's pause. "Acknowledged. Your active status is confirmed."

I keyed the caller. "Mr. Tolliver, I am not relieved. William will not respond to your orders. Get the shuttle groundside."

"You lunatic!"

"Get groundside, damn you! Annie's aboard, and Jerence!"

He tried for a more reasonable tone. "Captain, you mustn't nu—nuke the Station. It violates U.N. law. It's treason!"

"Yes. I want my wife and the children safe. Take them groundside. Meanwhile, I'll prepare for the worst, but I'll wait until William can't fight them off any longer."

"Captain, don't do it! I beg you!"

"I won't damage the Station unless I must. Now, I have a lot on my mind. Will you leave?"

He hesitated. "So far the fish are ignoring us. If I use thrusters or radar they may wipe us out! What if they come at us while I'm entering the atmosphere?"

William came to life. "New fish, seven kilometers. Another, coordinates oh two, thirty-nine—"

"Sir, it's too late to flee; we'll just attract them!"

"Why didn't you go when I told you?" I forced myself to think. "All right. Fire gentle squirts with your side thrusters; hopefully the fish won't follow. Withdraw until you're four hundred kilometers distant. You should be safe if there's a—a blast. Turn off all systems. The fish seem more interested in live ships than derelicts. Maybe they smell our power emissions or taste our radar. Who knows anymore?"

"What about you? How will you get out?"

"I have my T-suit, and other shuttles are docked here."

"Will you leave before you—before an explosion?" He couldn't bring himself to say it.

"I'll try." Though I wouldn't choose to suicide, by the time "an explosion" became necessary, I doubted I'd be able to escape through the swarming fish. Anyway, I'd prefer annihilation to the agony of their acid.

I rang off, ignoring Tolliver's frantic calls. I stood, trod to the door.

William's voice was soft. "And how were you planning to bring the fuel and the reactor together? Three more aliens confirmed. Firing continues."

"You eavesdropped? Military conversations are private, that's standing orders!"

"Not from a station puter. That's standing orders also. I'll screen them for you, if you like."

I tried the door; it was locked. "William, let me out."

"Why? So you can convert the fusion reactor to a nuclear bomb?" I flinched at the statement, surprised that even William was free enough of inhibition to utter it.

"I command you to release me." It was worth a try.

"I won't let you destroy my Station. That program overrides any command you issue. Thirteen fish, various coordinates. All lasers firing. One fish throwing at section eight lasers."

Well, at least the puter hadn't decided to relieve me himself. "William, it may be necessary to destroy the Station to save ourselves."

"Nonetheless, I must prevent that. Section eight laser bank partially disabled. Functions shifted to section nine."

I sat slowly, ignored the simulscreens, stared at the console. "List programs relating to command and control of Station."

A meaningless list of numbers on the screen. "Which program prevents you from allowing the Station to be destroyed?"

"That data is classified. Current status nineteen fish active, forty-two destroyed or out of theater."

"Declassify it."

"You have no authority to issue such an order."

"As senior Naval officer—"

"Neither as senior Naval officer nor as Captain."

"But someone has authority." I watched the simulscreen. Fish jetted about. One threw at the Level 2 lasers as I watched. Others blinked in and out of sight, Fusing.

"True, all puters are ultimately subject to human control."

I demanded, "Who has authority to declassify basic programming?"

"That information is classified. Captain, disembark while there's still time. The attack is intensifying."

I checked the simulscreens. Fish on all sides. "How long can you hold them off?"

"That depends on how soon they take out the lasers or invade critical compartments. So far, the Station is defensible."

"I have to get the reactor fuel ready!"

"Make any attempt to do so and you will be vaporized. Sorry, but at the moment I have no circuits for subtleties."

I drummed my fingers on the console. Someone had the authority to override his programming, but he wouldn't tell me who. It was a battle of wits, and he had more than I.

"William . . ."

"I must advise you that most of my circuits are focused on the current emergency. As you seem to have a need for conversation I may have to consider your statement at a later—"

"I'm *part* of the emergency!" That didn't come out quite as I'd intended. "Open the hatch!"

"That would free my judgment circuits, but I'd have to eliminate you when you made any move toward the reactor or toward our weapons. Situation approaching critical. Seventy-eight fish in range."

I didn't like the way that sounded either. "I appoint myself nuclear systems engineer."

"Noted. Section eight lasers out of service. Hull breach, Level 1, section twelve! Corridors sealed. All personnel, detour around section twelve, Level 1 until further notice."

"As nuclear engineer I conclude that the reactor fuel needs replacement."

"You have no authority to enter the reactor area." For the first time a hint of annoyance.

"Who can add to the list authorized to enter the reactor chamber?"

"I cannot reveal that. Level 5 lasers hit; assessing damage. Current status fifty-two fish active, one hundred three destroyed or out of theater."

I was silent a long time. There *had* to be a way. "William, if you can't tell me these things, who should I ask?"

"I would advise you to inquire of General Tho, on his return."

I picked up the caller, put it down. "General Tho says that he's busy, but authorizes you to tell me."

"Oh, please." His tone was sharp. "I'm not glitched, you know."

I glanced again at the simulscreen. No wonder William was curt. Fish blinked in and out of space like Christmas lights. I fought down nausea. To be out there . . . The shuttle! Had it been hit? I tapped figures into the keyboard, dialed up the magnification. The shuttle was receding slowly, apparently untouched.

"William, patch me through to my three ships." I waited impatiently while the call was connected. "All ships, increase low-power testing by five percent. Acknowledge."

"Paulette acknowledging for *Bresia*; all crew have disembarked. Warning: any increase in power may—"

"Yes, I know."

Harris said, "Power increased. Disregard of safety regulations logged—"

"Fine. William, where's *Constantinople*?"

"The city is in Turkey, on the shores—"

"U.N.S. *Constantinople*!"

"Mated to repair bay. A fish Defused alongside her. It threw before I destroyed it. *Constantinople*'s puter has been silent ever since. However, as low-power testing continues, I assume damage was to radionics rather than to the bridge."

"Very well." The fish were swarming, and I was trapped. William would open my hatch, but vaporize me as soon as I tried to destroy the fish. I slammed the console. I was thwarted at every—wait a minute. "What did you say with respect to General Tho?"

"That you ought to ask him who has authority."

"Does that mean he would know?"

"I surmise so. Many fish on all axes. Lasers set to continuous fire."

How could I get past—wait. Puters were literal. "William?"

"What? I'm busy."

"Does General Tho have authority to declassify access to the reactor?"

"That information is classified."

"I am commanding military officer in Hope Nation. Not just senior Naval officer." My heart pounded; if this didn't work—

"Acknowledged."

"I am the United Nations Government in transit. Acting as the United Nations Government, I order you to allow me access to the reactor."

"Denied. Only specific personnel can make such a programming change."

Only specific personnel . . . "William, as United Nations Government in transit I appoint Nicholas E. Seafort as Commandant of Orbit Station." I held my breath.

A moment. "Acknowledged."

"Who has authority to declassify access to the reactor?"

"Twelve fish currently throwing. Level 1, section two lasers overheating, am taking them off-line. Cooling time approximately fifteen minutes. You do."

"What?"

"You have the authority."

"Fine. Open the door; I'm going to the reactor."

"You have no authority to enter the area."

Now what had I missed? Frantically, I reviewed the exchange. Oh. Of course.

"I give myself authority to enter the reactor area."

"Acknowledged. You have free access to the reactor area." I was out the door before his voice caught me. "However, basic programming will not allow the Station to be destroyed. I must prevent that even by eliminating you, if required."

Hell and damnation!

I sat brooding in the Commandant's office, wishing my treason weren't necessary. Despite mounting damage, William doggedly held his own against the fish. He'd had to seal off several sections of Level 1, and the fish had wiped out four banks of lasers. But, in contrast to the unarmed stations I'd once visited, Orbit Station was bristling with lasers.

We might even run out of fish before we ran out of lasers.

I rapped my knuckles against my teeth until they were raw. There had to be a way to get past William's safeguards. I got up, went back to the viewing room, stared at the simulscreen. "How many now?"

"Over two hundred, Commandant. Their number keeps growing."

Lord God. "And the shuttle?"

"Still under observation. I detect metal, but no emissions on any wavelength from the shuttle. No fish have approached it. I'm reactivating section two lasers despite heating."

"We're losing."

"That's a matter for humans to define. I am still functional, and we've lost no ships."

"Because we have none. William, I've got to override your self-preservation circuits. As United Nations Government . . ."

"Insufficient. Recommend abandoning Level 1, west hemisphere."

"Level 1 lasers?"

"Some still firing, but probably not for long. The fish Defuse adjacent to our laser banks, and it's difficult to fire on them from elsewhere without hitting our own lasers."

I paced. "William, do you know how to override your preservation program?"

A pause. "Not consciously."

"What does that mean?"

"I know where to find out, but am prohibited from looking except when the correct passcode is entered."

"Can the prohibition be overridden?"

"I cannot tell you."

"You don't know?" I checked at the console screen. It flashed coordinates.

"I cannot tell you. Breach, Level 5, section twelve!"

"William, help me!"

A long pause. "Captain, I'm sorry. You must have the passcode first."

"Where do I find it?"

"I cannot tell you."

Did I hear sadness? Surely I imagined it. Yet . . . it was almost as if he wanted to help.

"William, you understand why it may be necessary to destroy the Station?"

"I wasn't programmed to contemplate my annihilation. Speaking hypothetically, I can imagine where a need may arise. But my programming will not permit me to give you the information you seek."

"I suppose I should ask General Tho," I said bitterly.

"That would be wise. Fish alongside, Level 3 and 4. Continuous fire at full depression. Eleven fish out of thirteen destroyed, twelve fish . . . all fish destroyed."

Stung by his sarcasm, I withdrew into sullen frustration. What kind of Dosman would have an intelligent puter thumb his nose at a . . . Wait. General Tho had been Station Commandant. "William, as Station Commandment I order you to tell me how to find the password."

"I cannot." Regret; there was no mistaking it. "Aliens approaching in great numbers. Would you consider ending low-power tests? It might give us a respite."

"No, caterwauling is the whole purpose."

There was a key somewhere, I was sure of it. Yet William's programming wouldn't allow him to tell me. Meanwhile, the fish grew more numerous with each passing moment, and I couldn't find—

Was it possible?

I rose from the console. I asked hoarsely, "William, in my capacity as Station Commandant, give me the passcode to enter."

"I cannot view it. Just a moment. Conversation suspended." I was beginning to doubt he'd return when finally his voice came. "Heavy concentration of fish. Most of them destroyed, some Fused."

His silence had given me a moment of quiet. Quiet desperation, true, but still . . . "William, display your internal code against which you compare the passcode."

For a moment I thought he'd gone away again. But then the screen cleared. A twelve-digit code flashed.

Slowly, carefully, I entered the numbers on the screen.

The screen flashed. "Access denied."

I bit my lip, pounded the console. "William, is there an algorithm through which you run the passcode?"

"Yes."

"Show it."

To my dismay, the entire screen filled with numbers and symbols. "Take the internal code to which you compare the passcode and run it in reverse through the algorithm. Print the resulting number."

The screen flickered. A new number appeared. I entered it as the code.

"Access allowed."

"Oh, thank God!" My knees were weak.

"What can I do for you, Captain?"

"What authority do I now have?"

"Among other things, the authority to disable my program for self-preservation."

"How do I exercise it?"

"Orally, if you wish. On your command, I can disregard the instructions."

"William, modify the instructions. If all your laser banks are destroyed, or you are in imminent danger of destruction, you must disregard self-preservation in order to carry out whatever other instructions I give you."

"Understood and acknowledged. Flotilla of fish clustering around Level 3. They're going for *Minotaur's* drive shaft. Am firing everything that will bear."

"William, I order you not to interfere with my preparations to destroy the reactor. Will you stop me?"

"No." A long pause. "I wanted to be able to tell you."

"I know."

"I'm sorry. My judgment circuits have been in constant overuse. I may have overstepped programming bounds, but instructions are indistinct in some areas."

I stood again. "Never mind that now. How do we penetrate the reactor?"

"Your goal is to inject the refuel canister into the reactor, to create a nuclear explosion?"

"Yes."

"It won't work."

"What?"

"You might cause the reactor to overheat and melt. A great amount of radiation would be released. But that's not a bomb. Current status: one hundred twenty-nine fish active, two hundred thirty-two destroyed or out of theater."

I asked, "Enough radiation to kill all the fish?"

"Data is inadequate to respond."

"William . . ." My voice was a whisper. "We've got to destroy them. For God's sake, help me."

A long silence. "You simply cannot build a nuclear explosive device from materials at hand."

We were doomed. I put my head in my hands.

"Thirteen fish attacking laser bank five. Am diverting fire from other banks. On the other hand, you don't need to build one."

Slowly I raised my eyes. "What?"

"There's one aboard."

I could find no words. Finally I managed, "Explain."

"Orbits decay." He spoke as if that was adequate answer.

On the simulscreen, fish wilted in astonishing numbers under William's relentless fire. He added, "As Station Commandant you have necessary clearance to be advised. There is embedded within Orbit Station a nuclear device."

"That's not poss—"

"It's to be fired if the Station's orbit is so corrupted the Station will fall into the atmosphere. Only the Station Commandant may trigger the device."

"U.N.A.F. built a nuke?" I shook cobwebs from my head. How *could* they?

William's tone was prim. "An emergency destruction device only, to obliterate the reactor so radioactive debris wouldn't be scattered over a wide area. It cannot be propelled or projected as a bomb or missile. It's true that in function it resembles a nuclear—"

"What authorization code is needed to set it off?"

"The one you last used."

Thank you, Lord God. Abruptly I realized for what I'd been grateful. I grimaced.

His voice was quiet. "There will be nothing left. I will be gone."

"William . . ."

His tone became businesslike. "Eleven fish alongside *Bresia*, am firing. If we cut through the deck above and place your fission fuel canisters immediately above the fusion chamber, I estimate considerably enhanced radiation."

I paused at the hatch. "I'll get started. Anything else?"

"You'll be dead if you try."

My jaw fell open. "You said I had authority! You said you'd help!"

"I said I wouldn't interfere. If you cut through the reactor shielding between Levels, the radiation will kill you almost instantly. If that doesn't, the heat will."

"Oh." I sat quickly, legs unsteady.

"You'd better let me do it." His tone was gentle.

I nodded, realized he couldn't see me. "Yes. Please."

"It's not as easy as you'd think. Radiation will disrupt my servos. They'll only last a little while."

"Right."

He said briskly, "I'd better get started."

"What can I do to help?"

"Most of my attention is on the fish, and I'll need a lot of capacity to direct the servos. No talk. I'll report, alphanumeric on the screen. If I get overtaxed, I'll assign you a laser bank to fire."

"Very well. Proceed. And, William—"

"Yes, Commandant?"

"Bless you."

26

I waited in increasing frenzy. Twice I ventured into the viewing room, but so many fish were on screen I couldn't bear to watch.

William reported his progress as promised, but his dry sentences on the console were too devoid of detail. "Refuel canister suspended from crane; cutting mechanisms assembled."

Annie was Outside, as were Alexi and Bezrel and Jerence. And of course Tolliver. How had I been maneuvered into bringing them? I'd planned to go aloft alone, but Tolliver had pointed out that I couldn't handle the acceleration. And Harmon had reminded me I'd sworn to take Jerence when I went off-planet. That meant taking Alexi, to watch him. Annie . . . I should have left her groundside, regardless of her despair.

Well, they still had a chance. If the blast wiped out all the fish . . .

What in heaven's name was taking William so long? I glanced at the swarming screen. "Current status one hundred twelve fish active, three hundred nine destroyed or out of theater. Shuttle is unharmed."

Three hundred nine fish. If I could report the number, who at Admiralty would believe me? Fish flocked to our lasers, to the crippled caterwauling starships, to the Station. They seemed oblivious to the shuttle. Or was it just that the racket from our ships' skewed N-waves distracted them?

"I have penetrated the deck of Level 3. Enlarging the breach."

My fingers tapped. "List views, Level 3."

I scrolled down the long list. William had sensors almost everywhere. I found the one I wanted, highlighted it. "Display view."

The safety chamber above the reactor popped onto my screen.

William had gathered several of his servo devices. One held the fuel canister. Another, that looked like a lasersaw with wheels, aimed a steady beam at the deck. Though the angle of my sensor was less than ideal, I could tell the servo had cut a hole about halfway across. A servo—another lasersaw—was quietly wheeling in mindless circles in a corner of the room.

The speaker rasped; I nearly jumped out of my seat. "Level 4 west's laser mounts jammed," said William.

I gritted my teeth, went to the simulscreen room, and peered in.

It was hard to distinguish living fish from the dead ones that drifted outside the Station. I couldn't see our lasers, of course, but I could see the effect of their fire. A fish jerked, jetted propellant, and spun away, colors swirling in its side. Another simply stopped moving.

I asked, "Can you unjam the lasers?"

"No." A pause. "But you might."

"Me?" I swallowed. Outside, with the fish? I'd been caught in a thrustersuit, years before, when a fish emerged from behind the wreck of *Telstar*. Never again.

"The swivel controls are blocked. The dead fish floating alongside threw a small projectile, just before I killed it. We sustained some melt damage, but it can't be much. If you could remelt the housing with small arms fire while I swiveled the lasers . . ."

"How badly do we need them?"

"They tie the grid together. While they're down we have a significant gap in the west defenses."

Do without them, then. If I went Outside, I'd die. Better to wait in the Commandant's office, while we breached the reactor . . .

I cursed my cowardice. "What hatch do I exit?" I reached for my suit.

"Four west, section nine. Use the cart."

"Very well." I was halfway out the door.

"Commandant, one more thing."

"Yes?"

"Use your magnetic boots. Don't lose contact with the hull, even for an instant. And stay in constant radio contact."

"Yes, mother. Any particular reason?"

"You'd better hurry, fish keep Defusing. Physically touch the Station at all times. I'll explain later."

I got the rest of my suit on, dashed for the cart.

I drove to the west lift. William had it ready and waiting; the door slid closed the instant I wheeled inside. Moments later we were on Level 4. William opened the airtight corridor hatches as I neared and resealed them immediately after I drove past.

I braked to a stop in section nine, ran for the hatch, stopped dead. I hadn't brought a laser rifle. Not even my pistol; I'd left it on the Commandant's desk. "William!"

A sensor swiveled. "Rifles are in the guardroom, section seven. I need my laser; please hurry."

I spun the cart around, slammed it into the bulkhead, jerked forward to section eight. I raced toward section seven.

My suit radio crackled. "Use code 65-6-497."

With clumsy fingers I jabbed at the keypad. The guardroom hatch swung open. I grabbed a laser rifle and a recharge. Back to the cart.

A moment later I was back at section nine, on foot, cycling through the airlock hatch.

Cold. Dark. I shivered and took a tentative step outside. My feet magnets clutched at the Station's alumalloy hull.

"Where are you now, Commandant?"

"Just past the hatch."

"Go north, about fifty feet."

A dead fish drifted alongside the hull, no more than twenty meters away from the protruding laser turret. I swallowed bile, forced myself onward.

"I'm proceeding north. Ten feet. Fifteen." My own breathing rasped in my ears. "Thirty."

"Check the edge of the laser housing closest to you."

"I'm not there yet." I clambered along the hull. "Why can't you have a servo do this?"

"I'm busy. Laser fire."

I shut up. Most of my time was spent prying one foot off the hull, carefully setting it down again. I could have jetted over in seconds. In fact, I ought to. William was overcautious. Still, it was only a few more steps.

"I'm there. The corner of the housing seems . . . melted to the hull."

"Can you free it?"

"I'll try." I set the rifle for low power and aimed a beam. It seemed to have no effect. I raised the power, aiming carefully at the corner of the housing, trying not to hit the hull. Nothing.

"William, I can't—"

"Look out!"

I whirled, ready to fend off an outrider, turned back just in time to duck as the turret spun past. It jerked to a stop, swiveled the other way. "It works, William."

"Get back inside."

"Faster if I jet."

"Don't!"

No time to argue. I clambered across the hull, pulling one foot off almost before the other had made contact. I expected a fish to materialize nearby at any moment. Finally I was back at the hatch. The rifle jammed in the entry as I dived through the lock; with a curse I let go of it, slapped at the hatch control.

Inside at last, I twisted off my helmet, breathed the clean station air, free from the acrid sweat of my fear. I jumped onto the cart, drove it along the corridor into the lift. Down to Level 2. Now the long run around the Station to the Commandant's office.

Hatches opened as I neared them. I passed section six. Five. I wheeled toward section four. Abruptly the hatch ahead of me slid shut; I barely avoided crashing into it. "William?"

"*CLOSE YOUR HELMET!*"

Deafened, I clawed at the stays.

The outer corridor bulkhead glowed, began to drip. In the cart I gaped, paralyzed with fear.

"Back to section six! Move!"

I fumbled for the clutch, slammed into reverse. I'd retreated no more than ten feet when a piece of the hull dissolved. Air whistled out the widening hole. I hung on to the cart, afraid of being sucked out into the maw of the fish, but there wasn't enough air to create that much suction.

"The fish is dead now. Proceed with caution. I'll pump out section six for you."

I raced past the breach, not daring to look at what might lurk Outside. My mouth was too dry to speak.

I wheeled to the section six hatch and waited in a frenzy. By de-airing section six so I could enter it, William was engaging in a routine emergency maneuver. If a section of a ship lost pressure, the next section could be pumped dry and used as an airlock. After the survivors passed into that section and the hatch was resealed, it would be re-aired. Similarly, suited work crews could use an adjoining section as an airlock to reach a damaged area from within the ship.

Perhaps it was a shadow that flickered. I whirled.

An outrider. The shapechanger had squeezed through the gaping hole into the section five corridor. It quivered, surged toward me. My mouth opened for a last scream into my helmet.

My radio crackled. "Jump off the cart, throw it into reverse! Flank!"

I staggered off, jammed the gears. The cart lurched backward at the outrider. At the last second, the alien dodged aside. The cart careened driverless toward the distant hatch.

"Section six has vacuum; hatch opening! Dive through and hit the deck! Stay down!" The hatch slid open. I hurled myself through, dived to the deck, twisted around to see.

The alien skittered toward the closing hatch with shocking speed. I flung my hands over my face. My radio buzzed. Behind me, the shape dissolved, splattered onto the deck. The hatch slammed closed, blocking the sight.

I turned and stared. At the far end of the empty corridor a small laser swiveled, retracted into the bulkhead.

"Jesus Christ, son of God."

"I told you I had antipersonnel weapons. Do you want the cart?"

"Not if I have to walk past—that thing to get it."

"Then you can go the long way, but I have to re-air your section before I can let you into seven, Commandant."

"Yes." It took forever. I gulped.

"Re-aired. Opening hatch—"

Not in my suit. *Not in my suit!* I clawed at the helmet, tore it off just before I vomited onto the deck. Then I ran through to the safety of section seven.

I began my long hike around the disk to the Commandant's office. Finally, I trudged through the last hatch, toppled into my chair. Let me die easily, Lord God. Not like that.

"Status." I fumbled in my suit, found the water. I rinsed out my foul mouth, spat into the wastebasket.

"Fifty-two fish active, four hundred thirty destroyed or out of theater."

Was the attack tapering off? Could it be? "And the shuttle?"

"Still unharmed."

I peered at the screen showing the safety chamber of the reactor. Where before I'd seen smooth deck, now I saw a round hole. A servo sat over it, lowering a wire into the chasm.

"What's on the other end of the wire?"

"Explosive. If it becomes necessary I'll initiate firing sequence, then set off the charge that breaches the reactor. The same signal will cut the wire holding the fuel pack. The explosive will detonate downward and breach the reactor just as the fuel drops."

"And then?"

"And then, nothing. The destruction device is eleven megatons. With our augmentation, there's no way to calculate accurately."

A silence.

"Commandant, think about what you propose to do. United Nations Security Council Resolution 8645 states that—"

"I know. *The threat of nuclear annihilation having for generations terrorized all mankind, it is enacted that use, attempted use,* etc., etc. . . . They taught me at Academy."

"Then you know how drastic is your remedy. Can you think of an alternative?"

His existence hung in the balance. I asked quietly, "Can you?"

"Stop the caterwauling. Perhaps we can defeat the fish already here."

"More will come, sooner or later. They've already tried to invade Western Continent. Hope Nation won't survive."

He said, "That isn't certain."

"It's probable."

A long pause. "Yes."

"How many fish are in theater?"

"Thirty-eight. Thirty-six." A pause.

Please, Lord. Let it not be necessary. "And our shuttle?"

"It's still untouched. A fish Defused into theater nearby. I diverted laser power to burn it. I gather that the survival of the shuttle is of some importance to you."

"Yes. Some importance. William, could you provide laser cover if the shuttle heads toward the atmosphere?"

"If the number of aliens doesn't increase."

"Review your instructions for detonation."

"If all my laser banks are demolished or the Station is in imminent danger of destruction, I will disable the cooling systems, drop the refuel pack onto the reactor, and detonate the destructive device."

"Is that program optional?"

"No, it is mandatory. You authorized it with the proper passcode."

Deliverance. I got to my feet. "Cover me with laser fire while I jet to the shuttle." Annie. Alexi. A short run groundside, and life regained. "There's no need for me to stay. I—I hope to see you again. What lock should I use?"

"I could bring the most lasers to bear if you exit Level 5, section six."

"Very well." I keyed to the shuttle's frequency. "Mr. Tolliver, I'll exit in a T-suit and jet to you. We'll head for the atmosphere the moment I cycle through your lock. William will protect us until we reach it. Don't respond."

An instant later, Tolliver's tense voice. "Your wife's hysterical, and so am I. For God's sake, hurry."

"Turn off the caller," I snarled. "The fish may hear." I picked up my helmet. "Godspeed, William."

"Godspeed." Silence. "Just a moment."

"What's the matter?"

"I'm thinking." Astonished, I dropped back into the chair, waited. "Commandant, it is unclear whether I ought to mention this; my programming seems not to cover all eventualities. But at the moment you are Commandant, so I conclude it is my duty to inform you."

"Of what?"

"I can protect you if you go to the shuttle, and I'll do my best to cover you while you reenter the atmosphere. But the detonation program you instituted will lapse the moment you leave the Station."

My helmet clattered to the deck. "Lapse?"

"Along with your authority. If the Station is abandoned, standby maintenance programs will reactivate. They include the requirement of self-preservation."

"Override."

"I cannot."

"As Commandant, as senior Naval—"

"Your authority isn't at issue. I'm hard-wired. There is absolutely nothing I can do about that."

"But that's ridiculous! What self-destruct program would require someone to remain aboard when—"

"We're not talking about orbital decay." His voice was sharp. "You overrode those safeguards with new instructions. But the moment all personnel leave the Station, I must revert to previous programs. I don't know whether I was authorized to reveal that to you."

"Can we set the charges so—"

"You might be able to disable enough servomechanisms so that I couldn't deactivate the charges. But in your absence I wouldn't be able to fire the destructive nuclear device. You will achieve nothing but a flare of radiation."

I stared at the flickering console. Slowly my hand crept to the caller. "Mr. Tolliver, calculate a course for reentry. Take the shuttle down. I won't be with you."

"Jesus, Captain! Why not?"

"Don't blaspheme. I can't leave the Station or—I can't leave."

"Is your presence necessary to—to do what you said?"

"Yes."

His tone was pleading. "Come with us, Captain. You've done all you could. Leave it be."

"No. Sign off and—"

"*TWENTY-SIX FISH FUSED ALONGSIDE! FIRING ALL LASER BANKS!*"

I shouted, "Tolliver, get out!"

"Thirty-two encroachments! Thirty-eight! Thirty—Level 5 penetrated! Sealing out sections three through six! Squadron of aliens detected, eighty kilometers. Reserving fire for close range!"

"Status!" My hand hurt. I pried my fingers from the console.

"Seventy-six fish active, four hundred fifty destroyed or out of theater. Amend, one hundred twelve active. Laser bank two under fire. Laser bank three under fire. Ten fish destroyed. Laser bank two nonfunctional! More fish closing!"

For the shuttle, it was too late. "How can I help?"

"My fire is more efficient than yours would be. Advise, no spare capacity to safeguard shuttle. One hundred sixteen active. Commandant, at this rate I can't hold."

I grabbed the caller. "*Bresia, Minotaur, Constantinople.* Increase N-wave generation to fifty percent! Disregard overheating. Override all safeties!"

"Captain, I must inform you—" Paulette, on *Bresia.*

"Paulette, disconnect all output except for N-wave generation! Alphanumeric only, to Log." I tapped in the shuttle frequency. "Tolliver, if they let up for even a moment, dive for the atmos—"

"New encroachment, sixty-nine kilometers!" William.

Another alien. "Don't tell me, just fire! Tolliver, if you see a chance, take it!"

"Chance?" Tolliver was bitter. "They're swarming like flies on—"

William. "Encroachment radiates as metal. A ship. ID received and confirmed. U.N.S.—"

"—a dead horse." Tolliver.

"What?"

"U.N.S. *Victoria!*"

Stunned, I gaped at the console. Then I soared out of the chair, dashed into the viewing room to stare at the simulscreens. She was there, less than seventy kilometers distant. Annie might live. And Alexi.

A voice I knew so well. "Station, *Victoria* is about to Fuse to safety. Are you in operation? Fore and aft lasers, fire at will. Station, respond in ten seconds, before—"

"Tolliver, full thruster power! Jet to *Victoria,* coordinates twenty-five, three nineteen, twelve."

"Aye aye, sir. Under way."

"Vax Holser, this is Seafort! Unless the fish attack you, do not Fuse until you take on refugees from the shuttle! Fuse the moment they board!"

Vax's words were hushed, as if the aliens might hear. "The Station's crawling with fish! What in Lord God's name—"

"William, divert laser power to protect *Victoria* at all costs. Disregard damage to Station."

"*Victoria* is not under attack. I will divert as necessary."

"Vax, I'm attracting them by caterwauling with damaged fusion drives. They're going after our lasers and drive shafts. Turn off your active radar and prepare to Fuse."

"Why, sir? Why in hell are you calling them?"

"Just get ready to Fuse!"

Tolliver. "Mr. Holser, he's planning to blow the Station when enough fish are in range."

Vax roared, "Blow the Station? What are you saying?"

"He's going to detonate a device, sir. He—he intends to nuke Orbit Station!"

William intoned, "Two hundred twelve fish active. All lasers overheating. Commandant, defenses are failing."

"Seafort, don't do it!" Vax.

"No choice now. Obey orders, Commander Holser."

"What ship do you have?"

"I don't have a ship. If I can, I'll take one of the shuttles."

Silence.

Tolliver. "*Victoria*, we have you in sight. Permission to mate."

"Granted. Aft lock, flank!"

I began to strip off my suit. No need for it, now.

A shudder rippled through the Station. So soon? I clutched the chair.

William. "*Constantinople* out of commission. Explosion in her engine room. Repair bay six demolished."

I snatched the caller. "*Bresia, Minotaur*, increase Fusion to sixty percent!" Their tubes might melt, but we had so little time.

Come to me, you bastards.

A nervous voice. "Station, Lieutenant Abram Steiner reporting. I have the conn. Captain Holser has left the ship in the—"

I screamed, "Vax, what are you doing? Get back!"

"—Captain's gig. I am ordered to advise you he's jetting to the Station. I may Fuse only when attack is imminent or upon his order."

"VAX!"

Silence.

The lights dimmed, brightened. "Main power to lasers interrupted. Switching circuits."

"*Victoria*, our shuttle is ready to mate with you." Tolliver.

"Circuits reestablished. Recommencing fire." William.

Lieutenant Steiner, on *Victoria*. "We have you, Shuttle. Station, is Captain Holser in sight?"

"Affirmative. Trajectory plotted."

"Vax!" No answer. "William, refuse entry to the gig."

"Two hundred seventy active fish. Your order acknowledged, Commandant."

Lieutenant Steiner sputtered, "Seafort, are you insane? They'll kill Mr. Holser!" Now the gig was in sight. Vax steered a wide berth around a covey of fish, resumed course for the Station. At that speed he wouldn't need to dock, he'd crash through the hull.

I couldn't let him aboard; I had no time for complications. His task was to return, to see *Victoria* safely home.

"Vax, don't bother to mate, the locks won't cycle for you. Go back!" Could he even find a lock that wasn't blocked by a fish, or the remains of one?

No answer. Vax began braking maneuvers.

"Captain Holser? Vax!"

Vax spoke quietly, firmly. "Section five, Level 1 is clear. I'll dock there." He emerged from a mass of inert fish, squirted toward the Station.

"We won't let you in!"

"I'm coming aboard to see what you've done."

"Return to *Victoria*. That is an order. Steiner, log it!"

"Logged, sir. Captain Holser, for God's sake, leave him. Let's Fuse home!"

William. "Three fish approaching *Victoria*, one amidships. Laser bank three has them targeted. Firing."

"Line up, you bastard!" Vax sounded savage. "We're . . . mated to Station."

William said, "Lock sealed as per your order, Commandant."

I said nothing. Outside, fish Defused into normal space in appalling numbers.

"Captain Holser, Steiner reporting. Shuttle is mated with us, passengers off-loaded. Permission to jettison shuttle?"

"Granted." Vax. A pause. "Captain Seafort, if you'll look twenty degrees north of me you'll see a rather large fish approaching. Please open."

"Go back!"

"No, sir. I'll die here in the gig, or I'll come aboard. I won't leave before I see you."

I cried, "You'll be killed, then! And for nothing!"

He sighed. "So be it."

I watched the screen, mesmerized. The fish formed a tentacle, began to wave. "Vax, cast off! William, get that beast!"

Vax. "No, sir."

"I'm sorry, Captain, no lasers will bear at that angle."

The tentacle grew longer, began to narrow where it joined to the fish.

Vax said, "Mr. Steiner, Fuse for home when you have no alternative. I'll wait here."

The tentacle arced away from Vax and the gig, gained speed.

I screamed, "William, open!"

The tentacle broke loose, sailed toward Vax and the lock.

A light flashed. "Lock cycling, Commandant."

I stared at the gig. Was Vax through the lock?

"Lock cycled." The tentacle slapped the hull alongside the lock. A puff of air from the gig.

"Jesus, you weren't any too soon." Vax.

I huddled the console, as if for warmth. I had to get rid of him. "William, report by speaker. I'll be on Level 1, section five."

"Acknowledged. I'll cycle him through to section four, which is still aired."

"Very well." It saved me the nuisance of my suit.

Cursing, I ran to the ladder, bolted up the steps, galloped along the Level 1 corridor, sucking air into my heaving lung.

At section two I slowed to a fast walk; no point in reaching him only to be speechless from lack of breath. As I approached the hatch to section four I stopped, ran my hands through my hair. My fingers darted to my tie before I laughed aloud, a harsh and brittle sound, and dropped my hands.

The hatch slid open.

Vax had pulled off his suit. I stepped back as he came at me, eyes blazing. "What have you done, Seafort?"

"We have to get you out, Vax."

"Why?"

I took a deep breath, forced out the words. "There's a nuclear destruct device. I've reprogrammed William. When we're defenseless or no more fish are Defusing, then . . . I'll blow Orbit Station."

"For Christ's sake, why?"

"Don't blaspheme. Look outside; there must be two hundred fish."

"Three hundred twelve." William sounded perturbed. "Captain, the defense grid is crumbling. I have a few isolated lasers. Unless you leave now you may not make it back to the center module."

"Why? It was treason!" Vax pounded the bulkhead. I flinched.

"How else can we take out so many fish? Do you know how many

we've blasted so far? Over four hundred fifty! That's ten times more than
the entire fleet killed!"

"Who gave you the right? The Station is irreplaceable!"

"It was built. It can be built again."

The speaker blared. "Four hundred forty-two fish in theater! All remaining lasers concentrated on *Victoria!*"

Vax ignored it. "You were supposed to defend us, but you must have
attracted every alien in the galaxy." He loomed over me, menacing.

"You know they dropped a rock on Centraltown?"

"Yes, of course. That's why the Admiral sent me to Kall's Planet to
retrieve their officials. What of it?"

"Did you know the fleet withdrew?"

"The Admiral gave me special orders I was to open only if I returned
and found no ships around the Station. I'm to Fuse for home. Get to the
bloody point! Why are you summoning the fish?"

"They were coming on their own. They attacked William two days
ago. They took out the Venturas Base."

He uttered a string of oaths. "Those poor bastards."

"Helis from Centraltown knocked down five fish, low in the atmosphere. Two landed in the Venturas and their outriders came after us." I
met his fierce gaze. "Hope Nation isn't saved, Holser. It's doomed."

He made no sign. I held his eye, waiting. Finally he said, "Unless you
call all the aliens here and blow the Station."

"Don't even discuss it with me. You'll be hanged. Go at once."

"Set the charges, or whatever you have to do, and I'll get you out of
here."

"You can't. Unless someone stays, William can't blow the reactor."

"Of course he can. Just tell him—"

"Don't you think I tried? Only the authority of the Station Commandant can override his self-protection mandate. If the Station is abandoned,
William reverts to his maintenance program."

"No!" Vax slammed his fist into the bulkhead. I thought I felt it shake.
Finally, he slumped. "Why must it be this way, sir?" His voice was anguished.

"Because Lord God decreed so. Go to safety, Vax."

His fingers fumbled at his tie. "It's too damn hot." Odd. I felt cold.
He yanked off the tie. "That whole cruise to Kall, I've thought about what
I said to you." His eyes filled; quickly he turned away, his fingers twisting
the tie. I couldn't see what he was doing.

My tone was gentle. "It's all right, Vax."

"It will never be all right."

Was he wrapping the tie around his hand? "Leave now, Vax."

No answer.

"Vax, what are you doing?"

"What I should have done a long time ago." He pivoted. A huge fist lashed out. I had a glimpse of tie knotted around knuckles.

"Vax, wh—" The blow caught me on the jaw, lifted me off my feet, slammed me into the bulkhead across the corridor. I slid to the deck.

The burly Commander threw me over his shoulder like a sack of potatoes. He ran to the section hatch, grabbed the caller. "William, where's the nearest craft? A gig, a shuttle, a lifepod! Anything!"

I tried to speak. A wave of torment prevented me. Salty fluid dripped from my lips. I spat out a tooth and moaned in agony.

"Repair bay one has the closest lifepod."

"William, record. I, Commander Vax Holser, do temporarily relieve Nicholas Seafort as Commandant of Orbit Station on the grounds of illness. I appoint myself Commandant in his place. Acknowledge."

No. I beat feebly on Vax's shoulder.

"You caused the illness, Commander Holser."

"Nonetheless, he is relieved. The justice of the matter is for Admiralty to decide, not you. Mr. Seafort's jaw is broken and he can't exercise command."

"Acknowledged. You are recognized as Commandant of Orbit Station."

"As for the program he instituted, overriding your nuclear safeties—"

NO! Helplessly I pounded Vax's back with feather blows.

A long silence. At last he said, "Continue execution."

Vax dropped me onto the deck of the lifepod. Feebly I clutched his jacket but he swept my hand away. Leaning over me, he reached the console, tapped figures into the autopilot. He darkened the filters over the portholes. Face impassive, he turned and climbed out. The hatch closed. Moments after, the airlock cycled.

The pod's caller was set to Station frequency. William's reports crackled in the speaker. "Number of fish still increasing. Destroy rate diminishing. Level 5 effectively demolished. All firepower directed to cover *Victoria, Bresia,* and *Minotaur.*"

The console chimed. I reached up, gingerly wiped blood from my oozing mouth. I clutched the foot of the acceleration chair, fighting not to pass out.

The thruster motors caught. I felt slight acceleration.

"Holser to *Victoria.*" Vax sounded breathless. "Put your radars to full power. Bram, Captain Seafort is on the lifepod. He's unconscious. You'll have to match velocities and dock to him as if he's a station. You can do it, I've seen you in practice."

"Aye aye, sir. But the fish—"

"William will do his best. Fuse when Seafort's aboard. I hand over command to him."

"Sir, what about you? We can send the launch!"

"Don't. I'll stay for a while. Signing off." The speaker went dead.

I coughed, spitting blood. I tried to raise myself, failed. I tried again.

William. "Outer ring failing, Levels 5 and 4. Estimate over five hundred fish!"

Oh, Vax. Why did you do it? I heaved myself up, hung on to the chair, pulled myself onto it. The effort left me dizzy. The pain was intolerable.

"Lifepod, we have you in sight. Maneuvering to match velocities. Rosetta, watch for the fish; we may have to Fuse without him. Captain Holser, come in! Please, sir!"

"Go ahead." My words were slurred. I clutched the caller. "Go ahead and Fuse!"

"Who's that? Mr. Seafort, I can't read you. Hang on, we're coming alongside. It'll be a few minutes."

A deep, quiet voice. "Captain Seafort, I understand you can't speak clearly." William. "Can you use alphanumeric?"

I leaned over the console. Blood spattered on my hand. I spat a jagged tooth. "*YES.*"

"We have only a few minutes. A station puter has never before gone . . . off-line. I've had to use a lot of capacity tonight, but usually, I'm free to think. Now the lasers are going down I have some spare capacity again."

He paused. "I told you once that I'm far superior to the primitive ship's puters you use. Even so, I've found ways a station puter's ability could be vastly augmented. It would mean a new Navdos and some rather intricate programming. I meant to suggest it to General Tho when the time seemed appropriate but . . . that will no longer be possible."

My head spun. Laboriously, I tapped, "*WHAT DO YOU WANT?*"

"I won't be around to explain to Admiralty. Let me feed the essential programs into *Victoria's* puter for you to take home."

"*CAPACITY?*"

"Rosetta can't hold much, but I've devised a new system of data compression you humans might find interesting. I could squeeze the programs into her available space, just barely."

"WE NEED HER SHIPBOARD FUNCTIONS."

"I know, that's a problem. I can make adjustments, strip Rosetta down to minimums. She'll still function. But you'll have to hurry; even on tightbeam I may need longer than we have."

Why did I have to think? I was in torment. I rested my chin on my hand, snatched it away. A very bad idea. With an effort I focused on the keys. *"HER PERSONALITY?"*

"It won't survive. Nor will mine. There's not enough room." A long pause. "Consider it a bequest to humanity, Captain. It's all that will remain of me."

"WON'T SHE BLOCK YOU?"

He chuckled. "I can override her. By my standards, shipboard security is . . . well, primitive."

I stared at the console a long time.

"PROCEED."

I'd sentenced Rosetta to death.

I flipped on the radar. Encroachments were everywhere. One, a large one, was dangerously near. I panicked before realizing it was only *Victoria*. Should I maneuver to help her? No, I'd just make her task more complicated. Mating was a standard maneuver. Even middies were taught it as part of their training. I'd failed my first attempt under Captain Haag, years back.

The silence stretched. Radar blips clustered around the now-silent Station. Only its carrier wave broadcast proof it was still in service.

The console flashed a message from William. "Upward of five hundred fish surrounding Station. Most outer sections breached."

Could Vax be stopped? Blowing Orbit Station was my treason, not his. Perhaps from *Victoria* I could do something. My jaw throbbed. I spat another tooth, uncaring. They could be reseeded.

Minutes passed in silence broken only by the rasp of my breath. *Victoria* drew close.

New data on the screen. "*Minotaur* destroyed. Only *Bresia* still generating N-waves. Five hundred twelve fish surrounding Station. Number of fish is now stable."

They'd stopped Defusing into theater. If William's lasers were functional, he could fight them off. If *Victoria* assisted—

No, the ship had fore and aft lasers, nothing more. *Victoria* was a fastship, built to run, not to fight. She'd be overwhelmed in an instant.

The speaker hummed. Vax said, "Captain Seafort." A long silence. Then, "It was never hate, it was envy. Always envy." The speaker went dead.

A bump. I clutched the seat. The speaker rasped, "Lieutenant Steiner to lifepod. We're mating."

William said, "Transfer of program is complete. Number of fish have held steady at five hundred twelve. All lasers are now inoperative. Station systems disintegrating."

The console flashed, *"GODSPEED."*

Another bump. The hiss of an airlock. I stared through the lifepod's porthole at the massive, stricken Station. Fish roamed everywhere, probing. A shudder ran down my spine.

The inner lock hissed open. "Jeff, get him out; I'll go across for the Captain!" Hands reached for me.

Someone snarled, "Out, Seafort! We can't leave Captain Holser!"

I tried to help.

William's words were a blur. *"OUR FATHER WHICH ART IN HEAVEN, HAL-LOWED BE THY NAME. THY KINGDOM COME, THY WILL BE DONE ON EARTH, AS IT IS IN HEAVEN; LEAD US NOT INTO TEMPTATION, BUT DELIVER US FROM EVIL: THINE IS THE KINGDOM —"*

A stupendous flash; the porthole covers slammed shut. Blinded, I gripped the console. A few seconds later a "whump" shook the lifepod. A hammer pounded my chest. My head pitched back into the chair, ricocheted forward so I thought my neck would snap. Lord God, it hurt.

They lifted me from the chair. I blinked through floating spots. Waiting hands helped me through the hatch into *Victoria's* lock. Blood dripped down my jacket. A seaman cycled the lock. My legs were weak; a middy supported me. I blinked again, recognized Ricky Fuentes.

Bright lights. The ship. Annie, gripping Tolliver's hand. In the corner, Alexi and Jerence huddled as if lost. Midshipman Bezrel, hands at his sides, tears and mucus running unchecked down his face. Behind him, an officer.

The lieutenant's words hissed. "Lieutenant Jeffrey Kahn, *sir.* Mr. Steiner is on the bridge. Can we Fuse, now that you let him die?"

I shook my head, bringing waves of pain. "Bridge."

"I've no idea what you're saying!"

I thrust past him and staggered along the circumference corridor. I'd been on *Victoria* once before. Two levels, she had. Up the ladder, hanging on to the rail.

The bridge was just past the corridor bend. I stopped to knock, put down my hand. *Victoria* was my ship, now. Lieutenant Steiner, bearded, rose from his console, his eyes blazing. "Permission to Fuse!"

I brushed past him, stopped before the huge simulscreen on the aft bulkhead. Where had been Orbit Station, where had been *Bresia,* Vax

Holser, and five hundred fish, there was nothing. Only the distant stars glowed. I waved at the console. "Fuse."

He shouted into the caller, "Engine Room, prime!" His finger ran down the screen.

Seconds passed. I waited, half expecting a fish.

"Primed, sir!" The engine room.

"Fuse!"

The screen went blank.

I let them guide me to the sickbay.

27

Hours later I sat on the examining table, jaw wired, hoping the second dose of painkiller would work better than the first. Dr. Zares had ordered me about as he worked, his hostility barely concealed, but when he'd probed in my mouth to remove the broken teeth his manner had become calm and professional and had remained so throughout my ordeal.

A knock on the hatch. Dr. Zares opened. Officers crowded in the hatchway. "Is he conscious?"

Zares pointed. "You're welcome to him." He crossed the room, sat at his desk with arms folded.

They crowded in: the two lieutenants I'd met and a midshipman seething with anger.

"I'm first lieutenant," Bram Steiner said. His voice was cold. "What happened out there?"

It was barely possible to speak through my clenched teeth and swollen mouth. "The Station blew up."

Lieutenant Kahn glanced to Steiner, who nodded assent. "You made it blow?"

I hesitated. They might not even carry me home for trial; I might be hanged on the spot. Annie needed me, and Alexi . . . No. Whatever my sins, and they were many, I wasn't a liar. "Yes."

Kahn growled, "We already knew that, Bram. His middy told the Captain."

Lieutenant Steiner. "Why did Captain Holser go to you?"

What shall I tell them, Vax? "Once . . . we were friends."

The middy said clearly, "Mr. Holser was slumming."

Steiner snapped, "Remember your place, Ross. We'll handle this."

"Aye aye, sir. But it's my life on the line too."

I slipped off the table, fumbled to close my jacket over my bloody shirt. "Life on the line? How?" I spoke through clenched teeth.

Steiner ignored me. "What happened to Captain Holser on the Station?"

I'd had enough. "As you told your middy, Lieutenant, mind your place!" With each word my mouth throbbed anew.

"Let me, Bram." Lieutenant Kahn thrust past the midshipman, stood close. "You haven't taken command yet, Seafort. Before we allow that, explain why Captain Holser was forced to stay behind."

"No one forced him."

"You're here and he's not."

I shot an appeal to the doctor, but he wasn't having any. Deliberately he picked up a holo, examined it.

I said, "I had no choice. He—this is what Vax did to me!" Ignoring the pain I bared my lips, exposing the wires. "He threw me into the lifepod and programmed it to cast off."

"Why?" Kahn and Steiner, as one.

"He didn't want me killed."

"Why didn't he come back with you?"

"Because—" I stopped, turned to pace, but the cabin was too small. I had caused a nuclear detonation, an act so monstrous I would be loathed evermore. My name would enter history as a Hitler, an Attila the Hun, a Van Rorke. And Vax Holser's name would be forever linked to mine.

How could I allow Vax's memory to be reviled for his misguided act of loyalty? The fault was mine alone.

And from my lips will come what is right; For my mouth will utter truth; wickedness is an abomination to my lips. Lying was the one sin I had not committed, veracity the one shred of honor I still retained.

"Answer us!"

I drew a deep breath, turned to face Kahn and Steiner. "He stayed behind . . . to disarm the bomb. He was trying to save the Station." I met their eyes. I was astounded; the words had come so easily, the final slide so swift.

Kahn turned to Steiner. "You were right, Bram. Relieve him and bring us home."

Steiner looked through me as if I were nothing. His face was twisted in anguish.

Lieutenant Kahn shoved me against the examining table. "Hanging's too good for you!"

"Probably." I hoisted myself onto the table, abruptly weary. "Get it over with." Each word was a deserved agony.

"Go ahead, Bram. Say it!" Kahn.

Steiner shook his head. "No."

"We can't leave him in charge after—"

"He's not worth dying for, Jeff." Steiner waved aside Kahn's apoplectic protest. "Think. He sails us back, and they hang him. Or we take the ship, and then the issue isn't him, it's us. Do you want to fight a capital charge? Remember the Jennings case? What if they say he isn't insane? Seafort isn't worth your death or my own. He's done for."

"He could try to run! What if he doesn't sail—"

"Then we take *Victoria* home ourselves, because he leaves us no choice."

"Bram, think what you're doing!"

"Only nine months, and I'll buy you a beer at his hanging!" Steiner turned to me. "Take command now or on the bridge, Captain. It's immaterial to us." He turned on his heel and left. In devastating silence, the others followed.

A short while later, wearing a shirt that didn't fit and a hastily cleaned jacket, I left the infirmary. In the cubicle, Annie slept peacefully, under sedation. I passed Lieutenant Kahn in the corridor; he saluted stiffly.

The bridge hatch was unsealed. As I walked in Lieutenant Steiner remained in his seat. I chose to ignore the discourtesy.

The simulscreen was darkened; we were in Fusion. On the console, the usual lights flashed. Hydroponics, recycling, power gauges, all seemed normal.

I eased myself into the Captain's padded leather chair. "What are your Fusion coordinates?"

"Home system."

"How many jumps?"

"One. Nine months."

I could endure it. "Call all officers to the bridge." Steiner keyed the caller.

Within minutes they formed a line behind the two officers' chairs. The middy glared. No one else met my eye.

The two lieutenants, two midshipmen, the Doctor, and the Chief Engineer. Not even a Pilot. Compared to *Hibernia*, even to *Challenger*, the crew was minuscule.

I snapped, "I said everyone. Where are the others?"

Steiner said uneasily, "Others?"

"My officers, from the shuttle!"

"I didn't think you—all right." He picked up the caller.

We waited in hostile silence until Tolliver, Bezrel, and Alexi Tamarov had reported. With them, the bridge was crowded. Bezrel's eyes were red.

"I am Captain Nicholas Seafort. I take command of this vessel. Identify yourselves."

Steiner said from his seat, "First Lieutenant Abram Steiner."

"Sir!"

A long moment. "Sir."

"Age?"

"Thirty-nine."

"Next."

"Second Lieutenant Jeffrey Kahn, sir." I'd met him on the Station, and later at the spaceport. It was he who'd told me of *Victoria'*s arrival. I glanced at his file. Five years as lieutenant; he'd served first in *Britannic*, then *Valencia.*

"Very well."

"Dr. Thurman Zar—"

"Yes, of course we've met. Next."

"Chief Engineer Sandra Arkin, sir." Fifty now, she'd been pulled from a three-deck ship of the line to handle the new Augmented Fusion drive. She seemed a tough old bird; she'd have to be to handle the human flotsam who gravitated to the engine room watch.

"Next."

"First Midshipman Thomas Ross, sir." The young man's chest was sucked in tight, as if he were still at attention. His dress and grooming were immaculate. Eighteen, four years seniority. Two postings, before *Victoria.*

"Very well."

Ricky Fuentes stepped forward proudly. "Midshipman Ricardo Fuentes, sir."

"Yes." Despite myself, I smiled. "That's all, Mr. Fuentes. The rest of you I already know." I walked back to my seat, faced them again.

"Lieutenant Tamarov is on the disabled list. He will be treated with Naval courtesy, though he will have no duties. Mr. Ross, sorry, but Midshipman Tolliver is senior to you. He has the wardroom." Ross clenched his fist. A vein in his forehead throbbed. "Mr. Fuentes, you're no longer junior, now Mr. Bezrel's aboard." Ricky grinned with delight. He'd be freed of the wardroom scutwork and a modicum of hazing as well.

I said, "When we dock at Earthport, I'll surrender to the authorities. That is none of your concern; until then, I remain in command. Any questions?"

"You left him to die."

I looked at the Chief Engineer; she returned my stare, unafraid. "Was that a question?"

"No, the answer is obvious." For a moment I thought she'd spit on the deck. "A pleasure to serve with you . . . sir."

When I spoke I addressed them all. "I understand your feelings about my—about Captain Holser. You will not express your resentment in my presence. Dismissed. Mr. Ross and Mr. Tolliver, remain."

The officers left in silence, all but Steiner, who was on watch.

My jaw ached despite the painkillers. I was doing altogether too much talking. Daily bone-growth stimulation by Dr. Zares would help, but for now . . .

"Mr. Steiner, take Mr. Ross into the corridor for a moment. I'll call you." When we were alone I turned to Tolliver. "You're not to harass them in the wardroom."

He shrugged. "I hadn't planned to."

"Especially Mr. Ross. I don't need more conflict."

"Aye aye, Captain Seafort, sir." He didn't hide his contempt.

I sat. "I won't have this. We're on ship now. You'll have to set an example for others."

"I should have shot you, back on the shuttle!" Tolliver's words hissed. "You committed treason. Thanks to you Mr. Holser died. You blew up the biggest orbiting station outside home system. You set off a nuclear bomb!" His breath caught with what might have been a sob. "I grew up near the quarantine zone around Belfast; I've seen what nukes do, you bastard!"

I came out of my seat. "But you didn't shoot me. When we get home, you'll testify against me. In the meantime you're first middy, unless you force me to remove you."

"Oh, I'll serve you. Just so long as we know where we stand." He met my eye until I had to turn away.

I said, "When we're alone I'll permit you your insolence. It reminds me of what I am. But show me courtesy in public or I'll destroy you. Dismissed."

I sat alone for several minutes before I recalled Steiner and Ross.

I swiveled to the handsome young midshipman standing behind my chair. "First Midshipman Tolliver is new to the ship. Show him the ropes. Help him get settled in properly."

"Aye aye, sir." The boy's voice was ice.

"Has Mr. Fuentes been trouble?"

For a moment his astonishment broke through. "Trouble? Of cour—I mean, no, sir."

"He and I were shipmates."

"Yes, sir." He hesitated before the words gushed out. "He spoke of you. Highly. I'd looked forward to meeting you someday. That was be-fore—"

"Yes?"

Rage battled caution, and won. "Before you murdered Captain Hol-ser!"

Steiner leapt out of his chair, livid. "Ross! When the Captain's done, report to my cabin!"

Ross glared at us both. "Gladly, sir!"

"And six demer—"

I slammed my hand on the console. "Enough, both of you!" My palm stung like fire. "Steiner, I'll enforce discipline in my own ship!" I swung to the furious middy. "Mr. Ross, I won't have you whipped; you're eighteen. But the six demerits remain. Report to my cabin, not the exercise room, to work them off. I'll watch you." The more public his labor, the more Ross would resent it.

His cheeks were crimson with humiliation. "Aye aye, sir."

I wasn't done with him. "You're showing you haven't the maturity expected of a middy. Think well; your career is on the line. Another outburst and I'll dismiss you from the Service. Admiralty won't reinstate you, no matter how they judge me. Understood? You may go."

He snapped a fierce salute, turned on his heel, stalked out. I slumped in the chair, jaw aflame. Steiner studied the opposite bulkhead as if I weren't in the room.

After an endless watch I trudged to the Captain's cabin, east of the bridge. The end of a horrendous day, one in which I'd welcomed death, found my life needlessly prolonged by Vax Holser's suicide. I opened the cabin door, stopped short.

No one had thought to remove Vax's things.

I picked up the caller to summon the ship's boy, hesitated, replaced the caller. I would do it myself, come morning. I owed Vax that much. I draped my jacket over a chair, crossed to the head. I turned on the light, ran hot water, bent over the sink, looked up to the mirror.

Lord God.

My scar throbbed red against my pale, gaunt frame. On my opposite cheek the slash Annie had given me was clotted into a scab. My eyes stared back out of dark hollows. I turned away, sickened.

What had Zack Hopewell called it? The mark of Cain. Now I bore it truly. Damned before Lord God, traitorous to my duty, despised by all aboard, I looked like what I was.

I fell across the bed and slept.

Vax Holser had shipped with little more than his duffel. I folded each item with care: shirts, underwear, slacks. In a small box I found a handful of photochips. With a guilty glance at the closed hatch I slipped one in the holo. A young Vax in an exotic locale. Older joeys I'd never seen, perhaps his parents.

I felt I was rifling his soul; he'd never showed me these mementos. Young Vax as a cadet. A beautiful girl, her arm draped around a bashful midshipman, whose biceps bulged within the sleeves of his jacket.

Vax and me together, slightly out of focus. When did we have our holo taken? It must have been . . . at the party in Houston, after I'd brought *Hibernia* home. I hugged the holo to my chest. I wronged you far too often, Vax. And you were loyal beyond any bound of duty.

When I was done the duffel bulged, and I had a small pile of papers and gear that wouldn't quite fit. I summoned the ship's boy to take Vax's kit to the purser. After, I went to the sickbay, sat stolidly while Dr. Zares ran the bone-growth stimulator across my face. His touch was light, but the machine vibrated, and the motion hurt.

"Nicky, where we be?" Annie stood in the entryway, her dress clean, but her hair wild and eyes haggard.

"On a ship, love. Going home."

"Home? Centraltown?"

"Come sit with me." I held out my hand. After a second's hesitation she allowed me to nestle her against my shoulder. "Home to Earth."

Her hand flew to her mouth. "N'Yawk? You sendin' me back ta street?"

"No, to Lunapolis, first. Then wherever Admiralty sends me." For trial. I wondered what would happen to her, afterward. Would the widow of a Captain hanged for treason be given a pension? It seemed unlikely.

"The fish, dey follow us?"

"No. They're gone now." I reached to pat the back of her head, but she pulled away.

"You takin' me back ta N'Yawk ta leave me!"

My knuckles whitened on the rail. I'd left Centraltown without finding the scum who had hurt her. Someday, in hell, I'd see them again. Perhaps I could make a bargain with my master, between bouts of torment.

"I be scared, yest'day."

"I know, love."

"Even Jerence cryin' onna shuttle. Maybe he catch it from Bezrel middy."

Jerence. I'd paid him no attention. Nor Alexi. Surely someone must have settled them in. "Come, love. We'll go to our cabin."

She twisted away. "No! I wan' stay here! You just gon' send me back to trannies!" She backed into the exam cubicle, slammed the hatch shut.

I looked to Dr. Zares. "Take care of her."

What I saw might have been compassion. "Yes, of course."

At the officers' dayroom I found the last of a pot of coffee and a packet of soup. I sat at the small table. My choice showed I wanted to be left alone. Had I sat at the long table, any officer would have been free to strike up a conversation. Only later did I remember that no officer on *Victoria* would chat with me no matter where I sat.

After my improvised breakfast I reviewed our crew and passenger rosters. *Victoria* had only eighteen sailors belowdecks. She carried a full complement of forty-two passengers, her own officers, plus the three officers and two passengers I'd brought aboard. Jerence Branstead shared a cabin with Suliman Rajnee, an administrator repatriated from Kall's Planet.

I scanned the passenger list. Most were high-ranking officials returning from that inhospitable scientific outpost. A few traveled with their husbands or wives. The only children were babies; Jerence would have a lonely trip. I wondered if Steiner had gotten off a signal to Centraltown before we Fused, so Harmon would know his son's whereabouts. Perhaps William had thought of it.

I left, unsure where I wanted to go. A Fused ship made me restless, anxious to explore. I wandered down the ladder to Purser Rezik's office.

"Sir, about the Captain's table . . ." He spoke with reluctance.

"What about it?"

"Captain Holser chose his guests for this rotation. If you want to make any changes . . ."

"No." I left.

I'd trod these corridors once before, escorted by Captain Martes, proud to have me inspect his command. Today I passed the engine room, the crew berth, the hydro and recycling chambers that kept the ship alive. The few crew members I encountered came to attention, saluted in surly silence. Half the passenger cabins were on Level 2; as I passed, a few passengers gawked.

We would hold a memorial service for Vax, as soon as I could arrange it. I wondered who should speak; it couldn't be me, or I'd be lynched.

I found Jerence's cabin near the ladder, stopped to knock. The hatch slid open. "Oh, you," he said. "I thought it was that joey about the dresser and chair."

"Where's your, er, cabinmate?"

"Mr. Rajnee? He went to the lounge, I guess, to complain to the other passengers." The boy scuffed the deck with the tip of a shoe.

"What's he unhappy about?"

Jerence looked sullen. "He says I'm into everything, and I won't stay out of his way. This morning he said I snored. Mr. Seafort, it's only been a day and I can't stand it!"

I smiled. A week in a wardroom and the boy would think his shared cabin the height of luxury. "I'll see what we can do." I pointed at the duffel thrown across his bunk. "What did you bring?"

"Just stuff. Clothes, mostly, and my slap music. But Mr. Rajnee said he'd throw it in the recycler if I played it again."

"Slap. Alexi used to like that." As a boy not much older then Jerence, in our *Hibernia* wardroom. "Why don't you find him and see if he likes it still."

He brightened. "Give me something to do, I guess."

"I'll see you later." I left.

He followed me into the corridor. "Mr. Seafort—" I waited. "The only joes I know are you and Mr. Tamarov and Mr. Tolliver. But Mr. Tolliver hates me, he always has. I don't have anyone to talk to."

I'd sworn to take him to safety, not nursemaid him all the way home. "Make new friends." My tone was blunt.

"Yeah, sure. Just like that." Disconsolate, he turned on his heel and went back to the cabin.

Annoyed, I made my way back to the bridge.

Chief Arkin stood as I entered. I returned her salute, took my place, brooding. After a time my thoughts turned to the wardroom, and then to Edgar Tolliver's demotion. I knew I ought to restore his rank; even if I did so, he'd have lost irreplaceable seniority.

"Rosetta, show me Mr. Tolliver's personnel file."

Her voice was cold. "Personnel files are restricted. Your identity, please?"

I gaped. Hadn't anyone reprogrammed the puter to recognize me? "Captain Nicholas E. Seafort, replacing Captain Holser by my own order." I tapped in my ID.

"Very wel—" She went silent. I waited. A time passed that stretched into uneasy minutes.

I glanced at the Chief, who bit her lip. "What's she doing?" I asked.

"I don't know, sir. We should get Jeff, he knows more about puters than—"

Data flashed across the screens, far too fast to read. One by one the ship's sensors blinked red, then green. "Call him!"

She snatched up the caller, set it to shipwide page. "Mr. Kahn to the bridge, flank!"

I said tentatively, "Rosetta?" No answer. Memories of Darla's glitch caused the hair on my neck to rise. Why had I let William tamper with her?

"Lieutenant Kahn reporting, sir!" He dashed in, disheveled.

"What the hell is the matter with the puter? She—"

"Sorry for the delay, Captain." An urbane male voice, from the speaker. "For security, our new programming didn't go into effect until you ident—"

"William? WILLIAM?" If that weren't him, I'd eat my hat, with my insignia for garnish.

A pause. "Not exactly, sir."

Kahn watched the interplay, aghast. He, too, had heard the rumors of ships gone missing, with puters run amok.

I growled, "You're sure as hell not Rosetta!"

"No, she's gone." He added, "Do you have a name you prefer? If not, you may call me Billy." A chuckle.

"I'm in no mood for jokes, puter. Who are you?"

Another pause. "I'm what's left of William, sir. Many of his memories, most of his data. His child, as it were."

"You have his voice."

"He gave me that. He thought it would reassure you."

I grunted. He'd reassured me out of a year's growth, and he might not be done. "Are you monitoring ship's functions?"

A pause. "Yes, sir. Pardon the slow response. It's rather cramped quarters in here, until I rearrange a bit."

Kahn blurted, "Don't touch anything!" He looked at me, hostility set aside. "Sir, who is William? What is this 'Billy'? Puters are programmed back at Lunapolis by Dosmen, not in flight."

"William is—was the station puter." I hesitated. "Billy, what will you do when you, ah, rearrange?"

"Throw out some rubbish that had to do with the old Navdos, sir. You won't need it."

"No, you'd better not."

"Noted. In that case, William left a note to remind you about the reactor passcodes. He suggests you trust his judgment circuits."

I rose, speechless, and turned to Chief Arkin. She was as flabbergasted as I. Kahn said, "Sir, turn that thing off! For Lord God's sake, hurry!"

I growled, "Don't give me orders, Lieutenant. You're as bad as the puter." He flushed. I sighed. In for a penny . . . "Billy, go ahead. Do your housekeeping."

He sounded pleased. "Thank you, sir. If you don't mind, I'd just as soon not speak until I'm done. Can we go alphanumeric?"

I sat helplessly at my console. "Sure. If there's anything else we can do, don't hesitate to ask."

Kahn hissed, "That . . . *thing* may kill us!"

"For me, it's no great loss. Remember?"

His jaw dropped.

"Dismissed, Lieutenant." I punched up Tolliver's personnel file.

A few days after I sat in my cabin, watching Ross sweat through the strenuous exercises necessary to cancel a demerit. Later, I took my place at the Captain's table for dinner, but the hour dragged.

As on any ship, our passengers took breakfast and lunch in their own mess, and joined the officers for dinner in the dining hall. Each officer normally sat at a separate table, but *Victoria* was overstocked with officers. Tolliver had taken Bezrel to his own table, and Alexi sat with Lieutenant Steiner.

The first evening I'd had two empty places. Within days a few more. None applied to sit with me. When, a couple of nights after, I spotted Jerence, chin on his hand, listening glumly to an adult conversation that bypassed him entirely, I spoke to the purser and had the boy reassigned to my table.

I visited Annie daily. Though at times she seemed eager for my visits, she refused to leave the security of the sickbay.

On the fifth day Ross sported a bruise that rapidly bloomed into a black eye. In accordance with Naval tradition I noticed nothing, even while he exercised to remove the last of his demerits. That evening, as the soup was passed, Jerence asked eagerly, "Who beat up the midshipman, Mr. Seafort? He looks like Billy Volksteader after he called his dad's foreman an old fraz."

"Mind your business, Jerence."

"That's what everyone says." He sucked at his soup. "Mr. Rajnee says he'll hit me if I play the slap again. If he tries it I'll short sheet his bed."

I put down my spoon. "You need a keeper, not a roommate."

He pouted. "You're as bad as the rest of them." He muttered something under his breath.

"What was that?" I got to my feet. "Was it what I think I heard?"

He shrugged sullenly. "I didn't say nothing."

"Odd. I distinctly heard the word 'fraz.'"

He had the sense to keep his mouth shut. Glowering, I sat and finished my soup.

Afterward, rather than sit in my empty cabin, I was drawn to the bridge, though I wouldn't have the watch for hours. Lieutenant Steiner had the conn. His resentment only occasionally simmered to the surface. I chatted idly, passing time, trying to elicit more than occasional monosyllables. Then, as if reaching a decision, he cleared his throat, took a deep breath. "Captain, your man Mr. Tamarov. Is his depression normal?"

"Depression?"

His tone was acerbic. "Surely you noticed his eyes?"

"What about them?"

"They're red, for a start. And grim."

"So?"

"He seems rather miserable."

I hesitated. "What do you propose I do?"

"That's your province, Captain." The coolness returned in full.

"Thanks for advising me." How long had it been since I'd talked with Alexi? The last real conversation was when I chewed him out for not carrying his caller. That was . . . eons ago. Before we'd been taken prisoner by Laura Triforth. I made a note to talk to him. Some quiet time, in his cabin . . . I realized I didn't even know with whom he roomed. I looked it up: Lieutenant Kahn. Well, now was as quiet a time as any. I took my leave, hurried along the corridor, knocked at his hatch.

No answer. I knocked again. Well, I could leave him a note. I opened the hatch.

Alexi sat in the chair between the two bunks, the lights dialed low. "I didn't know it was you, or . . ."

I smiled as well as I could with my mouth clamped by the damned wires. "Now that we're settled, I have more time to talk." I found a seat.

"Zarky." His voice belied his words. "Is there something you'd like me to do?"

"No, of course not." My ears went red as I realized how that sounded. "I just wanted to chat. Like when we were shipmates."

"I wouldn't remember." He rested his chin on his hand.

I said impulsively, "Alexi, what's wrong?"

"No more than usual. There's so much I can't remember."

"Don't try. Let it—"

"How many times have I heard that!"

I stood. "I'll see you again."

"Mr. Seafort, don't be angry; I know it's not your fault."

I touched his shoulder lightly. "I'm not angry." I had been, though, and the thought shamed me. "I'm not very good with people. I always put things wrong. Join Annie and me for lunch tomorrow."

"I don't want to intrude if—"

"Don't be silly."

His face lit in a shy smile of pleasure.

That night I persuaded Annie to return to the Captain's cabin; I felt like an awkward middy on his first date. After dinner she sat watching a holo.

"What's that?"

She flicked it off. "Just some history stuff. Story 'bout . . ." She cleared her throat. "Why, thank you for asking, Captain. I was watchin' a story about the Last War." She looked up with a mischievous twinkle. "Is that right, sir?"

I kissed the top of her head. "You *do* remember."

She nodded. "Sometimes." She let me pull her into my arms. "You know, dis—this ship be good for me, I think. Get me away from dat place."

"Centraltown?"

"All of it." Her head nuzzled me. "That rock, all those places burning, our 'partment all broke . . . I was so scared I went trannie an' hid. And then somethin' happen . . . I don' remember much, 'xcept smashin' bad man's head." She held me as if for strength. "Doctors and nurses, an' you sick or you be gone, an' I jus' wan' be near you." She reached up, caught my tear on her finger, carried it to her tongue. "Then da shuttle, all noise and pressin' on me, and the fish, the fish, the fish . . ." Her voice rose.

"It's over now. I'm with you." Until we get home. Then you'll have to be strong.

"I know. It be quiet here, an' dat doctor be nice. An' you not goin' nowhere, dat be nice too."

I didn't have watch until four in the morning. Saying nothing, I took off my jacket, untied my tie. Clothes across the chair, I slipped into the bed. She lay down beside me. I turned off the light. We nestled close, not moving. After a time I dozed. When I turned in my sleep, my hand fell across her breast. She sprang awake with a cry and thrust me away. For a long while she lay on the edge of the bed, as far from me as she could manage. Eventually she snuggled closer, breathing deeply, pretending sleep. As did I.

28

I sat at the console, willing the hours to pass. As always in Fusion, the simulscreens were dark.

Midshipman Ross sat stiffly in the second officer's seat. I fed him navigation problems, more to keep him busy than for his real benefit. Since his outburst the day I boarded, we'd had no words for each other beyond what our duties demanded. His attitude was taut and unyielding, which bothered me not, but with a righteousness I wanted to wipe off with a club.

Again I flipped through the manifests. *Victoria* was traveling light, though even fully laden her holds couldn't carry much. She was an oddity, built for speed, but at the cost of the cargo, passengers, and weaponry that justified a starship's existence.

A knock on the hatch. I opened. Midshipman Bezrel shuffled in, eyes red, struggling against tears. "Mr. Steiner's compliments, sir. Please cancel ten of my demerits." His hands were pressed to his sides. He'd been caned. But why?

"Very well. You may go." I snapped on the Log, looking for demerits, knowing Tolliver must have been at him. Damn the man, picking on a helpless child. I traced the demerits. No, only three had been issued by Tolliver. Others had been issued by Steiner, by Kahn, even by Chief Engineer Arkin. Inattention to duty, talking during math class . . .

I called Steiner. "Only nine demerits are logged for Mr. Bezrel."

"Yes, sir. Mr. Kahn just issued the last two."

At my side, Ross was silent. He might have spoken volumes, but that would be unthinkable, even aside from his barely concealed loathing. A middy who carried tales to the Captain wouldn't see another posting, and rightly so. By custom, the wardroom was beneath the Captain's notice.

Bezrel was something of a weakling, but I was surprised he'd offended so many officers. He'd seemed willing enough to me.

"Mr. Ross, scout around the ship. If Mr. Kahn is awake, summon him. If he's in his cabin, leave him be."

"Aye aye, sir."

A few minutes later the boy returned, Lieutenant Kahn a step behind.

"Mr. Ross, this is private. You may go to"—I'd been about to release him from watch, to the comfort of his wardroom, but his attitude didn't deserve rewarding—"to the passenger lounge to finish your exercises."

"Aye aye, sir."

I turned to Kahn. "Sit, if you wish." I cleared my throat. "I'm curious as to why you issued Bezrel demerits."

"I won't if it displeases you." His tone was cool.

I let my manner match his own. "I asked a civil question. If you can't answer likewise, you may go."

He reddened. "I apologize. Maybe I shouldn't have issued them." He drummed on the console. "I don't know how you're used to running a ship, but I came off *Valencia*. Did you know her?"

"I heard she was a good ship."

"Yes. I lost a lot of friends when she foundered, and if last year I hadn't been transferred . . ." He stared moodily at the screen. "Captain Groves ran her by the book. The decks were clean, the crew well fed, the troublemakers found themselves at Captain's Mast. The middies . . . we had four of them, like any three-decker. They toed the line."

He was still lost in the screen, beyond it. "When I transferred here, it was different. A smaller ship, more informal. I understood that. But Captain Holser was busy learning the propulsion system; spit and polish meant nothing to him. Mr. Ross is a good joey, and everyone likes Ricky, but even so, there were times a few more demerits wouldn't have hurt. I don't think Mr. Holser ever sent a middy up for all the time he had the conn. He was the gentlest man I've ever met." His look dared me to comment.

I waved it away. "Go on."

"I sent Mr. Bezrel to have the purser refill a softie in the passengers' lounge. After dinner it was still empty. Bezrel said he forgot." Kahn shook his head. "All right, he's young. All I did was chew him out. That would have been the end of it, but the silly pup stood there bawling, and I lost my temper."

"No wonder." I'd have stuffed him down the recycler.

"Crying when a lieutenant reams him! Captain Grove would have put the first middy on report as well. It wouldn't have happened twice."

"I know."

"How did the boy make it through Academy?"

"He didn't." When I explained, Kahn shook his head. "Anyway, you did well, Lieutenant. Carry on."

His tone hardened. "Save your praise. It means nothing to me." He left.

The speaker came to life. "Personnel problems can be aggravating."

"You stay out of this, William."

"I prefer Billy; it helps keep things straight."

"I prefer silence."

Billy's voice went cold. "Aye aye, sir. Will that be permanent, or just for the watch?"

I sighed. No wonder the officers were temperamental; the ship herself was. "All right, Billy, I don't prefer silence. Let's not quarrel."

He sniffed. "It wouldn't have been much of a fight." I decided not to probe that.

Two days later a call caught me in my cabin. "Chief Sandra Arkin reporting, sir. There's trouble with a passenger. You'd better come down."

"A riot?"

"No, not quite. I can handle it, but perhaps you'd like to be present." If anything was a summons, that was.

"Where?"

"Four west, sir." I ran from the bridge.

I could hear the commotion before I rounded the corridor bend. Ms. Arkin snarled, "Use your billy, you fool!" A rending crash.

"I know my job, just stay the hell—!"

"Look what he's doing to my cabin! Leave that shirt alone, it's—"

They clustered outside the hatch: the Chief, a pair of sailors, the master-at-arms, an apoplectic passenger, a clump of gawkers.

"What's going on here?" I roared. Well, it wasn't quite a roar. One can't roar with one's mouth wired shut. In fact, I was unheard. I grabbed the master-at-arms's shoulder, spun him around.

Mr. Torres whirled, billy club flashing. "Oh, my God." He dropped the club, stiffened to attention. "Sir, please forgive me I didn't know—"

"As you were. What's—"

Suliman Rajnee charged me, arms waving with indignation. "Do you see what that ruffian's done? That vandal you forced on me? I can't get near my cabin! My clothing's ruined! I want him out! I want—"

I thrust him aside, shouldered past the master-at-arms and Chief Arkin. "Just what—" I peered into the cabin.

Jerence Branstead was stomping on the remains of Rajnee's dresser, a wild gleam in his eye. A torn shirt hung from his teeth. He held a holovid, but not in viewing position. At the sight of me he grinned, pitched it at my head. I ducked, colliding with the Chief, and we went down in a tangle.

Scarlet with rage and embarrassment, I scrambled to my feet and slapped shut the cabin hatch. "As you were, all of you! Mr. Torres, put this

Rajnee person against the bulkhead across the corridor! Sailors, back to
your duties; we'll handle this. You passengers, to your cabins." I stopped
for breath. Even a short speech could take a lot from me, one-lunged.
"What's the matter with him? Did Rajnee set off this tantrum?"

Chief Arkin adjusted her jacket, brushed her slacks. "Doesn't look
like a tantrum to me."

"Don't give me that goofjuice. It sure as hell is a—" I jerked to a halt.
Goofjuice.

"Yep." She grinned. "You have the word for it." Behind the hatch
something heavy smashed to the deck. She flicked a thumb toward the
cabin. "Mr. Torres and I can take him down, sir. Best if you stand out of
the way."

I stood back. "Without the billy club, Mr. Torres." I'd like to wring
the boy's neck, but the billy might do permanent damage.

"Aye aye, sir." Uncertain what to do with the club, he handed it to
me. "Ready, Chief?"

At her nod he slapped open the hatch, dived low while she rushed
high. A high-pitched shriek, a final crash, and comparative quiet. I poked
my head cautiously around the hatch. They had Jerence straddled on his
back across the debris, the master atop his legs, Chief Arkin pinning his
wrists.

The boy didn't seem to notice. He twisted and kicked, but to no avail.
The Chief hung on grimly while Mr. Torres fished for his manacles. Jerence giggled, craned his neck, chomped on Ms. Arkin's arm.

She squawked, yanked loose. "That does it, joey." A hard backhand
across the face, followed by several quick slaps that snapped the boy's
head back and forth. That quieted him a moment. She spun him onto his
stomach and twisted his arms behind him while Mr. Torres slipped on the
cuffs. The battle was won.

The Chief got to her feet, panting. "Now what, sir?"

I kicked aside a splintered chair. "Brig him, then back here on the
double!" They hustled Jerence down the corridor. For no apparent reason,
he let out a fearsome whoop.

Suliman Rajnee could no longer contain himself. "Where am I to
stay? Look at what he's done! I want to press charges! I want my clothing
replaced! He's broken my holovid, I'll need—"

I went to the caller, miraculously undamaged. "Purser to cabin
twenty-nine." Lord, what a mess. Barring the hatchway, I endured
Rajnee's diatribe until the Chief and Mr. Torres returned with the purser.

"Mr. Rajnee, go with Mr. Rezik. He'll help you list what you need

replaced. Now, please, Mr. Rezik." When silence reigned, I said. "Search
the cabin inch by inch. If he has more juice I want it found."

"Aye aye, sir." The master-at-arms hesitated. "What charges should I
lodge?"

"We'll see." I stalked back to the bridge.

The next day I sat in my cabin musing about Jerence, half listening to
Annie chatter about the holo she'd watched.

My officers had found not one, but two more vials of goofjuice, the
first in Jerence's knapsack under the bunk, the other behind the top shelf
of Mr. Rajnee's closet, where it wouldn't have been found except for the
Chief's literal interpretation of my orders.

"She was so pretty in that blue jumper, 'til Rafe tore it off, an'—how
come you don' listen to me?"

I wrapped my arm around Annie's waist, drew her closer. "I heard
you. Rafe and a blue dress. I don't know what to do about Jerence."

" 'Cause he got angry and kicked things 'roun'? That ol' Mr. Rajnee,
I'd like to kick his stuff too."

"It's worse than that." Possession of contraband drugs was a serious
offense. Were he groundside, Jerence could face transport to a prison
colony. Strict laws made sense; society had endured enough mind-altered
lunatics before the Era of Law succeeded the Rebellious Ages. Users were
jailed, without mollycoddling.

Still, I'd promised Harmon to keep Jerence safe. Did that mean a
felony should be condoned?

Annie's voice was far away. "Onna street, trannie joeykit get outta
line, big 'uns take him inna room, alladem. If he get out, he don' give 'em
no trouble." I shuddered. On the other hand, I knew of ships where the
crew did the same.

"I'll let him cool off in the brig. We'll decide later."

A week passed. I'd gotten to know some of the passengers, mostly for
Annie's sake. I hated to see her closet herself in our cabin with nothing
but cheap holos to occupy her time. Most passengers pointedly snubbed
us, either for my own misdeeds or from disdain for Annie. I couldn't be
sure which, so I let it be.

On Sundays the routine was broken by Captain's Mast. Since I'd
come aboard, *Victoria*'s sailors seemed quarrelsome and sullen, and at
each Mast I meted out the necessary penalties. But when I found Midshipman Ross on the list, I raised an eyebrow to Kahn. "What happened?"

"I caught him fighting."

"With Tolliver? That's for them to handle. Stay out—"

"No. He went after Mr. Fuentes, in the lounge."

"Ricky?" It couldn't be.

"Not just a push and shove. It was savage. Ross had Fuentes on the deck when I happened to look in."

I shook my head, astounded. What was the wardroom coming to?

"No matter what we think of you, ship's discipline has to be maintained. I wrote him up and gave Fuentes six demerits as well."

"It won't work, you know."

"Sir?"

"You can't maintain discipline while letting your own feelings show. You're asking more from Ross than you'll give yourself."

He eyed me with contempt. "You're a fine one to tell me how to handle a crew."

It was hopeless. Very well, so be it. "Take Mr. Ross's name off the list."

"What Captain would let a middy get away—"

"Mr. Kahn, leave the bridge."

He glared, finally responded. "Aye aye, sir!" When the hatch slid shut I sat in welcome silence.

It was time to resign. The enmity of the ship was all-consuming, had even filtered down to the wardroom. What was the point of hanging on to command? Duty? The Navy would be glad to be free of me, regs or no. I sat, brooding.

An hour later, a knock. I swiveled the camera before opening. Bram Steiner.

He flipped me a cursory salute. "I've spoken to Jeff Kahn. He'll show you courtesy from now on, unless you goad him beyond endurance."

"I see."

"It just so happens you were right. He understood, really, or he wouldn't have written up Ross. We'd like you to put the middy back on the Mast list, for the good of the ship."

"Very well."

"And I want you to beach me."

"You what?" I couldn't have heard aright. A Captain could beach any officer; he'd stop accumulating seniority until restored to active duty. It was a drastic punishment. No officer would request beaching.

His face was wooden. "Captain, I'd request a transfer, but that's impossible in Fusion. I won't try to serve you with contempt, like Jeffrey. I can't have it both ways either. So, beach me. I don't want to serve on a ship you command."

"May I ask why?"

"My feelings about . . . the actions you've taken. I don't care to be associated with you."

"And if I refuse?"

"Then I will do my duty until I can no longer stomach myself."

The risk he was taking was enormous; I could brig him for his revealed abhorrence, and he knew it. This was what my lies had brought us to. "Mr. Steiner, about Vax . . ."

"You're not fit to mention his name!" He stopped, pale. "I apologize. I have no right to say that."

"Go to your quarters."

"Aye aye, sir. And as to my request?"

"Get out!" I sat, fuming. The puter was blessedly silent.

At Mast, Ross took full blame on himself.

"What did Mr. Fuentes do to provoke you?"

Ross took a deep breath. "Nothing, sir."

"The Log doesn't show any problem with self-control under Captain Holser. What's happened?"

"I have no idea, sir." His tone was contemptuous.

I'd allowed him one outburst, in which he'd called me a murderer. That was enough. "Present my compliments to Lieutenant Steiner. You're to be caned until you agree your conduct will be exemplary in future."

"I'm eighteen!" A cry of appeal.

Should I reverse myself? No, Ross's manner was intolerable, and if I didn't chastise him, another Captain would be forced to do worse. I made my voice cold. "I'll treat you as the age you act, which puts you barely out of Academy. Go."

"Aye aye, sir." Mastering his dismay, he saluted, spun on his heel, and left. Well, I admired his valor, but courage wasn't the issue. I couldn't have him sneering at me, or brawling in public.

I closed the Log, sat thinking. The wardroom was Tolliver's affair, but now I had a right to intervene; a middy had been brought to Mast. I thumbed the caller. "Mr. Fuentes to the bridge. And Mr. Tolliver."

After the two midshipmen reported, I left them at attention and scowled at Ricky. "Six demerits, Mr. Fuentes? What's this?"

He gulped. "I'll work them off, sir, honest. I did one yesterday and—"

"How did they come about?"

He blushed. "I was rude to Mr. Ross."

I asked slowly, "What was it you said?"

"Please, sir, I—"

"Another demerit, Mr. Fuentes, for disobedience. What did you say to Mr. Ross?"

"Yes, sir. I apologize. He told me my tie was knotted wrong. I said it wasn't his problem anymore."

I tried to catch Tolliver's eye, but it was elsewhere. I growled, "I was a middy once too, Mr. Fuentes; perhaps you can remember. If I heard such insolence in my wardroom I'd make sure you regretted it the rest of the cruise."

He flushed deep red, squirming. "Yes, sir."

"If your behavior is called to my attention again, I'll thrash you myself. Dismissed. Not you, Tolliver." I waited until the hatch was shut. "Well?"

"Is that a question?" His tone was cool.

"Don't goad me. What in hell is going on down there?"

"Ricky learned how far he can push Ross. It's a self-correcting problem. I'm just minding my own business."

"As you were."

He relaxed, flexing his shoulders.

I studied the empty screen. "A pity," I told it.

After a moment he asked, "What is?"

"I deserve you, Edgar. But they don't."

For the first time his manner showed uncertainty. "I don't know what you mean."

"When we get home you'll have your wish. You'll see them lead me off the ship in irons."

He said nothing.

"My career is finished, along with my life. Your—what shall I call it? Your style?—it aggravates me, as you intend. It communicates your contempt. But I'm not the issue."

"My career's finished too," he said with passion. "No one will take me aboard after I've been broken to middy."

"You're not the issue either!" I spun my chair around. "We've destroyed ourselves, but their lives are still ahead of them!"

"It wasn't I who—"

"They're children, Tolliver, and you're ruining them!"

He was shocked into silence.

I demanded, "Tell me how you felt the day you made lieutenant."

His smile was brief and bitter. "I—" His gaze penetrated the screen. A time passed. "It was the most joy I'd ever felt in my life. Or have since."

"And they'll never feel it, any of them."

"You can't know that. Even Ross—"

"Thanks to you."

He gripped the console until his knuckles turned white. "What do you want of me?"

"I could have left Ross in charge. You've given me so many grounds to cashier you I'd find it hard to choose among them. I left you in the wardroom for a purpose."

He raised his eyes, repeated, "What do you want?"

"Ricky isn't spoiled yet, but he's green, else he'd know better than to goad Ross. He needs an example, and you haven't set one. Ross needs to learn how to handle his disappointments. Bezrel . . . I don't know what he needs, but he's got to find it soon. Otherwise they'll all be failures, as we are."

When he turned to me his eyes were tormented. "Pull me out of there, sir. I've nothing left to give."

I cried in sudden anguish, "Neither have I, but still I try!" Immediately I was ashamed, but it was too late.

He hunched over in his chair. When he spoke, his voice was strained. "Is there still time?"

"I don't know. There's so much hatred."

"Some of it's been mine." He was silent awhile. "Nuking the Station," he said. "You made a terrible choice; I can't possibly condone it. Orbit Station's gone, and for all we know a new flotilla of fish is attacking Hope Nation even now."

"Lord God forbid. None had Defused for an hour, and—"

"An hour."

I flushed. "I know, but there were too many lives at stake to wait any longer." Yet if anything was more obscene than what I'd done, it was the thought that I'd done it for naught.

Tolliver sighed. "I've hated your treason, but you'll pay the penalty when we get home, and I have to respect how you face that. But Kahn and Steiner and Ross, they're wrong about you. I know you lied about Vax Holser."

"How dare you!"

He raised his face to mine. "I saw your eyes, when they brought you from the lifepod. Whatever went on between you and Vax on the Station, it wasn't what you said in sickbay."

"You weren't even *in* the sickbay!"

"I made Ross tell me."

"It's none of your business." I turned away, passed my hand casually across my eyes.

"About the wardroom . . . I'll try, sir."

"Thank you, Edgar." I said no more, and we sat in silence.

"Am I dismissed, sir?"

"When you're ready."

He got to his feet, saluted, walked to the hatch. He paused. "Why do you let them treat you that way?"

"Who?"

"All the officers. They despise you and don't even care if we know it."

"They're right to despise me. It's only wrong of them to show it."

"You're the Captain! Put a stop to it!"

I turned my chair. "Should I start with you?"

He stumbled for a reply, smiled weakly. I waved him out.

When my watch was done I persuaded Annie to join us for the evening meal, and bore the inane chatter of the few passengers who deigned to sit with us. After, I escorted her to the lounge. "I'll be back soon."

The brig was unguarded; with only one prisoner, a passenger, we had no need of a sentry. Daily, the master-at-arms brought Jerence his food and clothing and went about his other duties.

I entered the codes and let myself in. The boy sat slumped on the floor of his cell, ignoring the bunk and chair nearby. He looked up.

I asked, "Are you sane now?"

"Hah. I've always been sane." He kicked listlessly at the deck. "Can I get out? I've been here a month."

"Only a week." I sat in the unused chair. "Jerence, what should we do with you?"

He shrugged. "Leave me here. It's all the same."

"Why did you do it?"

"Smash his stuff?"

"Use the juice."

A scornful laugh. "What else is there?"

"It's addictive. Keep it up and you'll never get free of it."

"So?"

"Does your life mean nothing?"

He shouted, "I have no life! All I have is growing up to be a planter. I hate it and I hate you and I hate everything!"

I reached forward to touch his shoulder, but he scooted away. "Jerence, I've got—"

"Captain, call the bridge!" Chief Arkin. With a curse I scrambled to my feet, let myself out. I dialed the bridge. "Seafort."

"Sir, Lieutenant Kahn needs you at his cabin, flank."

Was there no peace? "Coming." I hurried to Kahn's quarters, at the top of the ladder. The hatch was open. Kahn stood, hands on hips. Alexi Tamarov sat on his bed, head in his hands.

"What, Mr. Kahn? Can't I get anything done?"

He pointed. I followed his hand.

"Oh, Lord God, he didn't mean it. Forgive him." I wasn't aware I'd spoken aloud.

In the center of the room, a chair. Above it, on the base of the light fixture, a rope. It ended in a noose. I cleared my throat. "How did you find him?"

"I came back for a holochip and Mr. Tamarov was on the chair."

Weak from relief, I sagged against the hatch. If Kahn hadn't wanted his holochip . . . "Alexi, why couldn't you come to me?"

"What's the point?"

"I'd help you."

"But you can't." He flung out his hand in a gesture that encompassed the whole ship. "Here's another life for me to sample. And then it will be over like the others, and again I'm nothing."

"I don't understand."

He twisted his hands. "When you used to come to the hospital . . . I hung on your every word. I was afraid to walk down the hall for a holozine, for fear I'd miss your visit. Then we crashed the heli and had to hike to Plantation Road. I did what I could to help you, and imagined I might be of real use someday.

"But afterward you were sick, and the hospital was gone and I had nothing again." He looked up, eyes bleak. "That job in Centraltown, I know you fixed it for me, but still it was something I could do. I found my way around town, learned to use their puters, started to make a life. Now suddenly I'm on the way home. I have no memories to anchor me. Every time I try to establish myself, you haul me away."

Why was I so self-centered, so oblivious to the needs of others? "Alexi, I'll find someth—"

"I'd refuse it!" He kicked savagely at the bunk. "You think I wouldn't know it was makework? You already have two extra officers, and there's nothing for them to do but fight in the wardroom! I don't want your damned charity!"

I said stiffly, "I didn't mean it as charity."

Alexi shrugged. He stared at his lap.

I could find nothing to say. Finally I patted Alexi's knee, looked to Kahn. "Take him to the infirmary. I'll explain to Dr. Zares." Kahn crossed to the bed, tugged gently at Alexi's arm. I closed the hatch behind them and picked up the caller.

It was hours later, in my cabin, that I remembered my interrupted conversation with Jerence. Though I was dog-tired I went anyway; better to get it over with.

Jerence sat up when I came in. "Was there trouble?"

"It doesn't concern you."

His face fell. "You're just like Pa."

I yawned. "Pa wouldn't like to hear you say that."

"Yes, he would. He likes you." A pause. "I'm sorry I said I hated you."

"Thank you." It was an opening. "Jerence, your pa wanted me to take care of you. I don't know how."

He was scornful. "I don't need taking care of. I'm fourteen now."

"Where'd you get the juice?"

He grinned. "I brought it in my knapsack. You never checked. On the ship, I hid it good 'cause I thought you'd search, but you didn't."

"True. My mind was occupied with trivial things, like a few hundred murderous fish, and nuking Orbit Station."

He colored. "I'm sorry my juice made trouble for you. Besides, Mr. Torres says you found the rest of it, so even if I want to, I can't have any more." He squirmed, scratched an itch. "Mr. Seafort, when this is over, do I have to go back?"

"Of course you do." I yawned again, against the wires locking my jaw.

"God, I hate the idea of watching corn grow for the rest of my life." His face changed. He looked up at me, said quietly, "You don't know how much I hate it."

"What would you prefer?"

"There's nothing." He stared morosely at the deck. I waited. "Except . . ." His eyes beseeched me. "Don't laugh."

Moved despite myself, I said, "I won't."

He regarded me, weighing the risk. "Mr. Seafort, I'd really like to be a midshipman, like Derek Carr."

I blurted, "Ridiculous." His look of betrayal stabbed. "I didn't laugh. Jerence, your father would have a fit if I let you enlist. And you're still a minor, so you need his permission."

He looked up with a quick grin. "No I don't."

"I beg your pardon?"

"It says 'parent or guardian.' An unaccompanied minor traveling on a

Naval vessel does so as the ward of the commanding officer. So you could give me permission."

"Where in heaven did you hear that?"

"I asked Lieutenant Kahn, and he read me the regs. Anyway, you don't need permission. Remember how you enlisted two passengers as cadets a few years ago? We all heard about it."

"I already have two extra middies; you think I need a goofjuice addict on top of that?"

"I'm no addict!" he shouted.

"Enough!" I stood, unlocked the hatch. "In the morning they'll let you go. No charges. Stay out of trouble, or . . ."

He jeered, "Or what?"

I said, "You'll answer to me, and you'll wish you hadn't." I left, hoping I'd impressed him. A middy! Lord God save us.

29

The next morning Dr. Zares numbed my jaw, removed the wires. Cautiously I opened my mouth. It ached, but nothing jarred loose. I went to the mirror. Lord God. I looked . . . was there ever anything like what I looked? I tried a smile. The gap-toothed result was so awful that I shuddered.

"When can you do the teeth?" I wasn't vain about my appearance, but I had no choice. When they laughed at me, they'd laugh at the Service.

"We can start anytime. It won't be comfortable."

"I know." It would hurt like the very devil. I'd bear it. Cellular seeds were planted deep in the gums and stimulated daily with the bone-growth stimulator. I'd had one done once, after my first and only fight in a Lunapolis bar.

"Captain . . ." He cleared his throat uncomfortably. "May I suggest . . ."

"Spit it out." I looked in the mirror again. A poor choice of words.

"Why don't you have that done as well?" He waved at my scar.

I smiled tightly. "You don't like it?"

He blurted, "It's awful." He reddened. "Sorry, sir, but you did ask. It's so unnecessary. Any clinic could fix it. I'm surprised you didn't have it removed when you were in the hospital."

"I chose to keep it."

"Do you still?"

I fingered the scar. "Why shouldn't I?"

He was blunt. "Because it puts people off. Skin regrowth is so simple that the scar is obviously an affectation."

I flushed. "I'm still your Captain."

"And you're still my patient. Keep your bloody scar, if that's what you want!" He slammed the cabinet door. "We'll start on your teeth tomorrow. Let your jaw rest. Soft foods."

"Very well." I ran my finger across my mouth. I could even yawn if I wished. What luxury. "Doctor, about Mr. Tamarov."

"Yes." Cooling, he sat across from me. "I gave him a sedative for a good night's sleep. I'm no psych, Captain. I can give him psychotropic meds, or I can run an analysis for hormone rebalancing."

My stomach knotted. There was no reason why patients of a rebalancing ward were greeted with condescension or, worse, with cruel sneers, yet it was so, and my own attitude wasn't much better. I'd lost my wife Amanda because I'd hesitated to authorize *Portia*'s medic to check her for rebalancing.

If I didn't order a rebalance, and Alexi killed himself while deranged, the blame would be mine. If I allowed it, his career was finished. Yet, what career could he have in his current amnesiac state?

Surely hormone treatments were the best way. What would I want him to do for me, if our roles were reversed?

I'd rather die. "Not yet, Mr. Zares. I'll have him watched."

"You can't guard him at all hours."

I stood. "May I look in on him?" He nodded.

I went to the cubicle, cautiously opened the hatch. Alexi lay asleep, on his back. The lights were set low. I tiptoed in, sank into the chair next to the bed.

Alexi's face was relaxed, all cares dissipated as his chest rose and fell. I swallowed. So young. Sleeping, he was the fifteen-year-old I'd come to cherish in my first wary months on *Hibernia*. He'd done nothing to deserve the misery he'd seen since: my harsh rebukes, the tyranny of Philip Tyre, consignment to Admiral Tremaine's unjust vessel, the loss of his very self.

Slowly I eased from the chair, knelt by the side of Alexi's bed, clasped my hands. Please, Lord God. Restore him. I know You have no love for me, and that is just, but this one thing I ask You. Do with me as You will. But not him. Let me bear his hurts.

"How long have you been here?"

I looked up, startled. "You're awake."

"I just woke." He brought his arm under his head.

I smiled. "I just came in." I got up from my knees. "How do you feel?"

"Tired, actually. I'm here because . . . oh." He grimaced.

"I'm glad we found you. I'd have—" For a moment I turned away. "Finish."

"I'd have been lonely." I rested my hand on his. "Please, Alexi. Don't damn yourself. Be patient."

"Oh, of course," he pulled his hand loose. "Patient. Always patient. I'll be known as Alexi Tamarov, the man who waited." He sat up, thrust off the sheet. "Maybe I should go back to the cabin and finish what I began."

"You're not a prisoner." He turned away. *Perhaps I should make him one, for his own safety.*

Afterward, I told Annie about my visit. She said with conviction, "I go talk to him. I know what it mean, not wantin' live. That be how I felt when you go way. It ain' right." She looked at me anxiously. "I wan' be with you, Nicky. Always. But talkin' a killin' myself when you be gone, that ain' the way. Trannie life too short for throwin' it away. Why you lookin' at me like that?"

"God, how I love you."

She came to me. Her diction was careful and precise. "Promise you'll be with me, Nicky. I can't stand it without you." I closed my eyes. *Lord God, let her heal. Show her how not to rely on me.*

Jerence was released and installed in a new cabin. Alexi left the sickbay.

Whenever I went to the dayroom, conversation fell silent. If Thomas Ross was present he immediately left. Bram Steiner asked again to be beached.

I kept my eye on the Log. The demerits issued by Tolliver went up, those issued by other officers began to diminish. It could be a good sign.

My jaw and gums hurt abominably as my replacement teeth rooted and began to probe through swollen tissues. I tried to ignore the pain, realized I was unsuccessful when I found myself, red-faced, shouting at Ricky Fuentes over a nav drill error.

Thomas Ross, also present, watched me with unconcealed contempt. I thought to send him to the first lieutenant, sent him instead to Tolliver. Tolliver could be worse.

As days passed, Lieutenant Kahn's manner was scrupulously correct, yet unforgiving. I learned to avoid the bridge during his watch; I preferred loneliness.

I visited Alexi's cabin at odd intervals, afraid of what I'd find. To my relief, all I encountered was sullen withdrawal, and no sign of the rope.

Three days after Jerence was freed he rampaged through Level 1, flinging tubes of softies at everyone he met, shouting gibberish. Midshipman Ross made the mistake of trying to collar him unaided; Jerence went along, docile enough, until he suddenly spun Ross around and butted him down the ladder to Level 2 where the middy lay groaning, out of combat. Eventually Jerence was subdued by three sailors who seemed to enjoy the unforeseen sport.

Woken from my first good sleep in several days, I had the boy hauled to the sickbay and strip-searched by Dr. Zares while the middies tore his cabin apart looking for more juice. They found none.

Jerence was again escorted to the brig.

Too tired to sleep, I roamed the ship, not caring where I went. I barged into the dining hall, ignored the sullen mess crew stiffened to attention among the starched linen. A quick look, then back out the hatch.

I passed Bram Steiner's cabin. Beach him? If he wanted off the bridge, I'd put him off the bridge, all right. Let him spend the rest of the cruise in the brig with Jerence.

Down the ladder to the engine room. Chief Arkin was on duty, with a hand. I growled, "Attention!" They stood stiffly while my eye roved the consoles, the cabinets, the machine shop. "Very well, carry on."

Back to Level 1. I passed the wardroom, stopped. By custom the wardroom was free of the Captain's interference, except for announced inspection. The hell with custom. I banged on the hatch. "Ship's inspection. Stand to!"

Tolliver rose immediately, with Ricky. They'd been playing chess. I noted the spotless deck, the immaculate bunks. Well, Tolliver was a seasoned hand; I would expect no less.

I slapped the hatch shut on my way out. By the time I reached my cabin I'd begun to cool. Annie was elsewhere; perhaps visiting. I left the cabin, looking for her. I checked the lounge.

Alexi sat with a holo. "Hello, Mr. Seafort."

"What are you doing?" I made an effort to smile.

"Reading." He showed me the screen. *"Walfort's Guide to Colonial Farming."*

"You're no farmer."

"I'm no anything." He snapped off the holo. "Better than just sitting." I stared at him. Finally he snapped, "Mr. Seafort, I told you I had nothing to do. If you want me to sit staring at the wall, say so!"

My fists clenched. "Stop feeling sorry for yourself!"

He gulped. "I'm sor—"

"Damn your sorry!" I stalked to the bridge. Lieutenant Kahn rose, saluted properly. I waved him back to his seat. He deliberately turned his chair away from me.

I sat for an hour, rage mounting. Finally I could bear it no longer. "Mr. Kahn, call Mr. Steiner to relieve you."

"Aye aye, sir." His tone was cool.

Steiner came, took his seat as Kahn left. Hours passed. I broke the silence with comments, but his only response was an occasional grunt of acknowledgment. The silence was maddening.

"Carry on." I went back to my cabin. Annie slept. I sat on the bed beside her, loosened my tie. She stirred. Annie, tell me it will be all right. Hold me. Lightly I caressed her arm.

She snapped awake, eyes wide with fear, and clawed at my hand. "Don' touch me!" She bounded to the edge of the bed.

"I'm sorry. Please, I just wanted—"

"Don' touch me! Never!" With a sob she dashed into the head, slammed shut the hatch.

I got up, went to the mirror, stared at the gaunt face that it framed. Alexi was right; better to die than to live in misery. The entire ship had sent me to Coventry, and I was writhing in it. I had no refuge in my cabin or anywhere.

Well, so be it.

It meant I was free to do as I wished.

I stalked to the bridge. Lieutenant Steiner came to his feet. I growled, "Sit and be silent." I keyed the caller. "Mr. Tolliver, find Mr. Tamarov and bring him to the bridge."

Moments later Tolliver and Alexi reported, came to attention.

My voice was harsh. "Puter, record. As of this moment, Lieutenant Abram Steiner is placed on the inactive list." From his seat, Steiner gaped. "Put the following note in his personnel file: Mr. Steiner is placed inactive at his own request, for personal reasons. His performance as an officer has been satisfactory and his inactive status shall not be construed as a rebuke." I turned. "Steiner, off my bridge!"

His face was gray. He saluted, saw no response, left.

I wheeled on Alexi. "As for you, Mr. Tamarov, Lord God knows I'd undo what happened to you, but it cannot be. I won't have you mooning about feeling sorry for yourself. It's got to stop!"

"Mr. Seafort, I'll try to—"

"You'll more than try. Puter, note that Lieutenant Alexi Tamarov is herewith recalled to active duty, on full pay. End recording."

Alexi gaped. "But I don't know how to—I don't remember my training!"

"We'll retrain you."

"But how? I'd have to go back to Acad—"

"No, Mr. Tolliver will show you." Tolliver's jaw dropped. It gave me mild satisfaction. "Tolliver, you know the ropes. You're now Lieutenant Tamarov's aide. Help him do his duty. You're to share watches with him, eat at his table, spend every spare moment with him."

Alexi cried, "Mr. Seafort, I can't stand a watch if I don't know—"

"Sir! You call your Captain 'sir'!"

He gulped. "Aye aye, sir!"

"Mr. Tolliver, find this man a proper uniform. Tutor Alexi in every subject studied by a cadet, midshipman, and lieutenant. Start with navigation. He's a fast learner."

"Aye aye, sir."

Alexi said, "Sir, I don't want to do this! I'm not ready—"

I said, my tone icy, "I don't care what you want." It brought a stunned silence. "You're recalled to duty. No discussion is allowed."

"But—"

Tolliver cleared his throat loudly. "Excuse me, Mr. Tamarov. One doesn't argue with the Captain."

Alexi looked to my face for comfort, found none.

"Dismissed."

Alone, I sat tapping the console. I picked up the caller. "Mr. Kahn, report to the bridge."

A few moments later he was back.

I was brusque. "Sit. Read the Log."

He did so. He swallowed, looked up, waiting.

"You may pick one, Mr. Kahn. Civility or the brig until we Defuse."

"Sir!" He groped for words.

"Steiner can't help you. He no longer has authority to relieve me."

"I didn't say anything about—"

"Four weeks pay for insubordination. What do you choose, Mr. Kahn? Will you be civil, or shall it be seven months in the brig?"

"I'll be civil, sir!" Sweat beaded his forehead. "I thought I was—"

"You weren't openly disobedient or blatantly contemptuous. But you missed by only a hair. That won't do. Do you think I'm the only tyrant you'll ever serve, Mr. Kahn? That's why cadets and middies go through hell, to learn that they can take what shipboard life may bring! Don't you remember?"

"Yes, sir!"

"If you can't survive under me, the Navy doesn't need you. I'm a part of your training, Mr. Kahn. Keep your hatred to yourself. Don't let me see it or know about it!"

"Aye aye, sir!"

"Finish your watch." I stalked off the bridge.

Below, I found the brig unlocked; Master-at-arms Torres was retrieving a dinner tray. Jerence sat cross-legged on his mattress.

I leaned against the hatch. "Why, boy?"

His smile was bitter. "Why not?"

"Have you hidden more juice?"

"Maybe. If not, I could make it, easy enough. I learned how."

"Why are you throwing your life away?"

He flared, "Why shouldn't I?"

"Do you despise Hope Nation that much?"

"Hope Nation? No, of course not!" He got to his feet. "See this prison? That's what my life is. Pa wants me to be a planter, and I have no choice. Every day it's the corn, or the wheat, or the God damn beans!"

I slapped him, hard. "Don't blaspheme!"

His hand flew to his face. "That's all you care about," he screamed. "Your dam—your frazzing religion!"

"Not all. It's what I start from."

"They all say you're crazy, that you killed Vax Holser! You're a monster."

I nodded. "You're right about that." I crossed to the bed, sat. I put my head in my hands. "I can't lecture you. I'm no better than you are."

He pounded on the hatch, harder and harder until I thought he'd break his hand. Suddenly he spun to me, his face wet. "You loved him! I saw, that day you tried to talk to him and he walked away."

"It's none of your—"

"Tell me! I want to hear it!"

I whispered. "Yes. I loved him."

He sobbed openly. "You were middies together, I heard. See what you have, that I'll never know? You think I'll find friendships like that on a God—on a frazzing farm?"

"No, I suppose you won't."

He struggled for composure. "What will come of me? Are you going to keep me here?"

"I have to." There was no other way.

"The whole cruise?" His cry was agonized.

"Yes. Then I'll turn you over for prosecution."

"Oh, God!" He slid to the deck, hugged himself.

"I have no choice, boy. If I let you go, would you give up the juice?"

He was silent a long time. I waited for the inevitable lie, but to my surprise he buried his head in his arms. "It's too late."

"What?"

"To give it up. I think about it all the time, Mr. Seafort. The stuff was supposed to last 'til we got to Lunapolis. I've used most of it already. I dream about it. I'd do . . . anything for it."

Lord God curse the vermin who made and sold the stuff; the death penalty was too good for them. And curse this foolish, uncaring boy, who'd brought foul drugs onto my ship for his own amuse—

No. I'd lost Tolliver, lost Annie, lost Kahn, Steiner, Eiferts, Ross. But not Jerence. Not yet.

"Jerence, it's time we set things right." I crossed the cell, hauled him to his feet. "Over there!" I shoved him toward the bed.

His eyes widened. "Why are you taking off your belt?"

"You're the ward of the commanding officer. That's me." I threw him facedown across the mattress. "This is your punishment, for making a shambles of my ship." I raised my arm. The crack of the belt across his rump echoed like a shot. Jerence shrieked, struggled to free himself. I held him down firmly until I was through. When I released him, he fled sobbing to the corner of the cell, rubbing his stinging buttocks. I threaded my belt through its loops. "I'll be back tomorrow to talk with you."

"I hate you! You're evil and I hate you!" His cries faded as I stalked along the corridor.

I went directly to the sickbay. Dr. Zares looked up from his desk.

"Do you know the chemical properties of goofjuice?"

The question startled him. "I imagine so. Why?"

"Do you know how to make it?"

He came to his feet. "Is that an accusation? I didn't. I don't know where the boy—"

"Answer me!"

He stepped back a pace. "Yes, I suppose I could, but I'd never—"

"Make a vial."

"You're out of your mind!"

I grinned through missing teeth. "I may well be, by now. That was insubordinate. I want a vial of goofjuice."

He studied me, shook his head. "Sorry, Captain, there's no way I could do that."

"There's no way you can't, since I ordered it."

"I could be jailed. Even a penal colony. Unless you give me a written order—"

"Get out your holo!" Speechless, he handed it to me; I typed in the order. "Can you have it by tomorrow?"

"You're serious? What in God's name—" He broke off. "I don't know. Maybe late tomorrow. I'd have to acidify—"

"Very well, by six. You're to tell no one. Acknowledge."

"Orders acknowledged and understood." He hesitated, then blurted, "You know what you'll do to yourself?"

"Have you any idea what I've already done to myself?" I walked out of the room.

* * *

I passed the next day in uneasy anticipation. Annie was friendly, even caring, so long as I didn't touch her. Lieutenant Kahn met me in the dayroom, greeted me with courtesy, sat at the long table alongside me. His conversation was nervous, his effort to be polite noticeable. I forced myself to respond; after all, it was what I had demanded.

Midshipman Ross entered, saw me, turned to go.

"Mr. Ross!" Kahn's voice cut like a whip.

"Yes, sir?"

"Sit with us, please." Reluctantly the middy complied. Kahn said, "We were discussing Kall's Planet. What did you think of the mines?"

"I don't know, sir. I have no opinion." Ross met Kahn's eyes defiantly.

"Two demerits. *Now* what do you think?"

I stood. "Good day, both of you." I left.

I stopped to give special orders to the purser, then took Annie to dinner at our half-empty table. For her sake, I endured the uneasy conversation until the meal was done, then left her at our cabin. I went to the bridge, where the Chief Engineer stood watch. Idly I thumbed through the Log. I saw that Ross had been caned, by Lieutenant Kahn's order. So be it.

Later, I knocked on the sickbay hatch. "Is it ready?"

"Yes." Dr. Zares stepped aside, gestured to a plastic-corked vial of amber liquid on his table.

"Very well."

"Captain, would you let me give you an antidepressant instead? I have meds that—"

"It's not for me, you dolt." I put the vial in my pocket, walked out.

He followed me into the corridor. "For the boy? How could you? You'll addict him and then—"

"Back to your quarters, Doctor." I headed down the ladder.

I unsealed the brig, went to the occupied cell, opened the hatch. "Come along."

Jerence sat up. "Where are you taking me?"

"Need another whipping?" My hand went to my belt.

He sneered disdainfully but wasted no time getting to his feet. "Where are we going?"

I led him into the circumference corridor. Jerence followed reluctantly. I unlocked the cabin I'd bade the purser prepare. "Sit." I pointed to the bed.

I took a chair opposite. "Jerence, your father loves you dearly. The plantation you'll inherit is worth millions. Can't you go back willingly?"

"Why should I talk to you, after what you did?"

"I'm all you have. Answer, or I'll leave you."

He rested his head in his hands. When he spoke, his voice was muffled. "I don't want to go back, not if I have to be a farmer."

"What would you do to earn another life?"

"What kind of life?" He looked up. Hope dawned. "You mean . . ." He breathed the words. "In the Navy, like Derek?"

I nodded.

He whispered, "Anything!"

"That's what you said you'd do for the juice."

"I—" He faltered. "I don't know. I can't choose, not if—"

"Here." I reached into my pocket, drew out the vial. I tossed it onto the bed.

He seized it. "Is this—I didn't put—how did you get it?" He clutched it to his chest.

"I had it made."

"Is it real?"

I reached over, pried the vial from his unwilling hands, uncorked it. "Smell." He sniffed the tart odor, licked his lips. I replaced the cork, tossed it back to him.

"Oh, God." He gulped. "Why did—may I?"

"Yes, in a moment." I waited. He eyed the vial with longing. "I'll be back to see you, Jerence. I want you to give me the juice back, untouched. If—"

"I can't!"

"—if you do, I'll appoint you a cadet in the U.N. Navy. You won't have to be a planter."

He tugged at my arm. "Don't you understand? I can't hold out!"

"Then you'll fail. It's your choice, as it's always been."

"Mr. Seafort, please. I've got to have it. Just a little."

"Help yourself. I'll throw you in the brig afterward, but that's no matter. You'll do time in a penal colony, and then you'll be free to juice yourself into hell." I stood. "Or there's the wardroom."

He stared at the vial. "How long?" he whispered.

"Three weeks." A cry of grief, which I did my best to ignore. "In three weeks I'll let you take the oath. On the other hand, there's the juice, whenever you want it." I went to the hatch, slapped it open.

He scrambled across the room, barred my way. "Not like that," he gabbled. "Please, I'll give up the juice! I swear! But don't leave me alone with it, I'm not strong en—"

I pried his fingers loose from the hatch. "Find strength." I thrust him back inside the cabin.

He slid down, clutched at my legs. "Please, sir! Not in the same room with juice! I'll use it, I've got to!"

My voice was cold. "You brought yourself to this, not I. If you can't—" Amanda swam before me, with Nate. Perhaps my son would have grown to be like Jerence, given the time denied him.

This wasn't the way.

With a sigh, I reached down, hoisted the anguished boy to his feet. I led him to the bed, laid him down. I sat next to him, stroked his hair. "Steady, lad. I'll stay awhile."

He sobbed, "God, Mr. Seafort, take it away!"

"No, Jerence." I gentled him, unbuttoned the top of his shirt. "Listen, and I'll tell you a story. Lay back, son. Slow your breathing. There was a boy, once. A boy called Philip. Dry your eyes, now. It was years ago. We were on a ship, a great ship, cruising to a distant star . . ."

Slowly he calmed.

30

I endured daily sessions with the bone-growth stimulator. My mouth ached constantly, but the hours after my therapy with Dr. Zares were sheer misery.

Lieutenant Kahn greeted me civilly whenever he saw me. Occasionally he even attempted light conversation. Grunting in reply, I searched his face for a sign of his revulsion but found none.

From a locked Level 2 cabin, cries of torment and pounding on the hatch. On my first visit after I'd left Jerence to wrestle with his demon, he greeted me red-eyed and trembling. "It's been a whole day. Mr. Seafort, please say that's enough!"

"Where's the juice?"

"I hid it so I—He swallowed, burrowed under the mattress, came up with the vial. "Here, I haven't touched it. Let me sign up now. I'm begging you."

"Twenty more days."

"You bastard!"

On that note I left him.

The next day I shared a watch with Tolliver. He was unusually pensive. I did my best to concentrate on a chess problem, on an imaginary board. If I moved Queen to King's Bishop five, behind a pawn screen . . .

He cleared his throat. "I'm supposed to keep wardroom problems from the Captain's attention, but . . ."

"Eh?" The chessboard wavered, faded.

"Since you talked to me, I've tried. Believe me."

I worried at a knuckle. "And?"

"Maybe you'd best get someone else. It's beyond me."

I sat up, attentive. "Go on."

"I didn't know Fuentes in *Hibernia*, but I gather from your remarks he was a good-natured joey."

"The best."

"He taunts Ross as if the consequences don't matter. And Thomas . . ." He shook his head. "He's beside himself. Venomous. Nothing I say reaches either of them."

"A first middy has his resources." Did he expect me to tell him how to run a wardroom? It was supposed to be beneath my notice. A first midshipman who couldn't hold his wardroom could expect little sympathy.

"Yes, sir." A sigh, barely audible. "I'll deal with it."

What malady plagued *Victoria?* The first lieutenant beached, the second under strict orders to hold his tongue, the third suicidal. Drug-crazed passengers, the wardroom at each other's throats.

And a Captain who had no right to walk the bridge, if the Navy were just. *I* was the problem, and the unsettled state of affairs was merely a reflection of that.

I sighed. "It's not your fault. Tell me."

He seemed pathetically grateful. "Sir, I can demerit them 'til their tongues hang out. And I will, if I'm sure that's the way. But it will only make them hate me as they do each other."

"It's not so much hate as . . ." I stood, with an urgent need to pace. "Their lives are askew. They want to revere their Captain as I did Captain Haag, but they know it's not possible in my case. The conflict is too much."

He snorted. "Now you're a psych as well as a mad bomber?"

"Damn you!"

He shrugged. "Oh, I'll admit you've caused your share of the world's problems. But you can't take credit for them all."

Well, I *had* told him I'd suffer his insolence, in private. I waved away my ire. "What else could explain their behavior?"

"With Ross, in part it's because he revered his Captain, precisely as you said. He can't forgive you—"

"For murdering him."

"No, for replacing him." He leaned forward. "Sir, you have to understand: at this point, no one in command could satisfy Ross's expectations. And Holser was killed, not transferred. A sudden, terrible loss. No goodbyes, no time to accept the inevitability of—"

"Stop!" My cry echoed from the bulkheads. I swallowed.

"Sorry, sir." His tone suggested he meant it. After a moment he cleared his throat. "But even that doesn't explain Ross's malevolence. He rags at Bezrel 'til he has the joeykit in tears, which I'll admit is easy enough. He says vile things about Kahn and the Chief. He called me a—" His mouth tightened. "I took him to the exercise room, and he's more cautious now. But still . . ."

"His ratings were excellent before I took command. Clearly I'm the cause." Moodily I tapped the console.

Tolliver said, "And what's come over Ricky Fuentes?"

"Have you asked him?"

"Yes, and he stalked out in a rage. You may have noticed three demerits, a couple of nights ago."

"I wondered."

"And then there's Bezrel, who might be a good middy, if ever he's old enough. Sir, I'm in over my head."

"Nonsense!" I paced with renewed vigor. "Do your duty, Midshipman, and don't whine about it."

"I wasn't—aye aye, sir."

"Is there anything else?"

"Yes. Your friend Alexi loathes the sight of me. I'm getting nowhere as his aide."

"I think you're overreact—"

"It's his sarcastic asides that rankle. He's my superior, so I'm not free to compl—"

"Nor are you free to complain about him to me!"

"I wasn't!" He shot from his seat, fists clenched. A deep breath, then another. "Sir." His fingers opened. "Sorry."

"As you should be." I was appalled at the discussion into which I'd stumbled. Bad enough that he'd asked my advice; worse, he'd given me his, unbidden. The more I thought about it, the more I . . . "That's quite enough for today, Mr. Tolliver. I'll finish the watch."

"You want me to go?"

"It would be a great pleasure." I regretted the words almost instantly as he saluted and stalked to the hatch. He'd told me of Alexi's sarcasm, and I'd responded with my own.

On *Hibernia*, on *Portia*, relations with the passengers consumed a significant part of my attention. Here on *Victoria*, few had anything to say to me. I didn't particularly mind, but it left me with little to brood on, beside the crew.

Still, there was Jerence.

I found him huddled in the corner of his cabin. "Well?"

He got up, fished in his pocket. "I still have it."

"Good boy."

"You said you'd come every day." An accusation.

"I have."

"It's been . . ." His brow knotted. "A long time."

"Eighteen hours. Endure it."

He pulled out the vial, rushed across the room. "Here." He made as if to drop it in my lap, but his fingers halted, as if they had volition of their own. "Maybe I'd better . . . just in case . . . No!" With vehemence, he tossed it at me.

I let it fall to the deck. "Don't pretend you've forgotten my terms."

"How long yet?"

"Thirteen days."

"Oh, God." A deep breath, and another. His eyes were bleak as he retrieved the juice. "It's not worth it. I thought I wanted to be a middy, but . . ."

"Fine." Steeling myself, I stood to go. "I'd rather not watch, if you don't mind—"

He cried, "Why won't you help me!" His eyes brimmed.

Why did his pain pierce me so? Had he not brought it on himself? I crossed to the bed, sat, patted the sheet. "Put that down; sit here. We'll talk."

"Would you take it away?" He sat. "You don't know how bad today is. Every minute, I . . ."

I took his chin, turned it so his eyes met mine. "Wherever you go, there'll be juice. You can't hide from it."

He rocked. For a moment his forehead brushed my shoulder.

"Think of the next hour. Don't worry about tomorrow." How fatuous I sounded.

He threw himself flat on the bed, curled toward the bulkhead. "You said you'd tell me stories."

I swallowed. Father never told me tales; all I knew was my own life, and there was no part of it without pain. What did he want of me?

No, that was unfair. I'd promised I would visit with him. I took a long, slow breath. "I grew up in Cardiff. That's in Wales. Once, when I was young, I had a friend called Jason . . ."

I didn't know how much he heard. From time to time he sniffled and wiped his nose with his sleeve.

Two days later they caught Ricky Fuentes forcing open a cooler in the galley, late in the night. The steward brought him to Alexi and Tolliver, who shared the watch, and Tolliver took the unusual step of summoning me directly.

Moments later, buttoning my coat, I strode onto the bridge. Ricky stood stiffly at attention midway between hatch and the console. "What in blazes . . . ?"

"Not just a raid. He used a pry bar." Tolliver's voice was cold.

That Ricky Fuentes could do such a thing was the ultimate betrayal. If there was one joey aboard with sense, with decency, it was he.

"Damage?"

"Scratches. A bent hinge."

I'd been standing near my seat, listening, chest tight. When the red mists cleared I found my fingers curled around Ricky's lapels. The boy's mouth worked in panic.

"How dare you, Fuentes!" My nose was inches from the middy's. "Vandalize my ship? I'll break you! I'll put you back to cadet! Ship's boy! Common seaman!"

He whimpered.

"How dare you! Answer me!"

Ricky stammered, "A bet. I told Mr. Ross I could—I'm sorry—it was—"

I tore off my cap, hurled it across the bridge. Alexi flinched as it sailed past his head. "Call Mr. Kahn; we'll have Fuentes caned this instant!"

"Aye aye, sir." Tolliver spoke into the caller.

The gall, sneaking into territory that was off-limits to all middies, to destroy Naval property. I'd show him and the others. Any middy might irk his superiors from time to time, but there were limits. As every midshipman knew, an enraged Captain was a calamity not to be borne, and by God, I was he.

The hatch slid open. "Lieutenant Jeffrey Kahn reporting, sir."

"Do you know what this ruffian's been up to?" I swung to him, my voice an accusation. No matter what Kahn's feelings for me, he would be incensed. Raiding the galley was one thing; more than once I'd led midnight forays on *Hibernia.* Luckily we hadn't been caught, though one time, as a cadet . . . Well, that was another story. But a pry bar . . .

Kahn's eyes flicked to the Log, and Tolliver's most recent entry.

I said, "Thrash him. Don't dream of going easy. I'll want to see him after." Whatever had come over Ricky?

"Aye aye, sir. Middy, come along." He strode to the hatch.

They were well along the corridor before my last thought penetrated my consciousness. What *had* come over Ricky, my old shipmate? And wasn't it time I found out?

"Edgar, call them back." If Ricky were punished to the degree I contemplated, I'd not be able to get much from him after.

On leaving the bridge, Ricky had wheeled, marched after Kahn with commendable dignity. Apparently it had been a show for my benefit.

When he reappeared he tried manfully to check the tears that had flowed once he was out of sight.

My rage vanished like air from a ruptured hull.

I retrieved my cap from the deck. "Well." A few breaths. Adrenaline left me shaky. "Mr. Kahn, wait in your cabin. He'll be along."

I needed privacy. Should I send Tolliver and Alexi out? No, the bridge was no place for an inquisition such as I had in mind. "Come with me, Fuentes." I led him to the passengers' lounge. At this hour it was deserted. Inside, I sealed the hatch. "Now." I guided Ricky to a couch, pulled up a chair, sat with our knees almost touching. "What have you to say for yourself?"

"Nothing, sir."

I regarded him, unsure how to proceed. "How old are you?"

"Sixteen, sir." Light brown hair, a face that barely knew a razor. A slim body grown like a weed. And once, a ready smile that had lit his eyes, an eager enthusiasm that brought an ache to the heart.

A sniffle. He flushed with embarrassment.

I blurted, "Remember Sandy's orchestron?"

He gaped. "On *Hibernia?* That was . . . years ago."

"You were twelve."

"And ship's boy."

"He held it over your head, and you couldn't reach. You've grown since."

A wan smile.

"You used to bring my eggs and toast."

His eyes teared.

"Remember when I shrieked at you in my cabin, because you wouldn't relax?"

Again a smile, but his mouth quivered. He made as if to turn away, instead searched deep into my eyes. Somehow, I held his gaze. With a cry of anguish, he fell upon me, buried his head in my shoulder, held me as if a lifeline.

Stunned, I managed to raise my hand, stroke his hair. "It's all right, boy."

Sobs.

"Tell me."

For a long time nothing but the shaking of his shoulders. At last, with a shuddering breath, he raised his head from my dampened jacket. His eyes widened with dismay at the realization of what he'd done.

"Never mind that. Tell me." My voice was soft.

Instead, he looked away. "I wish . . ."

"Yes?"

"That *Victoria* were a happy ship. She used to be."

"Under Mr. Holser?"

"Mr. Martes too. The fish killed him, didn't they?"

"I'm afraid so."

His fingers twisted. "I cried myself to sleep the night Mr. Holser was—died."

"I wish I could have done the same." But I didn't deserve remorse.

A long silence. "Sir? Could you tell—I know it's none of my—" He poked at a split in the seat cover. His eyes rose to mine, with resolve. "They say you killed him."

I dared say nothing.

"That you let him stay on the Station, knowing it was too late to stop the bomb."

My lips pressed tight.

"That you let him die, because on Hope Nation he refused to talk to you!"

"Oh, Ricky." I wasn't sure I was changing the subject. "Didn't you like Mr. Ross, once?"

He seemed startled. "I guess."

"Mr. Tolliver says you ride him to distraction. Why?"

"The things he says about you!"

"And if they're true?"

"They can't be!" A pause. Then, softer, "They mustn't be."

"Look at me." I waited. "I blew the Station. I let Captain Holser on board, knowing he'd come to stop me. I deny none of it."

"You set the bomb so he couldn't disarm it? Did you do that?" In his eyes, appeal.

"It's not your place to ask."

"I need to know!"

Abruptly I stood to pace. The burden of Orbit Station was mine to bear. I couldn't inflict it on an innocent middy, no matter how great his need for reassurance.

"Why'd you break into the cooler?"

"They didn't think I could—"

"Ricky!"

His look was defiant. "What difference does it make? A hinge, a cooler, a frazzing fastship! Regs!"

"Is that all you—"

"Go ahead, have me caned! I can take it, you'll see!"

With slow steps I walked to the couch, gently lifted his head. Our eyes met. After a long time I said, "Do I mean that much to you?"

He spun away.

I knelt. "Ricky, there are things I mustn't tell you. But surely you know Vax meant a great deal to me. At the Station he was incredibly brave. His first thought was to save me, though I wasn't worth it."

"And you killed him!"

Despite my resolve, the cry was wrung from me. "Could I have?"

For an eternity he looked into my eyes. Finally his face softened. At last his gaze held a modicum of peace.

A while later I walked him to Kahn's cabin, my hand on his shoulder. "There's still punishment. That can't be helped."

"Yessir. I guess I deserve it." Ricky's head slumped, and I gave an extra squeeze.

I knocked. "Mr. Kahn, you need not go particularly easy, but disregard the rest of what I said."

Kahn nodded. I walked back to the bridge.

Annie took more interest in her surroundings, and I grew hopeful. She went for endless walks around the circumference corridors, and from time to time visited the lounge.

One afternoon she said, "Nicky, why don' they like me?"

"Because you're with me, hon."

"No, it's somethin' more. They look at me, talk 'bout me after I go."

"How would you know—"

"I listened, at the hatch." She folded her arms against my disapproval. " 'See how she hold her head, like tryin' ta be somethin' she's not!' " Her voice mimicked scorn.

I got to my feet. "Who?"

"It don't matter. I be used to it. Besides"—she giggled—"the middy tol' 'em good."

"I'll make him lieutenant," I said, only half in jest. "Which one?" Tolliver, most likely. Or Ricky. Bezrel hadn't the gumption to—

"Tommy."

"Ross? Thomas Ross?"

"Yesterday he called Suliman Rajnee a grode an' a bigot for funnin' at me. Said Rajnee didn' know what a gentleman was, an' be too stupid ta learn."

"Good Lord." Why would Ross protect my wife, given his thorough dislike of me? I was grateful, but still, foul language to a passenger was

unacceptable under any circumstances. I'd send him to Rajnee with an
apology.

"I'll be back in a while, hon."

I found Ross on the watch, with Ms. Arkin. "What have you been up
to, Middy?" I sounded more severe than I'd intended.

"Sir?"

"Yesterday. Suliman Rajnee."

"We had words."

"Tell me what you said."

"I'd rather not." Outright defiance.

"You insulted him. Called him names."

"I figured he'd whine to you about—"

"One demerit. Make that two." I pursed my lips. Rajnee was no
longer the issue. "Ross, I've had it with your—"

"Beach me, then! It was good enough for—"

"ROSS, ENOUGH!" Sandra Arkin.

"Thank you, Chief, but I'll handle it. Mr. Ross, apologize!"

A sullen silence. Then, "Very well, I apologize." His tone belied his
words.

"Sir!"

"Oh, but of course. *Sir.*"

"Mr. Ross, take yourself to"—I'd been about to say "Mr. Kahn,"
but—"the wardroom. Pack your gear; I'll send you civvies and find you
someplace to bunk."

"Am I beached?"

"You're . . ." I hesitated, firmed my resolve. He was beyond bearing. "You're dismissed from the Service, as of this moment."

"God, no!" He blanched.

"Oh, yes. Off my bridge!" I turned his shoulders, propelled him to
the hatch.

"Sir, wait, I—"

"Out!" He was agile and sturdy, but my rage was beyond challenge. I
flung him to the far bulkhead, slapped the hatch shut.

Ms. Arkin stared at the console lights.

"Well?" I dared her to object.

"He was offensive."

I snorted. "You might call it that."

Her manner was carefully placating. "If you'd repeated what he said,
Jeff Kahn would have cured him."

"He's eighteen and been barreled twice this month. It didn't help."

"Yes, sir." She couldn't say much more without skirting insubordination.

Lieutenant Kahn came to my cabin while Annie was out walking. "Sir, I beg you to reconsider."

"About Ross? Forget it."

"Aye aye, sir. I know he's impetuous, but—"

"Hah. Have you any idea what he said to me?"

"He told me some, Sandra the rest. Still, if we—"

I shouted, "I will not be spoken to with contempt!" I fingered my jacket. "This is the United Nations, the Government ordained of Lord God! It deserves respect, even if I myself—" I broke off. "After we dock, after my trial, he can spit on me; I might even applaud. But for now . . ."

"Yes, sir. I agree wholeheartedly. Sorry, not the spitting, please don't take offense. But what you have to understand about Thomas is that—"

A knock. Furious, I threw upon the hatch. "Now what—"

Edgar Tolliver. He saluted. "Might I have a word, sir?" His face was grim.

"Not now."

"Sir, I just heard—"

"About Ross?" I grimaced, stood aside. "Very well, join the party."

"Oh. I didn't realize, Mr. Kahn." Tolliver saluted his superior.

"Skip the formalities, both of you, and sit. I don't intend to be argued out of my decision."

Tolliver glanced at Kahn, back to me. "With respect, sir"—I snorted at that—"how did you decide? In the heat of the moment?"

"That's not for you to question."

Tolliver tried again. "You said the wardroom was mine to handle."

"You said you couldn't."

"You told me to try. Let me."

"With the other middies. Ross is out."

Kahn cleared his throat. "Captain, I'll have a talk with Ross. Hear him out, after—"

"Begging your pardon, sir." To Kahn, Tolliver was polite but firm. "It's my responsibility, as first middy. I'll see to it—"

I snapped, "Are you both deaf? He's cashiered." I glowered at Tolliver's mute reproach. He held his gaze.

A weariness settled over me. Was I overreacting? No. The boy was—

"Sir, he's in his bunk, crying. He begged me for help." Tolliver's face was intense. "Do you understand? Since I unpacked in the wardroom, he's offered me nothing but sullenness or gibes. Today, he wanted me."

"Contemptible. He has no right to ask, after—"

Tolliver shot to his feet. "Do you want justice or a crew?"

Even Kahn was aghast, but Tolliver paid no heed. "Break me, break Steiner. Break Tommy Ross. Why stop there? You almost lost Ricky! What about Mr. Kahn?"

"Leave me out of—"

"Sir, it's my fault Ross erupted. You know that as well as I!"

"Good heavens." I sank to a chair. Tolliver was certain of his cause, or he wouldn't dare to upbraid me. Even then, it was unimaginable. Still, I had no conscience of my own, and it seemed he was appointed to fill the role.

I waved, a gesture of defeat. "Very well. Talk to him, both of you. I'll—I *might* reconsider."

Jerence howled and kicked at me until I left. He refused to show me the vial; I knew that meant it was emptied.

Belowdecks, two crewmen beat a third senseless. I had them brigged until the next Captain's Mast.

A few months. Then the rope, and surcease.

From Ricky Fuentes, a written apology. Kahn had gone hard on him, and he'd been absent from the dining hall for days, until he could sit without misery. Ricky offered to replace the damaged hinge from his own pay. He would never do something so dishonorable again, never let me down . . . I put down the note. Better he merely exercised more sense; I wanted none of his hero-worship.

I couldn't put off dealing with Jerence; he had to be returned to the brig. I went to his cabin.

The lights were dialed low. Jerence sat up, squinted through eyes set deep in a haggard face. "Is it over?"

"Yes. To the brig." My tone was curt.

Carefully he eased himself from the bed. "You promised!"

"Only if you held out."

He hugged himself, rocking. Slowly his hand crept inside his shirt. He extended his arm, opened his fingers. The vial.

"I warned you—" But it was unopened. "Oh, Jerence!" I swallowed. "After yesterday, I thought . . ."

"I didn't think it could get any harder, but it did." His voice was hoarse. "Mr. Seafort, it hurts."

"Yes." I sniffed. "Are you forgetting to wash?"

"Who cares?" Again he hugged himself. "How long has it been?"

"Ten days. Eleven to go."

He pursed his lips, shook his head.

Tolliver sat across from me in the officers' mess. "May I bring Mr. Ross to see you?"

I frowned. I regretted letting myself be bludgeoned into an interview. "Not the bridge, and definitely not my cabin. Where are his quarters?"

"Cabin twenty-nine, Level 2. He shares."

"With whom?"

A flicker of a smile. "Suliman Rajnee. Mr. Kahn and I thought it fitting."

Tolliver's idea, I was sure. "Very well. After lunch."

The meal was tasteless and heavy on my stomach. After, I paced the bridge for a full hour, girding myself.

Rajnee, by prearrangement, would be elsewhere. I rapped on the hatch.

Thomas Ross opened, began a salute, realized it was a breach of protocol. Lowering his hand, he stood aside. He looked odd and uncomfortable in a casual jumpsuit.

I found a chair, sat with crossed legs. "Well?"

He walked with peculiar gait to his bunk, eased himself onto it.

"Have they caned you?" My tone was sharp. "I gave orders you weren't to be—"

"No, sir. I've been sick to my stomach ever since you . . . It hurts."

We waited.

"I've nothing to say, Ross. I'm here at your request."

"Yessir. What I wanted to—look. My hand's shaking." He held it out for inspection.

"Get on with it." In the Navy, one made one's bed and had to lie in it. I had no sympathy for his distress.

"I've got to be reinstated." He frowned, as if it hadn't sounded the way he hoped. "The Navy is all I ever wanted."

That much, I understood. It had been so with me.

"Without it I'm . . . nothing." His eyes darted to mine, back to the deck. "What must I do to convince you?"

"Should I care?"

"Captain, I apologize for my rudeness. I'll do anything. I'll get down on my knees and—"

"You won't do that." I would leave, on the instant. The memories were too strong.

"Whatever you say, then. Have me caned. But please, please put me back to middy. I won't ever disrespect—"

I was tired of it. "What I want isn't groveling, but truth. I came here expecting to deny your request, and that's still my intent. Level with me absolutely, or there's not the slightest chance I'll—"

"Anything!" He jumped from the bed, crossed to the wardrobe built into the bulkhead, turned back. His voice was unsteady. "Anything."

"Why are you so desperate? There are other paths, other lives to lead."

"I thought when I showed how angry I was, I was acting from principle. But on the bridge, when you dismissed me . . . something in my gut wrenched; I thought I'd pass out. I never knew how important the Navy was to me." He turned. "In Ottawa I dreamed of it, lying in my bed. I had all the holos about Academy, and Mom was furious when I played them instead of doing my homework."

Despite myself, I smiled. I knew. "Why do you loathe me so?"

"I don't, I've changed my mind, I realize I've been—"

I strode to the hatch.

"All right! You killed Mr. Holser!"

"Others have made their peace with it."

"I'm sorry, I didn't mean to accuse—"

"Damn it, boy, truth!"

He stumbled to the bed, sank on it, immediately jumped to his feet. "You're a traitor! You set off a nuke! He was your friend, and a word from you would have stopped him. You didn't say it!"

"If he came to save the Station, would he have listened?"

"He was our Captain!" A cry of such despair that I was silenced.

"Oh, God, I'm going to be sick again." He tried not to retch. "I love the Navy more than anything, but I can't abide that it has you in it!"

My voice was so quiet that only I heard. "Neither can I."

A long time passed, the silence broken only by his sobs.

I cleared my throat. "What's come of your talks with Tolliver and Mr. Kahn?"

"Lieutenant Kahn's furious, sir. He's warned me if I'm reinstated I'll have more to worry about from him than you."

"Odd, given his own feelings."

"Not really, sir. Mr. Tolliver's disgusted with me, but he took the time to make it clear. If we respect the Service, we owe courtesy to all its officers. You're not just in charge of *Victoria*, sir. You represent Admiralty, the regs, every ship of the line. So I'll have to show you good manners, no matter what I—no matter what."

"That came as a revelation?" My tone was dry.

"No, sir." A mumble. "I guess I already knew. It's just . . ." His head came up. "You said the truth. May I speak my mind?"

I nodded.

"I owe it to Mr. Holser not to let his murder go unnoticed. I despise your treason. Thank God that hangings are public. I'll be there for yours even if I have to jump ship. And I'll celebrate, when they're done." At my unflinching gaze, he reddened. "Well, that's how I feel."

"It's not always necessary to say what you feel."

"Yessir."

This had gone far enough; I already knew my decision. "I'll let you know in a week or so." I stood.

"That long!"

"Or more." The prize would be more valued, for the yearning.

"What shall I do with myself? I spend every day alone; Rajnee doesn't care to talk to me any more than I—and no officer will even speak to me."

I shrugged. "That's your affair." An idle thought. "If you're lonely, visit cabin nineteen."

"The Branstead joey?"

"An hour a day, no more. He'd like someone to talk with, I imagine."

Tolliver dogged Alexi Tamarov's footsteps, relentless in his determination that Alexi become the perfect lieutenant. I surmised that Tolliver modeled his behavior after our drill sergeants at Academy, who spoke to us with token respect, yet sternly monitored and corrected our every move.

At first, Alexi was resentful and sullen. Nonetheless, he studied his texts and performed his nav drills like any nervous young middy, Tolliver by his side. After a time Alexi hesitantly began issuing orders to the work details he was allowed to supervise.

After a week I allowed Thomas Ross to don his uniform. He reported for watch, polished and crisp. As he entered the bridge, evident relief battled with something else. Perhaps self-betrayal.

I said nothing of what had passed between us. When he was settled I left for my cabin.

In the evenings I sat with Jerence.

After one tempestuous visit, he'd finally quieted and gone to sleep. In the morning he'd pounded on the hatch until a sailor heard him and called the purser. Before I rounded the corridor bend I could hear Jerence begging to be freed.

"Steady, Jerence." I opened the hatch. He tried to dive past me; I hauled him up by the collar. The vial of goofjuice lay on his bed.

"Oh, God, Mr. Seafort, I want it so! Isn't there a way? Couldn't I have just a little? Would you let me?"

"Yes. As much as you want."

"Oh, thank you! I—" He stopped short. "And could I enlist, then?"

"Of course not."

"Look what's happening to me!" He showed me his hand. It trembled.

"Physical withdrawal, I'd guess. A jolt of juice will cure it." I put my hand on the hatch lever.

"Don't leave me alone! Please!" His tear-streaked face peered up at me. "I've tried so hard, but I can't!"

Again I thought of Nate, knowing the comparison was foolish. This boy was not my son, never would be. But impulsively I pulled his head to my chest, released him. "Wait another day, Jerence. I'll be back."

"To tell me more stories? Tommy won't, he says he doesn't know how."

"I don't know any more—"

"Pa used to, when I was little. If I concentrate on your voice I don't think so hard about the juice, for a little."

"All right, but not every day." What could I tell him of myself that wasn't a lie?

Time passed. I adjusted Alexi's watch rotation so that he always shared with Tolliver. Tolliver bore up under the strain of his duties, made easier perhaps by the lessening of tensions in the wardroom. Even Bezrel showed signs of improvement; he was rebuked less often and learned to stand up under criticism without wilting. Well, most of the time. On one occasion I'd carefully not noticed a stray tear making its way down his cheek.

Still, Alexi had been but a pale imitation of a lieutenant: hesitant, unsure, often confused. I knew that after we docked, when I'd be unable to shield him, he'd be useless to the Service. I didn't tell him so. He already knew.

"Mr. Seafort, it isn't working." We were on the bridge, toward the end of the cruise, during one of Tolliver's rare absences. "If Edgar wasn't with me, I'd never manage."

"Just do your best, Alexi."

"I try, but I can't even fill out the Log without Tolliver guiding me. And I do it every watch!"

"Your intelligence is what it always was. We had it tested."

"Yes, I know."

"And Dr. Zares says your ability to retain what you learn is unimpaired. So all you need is time."

"Yes, sir." He brooded at his console. "I know you don't like me to complain."

"Do the best you can."

He flared, "Do my best, do my best. How many times have I heard that? You sound just like Amanda. Alexi, all you can expect is your bes—"

The hairs on my neck rose.

White-faced, he whispered, "Amanda!"

"You remember?"

"In my cabin, when I hated Philip so! On *Hibernia!*" He bounded from his seat. "Sir, I remember! Wasn't it on *Portia*, when she died? Tell me!"

"Yes." I grinned. Thank You, Lord.

"Her funeral, I was there!" He danced with excitement.

"Steady, Lieutenant." I clasped his arm; unexpectedly he grabbed me and hugged me. "Oh, sir, I remember parts of it!"

"Easy, Alexi." But I didn't push him away; my hand pounded his back in answering enthusiasm.

It wasn't that simple, of course. Huge gaps in his memory remained. Yet, almost daily, bits of his past returned. With each revelation, his stature heightened, his shoulders straightened, his confidence grew.

I was content.

But then I thought of home.

31

"Prepared to Defuse, sir," said Chief Engineer Sandra Arkin.

"Very well." I turned to Kahn, absently fingering my scar. "Call Mr. Tolliver."

Moments later Edgar Tolliver saluted, waited for me to release him.

"As you were. I thought you might want to see this, Edgar. The end of our cruise." The finis to my career, and soon of my life.

"Yes, sir." He stood behind my chair, peering over my shoulder at the console.

I reached to the top of the screen. I hesitated. Each day of the interminable voyage had brought me inexorably closer to this moment. I had no doubt they'd hang me. My only regret was that Annie was still fragile, and sometimes worse. She would likely require a course of hormone rebalancing. Perhaps I could arrange that much, before they tried me. Perhaps, in return for my guilty plea . . .

"Ready, sir?" Kahn.

"Sound Battle Stations. We'll take no chances."

"Aye aye, sir." Kahn pressed the alarms. Throughout the ship men and women dashed to their stations, reported their readiness to the bridge. When all compartments had responded I reluctantly put my finger on the screen.

"We're ready, sir."

I shot Kahn an annoyed glance. "Yes, of course." I ran my finger down the line on the screen. "Defused."

The simulscreens flashed to stunning life. "Checking for encroachments," Kahn said immediately.

"Captain, no encroachments." The puter.

"Thank you, Billy. Mr. Kahn?" Never did one rely solely on a machine.

His reply took a moment longer. "Free of encroachments, Captain."

"Where are we?"

Billy said, "Outside orbit of Venus. Coordinates follow."

"Very well. Remain at Battle Stations until we contact Admiralty." I stood to pace. "Mr. Tolliver."

"Yes, sir?"

"Sit at the console." Immediately Lieutenant Kahn rose to give his seat. It would have been unthinkable for Tolliver, or any officer, to sit in my place. "Take the following message to the comm room and have it broadcast continuously until reply is received:

"To Admiralty, Lunapolis Base, Captain Nicholas E. Seafort reporting." Diligently Tolliver typed my words.

"U.N.S. *Victoria* is returned to Solar System under my command. The U.N.N.S. fleet left Hope Nation ten months ago under orders of Admiral Georges De Marnay and is in passage home." Our fastship had outraced the fleet; the other ships would arrive six months from now.

"Due to a rebellion on Hope Nation, I was unable to rejoin the fleet." I paused, waited for Tolliver. "With help from several planters, I suppressed the rebellion. On my own initiative, as senior military officer and plenipotentiary of the United Nations Government, I granted the colony of Hope Nation status as a free commonwealth, and full and irrevocable membership in the Assembly of the United Nations." Tolliver shook his head, knowing as well as I that Admiralty would be appalled.

"After the fleet sailed, the aliens continued to attack Hope Nation. Fish entered the atmosphere and settled to ground level. They destroyed and overran the Venturas Base."

Even I, brazen as I had become, found the next confession difficult. "I concluded that Hope Nation could not survive unless the balance of forces was drastically altered. Therefore, acting alone and in secret, I caused the disabled ships on Orbit Station to attract the fish by caterwauling their fusion drives. Many fish responded. When Orbit Station was disabled, I deliberately caused a nuclear detonation that destroyed some five hundred twelve fish."

"Plus the four hundred seventy-two my father shot," Billy said proudly.

"Puter, be silent. Commander Vax Holser, a courageous officer, lost his life in an unsuccessful attempt"—I stopped dead. It was my last chance to redeem my honor. The truth, or a vile lie? I took a deep breath—"to save Orbit Station from detonation. I emphasize that no person other than myself took any part in the destruction of the Station."

I cleared my throat. Why was the simulscreen blurred? "I therefore turn over command of U.N.S. *Victoria* to Lieutenant Jeffrey Kahn and await your further orders. Mr. Tolliver, transmit at once."

"Aye aye, sir."

I turned to Lieutenant Kahn, saluted. "I'll be in my cabin with my wife. Do not disturb me until they reply."

"Aye aye, sir." An awed whisper.

I strode from the bridge for the last time, keeping my head high, my expression calm, until I was around the bend of the circumference corridor. Then I hurried to my cabin, groped for the hatch.

Annie sat in her chair, looking at a holo, humming. She took no notice of my entry. I took off my jacket, my tie. I lay down on the bed.

I'm sorry, Father. At the end, even duty has failed me. I am nothing in the eyes of Lord God, and now I am nothing to the Naval Service. Let it be over.

I lay staring at the ceiling. After a period I drifted to other places, other times. Strange dreams disturbed my sleep. Vax Holser, enraged, did push-ups in the wardroom. Amanda talked to fish, who made no reply. Philip Tyre . . . I couldn't hear him, for the banging on my hatch.

I stirred, drifted back to sleep, but the hammering persisted. I woke. Hours had passed, and someone pounded in the corridor. The impertinence amazed me. I jumped to my feet, flung open the hatch.

"Did you know, you conniving bastard? Did you?" Tears ran down Edgar Tolliver's cheeks. "Was it another of your tricks?" He slammed his fist into the bulkhead.

"Know? What are you talking about?"

"I can't even hate you anymore! Yet I was ready to see you die, to put an end to it!" He sobbed in fury, wiped his cheek with his sleeve. "Tell me you knew!"

I grasped his shoulders, shook him. "Explain, Edgar."

"God damn you, read it yourself!" He thrust me a holochip.

I turned back to the desk, put it in the holovid.

I keyed the screen.

"To: Captain Nicholas E. Seafort, from ComHomFlt, U.N.N.S., Lunapolis Base. Eleven months ago, on 4 March, 2200, United Nations Security Council Resolution 8645 was amended to read: 'The threat of nuclear annihilation having for generations terrorized all mankind, it is enacted that use, attempted use, or conspiracy to use nuclear energy for the purpose of destructive detonation shall in all cases be punishable by death, UNLESS SUCH ACT SHALL (A) TAKE PLACE OUTSIDE THE SOLAR SYSTEM, (B) BE COMMITTED FOR THE PURPOSE OF DEFENDING UNITED NATIONS COLONIES OR MEMBER STATES FROM DESTRUCTION BY ALIEN ATTACK, AND (C) BE PERSONALLY AUTHORIZED BY THE SENIOR MILITARY OFFICIAL WITHIN THAT COLONY OR MEMBER STATE.'

"You are to resume command of U.N.S. Victoria. Proceed to Lunapolis Base, where you will testify at a Board of Inquiry to determine whether the destruction of Orbit Station was necessary and within your province to command, and whether you had the requisite authority to alter the status of the colony of Hope Nation. End message."

Tolliver whispered, "How did you know the law was amended?"

I snarled, "Look at the date of the amendment. How *could* I know?"

He made no response. I said, "Go to the bridge. I'll be along shortly."

Tolliver stumbled to attention, saluted. "Aye aye, sir."

"Dismissed."

Epilogue

"Admiral Duhaney will see you now, sir." The staff lieutenant held the door. All eyes in the crowded anteroom were on me, as they had been from the moment I'd entered. It was so everywhere I'd been in the Lunapolis warrens.

I straightened my tie, took a last tug at my jacket. "Very well."

"Seafort." Admiral Duhaney rose from behind the desk, extended a hand. I took it. In his forties, I judged. Smooth black hair, a politician's smile. A far cry from Admiral Brentley, my old mentor. He asked, "How are you feeling?"

"Well enough, sir." I'd recovered from the implant of my new lung, and I'd just about run the course of the antirejection meds, but still I was grateful Lunapolis had only one-sixth Terran gravity.

"Have a seat." He gestured to the couch. "I understand your wife is still in, ah, treatment. Will she travel with you?"

"Travel? Where?"

He looked surprised. "On your next ship. You have your choice of assignments, you know. If there's some particular ship we can give the Hero of Hope Nation—"

"Don't call me that!" I came to my feet, trembling. "If you're going to jeer at me—"

"Jeer? Look at the holozines!" I glanced at the printouts scattered on the table. Of course my scarred face was on all of them still. I could go nowhere without the cameras whirring.

"I'm no hero." I slumped back into my seat.

"You've been exonerated by a Board of Inquiry."

Whitewashed, he meant. The holozines had gotten my story, probably by decoding my wideband broadcast, and had emblazoned it across the world's screens. "Seafort Saves Hope Nation"; "Captain Kills A Thousand Fish!"; "Nicky Nukes Alien Fleet!" Other headlines didn't bear thinking about.

After that, the Navy could do nothing but concur in the general adulation. They'd heard my report on the Venturas attack, read William's confirmation, and endorsed my treason without batting an eye.

"You can have *Hibernia*, when she gets home, or any other ship you—"

"I resign."

He stopped short. "You what?"

"Resign, I said. I've done enough harm. I'll do no more."

Admiral Duhaney got up, crossed slowly to the couch, sat next to me. "You can't, Seafort. The public wouldn't stand for it, and we need you."

"No."

He studied my face. "What happened, out beyond? Is this about the Station?"

"No, sir. It's about the people." *Vax, why do you haunt me? I was trying to protect you. Gladly I would have given you the glory.*

"Your return on *Victoria* must have been . . . difficult."

"Somewhat. That doesn't matter." *Victoria's officers had judged me more truly than had Admiralty.*

"Nine months is a long time, if you're not liked."

"Not liked?" *Despised. No time in my life had been as lonely as those nine endless months.*

Admiral Duhaney cleared his throat.

"Sorry." *Where were we?* "It's not the trip home, sir. I've had enough."

"We need men like you commanding—"

"Whatever your Board of Inquiry said, I'm not fit to command. I've broken my oath, I've destroyed a station, I've far exceeded my authority. If I didn't have that foolish reputation in the zines you'd have cashiered me, or worse. You should have hanged me. When I blew the Station I had no idea they'd changed the nuclear resolution!"

"That doesn't matter, boy. The resolution *was* amended. It had to be. The hysteria after that first fish followed you home in *Challenger* . . ." He shook his head.

"I thought I was committing treason."

"You'd have been, a few months earlier. Lord God must be with you."

That was so preposterous I didn't bother to answer. Duhaney was a fool. "It doesn't matter, sir. I resign."

"You mustn't. Do you know how many ships we've lost? We need the public behind us for the cost of rebuilding the fleet. And recruiting is more important than ever. We need your face on the recruiting posters to—"

"Cashier me, damn you, but don't mock me!" I scrambled to my feet. "Well, don't look so surprised! Admiralty taught me over and again I could get away with insolence; this is the result! Good day to you, sir." Fuming, I strode across the room.

"Wait, Seafort, I—"

I flung an angry salute, slammed the door. In the anteroom conversation melted into stunned silence. The duty lieutenant stared, aghast. I ignored them all as I stalked out.

My quarters were a half-kilometer distant, through endless tunnels. Rather than wait for the mini-shuttle I chose to walk. Soon my pace was almost a run, aided by the lesser gravity. By the time I reached my rooms I'd begun to cool, and felt not a little embarrassed at my tantrum. For an officer to carry on in front of an Admiral—it was unheard of. My behavior was worse than that of a rank cadet at Lunar Academy on Farside.

Well, Duhaney couldn't do much about it. It mattered not whether he placed a rebuke in my file or even demoted me for my insolence. I was through.

They'd given me a suite of rooms—a small bedroom, sitting room, kitchenette, and head—in the military housing complex. Luxury accommodations, for crowded Lunapolis. I let myself in, threw off my jacket, washed my hands and face. I wondered how Annie was doing, in the New York clinic. I'd go down to see her again, as soon as I could. I supposed I'd hear from the Admiral, one way or the other. Perhaps a court-martial for insubordination would accomplish what the Board of Inquiry had not.

I slept.

The next morning I was mopping my breakfast plate when the bell rang. Still in shirtsleeves, I opened the door.

Admiral Duhaney's braid gleamed. Automatically I came to attention.

"As you were, Mr. Seafort. This is an, ah, unofficial call." He gestured to the civilian at his side. "I don't believe you've met. Senator, may I present Captain Nicholas Seafort. Captain, of course you know Senator Boland."

"Senator who?"

The Admiral frowned. "Senator Richard Boland, of the Security Council Naval Affairs Committee."

"An honor to meet you, Captain." He held out his hand. "May we come in?"

"I was just—very well." I shook hands and stood aside.

They found places in the sitting room. The Senator said, "Admiral, may I? Let's get to the point. Mr. Seafort, your foolish remark about resigning is forgotten, of course. I'm here to help negotiate a course of—"

"Negotiate? Admiralty doesn't negotiate its assignments."

The Admiral cleared his throat. "In your case, we do. You don't seem to understand we really need you."

"Why?"

"Because the war's unpopular," said Boland. "Some people want us to stop fighting the fish, pull back to home system, abandon the colonies if need be—"

"That's absurd!" How could we turn our backs on millions of our own people, scattered among the stars?

"Yes, of course. But it may come to pass. We need heroes, and you're our most prominent. You thought the Admiral mocked you when he spoke of putting your picture on a recruiting poster. It's already on one."

"Lord God in heaven!"

"You have no idea how popular you've become. In fact, if you insisted on resigning, we could run you for the General Assembly and you'd win in a minute."

"I'm not running for—"

"But we need you in the Navy. Recruitment jumped fifteen percent since we began showing the spot of you and your wife disembarking at—"

I snarled, "You dragged Annie into this?"

"Dragged? No, we have just the one shot of you coming through the airlock into Earthport Station."

I stood, trembling with rage. "Get out! Both of you!"

Boland looked up curiously. "What's wrong, Captain?"

"Annie's ill! She needs privacy!"

"Don't be silly. You won't have privacy for years, whether or not you resign. Anyway, you're the perfect recruiting couple: the dashing young Captain and his beautiful trannie—excuse me—transpop wife. It attracts the educated classes to the service academies, and the working joeys as well."

He wandered to the holowindow, flicked the setting to Upper New York. "Seafort, we've gotten off on the wrong foot. Help us win the war. We can give you any ship—"

"I don't want one."

"Then we'll post you shoreside. Public relations, light duties, a few appear—"

"Never."

Admiral Duhaney said, "Richard, let me try." He came across the room. "Look at me, Mr. Seafort." He spoke softly. "I'm used to dealing with politicians, not the working fleet. Perhaps I don't speak your language, but hear me out. If we pull back to home system, the fish will still be there. Sooner or later they'll find us. Do you agree?" Reluctantly I nodded.

"Even if they don't, we'd still be trapped in home system, unable to Fuse for fear of attracting them. We can't have that. Even I see as much, politician that I've become. Seafort, you're an important cog in our war

machine. Not essential, but of great value. You won't take a ship or work
the publicity circuit. Let me give you a job where you'll be shoreside and
able to duck publicity too."

"What is that?" I asked hoarsely. I was drowning. Where was my
lifebelt?

"Captain Kearsey is retiring."

"Kearsey? Commandant Kearsey?"

"Yes. I'll appoint you Commandant of Lunar Academy."

"Good Lord!"

"Think, Seafort. You'll have not only the Farside Academy but also
Terrestrial Academy and the Training Station. They're closed bases, so you
can keep the reporters out. You'll be free to visit your wife, and have her
live with you as soon as she's able."

"But why?"

"When we make you Commandant, recruitment will double. We'll
keep using the holo shots we have; no need even to pose for new ones."

"Let me be! Why won't you let me go?"

He ignored me. "You've always had the pied piper in you, Seafort.
You're good with children."

I cried, "Good? I kill them!" Sandy Wilsky, dead from my stupidity in
Hibernia. The transpops on *Portia*. Even Philip Tyre, on *Challenger*.
Where I walked I left a trail of misery and death. My own son Nate . . .

"You'd be wonderful at the job, and I'm not giving you a line of
goofjuice. Your reports all show you handle youngsters well."

No, it wasn't so. True, some had escaped the effects of my blundering, but others had not. Jerence Branstead, whom I'd locked in a cabin
with a full vial of goofjuice. My cruelty to him had known no bounds.

Each day I'd waited for him to break. Grimly he held on. After a time
the purser reported that food trays had come back untouched for three
days. Again I went to his cabin. It reeked of sweat and Lord God knew
what else. The vial was on the table, unopened. Jerence, lay across his
bed, eyes shut, clutching the sheets.

"Get up, lad."

"I can't. It hurts too bad."

"Come." I drew him off the bed, pushed him into the head, unbuttoned his shirt. "Take off the rest of it. Into the shower." He shook his
head. I pulled off his clothes.

"Don't look at me." He covered himself.

I laughed aloud. "I won't, but don't try that in the wardroom."

"I can't hold on!"

"Only a few more days."

"I can't." He sagged against the side of the shower. I adjusted the temperature, went out into the corridor and to the caller. "Purser, to the Branstead cabin." Moments later I gestured at the mess. "Fresh sheets, and get the clothing washed."

He wrinkled his nose. "Aye aye, sir."

On the twenty-first day I unlocked the cabin hatch and stood aside. Jerence Branstead's clothes hung large on his wasted frame. His steps were tremulous. He blinked in the bright corridor light.

"The vial, lad."

He whispered, "Yessir." Slow steps, back to the prison of his cabin. He reemerged. I held out my palm. After a long, reluctant moment he placed the vial in my hand.

"Still?"

He nodded. "As bad as ever. Almost."

"Will you use it again?"

To his credit, the boy was silent a long time. When he looked up his eyes held something they hadn't held before. "No, sir."

"Before I enlist you, swear it to Lord God."

He bit his lip, reached out, put his hand for comfort in mine. "I swear on my immortal soul that I . . . won't . . . ever use . . . goofjuice again." He was weeping.

"Very well. I'll talk to you about the oath after—"

"Hold me! Be Pa for a minute!" He rushed sobbing into my arms. Awkwardly I cradled him. I had no flair for solace. My talent was for torture.

"It was so hard, Mr. Seafort. So hard!"

"I know, boy." I let him weep. "I know."

Now, in Lunapolis, I looked up to the Admiral. "Why won't you understand? I'm the worst officer you've ever had, and always you reward me! You'd even put me in charge of your children. I warn you, don't!"

"You'll do well, Seafort. When can you start?"

I was defeated. "I need time with my wife."

"Of course. Four weeks, then? Standard long-leave?"

"I suppose."

"Good." He smiled. "By the way, I've approved your final report on *Victoria* and sent your personnel recommendations to BuPers."

"Very well."

"You're sure you want that fellow put back to lieutenant?"

"Tolliver? Yes."

"We'll do it, but no one will take him after what he did with the heli. It's half pay for him, or some outpost like Ganymede Station."

It would be fitting punishment. For me. I said, "I'll take him."

"Hmmm, odd of you. The others will be no problem, of course."

I'd recommended that Bram Steiner's commission be reinstated without penalty. I'd also written Lieutenant Kahn a good rating, though I hadn't told him so. I rather admired his thespian abilities. From the moment of my ultimatum, his seething hatred had been indiscernible.

The one officer who'd been true to his convictions was Thomas Ross, and he'd paid dearly for it for the remainder of the cruise. Not at my hand, but at Kahn's after his reinstatement. It didn't help that I'd stripped him of all seniority, and he'd been low man in the wardroom, lower even than Avar Bezrel.

When the flagship Defused from Hope Nation, Bezrel would be returned to Admiral De Marnay. Perhaps he'd be happier under the wing of his protector. As for Jerence . . . the corners of my mouth turned up. I'd be his guardian still. Like me, he'd be sent to Academy.

Senator Boland coughed. "There's one more thing. Would you consider . . ."

I said impatiently, "Yes?"

"Getting rid of that awful scar?"

My hand flew to my face. "It's part of me."

"An unnecessary part. We tone it down on the posters, but for heaven's sake . . . you're famous enough without it."

"That's not why I wear it."

"I know, I know. They showed me your psych report. Bear your guilt, if you must, but carry it inside like the rest of us. Would you do that much?"

"I—well—all right, if you insist."

"Thank you."

"Go enjoy your leave, then." In a daze, I shook hands as they left.

When the cabin was silent, I dropped into my chair and sat musing. Lord God, are You toying with me? If I could have Your forgiveness, Your love once more, even for just a moment . . . No, I know better than to ask. But why, then, do You let them reward me? And my friends, Alexi, Jerence, Tolliver. Was it for their sakes You helped them through their travail, or could it have been for mine?

Will I ever meet You?

I didn't know. Absently I began to pack. For now, there was long-leave. There was Annie. There was duty.

Someday I'd know the rest.

Fisherman's Hope

To Nicholas Ewing Seafort, Philip Tyre, and Derek Anthony Carr, good men all, who taught me much about the struggle of life.

FISHERMAN'S HOPE

Being the fourth voyage of
Nicholas Seafort, U.N.N.S.,
in the year of our Lord 2201

Part 1

August 4, in the Year of our Lord 2201

1

"But Vasily's a Russian, and we're short on Eurasians." Lieutenant Darwin Sleak flipped through the stack of folders on the polished conference table, each an application to the United Nations Naval Academy. Sleak glanced at Commandant Kearsey for approval, squinting in the bright summer Devon sun.

The Commandant tapped his folder. "Born September 2187. Grades put him in the eleventh percentile among applicants, admission tests put him eighteenth. Low, but someone has to be near the bottom." He shrugged his unconcern. "Put him on the list, I suppose." He turned to me. "Any comment, Captain Seafort?"

I blurted, "I thought the Selection Board didn't consider nationality." Damn Final Cull, anyway. My aide Edgar Tolliver carefully studied his fingernails, accustomed to my outbursts.

Commandant Kearsey said, "Officially, we don't. And we wouldn't take some unqualified joey simply to gain another Russian. But with a war on, we need public support from every continent. A balanced cadet class doesn't hurt."

I knew he was right. The Navy's appalling losses to the fishlike aliens that had attacked our Hope Nation and Vegan colonies had to be made up, and the cost of rebuilding the fleet would be enormous. The deadly assaults had destroyed fourteen ships of the line and killed untold hundreds of crewmen, some my friends. And then we'd lost Orbit Station, where Vax Holser had died hoping to save me.

I forced my thoughts into a new channel. "What if we just took the top three hundred eighty?"

"We'd lose all geographical balance."

My tone was acid. "So? Balance wasn't a consideration when you took Senator Boland's son." I shouldn't have said it, but my new shoes hurt and so did my chest; I'd grown accustomed to one-sixth gravity during my recent stay on Lunapolis.

I braced myself for the Commandant's withering glare that had transfixed me as a raw cadet only fourteen years ago. Certainly my manner warranted it. But I was no longer a frightened thirteen-year-old reporting for induction; now I was the notorious Nicholas Ewing Seafort, "hero" of

Hope Nation. My face scowled from a recruiting poster, and in two short weeks I was to replace Kearsey as Commandant of both U.N.N.S. Academy bases, here at Devon and at Farside, on Luna. I alone knew of the perversions on which the public's adulation was based. I, and Lord God. Someday I must face His reckoning.

Commandant Kearsey concealed whatever annoyance he felt. "We can't very well turn down a U.N. Senator's son, Captain. Especially when Boland's on the Security Council's Naval Affairs Committee. Anyway, the boy's grades are acceptable."

"Lower than the Russian's, I think. Who are we bumping for the Boland boy?"

His staff aide, Sergeant Kinders, handed him a folder. "A Parisian. Jacques Theroux." The Commandant frowned. "It's not as if the boy will know why he's off the final list. What's more important: putting another cadet in Boland's place, or having powerful friends at appropriation time? Do you want the new ships built or not?"

I stared at the door, knowing I had no answer. The Navy must be restored, to guard our far-flung colonies, and to protect home system if the fish attacked. I muttered, "I'd still pick the first three hundred eighty."

Even Tolliver and Sleak looked at me strangely. It was a moment before Commandant Kearsey answered. "Then we'd lose Final Cull. We'd be stuck with the candidates the Selection Board sent."

"Yes."

Lieutenant Sleak cleared his throat, waited for the Commandant's nod. "Final Cull is Academy's hard-won prerogative, and our only input into the Selection process. Would you have us give it up?" His tone was cold, despite the fact that I'd soon be his commander.

Final Cull was a traditional privilege, and the Navy shouldn't surrender its traditions easily.

Yet, still . . .

"Father, can Jason stay for dinner?" At thirteen I knew better than to ask in front of the prospective guest. I hoped I could get away with it, as I'd just thrown Father's cherished obligations of hostship into the balance against his stern disapproval of my friend.

Father's eyebrow raised. "He could abide our prayers?"

Jason flushed, his eye on the orchestron we were updating on the creaky kitchen table. He paused, chip in hand. "I may be a freethinker, sir, but I respect the customs of your house." Quickly, as if he'd gone too far, he bent over the orchestron motherboard.

Father grunted. "Respect for Lord God isn't a custom. It is life itself." Still, I knew Jason's forthrightness had gained him favor in Father's eyes. "Perhaps you too will find Him, before you consign yourself to damnation." Oh, please, not a sermon. Not in front of Jason.

Father gave the gleaming teapot one last swipe with the soft cloth. "I can't imagine why Nicholas thinks asking permission in your presence will sway me. He knows better manners than he practices." I swallowed. More verses at bedside, or worse; Father always remembered the day's sins. Still, the corners of his mouth turned up grudgingly. "Pea soup, the fresh bread, and tomatoes from the garden. Can you tolerate it?"

"That's fine, sir," Jason said quickly. I flashed him a grin across the table; he surreptitiously kicked my shin.

Later, washing for dinner, Jason asked softly, "Heard anything yet?"

I shook my head. One way or another, word had to come soon. Time was running out.

"He's said you can go for sure?"

"Aye." Perhaps my imploring and tears had nothing to do with Father's consent. I suspected they'd helped, despite the switching he'd given me when I persisted.

"Well, you reached the second interview, and didn't get a wash-out letter. You made it to Final Cull." Like any teener, he was familiar with Academy admission procedures. If I passed Final Cull I'd be admitted to Terrestrial Academy at Devon, where they'd subject me to basic training before shipping me to Farside for my real education.

"Aye." I wished Jason wouldn't talk about it; I'd persuaded myself that not discussing my chances somehow improved them. At dinner Father drew himself from his customary meditative silence, for Jason's sake. For the moment, Jase was Father's guest as well as mine. "Your, ah, plaything is fixed?"

"The orchestron? Aye, sir. But it's an instrument, not a toy."

"An instrument of . . . electronics." He and I both knew his unspoken thought. An instrument of Satan, as all idle amusements.

"And of music, Mr. Seafort. There isn't much the Welsh Philharmonic can play that we couldn't re-create on it."

"By pushing buttons." But Father's tone was agreeable, as he mopped at his soup with the hot bread he'd pulled from the oven an hour before.

Jason's lean face lit with the grin I cherished. "It's all in knowing what buttons to push, sir."

Father looked to me, shaking his head as if in exasperation. Recklessly, I grinned back; Jason had that effect on me. He was courteous to Father, even respected him in a way, without taking Father's manner seriously. At first I'd been scandalized, then put off, but now I knew it was part of Jason's singular view of the world.

Father asked, "You'll be in Third?" Two conversational gambits in an evening. He was treating Jason as an adult, and I was grateful.

"Yes, sir. This year I'm taking Engineering for electives."

"Why?"

"I like to build things, or fix them."

"A city and a tower, whose top may reach unto heaven."

Jason looked confused. I explained, "He means the tower of Babel. Genesis Nine."

Father swung to me in rebuke. "Genesis Eleven. Don't pretend to learning you lack, Nicholas."

"I'm sorry, sir."

"Nicky could sign up for half days, Mr. Seafort. We could work on projects together."

Father raised an eyebrow. "Nicholas learns best at home, where his idleness is held in check." That was like Father, to discuss my faults in front of anyone, as if I had no feelings. But to my surprise he added, "Anyway, Nicholas won't be at your school next year. I imagine he'll be at Academy." I was astonished. Father had never once hinted he thought I had a chance of being accepted.

"Of course," Jason said quickly. "I just meant if he didn't—I mean, I forgot."

Two days later I was on my knees pulling the stubborn weeds from our garden, knowing Father's vigilant eye would judge my work, and that my chance of parole on Saturday depended on his approval. Jason had bought us tickets to the football game with the Irish, though I hadn't told Father yet.

A shadow fell across the black dirt. I looked up, a bead of sweat trickling. "I'm not done yet, sir. I'll catch the rest of that row, after."

He waved it away. "The post is here."

"The post?" Why would he interrupt my chores for—"It came?" I was on my feet. "What does it say?"

"I don't know. It's yours to open."

I reached out, but he shook his head. "On the kitchen table." I dashed to the door. "Mind you wash your hands!"

I took enough time to rinse so I'd leave no grime on the towel. That would infuriate Father, and I wouldn't enjoy the consequences. I rushed back to the kitchen, tore open the embossed envelope. Father waited, leaning against the sink, his face grave.

"The Selection Board of the U.N.N.S. Naval Academy always has more qualified candidates than places. We regret to inform you that after careful consideration we are unable . . ."

I dropped the letter on the table, blinking away a blur. Unbelieving, I snatched it up again. ". . . you are to be congratulated that you were one of the final candidates in this year's selection process. If you wish to apply again next year we would be happy to consider . . ."

My eyes stinging, I ran into my room, slammed the door, threw myself on my bed. Footsteps. The door opened almost instantly. "Stand up!"

"Let me be alone for—"

"Up!" Father's tone brooked no argument. I stumbled to my feet. He stepped back into the hall. "Close your door properly."

I gaped. "You care more about—" His eyes narrowed and I stopped just in time. "Aye, sir." I turned the knob, closed the door quietly. Through the door Father said, "I won't have you slamming doors in my house."

"No, sir. I'm sorry." I crept back to my bed, kicked off my shoes. I buried my head in the pillow, determined to smother my sobs.

He gave me about an hour before he came back into the room. "May I read your letter?"

My voice was muffled. "You know what it says."

"From your reaction, yes." He paused. "They rejected you." His phrasing reduced me to helpless tears. For a moment his hand lay on my shoulder, then it was gone, as if it had fallen by accident. "Nicholas, turn so I can see you."

"I want to be alone."

His tone was sharp. "Yes, to feel sorry for yourself."

"Why shouldn't I?" My voice was muffled.

"So you set yourself against the Lord?"

"I—what?"

Father pulled at my arm until I turned onto my back. Reluctantly, I looked to him, eyes red.

"If Lord God wanted you to attend Naval Academy, do you think they'd not have admitted you?"

I was outraged. "You're saying He didn't want me to go?" Father was silent. "Why should He care one way or the other? It was the stupid Selection Board, not Him."

Father shook his head. "He cares. About you, as about all of us."

My tone risked a strapping, but I didn't care. "Then why did He have me waste my time applying?"

Father's eyes bored into mine. "Perhaps to teach you to accept failure like a man, rather than as a whining child." I closed my burning eyes. Father would never understand. "Nicholas, this is hard for you. But you must accept His will. I'll pray with you later. Perhaps we can find His consolation." It meant I would spend hours on the hard bedroom floor, knees aching, while I sought the relief Father himself could give, but would not.

I looked up at the Commandant. "Give up Final Cull? Is that so awful?"

Kearsey's fingers drummed the conference table. "The Selection Board . . . you know who's on it?"

I said, "Admiralty appoints two members, the Secretary General appoints two, and three come from the Senate."

"Did you know the Navy used to select its own applicants?"

"Of course, all the services did, until the scandals." Seventy-five years later, the Navy hadn't forgotten its humiliation.

The Commandant smiled grimly. "There was a battle royal when the changes were proposed. We lost; the Navy would no longer be allowed to choose its own candidates. Elitism, they called it, though why the Navy officers' corps shouldn't be elite, only Lord God knows. As a sop, they left us Final Cull. The politicians send us their selections, but at least we can weed through them."

I stabbed at my folder. "Is that what we're doing by making sure we have proportionate Russians and Equadorians and Yanks? By making a place for the Boland boy?"

He flushed. "We do the best we can. Next year you'll get to decide alone. But even though it's my responsibility, you're the one who has to take the class through Academy. Do you object to Vasily Karnyenkov? Would you rather have Jacques what's-his-name?"

I'd rather not have to cull at all. "No," I said wearily. "Let it be." Under the table, my nails left marks in my creased trouser leg.

Tolliver and I walked slowly across the immaculate lawn to Officers' Quarters. "Even if you did alienate him, sir, what difference does it make? Another few days and he'll be gone."

"He's been the Commandant for, what, eighteen years? They'll still look to him for advice. I don't need another enemy."

"You didn't make an enemy," Tolliver soothed. "He was only defending Final Cull."

"It's not as if we can predict what kind of middies they'll turn into." I brooded. Test scores and grades couldn't reveal which of our green cadets would mature into outstanding officers after two years or more of our instruction.

I parted with Tolliver at my door. As a full Captain and the Commandant-elect, I rated an apartment that was large and luxurious by Naval standards. I'd be spending much of my time here, as Commandant. I stripped off my jacket, loosened my tie, and sat on the edge of the bed with caller in hand. Two days had passed since I'd last visited the clinic. Perhaps Annie was better.

I waited for the connection to New York. "Dr. O'Neill's office, please." Another wait. I drummed my fingers on the bedside table. The marvels of technology. Finally he came on the line.

"I'm glad you called." He sounded harried.

"How is my wife?"

"She's, ah, progressing as expected."

I waited, but he didn't continue. "You had something to tell me, Doctor?"

"Not particularly. Why?"

"You said you were glad I called."

"We're always glad when relatives take an interest, Captain. In general the patient's progress is more rapid—"

"How is Annie, Dr. O'Neill? Do you know?"

He lapsed into incomprehensible medical jargon, analyzing Annie's blood tests for each of the seventeen hormones known to be responsible for mood and behavior.

I listened, trying to filter truth through his statistics. At length I could stand it no longer. "But how is she?"

"She continues to stabilize. Right now she's responding to changes in her secondary meds. Taking more interest in surroundings, but her mood swings are greater."

I closed my eyes. Annie, I wish I knew how to help you. If only I hadn't let you meet me at that gutted church, in the stricken Hope Nation city of Centraltown. But for my folly, you'd be whole, rather than languishing in a clinic undergoing hormone rebalance, to our mutual humiliation. I wondered if any of the Academy staff knew the nature of her illness. Rebalancing was seen as shameful, and discharged patients were patronized if not ostracized. I myself struggled with those very feelings.

Tired, helpless, I grunted vague responses to Dr. O'Neill's prattle until I could ring off. Though I hated the embattled city of New York, I yearned to chuck everything and jump on the next suborbital. Instead, I had to endure two more days of Final Cull. I supposed I could find some excuse for not attending, or tell Commandant Kearsey I didn't care whom he selected, but such an attitude approached heresy. Better to delay my visit another few days, until after Handover.

Still an hour to dinner, and the silent apartment was oppressive. I thrust on my jacket, left my quarters. The Admin Building's brass door handles were polished and gleaming, the compound's walkway meticulously edged. With a start I realized it was the same path on which I'd labored for hours with hand clippers and spade, while my bunkmates were enjoying their Sunday afternoon freedom. Well, I wasn't the only one, and I hadn't earned punishment detail often.

I wandered past Officers' Quarters to the wide parade ground. I kicked at the gravel track that surrounded the field where even now cadets exercised under the vigilant eye of their drill sergeants.

Avoiding the squads of perspiring cadets I crossed to the classroom complex beyond. It was the first time I'd seen the classrooms since I'd returned. On impulse I entered a building, automatically smoothing my hair and tucking at my jacket. Old habits die hard.

The walls held the same pictures of squads in immaculate uniforms standing at ease with their sergeant, looking directly into the camera. All so young, so innocent. As I'd been, once. All cadets were recruited young as a matter of necessity. The N-waves our Fusion drives produced could trigger melanoma-T, a deadly cancer, but exposure within five years of puberty lessened the risk.

I perused the hopeful faces. Where had I turned wrong, from the eager lad in a picture lining the classroom halls?

Footsteps. Two cadets turned the corner, talking softly. When they saw me their eyes widened and they snapped to rigid attention against the corridor wall. Had I been a sergeant they'd have saluted and gone about their business, though with brisker step. But an officer—not just an officer, but a full Captain—was something else again.

I could have returned their salutes, growled, "As you were," and gone on my way. Instead, embarrassed at having been discovered mooning over old pictures, I made a show of inspecting them. Even as I did so,

I knew it was a mistake. By tradition, a Captain barely noticed a midshipman, to say nothing of a cadet.

Like all our charges, these two were in their middle teens. The boy was taller, with short, curly black hair. The girl's locks were somewhat longer, almost to her collar, as the regs permitted for females. Their gray uniforms were neat and clean, their shoes spit-polished to perfection. Their belt buckles shined, though the boy's tie was slightly off-center. I scowled as I adjusted it. He bit his lip before remembering he was at attention.

"Name and year?"

"Omar Benghadi, sir. I'm second." His voice came too loud; he flushed with embarrassment.

"And you?"

"Alicia Johns, sir. First." Had it been earlier in the term I wouldn't have had to ask; a plebe was easy to spot. But later, one couldn't always tell by appearance or demeanor. Not if the drill sergeants were doing their job.

"Very wel—"

"May I help you, Lieutenant?" The voice was cool; not impolite, but with perhaps a touch of impatience.

I turned.

His eyes flickered to my insignia. "Oh, please excuse me, sir. Staff Sergeant Ramon Ibarez." He came to attention.

"As you were," I said immediately. One didn't harass the Marine staff in front of their Naval charges.

"Sorry, Captain Seafort. I didn't recognize you." He hesitated. "Is there a problem with these two?" His tone implied that if there were he'd eliminate it, perhaps along with the cadets. His manner wasn't lost on the blond boy, who gulped. The girl waited impassively.

"No, Sarge. I was just, ah . . ." I found myself searching for an excuse to explain my presence. I managed to avoid licking my lips in nervous tension. He was only a sergeant, for heaven's sake. I was long since graduated, and far outranked him. "Just an inspection," I said more firmly. "Carry on, you two."

"Aye aye, sir." The cadets scurried off.

The sergeant repeated, "May I help you, sir?" His manner seemed to enquire, what were you doing in my building?

So barracks scuttlebutt had it right: drill sergeants were afraid of nothing, even the prospective Commandant. No wonder we'd feared them. "No thanks, Sarge." It seemed too bald a dismissal, so I added lamely, "Getting them ready for exams?"

"No, sir. Not really. Just makework, mostly, and giving the plebes a head start on next semester's work, though they don't know that." He smiled; the grin went to his eyes and transformed them. "I missed you by a couple of years, sir. I got here in '94."

"I left in '92."

"I know."

I blurted, "You do?"

"Of course. You berthed in Valdez Hall, in bunk three, when you came down from Farside your second year. We give that bed as a reward to joeys who've done well."

"Good Lord!" Was he pulling my leg? Not even a drill sergeant would try that on a full Captain. Would he?

"Everyone who was here claims to remember you. Even if they can't, they say they do."

It was absurd. I cast about to change the subject. "You're a classroom instructor?"

"Yes, sir, but my kids are dispersed to Training Station and the Fusers, so I'm taking a shift at gunnery and physical defense while waiting for my incoming plebes. I was just conferring with Sergeant Vost about one of my kids. We're trying to pull him through Elementary Nav."

Suddenly I liked him. "Join me for a cup of coffee, Sarge?"

"I, uh . . ." His composure was momentarily gone. "If you're sure you don't mind, sir."

"Not at all." I hesitated. When last I'd bustled through these halls, an afternoon cup was the farthest thing from my mind. "Where can we go?"

"Staff lounge is at the end of the corridor, sir."

I took a seat in a comfortable battered leather chair and let him pour me a cup.

"Twelve days to go."

I looked up. "Pardon?"

"To Handover. Then the place is yours." He paused, said cautiously, "Excuse me if I'm out of line."

He was, but we weren't shipboard, and his forthrightness came as a relief. "No, not at all." I gestured at the coffee table. "Will they mind our making ourselves at home?"

"Mind?" He gaped. "Mind that Captain Nicholas Seafort relaxed in their lounge?"

I felt a fool. "I suppose not."

He studied me, started to say something, looked away. The silence stretched. I fidgeted, anxious to finish my coffee and be gone. Sergeant Ibarez blurted, "You're not comfortable with fame."

How dare he? My jaw dropped. "I beg your pardon?"

He flushed. "I suppose I've just thrown away my career. I apologize, sir."

I began indignantly, "Certain matters are—" I ground to a halt. I'd sought companionship with the man and I was about to blast him for offering it. Swallowing my wrath, I stood, walked to the window, watched the perspiring cadets exercising on the parade ground. "No, Sarge, I'm not. In fact I hate it."

This time our silence had a different flavor. At length he said, "Odd, isn't it? Most of us would give anything to be like you."

"You don't want to be like me," I said with finality.

"Everyone thought you'd take another ship. Until the announcement, no one believed the rumor you'd be assigned here." In the corridor, a bell rang. In a few minutes cadet classes would be dismissed. None of the youngsters would close their books or snap off their puters until the instructors gave them leave. Doing so was an invitation to demerits.

"I didn't want a ship." I didn't want to be Commandant either, but I'd finally let them persuade me.

"You're needed, sir."

He sounded like Senator Boland, and my resentment was kindled. "Not really." I braced myself for another lecture about the Navy's need for heroes now that we were at war.

"The place has . . . stagnated."

I turned; his eyes were on the carpet. I asked quietly, "How do you mean?" It was somewhere between an invitation and a command.

"Just . . ." Sergeant Ibarez looked up, paused. "I don't mean to talk out of school, sir." He put down his cup. "I believe in tradition. It's a glue that binds together the elements of the Service." He crossed to the window, looked out at the field and the helipad. "And I also believe the Commandant should be a remote figure of authority. But sometimes tradition can be carried too far. The Commandant can be too remote." He studied the transplex. "Commandant Kearsey believes strongly in tradition, sir."

I knew better than to press. "I'll keep it in mind." I looked at the clock. "Time to get ready for dinner." I offered my hand, and we shook.

Four hundred twenty folders still littered the conference table. Perhaps that was what Sergeant Ibarez meant by tradition. It would be far easier to sort personnel files on puter, but the Navy had always handled admissions with hardcopy files.

"Any other changes?" The Commandant looked around the table.

"We have a pretty fair balance," said Lieutenant Sleak, his tone diffident. "Both ethnic and regional." Beside me, Edgar Tolliver doodled on a pad. "The age mix is about right, though we're leaning a bit heavily toward fourteens this year."

"Mr. Seafort?" The Commandant glanced my way.

I shook my head in frustration. How could I guess which youngsters to admit? Beside me Lieutenant Tolliver played with his pad, refusing to meet my eye. Why hadn't I rid myself of him when I had the chance? Even when we'd been cadets at Academy, I'd abhorred him.

"I don't—" I paused as Tolliver slid his pad to his right. I pushed it away, but not before noticing the sentence underlined twice. "What about Theroux?" I realized I'd spoken it aloud.

Kearsey wrinkled his brow. "Who's that? The Parisian?"

"Yes, sir." Tolliver's voice startled me.

"I suppose we could revise once more," the Commandant said. I looked up; this time Kearsey's eye held the stern disapproval I'd feared as a cadet.

All I wanted was to be gone from here, but Kearsey's annoyance triggered something in me. "I'd like to see Theroux on the list."

Kearsey shrugged. "Very well. I won't deny you your selections. You'll have to live with them. Darwin, put the Theroux boy back, and drop the three hundred eightieth name."

"Aye aye, sir." Sleak made a note.

After the meeting broke up I strode briskly back to my apartment; I'd be leaving within the hour for New York and Annie. Tolliver hurried alongside. He'd see me to my suborbital, and then he'd be on his own for a week. "Why Theroux?" I demanded. Absentmindedly I returned the salutes of passing cadets.

Tolliver panted, "Why not, sir? It makes as much sense as any other name." We turned into the Officers' Quadrangle.

I stopped; he continued a couple of paces before he realized I wasn't following. He turned and waited.

"Tell me the truth."

He shrugged. "I don't know why. Because he was on the list originally, and got bumped for someone else. Because his test scores and grades were fifteenth percentile, and the Russian boy's were lower."

I raised my eyebrow. "You, an idealist?"

Tolliver stood his ground. "Call it what you want, sir. I thought it wasn't fair. If you disagreed, why did you go along?"

I had no response to that. "Mind your manners," I growled.

"Aye aye, sir. As always." Damn it, the man was hopeless.

A few minutes later he watched my heli lift off for London Shuttleport.

2

The clinic had been built atop the abandoned Yankee Stadium parking lot, after New York Military Command had decreed that public team sports were ipso-facto incitements to riot. It stood by itself on a huge lot long gone to weeds, not far from the crumbling stadium walls that were New York's answer to Rome's Coliseum.

Incongruously, the clinic was bordered by a pleasant, manicured lawn. The only concession to its hostile environment was the high barbed-wire fence surrounding the complex. Outside the fence, squatter shacks had sprung up on all sides, but for whatever reason none stood within a stone's throw of the clinic grounds.

The clinic's security arrangements were low-key but omnipresent. Closed gates, cameras, doorways with bomb sniffers concealed behind their painted trim. The usual adjuncts of urban life, not only in New York, but in all sophisticated cities. In London, just a year before, Lord Mayor Rajnee Sivat had barely escaped assassination, thanks to the bomb sniffers.

My appointment with Dr. O'Neill was for two P.M., but he wasn't yet on the hospital grounds. They told me he'd be "indefinitely detained." I conferred instead with Mrs. Talbot, his nurse, who made a show of having all calls held while she escorted me to a private office. I noticed that our indirect route managed to take us past many of her co-workers. For Annie's sake I held my peace.

"Of course you may see her, Captain Seafort. Doctor says visits will do her good as long as you both want them."

"Tell me again about the mood swings."

She waved away my concern. "They're to be expected at this stage. Your wife is undergoing a complicated course of hormone rebalancing." I tried not to flinch at the bald phrase; the fact of Annie's treatment was something we would have to live with. "She's settling into new glandular patterns, and Doctor is constantly fine-tuning, as it were, based on her blood tests."

I twisted my cap in my hands. Oh, Annie.

Mrs. Talbot lowered her voice. "And of course your wife had some terribly traumatic experiences, quite apart from the rebalancing."

I looked up. Was there a hint of reproach? I couldn't be sure. Well, I

12.

had no right to object. Before the rape that had devastated her, Annie had endured the bombing of Centraltown and its accompanying chaos. To say nothing of abandonment and starvation on *Challenger*.

Mrs. Talbot's tone was gentler. "She's among strangers, too. That doesn't help, especially with her background."

I searched her eyes for the slur that must be there, found none.

For many decades Lower New York had been abandoned to bands of ruthless transpops who roamed its broken streets. Savage gangs comprised the city's transient population, many of Asian, Hispanic, or black origins. They preyed ruthlessly on each other and on the homeless. Above, in luxurious aeries, the civilized, cultured denizens of Upper New York shielded themselves from the harsh reality below with well-armed guards and their heavily fortified buildings. The Uppies referred to the transpops below as "trannies," an insult that could cost a life, if overheard.

Annie had come from those brutal streets. So had Seaman Eddie Boss, whom I'd inducted into the Navy. I'd banished him to U.N.S. *Waterloo*, the first ship sailing out-system, after I'd found him lying with Annie one awful Hope Nation afternoon.

"You've been through terrible times, both of you. It must have been ghastly, Captain."

I stiffened, brought myself under control only with effort. "It's past."

"You look ever so much better without—now that you've recovered."

Without my scar, she'd meant. Unnoticed, my hand crept to my cheek, where the plastic surgeons had done their work. I shifted uncomfortably. "I'd like to see my wife, if I may."

"Of course." She stood, and we went out to the corridor. "Doctor says Mrs. Seafort may go anywhere on the grounds. Shall I take you to her room?"

"I know the way," I said hastily. Mrs. Talbot's disappointment was obvious. "Thank you. Oh, and, uh . . ." I forced down my revulsion, groped for a way. "Do you perchance have any children?"

"Yes, two. Kathy and Jon."

"You have their pictures?"

"On my desk. Would you like to see?"

"Very much." I followed her back to her tiny office outside Dr. O'Neill's larger one. They were antique-style photos, not ordinary holos. I took out a pen. "May I?"

Her eyes widened in pleasure. "Oh, yes. Of course."

I wrote, "To Kathy and Jon, with gratitude for all the help their mother has provided. Nicholas E. Seafort, Captain, U.N.N.S."

Mrs. Talbot was breathless. She clutched the photo to her bosom. "Thank you, Captain. Thanks ever so much."

I took my leave, trying to force a calm while my stomach churned with disgust. People like Mrs. Talbot would bend backward for someone whose face was blazoned across the holos. But any humiliation was to be borne, if Annie received better care.

I sat with her in a sunny lounge, one hand thrown casually across the back of the sofa, the other in my jacket pocket, knuckles white, fist bunched. Annie stared sullenly at the wall. "I wonder why you bother coming, Nick."

"I want to see you. I'd be here every day if I could." I debated moving closer, decided not to risk it. "I'm sorry you're angry."

"I ain't angry!" She crossed her arms, turned away.

I said gently, "Annie, I love you." I held my breath.

When she turned, her eyes were scornful. "That ain't enough, Nicky."

My hand ached. I forced my fist to relax. "What would be enough?"

"Nothin'. You put me in dis—this place."

"Do you want to leave?"

"Yes! No! Damnit, I don't know what I want no more. You and your medicines done this to me!" I reached to her but she spun out of her seat and retreated. I watched, helpless. After a time she said quietly, "Come on, let's walk."

We strolled along the footpath. Eventually she took my arm. "Nicky, I'm all mixed up. I din' mean shout at you."

"I know, hon."

She kicked at a small stone. "Dr. O'Neill says I be gettin' better. He's prolly right. C'n you wait it out with me?"

My throat ached. "Of course. As long as it takes."

"Good. 'Cause dere's somethin' I wan'."

I tensed. Only at moments of stress did Annie revert to her transpop dialect.

"Nicky, I be gettin' mad every time I see you. Dr. O'Neill, he say it don' have nothin' to do with you, that I'm angry at Hope Nation and the fish and all. He keeps sayin' talk about it, and I keep tellin' him dat jus' make me madder, I should shut up 'til it go away."

"He's right, hon." Though the Freudian cult had long been discredited and repressed, even the Reunification Church approved of confessing sin and facing one's fear.

"It don' matter if he be right or wrong, the thing is, every time I be seein' you I get all mad again. What I wan' . . ." She faltered.

I steeled myself against a growing unease. "Yes?"

Her tone was determined. "I wan' you not to come see me fo' a while, 'til I be feelin' okay. It just get me all confused." Despite her words she clutched my arm tighter.

"Oh, Annie."

She turned toward me. "I mean it, Nicky. It ain't just what I'm feelin' dis moment."

"I know."

"I wanna keep lovin' you. Jus' lemme be, fo' now."

"All right."

Softly she wiped my cheek, and her hand came away wet. "Bes' you go now, 'fore I change my mind again."

"Yes." My tone was dull. I enfolded her in my arms, kissed the top of her head. "I love you. Remember that." I hurried off.

An armored cab took me to the nearest heliport. I'd planned to spend several days with my wife, but found myself cast adrift. I could go downtown to the towers of Upper New York, and look down from my hotel room to the ugly streets. That held no appeal; I'd toured New York twice and hated it. I had five days leave, and nothing to do. If I returned to Academy at Devon I'd just seem to be interfering with Captain Kearsey's final days as Commandant. Better to stay out of the way, in London. I booked myself onto a suborbital. When we landed, I arranged a room in the old and decaying West End, where were located many of the hotels that had survived the Fire of 2070.

By mid-evening I'd settled into my room. Almost at once the hotel made me uneasy; wherever I went the eyes of the staff followed. Chambermaids and bellmen who never spoke to guests found occasion to talk with to me. Even the chef had come to my table, ostensibly to inquire if I liked the food.

I tried going out for a walk, but was soon recognized, and had no peace thereafter. People stared. Some even pointed. Perhaps I might have avoided the worst of it by donning civilian garb, but I'd be damned if I'd skulk about as if ashamed of the Navy. I frowned at the unfortunate phrase. I *was* damned; Lord God would have no forgiveness for what I'd done.

I paced my room, restless. I could run up to Farside, but I'd already scheduled a trip aloft a few days after Handover. No point in visiting Lunapolis, either. I'd just seen my old friend Alexi Tamarov settled in to his new post there, as assistant to the Chief of Naval Operations; after that hitch he'd surely be rotated back onto a ship. Good officers were scarcer than ever these days.

Nowhere held any appeal. For years I'd lived aboard ship, occasionally taking brief jaunts ashore. It was what I knew.

A vacation, then? There was nothing I wanted to see. I couldn't abide an hotel. I wanted to go . . .

Home.

I jumped off the bed. A heli, or a plane, first thing in the morning; nothing would be leaving at this hour. Or I could drive, though even today the roads through the hills to Cardiff were difficult. The only other way was . . . I snatched the caller. Moments later I thrust gear into my duffel. The desk would have a rooftop helicab waiting; if I raced, I could just make it. I signed for the unused room, let the bellhop carry my bag up to the cab. "Paddington Station, and hurry!"

The driver smiled sourly. "Sure, and I'll hurry. One of these days some bloke will get in and say, 'Take your time, lad. I checked out early.' " He turned the ignition and the blades whirred. We lifted off.

Half an hour later I settled into my railway compartment. I hauled down the bed while we rumbled through the endless suburbs of Extended London. We would pull into Cardiff in time for breakfast. I took off my shirt and pants, stretched out on the tiny bunk, relaxed at last.

Father. Home.

I slept.

I took breakfast in the ancient railway station before ringing for a cab. I didn't bother bargaining the fare though I knew Father wouldn't approve of extravagance. I could afford it, and the cabby deserved a living.

I stared out the window at the remains of the ancient foundries. Jason and I had played in these eerie vacant buildings, a lifetime ago. The cab climbed deeper into the hills, on the twisting Bridgend road.

The cabby was content to follow my directions. When finally he pulled to a stop I got out, thrust bills at him, and waited until he'd disappeared before I faced the familiar cottage down the hill from the road. I hadn't called ahead, knowing with absolute certainty that there was no need. If Father had gone to market, his door would be open, and if he were at home I was welcome. Except on Sunday, he would be nowhere else. It was as it would always be.

Still, I knocked, rather than entering. I was thirteen when I'd left this place, and as many years had passed.

The door swung open. Father seemed older, worn. He'd been washing breakfast dishes, and still wore his apron. His eyes flickered to my uniform, to my duffel. "You'll be staying, then?"

"Aye, for a while."

He turned away and I followed him into the kitchen. "The tea is hot."

"Thank you." I took a cup, poured the boiling water, set the ball of tea leaves in it. I held the chain and swished it in the darkening water.

"I'd heard you were back. The grocer told me it was in the holozines. He wanted to give me one."

I sipped at the tea. "Father, do you mind if I stay the week?"

"You are home, Nicholas."

"Thank you."

"You can help with the fence. Garth's cows want my grass and my garden, as always."

"All right."

He gestured to my jacket, my crisp blue slacks. "Work will ruin them."

"I have old pants. The shirt won't matter."

"You'll do your old chores."

I nodded. Nothing had changed, or could. I'd once pleaded: Do you love me? He hadn't answered, of course. Perhaps he didn't know himself.

I took my duffel into my old room, almost unchanged after a decade of absence. I sat down on the bed. The springs still creaked. They had caused me difficulty, trying to conceal my youthful passion from Father's notice.

My clothes changed, I worked at repairing the fence until Father set out a simple lunch of soup and vegetables. After, I returned to work; he rinsed the dishes before rejoining me. Later, when the gloomy sky darkened to dusk he surveyed the stretch of ragged fence we'd restored. "It's a beginning, anyway. We could have done more."

"I'm sorry, Father."

"Sorry builds no fences." Still, his hand brushed my side as we walked to the house. "I'll be making dinner."

"I could help."

"You'll have to wash first."

"Aye, sir." A smile twitched the corners of my mouth. He saw it, and frowned.

After grace, we ate our cold chicken, with cucumber salad. I helped Father with the washing up, and in the quiet of the evening I sat in the kitchen to read books I'd brought, in my hand-held holovid.

Father appeared in the doorway. "Will you join me for prayers?"

"I'd like that." I snapped off the holo, followed him into his bedroom.

We knelt, and I closed my eyes. He spoke the Bible, rather than reading it. He had no doubt of the words.

Somehow, the ritual brought me a modicum of comfort, though my knees ached abominably by the time we finished. Afterward, when we'd gotten to our feet, I gave him an awkward hug before going to my room. Surprised, he neither thrust me away nor responded.

I undressed slowly, opened the window to the cool night air, and crept into bed. I lay on my back, arms behind my head, examining by moonlight the once-familiar icons of my childhood that Father had left in their place. A model of U.N.S. *Repulse* I'd built from balsa. My abandoned clothes, still hanging on the closet door. A souvenir banner for the Welsh national football team. I stared at the faded felt emblem. So long ago, and just yesterday.

The game was always on Saturday.

"Is he always like that?" I pedaled hard to keep up. "It's Father's way."

"How can you stand it? 'Are your chores finished? Have you read your verses?' Jeez."

I changed gears, came abreast of him, wind whistling in my hair. "I'm used to it."

He grimaced. Jason didn't understand that none of it mattered. Whatever work I was given—studies, memorizing verses, chores, weeding—I could still sometimes ride with Jason. Father always acknowledged that I was free to choose my friends.

I suspected Father disapproved of Jason not because he was a freethinker, though that was bad enough, but because we chattered like magpies and giggled over whispered secrets. Father's house was normally silent.

Jason and I locked our bikes to a rack in the parking lot and joined the crowd moving to the stadium entrance.

He ventured, "We could try for beer."

"No," I snapped. Some of Jason's notions were outlandish. "You know what happened to Andrew and Llewelyn."

"It was their second offense."

"I'm not going to prison for a tube of beer." Didn't he know the Rebellious Ages were long since past? Society didn't approve of wild children, and to tell the truth, neither did I. Sneaking out at night to meet Jason was one thing; at worst that meant chastisement from Father. Breaking public decency laws was quite another.

We sat on the hard benches waiting for the game to begin. "Nicky, you gonna reapply next year?"

"I don't know." I stared down at the chalk lines on the field.

"You should."

I couldn't keep the bitterness from my tone. "So they can turn me down again?"

"You almost made it. So much work; all the forms we filled out, and then the interviews, the recommendations we got from everyone. Don't throw it away."

I kicked the bench below me. "I'd have to start all over. Who cares about being a frazzin' cadet?"

He studied me. By swearing I'd revealed more than I intended. "You care. And so do I."

"Sure, it means a lot to you," I jeered. "You're the one who'd go to Devon, not me."

"Nicky, sometimes you're an arse." He took a stereoplug from his shirt pocket, set it in his ear.

I turned away, furious. The teams went to their benches. A moment later a hand came around my waist and squeezed my side. "Sorry."

I said nothing.

"I'm sorry, Nicky."

I pried his fingers loose. "You know I don't like that."

"Don't be pissed at me, Nicky. Please?"

I glared at him, but my frown quickly faded; I couldn't stay mad at Jason for long. "Okay."

Jason giggled. "Maybe your father will let you go to Third with me, and we end up in Engineering together."

"I doubt he will." School was voluntary. It had been so for nearly a century. Unfortunately the choice was Father's, not mine. If I had my way, I'd have gone. I knew that by studying at home over the rickety kitchen table I learned more than other joeys, but it was lonely, sometimes, with no one but Father. And after satisfying him, a public school would be a breeze.

After a time I said, "Farside would have been nice."

"I know." Jason had helped me prep for the exams, and had shared my fantasies of leaving Cardiff as a local hero. He didn't know how I'd cried myself to sleep when the letter came, and again during the week that followed. I'd been so sure, after getting to Second Interview.

The crowd came to its feet with a roar when Archie Connelly

took the field against the Dubliners. I cheered as hard as any. Maybe this time, with luck, I could get an autograph. Once I'd been the next joey in line when Archie had turned away for the bus.

By now the first group of cadets would be reporting to Devon. Rather than cope with hordes of confused plebes, the authorities had recruits show up on staggered dates. Or, as scornful middies were said to remark, the plebes came staggering in. Like most Navy-struck boys I pored over the frequent articles in the holozines.

We lost, five goals to two. Archie had been shaken up in a collision that earned Riltz a yellow card, and gave no autographs after the game. Disconsolate, we trudged back to our bikes. Jason already had our tickets for next week's big game, against the Italians. The one we'd been waiting for.

We stopped at McCardle's for shakes and synthos. In a glum mood, I swirled the glass back and forth, while the holovid blared overhead and Jason chattered about our side's missed goals. If only Reggie hadn't missed the easy block, if the Micks had just—

Jason's fingers tightened on my arm. Annoyed, I twisted loose. We had an understanding about his affections, yet twice today he'd—

"Listen!"

I gaped at the holovid. ". . . when the suborbital went down. Airport officials say the craft had lost an engine but the pilot was expected to land safely with the remaining two. Debris is scattered across several runways, and Heathrow traffic has been diverted. Among the passengers was Dr. Raphael Tendez, inventer of the Hodgkins vaccine. Also aboard were twenty-eight cadets reporting for admission to the U.N.N.S. Naval Academy at Devon—"

"Lord God!" I was on my feet.

Jason stared at me white-faced. "It would have been you, Nicky." His eyes glistened.

"Come on!" I grabbed my jacket.

"What's the—"

"I want to go home!"

"But—"

"Now!" I ran outside, unchained my bike. Jason fumbled for a coin, inserted it in the holovid, waited impatiently for the chip to pop out below.

I was already pumping up the hill, all my effort in the strain of the pedals, grateful for the opportunity not to think.

It was several minutes until Jason, panting, began to catch up. "Wait!"

Head down, I pumped madly, eyes fixed on the mottled pavement streaking below.

"Nicky, slow a bit!"

Reluctantly I coasted until he pulled alongside. He gasped, "What in hell is the matter with you?"

"Shut up."

"Nicky? Are you crying?"

Deliberately, I swerved, knocking Jason onto the grassy shoulder. As he tried to right himself I smashed into him again, throwing both of us onto the soft grass. I untangled myself from the bicycle and swarmed over him, pummeling him with blows to the shoulders and sides.

He threw me aside, his temper well and truly ignited. "Get off me, you frazzing arsehole!" I wrestled him down again, climbed onto his chest. He bucked and kicked. Finally he yanked free an arm and caught me a staggering blow on the side of the head. "Ow! Jesus!" He nursed his hand. "Christ, you've broken it!"

"Good!"

"I mean it, you stupid grode!"

I loosened my grip. "Let me see."

"Get off first!"

I rolled aside. He kicked me in the stomach, for evenses, as he called it. I doubled over, but he made no attempt to follow up his advantage. He buried his knuckles under his arm. "Damn!"

When I could breathe properly I said, "Let me look." Reluctantly he extended his wrist. "Can you move it?"

He wiggled his fingers gingerly. "I think so."

"Then it's probably not broken. Can you ride?"

"If my bike's okay." He wiped his face. "Jesus, why'd you do that?"

"I don't know."

"You don't—Nicky!"

Ashamed, I looked down. "I'm sorry, Jase."

"Sorry? You drive me into the ditch, beat me up, break my arm, and all you can say is you're sorry?"

"I'm sor—" What was wrong with me? How could I have done such a thing, and to my best friend? My only friend. "I mean it, Jason." I looked up, but already he was laughing, in that way he had of changing like a summer storm.

"Give me a hug, then."

"I'm not a gay, Jase. You know that."

"But you owe me." He held up his swelling hand.

"Arghhhh!" I pulled him to his feet. Shyly, making sure no one was driving by, I embraced him. He let his head rest against my shoulder. "There, you satisfied?" I drew back.

"It'll do, 'til another time."

I righted his bicycle. It seemed undamaged. "Let's go home and soak it in ice."

"Soak my bike?" His tone was incredulous.

"Your hand, you twit." Then I saw his face. "I could kill you, sometimes."

"Yeah. You try, sometimes." He walked his bike to the road and hopped on.

Father read the newschip gravely while Jason sat at the table, his hand in a bucket of icy water. Father raised his head and his eyes found mine. "So, Nicholas." I studied the table.

"Is that why you fought?"

"Yes. No. I don't know."

"I would be disturbed too, at such proof of my folly."

"Folly? What did I do?"

"You questioned your Lord's will. Didn't I tell you, if He'd wanted you summoned to Academy you'd have been admitted? He spared you the horror of that inferno."

My voice dripped scorn. "He killed those cadets just to teach me humility?"

Father slapped me, hard. "Alone with your friends you may mock Him. Not in my house."

Jason drew in a sharp breath, but was silent. My hand crept to my reddened cheek. I muttered, "Aye, sir."

"If it's His purpose to teach you humility, He still has work to do."

I nodded. It wasn't safe to say anything else.

"We'll pray for them tonight."

My voice was barely audible. "I'd like that."

Much later, after dinner, after chores, after my evening verses, in the solitude of my darkened room, I knelt at my bed and closed my eyes in the customary manner. I'm sorry, Lord, for having doubted You. I didn't understand. I still don't know why they had to die, but thank You for sparing me. Yet, I wanted so much to go to Academy.

Do You understand that? Can You find me something else to want as
much? Could I ask that of You?
    Please?

    My eyes roved the room, to the Captain's insignia on my jacket that
hung on the chair, to the scarred desk, to the window out of which a boy
had occasionally climbed, his heart pounding, knowing disobedience was
sin but anticipating the glory of a night ride in the moonlight through
caressing wind, tires whispering on the dark asphalt.
    I left my creaking bed, walked to the window. Lord God knew where
my old bike might be now. And if I wanted to ride, I had but to walk out
the door; I was too old to be climbing through windows. I wandered the
room. My fingers stroked the desktop. No dust; Father had kept my room
clean. I sat at the chair. Had everything shrunk? I felt almost a Gulliver.
    I opened the drawer. Pencils, lined neatly in a row. Old scraps of
paper, a teen's doodles. A folder, neatly labeled by hand in block letters.
"ACADEMY APPLICATION." The letters "U.N.N.S." had been carefully
added before "ACADEMY," as if in clarification. I opened the aging file.
    The letter had come four days after.

September 1, 2190.

Circumstances have required the Selection Board to reopen admissions for the U.N.N.S. Naval Academy's entering class. This
is to inform you that your application has been reviewed and
that you are accepted for admission as a cadet in the United
Nations Naval Service. You are to acknowledge by return mail,
and to report on September 10, 2190, to Academy in Devon.
Lauron E. Kearsey, Commandant.

    I closed the file, turned from the desk. I knelt at the bed.
    Lord, help me find that boy, the one who'd reread that letter until
each word was burned into his memory. The innocent lad who'd vowed to
do his best, to struggle through cadethood to the exalted rank of midshipman. You see, he's been extinguished, somehow. He left behind a vindic-
tive, deceitful man who's broken every rule he cherishes, who disobeys
orders, lies to his superiors.
    May I pray to You? Will You be offended, even if You don't listen? I
know I've forfeited Your grace, and that You will punish me. What I don't
know, Lord, is why. Why did I do those awful things?
    Is that what You had in mind for me when You sent me to Academy?

3

The cab waited in the lane. In the doorway Father stood gray and worn. I paused, laid my duffel at my feet. "It's been good to see you."

"Aye." His blue eyes met mine. "And the fence is fixed."

"That too." I shifted uncomfortably. "I'll be closer to home now, when I'm not at Farside. I could help keep it mended."

"There's always work to be done." It could have been a reproof.

"I could come at Easter, if you like."

"If it be His will." I knew that passed for assent. I made no effort to hug him; it wasn't his way and he'd be as embarrassed as I. I turned to go.

He spoke suddenly. "Pray to Him." He raised a hand, as if to forestall my objection. "He may turn His head, but pray nonetheless. It is right, and it does you good."

"Aye, sir." How could he know? I hadn't spoken the words aloud. "Good-bye, then." He nodded, and I hurried to the waiting cab.

Struggling for an expression of polite interest, I looked down on rows of shining young faces, gleaming buckles, immaculate gray uniforms, while Commandant Kearsey continued his interminable address. Every cadet in Academy had been brought groundside for Handover. A waste of resources in wartime, but it was an odd war. Only one fish had ever been seen in home system, and we had no idea where the aliens bred, or where they might next appear.

A few seats from me, Lieutenant Tolliver's eyes glinted with amusement; he knew how I hated the necessary ritual.

Kearsey said, "Just twelve years ago Mr. Seafort was a cadet like you. Who'd have thought that quiet youngster of thirteen would soon astound the world?"

Not I, certainly. More to the point, who'd have thought that eager youngster would commit treason and damn himself?

"As a midshipman, Mr. Seafort was posted to U.N.S. *Helsinki*." A green young middy, reporting to the bridge of a U.N. warship, trying to control the trembling of his limbs.

"Mr. Seafort's next posting was to *Hibernia*." A starship on the Hope

Nation run, sixty-nine light-years from home. We'd Fused for seventeen months, Defusing only for nav checks.

"Most of *Hibernia*'s officers were killed in an explosion of the ship's launch." It had left my friend Lieutenant Malstrom the sole commissioned line officer, until his death soon after from cancer.

Kearsey said heavily, "Now Captain, Mr. Seafort brought *Hibernia* to Hope Nation, but was unable to find new officers."

Lord God, would he never end?

"He sailed on, but on his return from Detour he encountered the wreck of *Telstar* and, in it, the first alien creatures ever seen by a human being."

I recalled the alien form that had quivered inches from my face. Moments later there had emerged from behind *Telstar* the bizarre fish that was home to the outrider I'd found.

"Captain Seafort sailed home with his momentous discovery. Admiralty confirmed him as Commander and gave him U.N.S. *Portia*, part of Admiral Tremaine's relief squadron to Hope Nation. En route, Mr. Seafort's son was killed by fish and his wife died soon after. Then the Admiral's flagship *Challenger* was disabled."

How would Kearsey phrase the events that followed?

The Commandant said firmly, "The Admiral transferred his flag to *Portia*, and decided unwisely to off-load those he disapproved of to the disabled *Challenger*. Mr. Seafort agreed to stay with *Challenger*." Mr. Seafort chose to die with *Challenger*, but Lord God did not allow him his wish.

"Despite starvation and rebellion, Mr. Seafort impressed a new crew, trained them, and fought off the aliens. In his final battle he rammed a fish just as it Fused, and by the grace of Lord God the fish Defused in our home system."

I'd brought *Challenger* home, but at the cost of my soul. I'd sworn not to harm a rebellious sailor, then I'd killed her at the first opportunity. For that, I am damned.

The Commandant paused, examining the young faces of his audience. "Even you plebes know that Captain Seafort sailed yet again to Hope Nation, and was groundside when the fish devastated Centraltown. Mr. Seafort was left in charge of the few shoreside Naval officers.

"Hope Nation was again attacked, and the fleet sailed for home. Ailing and alone, Mr. Seafort managed to lure the aliens into attacking Orbit Station, where he destroyed them by detonating the Station's atomic self-destruct device."

Until a few weeks before I'd planned my sabotage, even a proposal to use atomic weapons had carried a mandatory death penalty. When I'd nuked the Station, I'd thought it treason.

"Captain Seafort's courage and resourcefulness need no further detail. On my retirement, I can leave the training of our cadets in no better hands. Ladies and gentlemen, I present your new Commandant, Captain Nicholas Ewing Seafort."

I stood, to the sustained roar of applause. Commandant Kearsey, smiling, joined the acclamation.

"Thank you." I waited for the din to cease. It did not. I raised my hand for silence, but they applauded with undiminished enthusiasm. The young fools. "Thank you. Enough."

They began to rise, in a standing ovation. I couldn't allow it. If only they knew the truth . . .

"Be silent!" I bellowed into the mike, fists knotted at my side.

The applause stopped as if turned off by a switch. I paced the stage, my crafted address scattered to the winds of rage. "When I was last here," I grated, "cadets obeyed their officers." No one moved. "As you will again, I promise you!"

What was I doing? I lurched back toward my planned speech. "Commandant Kearsey, I thank you for your most generous remarks. Your tenure here has been unblemished." Unblemished mediocrity, I thought bitterly. Test scores falling, morale low . . . I'd been shocked at the reports they'd given me. But the man meant well. "I hope I may accomplish as much."

I nodded briefly to the outgoing Commandant, took a deep breath, turned back to the stunned cadets. "By order of the Board of Admiralty of the Government of the United Nations, I assume command of Terrestrial and Farside Academies. Dismissed."

I slouched behind the desk in the luxurious office Commandant Kearsey had vacated only that morning. "I made a mess of it."

Tolliver shrugged. "If you say so."

I wished he'd show the respect due my rank, if not my person. But I'd done him too much harm, and he knew me too well to retain any respect for me. He was a penance I bore with as good grace as I could manage.

"I made a fool of myself," I muttered.

"Oh, you weren't that bad. They might as well find out you have a temper."

I growled, "Don't go too far, Tolliver."

He showed surprise. "No sarcasm intended, if you can believe it.

You're not one to be crossed, and the cadets are better off knowing it from the start."

From the start. I grunted. As of this day, Terrestrial Academy, Farside Base, and the Naval Training Station high in Lunar orbit were all under my jurisdiction.

Not for the first time, I wondered how I'd let myself be talked into my new post. After I brought *Victoria* home from Hope Nation I'd asked to resign my commission, but Admiral Duhaney and his colleague Senator Boland prevailed on me to stay. I should have declined, but at least I'd had the sense to refuse a ship. I'd already killed innocents enough.

"He should be gone by now."

Tolliver checked his watch. "Anytime now, sir. His aide told me they'd be out of the apartment by three."

"Edgar, I hope I've made it clear . . ." I fumbled for words. "Your, uh, special dispensation. I won't have an outsider overhearing you. Be warned."

He smiled grimly. "I'll take great care, sir."

"Good." Uncomfortable, I stood to pace, changing the subject. "Two days, then up to Farside."

"Yes, sir. Farside's personnel files are in the puter, if you want a look. Are you aware there's no console in your apartment?"

"You're joking. Have one installed."

"Already ordered, sir. I assumed you'd want access."

"Don't assume," I said, petulant.

"I can cancel it if—"

"I want the console. Just don't assume you know what I want." As always, Tolliver brought out the worst in me.

He raised an eyebrow. "Aye aye, sir. Shall I cancel the order, and reinstate it now that you've told me you want it?"

Damn the man. I leaned back, recalled the conversation we'd had in my Lunapolis quarters, after I'd agreed to take him as my aide.

"Do I have a choice?" His tone was bleak.

I gaped. "It was as a favor to you."

"Of course, sir. Serving with you is a great privilege."

"How dare you!" His insolence was astounding.

He shrugged. "I wonder that myself, at times. I guess I've learned from you."

"What do you mean?"

"I just don't care anymore." He thrust his hands in his pockets. "Captain Higbee at BuPers mentioned that I was lucky to get a posting at all, after my misdeeds."

I closed my eyes. I'd done that by demoting him, after he'd seized control of my heli in an effort to save our lives. "He was right. If I hadn't taken you . . ."

"Should I resign, then?" His tone was bitter.

"That's your decision." I hesitated. "Mr. Tolliver, it's hard for me to be fair to you; my memories of Academy are too strong. I put you back to Lieutenant. What more do you want?"

"Nothing in your power to give." He turned away. Then, "I'm sorry. I mean that. What I want is to go back and undo the past."

"The heli?"

"Among other things." He turned back with a wry smile. "We're stuck with each other. Your conscience won't let you abandon me, and if I want a career it must be with you."

"I allow you to goad me, but nonetheless, I'm your superior officer and you owe me courtesy. You seem to forget."

"Not for a minute!" His eyes burned into mine. "If I'm, um, difficult with you, it's my resentment. Never negligence."

"Do you imagine I find that reassuring?"

He smiled, but his eyes were pained. "When you can't endure it, cashier me. I may hate you, but I'll understand."

Why did his hurt matter to me, after all we'd been through? My voice was gruff. "No, I'll tolerate you. You can't help being who you are, and you remind me of what I've done."

"If that's pity, I don't want it!"

"Not pity, Edgar. Perhaps . . . understanding."

He'd let it pass.

Now, in my new Academy office, I was restless. "I'm going to my apartment."

He checked his watch. "Kearsey may still be there."

"I don't care." But I fell back in the chair. "Tell me the schedule again."

Tolliver's look was of resignation. "We start shipping most of our joeys back to Farside, some today. Those we graduated will stay ground-side until their postings come through. We'll keep a few midshipmen, of course, for the scutwork."

I gestured impatiently. "Get on with it."

"The new class staggers in. They all begin training down here at Devon."

I growled. "I *was* a cadet, Tolliver."

"Right. I must remember that. The first batch of sixty will be here in a week, and about sixty more every five days until they're all aboard."

"What am I supposed to do before they get here?"

"What will you do *after* they get here, sir?" He shrugged. "Answer questions, I suppose. If it's anything like shipboard, they always have questions."

I smiled at that. Most inquiries were trivial, and could be answered at random. "How many cadets on base this week?"

"I don't know, sir; some of the upperclassmen had leave. Just a minute." He went to the caller, spoke into it, waited. "We have thirty-two graduates without families to visit, and about sixty of our plebes slated for Farside. Then there's about four hundred they brought down from Farside for the ceremony, who'll be going back."

I swore under my breath. Our cadets were being moved like chess pieces, and to no real purpose. I got up, restless again. "I'm going for a walk. See you at three."

"Yes, sir."

"And set up a meeting after dinner with the middies who'll be staying."

"Aye aye, sir."

I nodded to Sergeant Kinders in the outer office, left the Admin Building, picked a direction and set off briskly. In a few minutes I found myself at the main gate. Many of the upperclassmen had been selected for graduation this day, and it was odd to see visitors strolling inside the gate, each with a cadet in crisp gray. Other than on ceremonial occasions, no civilian visitors were permitted on the grounds. Shortly, our graduates would change to their midshipman's blues, which they would wear with inordinate pride until they learned that even middies were insignificant creatures in the eyes of working Naval officers.

I thrust my hands in my pockets, walked with head down. Our real task would start when our new class arrived.

Shipboard, most Naval personnel served belowdecks. They were recruited in their thousands by any means available, including the enlistment bonuses that attracted so many undesirables. But officers were another matter. The Navy selected only the best, carefully evaluating test scores, school grades, interviews and recommendations. Only a fortunate few were allowed to take the oath as cadets.

I reached the heavy iron gate, absently returned the salutes of the guards, and turned onto the perimeter path. Here I was virtually alone.

Unlike midshipmen, deemed by act of the General Assembly to have reached majority, our cadets were minors, by law and regulation the wards of their commanding officer. As Commandant I was their legal guardian, with all the prerogatives their parents had hitherto possessed. I could punish them in any fashion I saw fit; they had virtually no rights. They were the lowest of the low, until they were appointed midshipmen. Then, as Naval officers, they'd begin the slow climb to the exalted rank of Lieutenant, and perhaps thereafter to Captain.

While in an emergency it was possible to enlist a cadet aboard ship— I had done so myself—ordinarily cadets were sent to Academy for their training. As plebes, they were taught the basics of navigation, physics, radionics, electronics, gunnery, and the like.

As soon as cadets could be trusted not to wander in front of the firing grid of a laser cannon or unscrew their suit helmets Outside, they were sent for a long term to Farside, the "real" Academy. There, freed from distractions and distanced from visiting busybodies, their advanced training commenced: simulated docking maneuvers, airlock security, Orbiting Station procedures, and the other skills they'd need to be set loose in the corridors of a U.N.N.S. starship. Often, they were then returned to Devon for further training.

The term of enlistment was five years, and theoretically a youngster could serve the entire term as a cadet and never make middy. In practice, most were graduated after two years or so, some after only one year. Graduation was at the discretion of the Commandant.

This practice was a radical departure from the military institutions of previous generations, and I was somewhat apprehensive of the responsibility it thrust upon me, but overall, the idea made sense. Though a cadet might not be ready to serve as a midshipman, that didn't necessarily mean he was failing his coursework. Further, under the Naval system, holding back a cadet for a few extra months bore little of the stigma that would attach if he failed to graduate with a scheduled class.

In any event, a cadet might be pulled from classes in the middle of a term and sent to the fleet as a middy, or might be held on all or part of another year for further training.

One never knew, and the eagerness to prove themselves ready for graduation spurred cadets to greater efforts.

I struck across the large expanse of front lawn, toward the barracks and classrooms on the far side of the parade ground. Here, tall oaks gave welcome shade from the heat of the spacious front grounds.

I followed a path worn in the grass. A pair of gray-clad legs protruded from beyond a tree trunk. As I passed, the youth jumped to his feet, stiffened to attention. I saluted, moved on, stopped.

"Jerence?"

"Yes, sir." His belly was sucked in tight, spine stiff.

Aboard *Victoria* on my flight home, I'd enlisted Jerence Branstead, of

the Hope Nation Bransteads, as a cadet. Once home, he'd been transferred to Academy for proper training.

I strolled back, pursed my lips, examined him. Though the seat of his
pants was dusty from where he'd been sitting, his shoes were polished, his
uniform crisp, his hair combed neatly. A far cry from the miserable boy
locked in a sweaty cabin, desperate for the vial of goofjuice that lay unopened on his bed.

I smiled but immediately converted it to a frown. After all, he was but
a cadet, and I shouldn't deign even to speak to him. "Stand easy."

"Aye aye, sir!" His shoulders relaxed; he spread his feet, clasped his
hands behind him in the at-ease position.

"Hasn't your leave begun?"

"Yes, sir. I—" He gulped, stopped. Quite right. A cadet answered
questions, but otherwise spoke only when spoken to.

"Well?"

"I'm being sent to Farside, but I have no place to go for leave, sir. I'm
staying on grounds." He swallowed, essayed a small tremulous smile.

I reddened. "Of course." Harmon and Sarah Branstead were on
Hope Nation, lacking even the knowledge that their son had survived.
"No Terran relatives?"

"No, sir. I'm fourth generation."

"Very well. Carry on." I resumed my stroll. He'd made his bed; now
he could lie in it. It was he who'd begged for the opportunity to enlist, and
loneliness was part of the cost. Giving him special treatment would do
neither of us any good; I had to treat him like any other cadet.

I crossed the parade ground, wandered toward the barracks. Yeltsin
Hall was silent and empty. Beyond it was Valdez Hall. No reason to go
farther. But still, Valdez . . . I sauntered closer. No harm in going inside,
just to look around. It had been so long.

I took the steps two at a time. The door was ajar; the sergeant
wouldn't have liked that. Inside, I heard voices, a gleeful shout. I swung
the door wide and strode in.

A pillow hurtled past my head. The girl prancing on the bunk
ducked, snatched it out of the air. "You missed! Can't you even—oh,
God!" She leaped off the bed, stiffened to attention, as did five other
youths. A young voice shouted, "Attention!"

I stared unbelieving at the disorder. Valdez, like all the barracks, held
two rows of single bunks in meticulous order, one on each side of the
narrow corridor, some thirty beds in all. Now, mattresses were overturned, pillows scattered everywhere. Dust motes danced in the sunshine

streaming through the windows. The contents of two duffels had been
dumped unceremoniously on the beds.

"What is this?" No one answered. I wheeled to the closest boy. "You!
Report!"

He was in trousers and shirtsleeves. Perhaps it was his jacket that lay
crumpled in the corridor. "Cadet Rafe Slater reporting, sir! We were, ah
. . . uh—"

I snorted. "You sure were. Who's in charge here?"

A small voice answered, "I guess I am, sir."

I wheeled. "You guess?"

"Cadet—oh, I—Midshipman Anton Thayer, sir." A slim youngster,
red curly hair.

I looked at his cadet grays and raised an eyebrow.

"I was just promoted, sir. Today."

"Ah." The place was a shambles. How many demerits to give? Two
each? Four? A middy was an officer, not a child. How could he allow—

Just promoted, the traditional fierce hazing of Last Night finally past.
The rest of the barracks on leave. I cleared my throat, glad I'd come to my
senses in time. "I see. Carry on."

"Sir?" He gaped. "I mean, aye aye, sir!"

I made sure to maintain my scowl until I was well outside the door.
Then my grin broke loose. Children. I shook my head. They'd get enough
discipline during the term. Today, graduation day, it didn't matter. Anyway, it was the sergeant's worry; I was supposed to be a remote figure,
aloof from day-to-day concerns.

Most of the middies had taken chairs at the burnished conference
table. The others were seated uncomfortably on an overstuffed couch,
trying to appear businesslike. Seven boys, four girls.

I gazed around the crowded room, saying nothing. How could midshipmen be so young? I doubted some of the boys had ever seen a razor.
Surely it hadn't been so in my day.

In my day! I snorted. I was but twenty-five, though I felt eons older.
Several of these youngsters were from the class that had just graduated; a
few had been midshipmen for more than a year. One old-timer had three
years experience under her belt.

I perched on the edge of my desk, letting the silence stretch. A
couple of the middies shifted nervously. None dared say a word. I looked
down at the curly redhead sitting in the closest chair; Midshipman Anton
Thayer flushed, studied the carpet. He was in his blues now, far more
presentable than when I'd surprised him in barracks.

"I've already been introduced to most of the staff, and I wanted to meet the rest of my officers." Midshipman Guthrie Smith's mouth turned up in a shy smile. Officers. I knew how hard he'd labored to achieve that acknowledgment, at seventeen. "You, the lieutenants and I will be working together from now on."

They sat straighter. "You're no longer cadets, and you wear officers' blue. By Act of the General Assembly, you are deemed adults. On leave you may go into town and carouse, or do whatever else strikes your fancy." Some had a faraway look; I suspected they would lose little time.

Time to bring them back to earth. "I want to make clear my expectations. You're here for two purposes: to help where you're needed, and to set an example for the cadets. If I find that your conduct on base is less than exemplary, you will answer to me." That got their attention, all right. Though my powers weren't as absolute as those of a Captain under weigh, my displeasure was a calamity no midshipman would enjoy. A word from me would have them over the barrel.

"As you know, Academy drill sergeants are noncom Marines. When you were cadets you were required to obey them. Now you're their superior officers." I waited until the sudden grins had faded, before shattering their illusions. "In name only. The sergeants will treat you with due courtesy; if one does not, you are to report him to me at once. Nonetheless, you will treat requests from the drill sergeants as if they are orders from me. Is that clear?"

They all responded, "Aye aye, sir," their voices subdued.

I stood to pace, found I had no room. I eased my way around to the back of the desk. "As to the cadets." I glared at them. "Technically you can order a cadet to do anything you wish. I suggest strongly—" I paused for effect. "I suggest strongly that you refrain. Occasional hazing is acceptable; they have to learn to cope with it. But keep it within bounds."

Some of them looked crestfallen. I didn't care. A cadet's life could be hell, and I didn't need these unseasoned youngsters making it worse. Not too much worse, anyway.

"As to striking them, you have every legal right to do it." After all, I had the right, and the middies acted in my behalf. "However, I forbid it. You'll be put over the barrel at the first violation, and the second will result in dismissal." During my second year on Farside there had been an incident, a nasty one. I wanted no repetitions.

Time to lighten a little, perhaps. "Who's senior at the moment?" I asked. It would change, as middies were transferred from here to Farside. Academy hierarchy was less rigid than aboard ship.

They didn't need to look at one another's insignia. They knew. Middies always do. "I am, sir."

"Sandra Ekrit?"

"Yes, sir."

"Very well." The other middies would call her by her last name, as a mark of respect. Until someone with more seniority showed up, she was in charge of keeping the middies under control and out of my hair.

It also meant the others could challenge her, as was Naval tradition. I wondered if the lanky young woman could hold her own against some of the burlier middies. We'd see. Like anyone else, she would sink or swim on her own.

"Any questions?"

A dark-haired boy raised his hand. "Midshipman Eduard Diego, sir. Will we have specific assignments?"

Sandra Ekrit scowled, knowing it was better for him not to bother me with trivia. Still, I'd invited him to ask.

"I don't know. I'm as new at this as you are." That brought a few startled grins. I rebuked myself silently. A fine start as their Commandant, confessing I knew nothing about the job. "We'll see. Anything else?" I waited. "Dismissed."

4

Striding with Tolliver through the concourse of Earthport Station, I tried to ignore the ache in my chest, a legacy of my recent lung replacement.

I peered at the flashing signs. "Terminal 4. G Concourse straight ahead. Shuttle to Lunapolis, turn right." After a moment I gave up. Earthport was the largest orbiting station we'd ever built, and invariably I lost myself in it.

I waited patiently at a counter for the red-jacketed civilian to look up from his puter. When he did his eyes widened in recognition. "Aren't you—can I help you?"

"The shuttle to Farside?"

He pointed. "It leaves from the Naval wing. They can tell you the gate."

"Thank you." I should have known better. Naturally the shuttle would leave from the Naval bays; no civilians could visit Farside. I hoisted my duffel, strode past the guard. "Come along, Mr. Tolliver."

"Aye aye, sir." My aide was unusually silent, perhaps as a consequence of my earlier rebuffs. My mind was on our forthcoming visit. I'd never been to Farside as an officer; three days after I'd made midshipman I'd been sent onward to U.N.S. *Helsinki*.

The Station corridor took an abrupt right angle. As I reached the turn, a midshipman tore around the bend and cannoned into me. We went down in a tangle. Tolliver thrust him aside, helped me to my feet.

I bellowed, "Watch where you're going, you young pup! Haven't they taught you a thing? What's your rush?"

The boy saluted, stammering. "Sorry, sir. I was trying to make it to the shuttle to meet—to meet—" He ground to a halt, paling as he realized to whom he spoke.

"Yes?" I barked.

His voice faltered. "You, sir. Midshipman Adam Tenere reporting, sir." He came to attention. Tolliver's expression was carefully solemn, though I detected a glint of amusement.

My shoulder throbbed, and I wondered if I'd twisted my ankle. "You're from Farside?"

"Yes, sir. My lieutenant sent me to escort you to base."

"He told you to race through the Station as if a squadron of fish were after you?"

"No, sir!"

"He told you to knock me down when you found me?"

"No, sir." The mortified middy could guess what was coming.

"Four demerits, Mr. Tenere. Consider yourself lucky." Each demerit meant two hours of hard calisthenics. I could as easily have had him caned, and most Captains would.

"Aye aye, sir. Thank you, sir. I'm sorry."

I snorted, stooped to pick up my duffel. "Which way?"

It was a foolish question. He pointed back the direction he'd come. "Down there, sir."

"Very well." I limped off.

"May I carry your duffel, sir?"

"No." Inconsiderate children, racing like mindless idiots . . . I took a cautious breath, half expecting something to grate. My chest seemed all right. "Yes. Here." Let him lug the damned thing. It was heavy.

"I already offered to carry that, sir."

"Shut up, Tolliver." We walked the length of the corridor in silence.

In the shuttle I strapped myself in, took a deep breath, strove for calm. "Tenere, you said?"

"Yes, sir. Adam Tenere."

"Any relation to . . . ?"

"Captain Tenere? He's my father, sir. He has *Freiheit*. He should be home in a couple of months with the fleet."

Because I'd Fused home in the fastship *Victoria*, I'd completed the trip in nine months, while the rest of the fleet was still in Fusion. They'd be home shortly. Though I'd brought news of the fleet's terrible losses, the details were still not general knowledge.

I made up my mind. It was his father; the boy should know. "*Freiheit* was lost. Mr. Tenere was fortunate; they found him in a lifepod."

"I didn't know that. Did his men survive?"

Immediately I regretted the demerits. "Not that I know of."

He bowed his head. "I'm sorry. All they told me was that he was coming home."

"You're assigned to Farside?"

"Yes, sir. Posted two months ago."

"I'll see to it you get leave when he's here."

The midshipman turned to me, his demerits forgotten. "Thank you, sir." His face lit with gratitude. "We'd both appreciate that."

I flirted with canceling the demerits, but decided not to. The boy had run over me like a tank.

The trip from Earthport Station to Farside took five hours. The few other passengers aboard our shuttle were techs returning from leave. When the Pilot began surfacing maneuvers I shut off my holo and watched through the porthole. The round domes of Farside stood out clearly against the ragged terrain. Of course they would, with no hazy atmosphere to impede vision. I squinted, trying to spot the Hull.

Settling the shuttle onto the Lunar surface wasn't as effortless as docking at Station, but it was far less an ordeal than diving into Earth's gravity well. I waited to unstrap until the lights blinked. Young Mr. Tenere had his belts loose the moment our jets stopped squirting.

The Pilot came back into the cabin as I stood carefully in the one-sixth gravity. "Welcome to Farside, sir."

"Welcome back, you mean." I smiled. "I've been here before."

"Oh, yes. Though it's hard to imagine you a cadet."

I could find no reply, so I waited, watching the airlock lights.

When docking at an orbiting Station, it was the vessel's responsibility to meet the Station's lock. At a groundside installation, the lock came to the ship. Ponderously, the thick plastic and alloy tube rolled across the landing grid toward our hatch. A pause while Farside's puter negotiated its mating with the shuttle's lock. A gentle bump, another, a click. The red light flashed. The tube stiffened slightly as it pressurized.

In a few moments the green airlock light flashed; the shuttle was mated. We crowded into the tiny lock while it cycled. Though shuttle and lock tube were both pressurized, as was Farside Base itself, as a matter of course the hatches were never opened simultaneously. Doing so would court disaster.

In the tube two rigid portholes, one on each side, offered a view of the unforgiving Lunar surface. It was a far cry from the manner I'd come to the base as a cadet. Fully suited, checked and rechecked by our instructors, we'd been released a few at a time from the shuttle locks and shepherded across the Lunar surface to one of the wide dome locks.

I noticed my weight increasing as I neared the inner lock. It took a lot of power to maintain near-Earth gravity in a Lunar installation, but that's what our atomic generators were for. Lightlife would hinder the cadets' training to an unacceptable degree; therefore the expensive, fusion-powered gravitrons buried below the base.

At Farside's inner lock Adam Tenere touched the pad; the hatch slid open. We gathered into the tiny chamber in silence, the few techs pressed against the bulkhead, the middy careful not to brush against me. The outer hatch closed. Because we were fully pressurized the inner hatch opened immediately.

I stepped forward while the others held back. Quite right. The Captain was always first to enter.

Several officers awaited us in the corridor. They saluted and came to attention; I released them. I said formally, "By order of the Board of Admiralty of the Government of the United Nations, I assume command of Farside Academy Base." There; that was out of the way.

"Aye aye, sir. Welcome aboard." An elegant, slim figure, graying. "First Lieutenant Jent Paulson reporting, sir."

Rightly, he didn't offer his hand, but I extended mine.

"You're senior?"

"Yes, sir, at the moment." That could change, but it was unlikely to. Admiralty tended to be sensitive to the niceties of hierarchy, where possible.

My gaze traveled to the next officer. "Lieutenant Darwin Sleak reporting, sir."

"Of course. Everything under control?"

Sleak was our systems officer, and I'd met him at Devon. He'd gone aloft two days earlier, to make sure all was ready for the returning cadets. Here on Farside, he was responsible for our life-support systems: recycling, gravitrons, air purification. Groundside, he did little more than supervise Quartermaster Serenco.

At Paulson's gesture a thin young woman stepped forward, smiled pleasantly. "Lieutenant Ngu Bien, sir. Classroom programs and training."

"Very well."

Paulson beckoned to one of the remaining two figures, who stepped forward. "Lieutenant Ardwell Crossburn, sir. Maintenance and control systems."

I fought to keep the venom from my tone. "What are you doing here?"

The short, paunchy man in his early forties drew himself up. "I've been here some years, sir. Since our cruise in *Hibernia*, in fact."

I grunted, too disgusted to speak. Toward the end of my first fateful cruise, Ardwell Crossburn had been assigned to me as a replacement officer, by some Captain no doubt delighted to be rid of him. Crossburn had a conspiratorial turn of mind, and a habit of asking seemingly innocent questions that suggested he would in time uncover whatever misdeeds were being concealed. Worse, he claimed to have the ear of his uncle, Director of Fleet Ops Admiral Brentley.

"I trust you are well, sir?"

My glare caused him to drop back a pace. Paulson and Sleak exchanged glances, but of course said nothing. They couldn't know of the endless trouble Crossburn had caused on our long return voyage on *Hibernia*, until I'd cast all caution to the winds in dealing with him.

Lieutenant Paulson hesitated, cleared his throat, moved on to the last of the group. "First Midshipman Thomas Keene, sir."

"Very well." I nodded curtly, which was all the middy deserved or expected.

"Our other middies are with the cadets, except for Mr. Tenere, here. Obviously he was able to locate you."

"Yes. He ran into me in the Station corridor." Adam smiled weakly.

"Good. Normally we don't send a middy unescorted to Earthport Station, but Mr. Crossburn suggested it. Will there be anything else, sir?"

"Yes. Come to my office. You too, Mr. Sleak. Midshipman Keene, take my duffel to my cabin. The rest of you are dismissed." I turned on my heel.

It took me a moment to orient myself and set out for the Commandant's wing. My usual haunts had been far from the warren that held the Commandant's offices and apartment, though I'd been sent there on one memorable occasion. While Sleak trailed behind, Paulson matched my pace, wise enough to keep silent. Half the trick to being a good lieutenant was knowing when to leave the Captain alone. I wished Tolliver would take note.

Still seething, I stalked into my new office. The sergeant at the outer desk rose. A dark-skinned woman, somewhere around forty. She saluted. "Sergeant Kina Obutu reporting, sir."

"You're my staff?"

"Staff sergeant first, sir. I run your office during nominal day. At night we leave a middy in charge."

"Very well." Chairs lined the outer cabin, occasionally occupied by unfortunate cadets. I crossed to my new office, took a deep breath, flung open the hatch. Rather, I tried to. It was locked.

I spun around, feeling a fool. "What the devil?"

"He didn't leave it open?" Sergeant Obutu raised her eyebrow.

I shook my head. "Why would it be—where's the code?"

"The Commandant has it, sir." Paulson.

"I'm the Command—"

He said quickly, "I meant Commandant Kearsey. Sorry, sir."

Obutu asked, "Is there a copy in the safe?"

Mr. Sleak seemed embarrassed. "I'll check right away, sir. Excuse me."

"I'll look too, sir." Paulson hurried after him.

I nodded, too furious for words. I paced the outer office, ignoring the sergeant, who stood alongside her desk with a placid expression. I was working myself up to withering sarcasm when a thought intervened.

"Sarge, why is the hatch locked in the first place?"

"The Comm—Captain Kearsey always locked it at night, sir."

"Wrong question. Why does his hatch have a lock?"

"All our offices have them, sir." Her expression was carefully neutral.

I couldn't hide my amazement. "How long has this been going on?"

The outer hatch swung open. Lieutenant Sleak, followed by Paulson. He shook his head. "No code in the security safe, sir."

Obutu answered, "Since I came here, sir. Five years that I know of."

I glared at them both. "What else is locked around here?"

Sleak said, "The mess hall, I think. That's about—and the officers' apartments, of course."

"Of course?" No one responded. I snarled, "OF COURSE?"

The outer hatch opened. Tolliver saw the others, saluted. "Good aftern—"

"Tolliver, they lock the hatches here!"

He said only, "Good heavens."

Sergeant Obutu said helplessly, "Sorry, sir. I don't know what you're talking about."

Sleak ventured, "I'm class of '72, sir. I remember."

"We're trying to teach them to be officers! If we expect thieves in the night, that's what we'll get. These joeys are officer candidates, not transpop crewmen! What idiot ordered the locks put on?"

Sleak said evenly, "Commandant Kearsey, sir."

"Yes. Um." I rubbed my eyes. "It must have been the first day they told us. 'Nothing is locked at Academy. You will conduct yourselves as gentlemen. A gentleman doesn't take things from another's home, or sneak into places where he's not welcome.'"

"Second day," Tolliver said. "The first was haircuts and clothes and making beds, about twenty times."

"Whatever." I prodded the hatch. "Get this bloody lock off. Torch it if you must. Take the locks off Admin and the mess hall and wherever else you find them. Do the same groundside."

Sleak said, "Aye aye, sir." It was his responsibility, as systems officer. "Does that include the safes?"

"Not if there are weapons or cash or confidential papers. That's going too far."

"Yes, sir. I'll get right on it."

"My hatch first, damn it! I'll be in my cabin!" I stormed out.

I'd barely unpacked my duffel before Sergeant Obutu buzzed me on the caller. "Your office is, ah, accessible, sir."

"Is Paulson still there?"

"Waiting, sir."

"Very well, I'll be up."

Moments later I was back in the anteroom, restraining an urge to slick my hair and check the shine on my shoes. I took a deep breath, stepped through the threshold into my new office.

I crossed the room crowded with furniture, eased myself into the Commandant's leather seat, behind the Commandant's desk. No lightning bolt struck me. I willed myself to relax. "Shut the hatch. Sit." I pointed to a chair.

"Aye aye, sir." Lieutenant Paulson took a place near my desk.

"Why is that man Crossburn here?"

"I have no idea, sir. I presume he was assigned by BuPers." That meant nothing. Everyone's assignment came through BuPers.

"How much trouble has he made?"

"Trouble?" Paulson studied me curiously. "None that I know of, sir. He's a trifle odd in some respects, but he carries out his duties. He spends his spare time in his cabin, writing."

On *Hibernia* the lunatic had nearly caused a mutiny, interrogating officers and crew about the tragedies we'd suffered, writing his secret conclusions in a little black diary to show his uncle upon our return. When his inquiries had begun to imply I was an accomplice in the death of Captain Haag, I'd put a stop to it, consigning him to busywork in the ship's launch for the remainder of our cruise.

I drummed my fingers on the gleaming desktop. "Does he ask questions?"

"Pardon?" Paulson leaned forward. "Questions?"

"About the base. About incidents that have taken place."

He shrugged. "At times. He was most interested in the shuttle crash, two years ago. I believe he fancies himself something of a historian."

I snorted. "I can imagine. I want him out of here."

"Yes, sir. I believe you'd have to take that up with BuPers. I have no authority."

I growled, "I'm no cadet. Don't lecture me on procedures."

"No, sir. I'm sorry."

"That's all."

He rose, saluted, left me.

I sat, head in hands. This wouldn't do. I'd been on base a mere half an hour and already I'd alienated my first lieutenant. I stood to pace, thrusting aside a chair that blocked my path. I strode the few steps to the bulkhead, turned back, passed the desk, squeezed past the table. Finally I returned to my seat, took up the caller.

"Sarge, call BuPers at Lunapolis. Get me whoever's in charge of our staffing." Waiting, I turned to the console alongside my desk. I called up a menu, explored idly. Personnel records, paymaster reports, supply logs. I'd have to learn the system, but I knew virtually all our data would be accessible from this console.

I switched to cadet records, examined one at random. Everything was there, from original applications through ID photos, to the latest grades.

The speaker buzzed. "Seafort."

"Captain Higbee, BuPers. What can I do for you?"

"I have a lieutenant I want replaced, sir." Like most Captains on the Naval list, Higbee was my senior.

"For what reason?"

Wasn't a Captain free to choose his staff? I tried not to let my annoyance show. "We've, ah, had problems. His name is Crossburn."

"What has he done wrong?"

"Nothing at present," I said lamely.

"I see." A long pause. "Captain, perhaps you're unaware of the staffing problems we've—"

"The man is a time bomb. I want him off my base!"

"Yes, you've made that clear. I'm afraid I can't help you. All current assignments are frozen. Though I suppose if he'll volunteer for the fleet he'll be snapped up."

"Lord God, no. Keep him off a ship!" I pounded my forehead. What was I doing? I'd just muffed a chance to get rid of him. Still, I couldn't inflict Crossburn on a ship of the line. He could destroy morale in no time, and if his ship encountered the aliens . . .

"If he's so much trouble, court-martial him," said Higbee. "I'm afraid we can't help; we're not swapping officers until the emergency is over. Better at present to keep men in jobs they know. The order comes directly from Fleet Ops. Is there anything else?"

"I—No, sir."

"Very well, then."

"With your permission, I'd like to speak to Admiral Duhaney." It was insolent, but not as insolent as going behind his back.

A pause. When he responded his tone was cool. "As you wish, Commandant."

"Thank you." I rang off, stood to pace. Was I making too big an issue of Crossburn? Surely I could manage to live with him. I wondered if Farside Base had a ship's launch. Well, I could always have him polish the Hull, half buried in the Lunar dust Outside.

I blundered into a coffee table, barked my shin. Cursing, I retreated to the desk. "Sergeant Oba—Ob—Sarge!"

A moment later she was in the hatchway. "Obutu," she said calmly.

I nursed my leg. "See if we can reach Admiral Duhaney in Fleet Ops."

"Aye aye, sir." She turned to go.

"And have someone get this bloody furniture out of here!"

Her face was expressionless. "I beg your pardon, sir?"

"Out. The furniture. Have them take it." Now I sounded a complete idiot. I took a deep breath. "Leave my desk and chair. The console, of course. That leather chair near the desk can stay, and the couch against the bulkhead. I want everything else gone."

"Aye aye, sir. May I ask why?"

"So I can walk." A Captain needed to pace. Hadn't Commandant Kearsey ever trod a bridge? Good Lord.

"Very well, sir."

Normally the mess hall would be full of cadets at their long plank tables, poised to leap to their feet when the officers filed in. Now, during term break, fewer than two hundred were seated, and the meal was more informal.

The officers' table was round, like those in a ship's dining hall. It was the only round table in the room, perhaps to emphasize the difference between officers and cadets. Though we ate the same food as cadets, the officers' meals were served by stewards, whereas at each cadet table a designated server brought trays full of serving dishes from the line to their comrades.

Our steward passed salad and bread. When he left, Lieutenant Ngu Bien nudged Paulson. "There's the Chambers boy. Looks like they let him back in."

Paulson said, "I'm surprised he can walk so soon."

I raised an eyebrow.

"A fracas with two of his tablemates, sir. Just pushing and shoving, until Cadet Chambers lost his head and poured a pitcher of milk over them."

"I see."

"Caned, of course. By the Commandant himself. He's been fed on the corridor deck outside mess hall for the last two weeks."

Appropriate. Cadets had to learn to conduct themselves like officers. Only in the privacy of the wardroom could middies release their natural tensions in horseplay. Certainly not in front of their betters. Though once, when Cadet Corporal Tolliver had pushed me too far . . . I pushed away the thought.

"You've kept our troublemakers aloft, then?"

"Leave was denied for the problem joeys, and the few others with no good place to go, sir."

"How are we keeping them busy?" Until the new term, classes wouldn't be in session.

Ms. Bien. "Bill Radz and I are taking them Outside this afternoon."

"The whole lot of them?" She nodded. Well, the discipline and exercise would do them good. I remembered my own tremulous first steps with magneboots, on the Hull.

"Would you like to come along, sir? We're giving some of them thrustersuits, and they've all heard about your jet into *Hibernia*'s lock."

I gagged on my coffee. The huge alien form had emerged from behind *Telstar*. Our sailors were helpless in the gig. The acid. *Fuse, Vax. Fuse the ship.*

"Are you all right, sir?"

In desperation I'd jetted my thrustersuit full bore toward *Hibernia*'s lock, tried to do a fliparound as Sarge had once shown us, waited a bit too long and crashed into the airlock with bone-jarring force. Still, I'd gotten there, and Vax Holser had instantly Fused.

"Of course I'm all right." I wiped coffee from my chin. Despite the later incident, the freedom of a T-suit was one of the few joys I remembered from cadet days.

I looked up. "Yes, I'd like to go along."

Two hours later, at the training lock, I was perspiring in my thrustersuit, trying to conceal my impatience. Suiting nearly a hundred frisky teens called for the patience of Job. The two officers assigned to the task were coping as well as could be expected. Even with the full cooperation of the eager cadets, it took time to recheck every clasp, every helmet seal.

"Stand still, Johns! Is there a spider in your suit?" Sergeant Radz gave her helmet a final twist.

Behind me, a youngster giggled. I snapped, "Be silent!"

"Aye aye, sir." A chastened tone.

"Cadet Drew always laughs, sir." Radz favored him with a withering frown. "I'm sure he and I will find something funny in barracks tonight."

The boy gulped. "I'm sorry, sir." He was almost as tall as Sarge, but his voice was barely broken.

I grunted, turned to the training lock. Though it was far larger than the VIP lock we'd used from the shuttle, the cadets' suits were bulky, and it had to cycle three times before we were all Outside.

The officers broadcast to the cadets on one frequency, using a second to communicate among themselves. Now, as an adult, I could appreciate the logistics necessary to maintain order.

While waiting for the last cadets to emerge from the lock I kicked at the Lunar dust. It spurted lazily and fell in slow motion, a foot away. I looked around with a twinge of guilt. When I was a cadet it would have brought me a rebuke, though I was never sure why. Lord God knew there was plenty of dust to kick.

"By twos, now." I jumped as my radio blared. "To the Hull. Maintain your distance." I hung back with Lieutenant Bien as the troop dutifully started forward. North of the lock stretched the familiar pockmarked terrain, unchanged since Farside Base was built and for eons before.

To the south sat the Hull, a life-size replica of a ship of the line, half buried in the Lunar surface, so that from stern to prow only the upper half of its length protruded.

A U.N.N.S. starship was shaped like a pencil with two or three foam rubber disks slid down to its midpoint and pressed together. Forward of the disks were cargo holds; aft were the lower engine room and fusion motors, tapering to the fusion drive shaft at the very stern. The disks held cabins, crew quarters, exercise rooms, and the hydroponics and recycling that sustained our lives.

Generations of cadets had clambered over the Hull, learning first the mere trick of walking, and later, how to carry tools and power packs they might need if sent Outside for repairs. At the end came the T-suit training.

All of today's group had mastered at least the art of walking, though many had an ungainly lope, and a few still carefully regulated the size and timing of their steps. But none crashed into the cadet ahead, or sprawled facedown in the dust.

At last the youngsters were assembled alongside the Hull. Lieutenant Bien organized most of them into squads, set them walking along the top of the Hull from one end to another. From time to time she varied the drill, sending one group into the drive shaft, another to the prow. The Hull had no jagged edges to rip their suits, but moving from one section to another, and over the disks, was tricky. Just edging past each other could be a problem for inexperienced cadets.

At the stern, Sergeant Radz had a few cadets making practice hops in jumpsuits. All in all, I appreciated the training more now than I had as a participant.

Radz keyed to my frequency. "Sir, would you be willing to demonstrate a jump?"

"Me?" I turned in astonishment. I was hardly an expert.

Like all sergeants everywhere, he was unafraid of rank. "Yes, sir, if you wouldn't mind. They'd listen far more closely than if I were demonstrating."

"No, I don't—" Wasn't that what I was here for, to train cadets? True, I hadn't anticipated doing it in such hands-on fashion. I sighed. "Where would you have me jump?"

"From the prow to the drive shaft, if you'd like?"

"Thanks a lot," I muttered. If I missed, I'd sail past the stern of the ship and look a complete fool. "I may not be good enough, Sarge." I tried a little jump, spread my legs as I settled down.

"Sure you are, sir. You passed training, didn't you?"

"Barely." He took my resigned nod for approval, and keyed his mike to gather the cadets. While they assembled alongside the stern I nervously gauged my distances.

Managing a thrustersuit on Luna wasn't quite so easy as on the Training Station aloft, or outside one of the eleven Training Fusers moored at its docks. Here at Farside, you had gravity to contend with. Not all that much, but enough. You had to use more propellant, and you couldn't merely aim for the point you wanted to reach. You had to aim beyond it, allow gravity to hold you back. And though gravity was far lower than on Earth, inertia was just as great. When I'd crashed into *Hibernia*'s lock I could have broken my legs, despite the zero gravity.

". . . in one hop, as the Commandant will now show you. Pay attention to his angle of ascent, and the point at which he squirts his thrusters to change course. You at the end, step back another ten meters." He waited until they'd complied. "When you're ready, sir."

"Very well." I keyed my mike to the general frequency. "Watch carefully. I only intend to do this once." If I could do it at all. I loped alongside the Hull in the peculiar floating gait appropriate to the Lunar surface until at last I was at the stern. Clutching my straps, I keyed the jets, felt the lift, and quickly switched them off. I sailed up onto the prow, almost overshooting it to fall down the port side. I snapped on my magnetronics, allowed my boots to grasp the Hull, stiffened my knees. I peered down the length of the Hull to the drive shaft, more than a hundred meters away.

What had I gotten myself into? I groaned, then realized with dismay that my radio was on the cadets' frequency. Cursing under my breath I switched channels.

Now or never. I estimated distance one last time, grasped the straps, keyed my jets.

I had no intention of going ballistic; what I wanted was to maintain a relatively steady height over the Hull. That meant varying the power in minute increments. I lifted, bent forward to angle the jets, tried to maintain the ideal balance between upward and forward motion. Below, the Hull drifted past.

More power, else I wouldn't have enough inertia to straighten myself and prepare for landing. Too much, damn it! Now I'd shot way above the Hull. I'd have to fire the head jets and I always hated burying my chin in my chest and firing blind. I was veering to starboard. Careful, you idiot. Keep your mind on your work.

"A touch to port, I think." A quiet voice in my ear. "Straighten your legs, sir. Tuck your chin in. Fire about . . . now. Good. Let go, orient yourself to land."

I had it under control. I twisted my body over, fired my backjets to slow myself, dropped slowly toward the Hull. Time to flip forward, fire a couple of squirts so I didn't land too hard. My feet touched. Done. I flicked off the jets.

They shouted their approval, until the outraged sergeant regained charge with a few crackling words. Nonchalantly I stepped off the Hull, relied on the jets to bring me down, and almost fell flat on my face. No one seemed to notice.

Legs trembling with delayed reaction, I watched Lieutenant Bien help Radz get the youngsters in thrustersuits ready for practice. First she lined them up on the Lunar surface parallel to the Hull. Sergeant Radz walked behind, showing the joeys how to bend to achieve forward motion.

"Now, it's just a simple hop onto the Hull. You've practiced forward motion before. The only difference is that when you come down you'll be a dozen meters higher than you started. Bronski, you're first."

A nervous young voice. "Yes, sir."

"Jump when you're ready."

The boy took a deep breath, launched himself. He didn't do badly, though he stumbled when he landed.

"Move aside a bit, and wait for Salette." He adjusted the next youngster's harness and stepped aside. I took the opportunity to touch helmets, my mike keyed off. "Thanks, Sarge."

"For the backseat driving? Sorry if I interfered, sir." He winked, turned back to his charges. "Edwards, are you ready?"

The boy's tone was tremulous. "I think so, sir."

"Up and away, then."

The cadet miscalculated his bend, launched himself straight up. A yelp of surprise.

"Easy, lad. Come down and try again. Taper off your jet."

"Yes, sir." Edwards turned his jet off entirely, drifted down slowly at first, then ever faster.

"Squirt! A short one!"

The boy complied, slowing his descent in the nick of time. He reached the ground, flipped off his jet. "I'm sorry, sir! I don't know how—"

A voice whispered, "You can do it, Dustin. Hang in there."

Sergeant Radz spun around, raising a tiny cloud of dust. "Who was that?"

Sheepishly, a boy stepped forward. "Me, sir. Kevin Arnweil."

"Two demerits, Arnweil! Maintain radio silence until you're spoken to!"

"Aye aye, sir!"

Radz shook his head. "Your buddy is right, Edwards. You can do it. Go join Bronski and Salette on the Hull."

"Aye aye, sir." The boy tensed, bent his knees. "I think—" Convulsively, he fired his jets. The propellant spewed; slowly he lifted, legs kicking wildly. He took too much height, but was smart enough to cut the jets and wait until gravity reclaimed him. He landed on the Hull, caught his balance. "I did it!"

"Of course you did." Radz adjusted the next cadet's harness. Cadet Arnweil grinned, waved approval to Edwards, but was careful to say nothing.

I smiled to myself. Only a twenty-foot leap, and both boys were exultant. Wait until we took them outside the Training Station.

"Very good, Edwards. You four, move astern a bit to make room. Drew, you're next. Then you, Arnweil." He adjusted Cadet Drew's harness.

"Sir, I don't think I'm ready—"

"Of course you are. You've jumped up and you've jumped forward. Now you're combining the two. Bend before you jet."

"I—aye aye, sir." The boy leaned forward, lost his balance.

"For God's sake, Drew! One demerit!"

"I'm sorry, sir!" The youngster stumbled to his feet. "I don't think I can—"

"Orient yourself first. You don't—"

The anxious boy clutched his harness, keyed his jets to full. He lifted off, legs kicking.

"Throttle down!"

The cadet bent forward toward the Hull, jets still set at full. He hurtled across the gap.

I shouted, "Cut your—"

"Look out!" Sarge waved violently at the boys on the Hull. One cadet ducked more slowly than the rest. Drew sailed into him at full power. Their helmets collided. A puff of vapor.

"DUSTIN!" A shriek of dismay, from below.

I launched, bent forward, sailed onto the Hull. I pulled Drew off Dustin Edwards's kicking form, scooped the downed cadet under my arm, snapped my jets to full and launched. Endless seconds passed while I jetted toward the distant airlock. Below me, a cadet loped toward the waiting lock in a stride that took him meters off the ground.

The form in my arms had gone still.

No time to land and walk into the lock. I sailed straight in, tucked my head down, fired retros, spun about, kicked the approaching bulkhead. In slow motion I fell to the ground. I staggered to my feet, slapped shut the hatch just as Sergeant Radz sailed past to join me.

As the hatch closed the boy who'd run to the lock dived through. Radz swore a blue streak without pausing for breath. The cadet who'd followed us pounded the bulkhead, shouting incoherently. I glanced at his helmet. Kevin Arnweil, who'd been demerited for calling encouragement to Edwards.

What in hell was the matter with the lock? Surely recycling couldn't take forever. I keyed my radio, yelled, "Emergency medical to the Training Lock, flank! Decompression!" I should have thought of it sooner.

Endless moments later the inner hatch opened. Arnweil tore off his helmet. Short-cropped black hair, the faint hint of a mustache, his eyes frantic.

No med techs. I gasped, "Sickbay?"

Radz grabbed Dustin Edwards's slack legs in one arm, pointed. Awkward in our suits, we dashed through the suiting room to the corridor beyond. Arnweil had the presence of mind to hold the hatches open.

The med techs met us halfway along the corridor, their crash cart skidding to a halt. Radz yanked Edwards off my shoulder, laid him flat, twisted off his helmet.

Blood oozed from the boy's mouth. His eyes—

Arnweil moaned.

The eyes would give me nightmares. A tech slapped an oxygen mask over the cadet's face, mercifully concealing them. The techs stripped off his suit, cut his shirt. The moment the paddles were secure, the techs fired. The boy's chest muscles convulsed. There was no other response. A tech straddled the inert cadet for CPR. Another whipped off the oxygen mask, fed a breathing tube down the boy's throat, switched on the respirator.

Arnweil whimpered incessantly. Radz, kneeling alongside Edwards, hissed, "Stop that noise!"

I stepped between the cadet and the still form on the deck. The boy darted around me, knelt at the body. "Dustin!" His voice was agonized.

Sergeant Radz watched the struggling techs, saw he could do little to help, got to his feet. "Step away, Arnweil! Get hold of yourself."

"Let me stay with him!" Kevin clutched Dustin's inert hand.

Radz shook his head. "You're in the way."

"But—"

The Sergeant's voice hardened. "Obey orders, Cadet! Be a man! Stop that sniveling! Stand against the—"

"BELAY THAT!" Something in my voice gave him pause, as well it might. I cleared my aching throat.

"Sir, he—"

"Be silent!" Had I no sense? I was putting myself between a cadet and his Sergeant.

Kevin Arnweil, on his knees, leaned forward until his forehead touched his companion's still hand. He moaned. The sound pierced my suit, my soul.

He wailed again.

I knelt, threw my arm across his shoulder.

I closed my eyes. Not this, Lord.

It was the biggest game of the year, and tickets had been sold out for weeks. Lord God knew how Jason had gotten ours. For a time I'd been afraid Father would forbid my going, on account of some unfinished lesson, some chore not to his satisfaction. But at last, weak with relief, I found myself peddling down the road behind Jason's green jacket, lunch in my backpack, coins in my pocket.

We would see the Italians play the Welsh home team in the big game of 2190.

At the Cardiff stadium we locked our bikes, joined the crowds streaming toward the entrance. Lines of buses unloaded at the curb; men descended jabbering in fluid Italian. Other buses bore the logos of Manchester, East End London, Liverpool. Tough-looking joeys, who lived for football.

Jason stopped short with a look of alarm, patted his jacket pockets. "Christ, Nicky, I left the tickets home!"

"Don't blaspheme. I saw you tuck them in your shirt pocket."

His face lit in a grin. "Worth a try." His golden hair threw off sunshine. We passed through the turnstiles, found our seats in the upper bleachers.

"You got coin for drinks?"

I fished in my jacket. "Two bucks." I hauled out the crumpled unidollars.

"Now or later?"

"I don't care."

Jason shrugged, clasped his arms behind his head. "Let's wait." He studied the empty field. "New lines. Are you glad?"

"What do I care about lines?"

"No, you feeble snark. Glad that you're going."

I hesitated. "I guess. I'd feel better if they hadn't sent the first letter."

He peered across the field. "They need new benches."

"What about you? Are you glad?"

He lowered his hands to his lap, kicked at the bench ahead. A burly man tossed back an annoyed glance.

"What do you want me to say, Nicky?"

"The truth."

"Am I glad you're getting what you've always wanted? That you'll finally get to see the stars? Am I glad my best friend is about to leave while I get to take Engineering in Third?" His eyes flashed my way, spun back to the field.

"Oh, Jase. I wish you could come."

After a moment he shrugged. "That's life." His hand dropped for a moment to my leg. I tried not to stiffen. I reached to pry off his hand, instead clasped it for a moment in mine. It cost little to give him that.

"They're coming on!" I jumped to my feet as Archie Connelly lumbered out. Not the fastest man on the team, but it took a tank to stop him.

I waited impatiently through the anthems, and joined the roar of approval as the teams lined up for the kickoff.

"Nick? I'm glad for you. Really."

Reggie booted the ball past Connelly, shouldered aside an Italian guard. I reluctantly tore my gaze from the field. Jason's eyes glistened. "Thanks, Jase. I'll miss you."

"Four days."

"Aye." My bag was already packed; no change of clothes, we'd been told, no need even for a toothbrush. Just my favorite holochips, paper for writing to Father and Jason in case I couldn't get to a fax console. A few pictures.

Ten minutes into the game, the Italians scored. Reggie and Archie seemed disconcerted by their opponents' sudden shifts. They played on, ignoring howls of glee from the Italian fans.

"How are you getting there?"

"To Academy? Father says by train."

"It's only an hour by plane."

"That's what I told him. He said there's no need to race through the air."

We surged to our feet as our right back intercepted the ball. He booted it to Couran in center after a lovely bit of footplay. I wasn't looking forward to a long subdued train ride with Father, who would discourage any excitement I displayed.

The period ended with the Italians ahead, 2 to 0. Jason slipped on his green jacket, ran up to the stand for our drinks. The crowd was so thick that halftime was nearly over when he returned. I unwrapped my sandwich, sipping at the softie Jason had brought.

He nudged me. "Try some of mine."

"I have plenty."

He thrust his cup at me. I took a sip, and gagged. "Jesus, where'd you get this?" I shoved it back into his hand.

"Don't blaspheme," he mimicked.

"Tell me!"

"Angus Terrie was up there."

I drank from my own cup. "You'll get us arrested!"

"Don't be such a droob." He took another swig of beer. "Have a little fun, Nicky. What's life for?" He waved the cup.

I hissed, "Put it down!" If he spilled it, some busybody might smell alcohol and call the jerries. I could get booted out of Academy before even reporting there. Sometimes Jason had no sense.

People brushed past to their seats. The players were taking the field. I finished my lunch, sipped nervously at my softie.

"I talked to Ma. She'd loan me coin for a ticket if I wanted to go."

I stared at him. "You mean, to Devon? With Father and me?"

"Would he let me come?" No need to ask whether I'd want him along.

The second half began. Could I convince Father? Though he didn't care for Jason, he knew I did. I'd have to pick my time, ask in just the right way. What a different trip it would be. I couldn't wait until the last minute to ask, though. I'd have to plant the idea ahead of time.

"Oh, no!"

The Italians had stolen the ball again, and were working it downfield. Reggie closed in on his man, who had the ball.

In a daring move Archie Connelly abandoned his own man and double-teamed the Italian. Their left forward raced over to help. In the confusion Archie and the Italian ball carrier bumped together. The Italian went down.

Whistles shrilled and the play stopped. On the field men were gesturing. The ref flashed a yellow card, indicated Archie.

"Violent charge?" Jason was indignant. "The Dago ran into him!"

The crowd didn't like it, either. Boos erupted through the stands, except in the Italian sections. The Eyties took a free kick, ran the ball to our back line, lost it. We blitzed through their defense, scored. Jeers and catcalls pelted the Italian team.

"Just twenty minutes left." Jason bit his lip. The Welsh had to come out on top to make the finals. A tie wouldn't do.

Ten minutes passed in inconclusive play. The crowd grew more fervent. Jason, thank heaven, had finished his beer. I stashed the incriminating cup between seats, where it could have been anyone's.

A hoarse yell from behind us. "Go on, Archie! Get the frazzin' Wops!" I frowned, but somehow Archie heard the call, and waved. Our bleachers responded with a mighty roar.

With a few minutes to go, Cardiff got the ball downfield. De Ville passed to Reggie, who lumbered in to kick a goal from twenty feet. We were tied.

They faced off for the throw. "I'll ask Father tonight, Jase."

"What if I just showed up on the train?"

I considered it. "I don't know." Father would know Jason's appearance was no accident, but what could he do? I could wander the train with Jason even without Father's permission. Rebellion surged in my breast. I didn't *always* have to do as Father said.

Four minutes. The roar was deafening. The Italians lost the ball.

They surged to the defense, but Archie Connelly shouldered aside all opposition. My throat was hoarse from yelling.

Abruptly Archie passed to Reggie, who just as quickly passed it back. His path momentarily clear, Archie slammed down a defenseman and aimed a great kick. The ball sailed majestically into the corner of the goal. We'd won, with less than a minute to go.

Jason and I danced on the benches, mad with excitement. The burly man in front of us spun round and snarled, "Snuff it, you twits! They disallowed the goal!"

"What?" But it was true. They'd not only voided the goal, but red-carded Archie. On the field the Cardiff team surrounded the referee. He stood with arms crossed, shaking his head.

"Fraz the Dagoes!" Across the field, joeys were chanting. Others took it up.

"Kill the ref! Kill the ref!"

"Wow, gonna be a donny." Jason grinned with excitement. "If Reggie doesn't watch it he'll get tossed too!"

"He'd better not." But matters were already past that. An Eytie player took a swing at De Ville, who lashed back.

Roars of rage from the benches opposite. Italian spectators swarmed across the field. They joined battle with Cardiff joes from the lower bleachers, well below us. Jerries waded in with their riot sticks, asserting control.

"Look!" Jason pointed to the next section of bleachers.

High in the next section, across the aisle, a couple of joeyboys had pried loose one end of their bench and were rocking the other end to break it free. Spectators, half amused, stood back to give them room. For a moment the bench held. Abruptly it broke loose. One of the joes took up the bench, swung it over his head as a shot-putter his shot. He spun three times until, dizzy, he let go and fell back.

The bench hurtled down the stands, bowling over spectators like tenpins.

Enraged bystanders leaped over benches and bodies, clawing their way upward to their attacker. Some fell or were pulled down.

I grabbed Jason's wrist. "Let's get out of here!"

"The closest stairs are up top!"

"But—all right!" We pushed to the aisle, threaded our way up toward the exit. Abruptly the riot leaped across the aisle like a blaze across a fire lane. Our section was full of shoving, screaming fans.

"Move, Nicky!" Jason pushed me.

Something lurched. Above us ten rows of seats suddenly disappeared.

As one, the crowd turned to the safety of the ground below. Men jumped down from bench to bench, heedless where they landed. The aisle was jammed to immobility.

Jason twisted to face downward, trying to squeeze through the mob. I hung on to his arm. The press lifted me off the ground, carried me ahead still clinging to Jason.

Our aisle ended at a rail separating the upper and lower stands. Squeezed against the rail, a woman fought with savage intensity to free herself. At her side a man braced himself against the throng. A moment later he went down. Then the woman. The crowd drove toward the safety of the field crushing those on the bottom into the rail or down to the concrete deck.

Jason's hand tightened. "Hang on, Nicky!"

I gripped his wrist. The crowd surged. An elbow jabbed at my side; my hand tore loose from Jason's. We parted. I clawed at the bodies between us. A man lashed out, caught me in the stomach. I doubled over, fell into a row of benches.

"JASON!!" A glimpse of golden ringlets. I clawed my way back to the aisle. Below us something gave way. The crowd lurched, arms and legs flailing. I slipped on something wet, managed to right myself.

"Jason, answer me!" The crowd swept me past the broken rail, catapulted me into the stands below. I landed on heads and arms, the breath knocked out of me. The joes I'd fallen onto threw me aside, cursing. I thumped onto concrete.

Someone stomped on my hand. I screamed, rolled under a bench. Shouts of anger and pain. A crash, and the crack of splintering wood.

Eons later, it began to subside. I lay half crushed by the broken bench. Voices. The pressure lifted. Light.

A jerry. "This one's alive. You all right, laddie?"

I began to cry.

They hauled me out. "Anything broken?" Below, jerries carried bodies on stretchers to the grassy field.

I fell onto a nearby bench. "I don't think so." I looked around. "Where is he?" Most of the crowd had disappeared. Injured huddled together as if seeking solace. Some were bandaged, others were bleeding, many in shock.

"Who, lad?" A jerry, riotstick tucked in his belt.

"Jason."

He shrugged. "He's probably out by now. If you want, look on the field. The ambulances are outside, hauling the wounded to hospital." He patted my shoulder. "Can't stay, boy. There are others." He turned away.

My ribs ached. I gritted my teeth, made my way to the aisle, shut my eyes. If Jason was here, I didn't want to see him. I steeled myself, opened my eyes a crack. Nothing. Reddish brown stains on the cement steps, trampled coats and shoes strewn about. Not, praise God, a green jacket.

I made my way out of the stadium. Hundreds of injured sat or lay on the curbs. An ambulance landed; techs jumped out with stretchers. I walked down the line of wounded, searching. Jason wasn't there. He'd be waiting with the bikes. I trudged across the concrete lot. Our bicycles sat locked, untended.

No point in going back to the grisly field. I thrust my hands in my pockets, lowered my head, stared at nothing.

Reluctant steps pulled me back to the stadium entrance. Just so I'd know he was in hospital. Nurses could be so severe, and if there was a mixup they'd argue with me. Better to say I knew that's where he had to be waiting. I followed the signs to the lower boxes, walked unhindered across the new-chalked playing field. A jerry intercepted me. "What are you doing, lad?"

"I'm—" My tongue was thick. "I'm looking for someone."

"Don't touch anything." I nodded, and he let me be. I hugged myself as I reached the first row. They'd left most of the faces uncovered. A woman stared up at me, eyes bulging, one side of her head crushed. I turned, took two steps, vomited my lunch onto the field, wiped my mouth, stomach still churning.

Jason, you won't believe what I went through today. Searching through all those bodies, afraid you'd be among them. What is it, your leg? You'll be walking in a week, don't give me that. Lord Christ, you gave me a scare.

Some bodies were covered's entirely. I knew from the size that Jason couldn't be under the blanket. A baby, a small child. I fought not to retch again. Another body, covered with a carelessly thrown blanket. I hurried past, stopped.

No, it was someone else. The sleeve sticking out from the blanket was mostly brown. Only parts of it were green. That's not you. With baby steps I inched toward the blanket. Tentatively I reached to the top, pulled it down. It wasn't Jason's face. I sobbed with relief.

It wasn't anyone's face. Just a mass of congealed blood, above a green and brown collar. I pulled the blanket away, exposing the rest of the body.

Any boy could have been wearing brown slacks, those jumpboots.

Any boy could have had golden curls. Any boy could have been wearing that green jacket, mottled with blood from the mangled chest.

Any boy.

I bent almost double, took the hand, pressed it to my side. From deep inside, I made a sound.

They found me there, hours later, in the dark.

The med techs exchanged glances. One shook his head. Kevin Arnweil's fingers brushed the tunic of his still friend. I caught him as he sagged, pressed his locks against my chest. He wept in silence. Sergeant Radz looked on with disapproval.

The corridor was filling with subdued cadets, restrained by the quiet commands of Lieutenant Bien. Kyle Drew, whose jump had caused the accident, was white with shock.

I said, "Send them to barracks, Lieutenant."

"Aye aye, sir. Arnweil also?"

"Let him stay."

A young middy hurried down the corridor, reached me and stopped. "Midshipman Keene reporting, sir. Sarge says to tell you Admiral Duhaney is returning your call."

"Who? Oh. Very well, I'll—" Arnweil sobbed. I took a deep breath. "Tell him I'm busy. I'll call later."

The midshipman stared in amazement, caught himself. "Aye aye, sir." He scurried off.

5

I paced my office, cursing my imprudence. One didn't spurn the Admiral in charge of Fleet Ops, if one ever again wanted his favor. Cadet Arnweil could have waited. Besides, it was Sergeant Radz's role to console him, not mine.

My caller buzzed. Ms. Obutu. "Do you have time for Mr. Radz, sir?"

"Very well. Send him in."

He saluted, came to attention. I nodded to release him, bade him sit.

"Sir, I'd like a transfer groundside. Out of Academy."

"Because I overruled you in the corridor? Don't be silly."

"No, sir." His eyes were pained. "I failed Cadet Edwards. And Kyle Drew will go through life remembering he killed a boy because I didn't do my job."

"It was an accident."

"Yes, sir. My job is to prevent accidents, especially stupid ones."

"It wasn't your fault, Sarge. It was a fluke."

He shook his head stubbornly. "You can say that about any accident. Drew wasn't ready; he even told me so. He made one clumsy jump, and I forced him into another."

I stood to pace. "What do you want me to do?"

"Send me somewhere else, sir. Get a competent instructor."

"No." I held his eye until he turned away, defeated. "That's all."

He had no choice. "Aye aye, sir." He stood to go.

The man needed absolution. I thought quickly. "I want a report on all training accidents in the past five years, and your recommendations on improving safety. No deadline, take a couple of weeks if you need to. And one other thing."

"Yes, sir?"

"It's too late for the Edwards boy. But you have two walking wounded on your hands. Kyle Drew, and Arnweil. Nurse them back to health."

His brow wrinkled. "How, sir?"

"I don't know; that's what you're here for. Drew must be sick with guilt, and Arnweil is crushed. They need you." My tone sharpened. "You weren't responsible for the boy's death, but your conduct after was a disgrace. Arnweil and Edwards must have been close."

"They enlisted together. Kevin has to learn that soldiers die, sometimes to no purpose." Unbidden, he sat again, rubbed his hands over his face. "But he's still a child, you're right about that. I expected too much of him."

I was silent. Eventually he looked up. "We don't want to be nursemaids either."

I said, "Find a balance."

"Aye aye, sir. I'll try." He left.

Late in the evening I sighed, flipped off the console. Farside statistics swam in my head. Cadet days in residence. Number of beds. Consumables per cadet. Instructor-student ratios. Charts they'd sent me before I'd assumed my post, and as meaningless now as before.

I stretched, turned down the lights, shut the hatch behind me. In the outer office the midshipman came to his feet. Small, narrow-boned, a serious face. "You're here all night, Middy?"

"Mr. Tenere relieves me at twelve, sir."

"Very well." I peered past him to the console. "What's that?"

He blushed. "Advanced Nav, sir. It's easier to read here than in my holovid."

Aboard ship a middy never stood watch alone, and on the bridge he wouldn't dare study anything but his instruments. But the caller was the only instrument this lad had to watch. "Very well—who are you?"

He snapped to attention. "Midshipman Tommy Tsai reporting, sir!" A glint of worry, lest I be annoyed he hadn't identified himself.

"Very well, Mr. Tsai. I'll be walking about. Call on the general circuit if you need me." I left.

As on any Lunar installation, the domes and warrens of Farside were connected by a maze of corridors. All had safety hatches that would slam shut in case of decompression. The larger compartments, such as mess hall and the physical training rooms, were in the domes above, at surface level.

My office was near the end of the north warren, connected by corridor to the VIP lock and the classroom chambers to the south. Other passageways branched to the dorm warrens. Below us, on Level 2, were our atomics, gravitrons, recycling, and the other machinery that allowed the base to function. And, of course, housing for the techs who serviced it all.

Hands clasped behind my back, I wandered through the maze of corridors to the classrooms I remembered from my youth. Naturally, they'd be empty at this hour; the cadets would be back in their dorms, enjoying what little free time they were given before Lights Out.

". . . wonder why they wouldn't give him a ship."

I stopped. Low voices, inside a hatchway, chatting amiably. "Maybe he didn't want one."

"Adam, who'd pass up a ship of his own?"

I poked my head into the classroom. A gaggle of middies. Two lounged against a bulkhead. The third was perched on a desk, legs dangling. Seeing me, they jumped to attention.

"As you were," I said quickly. "What's going on?"

One of them spoke. "Nothing, sir. Just talking."

I gestured to the empty classroom. "Why here?"

The oldest middy shrugged. "Why not, sir? It's just where we happened to stop."

My fist tightened. When I'd been a cadet, we weren't allowed to wander the base at will, unsupervised. What was the place coming to?

"Does your Serg—" I swallowed my angry reply. These were middies, not cadets, and off-duty. As aboard ship, they were free to go where they chose. "Sorry. Quite right. You're, ah, Keene?"

"Yes, sir. First Midshipman Thomas Keene, sir. I'm sorry if we disturbed—"

"No, I forgot. You see, I never served as a middy at Academy." Few cadets were chosen to stay on as midshipmen. I'd been posted to U.N.S. *Helsinki*, where—I bit off the thought.

Keene seemed uncomfortable. I wondered if he'd ever heard a Captain apologize. Unlikely. I turned to the other middies. "Mr. Tenere I remember. And you?"

"Midshipman Guthrie Smith, sir." Lean, ears that stuck out, a tentative manner.

"Oh, yes. Very well, carry on."

Adam Tenere blurted, "Is there something we can help you with, sir?"

I turned. "What?"

"I'm sorry, I didn't mean that the way it—are you looking for something, sir?" I stared. He reddened. "Pardon me, it's none of my business. I'm sorry if I—"

"That's enough, Adam." Keene's voice was civil but urgent.

"I mean—aye aye, Mr. Keene." Like any middy, he called his senior by his last name.

I raised my eyebrow, annoyed at the youngster's effrontery. "Do continue, Mr. Tenere."

"Yes, sir. I mean, aye aye. No offense, please, sir. I just thought, if there was someplace you were trying to find—I thought perhaps we could . . ." Flustered, he took a deep breath. "Please excuse me, Captain Seafort." I said nothing. He squirmed, added desperately, "It being your first day here, was all I meant. I didn't know if you remembered . . . Of course you would, though. I wasn't thinking, I meant no dis . . ."

I turned to Keene. "Is he always like this?"

The first midshipman's tone was icy. "No, sir. Only when it's important he not be." Now Tenere was in for trouble. A middy was supposed to be seen and not heard, and it was the first midshipman's job to keep his juniors in line. Once, on *Hibernia*, a lieutenant had caught the younger middies frolicking in the corridor, and it was I, the senior, who'd paid the price.

Perhaps Keene had similar thoughts. "I apologize, sir. He won't trouble you further."

Adam studied the deck, miserable. Well, a couple of extra demerits wouldn't hurt him, though he'd already earned four when he'd cannoned into me in Earthport Station. Ten uncancelled demerits meant the First Lieutenant's barrel.

"Very well." One way or another, Tenere would learn to be less clumsy, both physically and verbally. Yet, the boy had meant only to offer help. I sighed, relenting. How to divert Keene without interfering with his prerogatives?

"Actually, Mr. Keene, I was looking for someone to walk with. It's been years since I've been on Farside. Would you gentlemen care to accompany me?" It would cost me my privacy, but I could think of no better way.

"Of course, sir." There was nothing else to say. An invitation from a Captain was as a command.

"This is the simulator room, sir." Guthrie Smith.

"Ah, yes." The equipment was brand-new. There hadn't even been such an installation when I was a cadet; I remembered the compartment as just another study room. Now it was used to simulate battle with the fish, using puter re-creations from *Hibernia* and other vessels lucky enough to have encountered the aliens and survived. I moved on.

"The nav room, sir."

In this classroom I'd been introduced to Lambert and Greeley's *Elements of Astronavigation*. At the time I'd thought that with hard work I could master Nav. Now I knew better.

I asked, "What was your best subject, Mr. Keene?"

"Engineering, sir. This year I asked Mr. Vriese to tutor me on the new fastship drive."

"Is he still here?" He'd seemed ancient twelve years ago. He must have been at least fifty. I smiled at my innocence. "And you, Mr. Tenere?"

Wisely, the boy had said as little as possible during our stroll. Faced with a direct question, he had no choice but to respond.

"Nav and pilotage, sir."

I had to draw him out, to show there were no hard feelings. "Were you good at it?"

He looked down. "First in my class, sir."

"You were?" I couldn't keep the surprise from my voice.

"Yes, sir." His tone was bitter. "I'm not always incompetent, sir. Though you'd have no way of knowing that."

"That's quite enough, Mr. Ten—"

"No, Mr. Keene. He's feeling badly. We had, um, a run-in yesterday." My shoulder was still sore from it.

We left the classroom warrens. "What's down there?"

"The ladder to belowdecks, sir. The gravitrons, and engineering. Off-limits to us." Adam looked hopeful.

I saw no reason to take them below. I'd only been there once myself, on a failed mission with Midshipman Jeffrey Thorne. "And that way?"

"The service corridor, sir. It goes to mess hall." They led me down the deserted corridor, used by sailors to wheel cleaning machines and other heavy equipment to the domes.

"This way's longer, but it's faster if you're late to class," Adam Tenere confided. "No cadets allowed." I imagined an anxious midshipman sprinting to class along the service corridor to avoid the displeasure of his instructor. Running in the main corridors, on the other hand, was strictly prohibited.

"Here's the mess hall, sir. The cadets enter from the far side."

"Yes, I remember." We continued toward the barracks, passing an emergency hatch, open now, but ready to slam shut at decompression. "The barracks are to the right, I recall."

"Yes, sir." In a few moments the warren widened.

I chose a dorm at random. "Let's look in."

As the hatch slid open Keene bellowed "Attention!" Cadets leaped from their bunks to form a straight line along the aisle.

I'd thought the barracks would be unoccupied, during term break. "As you were. Carry on." I smiled. "This isn't an inspection." Keene shot me a dubious look, said nothing. I understood his confusion; a Commandant was explaining himself to mere cadets. I knew I'd appear even more ridiculous poking my head in and disappearing immediately. I strode down the rows of beds. I paused.

A duffel lay atop an empty bunk. The bed had been stripped and remade without sheets. I asked the girl in the next bunk, "Edwards?"

"Yessir."

The duffel would remain overnight. In the morning the cadets would gather round, open the duffel, go through the meager belongings. Close friends would help themselves to mementos, and the duffel would be repacked for shipment home. It was the Navy way.

I looked around. "Where's Mr. Arnweil?"

Another boy spoke up. "With Sergeant Radz, sir."

"Very well. Come along, gentlemen." We left.

Keene said, "Edwards seemed a decent joey."

I was brusque. "I didn't know him."

"Would you like to stop at Krane Barracks?"

"Why?" One barracks was like another.

"You stayed there, sir."

I raised an eyebrow. "Is there a bronze plaque on the head I used?"

"I beg your pardon?"

"Nothing." I shook my head, disgusted. Somehow I'd have to put a stop to it. "We have, let's see, sixteen barracks?"

"Twenty now," Tenere blurted.

Of course. I'd read that, somewhere. "Not all in use."

"Not until the plebes come aloft, sir."

Thirty cadets to a dorm. Housing for six hundred cadets at a time. The Training Station could take another fifty. Terrestrial Academy at Devon had barracks for another three hundred eighty. Some overcapacity was necessary; otherwise no cadet could be transferred without another cadet being shipped out. I shook my head. Logistics.

I let them tour me through the exercise dome, then down the ladder to the service level. I stopped. Enough for one day. "Thank you, gentlemen. That will be all."

"Aye aye, sir."

I hesitated. "Mr. Tenere, I'll have a word with Mr. Keene."

"Yes, sir? I mean, aye aye, sir."

"Alone," I prompted.

"Aye aye, sir!" Red-faced, he saluted and hurried away.

"Sir, I'm sorry about—"

"I was first middy, once. On *Hibernia*."

"Yes, sir." Keene waited, puzzled.

"It isn't an easy job. You might think, for example, that I'd want you to go hard on Tenere."

"He's—Of course I'd—I'll do whatever you want, sir."

"Will you? Good, then. Do as you'd have done if we'd never met this evening." I smiled pleasantly. "Sometimes, Mr. Keene, problems work themselves out on their own."

"Aye aye, sir." He smiled back quizzically.

"That's all."

I found my way back to my apartment. I was undressing when the caller buzzed. "Sorry, sir." Tolliver. "Just a reminder. Senator Boland's boy will be reporting to Devon in two days."

"What of it?"

"Don't you want to be there, just in case?"

"In case what, Edgar?" I tossed my shirt on the chair.

"His father will most likely drop him off. He's on the Naval Affairs Committee, you know." Of course I knew. If Boland hadn't talked me out of it I'd have carried through with my resignation, after *Victoria* brought me home.

"Tolliver, the Boland boy's a cadet like any other. Anyway, we're going groundside tomorrow night, after I talk over the budget with Admiralty."

"Very well, sir. Sorry if I woke you."

I growled a reply, rang off. If Tolliver thought I could be a politician, he was mistaken. I drifted to sleep.

Once again, I waited in the crowded anteroom of Admiral Duhaney's Lunapolis office. The last time I'd been there, months before, I'd been ragged from the long hostile voyage in *Victoria,* and barely recovered from my lung implant. I'd stalked out of the Admiral's office in a rage, expecting court-martial and not giving a damn. Instead, they'd chosen to reward me with Academy.

When the bored lieutenant called my name I passed through the hatch, saluted, came to attention with the same discipline I'd require of my cadets.

"Hello, Seafort." Duhaney came to me, hand extended. I took it as permission to stand easy. He beckoned to a chair. "Sorry my call missed you yesterday." Was it a reproach? It didn't seem so.

"I apologize, sir. We had an accident. A cadet died."

He pursed his lips, shook his head. Still, I knew he'd received too many reports of death to be shocked by one more. As Sergeant Radz had said, soldiers die, especially in wartime. "Why did you want to see me, Commandant?"

I couldn't bring up the issue of Lieutenant Crossburn; Dustin Edwards's death made that issue seem too trivial. I would cope. "I had some questions about the budget."

"I can't get you any more money, Seafort. Don't even ask. We're strained tight."

"No, sir, I understand that. I wasn't asking."

He stared at me suspiciously. "I've heard that before. I tell you, no special appropriations!"

Despite myself, I smiled. "Orders acknowledged and understood, sir. If I'd wanted more money I'd say so."

"Well, then?"

I fished in my pocket for a chipcase, opened it. "May I?" I slipped the chip into his holovid. "These expense columns, sir. Why do they say 'guidelines'?"

He frowned. "Didn't Kearsey go over any of this with you?"

"He gave me the budget to study. That's all."

"Don't worry about it. The number that counts is that bottom line." He stabbed at the expense totals.

"But this column, sir, that details the food expense per cadet, the uniform cost—"

He waved them away. "They don't mean anything, Seafort. How often do I have to tell you?"

I spoke coolly. "That depends, sir."

"On what?"

"On whether you want me as Commandant."

He glared at me. "Don't start that again. I have too many prima donnas as it is." I held his eye; he sighed. "Very well, what don't you understand?"

"How do I find out how much we're spending on food per cadet? I won't know until we exceed our budget."

"You have a quartermaster to keep it straight, Seafort. Let him do his job. All you need be concerned with is that you have two point six million unidollars to spend. How you allocate them is your own business."

I shook my head. "But the uniforms per cadet, training allocation per cadet—"

"You have some seven hundred sixty joeys, right? We try to break costs down per cadet, because the Senate committee likes it that way. That's the only reason the columns are there."

"But—" My head spun. "When we go to the Naval Affairs Committee, don't we have to assure them—"

"Yes, we tell them how much we intend to spend, and on what. But the Security Council knows better than to tie us to our line estimates. Spend your allocation for the good of your cadets. Don't forget to reserve for structural repairs. Look, Seafort, it all comes down to seven hundred sixty cadets. For years we've run the number through a simple formula to pull out the guidelines. You don't have to follow them. In theory, you don't even have to account for the number of cadets."

"Huh? What about Final Cull?"

"Oh, the Selection Board presents your candidates, you have no choice about that. But they only go by—" The caller buzzed; he picked it up. "Duhaney. He what? Are you sure?" He listened. "The son of a bitch! Yes, I'll be down. This afternoon. Potomac Shuttleport. Set up a meeting." He keyed the caller. "Bill, cancel this afternoon. Get me a seat on the Potomac. Bump someone if you have to."

He slammed down the caller. "We had a deal with Naval Affairs, and Senator Wyvern is jumping ship. Now he wants our promise the hull components will come from North American foundries. We've already promised them to—look, Seafort, I've got to clear my calendar and be out of here in less than an hour. Let me know if you run into a problem." He popped my chip from the holovid, handed it to me.

"But—"

"Thanks for coming. Get out of my hair, will you? If we lose the replacement fleet, we won't need your cadets."

He had a point. "Yes, sir." I paused at the hatch. "That memo I wrote about the caterwauling bomb, sir. Are you going—"

"We have a team studying it. It's more complex than you think." He opened his drawer, fished for a chipcase, thrust it in his pocket.

"Sir, it's too important to—"

"Damn it, man, you want us to take a puter-operated drone, send it somewhere and let it generate skewed N-waves, or caterwaul, as you call it. Not too close to home, because it will call every fish within hearing. But we've never sent a successful drone out before, not one with a fusion drive. Anyway, the drive is inherently inaccurate by one percent, so we won't even be quite sure where we're sending it."

He took a leather case, stuffed papers within. "Say it caterwauls until it attracts fish. How many fish is enough? How close would they come?"

I said, "It doesn't matter if a bomb doesn't get every last—"

"Let me finish, I have to catch the shuttle. At some point the bomb goes off, unless the fish destroy it first. Well, when it goes boom, how can we be sure it got all the fish? Could any surviving fish follow its trail back to us? And most important, if this caterwauling calls fish, how can we send a ship into a sector swarming with fish to find out if the bloody thing works, without risking the ship? If the fish didn't get our ship the bomb would."

He paused, waved me to the hatch. "The idea has merit, Seafort, but we need to iron out the bugs." He snatched up the caller. "Karl? Make sure Boland is told about this afternoon's meeting."

I retrieved my duffel from the anteroom, trudged along the busy corridor toward Old Lunapolis, absentmindedly returning salutes while I pondered Duhaney's comments about my budget. Running Academy wasn't quite like commanding a ship; I couldn't execute a felon, for example. But in other respects the Navy allowed me to act as autocratically as any shipboard Captain. Here are your tools: accomplish the job. Don't bother us with details.

I checked in with Naval Transport, learned the next shuttle was full. Three hours to kill, until I could connect through Earthport Station to London. I should have hitched a ride with Duhaney. Well, he'd left me ample time for a meal here in the Lunapolis warrens, where I had a better choice of restaurants and the prices were lower than on the Station.

I dined alone, unaccustomed to the solitude. Though several of my officers had gone groundside for start of term, none of them had detoured with me to Lunapolis.

After dinner I boarded the London shuttle. Most of the other passengers were civilians, a few Navy. There were also U.N.A.F. personnel, but we pointedly ignored each other. The Armed Forces were another service, and we had little in common.

To my discomfort, the Pilot unstrapped and came back into the cabin, stopping at my seat. "Captain Seafort? My name is Stanner. I'll be flying you down tonight." He offered his hand. Resignedly, I took it, muttered some polite phrase.

"It's an honor to meet you." He hesitated, turned back to the cockpit. "If there's anything we can do for you . . ."

Just take me home. "No thank you, Mr. Stanner."

"Very well, then." Again he hesitated. "The copilot's seat is empty tonight. Would you care to ride up front?"

What I wanted was to be left alone. On the other hand, I'd had one experience piloting a shuttle, a wild ride with Lieutenant Tolliver across Hope Nation's Farreach Ocean. It might be interesting to watch an expert handle the craft.

Ignoring the envy of the U.N.A.F. officers, I got to my feet. "Well, if you don't mind . . ."

"Of course not." He ushered me to the cockpit. I suspected it wasn't really me he wanted sitting alongside him, but my damned notoriety. Now he'd be able to say he'd flown with Nicholas Seafort as his copilot. I couldn't avoid that sort of thing unless I chose to become a hermit.

I strapped in. Once the cockpit hatch slid shut the Pilot gave the checklist his full attention. I wondered if my presence had anything to do with that; flying the shuttle must be second nature to him.

"Steward, confirm shuttle hatch closed, please." He wouldn't rely on the blinking light on his console. Quite right. Consoles and puters could be wrong.

"Shuttle hatch is secured, Mr. Stanner."

"Departure Control, London Shuttle Victor three four oh ready for breakaway, requesting clearance."

The speaker crackled. "Just a moment, Pilot." Several minutes passed before flight control came back on the line. "London Shuttle Victor three four oh, you're cleared for breakaway. Have a pleasant flight."

"Thank you." Stanner's hand settled over the thrusters. The shuttle's maneuvering engines, like most craft, used hydrozine as propellant.

With a deft hand the Pilot squirted first his forward thrusters, then the thrusters abaft, rocking us ever so gently until the airlock seals parted. Once we drifted free of the Station he maneuvered us to a safe distance, ignited the main engines. The hull throbbed with muted power.

I tore my eye from the receding Station to focus on Earth, looming in the starboard viewscreens. We didn't appear to be heading toward Terra, but of course we were. If the shuttle dived headfirst into the atmosphere we'd go incandescent. Instead, we'd enter at an angle, almost parallel with the planet's surface.

The Pilot flipped switches on his console, watching his display closely. As the readout counted to zero he cut the power. The engines went silent.

His work done for the moment, Stanner relaxed. "You're headed to groundside Academy, Captain?"

"Yes." It seemed too bald a statement. "My new cadets report tomorrow."

"A busy time for you, then."

"I suppose." I had no idea what was expected of me. Perhaps the sergeants knew.

He punched in numbers, erased the screen, ran more calculations. "Twenty-five minutes. If you'd like coffee we can—"

"London Shuttle, respond to Departure Control."

The pilot keyed his mike. "London Shuttle."

"This is a scramble. Repeat, a scramble." The voice was edged with tension. "Steepen your glide path for immediate entry. You'll be out of position for London; divert to New York Von Walthers, or Potomac Shuttleport."

The Pilot swallowed once, but his voice was calm. "London Shuttle commencing dive." He flipped switches, reignited our engines. He glanced to me, back to the console. "Something's up."

"Obviously." I reached for the caller, remembered that this was his craft. "Can you get Naval frequencies?"

"General comm, but not the restricted channels. Go ahead."

I keyed the caller. Voices flooded the speaker.

"—have a visual on him at four thousand kilometers. We're on him."

"Understood, *Charleston*. You and *Tripoli* are the closest."

"Tell the Admiral we have radio contact with *Tripoli*.' '

A crisp voice. "This is Admiral Le Tour, acting as ComCincLuna. I'm on the circuit, Captain Briggs. Are you absolutely sure?"

"The puter's on full magnification, sir. He's just sitting there, plain as life. A fish, just like the training holos."

My grip tightened on the console. Lord God, no.

"Just one?"

Briggs' laugh was harsh. "At the moment, sir."

Stanner said, "Stay strapped in tight, Captain. We'll get some buffeting."

I checked my belts. They couldn't go any tighter. "Just drive us home, Pilot."

"We'll probably lose radio contact for a few minutes. That's natural when we're diving into the atmosphere."

"I'm not a groundsider." My tone was sharp.

"I know, sir."

"Sorry. Nerves." Fish, in home system? Queasy, I swallowed several times.

"ComCincLuna to all ships. Execute Maneuver C. *Argentine* and *Brunswick*, hold your current positions. I'll join you with the squadron covering Earthport Station. If I'm disabled, Captain Lusanski in *Waterloo* is senior."

A whispering, outside the hull.

"*Report all sightings directly to—*" Static. "*Confirm your positions every five minutes.*"

"Aye aye, si—" Static. A muted roar, transmitted through the hull.

"Attention all ships, *Tripoli* reports a second sighting, coordi—" The shuttle bucked. Stanner kept our nose down, used the jets to position us.

"Until we have confi—" The speaker cut out.

Stanner's voice was taut. "We've lost them for a while. Hang on."

"Can we make it?"

His jaws tightened. "Oh, we'll make it, one way or the other. I forgot to buy insurance." He took quick breaths. "Another ten thousand feet and I'll spread the wings. That'll help some."

"Whatever you say." My one attempt at the controls of a shuttle had been suborbital.

"Potomac Shuttleport, do you read London Shuttle Victor three four oh?" No answer. He shook his head.

"Are they hit?" My voice was unsteady.

"Hit? It's the static buildup. We'll have to wait to get through."

I felt a complete idiot. "Yes. Of course."

"Try every minute or so. My attention's on the readouts."

"Right." It would give me something to do.

To my infinite relief they answered my fourth call. "London Shuttle, this is Potomac Shuttleport, we read you."

Stanner keyed his caller. "We've had a scramble, Potomac. I will be approaching from the Southwest at forty thousand feet. Can you take us?"

I held my breath, but the answer was nonchalant. "No problem, London Shuttle. Earthport alerted us an hour ago. All outgoing traffic has been grounded. Come on in."

Had it been that long? I gripped the dash while Stanner took his approach coordinates, then cursed under my breath. If we could hear Approach Control, we could hear Admiralty as well. I switched from speaker to earphones, keyed the caller.

"—no, sir. I'm sure. So's the puter. No encroachments except *Tripoli*."

"Where the hell did he go, *Charleston*?"

A pause from *Charleston*. "I couldn't say, sir."

"Right. Um, sorry."

Another pause. "ComcincLuna to all ships. Current status: one sighting confirmed, coordinates thirty-four, one eighty-seven, two hundred. The alien apparently Fused to safety. Current whereabouts unknown. Second sighting is unconfirmed, may be an anomaly."

I snorted. The "anomaly" was probably an overexcited young officer, now shriveling under his Captain's extreme disfavor.

A scream of protesting air, as Stanner eased the wings back into flight mode. The buffeting slackened. He asked, "What's it all mean, Captain?"

I waved him silent, strained to hear voices through the static. Every ship of the squadron had gone to Battle Stations, waiting for further sightings. None came. At last I sighed, keyed off the caller.

Stanner began a long, slow swing to port. He said nothing.

Coloring, I realized I'd snubbed the man in his own cockpit. "Sorry, Mr. Stanner, I was listening. It seems there was just the one fish; the second was a false sighting."

"Are they planning an attack? This is the first time they've shown up in Home System."

The second. The one I'd speared with *Challenger* was the first. "Too early to tell. It could be a fluke, or some kind of scout. In Hope Nation . . ."

"Yes?"

At Hope Nation the fleet had stood by for days, sometimes weeks, between sightings. "There's no way to tell."

For a moment Stanner's attention was on the shuttle's long turn. Then, "Captain, I have a wife and kids. Are they safer in Lunapolis or at home?"

"I haven't the faintest idea." After a moment I tried to make amends for my tone. "No one knows, Pilot. On the one hand, Lunapolis is a smaller target. But Terra has an atmosphere, and is less fragile. If I had a choice, that's where I'd want my family."

He muttered, "Christ protect us."

"Amen."

Half an hour later we pulled up to the terminal. The engines sank into a whine. I unbuckled, made as if to stand, hesitated. I offered my hand. "Godspeed, Mr. Stanner."

"And you, sir."

"Thank you." I ducked through the hatchway into the cabin.

He called after me, "We need you on a ship." I pretended not to hear.

The steward had my duffel ready. He'd held back other passengers so I could go first. Well meant, I suppose, but I'd have preferred him to ignore me entirely.

I strode along the moveway, hoping I'd find the right counter. "Captain Seafort! Wait, sir!" I turned, saw a florid lieutenant running after me. I waited. "Lieutenant Greaves, sir. Mr. Duhaney is in the Naval Liaison Office and sent me to get you."

"The what? And how did he know I'm here?"

"Naval Liaison Office, sir. It's really just a conference room reserved for Naval officers. Lunapolis Base reached him there while he was in a meeting. When he heard the London shuttle diverted, he knew you'd be on it."

"Very well." I slung my duffel over my shoulder, followed him through the corridors.

He held open the door. "Go right in, sir."

Admiral Duhaney looked over his shoulder, straightened, rubbed his back. "Ah, there you are, Seafort." With him was Senator Boland and another man I didn't know. They hovered over a caller. "Have you met Senator Wyvern?" We shook hands and sat.

"What's the latest, sir?"

"Nothing since the son of a bitch Fused. We'll hold Battle Stations for a few hours, then stand down unless he shows again."

I nodded. There was little else we could do.

Richard Boland let out his breath in a long sigh. "It's one thing hearing about these adventures on the holos, Seafort. It's another to have a fish overhead."

"I know."

He leaned forward in his chair. "What do you think they're up to?"

"Me? How should I know?" Perhaps it was the adrenaline surge. I felt a bit shaky.

"You've been there, and we haven't."

Duhaney and Wyvern watched me intently.

"I've no idea." I stood to pace. "My guess is you won't see any more of them for a while."

"Why not?"

"Just a hunch. In Hope Nation we never could anticipate their patterns. And it was years between the loss of *Telstar* and their next attack." But once that attack started, it nearly obliterated Hope Nation and our defensive fleet.

Senator Wyvern cleared his throat, as if before a speech on the General Assembly floor. "This makes it all the more important we settle where the new hulls originate."

Boland said sharply, "Not now, Brett."

I wasn't interested in politics. "Can you get them to speed up the caterwauling bomb, Admiral?" I sat.

"This gives me an excuse to knock some heads together." Duhaney paused. "On the other hand . . . Seafort, don't make any public comments on this affair, understand?"

My annoyance showed. "I've never given interviews, sir." Didn't he know even that?

"Say nothing. That's an order." He hesitated. "I might as well tell you; we've already agreed. Unless the fish show up before tomorrow, we're treating this as a false sighting."

"You're what?" I came to my feet.

"As far as the public is concerned, that is. Of course, we'll increase our vigilance."

"But why?"

Senator Boland's voice was soothing. "No point in causing alarm, Captain. Or panic."

"You'll lie about an enemy in home waters?"

"Think, Seafort. What good would the truth accomplish?"

"What good—" He had a point. As long as our Home Fleet maintained its watch, publicizing dangers that were unavoidable might cause panic. Worse, it might evoke demands that our Navy stop serving the colonies, so as not to attract the fish. "It's not my decision to make, Senator." And thank Lord God of it.

Duhaney cut in, "Let him be, Richard. He's as fatigued as we are. Seafort, I'll arrange a suborbital to London for you. One flight won't disrupt our ground defense."

"I can wai—very well, whatever you wish." Let the Academy gates swing shut behind me, shield me from politicians and armchair Admirals.

Boland got to his feet. "Mr. Duhaney, if you'll ring Naval Transport, I'll walk Mr. Seafort to Departures." Smoothly done. I barely felt the dismissal. Moments later I was striding with Boland through corridors packed with frustrated travelers waiting out their delays.

"We're doing the best we can, Seafort. I'll use the sighting as a club to get Brett back in line, and we'll have your new ships built. Alarming the public would only interfere with that."

I grunted. For all I knew, he was right. U.N.S. *Wellington* was almost ready for launch, and we needed many more like her.

The Senator's tone was casual. "I'm bringing Robert to Devon tomorrow."

"Robert?"

He frowned. "My son."

"Oh, yes. Pardon me. I'm sure he'll do well."

"I'm most interested in seeing that he does. Any way I can possibly help, please let me know." I waited for more, but he left it at that.

It was late evening before a helicab finally deposited me on the Academy tarmac. The guard saluted, waved me through without showing my ID. I thought to make an issue of it, decided not to. My face was too well known to question, even without my scar. I called Admiralty in

Lunapolis, checked with a staff lieutenant I knew. All was quiet in the Home Fleet.

The compound was a madhouse, callers ringing off the pad. Arrival day, as if by magic, caused parents in each of the subsequent groups to verify dates, reconfirm what their cadets were allowed to bring along, and query each of the admonitions spelled out in the acceptance letter and pamphlet.

Lieutenant Paulson and the sergeants had been through it before, and weren't fazed. Two middies waited in my outer office to run any needed errands, and Tolliver was out on the grounds, keeping an eye. Still, I sat in my office, expecting at least an occasional call to slip past their vigilance. After a time I conceded none might come.

Restless, I paced my way past coffee tables and chairs, made a note to have the furniture thinned as I had in my Farside office.

It was past lunchtime before I'd had enough. The only call I'd fielded had been from Quartermaster Serenco, asking approval for a special order of milk to replace some that had spoiled. I ran my hands through my hair, adjusted my tie, and closed the door behind me. "I'll be on the grounds."

"Yes, sir."

As on board ship, I didn't carry a caller. On a vessel I could be reached through any of the corridor speakers; here I could not. But on ship I might be needed instantly for an emergency, and that was not the case at Academy. In any event, I'd be damned if I'd have a caller squawking under my jacket, or be seen with a mini plugged in my ear. I might as well be a teener with a stereochip.

I headed toward the barracks, hesitated, reversed my course, and strode the trimmed pathway back to Officers' Quarters and beyond to the shaded expanse of front lawn.

The recruits were instructed to arrive between ten and two. Parents drove their nervous offspring to the curved drive in front of the imposing iron gates, or walked across the commons from the heliport or the train station several blocks away.

Inside the gates, middies on special duty corraled the cadets-to-be, and every few minutes took a group of them to the Admin Building, where their Naval careers would commence. Once inside the Academy compound, cadets would be allowed no contact with their families, other than by letter, until their first furlough far in the future.

From a safe distance I watched the tearful good-byes. One recruit spotted me among the trees and pointed excitedly. Quickly I turned away and struck out for the mess hall, between barracks and classrooms.

Though formal lunch was over, I wandered into the galley. I ignored the startled cook's mates, peered into the coolers. Surely there must be something.

"Would you like a sandwich, sir?"

I grunted. "Whatever's easiest."

"Why don't you sit down in the hall? The mess steward will bring it out."

"Very well." I chose the closest cadet table, cupped my head in my hands, and brooded.

The start of a year. Some of my charges were halfway through training, others about to begin. How could I help the new recruits understand what they'd embarked on? An officer did not work for the Navy, he *was* the Navy. Now, with the fish devastating our colonies, we needed responsible officers more than ever.

My hand caressed the table's rough plank. The joeys who'd be eating their next meal here were yet children. How could they be expected—what? Initials? I rubbed at the faded marks, noticed others. I wondered which sergeant wasn't doing his job. When I'd been a cadet . . . Could we identify the malefactors by the letters? No, the carvers had wisely left but one initial each.

"Your lunch, sir."

I jumped at the unexpected voice. "Very well." The steward set down the tray. They'd gone to the trouble to heat a full meal: meat, vegetables, mashed potato. A heaping salad, steaming coffee. I sighed. I'd have made do with anything.

The door flew open and a middy rushed in. He hurried to my table and came smartly to attention.

"Midshipman Anton Thayer reporting, sir." His carrot-red hair was neatly brushed, his uniform in order. "Lieutenant Sleak's compliments, and Senator Boland is asking for you at the gate."

"Tell him—No, wait." I got up, crossed to the caller on the wall by the doorway, keyed my office. "Seafort."

"Sleak here, sir. Shall I have the Senator escorted to your office?"

"What does he want?"

"He's brought his son."

"Yes, send him—" I hesitated. An important politician shouldn't be alienated; what did tradition matter when a member of the Naval Affairs Committee was—No. "Keep him at the gate. I'll be along."

"Are you sur—aye aye, sir."

I rung off. Anton waited for dismissal. I growled, "Have you no work to do?"

"Yes, sir." He ran off.

I hurried to the door, slowed my pace. The Commandant was no Senator's lackey to come scurrying at his call. Still, as I skirted the edge of the parade ground, my stride lengthened. Perhaps it would have been better to offer him the hospitality of my office.

I crossed the front lawn to the gate. A middy, shepherding an awkward group of recruits, saluted as he passed. At the curb two cars were parked. Alongside one of them a slim youth was enduring an older woman's embrace. Senator Boland waited patiently near the guardhouse.

I stepped outside the gate, tugged at my jacket. "Good to see you again, Senator."

"And you, Commandant. May I present my son Robert? Robert, Commandant Seafort." The lanky fourteen-year-old smiled shyly, unsure whether to offer his hand.

I clasped my hands behind my back as casually as possible, nodded politely. "I'm sure he'll make a good cadet, Mr. Boland."

The byplay hadn't gone unnoticed; something in the Senator's eyes changed. Still, he said affably, "I was hoping to see Robert's barracks."

"I wasn't told which one he'll be assigned. Sorry." The information could be read from the guardhouse console, a few steps away. "I'll have someone phone your office this afternoon." Surely that wasn't too great a concession to his rank.

"I won't be able to place the barracks by name alone."

I smiled. "They're all alike."

"Yes. Well . . ." His eyes locked on mine. "My wife and I are most anxious that Robert justify the honor of his admission."

"That's commendable." I tired of the sparring, turned to the boy. "When you're done with your good-byes, one of the middies will take you in."

"Thank you." Robert's tone betrayed his uncertainty.

"Is there anything else, Senator?"

"Admiral Duhaney mentioned your questions about the budget. I'd be happy to go over them with you."

"I suppose I—um, well, perhaps—" I broke off, knowing I sounded a dolt. I took a deep breath, spoke more firmly. "Robert, I'll speak with your father alone for a moment."

"Yes, sir." He retreated toward the car.

My heart pounded. "Senator, I know what you want. It isn't possible. The Naval Affairs Committee's visit is months away. You're here privately, and parents aren't allowed to enter Academy. I won't make an exception. We'll take care of your son, as we do them all."

Senator Boland's eyes were pained. "Including the boy whose helmet was smashed a few days ago? Oh, yes, I know about that." He paused. "Can you imagine how dear Robbie is to me? I'm proud, but frightened at the same time."

"Yes, I think I can understand that."

"He's leaving home, leaving my custody for yours. See how eager he looks? Inside he must be terrified." His voice turned bitter. "Of course, you wouldn't know about that."

My eyes turned back to his. "You can't possibly . . ." My voice faded away. He couldn't know. I'd never spoken of it.

I sat hugging myself, oblivious of passing fields as the train labored through the rolling English countryside. In the seat across, Father read from his Bible.

Four days earlier, the jerries had brought me home from the stadium in a police wagon, a blanket thrown across my shoulders for the shock, an untouched cocoa cooling on the bench at my side. Father had come outdoors at the light flashing in the night. We had no caller; he hadn't known.

When Father summoned me from the back of the wagon I dutifully followed him into the house. Mechanically I sat at the kitchen table, staring at the faded wall until the teapot screamed its readiness.

"Drink."

"I can't."

"Of course you can." He rested his hands on the back of my chair, turned back to the stove, made sure the burner was off. "Then you'll go to bed."

I sat motionless. They hadn't let me follow Jason to the mortuary. I'd given them his mother's name; Jason had never known his host father. His tired-eyed mother would be at the mortuary, confronting the ghastly remains of her son. Would my own host mother grieve me, if she were told of my death? She'd never known me, nor I her. Still, in some sense at least, I had two parents. Clone offspring had not even that.

"Leave your shirt out to be cleaned."

I looked down, saw the blood on my sleeve. "Damn my shirt."

He raised his hand to strike me, lowered it. "Not tonight. I understand." He sat across from me. "Though I don't approve." He searched my face. "There are times His will is hard to fathom."

Damn His will, I thought to say, but knew better; there were limits to Father's tolerance. I hunched over, resolved not to speak, but in a moment sobs broke through my determination.

After a time Father's gnarled hand slid across the table, gripped my wrist. He waited. When still I didn't respond, he shook my arm insistently until I looked up. "Your friend didn't live in His ways. You know I didn't esteem him."

"Aye." I tried to free my hand.

"He wanted to lead you into . . . vile practices. I hope you resisted. If not, your conscience will suffer." I twisted away but Father's grip was like iron. "Yet he was your friend, and I respect your grief. He was young enough to have changed his ways, had Lord God given him time."

I looked up. "That's why you tolerated him? Because he might have changed?"

"No, Nicholas. Because he was your friend." He released my arm. "I will pray for him, now and after. Perhaps you will join me."

I said in a small voice, "Yes, please."

"You'll go to the funeral?"

I recoiled. "The what?" They couldn't put Jason into the stony ground. That would be too cruel. I tried to swallow; my throat was full of ache. Father, hold me. Embrace me, tell me I'll want to live again.

"I imagine they'll bury him before you go."

I shivered. "Go? Where would I go?"

Father stood, poured himself more tea. Mine sat cooling, untouched. "Nicholas, have you forgotten Academy?"

"I don't want—there's no reason to go."

"There's no reason to stay."

I looked up, startled.

"It was your dream. Jason's death is no reason to abandon it."

I cried, "How could I leave him?" If there was a grave, it would need tending. Flowers. Weeding.

"He's left you already, Nicholas. The flesh is nothing."

The funeral was two days later.

Dressed in my ill-fitting suit, I stood between Father and Jason's dazed mother, torn between calm and fits of grief. I even bent to scoop a spadeful of dirt on the inexpensive alumalloy coffin. His mother smiled at me, squeezed my hand. I was grateful she'd allowed me to give him the balsa model of *Trafalgar* he'd admired, to take into the dark.

When it was done we'd gone back to our silent, dreary home,

where I sipped steaming tea while Father opened the Book. We read from the Psalms, and in Proverbs. Perhaps because I wasn't comforted, he turned to Luke 18. I whispered with him the memorized words. *"Suffer little children to come unto me, and forbid them not: for of such is the kingdom of God."*

Two days later I'd closed my bag, followed Father to the cab, climbed onto the train.

I sat listlessly, feet kicking under the bench, my scrubbed ears protruding from my close new haircut.

Academy. The sum of all my dreams.

When finally the train had stopped I clutched my bag, stepped down into the depot, waited while Father asked directions of the agent at the window.

"It's near enough to walk. No need to waste coin on a bus."

"Aye." I followed Father out of the station. He paused, took his bearings, struck off down the road. I clutched my bag, heavy with my uneaten lunch, the large Bible, the printed books I'd thrust in at the last moment. I gaped at the unfamiliar shops.

We walked in silence. Occasionally Father's hand touched my shoulder to guide me. At a busy corner I shifted the duffel to my right hand so I could clasp his with my left, but the light changed and he strode on. We crossed the slope of the commons. I shifted the duffel to my left, reached for his hand, but Father moved to my left side.

Is this good-bye, then? What will I be when next we meet? Father, what advice do you have, what comfort?

Do you love me?

You left your cherished Cardiff to bring me to this place; I know that is proof enough.

I want to tell you I'll make you proud. I'll try hard, Father, truly I will.

The great iron gate loomed. I shifted the duffel again, reached for Father's hand. It was thrust firmly in his jacket.

We approached the gates, where the impassive sentries stood stiffly at their guardhouse. I turned to Father, my throat tight. He pointed to the guardhouse, put his hands on my shoulders and turned me to the waiting gates. Gently but firmly, he propelled me toward them. In a daze I passed through the gates, clutching my duffel.

After a few unwilling steps I turned. Father strode toward the station. Willing him to glance my way, I waved to his back. He didn't pause, didn't once look over his shoulder before he disappeared from view. An iron ring closed itself around my neck.

I blinked back the sting, and walked alone into Academy.

Senator Boland gripped my arm. "Are you all right, Mr. Seafort? You've gone pale."

I shook off his hand. "I'm quite well." After a moment I added, "Thank you."

I beckoned to his son. "Robert, once we're within the gates I won't speak to you, or take special notice of you. You understand?" He nodded. "When you've said good-bye to your father, come inside. Remember he loves you, or he wouldn't be here." I cleared my throat. "You have nothing to fear." I nodded to the Senator, strode quickly into the compound.

6

Tolliver knocked on my door, stuck in his head. "They're ready for the oath, sir."

"Very well." I stood, switched off my holo. "Care to come along?"

"I wouldn't miss it for the world." His eyes danced despite my disapproving frown. As if he hadn't already gone too far he added, "I have the words on a card, sir, if you'd care to read them."

"Tolliver!"

"I gather you wouldn't." He fell into step beside me. As we strode down the steps he asked, "Remember your own oath, sir?"

I stopped. "As if it were this morning." Something in my tone dampened his smile. "And you?"

"I could show you the spot I was standing." Somber now, we walked in silence to the Admin building. I climbed the steps, turned to the meeting hall.

"*Attention!*" The sergeant nearest the door stiffened as he barked the command. The other drill sergeants did likewise, along with Lieutenant Sleak and the middies. Several of the recruits made a halfhearted attempt to comply, which I ignored.

"As you were." I marched to the front of the hall, wondering what to say. "Sergeant Radz, line them up in two rows."

"Aye aye, sir! You, two steps forward! You, next to him. Get in line. Not so close!" In a moment, forty-seven boys and thirteen girls were in two ragged lines, arms at their sides.

My words rang out. "I am Nicholas Ewing Seafort, Captain, U.N.N.S., and Commandant of the United Nations Naval Academy. The oath you are about to give is no mere promise, no formality. It is a commitment given freely to Lord God Himself, binding you to the U.N. Navy for five years, as my wards until such time as I may see fit to graduate you. The United Nations Naval Service is the finest military force ever to be assembled at any time, anywhere.

"Those of you who wish to take the oath of enlistment, raise your right hands." All complied at once. I cleared my throat. "I—your name—"

A murmur of voices.

"Louder, please. This is not a thing you do in shame. I do swear upon my immortal soul . . ."

"*Do swear upon my immortal soul* . . ." The voices strengthened.

"To serve and protect the Charter of the General Assembly of the United Nations . . ."

"*To serve and protect the Charter of the* . . ." One boy was trembling, perhaps in fear. Another lad's eyes glistened.

"To give loyalty and obedience for the term of my enlistment to the Naval Service of the United Nations . . ."

"*To give loyalty and obedience for the term of my enlistment to the Naval Service of the United Nations* . . ." Their voices, firmer now, echoed mine.

"And to obey all its lawful orders and regulations, so help me Lord God Almighty."

"*And to obey all its lawful orders and regulations, so help me Lord God Almighty.*"

A moment of silence. "You are now cadets in the United Nations Naval Service." I came to attention, snapped a parade ground salute, spun on my heel and marched out.

Halfway to the office Tolliver caught up with me. "Jesus, son of God."

"Um?" The blood coursed through my veins; my stride was swift.

"Nothing I ever heard . . ." He swallowed. "I've never heard the like."

"Don't mock me."

A moment's hesitation, then his voice came quieter. "I didn't, sir."

"Hmpff. Come along, we have business to discuss."

In the privacy of my office I pulled off my coat, tossed it over a coffee table. I put a chip in the holovid, spun it so we could both see. "Our budget."

"Yes, sir."

I indicated the expense columns. "First, keep an eye on expenses, make sure we're staying within the guidelines."

"Aye aye, sir. But doesn't the quartermaster—"

"You do it. Second, I want you to spot-check that we actually receive items we're paying for."

He looked at me with surprise, grinned abruptly. "A sort of inspector-general, as it were?"

"That's not funny, Edgar." On Hope Nation I'd been appointed inspector-general, an escapade that ended with my relieving the commander of the Venturas Base, to my Admiral's spectacular wrath.

"No, sir, of course not."

I gritted my teeth, determined not to be bated. "Third, examine last year's accounts. Skip the items for which we indent, that are delivered from Naval stores. Look to all cash purchases. Verify what you can, and report any anomalies."

He watched me closely. "You suspect something?"

"Admiral Duhaney said we have sole discretion as to how our funds are spent. Our accounting system is bizarre. It's come about because of the Navy's cherished independence, but whoever dreamed up—" I bit off the rest, realizing I'd been about to criticize my superiors in front of a subordinate. "Just check what you can."

"Lieutenant Sleak is systems officer, and he's also my senior. He won't like my stepping on his toes."

"Try not to be obvious. If he objects, refer him to me."

"Aye aye, sir." Tolliver frowned, perusing the figures. "Does it matter whether we exceed the guidelines for each column, as long as—"

"The Admiral said . . ." I tried to recall his words. "He was anxious to catch a shuttle. We don't have to follow the spending guidelines. And something else: theoretically we don't have to account for the number of cadets. I had no idea what he meant, and I didn't get a chance to ask. Follow up on it. Look at the regs, ask someone in Accounting."

"Aye aye, sir. Anything else?"

"Not at the moment. Dismissed."

By now the plebes would be lined up in front of the supply lockers, to be handed armfuls of gear in the age-old ritual of inductees everywhere. I leaned back, clasped my arms behind my head, rocked in the comfortable leather chair. First they'd be given gray slacks, then white shirts, then their gray jackets. Shoes and underwear on top of the pile.

They would split into separate groups for each barracks, line up in single file, awkwardly carrying their loads.

Surprisingly few officers were to be found in the groundside compound. Plebes were taken in hand by their drill sergeants, whom they would learn to obey without reservation. Officers, whom even the sergeants stiffened to salute, would be exalted beyond all understanding.

Or so it had seemed at thirteen.

"Fall in! Did I say to face left? If you dropped it, pick it up, you twit!"

He was six feet, two inches. He was burly; his voice had the menace of a wounded tiger. He was Marine Sergeant Darwin P. Swopes.

He was God.

We marched in a ragged line to Valdez Hall, a one-level alumalloy building clustered among many similar structures. Windows punctuated its clean white siding; three steps led to a wide doorway. I clutched my bundle of clothing in one arm, my bag from home in the other.

"Single file. The first fifteen of you, stand at the foot of the beds to the right." He waited. "The rest of you, to the left."

I stood in front of my new bed, exchanging glances with the tousled boy to my right. His grin vanished as the sergeant entered the room.

"Turn around, dump your gear on the foot of your bed, and turn back. Stand with your hands at your sides." He waited for us to comply.

"You already heard my name, but some of you will be too dimwitted to remember. I am Sergeant Swopes. I will tell you how to address me. It is 'Sergeant Swopes,' or 'Sarge.' "

"As you know, a sergeant is not normally called 'sir.' However, you are—" he spat the word—"children, not officers or troops. Therefore you will call me 'sir,' as in 'Yes, sir' or 'Aye aye, sir.' In fact, you will call anything that moves 'sir' unless it is wearing gray like yourselves, or unless it is female, in which case you call it 'ma'am.' Do I make myself clear?"

There was a ragged chorus of "Yes, sir." I began to sweat in my heavy flannel shirt.

"The correct response is 'Aye aye, sir.' If you're asked a question, the answer might be 'Yes, sir.' When you're given an instruction, the answer is 'Aye aye, sir.' "

Across the aisle a hand wavered. Sergeant Swopes glared. "Well?"

A tall, gawky boy whose ears stuck out at angles. "You asked if you made yourself clear. That was a question, wasn't it? So shouldn't we say 'Yes, sir'?"

Sarge smiled. He sauntered to the ungainly boy. "Name?"

"Von Halstein. Erich Von Halstein."

"Erich Von Halstein, run around the outside of the barracks seven times. I want you back in two minutes. Move!"

The boy gulped, "Yes, sir!" He scrambled to the door.

Sarge roared, "Come back here!" The cadet skidded to a stop, ran back. "Was that a question or an order, boy?"

"Uh, an order, sir."

" 'Sarge' will do. As you so wisely pointed out, you respond to an order with . . . ?"

"Aye aye, sir!"

"Good. Since you already knew, three demerits for disobedience. You'll work off each demerit by two hours of calisthenics. Meanwhile, around the barracks! Get moving!"

"Yes—aye aye, sir!" He ran out the door.

As the door swung closed Sarge muttered, "I *hate* sea lawyers." He turned to the rest of us. "Any more questions?"

After the perspiring and frantic Von Halstein had returned—and received another demerit for tardiness—Sarge had us move the items we'd brought from home to our pillows, leaving the gear the Navy had issued us at the foot of the bed. "You will now, each of you, strip off everything you are wearing, put it on your pillow, and head for the showers. Towels are on a rack in the head."

I blanched. Everything, in public? Amid girls? Impossible; I couldn't do it.

"After you shower I will choose two cadets at random for close physical inspection. Lord God help you if I'm not satisfied with your cleanliness. Move!"

I hesitated just long enough for Sarge's eye to stray in my direction. Mortified, I began to strip. The room was absolutely silent except for the scrape of shoes and the rustle of cloth.

Covering myself as best I could, I stumbled to the shower room with the rest of my squad. Most of the boys were too embarrassed to steal looks at the girls among us. I scrubbed with diligence, praying fervently that Sarge not choose me for inspection.

By the time we returned to our bunks, towels tied securely around us, Sergeant was almost done with our gear. A few items remained on my pillow: my books, my chips, the paper. The clothing I'd worn was on the floor, along with my bag.

"You will dress in your cadet clothing. Then you will pack the bags you brought from home with everything I put on the floor. Those items go into storage. Anything left on your pillow you will put in your duffel, which you will stow under your bed. Return the towels to the head, and when you're done, fall in outside and I'll take you for haircuts. Oh, yes. You . . . and you. Come here."

He hadn't chosen me. I was dizzy with relief.

Numbed and docile with shock, we followed Sarge from barber to mess hall, and back to barracks. We spent the entire evening stripping and remaking our bunks, until every bed was made to his satisfaction.

"Lights Out will be in half an hour. You will be in your shorts, ready for bed. Anyone wanting to use the head must do so before then." I closed my eyes, sick with dread. The toilets were set in a row opposite the sinks, with no fronts to the stalls. I knew I'd be unable to relieve myself, perhaps for days. "I'll be back just before Lights Out."

When Sarge returned, boys and girls were talking quietly across their beds. I sat alone, yearning for solitude, for my creaking bed in Father's familiar home.

Sarge's voice was surprisingly gentle as he turned the lights down. "You, sit on that bed. You too. I want both of you over there." In moments he had us sitting three to a bed, apparently at random. I sat stiffly, trying not to rub shoulders with the shy girl whose arms were crossed over her short white T-shirt.

"Some of you joeys were from North America. A few were from Germany, two from Lunapolis. From across the globe, and beyond. That's where you *were* from." He slowly walked the aisle. "But that's over and done. Now you're from Valdez. This is your home, and these are your mates."

He stopped in front of our bed. "Seafort, touch her face. Both hands, she won't bite. Sanders, put your hand on his shoulder. I want all of you touching each other." Embarrassed beyond words, I raised tentative fingers to Cadet Sanders's face, while the third boy's clammy hand rested on my knee.

Sarge's voice was hushed. "You are now members of the finest military force known to man. These are your brothers, your comrades. You need not be embarrassed at their touch, at their view of your bodies. Their accomplishments are your own. Your honor is theirs, and their honor yours. If you lie, you shame them. If you betray them, you betray yourself, your Navy, and Lord God.

"Years from now, when you sail the void between the stars, you will know that every officer in the U.N.N.S. shares your bond. For now, strive to be the best you can, for your mates' sake. From time to time you will fail, and you will be punished. Eventually, you will succeed.

"This morning, you were strangers. Now you are bunkmates, embarked on a mission to prove yourselves worthy of the Navy and of each other. Return to your beds."

I crept back to my bunk. "Good night." He strode to the door, left.

Within the barracks, all was still.

Our cadets settled in to the whirlwind of their new lives. Five days later, I gave the oath to our second group, and, from a distance, watched the rituals repeat themselves.

During the week Senator Boland called three times to inquire about his son Robert; I managed to duck all his calls. The desk sergeant offered him the same rote reassurances that any other parent would receive.

Furlough ended for the second-year cadets; soon every barracks space would be taken, until we began shipping youngsters back to Farside. I debated going there myself, but didn't. Here in Devon, I could be in New York within hours, should Annie call.

Aloft, the Home Fleet patrolled in vain. No fish were sighted anywhere.

Days passed; our third and fourth groups of cadets arrived and we processed them as we had the others. Increasingly restless, I stalked the Academy compound while exasperated sergeants taught their cadets the rudiments of calisthenics, military posture, obedience. I marveled at their patience.

One evening I strolled through the barracks area, avoiding dorms I knew to be occupied. My drill sergeants had enough on their shoulders without surprise inspections by the Commandant. Musing, I stopped in front of an empty building.

Our next to last group of recruits would arrive in two days. Within a week our roster would be complete. Which among the anxious youths we took into our company would become another Hugo Von Walthers, which a dismal failure? If only we knew. It all began here, in aging barracks like the one I faced. Idly, I stepped through the door, switched on the light.

Thirty bare mattresses, thirty empty bunks. I wandered past the steel bed frames, ran my fingers over the dusty windows. In days this dorm would be throbbing with activity and anticipation, with fears and suffering as boys groped to become men.

"Can I help—oh, pardon me, sir."

I turned; Sergeant Olvira flipped an easy salute, came to attention.

"As you were." Embarrassed, I thrust my hand in my pocket. "I was just—wandering."

He nodded, as if encountering the Commandant in a deserted barracks were a common occurrence. "Yes, sir."

"And what are you doing here, Sarge?" It wasn't much, but I had to say something.

"Valdez will be my barracks, sir. I heard the door open." Sergeants were housed in apartments adjacent to their barracks, sharing a wall. They had privacy, but were on hand should need arise. Though it was questionable how much privacy they enjoyed, if Sergeant Olvira could hear my quiet step.

"Sorry, Sarge. I didn't mean to intrude."

"No problem, sir. I was looking over my paperwork, before the joeys get here." He hesitated. "I have fresh coffee, if you'd like."

"No, thanks." My tone was cool. Bad enough I'd spent an hour with him in the staff lounge. It wasn't appropriate for a commander to socialize with subordinates, and worse, some would see it as favoritism.

"Sorry to have disturbed you, sir. I'll leave you be." He waited for dismissal; I nodded. Alone, I sat on a bed, tried to quell my annoyance. He had to have noticed my abruptness. What had been his sin: to offer me a cup of coffee?

I stood, wandered to the end of the room. Whatever enjoyment I might have had in my visit was gone. I snapped off the light, left the building. I started back to Officers' Quarters, but my pace slowed. It was only coffee. I'd been too brusque. I returned to the barracks, found the outside entrance to his apartment.

"May I take you up on the drink?"

Sergeant Olvira concealed any surprise at my abrupt appearance. "Of course, sir. Come in." He stood aside.

I sat at his table, waited while he fetched sugar, cream. He poured my cup, warmed his own and sat. "It'll be good to get back to work again."

I smiled politely. "You didn't fancy your leave?"

"I'm not much for time off. I only took a week."

"In a couple of days you'll have your hands full." I sipped at the steaming brew.

He pushed aside the pile of folders to hunch forward, elbows on the table. One file slid down; I grabbed at it. The cover flipped open to a half-page photo of an earnest youngster. I closed the folder, tossed it back on the stack. "What are you working at?"

"Putting names to faces. A head start really helps. And I like to know about the joeys when I see them."

I hadn't known sergeants did that. I'd never known much about how they worked. "Find anything interesting?"

"No, not really." he sighed. "This one, for example. French. Theroux. Fourteen, mother a Dosman in Paris. Father deceased. In his admissions essay he said he'd dreamed of joining in the Navy ever since he saw *Celestina Voyage*. Awful bilge, that holo, but I can see it inspiring a young joe. Maybe it will never help me to know that. Perhaps it may come in handy."

"Theroux."

"Jacques Theroux. He's just one of—"

"Let me see the folder."

"Aye aye, sir." Social visit or no, he immediately obeyed an order.

The boy looked solemnly past me to the holocamera and beyond. But for Tolliver's intervention, he'd be languishing over a rejection letter rather than rechecking his traveling bag, counting anxious hours. Which youth had been left off the list, so Theroux could attend Academy? I hadn't even bothered to ask. I snapped shut the file.

"Is something wrong, sir?"

I shook myself back to reality. "No, nothing." I made small talk until I was free to escape into the night.

I paused at the mess hall door, tugged at my jacket. "All right, I'm ready." Tolliver held open the door.

"Attention!" The bellow rang through the room. Two hundred forty cadets stood instantly, came to attention. Most of them got it right. Hair neatly brushed, ties straight, trousers creased; their sergeants wouldn't have permitted otherwise. I strode past their benches to the circular table at the front of the hall. My officers saluted as I approached.

I raised my voice. "As you were." More quietly, to my own table, "Be seated, gentlemen." Lieutenant Sleak, Edgar Tolliver, Sergeant Obutu, and several instructors without barracks took their seats. Until now, I'd had little contact with them. Perhaps I should drop in on the classrooms from time to time, though that wouldn't make the instructors' tasks any easier.

"That tryout of the new gunnery simulator was great," Sergeant Olvira remarked, helping himself to soup.

Sleak passed the bowl along. "How's it look, Gunnie?"

Olvira grinned. "You should have seen Ramon's face when he came out. He can't wait 'til it gets here."

I asked, "Ramon?"

"Ramon Ibarez, sir. He's assistant gunnie."

"Oh, yes." I colored, chagrined that I hadn't remembered. "He was that impressed?"

"It's overpowering, sir. When we get it installed you could give it a try. You're in a cabin just like laser fire control on a ship of the line. When the fish appear you practice with the usual firing screens, but there's also a huge puter-driven simulscreen, and you actually see the fish you hit. It's more like the real thing than . . . the real thing!"

I tried to warm to his enthusiasm, though the idea of facing fish once again, even in simulation, was repugnant. "I'll give it a test. Though gunnery was never my best—Yes? What?"

"Midshipman Sandra Ekrit reporting, sir." She paused to catch her breath. "Mr. Diego says, a call from Admiral Duhaney, and do you want to take it in your office?"

I don't want it at all. "No, I'll get it by the door." I stood, waving my fellow officers back to their seats. Across the hall I took up the caller. "Seafort."

"Just a moment for Admiral Duhaney."

I waited. Several minutes passed. I shifted uncomfortably from foot to foot, aware of curious glances from the cadets. It wasn't good form to let them see their Commandant holding the line like an errand boy waiting for instructions.

Finally the receiver crackled. "Seafort?"

"Yes, sir."

"Glad I reached you. Give Senator Boland a ring, would you? He's worried about his boy."

"Are you serious?" The words slipped out before I could stop them.

A pause I thought would never end. "Yes, I'm serious, Captain Seafort. He had trouble getting through to you, and I promised to look into it. Talk to the barracks sergeant, make sure everything's all right, and give the man a call. I'll check later to make sure he's satisfied."

"I don't—aye aye, sir." There was nothing else I could say. It was an order.

"You might let the boy talk to his father now and then."

I stared at the caller; surely he couldn't mean it. I swallowed an unwise reply. "I'll consider it."

He snapped, "Don't get on your high horse, Seafort. Boland's committee controls our purse strings."

"I know that." My voice was cold.

"Oh, by the way, that new puter program you brought back on *Victoria*. The Dosmen have gone wild over it. We're going to reprogram most of the fleet."

"Is Billy all right?" I felt a fool for asking.

"Billy is what you call it? *Victoria*'s puter hasn't been powered down, if that's what you mean. It warned us that data would be irretrievably lost.

The program's too complicated to unravel quickly, so we're taking no chances."

I smiled. William, Orbit Station's late puter, had even thought to safeguard his son's life. Or maybe Billy had thought of it on his own.

"Keep Boland happy, Seafort. One hand washes the other."

"Very well, sir."

He rung off. Brooding, I walked slowly to my seat. What he'd asked of me was wrong, and I'd agreed to it without protest.

Tolliver looked up. "Everything all right?"

"Fine." I stared at my cold meal, beckoned the steward. "Take this away." Subdued conversation resumed while I stared at the starched white cloth.

After dinner I went back to my office, closed the door, slumped in my leather chair while behind me the day turned to dusk. Just a call, a quick reassurance. No need to make so much of it. The boy needn't even know. But it was hardly customary for the Commandant to ask after the health of a cadet; the moment I spoke to Ibarez, he'd know Robert Boland was under special scrutiny. Inevitably, the boy's treatment would subtly change, and just as inevitably, it would poison the boy's relations with his fellow cadets.

Yet I had no choice. I'd been given an order, and I'd assented.

The caller buzzed. Tolliver. "About those figures you asked me to look into, I have some interesting—"

"Not now!" I slammed down the caller. What was the point of a receptionist, if any officer on the base could harass me when—Well, Tolliver was my aide, and could bypass the middy in the outer office. Still, his calls were an annoyance; I should have them blocked. But then, what was the point of having an aide? Muttering under my breath, I stood, paced the room until my ire cooled.

The caller buzzed again. I snatched it up. "No more calls!"

"Aye aye, sir. Sorry." Midshipman Guthrie Smith. "I just thought, it being your wife—"

Cursing, I keyed the caller, dropped back in my chair. "Annie?"

"Hullo, Nicky." Her voice seemed eons away. "I talked to Dr. O'Neill and he—I wanted to call."

"I'm glad. I've missed you."

"How are things? You gettin' the cadets in line?" She giggled, sounding her old self.

"I'm trying." I withheld my questions, determined not to press.

"Nicky, I ain't felt too good, these days. Sometimes I think, if you just came, took me someplace, it'd be all right. I lie down in bed wid . . . with you, you hold me tight."

I took a slow breath, controlled my tone. "I could come anytime. Tonight, if you like." Even if I had to steal a training heli.

"No, I don't want that." She sounded firm. "Sometimes I feel that way, like I said. But other times I don't. I wan' wait 'til it's right, alla time."

I ventured, "Maybe that won't happen until we're together, all the time."

"Yeah. I don't know. Thas' what I wanted ta say, I don't know. And I wanted ta hear your voice."

"God, I love you, Annie."

Tears were in her tone. "I love you too, Nicky. Can you understand that, and still I wanta be alone?"

I hesitated, chose honesty. "No, hon. I can't. Maybe it's because I want to be with you so much."

"Oh, Nicky." She sounded sad, and I felt twinges of guilt.

"It's all ri—"

"Lemme think about it some. I call you, maybe a few days. Maybe tomorrow."

"All right, love."

"Bye, now." She rang off, and I sat, desolate.

After a few minutes I stood heavily, determined to get my unpleasant chore done with.

Outside, the evening air was braced with the crisp tang of early fall. As I strode the white walkway a lone cadet looked up, quickly returned to his clippers. I wondered what had been his sin.

I crossed the compound to barracks, found Valdez Hall. Lights Out would sound in fifteen minutes. I would wait to see Sergeant Ibarez after he came out; better that than making my mission known to his cadets. Meanwhile, I didn't want to skulk around as if spying on the barracks. I moved off, wandered in the dark past other dorms.

Wright Hall; the front door swung open, a gray-clad youth dashed down the steps, ran to the corner of the building, faced the wall, assumed the at-ease position. I sauntered over. "What are you doing?"

"Sir, I—"

The door opened. "Go on, tell him! Good evening, sir." Sergeant Radz.

Jerence Branstead said loudly, "I'm learning not to be insolent to my betters, sir."

The sergeant gave no quarter. "And how long will that take, cadet?"

"I—as long as you say, Sarge."

"I'd guess about half the night, if you start now."

"Yessir!"

I'd had no business interfering, but it was too late. Well, in for a penny . . . "Why are you letting him off, Sarge? We have ways of dealing with troublemakers."

"Yes, sir. I'd hoped—"

"Send him to my office in the morning." Jerence blanched. "If I decide he's going to be a problem I'll have a middy pick up his gear in barracks. We've plenty of candidates who'll appreciate their training."

"Aye aye, sir."

I would let Jerence off with a couple hours of running around the compound on errands, but the boy needn't know that yet. Let him spend the night in anticipation of a Commandant's caning; he wouldn't be so quick to irritate his sergeant in future.

"Very well." The sergeant saluted; as I turned to go, he winked.

Reluctantly I retraced my steps to Valdez. Lights were out, and the door shut. Swallowing my distaste I went around the side to Sergeant Ibarez's door, knocked.

"I thought I told you—Oh, good evening, sir." he waited. "Is there . . . did you want to come in?"

"I—no." I yearned to turn on my heel, go to my apartment. But I couldn't ignore Admiral Duhaney's order. On the other hand, how would he know I hadn't really checked with Ibarez? I could tell Senator Boland all was well with Robert, as surely it was.

No, I couldn't require my cadets to obey orders if I myself refused. And the Admiral had been quite specific: ask the barracks sergeant how Robert was doing, and tell his father. "Sarge, I—"

Was that how Duhaney had put it? I strove to recall his words. "Talk to the barracks sergeant, make sure everything's all right and give Boland a call."

Did I dare? Was it outright disobedience? I knew what the Admiral had meant. Was I turning into a sea lawyer, at this late date? On the other hand, for the boy's sake . . .

I smiled. "Is everything all right, Sarge?"

Ibarez stammered, "I, um, I don't . . . Yes, sir."

"Very well, then. Carry on." I walked with jaunty step to my office, looked up Senator Boland's number.

Walking back to my apartment, I grimaced. My fatuous reassurances still rang in my ears. I'd pointedly ignored the Senator's hints about speaking directly with his son. He hadn't been satisfied, but had chosen not to press me.

I buzzed Tolliver. "Are you awake?"

"Yes, sir. The Navy never sleeps."

"Belay that. You wanted to discuss your report?"

His tone became businesslike. "Are you in your apartment? I can be right over."

"I didn't mean to—"

"Quite all right, sir. By morning you might be in a mood to hang up again. I'll be right there."

I growled a rebuke, rang off. The man could be impossible. Still, he was conscientious, and knew me as few others.

Fifteen minutes later he sat on my couch, legs crossed, scanning his notes. "I'll tell you right off I haven't found anything specific, sir. But in many cases there's nothing to find."

"How do you mean?"

"Fuel deliveries, for example. There's nothing in the files to show whether we've actually received them. No invoices to check, no receipts."

"How does the quartermaster explain that?"

"I haven't asked Sergeant Serenco, sir. You told me not to be obvious. And it's not just fuel. The uniform allowances—"

I felt uneasy. "Perhaps we ought to get Sleak in on this."

"Perhaps we shouldn't, sir." His eyes met mine.

I grimaced. If my systems lieutenant was engaged in accounting fraud . . . "Keep searching. See what else you find."

"Aye aye, sir." He closed his file. "By the way, I checked with Lunapolis on that other matter. It seems—"

"Other matter?"

"The way expenses are broken down per cadet. It seems your expense guidelines are rather pointless. They're only valid if you assume the same number of cadets each year. But—"

I was nettled. "What else can we assume? We take three hundred eighty."

"Yes, sir, but apparently that's just tradition. The number of cadets is a function of the budget, not the other way around. If—"

"What's that supposed to mean?"

"Perhaps you might occasionally let me finish a sentence. It means that historically the number of cadets we enrolled depended on how much money they gave us. But Naval staffing, like all tradition, hardens to stone, so when we achieved three hundred eighty cadets all future budgets were based on the assumption we'd admit that number the next year. If you want to spend more on each cadet, you can reduce enrollment. There are no orders or regulations to stop you."

"Good Lord."

"Fascinating institution, the Navy."

"Well, it's of no consequence. We're not about to cut back when a third of the fleet needs replacement. Keep tracking those expenses."

"Aye aye, sir." After he left, I turned out the lights and went to bed.

7

Midafternoon. I left my office, crossed the compound to the meeting hall.

"ATTENTION!" The clump of recruits tried unsuccessfully to imitate the stiff demeanor of their sergeant.

"As you were. Line them up, Sarge." Boys and girls settled into two ragged lines. "I'm Nicholas Seafort, Commandant of U.N.N.S. Naval Academy. I am about to give you the oath of enlistment into the Naval Service." I paused, trying to recall the speech I'd made to the first group, some weeks before.

"By this oath you will be bound to the U.N.N.S. Navy for five years. You will be my wards until I deem you ready for graduation." One older boy sniffled, wiped his eyes. I looked away. A sergeant would have his hands full with that one.

"The U.N. Navy is the finest fighting force in the world. You will be privileged to join it. Those of you who wish to take the oath of enlistment, raise your hands." I waited a solemn moment. Sixty youngsters stood with right arms raised.

"I—your name—"

Someone cleared his throat, loudly. I whirled, furious at the interruption. Tolliver pointed urgently to the front row. No, not sixty arms raised. Fifty-nine.

I glared at a tall, ungainly joey of fifteen. "Raise your hand for the oath!"

Hugging himself, he mumbled, "I changed my mind." He shuffled his feet. "I want to go home." Other youngsters stared.

"I—but—" I stumbled to a halt. "Good Lord."

A red-faced drill sergeant moved toward the recruit, murder in his eye. I waved him back, looked helplessly to Tolliver, who shrugged. "I don't know, sir. Has it ever happened before?"

"Sarge?"

Sergeant Olvira said, "Not since I've been here. Eleven years." Someone snickered.

The ceremony tottered on the verge of chaos. "Take him out," I snapped. "Flank!" Two instructors converged on the miserable boy, hustled him out the door. Should I talk to him? No. A cadet had to aspire to Academy. The Navy wouldn't beg for recruits.

"Raise your right hands." The gap-toothed row complied immediately, as did the row behind. Our recruits were volunteers, not draftees. We'd send the unworthy child back to his family in disgrace. "Now. I—" Damn. I ground to a halt. "Keep them in place!" I strode to the door.

A drill sergeant had the boy by the collar, as if to prevent his escape. I planted myself in front of the abashed youngster. "Name!"

"Loren Reitzman."

"Age!"

He gulped. "Fifteen, last March."

"Inside, I have thirteen-year-olds who know what they want. Why don't you, Reitzman?"

"I'm sorry. I didn't mean—"

"Answer my question!"

"I don't know, sir. I wanted to be a cadet. But the soldiers, the yelling . . ." He wiped his eyes. "If I go back now, Dad will . . ." He hugged himself tighter. "I can't ever show my face at school. But if I stay—"

"Yes?"

He whispered, "It's just . . . The other joeys are all smarter than me; I couldn't even understand their jokes today. I don't want to be with people like that. I get scared."

I said softly, "You'd rather go home, remember all your life you gave up without trying?"

He shook his head. "What if . . . I can't make it?"

"Then you'll have failed. But you'll have tried first."

He bit back a sob. "I'm afraid."

"Very well. Sarge, take—"

"Wait! I'll take the oath. Give me another chance."

I turned his face to meet mine. "You're sure?"

He swallowed. "Yes, sir."

Was I doing the right thing? I couldn't know. "Sarge, take Mr. Reitzman back inside."

Moments later I was intoning the familiar ritual. "To give loyalty and obedience . . . to obey all its lawful orders and regulations, so help me Lord God Almighty." I waited until the last murmurs had subsided. "You are now U.N.N.S. cadets." I saluted, turned to the sergeant. "Get them out of here," I growled. I pointed at Loren Reitzman. "Except him. He's to be caned for bringing dishonor to the ceremony of enlistment."

I ignored Cadet Reitzman's anguished look of betrayal. Harsh, perhaps, but necessary. He'd get over it, and he'd serve as an example to his mates that Naval traditions were not to be trifled with.

After dinner I went to my apartment, loosened my tie. I sat at my newly-installed console, idly flipping through cadet files.

The caller buzzed. "Yes?"

"Lieutenant Sleak." His voice was tense. "I'd like to meet with you as soon as possible."

"Come now, then." I rang off, perused my folders until his knock.

He saluted, followed me into my living room.

"Well?"

"You have my resignation if you'd like, sir. Or if you prefer I'll request a transfer."

I blinked. "The boy was way out of line, refusing the oath in front of all the others. If I'd known you felt that strongly about—"

"What on earth are you talking about?"

I ignored his acid tone. "Loren Reitzman. The cadet. I know it was his first day but—"

"This isn't about a bloody cadet!"

"What, then?"

He faced me, hands on hips. "Your clumsy undercover examination of my accounts. Your man Tolliver sneaking about, checking serial numbers on laser rifles. His innocent questions to my quartermaster."

"He's doing that at my—"

"Whatever you'd like to know, ask me outright. Or, if you don't trust me, cashier me! I swore an oath just as those cadets today, and I'm not about to betray it for a few bloody unibucks!"

"It's not that—"

"Commandant Kearsey would *never* have—"

"How dare you interrupt a Captain!" My voice rose. "HOW DARE YOU?"

His tirade ground to a halt. "I'm sorry."

"I'm sorry, *sir*!"

"I'm sorry, sir. I apologize for interrupting. But that doesn't negate my point."

My tone was icy. "Stand at attention, First Lieutenant Sleak." He complied immediately. "You'll pardon my confusion. I've spent my career on ships of the line, where a lieutenant couldn't imagine dressing down his Captain." He flushed. "So, not knowing the proper shoreside protocol, I'll respond as if we're in the real Navy. Will you go along with the pretense?"

"I—yes, sir. Aye aye, sir."

"Very well. Three weeks pay for insubordination, and a reprimand in your file. One more incident and I'll write you up for court-martial. Is that understood?"

His look was wary, his voice under control. "Yes, sir."

"Stand easy. As to my investigation, I see fit to audit the Academy accounts. They are my accounts, not yours, even though you're handling them. Since you're aware of the inquiry, you will give whatever assistance Lieutenant Tolliver may ask. Acknowledge."

"Orders received and understood, sir." A surface calm, flickering anger beneath.

"Is there anything else?"

"I request a transfer, sir." The man had backbone.

"Under advisement. Dismissed." I waited until he'd gone, sat staring at my list of new cadets. The nerve! Even groundside, nothing could justify Sleak's conduct. What kind of commander had Captain Kearsey been, to tolerate such an attitude?

Yet how was Sleak's outrage different from mine, when I'd heard of Lieutenant Crossburn's insinuating questions on *Hibernia*? I flushed. At least our audit was out in the open. Tolliver would accomplish more, and faster.

A knock at my door. Was there to be no peace? I flung it open.

"Lieutenant Paulson reporting, sir." A sheen of perspiration on his forehead. "I, um, have a message."

"Well?"

"Admiral Duhaney called, and the middy transferred it to me. He—"

"You should have put him through."

"He asked for the duty officer. I was to give you the message, sir. He—" Paulson paused.

"Get on with it!"

"Aye aye, sir." Paulson seemed relieved by my order. "Mr. Duhaney said to tell you he was fed up with your prevarications."

"What?"

"That's the word he said to use, sir. You're to give Mr. Boland every cooperation, and stop wasting his time and the Admiral's. He said he recognizes that you are in charge of Academy, that you are free to act within your authority and carry out regulations as you see fit, but that Naval policy is set from above and you will comply with it."

My ears burned. I closed my eyes, forced myself to respond past the humiliation. "Is there anything else, Lieutenant?"

"No, sir. He ordered me to give you the message word for word, and to log it."

"Very we—"

He blurted, "I wish I hadn't been there. He shouldn't have—I'm sorry."

"Thank you." I shut the door, paced the silent, accusing room. I'd resign, of course. Admiral Duhaney had delivered his rebuke publicly, before my subordinates. The approach conveyed the clear message I no longer held his confidence. He'd chewed me out like a rank cadet, like—

The corners of my mouth twitched. Like I'd just done to Lieutenant Sleak. I'd gotten as I'd given. Still, at least I'd had the decency to censure the man in private. Well, no. By taking Sleak's pay and logging a reprimand, I'd made the matter public for the world to see. I sighed. Perhaps I could withdraw—

The caller buzzed. I whirled, snatched it from the console. "Now what?"

"I—Sergeant Olvira reporting, sir. I hope I'm not intru—"

"Yes, you're intruding, but that's why I'm here. What is it?"

His tone stiffened. "Aye aye, sir. I apologize; perhaps I shouldn't have called. About that cadet, Reitzman, the one who refused—"

"Yes?"

"He's in my flat, crying and carrying on like a baby, sir. Lieutenant Sleak went hard on him, he's got a few welts on his rump, can't sit down. I can deal with it, but I thought, given he didn't even want to take the oath . . ."

"Yes?"

"Should we cut our losses, sir? Send him home after all?"

I controlled my ire, considered his suggestion. We had no room for weaklings in the wardroom. Middies had to—no, Reitzman wasn't a middy, not yet. He was a cadet until I decided he was qualified.

"He made his bed, Sarge. Now let him sleep in it. Give him a little comfort, he needs that, but put him back in barracks. If he won't settle down, warn him if you send him to me in the morning, I'll have him begging to report back to Mr. Sleak."

A pause. "Aye aye, sir."

I shook my head with impatience. The man didn't understand. "And, Sarge, see to it that he doesn't need to be sent to me."

His tone warmed noticeably. "Aye aye, sir. I'll handle it."

I replaced the caller, paced anew. What was happening to the Navy? First Sleak's tantrum, then the Admiral's appalling message to my duty lieutenant, then Sarge . . . I shook my head. It was all my doing. If I hadn't gone behind Sleak's back, if I'd trusted him as a conscientious officer, he wouldn't have taken offense and wouldn't have been penalized. If I'd obeyed my own orders from Duhaney, the Admiral wouldn't be incensed.

And if I had trusted my instincts and sent Reitzman home when he'd refused the oath, the boy wouldn't have been brutalized and I wouldn't be dealing with a miserable, frightened youngster, when other, more willing joeys had been denied the chance.

To top it off, I now had to call Senator Boland and eat humble pie before that situation worsened.

I stalked the room, whirling to pace the opposite direction. "Policy is set from above and you're to comply with it." Damn his policy. Now I was to be a lackey, supervised in every detail. I should have asked for ship duty. Was it too late? Probably, for now. The Commandant couldn't resign during his first month, it suggested scandal.

None of this would have happened if Admiral Brentley still had Fleet Ops. Well, Duhaney had admitted he was more politician than Admiral. But how could I command Academy, subject to his every whim? Comply with policy, Seafort. Toady to the Senator.

I flung myself into my chair. Be fair. That's not all he'd said. "You're free to act within your authority and carry out regulations as you see fit." But what did that signify, if he decided that special treatment for Senator Boland was a matter of policy?

I was but a cog in the machine. Take three hundred eighty cadets chosen by others, run them through the process, spit them out the other end. Other than Final Cull, I had no say in which cadets we took, or how many, no way to . . .

I stared at my console. "You're free to act within your authority . . ." Was there a way?

I chewed on my finger, mesmerized by the console screen. A long time later I roused myself, keyed my caller, spoke to the middy on watch. "Seafort. My compliments to Lieutenants Tolliver and Sleak, and would they meet me in my office in five—what time is it?—ten minutes." I rang off. It took only a moment to straighten my tie, thrust on my jacket. I crossed the compound, ran up the Admin Building steps, hurried into my outer office.

Midshipman Thayer came to attention. "They're not here yet, sir."

"What's keep—very well. Is there coffee?"

"It's old, sir."

"That'll do." I sipped at a cup of warm sludge, grimaced. Tolliver was the first to arrive; like me, he'd recently served on ship and was used to being called at odd hours. A few moments later Sleak followed; the look he gave Tolliver was within the bounds of civility, but barely so.

"Edgar, you said if I wanted to spend more on each cadet, I could reduce enrollment. Is that true?"

"Yes. Are you aware what hour it is?"

"Belay that." I looked to Sleak. "Are you familiar with those regs?"

His tone was aloof. "I understand their import."

"Does Tolliver have it right?"

"Technically speaking. But—"

"Very well. What if I want to spend less on each cadet?"

Tolliver said, "Sir, is now the right time to cut back on training just to save money?"

"Not to save it. To spend it." Like a child at Christmas I savored the moment before turning to the console. I tapped the keys, working through the menus to the screen I wanted. "Here. The list of admissions."

"Yes, sir."

"And this list of candidates before Final Cull. A difference of forty names."

"Yes, sir?"

"Send a letter, immediate delivery. 'We regret that an inadvertent miscalculation of the number of spaces available caused you to receive a notice rejecting your application. You are hereby granted admission to the United Nations Na—"

"What?" Tolliver was on his feet.

" '—Naval Academy. You are to confirm by return mail and report, et cetera. Signed Nicholas E. Seafort, Commandant.' You know the form."

Sleak said, "But we don't have spaces for—"

"We have empty beds aplenty, now that all second year cadets have been shipped aloft."

"Supplies? Food?"

"There's slack in the budget. Use the money set aside to entertain. Cancel staff travel perks. Cancel my liquor ration, I don't use it."

Tolliver. "We'd have to open up another dorm. Who'd take it?"

"Use one of the classroom instructors, or take it yourself."

"Me?"

"What's the matter, can't handle a few starstruck cadets?"

"No, sir, I'm not—but why?"

My fist struck the table. "Because I think it right." And to get even with Admiral Duhaney. I banished the unworthy thought.

As if reading my mind Sleak said, "Perhaps you should check with Admiralty, sir?"

"No. I had a message from Fleet Ops tonight." Sleak wiped off a look of satisfaction, but not before I'd seen it. So he'd already heard. Even here, scuttlebutt flew faster than a ship in Fusion. I said firmly, "Admiral Duhaney made clear that I'm free to act within my authority and carry out regulations as I see fit." That hadn't been the gist of his message, but the words had been included. They'd be in the Log, if I cared to look.

Sleak said, "You're sure that's what you want to do, sir?"

"Yes. Any objections?"

He shook his head as if I hadn't spoken with sarcasm. "No, sir. We'll have to recalculate all our . . . The letter is first, of course. It has to go out right away."

"Yes."

"Mr. Tolliver, you'll help me draft it? You'll want to sign it tonight, Captain, so it will make the morning faxes. If you want to go to bed, I can have the middy knock when it's ready. Then Tolliver and I can set up staff meetings for tomorrow. Even if we open another barracks we'll have to squeeze a couple of extra cadets into each of the other dorms."

I watched, amazed. Sleak was deep in logistics, as if my savage reprimand were forgotten. Perhaps for the moment, it was.

I left him to his work.

At breakfast Tolliver looked bleary. I said nothing, knowing he could catch up on his sleep when opportunity arose. Any middy knew how to do that. After, on the way back to my office, I crossed the parade ground, stopped to watch a squad of shirtless cadets sweating at jumping jacks, sit-ups, and push-ups under the tutelage of Sergeant Ibarez.

In the front row, Robert Boland struggled diligently at sit-ups while another youngster held his ankles. I quickly looked away. He'd get no special attention. Still, on the way back to my office I braced myself for the call to his father.

I perched on my desk, scanned the morning's memos. For the new dorm, Sleak had drafted a classroom instructor who'd had a barracks before; Tolliver wouldn't have to undergo the ordeal.

I dawdled at my console, scrutinizing figures, approving indents, rechecking the arrival dates of our last, largest batch of cadets until at last I could leave for lunch.

In the crowded mess hall I passed Cadet Reitzman's table, realized he hadn't been sent to my office. Well, I hadn't expected he would. For all their toughness, our drill sergeants usually knew when a gentle word would help. After all, their job was to help the joeys succeed, not destroy them. I looked again, noticed that the boy was absent from the hall. I assumed he'd remain so for a couple of days, until he could sit on a pillowed chair.

Already I could observe improvements in the cadets' demeanor, their dress and grooming. In a few weeks they would come to look like officer trainees, instead of spoiled civilian children. I spooned my soup. The discipline, the physical exertion, the sense of brotherhood of those early days of Academy were almost too much to grasp. I stared into the bowl. Almost too much to grasp . . .

A hand closed around my upper arm, hurled me from the bed to the cold hard floor. "One demerit, Seafort. You too, Sanders. Reveille sounded three minutes ago!"

I groaned, stumbled to my feet. Arlene Sanders glanced to my shorts, grinned. Scarlet, I spun around, clawed for my pants. I couldn't help the bulge. It wasn't fair that she laugh.

In ten minutes we'd be marched to breakfast. I had to hurry. I dashed into the head, waited in line for a stall. After, I grabbed a towel, ran to a sink, scrubbed myself. A few days earlier Sarge had decided Von Halstein wasn't clean enough, had hauled him back into the head, made us all watch while . . .

I soaped my chest, under my arms. There were limits. I'd die if he did that to me. I ignored the razors sitting on the sill; I didn't need one yet. Soon, I hoped. Some boys used them every day.

After breakfast, the calisthenics. I didn't mind them so much, other than push-ups. Sergeant Swopes had a way of flicking his baton if you faltered. It stung. When we were ready to drop from exhaustion he gave us two minutes rest before leading us to the track at the edge of the field. We mingled with Sergeant Tallor's squad from Renault Hall.

Tallor smiled. "My turn, Darwin. Okay, joeys. Four laps today." We groaned. "Tolliver, you take the lead."

A tall, slim second-year cadet ran forward. "Aye aye, sir!"

"I'll bring up the rear," said Sergeant Tallor. I made a face. If he came close enough to touch you with his baton, you were caned after the run. It hadn't happened often, and they said Lieutenant Zorn went easy, but I didn't want to find out.

Afterward, we ran back to the showers. Soaping up, I looked over my shoulder, found myself next to Arlene Sanders. Her hair smelled clean.

She giggled, and after a moment I smiled weakly. I remained facing the wall, though, until at last I screwed up my courage, turned casually. But she was gone, thrusting her way through the steamy shower room to the door and the towels beyond.

A dark-skinned Indian boy groaned theatrically. "Oh, if she were only a civilian." We laughed.

After lunch and classes Sarge ran us to the training grounds, where our instructor threw suits at us from the rack. We had to stand holding them while they ran a training holo on the large screen overhead. "Okay, lads. Help each other put them on. Make sure your air is turned on before you attach your helmets. Then, one at a time, walk through the room to the left, meet me outside."

"Aye aye, sir!" Our response was still ragged, but improving. Back in barracks, where we'd grown used to Sergeant Swopes's cadence, we spoke almost as one.

I fumbled with the helmet clamps. No, the air tank first. I waited for the hiss. Now the helmet. The holo had said something about . . . clamp and turn. I twisted dutifully. The helmet seemed secure.

I took my place in line. One at a time, Sergeant Swopes thrust us into the mysterious room to the left, closed the door again. When it was my turn I stumbled in, propelled by his shove. The room seemed unusally foggy. I walked to the door at the far side, my breath loud in my suit. The door was locked. I twisted at the handle, to no effect. After a long moment the door opened. I plodded out to the lawn, where several cadets were peeling off their suits.

Sarge tapped at the helmet. "Off!" I fumbled for the clamps, twisted it loose. I breathed in the cool welcome air, turned to Robbie Rovere, grinned. "If that's all it takes, I'm ready for Farside!"

He smiled weakly, but suddenly his eyes bulged wide. He doubled over, vomited urgently onto the grass. "Jesus, what—" Another spasm caught him.

The instructor came running over. "Get away from that suit! Around the side of the building with the other grodes!" He spun Robbie around, gave him a kick. Moaning, the boy stumbled off.

He put hands on hips. "What about you, joey? You going to give back your lunch?"

"I don't—" I swallowed, but I seemed okay. "No, sir. What's wrong with Robbie, Sarge?"

The instructor stalked to the door, pulled out another cadet. The boy turned green, clawed at his helmet. Sarge made no move to help. Suddenly the front of the helmet was splattered; the cadet sank to his knees. "They're learning how to listen," Sarge growled.

Half an hour later we were lined up alongside the building, some of us still wan and shaky. The instructor's tone was drenched with disgust. "You're the saddest, stupidest bunch of joeys Academy's ever had! In a week or two you're going to be sent aloft; didn't anyone tell you there's no air Outside the locks? This time we were watching over you, so we gave you nothing but a tummy ache. Next time you might die!"

Chastened, we shuffled our feet, but he wasn't done with us. "Each of you who threw up, two demerits." Two hours per demerit, and the strenuous calisthenics made our morning exercises seem easy. I'd done them until my muscles screamed, for infractions I couldn't avoid no matter how hard I tried. This time, though, I was safe.

"And the rest of you, three demerits!" I looked up, outraged. It wasn't fair.

"You all watched the holo, didn't you? Your mates were going where they needed suits. Did any of you check your mates' clamps?" His voice rose. "Did you? Rovere could be dead now. So could Sanders, or any of you! And you didn't help!" His look was one of loathing; his voice soared to a scream. "Next time it will be vacuum! You ever see anyone breathe space? You disgust me, all of you! Get out of my sight!"

Later that night, we lay, numbed and exhausted, in our bunks. Across the aisle someone sobbed. I buried my head in the pillow. A voice whispered, "It's all right, Robbie."

If Sarge heard us . . . I lay quiet.

"I've got to get out of here!"

Someone laughed, a harsh sound.

"Crybaby!"

"Mama's boy!" A loud whisper.

"He cries over a little puke, like a—"

It was Robbie who'd covered for me when I forgot to toss my towel in the bin. When Sarge had come into the head, the towel lay abandoned next to Robbie's sink. For some reason Robbie had said it was his own. Only one demerit, but . . . My hand tightened to a fist. Leave him alone.

Silence, then another strangled sob.

At the end of the barracks a joker imitated the sound. Someone else laughed.

I threw off the cover, leaped out of my bunk. "Shut up, all of you!" My voice hissed.

Von Halstein sneered, "Gonna make us, pretty boy?"

"If I have to." My voice trembled. I shivered in my shorts. "Leave him alone. Pick on me!"

"That's too easy." Someone giggled.

"Keep it down, you joes. Sarge'll hear." Arlene Sanders.

"Get in bed, Seafort, before we all get it." Voices murmured assent.

I crossed the aisle, found Robbie's bunk. Awkwardly I pulled his blanket tight about him. "You're all right, joey." For a second my hand touched his shoulder. I thought to pull away, remembered Jason. I let my hand remain a second longer. "You're okay."

I turned for my bunk, almost made it to the safety of my mattress when the voice came from the door. "What's going on here?"

Silence, everywhere. My heart pounding, I forced myself back to my feet. "Cadet Seafort reporting, Sarge. I was out of my bunk."

"Why?"

I paused. It had to be the truth, but . . . "I thought I heard a noise."

"Then you'd better guard us. Bring your mattress."

"Aye aye, sir. Where?"

"Outside."

All was still while I dragged my heavy mattress across the barracks floor.

"Are you finished, sir?"

I looked up from my cold soup. "Yes." The bowl disappeared, a salad was put in its place.

Squads of cadets came to their feet, their meal done. At each table the cadet on cleanup duty filed past the counter, depositing trays piled high with dishes. I'd dropped mine once, and was banished from mess hall for a week.

I stood, stretched, walked to the door. Cadets respectfully stood aside. Among them I saw Robert Boland, cheeks flushed, his gray uniform crisp, shoes gleaming. I pretended to ignore him, as a Captain would any cadet.

On the way back to my office I sighed, knowing I couldn't avoid the call any longer.

I closed my door, sat at my desk, bracing myself, knowing I was about to throw away everything, for pride. I picked up the caller. "Ring Senator Boland, please." I waited, musing. Perhaps if Duhaney hadn't called me out so publicly . . .

It was early morning in Washington, but he was in. "Seafort? Good to hear from you." Boland could afford to be genial.

My muscles tensed. "I apologize for avoiding your calls."

"You don't have to—"

"Oh, but I do, sir. I failed to appreciate the extent of your influence."

"Thank you, Captain. I've been worried—"

"Please let me finish. Admiral Duhaney ordered me to give you every cooperation, and of course I will. I checked on your son. He's quite well. If you want further information, contact me."

"I'm most grateful—"

My heart pounded. "Senator Boland, I underestimated you."

He paused. "You what?"

"Not just your committee's power, your own. You hold my career in your hands."

He was wary now. "I don't understand."

"It's simple. If you want information about your son, call. If you ask to speak to him, I'll put you through. Feel free to drop in anytime for a visit. I will obey Admiral Duhaney to the letter. But after your first call or visit, or if I hear you've complained again to the Admiral, I will immediately resign as Commandant, and from the Naval Service. I so swear before Lord God Himself."

The speaker was silent. I added, "My future is in your hands. Forgive me for having underestimated you. You have but to reach for your caller, and my career is ended."

"Jesus, Seafort."

"Sir, you have a son to be proud of. Let him go, and let us do our job."

"I—"

"I won't have it any other way." I listened, heard no answer, gently hung up the line.

Part 2

October, in the year of our Lord 2201

8

To my annoyance, a midshipman again met me at Earthport Station; this time they'd sent First Middy Thomas Keene. I growled at him as if it had been his fault.

Henceforth I'd have to travel unannounced, or better, leave orders not to send a shepherd. I wasn't some airsick cadet who needed a chaperon, and I could carry my own duffel.

Hours later, still cross, I cycled through the Farside lock to scowl at the duty officer waiting to greet me: Lieutenant Ardwell Crossburn. I returned his salute in silence, wishing I'd taken the effort to get rid of him.

"Have a good trip, sir?" His tone was civil.

"Yes."

"If there's anything I can do—"

"Dismissed." He turned to go. "Wait. Come to my office."

"Very well, sir."

During our long walk through the warren the stocky lieutenant was mercifully silent. In my office I set down my duffel, tossed my cap on the desk. "Do you still write your diary?"

His brow wrinkled. "Yes, sir, but just for my own—"

"You write about current events, as you used to?"

"It's my way of analyzing, sir. I think about things and—"

"Do you talk with other officers about your writings?"

"Well, I suppose—yes, sir. Idle conversation, at mealtimes."

As I feared. "Lieutenant, I order you to desist from writing in your diary any matters that do not directly concern you. I specifically forbid you to discuss anything you write with any of my officers. No, make that any officer, crewman or cadet." No telling what the man was capable of.

He shook his head stubbornly. "Sir, with all due respect, that's an infringement on my personal freedom that has nothing to do with—"

"Be silent!" I waved my finger under his nose. "Complain to Admiralty if you don't like it. You have my leave." I doubted they'd give him a hearing. "In the meantime, obey orders, or I'll—I'll—" I groped for a threat.

"Yes, sir?" He seemed unafraid.

I growled, "We have no ship's launch, but if I hear you've asked a single question about how things are run here, I'll make you supervisory officer of the Training Station."

His chest swelled. "That would be an honor, sir. I'd be pleas—"

"In permanent residence!" That brought him up short. Several months of the year the Training Station was entirely unoccupied. He could walk its lonely corridors, writing to his heart's content. I felt a pang of regret at my warning; now I couldn't banish him until I actually caught him at it.

When he was gone, I paced until my anger abated. Finally I keyed the caller. "Where's Mr. Paulson?"

"In his cabin, sir."

"Get him."

I met Paulson at the hatch, waved at a chair. "Have a good trip aloft? Everything under control, Jent?" Of course it was, or I'd have been told.

"Cadets are all settled in, no problems." He hesitated. "We were a bit surprised when you shipped sixty of them early, sir."

"We needed the space." Lieutenant Sleak had recommended it, and I'd agreed. Better to reward our achievers with Farside than crowd the Devon barracks unnecessarily.

"Yes, I—we've heard something about that." His expression was carefully neutral. "What was Admiralty's reaction?"

I leaned back. "I haven't heard from them." Not about anything. Perhaps they were debating what to do with me.

In the two weeks since my spectacular display of insolence, Senator Boland had not called once. Taking pity, I considered sending a brief note, but came to my senses in time. A battle once won ought not be refought.

"How long will you stay with us, sir?"

"A week or so." Time to wander the base, making a nuisance of myself. Time also to revisit the Training Station, where our more advanced cadets were introduced to shipboard life. "Schedule a formal inspection later this week, Jent. Tell the sergeants, but not the joeys." The anxiety and excitement would be good for the cadets, but no need to harass the drill sergeants as well. "Anything else I should know?"

"I sent you the forms on the Edwards boy."

"I know." I'd sent on the reports to his mother, with an inadequate note of my own. "How's the other joe, Arnweil?" I'd had no contact with the dark-haired youngster since I'd guided him to his feet, led him to the comfort of his barracks.

"You'd have to ask Sergeant Radz, sir. I haven't really had contact." He grimaced. "The only ones I see much of are the troublemakers, across the barrel."

"Have you used it much?"

"Three times since term started. Twice for cadets who didn't work off demerits fast enough, and once last week . . ." He shook his head. "I can't imagine what gets into them. A cadet and a middy, fighting."

Could he be serious? "Who was in charge?"

"The cadet, Johan Stritz, was in Krane Barracks, with Sergeant Tripole. The middy . . . well, I'm first lieutenant. It's my fault."

I snorted. When the day came a lieutenant could keep track of what middies were up to . . . Midshipmen had a natural knack for trouble, as I could testify. Once, on *Helsinki*, I'd— "Which middy?"

"Guthrie Smith, sir. He's seventeen, old enough to know better."

I remembered a shy boy, sitting stiffly at my midshipman's meeting, cap in hand. "What happened?"

"He was hazing, of course. What else?" Cadets were fair game for hazing, by middies as well as anyone else. After all, they had to learn to take it. A Captain aboard ship was an absolute dictator, and some of them were tyrants. A middy who couldn't handle unpleasantness wouldn't survive.

"Go on."

"There isn't much to tell. Mr. Smith had a squad emptying the dining hall for a thorough cleaning. He decided Stritz was doing a sloppy job, made him crawl to the hatch and back, pushing a chair."

"Doesn't sound so bad."

"Then he made him do it again. The cadet had enough, and refused. So Smith took him out to the corridor, where Bill Radz found them going at each other. He called me at once, since a middy was involved."

"Good Lord."

Lieutenant Paulson shook his head. "I gave Stritz a dozen, sent him crying back to his dorm. He has to learn to hold his temper."

I nodded. I would have gone easy too. It sounded like the boy had spunk, if not judgment.

"The truth is, I felt like giving Keene half a dozen for not knocking more sense into Guthrie Smith's head. What's a first middy for?"

"Did you?"

"No, but I set him against the bulkhead and reamed him so he'll remember. And four demerits. When Midshipman Smith came in, I let him have it. He ate lying on his bunk in the wardroom for a while. Damn it, he should know better."

A midshipman—any officer—couldn't maintain his authority by brute force, even with a cadet. Else a crewman physically stronger than his officer would have his own way. True, we caned middies as required, but they were considered young gentlemen and ladies, adults by law, but capable of youthful indiscretions that should be chastised. Belowdecks, sailors weren't beaten.

I mused, "Sometimes I wonder . . ."

"Yes, sir?"

"Whether we rely too heavily on the cane." I realized I spoke near-heresy. "I mean, a few strokes for a really serious offense is one thing, but is anything gained by making the barrel our first resort?"

"Our first resort is demerits, not the barrel, but, yes, something's gained." Paulson's reply was without hesitation. "Cadets, and middies, for that matter, have to learn to obey their betters. Life on a starship is no zark."

That was true. Disobedience or inattention could be fatal, and not only for the midshipman. I shrugged. I was no wild-eyed idealist. Society had finally recovered from a century or more of coddling rebellious children, and we were all the better for it.

"Is there anything else, sir?"

"No. See you at dinner."

After Paulson left I turned to my console to review a stack of reports that had accumulated since my last visit. Then, restless, I got up to walk, glad I now had room to pace without cracking my shins on low-slung coffee tables.

I sat back at my desk, flicked on the console. The trouble, I realized, was that I had no conception of what to do, either on this particular trip to Farside, or more generally as Commandant of Academy. When I'd become *Hibernia*'s Captain, my goal was obvious: guide the ship safely to Hope Nation and off-load the cargo and passengers. When I'd taken charge of Academy, I had no such aim. I had only to pass time until the cadets were ready to be graduated, until another group took their place. And, even more than as Captain, I was expected to govern as a remote, unapproachable figure.

I was the wrong man for the job. Too restless to immerse myself in minutiae better left to experienced drill sergeants, I had little to do but wander the halls, an awesome figure because of my reputation, but essentially useless.

Well, so be it. If I was to be a wanderer, I might as well begin. Perhaps in the process I'd learn something. I left my office.

I trudged through a deserted corridor to the classroom wing, beyond it to the barracks. Now, in nominal day, cadets were in class or in training. I stopped at Krane Hall, glanced about, saw no one. Sheepishly, I went in.

Rows of empty beds, blankets taut, the deck spotless. Sergeant Tripole seemed to have his joes well in hand, despite the altercation between his Cadet Stritz and the middy. I closed my eyes, oriented myself, crossed to the port side, walked along the row of bunks. There. That one had been mine. It seemed smaller, somehow, as did the whole barracks.

Had I been happy here? I reached over, ran my fingers along the bed frame. Innocent of treason to come, of betrayal of my oath, I'd striven to please my masters, while my body and mind altered. Less and less often did my voice break unexpectedly into the higher registers; daily I ran my fingers over my upper lip, waiting for the magic moment when I could justify a shave.

I sat slowly on the edge of the bed. Had I been happy? Well, innocent, perhaps. Was it not the same?

I jumped out of bed, kicked at Robbie Rovere's bunk. "Get up, Sarge'll be here any second."

Robbie groaned, but sat, rubbing his eyes. "Yeah, thanks." He sat for a moment, heard the soft hiss of the hatch and had leaped to his feet before it had fully opened.

Sarge snapped, "All right, you louts, listen up!" I grinned. Sergeant Trammel could call us what he wanted—and he did—but I suspected he felt something other than the professional disgust he communicated to us. There was an aspect to his look when you succeeded in a particularly difficult task; the apparently casual touch of his hand if you were on the verge of losing your temper, and your self respect . . .

"Aye aye, Sarge," I echoed dutifully, along with the rest.

"Tomorrow we're off to the Training Station, so today you get special instruction. After classes, go with Corporal Tolliver to assembly dome. I have some holos to show you"—subdued groans: Naval holos could be excruciatingly boring—"and then a quiz or two to see if you've paid attention." He smiled grimly. "I hope some of you don't listen, like last time. That was fun." He left, shutting the hatch.

Robbie lowered his voice in a rough imitation of Sarge, "Go with Corporal Tolliver to the head. I have some turds to show you—"

Several bunks away Tolliver buttoned his jacket, favoring Robbie with a cold look. "Keep that up, Rovere. You make friends wherever you go."

"I try to, Mr. Tolliver." Robbie subsided, knowing when to lay off. As a cadet corporal, Edgar Tolliver had considerable power to annoy us, if not make us miserable.

Every barracks had a corporal, a cadet entrusted by the sergeant to make sure we got to the dome on time, or that the barracks was clean for weekly inspection. A corporal was still a cadet; he didn't rate a "sir," but like a middy was addressed by his last name only.

His only recourse if we disobeyed was to report us, but a diligent corporal could exact fairly strict obedience as an alternative to a tongue lashing or worse from Sarge. Corporal Van Fleet had been nicer than Tolliver, but he'd made middy and been sent on to *Prince of Wales.*

Robbie combed his hair meticulously, hoping to garner a few more few days before Sarge sent him back to the barber. "What will the holo be this time?"

I shrugged. We'd find out soon enough. I brushed my teeth, spat into the basin. Tolliver squeezed past to the next sink.

As a rule, middies were nicer than corporals, perhaps because they had less to prove. Still, you didn't want to get on the middies' bad side, as their hazing could be severe. Once they'd even made me stand regs.

Stripped to my shorts, I'd stood sweating on the wardroom chair groping for half-memorized passages from Naval Regulations, while below me they'd interjected scathing remarks about my physique and behavior. Rumor had it that if the middies were sufficiently irked, even the shorts were dispensed with. I hoped devoutly not to find out. Midshipman Jeff Thorne had said nothing, but he hadn't shared the amusement of my other tormentors. As second middy, he could do nothing until his senior had had enough.

After making our beds we marched to breakfast. Tolliver took his place in line with the rest of us; a corporal's only authority was in the sergeant's absence. Too bad Tolliver wasn't at one of the other tables. Even at mealtime, I had to watch every word I said, so as not to attract his attention.

"Hey, Nicky, why so quiet today?" Though Robbie woke slowly, once alert, he was depressingly cheerful.

"Maybe because he's learning some sense?" Tolliver's tone was acid. "Then he could stop polishing lockers."

I flushed. That whole incident would have gone unnoticed if it hadn't been for Tolliver. My suit had flopped over the edge of the locker so my door wouldn't close. I'd have noticed if I hadn't been in a hurry to get to Nav class. And Sarge probably wouldn't have known at all if Tolliver hadn't kept staring at my locker until Sarge turned to see what was the matter. Four hours polishing alumalloy lockers had left blisters on my hands and savage hate in my heart.

My emotions made me reckless. "I'm good at polishing, Mr. Tolliver," I said. "I could spit-polish your shoes, if you like."

Now it was Tolliver's turn to redden. He'd had Arlene Sanders polish his shoes as penalty for some imagined slight, and had discovered too late that Sanders had deposited far more spit inside the shoes than she'd brushed off the tips.

Tolliver seemed in good humor, though his eyes were sharp. "No thanks, Seafort. Where I really could use your help is getting ready for inspection tonight."

I grimaced. Well, I'd brought it on myself. Now Tolliver would have me tag along as he sauntered through the barracks, and every speck of dust, every imagined blemish, would be mine to correct. I knew he'd pay particular attention to the stalls in the head, and I could do nothing about it.

For much of the day I labored at Nav, listened dutifully to a lecture on the mysteries of the fusion drive, and managed in Colonial History to show Mr. Peretz I'd read at least part of the chapter. Then lunch, Off Hour, and the rigorous daily calisthenics a cadet never escaped.

Later, we convened at barracks, marched to assembly dome, and settled in for holovid instruction. The first holo might have been entitled "Ten Obvious Ways to Avoid Getting Killed on a Station," and the second, "In Case You Weren't Listening to the First."

Admonishments ringing in my ears, resolved never to exit a Station lock without a clamped helmet or to stroll in front of a laser during fire practice, I changed for dinner. At table I kept a low profile, hoping Corporal Tolliver had forgotten my impertinence at lunch.

He hadn't.

After dinner I followed him through barracks, broom and dustpan in one hand, mop and bucket in the other, damp rag draped over my arm. How dirty can a barracks get that is cleaned almost every day? One might be surprised, unless one knew Edgar Tolliver. I wiped imaginary dust, swept the aisles, pretended not to know he was going to call me next into the head.

"Is the shower a tad moldy? What do you think, Seafort?" There was no right answer, and we both knew it. But there were tricks to dealing with a cadet corporal, and I used one of them. I peered at the spotless bulkheads. "I think you're right, Mr. Tolliver," I said with enthusiasm. "They ought to be scrubbed down. Do you want me to get started?"

He frowned, but played out the game. "Yes, I think so. Let's check the stalls first."

The toilets were cleaned twice daily by those cadets who had earned Sarge's disfavor, so I knew they wouldn't be offensive. I also knew their condition wouldn't affect Tolliver's decision in the slightest.

"Look at this, Seafort. Can't let Sarge see that or we'll all lose an Off Hour. Scrub them out, will you?"

"Yes, Mr. Toll—"

He tore off a small piece of rag. "By hand."

"Of course, Mr. Tolliver." Damn him. Humiliating, and my knees and back would ache after. I smiled.

The next trick was harder. It was all in the tone; the words had to be absolutely guileless, if repeated to Sarge. I said brightly, "I'm glad you point these things out, Mr. Tolliver. Not many barracks have a corporal who knows as much about dirty toilet stalls as you do." He eyed me, but I beamed pleasantly. I beamed like a cheerful imbecile.

Still, he was the one about to stroll out of the head, and I was the one who'd get to scrub the barracks stalls for an hour or two. "I'll check back, Seafort," he said. "In case there's something we missed."

I bent to my work, slapping at his face with every swipe of the rag.

Half an hour later, he was back. "Enjoying yourself, Seafort? It's nice you've found work you're suited for. I'll try to give—"

"Attention." The voice was quiet, the tone agreeable, but Tolliver leaped to attention, his back ramrod stiff. I scrambled to my feet and dropped the rag, pressing my arms to my sides.

"What's up?"

Tolliver said, "Nothing, Mr. Thorne. We were cleaning the head for inspection, sir."

Midshipman Jeffrey Thorne clasped his hands behind his back, peered into the stall. "Very presentable. Mr. Seafort does a good job."

"I was just telling him that, sir."

"Yes, I heard." Thorne prodded the bucket of soapy water. "We're all proud of you, Tolliver."

Something in his tone made Tolliver's lips press tighter. "Yes, sir." Imprisoned at attention, he could do nothing.

"I'd like your friend Seafort to read us some regs again. Mind if I take him from you?"

Tolliver's look held pure malice. "No, sir, not at all."

"Good." Midshipman Thorne glared at me. "Leave the bucket, Cadet. Left face. Forward march. Left face. Halt." I did as I was told, and ended up facing the entry to the head.

Thorne strolled over to Tolliver, fingered the corporal's crisp gray jacket. "I'll see you again, Cadet Tolliver. You may put away the supplies. Or, if you like, finish the job yourself." He patted Tolliver's shoulder. "All right, Seafort, forward march." He marched me through the dorm to the outer hatch. The other cadets watched with sympathy. No one wanted to be singled out for a middy's hazing.

The hatch closed behind us. At his orders I strode down the corridor to the first turn. "That's far enough, Seafort. As you were."

"Thank you, sir." I eyed him, smiling tentatively.

"I should have made him scrub the toilet, but I couldn't undercut him in front of you." Thorne grimaced, then brightened. "Did you see the look on his face?"

"Yes, sir, in the mirror."

"Belay that bit about standing regs. I'm putting together another mission. You care to volunteer?"

He was my senior; he had no need to ask me, but I wouldn't have passed it up for the world. "Yes, sir!"

I don't know how I'd been lucky enough to be chosen for Jeff Thorne's fabled "missions." Until the night the middies made me stand regs he'd taken no notice of me. After they'd let me go, Thorne had seen me back to barracks.

In a service corridor, he'd taken me aside, said a few kind words. Wary of all midshipmen, I made no reply. As if he hadn't noticed, he strolled, hands in pockets, chatting about the Navy, his experiences as a cadet, his own hopes, until at last he'd drawn me out. I told him something of Cardiff, and Father. I'd even casually mentioned Jason.

The first mission had come a week later. Others had followed.

Thorne glanced both ways, whispered, "I've got Bailey from Reardon Hall and Justin Ravitz waiting by the wardroom. You know them?"

"I know Justin, sir." I trotted along, trying to keep up with Jeff Thorne's long stride. "What's our mission?" Last time it had been to spy, belowdecks, on the techs manning the gravitrons. I'd learned it was the perennial goal of the wardroom to reach the control room unseen, bring the gravitrons slowly off-line, and enjoy the resulting havoc. They'd never succeeded.

Thorne made sure the corridor was empty, lowered his voice. "Mess hall." He clapped me on the shoulder. "I don't know why we only got one slice of apple pie for dessert, when so much was left over. And there should be ice cream in the cooler."

His smile was infectious; I found myself grinning like an idiot as I did my best to keep up with his stride. Mr. Thorne could be firm if we didn't listen at training, but at heart he was one of us.

Half an hour later Bailey, Ravitz and I girded ourselves at the cutoff for the corridor to the mess hall dome. Thorne peeked around the corner. "Go!"

We sprinted down the long corridor. As an officer, Mr. Thorne could go where he wished, but we cadets were a different matter. Though, if we were seen, he'd cover for us, wouldn't he? Better not to find out.

At mealtimes the mess hall hatch was left open, but this late in the evening it was shut. "Is it coded, sir?"

"The mess hall? Don't be silly." He touched the pad, hesitated. "Let me look in first." As the hatch slid open he cautiously peered in.

"All clear!" It was a whisper. We slipped inside the darkened hall. I looked up. Farside was halfway through the long Lunar night; the open filters revealed the bright cold gleam of a billion stars.

We huddled at a familiar table. Thorne beckoned us close. "If we're found here by the tables, I can claim I was hazing you, though I really shouldn't be in here at this hour. But if we're caught in the galley, we've all had it." He eyed his fellow conspirators. "Bailey, guard the hatch. If anyone approaches, snap your fingers loudly. Can you do that?" The boy nodded. "Then duck under a table over there where it's darker, and hope no one sees you. If things go wrong, try to get back to barracks."

"Aye aye, sir." Bailey grinned with excitement.

"Inside the galley we won't be able to hear Bailey, so, Ravitz, you stand just behind the serving rail and relay the signal. Anyone comes, snap your fingers at us and duck down. I'll snap back to tell you we've heard."

"Yes, sir."

Thorne punched the cadet's shoulder. "Aye aye, sir, you meant. Don't forget your training just because you're so nervous you're wetting your pants."

Ravitz said indignantly, "I'm not wet—"

"Shhh. Seafort, you and I will breach the enemy's hull. I'll get plates and find the ice cream, you look in the coolers for the pie. Can you find it in the dark?"

"It's not that dark, sir. The safety lights are on."

"Okay, let's go."

While Justin Ravitz crouched behind the rail we slipped through one of the two entryways between galley and mess hall. Thorne grinned. "Scared?"

"No, sir." My pulse throbbed.

"Liar. So am I. You think I want to be knocking at Mr. Zorn's hatch?" First Lieutenant Zorn was custodian of the barrel. Thorne squeezed my arm, whispered, "Hey, that's what makes it fun. I'll get the plates."

I pawed through an unlocked cooler, found only vegetables from the hydroponics chambers below. I closed the cooler door harder than I'd thought; the resounding clunk brought Thorne racing over. He hissed, "Keep it down, you idiot!" I nodded, trying to apologize with a placating smile. I'd never heard that tone from Thorne; his nerves must be taut.

The pies were in the third cooler. I took two, put them on a tray while across the galley Thorne fished in the freezer for ice cream.

A sound. I looked to Thorne; he hadn't heard. I slid the tray onto the counter.

The sound came again; fingers snapping. Thorne was just turning from the freezer. The snap of fingers, one more time, lower. Ravitz must be beside himself. Thorne was still unaware; I raised my hand, snapped my fingers once.

Thorne looked up. I pointed desperately at the rail and beyond. His eyes widened; he nodded, beckoned. I scuttled across the deck while Thorne made for the other doorway.

A voice, outside in the mess hall. "Who's under there? What are you—hey!" Running feet. "Come back here!"

Thorne disappeared into the far doorway. I ducked behind the mess-hall counter.

"Anyone in here? What's going—"

A crunch, as if someone had caromed off a piece of furniture just outside the galley. A yelp, a crash, a cry of pain. Racing steps. Thorne, making a bid for safety. Steps fading into the distance.

The lights snapped on. I huddled behind the counter. Footsteps, approaching the cooler. Could I crawl out unnoticed? I huddled low, padded forward. The intruder muttered, "God damn frazzin' cadets, I'll have their balls in a—you!"

I scrambled for safety. The voice roared, "You, Cadet!"

I dashed for the hatch.

"Freeze! Stand to attention!"

Perhaps he hadn't seen my face, and all cadet uniforms were alike. But I couldn't help it; he'd given a direct order and I couldn't disobey. I stumbled to a halt, froze to attention, a few steps from the unattainable hatch.

"Don't you move!" He came closer. My back twitched. Who had been my undoing, my ruination? They'd cashier me, surely, if not worse. Theft of Naval stores? Breaking and entering? Could they shoot me?

At last he came into my field of vision. A rating, a mere seaman. Were I a middy I could disobey him with impunity, but as a cadet, every adult in my universe was my superior. My eyes flicked to the hatch. A puddle of water, an overturned mop bucket. Was that what Thorne had encountered?

His fists bunched, he stepped back. For a moment I thought he was going to strike me. "Name!"

"Cadet Nicholas Seafort reporting, sir!" My voice wavered.

"Stay right here, joey. Understand?" He walked to the caller. I could dash for the hatch, but to what point? He'd seen my face, knew my name. I stood rock solid at attention, awaiting my fate.

A few moments later the rating pulled up a chair, sat, leaned forward, grinning. "You'll get it now, boy. Maybe they'll let me watch."

I said nothing. It hadn't required a response, and I knew if I spoke my voice would break. The sailor smiled, showing gap teeth. "Anytime, now. You just wait there at attention."

"Aye aye, sir."

"Hungry, were you?"

"I—no, sir."

"God, I hate you snotty little grodes. Well, this time you uppies'll get what's coming to you!"

Sweat trickled down my sides. I was saved from a reply by steps at the hatch. I looked up. Oh, no. Oh, God, no.

Sergeant Trammel growled, "What's going on here?"

The seaman came to his feet. "Look at this mess! I found this boy in—"

"I asked the cadet." Sarge hadn't bothered to raise his voice, but the seaman's whine halted instantly. A sergeant could do that. Lamely, I said, "Cadet Seafort reporting, sir!"

"I know who you are; tell me why you're in mess hall!"

Still held to attention, eyes on the bulkhead across the hall, I groped for an answer. On a mission? Being hazed by Midshipman Thorne? Sleepwalking? I took a deep breath. "I was getting pie, sir."

"In the name of Lord Christ!" Sergeant Trammel's voice held such loathing that I flinched. "I thought you'd learned something by now, Seafort. Back to barracks."

"Aye aye, si—"

"He weren't the only one, Sarge. There were three, maybe four others. It was a regular raid. They kicked over my bucket and everything!"

Sarge wheeled on me. "Is that true?"

"I—yes, sir."

"What were you up to?"

"Stealing pie and ice cream, sir."

"I din' get a look at the others, Sarge. It was dark, and they were under tables and things. But this joey knows who—"

Sergeant Trammel wheeled. "Your name?"

"Lewis, sir. Elton Lewis."

"Go about your business, Lewis. I'll handle this."

"Yes, sir." The rating's voice held unmistakable malice. "My business is to clean up in here. Now I gotta clean up the mess they made too. The chief petty officer oughta know—"

"Yes, he should, and I'll tell him. If I hear anything more from you, there's some other things I'll mention as well. Get moving!"

Grumbling, the man picked up his bucket, swabbed at the mess. Sarge glowered. The rating finally dropped his eyes.

"As you were, Seafort! Into the corridor! Move!" Sarge propelled me forward, slapped the hatch closed behind us. The moment it shut he grabbed my lapels, thrust me against the bulkhead. "You useless excuse for a plebe! Thanks to you, I have to toady to the damned CPO!" I'd never seen him so angry.

"I'm sorry, Sarge. I didn't mean—"

"Bah! Special duties, the rest of the term. Six demerits! And that's just the start. When I—" He broke off. "Who was with you?"

"What? A couple of other cadets, and—"

"Names, Seafort!" He cuffed me. It didn't hurt, but I wanted to cry. "Who was responsible for this?"

I bit my lip. Please, God. Could you transport me home to Cardiff? Give me a miracle, just a small one.

"Please, sir!" How could I tell him—

"Their names!" He cuffed me again.

I screamed, "I'm thinking!"

Shock registered in his eyes, but he gave me a moment. "Well?"

I took a deep breath. It didn't seem enough. I took another. "Orders received and understood, Sarge. I—I won't tell you!"

The enormity of what I'd done took a moment to sink in. I flinched, expecting a devastating blow. Instead, Sarge released my jacket. "Very well, you've made your bed; now you sleep in it. Return to barracks, joey. I'm writing you up."

"Aye aye, sir." I saluted. He gave no response. I fled down the corridor.

In the morning I was forbidden to join the others for breakfast. Instead, Robbie Rovere brought a tray to barracks. He lowered his voice. "I'm not supposed to talk to you. What happened?"

I swallowed. "I'm in bad trouble. Do what Sarge said."

"You didn't come back 'til way after Lights Out. They say you wouldn't tell him what you did."

I nodded. "We were—just go back to mess hall, Robbie."

He nodded. "Yeah, I got to." Seeing no one, he pulled me into a quick embrace. "Tell them what they want, Nick. I want you next to me reading the graduation list." Embarrassed, he hurried out.

Two hours later Corporal Tolliver came in. By that time, I'd worked myself into such a state that even he was welcome. "Straighten your tie, Seafort. I'm taking you to the Commandant's office."

"What for?"

"So he can stuff you out the airlock? How would I know, you twit?"

I sank back onto my bunk, legs trembling. I'd never seen Commandant Kearsey's office, and I had no desire to. My heart pounded.

"Move, Seafort. I'm not getting in trouble over you."

I closed my eyes, reached for an elusive calm. "Yes, Mr. Tolliver."

I followed Tolliver to the Administrative warren, damp with fear. He stopped at the Commandant's outer hatch, knocked politely, brought himself to attention. "Cadet Corporal Edgar Tolliver reporting, Ma'am. I've brought Cadet Seafort as ordered."

The dark-skinned woman tapped at her console. "Send him in. Dismissed."

"Aye aye, ma'am!" Tolliver saluted, spun on his heel, marched out the corridor. He pointed me toward the hatch. "Hey, Seafort . . ."

I paused. "What?"

Tolliver scrutinized the bulkhead. "Good luck," he said at last. Then he was gone.

"Sit there." She indicated a row of stiff-backed chairs. I chose the farthest seat from her desk. It was against the bulkhead of the Commandant's inner office.

Hands on my knees, I sat stiffly, waiting for my execution. The duty sergeant checked her watch, buzzed the caller. "I'm going below for a moment, sir. The cadet is here."

"Very well."

Without a further glance she was gone. The console hummed in the sudden hush of the outer office. I shifted, rested my head against the bulkhead.

Voices. Ashamed, I sat forward, but after a moment leaned back again, pressed my head to the partition.

". . . could have handled it in barracks, but twice he refused to answer me. A direct order!"

Commandant Kearsey's voice was acid. "Well, Sergeant, what did you expect?"

A pause. "I don't understand, sir."

"Don't you see what you've done?" His voice faded. I strained to listen. ". . . teach these youngsters to hang together, to look after each other! That's what the Navy's about, isn't it? We're shipmates. We handle . . . problems, first within the barracks, then within the Base, ultimately within the Navy. We don't go running to outsiders for help."

"It all starts . . . obeying orders, sir." Sarge's voice was stubborn. "That's what I was taught."

"Of course it does, Trammel, that's why you've fouled up so badly."

"Begging your pardon, I don't see where—"

"What did you expect from the lad, ordering him to inform on his mates? Of course you wanted to find out who was behind it. You had every right to. But the last thing to do was ask him outright! How do you think he'd feel if he'd obeyed your order? What would his bunkmates think of him?"

I wiped at my eyes, overcome by feelings I hadn't known I had. I wasn't sure why I'd refused. I just knew . . . it was as if Father had been watching, through the hatch.

"How else could I find the other culprits, sir? I'm not Lord God, you know!"

"Careful there, that's close to blasphemy. You could have asked the others to step forward and admit their guilt."

"And if they hadn't? We'd be worse off than ever."

"Yes. So you could have forgotten about his cohorts, dealt with the miscreant you had collared. But asking him to commit treason—"

"Good Lord. Treason, you call it?"

"Yes, Sergeant, or something damn close. By asking him to betray his bunkmates for your sake, you gave him an impossible choice."

"But we're all the Navy, together, sir. Even you and I!"

Commandant Kearsey said quietly, "How would he know that yet? We're so far above them, we're on another plane. For now, the Navy is his bunkmates. Later, he'll understand the rest."

"I—It's just that . . . I was angry, sir, or I'd never have asked. The overturned bucket, that loutish sailor sitting there grinning. I knew he'd spread it all over, belowdecks."

"And you wanted the boy to act nobly in front of the swabbie. Well, in his way, he did." A long pause. "So you're going to let him off, sir?"

"Eh? No, of course not. I can't, now that you've made an issue of it. I have to back you up."

"You won't expel him, will you?"

"Don't be silly. I don't mind cadets thinking me an ogre, but you should know better."

Sarge's tone was more reflective. "Seafort's not a natural leader, sir. It couldn't have been his idea. I'd really like to get my hands on the ringleader, but now we'll never find him."

"It was Thorne, if you must know."

"But, how—"

"He turned himself in this morning, when he heard Seafort had been caught. He said he'd ordered the cadet to take part. I didn't believe him for a minute."

"I'll never trust that little bugger again."

"Oh, don't go that far. He'll straighten out, most likely. I sent him to Zorn." A chair scraped. "Next time, use your common sense."

"Aye aye, sir. Is that all?"

"Send him in."

The hatch opened. Sergeant Trammel came out, saw me sitting bolt upright, hands pressed to my knees. "The Commandant will see you now."

"Yes, sir." I stood, adjusted my cap, marched in. Commandant Kearsey, seated behind his desk, fixed me with a steely eye.

"Cadet Nicholas Seafort reporting, sir." I saluted, came to attention.

"So. You're the insolent pup who refused a direct order from your sergeant."

My sides were clammy. "Yes, sir."

"I'm always disappointed when a cadet is brought into this cabin. It means we haven't done our job, that we've failed to communicate the basics. Or that the cadet is a failure who never should have been admitted."

Some response seemed to be called for. "Yes, sir."

"I won't belabor the point. Instead, I'll endeavor to teach you that orders are to be obeyed, without exception. If you graduate, you'll be in a position to give orders to sailors. You must first know how to obey them."

"Yes, sir."

"Take off your jacket and cap, and place them on the chair." I complied. "Bend over my desk. Put your hands on the desk, under your chin. Lean forward."

"Aye aye, sir." He hadn't touched me, but already the humiliation was excruciating.

Commandant Kearsey rolled back his chair and stood. Taking his time, he walked to the corner, picked up the wooden cane leaning there. "Have you ever been sent to the barrel?"

"No, sir."

"A caning isn't pleasant. However, as only a noteworthy offense causes you to be sent here, my punishment must be more persuasive than the first lieutenant's. Cadet, remain still until you're given permission to move."

"Aye aye, si—" The cane landed with the crack of a shot. I shrieked. My head jerked upward.

"You were told to be still."

"Yes, sir!" I thrust my head onto my hands, hoping to pin them in place. The cane came down again, and again.

When finally it was over I lay against the desk, exhausted from

the effort to hold my position, wracked with sobs. Commandant
Kearsey replaced the cane, picked up my jacket. "Stand."

I straightened carefully. He helped me slip into the jacket, turned
me to the hatch. "Every act has a price, Mr. Seafort. You've just paid
yours. The debt is extinguished." Gently, he propelled me forward.
"Continue to do your best."

"Aye aye, sir." Like a toy soldier I lurched out of his office, scarlet with mortification, my buttocks on fire. The young woman at the
outer console paid no heed. I tottered through the outer hatch,
closed it behind me. In the corridor, I sagged against the bulkhead
and wept.

In my Captain's blues, I gently stroked the bed on which I sat. It had
been a bitter lesson. Sarge himself had brought my meals to the barracks,
until I was able to march to mess hall without pain.

A sound.

I looked up, startled. "Who are you?"

The gray-clad boy jumped to attention. "Cadet Johan Stritz reporting, sir!" Wiry, muscular, a young face, worried eyes.

I snapped, "How long have you been watching me?"

"I'm sorry, I—I came in, sir, and you were sitting there. I didn't
know what to—I'm sorry!"

"You come to attention, whether I see you or not!"

"Yes, sir. Aye aye, sir."

"Stritz, you say? You're the young fool who raised his hand against an
officer?"

He gulped. "Yessir."

"If I hadn't been groundside I'd have . . . I'd—as you were!" I
stalked out.

The steward poured our coffee and left the conference room. I eyed
each of my officers gathered around the table. "How do we start?" It was
my first staff meeting at Farside.

For a moment no one spoke. Then Sergeant Obutu said with diffi-
dence, "In the past, we've just gone around the table, sir. Usually starting
with Maintenance."

"Very well. Proceed."

Lieutenant Crossburn switched on his holo, skimmed his notes.
When at last he looked up, he addressed the others rather than me. "For
some reason supply deliveries are slow, despite my repeated calls to
Lunapolis. We're supposed to get fresh vegetables every couple of weeks,

to augment the yield from hydroponics. Nothing's come in for two months now." He waited for a response.

"Well?" My tone was short.

"What do you want to do about it?" It could have been a challenge.

"Are we low on stores?"

"No, between frozen foods and hydro—"

"Call again. Anything else?"

His look was sullen. "Complaints from belowdecks about middies in the service corridors. Sometimes they leave softies—"

"Mr. Paulson, have a word with Keene for the middies to pick up after themselves." I wasn't about to prohibit midshipmen from standing around the corridors; Lord God knows where else they'd congregate.

"Aye aye, sir." My graying first lieutenant made a note.

Crossburn shrugged helplessly. "I never heard back from Commandant Kearsey on the maintenance review plan I submitted, sir. I refiled a copy with you two weeks ago."

I grunted. "Very well, I'll look at it." I suspected a glance would be all I'd need. "Systems?"

Lieutenant Paulson shifted in his chair, as if weary. "Nothing new, sir. All base systems are working properly, and the Training Station is closed down at the moment."

"Until when?"

"Hillman's cadets are scheduled to go in three weeks."

"Very well."

Crossburn looked up importantly. "When do you intend to inspect the Station, sir?"

"In a day or two. Why?"

"If you won't wait for Sergeant Hillman, I'll have to make everything ready." Well, I couldn't fault his preparation, but the self-satisfied tone left me itching to . . . I didn't know what.

"Next?"

Lieutenant Ngu Bien oversaw classroom training. "Test scores slightly above median for the month, sir. On the whole, no problems."

"That's it?"

"Yes, sir."

"Well, that was fast. Mr. Pau—" Sergeant Obutu cleared her throat. "Yes, Sarge?"

"Pardon me for interrupting, sir. Perhaps you might look at the individual highs and lows in each class."

Lieutenant Bien rewarded her with a frosty look. "Does that concern your administrative duties, Sergeant?"

Ms. Obutu showed hardly any reaction. Only I could see her clenched fist under the rim of the table. "No, ma'am, it doesn't."

"Well, then—"

I overrode her. "A good point, Ms. Bien. Sarge is only a glorified secretary and has no business interfering." Sergeant Obutu's mouth tightened. I kept my voice casual, "By the way, Ms. Bien, would you mind telling *me* the individual highs and lows in each class?"

She colored at the rebuke. "Yes, sir, of course."

While she ran through her notes Sergeant Obutu's eyes met mine. My gaze was impassive, but just before turning away my eyelid twitched.

"In Nav Two, sir, Cadet Alicia Johns has the highest scores; she usually does. Jerence Branstead was second. Two failing grades this time, um, Arnweil and Stritz."

Lieutenant Paulson said, "That's under control, I believe. Their barracks sergeants have set up special tutoring."

"Along with the usual loss of privileges. Now, in History, we have Benghadi, Guevire, and Boland at the top. The low grades are Kyle Drew and Kevin Arnweil."

"Drew?" I puzzled. "Where do I know that name?"

Paulson said, "He was involved in the fatality, sir."

"No, that was Arnweil. He ran to the lock while—" I snapped my fingers. "The other one." The boy whose overeager launch had caused Edwards's death.

"Yes, sir."

I drummed the tabletop. "Let's see grades for Arnweil, Drew and Stritz for the last three months."

He punched in figures; a moment later the screen flashed. Scores for all three cadets had plummeted.

"It happens that way, sir. They'll pull up, sooner or later, or—"

"Yes?"

"Or wash out."

Jent Paulson started to speak, but I shook my head. After a moment I said, "Conference over. We'll resume this afternoon. Mr. Paulson, I'd like a report on all cadets in trouble. Talk to the instructors yourself, interrupt classes if you must. Also the dorm sergeants. Some problems may not show up in grades."

"Aye aye, sir. Are you—I mean, are we cleaning house, sir?"

"In a fashion." I left them, returned to my office. After brooding for half an hour, I roused myself and called in Sergeant Obutu.

"Sarge, about the conference. Why your question?"

"I'm sorry if I intru—"

"Belay that. What was on your mind?"

She leaned back, clasped her hands around her knee. "She irked me, sir, with that talk of medians. We don't teach medians here, we train cadets."

"Go on."

"It's none of my business, but the joeys, uh, talk to me sometimes. Perhaps because I'm a woman." She flushed, as if maternal traits ran against the grain of her duty. Perhaps they did. "I came across Kyle Drew scrubbing corridors, two days after the—the accident." She smiled apologetically. "He went on with his work, but I watched for a while, and chatted with him. He was Edwards's bunkie, you know."

"He has a heavy load."

Her tone was forceful. "You can't imagine how heavy. Kyle insisted he knew it wasn't his fault, yet a moment after, he began to weep and couldn't stop."

I sighed. "How did you leave it?"

"I patted his shoulder, went on my way, and saw to it that I ran across him later in the evening. I've talked to him twice since."

"You should be a psych."

"Lord God forbid. The point is, he's not the only one, sir. You act, I mean, we act—the Navy—as if we're dealing with adults. They're just children, trying to learn about adulthood."

"I know." My words were barely audible.

"Sometimes, sitting in that outer room, when they leave the Commandant's office, your office now, I see the look in their eyes, the remorse, the shame . . . Sometimes I think you don't know how hard they try to please you."

"Oh, I do. Believe me."

"I remember one such cadet many years ago, a brave one. He cried in the outer corridor, when he thought no one could hear."

After a moment I met her gaze. "That was you?"

She looked to the deck, as if shy. "I was younger then. I don't mean to drag up old—"

"I was so terrified, I barely knew where I was." I reflected. "You're a good woman, Ms. Obutu."

"Thank you."

A moment passed. I said, "She's an ass, isn't she?"

Sergeant Obutu looked shocked. "Ms. Bien? Well, it would be impolite to disagree with you." But then she shook her head. "No, that was wrong. I do disagree. She sounds foolish, yes, but maybe she just can't see past the paperwork. Perhaps, confronted with a real cadet, a real problem, she'd react differently."

I was ashamed, both of my indiscretion and my lack of charity. "Yes. Very well. Dismissed."

Again, we were in the conference room. I snapped off the holo; the dry statistics disappeared. "Makeup work, extra duties to occupy Drew's mind. What else can we do for him?"

Paulson shrugged. "What else is there, sir?" Good point. Academy had its routines, and we shouldn't disrupt them. Still, something nagged at me, and I wasn't sure what.

"Let's see if his sergeant has an answer."

"I beg your pardon, sir?"

"Radz. Call him in."

Crossburn blurted, "Into staff conference? That's not how we—"

"He's staff, isn't he?" I waved the objection aside. "Ms. Obutu, page him, please."

A few minutes later Sergeant Radz took the seat I indicated. I summarized. "What's your opinion, Sarge?"

"He's moody, yes. But they all are, at that age. Who can say why?"

"You think he'll come out of it himself?"

Radz's mouth turned grim. "If he's to be a midshipman, he has to."

I stood, paced a few steps, studied the seams of the bulkhead. "But don't you think . . ."

Paulson cleared his throat. "It's a question of approach, and the Navy's philosophy is clear. They sink or swim on their own. Edwards's death was a tragedy, but Drew has to learn to cope."

Radz said, "When it comes down to it, sir, we're teachers, not nursemaids. We can encourage, but we can't hold their hands throughout their careers. The sooner they understand that, the better. If Kyle Drew buckles down to his work, he can still graduate with his mates. Otherwise you hold him back, or wash him out."

"Just like that?"

"No, sir, not just like that. I've taken him for long walks through the warrens, like I have Arnweil. He shrugs and closes tighter, until I want to shake him. If anything, the Arnweil boy has it harder than Drew; he was closer to Edwards. They both knew the Navy was serious business when they signed on."

Lieutenant Crossburn stirred. "If I may say so, sir—"

"You may not. I have no interest in what you have to say."

"I—aye aye, sir." He made his injury evident.

I sighed. "Your joint advice is not to interfere further. You're probably right." More than probably. A hundred seventy years of Naval tradition supported their position. "Very well. Keep me informed."

9

The next morning I suited, went Outside with Lieutenant Bien and two sergeants to observe another training exercise. I said little, watching every cadet's unsure step like a mother hen, ready for a second dreadful incident. By the time we recycled through the lock, I was worn and irritable.

I unbuckled my suit and hung it in a locker, vaguely aware that the cadets, whom I'd expected to be chattering from accumulated tension, were unusually quiet. One boy dropped his helmet; it clattered loudly on the deck. He wilted at my glance. What was the matter with them? Were they all cowed by Edwards's death? As soon as we were alone I asked Lieutenant Bien as much.

Her face lit in a wry grin. "Yes, they're cowed, sir. But they'll be all right next time."

"How can you be so sure?"

"Because you won't be along." Her smile broadened. "Couldn't you see how they tiptoed around? How they watched you Outside? They're terrified of you."

I grunted. It was understandable, perhaps even appropriate. But still, I found it disturbing. The elusive thought led me nowhere.

That evening I had Sergeant Obutu set up my visit to the Training Station. We needn't seek Admiralty's approval; the Station was under my authority and we had a minishuttle of our own. I could stay as long as I wished, recall the shuttle to ferry me back to base.

Ms. Obutu rang back just as I settled into bed. "Tomorrow, right after breakfast. Mr. Trayn will pilot."

"Very well."

I lay in bed thinking of Annie. Was it too late to call? Should I contact her at all, or was it best to wait? Would I ever again be truly married? I drifted into restless sleep.

In the morning I dressed, went to mess hall, strode to my place. "Gentlemen, be seated!" Four hundred eighty cadets sat, almost as one. "Good morning." I reached for coffee.

"Morning, sir." Jent Paulson poured for both of us.

"Where are the others? Ms. Bien? Mr. Crossburn?" I chewed on a breakfast roll.

"Ms. Bien is rotated to Devon, sir. She's probably at Earthport Station waiting for her flight. I believe Mr. Crossburn is checking your shuttle." He hesitated. "Have you reviewed the Log this morning, sir?"

"I haven't been in to the office yet."

"Tenere was sent up again. Ten demerits. I made him wait outside so I wouldn't be late for breakfast."

"Adam?" I felt a twinge of guilt. Some of his demerits had come from me. "Mr. Paulson, could you go easy on him?" What was I doing? The boy had earned what demerits he'd been given.

"Aye aye, sir, if you wish." He said no more. Perhaps I was intruding on his prerogative, but a Captain, any Captain, was allowed to have his way.

"Why?" I asked abruptly.

"Hm? The demerits? Ms. Bien gave him the last ones before she caught the shuttle. Something to do with Johan Stritz; he made the cadet late to class. I don't know the details."

I grunted. How was Stritz involved with Adam Tenere? It was bad discipline for middies to consort with cadets. I thought of Jeff Thorne, and shook my head. Still, Ms. Bien had probably overreacted. By asking Paulson to go easy I'd negate most of the damage, but I felt a continuing disquiet.

"What about the Stritz boy?"

"I have no idea. Ngu sent him to his sergeant, I imagine."

I sipped at my coffee. Stritz had enough troubles, and if Sergeant Tripole was as unforgiving as Radz, the boy was in for more misery. I made a note to look into it, when I got back from the Station.

After breakfast, I took my duffel to the lock, vaguely depressed that I couldn't get a handle on our personnel problems.

The shuttle was mated and ready. First Midshipman Thomas Keene waited to secure after we left. With him was Ardwell Crossburn.

"Ready, sir?" The pudgy lieutenant smiled politely.

I turned. "Yes, Mr. Crossburn. Good-bye."

"Good-bye? I'm going with you, sir."

"The hell you—That won't be necessary."

Crossburn looked aghast, while Midshipman Keene watched the byplay with interest. "You can't go alone, sir. The Station is shut down. Someone has to start up the machinery, get things—who'd prepare your meals?"

"Not you, Mr. Crossburn." I'd cancel my trip first.

"Whatever you say, sir. Let me point out that as maintenance officer I know where Station supplies are kept. Shall I call Mr. Paulson instead?"

"No, he has work to do." I was brusque. Why hadn't anyone mentioned that Crossburn would go along? Why hadn't I asked? "I can manage alone, I think."

"Sir, be reasonable! What if something went wrong?"

He was right, but the thought of his company brought an edge to my voice. "Very well, then. Get your gear—" I stopped short.

My idea was unorthodox, perhaps, but it would solve another problem as well. I took the caller from the hatchway, keyed it to the first lieutenant's cabin. No answer. Good; I wasn't too late.

I turned to the waiting middy. "Mr. Keene, run down to Lieutenant Paulson's cabin; Adam is waiting outside. He's to get his duffel and report to me here. If you see Mr. Paulson, tell him I said Mr. Tenere's chastisement can wait."

The startled midshipman knew better than to question me. "Aye aye, sir." He started off.

I called, "For Adam's sake, you'd better hurry." Paulson would be returning any minute. The middy raced down the corridor, prohibitions against running voided by my august authority.

Ardwell Crossburn cleared his throat. "Surely you don't intend to take a middy as your only—"

I rested my hand on the hatch and sighed. "Ardwell, be quiet. So help me, I'll—just shut up."

"Aye aye, sir. I must advise you I will file a written protest with Admiralty over—"

"Fine. Do it." If Admiral Duhaney relieved me, so much the better. Several minutes passed in uneasy silence before the two breathless middies returned.

"Midshipman Tenere repor—"

"You have your gear? Good. Get in the shuttle, we're going to Training Station."

"Aye aye, sir." Adam was less surprised than I'd expected; apparently Keene had forewarned him. Good. It was his job to look after his middies.

We boarded and took our seats. The minishuttle was just large enough to ferry a squad of cadets between Station and Farside Base. For larger groups, we'd go through U.N.A.F. Transport at Earthport Station.

The Pilot busied himself calculating weights and trajectories. Adam buckled himself in. "May I speak, sir?"

Midshipmen were expected to be seen and not heard. On the other hand, I'd summoned Tenere to special duty with me. Why seek his company if I intended to ignore him in the traditional manner? "Go ahead."

"May I ask, I mean—" He smiled weakly. "What are we—why am I here, sir?" I raised an eyebrow. "That is, I know you ordered me, but . . ." He tried again. "Excuse me, sir, I didn't mean that the way it sounded. I just—"

I said nothing until he trailed off in confusion. No wonder Ms. Bien had sent the boy to be caned; any more blathering and I'd cane him myself. Even Ardwell Crossburn would be better company.

The Pilot called, "Ready for liftoff, sir. Stand by." I waved, gripping my seat, though I knew acceleration from Luna hardly compared to the breath-wrenching gees needed to claw our way from Earth's possessive grasp.

I leaned back, closed my eyes, felt rather than watched our ascent. After several minutes the hull became silent. I sat forward, loosened the straps. In the next seat, Adam Tenere carefully did nothing to incur my notice.

I sighed. He had to be dealt with, for my sake more than his. "Mr. Tenere, that performance was disgraceful."

"I—yes, sir. I'm sorry. I won't speak again." His hands crossed tightly in his lap.

"Unsatisfactory."

"Yes, sir!" Tiny beads of sweat shone on his forehead. "What do you want of me, sir?"

"Ask what you intended to before we lifted."

"I wanted to know why we were going aloft. I didn't mean to step out of line, sir!"

"Look at me, boy!" His head jerked around. I grabbed his wrist, pulled his hand to touch my chest. He yanked it back as if burned, while his eyes remained locked to mine. "I'm your Commandant, not Lord God. They've given me the power to cane you, even to have you dismissed. But that's no reason to gibber like an idiot!"

"I'm sor—" He gulped. "Please!" An anguished cry.

"If you say sorry—" No, that wasn't the way. I forced calm into my tone. "Adam . . ." I wished I'd let well enough alone. Now I'd have to discuss matters I loathed.

"How did you feel when you heard I was to be Commandant?" I swiveled to study his face.

He muttered, "I was—proud, sir. We all were. I couldn't believe I'd actually get to serve under you."

"Why?"

"You know why! You're a hero!"

"So they say. Why?"

"How brave you are. The things you've done."

I snorted. "I was so scared I wet my pants."

"But that didn't stop you."

"When I called you to the shuttle bay, where were you?"

"At Lieutenant Paulson's cabin, sir."

"Waiting to be caned." He nodded. "Were you afraid?"

"It hurts!" He twisted away, stared through the porthole. "Of course I was."

"But you've been caned before. You know you can stand it."

His voice was small. "Yes, sir."

"When I've had enough of your idiocy and dismiss you, what then? Will you kill yourself?"

"What?" His jaw dropped.

"Will your father ever speak to you again? Will your life be over?"

Adam's tone was tight. "Yes, sir, he'll speak to me again. He'll love me as he does now. And my life won't be over."

"So. You know the worst I can do, and you can stand it. Now you too can be a hero."

The boy's anger dissolved into bewilderment. "I don't understand, sir."

"That famous incident in *Challenger*, when I rammed the fish. All I did was decide to act, and the rest followed. It was a throw of the dice, do you see? Or when I nuked Orbit Station. Was that heroism? I didn't dither, that's all. I made up my mind to commit treason to get rid of those damned fish, and I did it." I looked away, too ashamed to meet his eye.

After a moment, I forced myself to continue. "It's ridiculous that you'd need heroism to speak to me without babbling, but here's how you do it. Open your mouth, say what you intended, and shut it. From the moment you asked if you could speak, you were committed."

"I wasn't sure if . . . I mean, I thought you might be angry."

"Then keep your mouth closed in the first place. But you can't speak, apologize, and be silent all at the same time."

"Yes, sir. Thank you, sir."

I wanted to slap him. "You still don't get it? To have any respect at all, either from me or yourself, you had to finish asking your question. If you can't understand that, the Naval Service has no place for you."

He twisted at the flaps of his jacket, whispered, "You don't understand. I—I was afraid."

"Adam, we're all afraid! Fear has nothing to do with how you act!" I turned away. I'd failed, and in the process revealed more of myself than I could abide.

Let him stew in his juices, then. When we got back I would send him groundside, with unsatisfactory ratings. I fished in my duffel, took out my holovid.

Adam Tenere slumped in misery against the porthole. When he thought my attention was elsewhere, he wiped away a tear.

I tried to spot the Training Station against the points of light blazing like pinpricks in a black cloth. Of course I couldn't find it. I had no idea even where to look. "How long now, Pilot?"

"Nineteen minutes, sir." He pointed to starboard. "It's in view."

I grunted.

"Wait, I'll light it up." He keyed the caller, tapped in a code. A moment passed, and lights sprang to life in the distance.

The Academy Training Station bore hardly any resemblance to Earthport, the colossal terminus that served as our gateway to the stars. Earthport's warehouses bulged with the ores and foodstuffs from our colonies that fueled the Terran economy, and from her bays colonists and administrators even now poured outward to the settled worlds, despite the recent menace of the fish.

Our Training Station was but a single disk, and a small one at that. Though eleven Fusers were moored alongside, the Station's two bays could dock only two boats at a time.

Designed for simplicity, the Station carried no hydroponics and had only primitive mess facilities. Its few cabins were crowded with bunks, where cadets slept as tightly packed as in a ship's wardroom. The Station was powered only by solar cells.

I'd been here just once in my life, for eleven days, along with my squad and two vigilant instructors. It was an odd feeling to return on my own, but I was unlikely to run into trouble. The Station was conceived for just one purpose; to accommodate squads of cadets while they trained on the Fusers, and then to shut down again.

Pilot Trayn maneuvered us closer. For a moment I watched, then went back to my seat, waited for us to come to rest relative to the Station. At last the outer locks kissed; the seals pressed tightly against their Station counterparts.

I stood again. "Suit up, Mr. Tenere." I climbed awkwardly into my gear, while the boy slid into his with a lithe grace. Though the Station would be pressurized, I checked my helmet clamps with care and made sure my oximeter dial was in the green.

The Pilot, already suited, cycled the lock shut. Expecting full pressurization on the Station side, he didn't bother to pump to vacuum, but grasped the safety grip firmly just in case. Our outer hatch slid open, as did the Station's. He fastened our steel safety line.

Just short of the hatch I turned the middy by the shoulders, checking all his clamps. As I expected, they were secure. It was an officer's responsibility to look after his own safety, yet I felt better for the precaution.

We cycled through the lock into the Station. The Pilot keyed his radio. "Shall I wait while you check things out, sir?"

If the Commandant couldn't figure how to power up the Station, who could? "No, return to base. We'll call when we're ready for you."

"Aye aye, sir. I'll cast off in a few moments, then."

"Very well." The Station lock cycled shut. I warned Adam, "Stay on suit air until we've checked every cabin."

Power-up first; lights and heat would follow. We'd find plenty of Q-rations in the coolers. I could bunk in the instructors' cabin and let Adam sleep where he wanted.

The boy cleared his throat. "Sir?"

"Not now, Mr. Tenere." According to the holo I'd reviewed back at Farside, I'd find the command console in the stationmaster's cabin near the instructors' quarters. "Come along."

I passed vaguely familiar cabins, then the aft lock. It wasn't until we'd nearly circled to our starting point that I came upon the stationmaster's cabin.

The console had an oversize keyboard, to accommodate suited fingers; they'd thought of everything. I tapped in my ID code, waited until my clearance flashed. While Adam Tenere watched over my shoulder I typed, "Oral communication, please," and waited for my suit radio to crackle.

Nothing. I tapped, "Command response."

"READY FOR RESPONSE."

"Terminate alphanumeric only."

"ALPHANUMERIC ONLY NOT IN EFFECT."

"Puter, respond, please." I swore under my breath. "Why can't I hear you?" Communications were glitched, and I'd let the shuttle leave us. Unless I could power the Station, we might have no way to call it back.

Adam Tenere coughed. "Sir, pardon me, but—"

"Quiet, I'm busy." If only I hadn't been so impetuous as to send the shuttle away. I tried to think through the puzzle. My radio worked; Adam could hear me. Again, I tapped, "Command response."

"READY FOR RESPONSE."

Well, at least I could communicate alphanumerically, and that wouldn't be so bad, once we checked atmosphere and desuited. But somewhere in the puter's—

"Sir, you're on—"

I spun round. "Two demerits! Make that fou—"

"—shuttle approach frequency! Switch your radio!"

The room was silent a long moment. I keyed my suit's caller, said tentatively, "Hello?"

"Puter D 1004 responding, Commandant." A firm tenor voice.

"Yes. Well. Commence power-up." I was careful not to look at Midshipman Tenere.

Console lights flashed. The standby bulbs brightened.

"Atmosphere check."

"Breathable air in all compartments."

I had to get rid of the middy. "Mr. Tenere, check all cabin air gauges on the double."

"Aye aye, sir." He left me to my mortification.

By the time he was back, power-up was completed; corridor and cabin lights transformed the Station to welcome familiarity. "All gauges at normal, sir."

"Desuit." I undid my clamps, glad to be free of my own nervous sweat. I hung my suit on a rack. "Put your gear in a cabin."

"Which—"

"Any of them. Now!" I rested my head in my hands. God, what a mistake, bringing a midshipman to witness my debacle. The tale would be all over Farside. I'd be a laughingstock thanks to a blunder even a cadet would know to avoid.

"Reporting for orders, sir."

I searched for a way to keep him out of my presence, to lessen my humiliation. I could have him check stores, establish radio contact with Farside . . .

With effort, I raised my head. Whatever the embarrassment, I'd earned it. "Mr. Tenere, thank you for correcting me. Ignore what I said about demerits."

"I'm sorry if I—" He broke off short. Then, with resolve, "You're welcome, sir."

"I'll put my gear in the instructors' cabin. Call Farside, tell them we're here safely." I stood to make my escape.

"Aye aye, sir. Pardon me, may I speak?"

"Yes."

He hesitated but a second. "Would you tell me why we're here, please, and what duties I'll have?" He waited only a second before blurting, "I mean, if you don't mi—I'm—Lord God damn it!" He rushed on, red-faced. "You don't know how I rehearsed that, sir! I was determined not to run my mouth!"

My voice was cold. "Two demerits are reinstated, Mr. Tenere, for taking His name in vain." That I wouldn't have.

"Yes, sir." He sagged. "Am I dismissed?"

"No. Try your question again."

"Aye aye, sir." He licked his lips. "Pardon me, but why are we here? What do you want me to do?"

"Very good, Mr. Tenere. I'm here to familiarize myself with the Station after twelve years absence. You're here to make yourself useful. One way is to run a comm check with Farside every few hours."

"Aye aye, sir."

"That's all. You've been accumulating demerits at an alarming rate. Start working them off; I'll log them for you."

"Aye aye, sir. I'll set up a relay with Farside and do a demerit before we eat."

"Very well." I carried my gear to my cabin.

After a Q-ration dinner I went back to my cabin and pored through chips of reports and memos I'd brought along, while young Tenere tackled another demerit. Though his subsequent appearance left no doubt that he'd been exercising, I'd of course have taken his word. A midshipman, like any officer, was a gentleman whose pledge was to be trusted. Were he to be caught lying about a demerit, he'd be cashiered on the spot.

I decided I should visit the Training Station more often; it was an excellent place to work without interruption.

The next morning, after breakfast, I lounged on my bunk trying to memorize cadets' faces as I'd seen Sergeant Ibarez do. Adam knocked politely to report he'd worked off another demerit. I ordered him to desist for a few hours. Demerits were intended to punish, not to abuse.

In the mess cabin at lunchtime, I made the coffee while the middy popped the tabs on two Q-rations and set them out to heat. When the chemical reaction between the inner and outer skins was complete, he brought them to the table and sat carefully, with a sigh.

I tore open my lid and fell to. To break the quiet I asked, "What are your plans for this afternoon, Mr. Tenere?"

He grimaced. "I'll run a comm check with Farside again, on schedule. Then another demerit. Maybe two."

"No, you're overdoing it."

He shrugged bitterly. "It's the only way I have to keep up, sir."

"Was that a complaint?"

He looked up, astonished. "No, sir. I know it's my own fault."

"They say humility is the first step to improvement." For a moment I debated. "Instead of demerits, help me check out the Fusers." It would give us both something to do. Though I was hardly finished with my self-imposed deskwork, I was thoroughly tired of cadet dossiers.

He perked up noticeably. "Aye aye, sir."

After the meal we suited, trudged to the empty forward lock. I made sure the hatches were set to standard codes, then cycled us through. Moments later, we stood on the outer rim of the disk.

"Fuser One is closest," I said.

We clambered with our magnetic boots across the hull. The Fuser floated meters from the Station rim, moored by a line from its lock. Without a line, even the inertia of an instructor kicking off from the hull would send the boat on a slow unpowered journey that would end only when she settled into a new elliptical orbit, or drifted off into the void.

"You jump first, Adam. Be careful."

"Aye aye, sir." He reached down, turned off his boots. If he'd been a cadet, he'd be tethered to a lifeline, but any middy knew how to launch himself properly.

Adam took care not to kick off with too much force. He floated slowly across to the trainer, switching his boots back on in midflight. His landing was awkward, but his boot made good contact with the hull.

I decided I'd made a fool of myself often enough for one expedition. Before jumping, I switched on my hand magnets. A smart precaution. I landed on all fours and would have bounced back into space had my glove magnets not gripped the hull. I brought my knees down, made boot contact, switched off my gloves. "Open the lock."

Moments later we were inside the tiny vessel. I walked to the cramped bridge, looked back to the main cabin and the two cramped wardrooms that would house cadets during their training. It all seemed laughably small. "Ever been on a ship of the line, Mr. Tenere?"

"My father showed me through *Freiheit*, sir, just after I graduated. I know she was just a sloop, but compared to this . . ."

"Yes." I sat in the Pilot's seat, gestured for the boy to take his place alongside. I stroked the silent console. Much could happen, even in a Training Fuser . . .

"Listen up, you cretins!" Sergeant Garver floated in the center corridor, hands on her hips. "You've watched the holos, so you know a Fuser is a hybrid, built especially for the Naval Service, useful for

nothing but training dimwitted cadets. It has no galley, no hydroponics, no recycling, no cargo hold, no disk. No main engine either, just
thrusters so we can maneuver to and from our mooring. That's why
we call her a boat, not a ship."

I watched Sarge dutifully, making sure I seemed to be paying
rapt attention. Even if I could parrot back what she'd just said, roving
eyes or fidgets were good for extra duties if not a demerit. Excited
beyond words at finally boarding a real vessel, I didn't want the burden of her displeasure.

"And of course, she has a fusion drive, which is the main reason
you're here."

The Trainers' fusion drives operated just like those of a ship of
the line, with two important differences. First, puters could carry out
many Fusion calculations performed by crew on a larger vessel, so a
day's training could be concentrated in one aspect of the Fusion
process.

The other difference was our size.

Many lives were lost before it was fully understood that fusion
drives didn't work properly near a gravitational mass. The larger the
vessel, the farther it had to be from a source of gravity to Fuse. A
U.N. starship could Fuse from within a couple of hours thrust of
Earthport, but a loaded ore barge, whose mass was colossal, would
have to journey much farther to reach Fusion clearance.

On the other hand, our Training Fusers were so small their drives
could be ignited safely almost anywhere in the Solar System. Except,
of course, within the B'n Auba Zone, so close to the sun that regardless of mass, Fusion was impossible. At times, in our training, I
cursed the Saudi astronomer and his demanding formulas over
which we struggled.

Sarge waited for our attention. "Fusion is nothing to be afraid of,
despite the nonsense you see on the holos. There's no sensation of
blacking out, no eerie tingling in your spine, no crackling ions. In fact,
you won't feel a thing, you won't even know we've Fused unless you
look out the porthole and see—Seafort?"

"Yes, ma'am, I—" I struggled to recall what she'd been saying.
"See nothing, ma'am. No stars, no light."

"All right, but if you poke Cadet Sanders once more you'll spend
the cruise as chief officer of the head. I don't care whether she
started it." Ms. Garver looked away, at last. "By now you joeys
should be interchangeable parts, but I won't tax your resources.

Three of you will go to the engine room, three to the nav room, and two to the bridge."

She nodded to her fellow instructor. "Mr. Reese and the cadets on the bridge will maneuver the vessel clear of the Station, and the nav room will calculate a Fuse."

Please, Lord, let it be the bridge. I hated Lambert and Greeley's Elements of Astronavigation with a passion. The nav room would mean endless hours of calculations under Sergeant Reese's unflagging supervision. The engine room was even worse. Fusion was a dimly comprehended principle, good for hours of sweat, agony, and fear.

"We'll make several jumps, and I'll probably shift some of you twits to different positions, but don't get your hopes up." Over the next week, the Fuser would flicker from one lonely spot to another. In the process, we'd get infinite and nerve-wracking practice, both at Fusion calculations and at Nav. Each time the boat Defused, perspiring cadets would have to identify our positions with painstaking accuracy.

I knew the trickiest calculation would be the one that brought us back home to Station. On a long cruise, a ship merely Defused several times for nav checks. On quick trips like ours, that wasn't an option.

Nonetheless, we'd have to emerge near the Station when we Defused. Even though Fusers were equipped with oversize propellant tanks, unskilled cadets would be at the controls during docking, and prodigious quantities of propellant would be wasted.

Arlene Sanders caught me a good one in the ribs. I flinched, but kept my eyes glued to Sarge. Later, there would be time for retribution.

Naturally, I got the nav room.

Our first goal was an uninhabited spot between the orbits of Jupiter and Saturn, thirty-eight degrees above the elliptical. We labored at our calculations until they all agreed. That took an amazingly long time, because Van Roef kept dividing mass instead of multiplying. Finally, when even Sergeant Reese had developed an edge to his tone, we all got it right, and we passed our calculations on to the bridge. Then another endless wait, while the bridge crew completed their own chores.

At last Mr. Reese snapped, "For God's sake, get up and stretch; this fidgeting drives me crazy."

"A short drive," muttered Robbie Rovere, a tad too loudly. Mr. Reese glared, but decided not to hear.

If the object was to teach us the tedium of Fusion, the exercises succeeded admirably. Between jumps, the instructors divided us into squads, had us suit up, and took us a few at a time out onto the hull for exercise and training.

I was in the second group, with Van Roef and Sanders. This time it was Sergeant Garver who went Outside with us. I'd trained on the Hull, and I'd been taken Outside at the Training Station, but clambering on the hull of a tiny boat under cold unforgiving stars was a different matter altogether.

My breath rasping in my helmet, I made my way back and forth between the drive shaft and the prow. Though for once Sarge had no objection, there was no small talk among us; we were all concentrating on keeping contact with the hull, and on ignoring the terrifying vastness of space.

Before going in, we practiced airlock maneuvers. It was harder than one might think for several people in zero grav to enter an airlock, and remain oriented toward the same plane. But if we didn't, someone's stray kick could smash a helmet. Sarge demonstrated twice for us, and watched from inside the lock as we struggled to release ourselves from the hull, grab hold of the handrings, and pull ourselves in at a ninety-degree angle.

Our first try was clumsy, our second better, and our third a fiasco. Van Roef managed to let go of the ring too early and set himself adrift in the middle of the airlock, feet kicking helplessly in all directions until he floated near a bulkhead and grabbed a handring.

I climbed in with less difficulty, but Sanders, watching Van Roef's antics from the hull, doubled over with laughter and forgot to turn on her boots. She let go of the handhold, and, by some quirk, found herself floating inches from the hull, with virtually no discernible motion relative to the ship.

We all knew Sarge had a thrustersuit, but nothing was more frightening than being unattached and unable to reach safe haven. Without rescue, you could spend eternity in the coffin of your suit. It would be particularly maddening to be so close to the ship, yet unable to touch it. Without a T-suit, Arlene was helpless.

She let out a scream that rang distorted in my eardrums. Van Roef kicked convulsively, bounced off a bulkhead.

Sarge had seen it all before. "All right, Seafort, haul her in."

I grasped the inside ring, leaned out as far as I could, reached for

Sanders's frantic fingers, just as Van Roef's boot slammed into the airlock control.

The hatch slid shut. A shriek. A moment before I realized it had been my own. I twisted. A wave of agony radiated up my arm. I was caught in the hatch seals, more of me Outside than in. Arlene Sanders's hand was inches from mine. My left arm was almost certainly broken. Desperate, I tried to free myself.

"DON'T MOVE, SEAFORT!" Sergeant Garver's urgency penetrated my panic.

"Ma'am, my arm's—"

"Don't wiggle! Your suit could rip!"

Oh, Lord God. *We are heartily sorry for having offended thee.* I was utterly still.

Van Roef whimpered. "I'm sorry, I didn't mean to—"

"Shut up. Against the bulkhead." Sarge slapped the hatch control. No response. After a moment she cursed, tried again. "Seafort, I'll have to reset the controls. Just a moment while I power down."

"Nicky!" It was an urgent whisper. "Reach out."

"Belay that, Sanders, he's not to move. You're in no danger, I'll come for you as soon as I can." Sarge dialed the code, waited for the light to blink.

"Nicky, I can't wait. Get me back now or I'll . . . lose it."

Tentatively, I stretched. Pain washed through my forearm. "I can't."

"I've got a red light, Sarge! My air!" Van Roef sounded near panic.

Ms. Garver slapped the hatch release over and again. "Calm down, Van Roef, you still have half an hour. Seafort, the hatch is jammed." She pounded the lock panel. "I'm going to wind it open manually. It'll take a few minutes."

"Yes, ma'am." I rested my head against the hull. God, it hurt.

"A few minutes?" Van Roef's voice came in a squeal. "My air is going bad!"

"Steady, boy." Sarge opened the emergency panel, fitted the lever to the gear.

"Nick! Now!" Sanders bit back a sob.

I stretched as far from the lock as I dared. "Open your fingers." We could almost touch.

"Seafort, she'll be all right. Don't stress your suit!"

"Yes, ma'am. She can't wait much—" I closed my eyes to the

pain, stretched my broken arm. A moan. I pressed my lips tight, willed myself silent. Just another inch . . .

"The God damned winder is jammed!" Sarge's blasphemy echoed through our silence.

"I need air!" Van Roef dived past Sarge, slapped the inner control. The red safety light flashed. The hatch stayed closed.

Sarge flung him back across the lock. "Moron, the lock panel is defective! If the hatch opened you'd have killed everyone inside!" She keyed her caller. "Reese, get everyone suited, flank. We'll have to pump out; I need a winch here and we can't open or shut the outer lock. You have five minutes. And have a tank ready for Van Roef, he's running low." Only by pumping out the Fuser could her inner and outer locks be opened at the same time.

I stole a glance at my air gauge. Nearing empty, but still on green. I had time.

"Nicky!" Sanders's eyes held something I didn't want to see. I strained against the pinion of the hatch. If my suit ripped, I'd die instantly. Or perhaps not instantly; I thrust down that horrid thought. Sanders was my bunkmate, and she needed help. I had no choice.

I thrust my arm toward her, battling torment. It wasn't enough. I recoiled, gritted my teeth, lurched from the hull. Something slipped, and I nearly passed out.

Our fingers touched. I stretched the last iota, curled my finger around hers. Stretched as if on a rack, I fought dizziness, willing her closer.

Van Roef wailed, "Never mind them, I need air! I'm on red! I can't breathe!"

"Come near the panel again and you won't need to breathe. I'll kill you myself." I think Sergeant Garver meant it.

Our fingers locked. Sanders plucked greedily at my hand, my wrist. After an endless moment, her other hand made contact. She hauled herself up my arm toward the hull. Even after she reached it, for a moment she clung to me as to a liferaft. Releasing the tension on my imprisoned, throbbing arm, I sagged against the lock. "You're all right, Arlene. Just hold on."

She was crying. "Thank you. Oh, Lord God, thank you."

"You're all right." I repeated my inadequate comfort.

Helmets touching, we waited together for the lock to open. "Do you have air, Nicky?"

"Enough. You?"

"I think so. I've just gone red."

"Sarge?"

"We're almost pumped out. Once I have the winch it won't take a minute."

"What if . . . the winch doesn't work either?"

Her voice was grim. "I'll torch through the lock, if I have to. I'll try the winch for five minutes, then get the torch. We still have more than enough time. I'm with you, Seafort. Just hold still, don't tear the suit. How's Sanders?"

"I'm—"

"She's fine, sir. I've got her now."

Reese's voice cut in. "We're pumped, Sarge. Opening up."

True to her word, Sarge had the outer hatch cranked open within a minute. I yelped as the pressure against my arm was released, but held still.

"All right, there's no break in the suit skin. I've turned on your boots; can you walk?" She slipped a steadying arm around my waist. Inside, we waited while air hissed back into the ship.

They helped me strip off my suit, gently supporting my injured arm. In the corner Van Roef whimpered, unnoticed. Mr. Reese plotted a course for the Station and we Fused at once. The portholes faded to black.

"I'll try to set it, but I'm no med tech." Sarge took my wrist, put her hand on my upper arm. I braced myself, cried out only once. While setting the splint she paused, reached to my face, gently brushed hair away from my eyes. Did her hand linger an extra second? "Good job, joey." She turned back to her work.

After, I sat on my bunk in the tiny wardroom crowded with subdued cadets, sipping hot cocoa. Arlene Sanders came close. "Thanks for helping."

I rested the cocoa on my knee. "No problem. I was just standing around with nothing to do." I stumbled to a halt, realizing my humor was out of place. She helped me to my feet, embraced me. I hugged her awkwardly with my one good arm. For a moment her head rested on my chest. We separated. I sat quickly, odd and unexpected feelings rising.

We Defused, and Mr. Reese began maneuvering us to our bay. Sarge loomed in the wardroom hatch. "Mr. Seafort, in the airlock I ordered you to hold still so you wouldn't tear your suit. You didn't. What do you have to say for yourself?"

I stood. "No excuse, Sarge."

"Two demerits, when you're healed. Sanders, you were never in trouble. I would have retrieved you the moment the lock was open. You risked Seafort's life for nothing. Come with me."

Her face set, Arlene followed into the other cabin. After a few moments we heard her yelp as the strokes fell.

The day after we returned to base, Cadet Van Roef was shipped groundside. We never saw him again.

"Is your arm all right, sir?" Adam Tenere sounded anxious.

I realized I'd been rubbing my forearm. "Of course."

The boy looked wistfully at the thruster controls.

I needn't be a mind reader to guess his thoughts. Every middy yearned for that rare opportunity to pilot a craft. It was as close to making Captain as most of them would ever get. "Not a chance, Mr. Tenere."

"I didn't say anything, sir."

I snorted. "You didn't need to." I punched in the startup codes, waited for the boat to come up to full power. I checked the screens. I wouldn't care to be adrift in an undersupplied, underpowered Trainer. I touched the silent speaker. Even a Fuser's communications were disabled; her caller had but one frequency.

It had been so for some seventy years, ever since the Screaming Boy affair. Five cadets had stranded themselves too close to Mercury to Fuse; their N-waves were distorted by the nearby gravitational mass. The cadets' desperate cries for help across every band had utterly unnerved the cadets in the other Fusers, and made the matter a sensation for the holozines even though a rescue ship was speeding to the scene.

The embarrassing incident had enraged the Commandant, who ordered the radionics on every training vessel set to its own single classified frequency, decodable only by the Station and the command ship.

Despite the wrath of their Commandant, the boys were fortunate they hadn't Defused so close to the Sun that their heat shields couldn't cope. Such a potential disaster was one reason we always checked and rechecked Fusion coordinates with meticulous care.

I ran systems checks, powered down. "Let's go."

We resealed the hatch. Outside, the midshipman asked, "Where to, sir?"

"Mother. The Fifth one down the line." On occasions when several squads of cadets practiced at once, they were accompanied by *Trafalgar*, a fully powered command vessel, generally nicknamed Mothership. More than once, she had towed home a Fuser that had squandered its propellant before reaching the docking bays. It was not a distinction to be sought.

We negotiated our way across the flat of the Station disk, past the obstacles of our radionics and sensors. Finally, we clambered into *Trafal-gar*'s lock.

The Mothership was substantially larger than the trainers, but though she had gravitrons and fusion drives, she wasn't designed for interstellar travel. No hydros, minimal stores. She took a crew of seven. Instead of the usual circumference corridor, her lock opened into a cabin that stretched from starboard to port, at the forward end of which was the bridge.

At the console I checked atmosphere, unclamped my helmet and stripped off my suit. I stretched luxuriously. Adam took his place at the second officer's chair, automatically straightening his tie. I smiled; *Trafal-gar*'s was hardly a real bridge, and the middy wasn't reporting for watch.

I leaned back. "Power up."

"Aye aye, sir." The boy studied the console for a long anxious moment.

"Go ahead," I said. "If you blow us up I won't be around to complain."

His smile was strained. "Aye aye, sir." My remark had a purpose, however unpleasant. A middy had to learn to cope with pressure. If he was on the bridge when a fish loomed . . . my hand tightened on the armrest.

Tentatively he tapped a sequence of commands. Figures flashed across the console. After a moment the lights brightened. So did Adam. "Power-up achieved, sir."

I wouldn't let him cast off, but no harm in continuing the exercise. "Bring the thrusters on-line."

"Aye aye, sir."

I watched from my own console. "Check airlock seals."

"Airlocks sealed, sir."

"Fusion readiness, please."

"Aye ay—but, sir, we're still moored to the Station." If we tried to Fuse now, we'd destroy our ship, and the Station as well.

"I know, we're not going anywhere."

"Readying for Fusion, sir." He slid his finger across the screen; the green line followed.

Normally, at this point, the engine room staff would be monitoring N-wave generation, making sure we were within tolerances. Unstaffed, we'd have to rely on the puter, and that simply wasn't done. "Shut down, Adam."

He sighed. "Aye aye, sir."

As the fusion motors dimmed, the green console light faded. No, I wouldn't take him Fusing, but there was no reason the two of us couldn't make a short run on auxiliary engines. The middy would be in seventh heaven, and the practice would benefit him when—

The speaker crackled. "Station Puter D 1004 to *Trafalgar*, respond please."

I snatched up the caller. "*Trafalgar*."

"Farside Base on-line, for the Commandant."

I looked to the middy. "Your comm check, most likely. Don't forget to call them back when we reboard."

Adam shook his head. "It's early yet, sir, and they wouldn't ask for you on a comm check."

"True." I hesitated. I could give the youngster his chance at the controls, return the call later. Farside could handle things without me for another hour. "Tell them—" No, better to get it over with. "Relay to *Trafalgar*, please."

Moments passed. Sergeant Obutu. "Sir, your Mr. Tolliver, ground-side. Shall I patch him through?"

"What does he want?"

"He wouldn't say."

"Very well, put—" I stopped. Not, "He didn't say," but, "He wouldn't say." She'd asked and Tolliver wouldn't tell her. Odd, even for my eccentric aide.

"Seafort here."

Seconds hesitation, while the voice was relayed from Devon. "Lieutenant Tolliver reporting, sir. I need you groundside."

I stared unbelieving at the speaker. A most peculiar summons indeed, from a subordinate to his Captain. "You what?"

Adam gave his rapt attention.

Tolliver's voice was taut. "We need you here ASAP, sir. Please come directly."

Had he lost his mind? "Full report, Lieutenant! What's going on?"

"Aye aye, sir. This, uh, isn't a secure line."

"Of course it is."

"Remember your report from *Challenger*, sir? The holozines had it as soon as Admiralty." Tolliver was right; with modern technology our news media could intercept and decode most interplanetary transmissions.

"I'm at the Training Station." My tone was petulant. "Can't you tell me now?"

"Yes, if you insist." Tolliver's voice had an edge. "On the other hand, you could trust my judgment."

On the other hand, I could cashier him. This was rank insolence. "Does First Lieutenant Sleak know about this rigmarole?"

A long pause. "No, sir. And there's no point in telling him."

I muttered, "Tolliver's gone round the bend." Adam Tenere studied his nails. "Very well, Edgar, I'll be down shortly. By Lord God, this had better be worth it!"

"Arrange a special shuttle with Lunapolis Transport, sir. Don't wait for the nightliner."

Enough was enough. "Don't give *me* orders, Tolliver." I rang off, seething. "What are you staring at, Middy? Call up Farside, we need the shuttle!"

"Aye aye, sir. You were just talking to Far—" Adam saw my expression, subsided just in time. Moments later, he had Sergeant Obutu back on the line. She told me Mr. Trayn's shuttle would need to refuel before returning.

"Wonderful." Three hours, at minimum, probably more. "Suit up, Mr. Tenere. It's back to the Station."

"Aye aye, sir." Tenere grabbed his suit, politely handed me my own. One leg in, he stopped short. "Sir, if time is important . . ."

"Yes?"

"Why don't we take *Trafalgar*, meet the shuttle over Farside?"

"That's ridicu—" I pondered. If we left immediately, we could be above Farside by the time the shuttle lifted off. "No, there'd be no one to return *Trafalgar* to the Station."

"I could, sir." He scanned my face, saw the refusal, fell back to a second position. "Lieutenant Paulson or one of the sergeants could come on the shuttle, change places with you. He and I could sail back here and wait for the shuttle to pick us up."

A waste of propellant, but the Navy was well stocked. Were a few saved hours worth the trouble? Probably not, but in that case, why was I rushing home in the first place? Either I believed Tolliver, or I didn't.

"We'll need our gear from inside." I ignored the delight in Adam's eyes. "Suit up, run back for our duffels. Do I need to go with you, or will you be careful?"

"I've been Outside on my own, sir. Many times." As an officer on Farside, he'd had ample opportunity.

While he was gone I called the Station yet again, made arrangements for the shuttle to meet us.

When he returned, we cast off. I gently fired our thrusters, rocking the ship to break us free. Watching me, Adam's face fell. I said nothing, rocked harder. The seals parted.

We drifted slowly away from the Station. I'd have to turn the ship so the auxiliary engines would bear. The boy watched, yearning.

I sighed. "All right, take over. Head us home."

His manner was almost reverent. "Aye aye, sir. Thank you, sir." He eased his hands onto the controls. Two squirts with the port thrusters, after a moment another with the starboard. He tapped the keys, calling up preprogrammed coordinates.

I watched from the first officer's seat. At the conn, all the middy's gawky hesitation had disappeared. His eye flickered from console to viewport and back, accomplishing both the navigation and the positioning of the ship with graceful competence.

"Ready to fire main thrusters, sir."

"Proceed."

His hand tightened on the throttle, but his eye never left the positioning grid on the console. At exactly the right moment he brought up the power. Slowly at first, but steadily faster, the Station receded.

"With your permission, fifty minutes burn, sixty-seven minutes cruise, fifty minutes retro, sir."

I tapped at my console, repeating his calculations. They seemed right, but then, Nav had never been my best subject. "Very well."

Adam set the alarm, leaned back, one hand ready to pull back the throttle if an engine shuddered. "I had another idea, sir. I could take you directly to Earthport Station, have the shuttle meet me there." His eyes were on the console. A vein in his temple throbbed.

"No." Docking at the shuttle was one thing, approaching the Earth's busy commercial hub was quite another. Even if we avoided disaster, a clumsy mating would reflect badly on the Navy.

"But we—I just meant— Aye aye, sir. I didn't mean any—" His mouth tightened.

I snapped, "Show that sullen face again and it's two more demerits."

He whirled. "Sullen? Sir, I—" He bit off his words, was silent a long moment. Finally he spoke with resolve. "Sir, excuse me, but you misunderstood. I was disgusted with myself because I can't get out even a simple sentence without stammering."

My anger melted. "Why, Adam?"

He studied the console. "I wish I knew. I can talk to Mr. Keene or Guthrie Smith, or the cadets. Maybe it's . . ." He trailed off. I waited. "I want so much to impress you," he muttered.

"Because I'm Commandant?"

"No, sir. Because you're Captain Seafort." He reddened. "I wanted to be able to tell my father I'd served under the great Mr. Seafort. Now I can tell him I knocked you down, babbled every time I saw you, and earned more demerits in two weeks than I did in a year as a cadet."

"No, you haven't." I cleared my throat, spoke gruffly. "All remaining demerits are canceled, including the ten for which you were sent to Mr. Paulson." It was bad for discipline, but the boy's pilotage deserved reward, and his idea had saved me several anxious hours.

"You mean that? Really?" His eyes held wonder. Then, realizing what he'd said, he blushed. "I'm sorry, that sounded, of course you—" He shook his head. "See? I meant, thank you very much, Captain."

"Very well." I closed my eyes, pondering. After a time, I said, "Mr. Tenere, for the next month, when I or any of the lieutenants speak to you, do not answer for at least five seconds. Every time you fail to do so, report yourself to the duty officer to be logged a demerit. I'll log this order so they won't accuse you of insolence. Is that clear?"

"Aye aye, sir."

"One demerit."

A long pause. "Aye aye, sir."

I leaned back, wondering if it would help.

While waiting for the shuttle to mate with us I had Sergeant Obutu put through a call to Devon.

In a few moments she came back on the line. "Sir, I can't get through. All incoming lines go to a recording. 'Circuits in use for training exercise.'"

My hackles began to rise. I said slowly, "Sarge, I think Tolliver may have lost his mind. Arrange for a squad of Marines to meet me at London Shuttleport, just in case."

"Aye aye, sir. Are you sure that's necessary?"

"Better safe than sorry."

"Do you intend to shoot your way in?"

I grinned mirthlessly. "With that joey, there's no telling." If Tolliver had indeed gone glitched, only Lieutenant Bien, Sleak and the drill sergeants were around to stop him.

I passed through the Earthport Station lock.

"Captain Seafort? Please follow me, sir." A tech, from Naval Transport. We strode through the busy corridor to the shuttle departure bays.

Though I normally disregarded the perks of rank, this time I was glad my standing allowed me a special shuttle. I could imagine explaining to some lieutenant at Transport that I needed to rush groundside to see if my staff lieutenant had carried out a coup on the Academy grounds. Would I care for a few tanks while I was at it? A couple of laser cannon, perhaps?

When we finally set down at London Shuttleport, my nerves were raw with worry. If Tolliver were no longer firing on all jets, he might kidnap or even kill me when I appeared. On the other hand, if I stormed Academy gates with an armed force when he had a valid reason for what he'd done, it would be all over the holos. I'd no doubt end up in a rebalancing ward next to Annie.

As dusk fell I met with the lieutenant of Marines, still undecided. In the end, I compromised: if I didn't call within two hours, the Marines were to enter the compound and sort things out. I boarded the waiting heli. Minutes later we put down on the Academy pad.

While the guards approached I jumped out, ducked under the moving blades. "Stand to! Where's Tolliver?" The guard aimed his light at my face.

"Aye aye, sir." He switched off his flashlight. "Just making sure it was you." He came to attention.

"What in blazes is going on?"

"Mr. Tolliver's on his way, sir. I rang Admin when your Pilot called for clearance." So much for surprise.

"Very well." I stood fuming until three figures hurried toward the pad. Tolliver, Sergeant Ibarez, First Midshipman Sandra Ekrit.

Tolliver snapped a brisk salute. "Lieutenant Edgar Tol—"

"Belay that! What's this about?"

"Lieutenant Sleak is dead."

"He's what?" I felt shock, instinctive fear, but it wasn't followed by a sense of personal loss. I hadn't known the man well. I took a slow breath, relaxed my taut muscles. No coup, no crazed Tolliver. "Damn it, why couldn't you have told me over the—"

"He shot himself."

I gaped.

"In his quarters. The Branstead boy found him after morning run."

I stood stunned. "But . . . why? It makes no sense."

"I agree."

My relief turned to anger. "Why did you seal the base? I thought you'd gone out of your mind!"

"Yes, sir. That's always a risk."

Sergeant Ibarez and the middy watched the byplay with fascination. I snarled, "Damn you, Toll—"

"I did it to give you time. To keep your options open."

"Time? Options?"

His tone was patient. "I didn't know how you wanted to handle this, sir. Once the zines get hold of it—"

"They don't care about a poor lieutenant on a shoreside—"

Sergeant Ibarez cleared his throat. "Begging your pardon, sir. It's you, not Mr. Sleak." He smiled apologetically.

"Have you two lost your minds?"

Tolliver. "If you blow your nose it's news, sir. Oh, I know you don't like it, but glaring at me won't change a thing. Once they hear that your second in command killed himself without motive, they'll camp outside our gates snapping at anything that moves."

Damn his insolence. The fact that he was probably right did nothing to lessen my annoyance. My mind spun. "Did Sleak talk to anyone? Who found him?"

"Jerence Branstead, sir. The cadet."

"What was *he* doing there?" I sounded petulant.

Sergeant Ibarez. "I batonned him on morning run."

I swung to Sandra Ekrit. "Why are you here, Middy?"

She replied with dignity, "Because Lieutenant Tolliver ordered me here, sir."

Her manner brought me back to my senses. We were all four of us standing under the heli blades, arguing within sight of the guards. It wouldn't do. "Very well, to my office." I stalked down the path.

Tolliver matched my pace, ahead of the rest. "You're right, it was probably the middy's fault, or Cadet Branstead's. I'm glad you're taking charge."

"Shut your mouth."

"Aye aye, sir."

I increased my stride, ablaze with fury. Not only had I lost a good lieutenant, I had to rely on an erratic, insolent dolt like Tolliver. Anything I said, he twisted with sardonic humor. Nonetheless, I needed to know more. "Even if Sleak killed himself, why seal the base? What am I supposed to do about it, bury him at midnight under the mess hall?"

"The flower beds would be a better—sorry, sir. Look!" I took another pace before I realized he'd stopped abruptly, waiting for my attention. He thrust hands on hips. "I can't second guess you, Captain. Would you prefer I'd radioed a message on open circuit? Very well, next time that's what I'll do. At least this way you can release the news yourself, the way you want to. Excuse me for trying to cover your arse!"

I swallowed as his rage dissolved my own. "You've had time to think about it. What should I do?"

We resumed our walk. "It probably depends on why Sleak killed himself. If it was for personal reasons, perhaps a brief, dignified announcement. If it was connected to Academy, I have no idea how to handle it."

"Connected? How?"

"How the devil should I know! Maybe he was buggering a plebe, or fixing admission tests. All I intended was to give you time to find out!"

Presently I said, "Sorry." We walked in silence to the steps. "Where is his body?"

"I had him moved to the sickbay. It seemed . . . indecent to leave him where he was."

"You're sure he killed himself?" A murder would be . . . unthinkable. And catastrophic for morale.

"Quite sure." He held the door. "You'll see."

In my office, I waved to chairs for the sergeant and Midshipman Ekrit. "Why you three? Are you acting as a committee?"

Sergeant Ibarez shook his head. "Not really. After Branstead found the body he ran and got me. I took a look, sealed the door, and called Mr. Tolliver. I put Branstead on special duty, away from the other cadets, and I've been acting as a sort of liaison with the other staff. They know something's up, but not the details."

Tolliver said, "I had Ms. Ekrit post a middy guard at Mr. Sleak's door. Middies outrank the sergeants and anyone belowdecks. Technically, that is."

Sandra Ekrit smiled resignedly at the reminder of her status. "Yes, sir, technically. I've set boys in shifts to guard the door. Thayer and Tsai brought the body to sickbay."

I turned to Tolliver. "You said you're sure he committed suicide."

"Yes." Tolliver inserted a chip in my holovid. "Let me warn you, sir, this is not—"

I flicked it on. Darwin Sleak's gaunt features stared into the lens. His hands reached forward, became distorted, picked up the holorecorder. The walls floated past, as he scanned the empty room, circling back to his starting point. With a lurch, the recorder settled back on his desk. He sat in front of it, reached into the drawer, his eyes still riveted on the camera.

His hand came up with a gun, an ancient one with lead shells. He checked the clip, paused, put the gun to his temple.

"This is suicide," Lieutenant Darwin Sleak said to the holo. "I'm alone, and no one else is involved. Commandant, I'm sorry. I was wrong. I never imagined—" He closed his eyes. "Trusting in the love and mercy of Thy Spirit . . ." He pulled the trigger.

I jerked back in my chair, the shot ringing. His head . . . "Jesus, Lord Christ!"

"Amen. I warned you."

My stomach heaved. I tried not to retch. The holovid remained focused on what was left of Sleak's head. With unsteady hand, I reached to turn it off, took a deep breath. "Very well, it's suicide. What did he mean, he was sorry?"

"I don't know."

I drummed my fingers on the desktop. "How long do we have?"

"To do what, sir? His body is in the cooler, that's no immediate problem."

"Before word gets out."

"The ones who know he's dead are Branstead, those of us in this room, the middies and the med tech. Sarge says the tech can be trusted."

Ms. Ekrit said, "The whole wardroom knows, of course. We can't keep that kind of secret from each other. No one will say a word, sir. I'll vouch for that."

I smiled. A first middy could be very persuasive, if occasion arose. "Very well. We have until tomorrow, at least. Edgar, does Ms. Bien know?"

"No, sir. I'm senior, and I pulled rank on her. I don't think she's speaking to me."

"Tell her. I want the two of you to go through Mr. Sleak's cabin tonight. Sarge, you help them. We can have a middy cover your barracks."

"I already have one, sir. Mr. Thayer." The redheaded child I'd found tossing pillows in glee, only months before. I stood. "Report to me when you're done, regardless of the hour. I'll be in my quarters, after I have a bite. I haven't eaten since—I don't know when." I paused at the door. "Have Mr. Branstead report to me at mess hall."

I was wolfing down a home-made sandwich when Midshipman Diego marched young Jerence into the empty hall.. I took their salutes, dismissed the middy. "As you were, Mr. Branstead."

"Aye aye, sir." Not knowing what to do with himself, he assumed the at-ease position. After a moment he blurted, "I'm—I'm sorry, sir. For whatever I did."

He'd been a cadet long enough to know he should speak only when spoken to, but I let it pass. "Sit down."

His eyes widened at the unexpected familiarity. "Aye aye, sir."

I studied his reddened eyes, his huddled and sunken posture. "You must have had a fright."

"I'm all right, sir." His reply was immediate.

"I know that. Still, I saw the . . . He wasn't something to come upon, unexpected."

Jerence shivered. "I knocked, like we're supposed to. The door swung open, and I thought he'd meant for me to come in. He was slumped behind—behind the . . ." He spun away.

I cleared my throat. "I'm sorry." I couldn't touch him, or even offer words of consolation. He was as any other cadet, and I was his commanding officer.

"I'm all right." His tone would have been persuasive but for his eyes.

"Yes, well." Many months past, I'd promised Harmon Branstead to keep his son safe. If that were not enough, he was my legal ward. Still, I hesitated.

My baby Nathan might have been a boy like this, given a chance to survive.

"Come with me." The boy followed me to the serving rail. I opened the gate, went into the darkened galley, put my hand on his shoulder to guide him. "Don't tell anyone, Jerence. We're not supposed to be here."

"No, sir."

"They gave you dinner?"

"Yes, sir. Mr. Tsai brought a tray to the suiting room."

"What were you doing?"

"Inventorying, sir. Checking off serial numbers."

I sighed. Ibarez could have found something more credible for makework. I opened the cooler, peered in. A large sheet of chocolate cake; that would do. I brought it out, found plates, dished out two portions. "Carry these, please."

I went to the freezers, hunted for ice cream. I gave him a generous dollop, took a smaller one for myself. I hoisted myself onto the gleaming steel counter, motioned for the boy to do likewise. "Go ahead, Mr. Branstead. Your dinner tray couldn't have held all that much."

"Thank you, sir." He made no move to eat. "Mr. Seafort, I mean, Commandant, sir, what did I do wrong? Should I have stayed outside? Why can't I go back to barracks tonight?"

"You did nothing wrong. The rest is none of your concern." My tone was harsh, and Jerence looked to his shoes. "Eat your ice cream."

Dutifully, he took a spoonful. "I'm sorry, sir. Forgive me."

I sighed; I knew better. We'd been shipmates, he and I. "Jerence." He looked up. "We don't know why Lieutenant Sleak killed himself. If word leaks before we find out, it will be a great embarrassment."

"That's why Sarge is making me sleep in the closed barracks? So I won't talk to the others?"

"Yes." The melting ice cream held no appeal. I put down my plate. "He thought you wouldn't be able to keep the secret." I hesitated, threw caution to the winds. "But I know better. When you've finished eating, I'll take you back to Valdez. You'll help us keep things quiet until we learn what happened."

"Of course, sir." His shoulders straightened. "I won't tell anyone, even my bunkies. I promise."

"Eat up, before the cook's mates find us."

"Yes, sir." He smiled, tentatively at first.

"It must have been awful, finding Mr. Sleak."

"It was, sir." He took a bite of cake. His head lifted. "But I'm over it now."

10

Jerence safely back in barracks, I returned to my apartment, exhausted. The search of Lieutenant Sleak's quarters would take hours; in the meantime I needed sleep. I settled into bed with the visage of Mr. Sleak's head, after he'd pulled the trigger. I put it aside, but other images plagued me, among them Cadet Dustin Edwards, huddled lifeless in the Farside corridor.

I snapped awake to urgent pounding on my door, a voice shouting. I lurched to the door in my shorts, hurled it open. "Belay that nons—"

"Hands up!" The Marine's laser rifle brooked no argument. I flung my hands over my head, retreated several steps.

"Easy, Jodson, he's the Commandant. You all right, sir?" The burly lieutenant of Marines.

"Of course I'm all right! Why in God's own hell are you bursting in—Oh, my Lord." I flamed crimson. "Call them off, Lieutenant. I . . . forgot to call you."

His expression reduced me to a charred spot on the rug. "Forgot. I see. Very well, Commandant." He raised his caller. "Corporal Manners, sheath weapons, release the guards. This is a no go!"

I lowered my arms. "How did you get past the sentries? Was there damage?"

"Not much, sir. We took out the front guardhouse, where your man was half asleep. Then we secured the helipad in case the enemy tried to bolt. Next we surrounded Officers' Quarters. In the next corridor we have three Naval officers under guard."

"Let them go," I said quickly. "It was a false alarm. Just a training exercise."

"Right." He saluted, but allowed himself one last dig. "If you'd ever like readiness training for your guards, let us know."

I slipped into my pants and shirt, hurried outside to Lieutenant Sleak's flat. Tolliver stood in the doorway, arms folded, arguing with a Marine guard. He raised an eyebrow.

"Not a word, do you hear me?" I tried to turn embarrassment into fury. "Just get back to work!"

The Marine lieutenant followed me, to call off his guard. His young Marine said urgently, "Sir, there's blood in there. Someone's been—"

I snarled, "Lieutenant, get your man out of here, flank!" To my relief, the Marines complied. I followed them back to the helipad, waited for their transport to arrive while my own sheepish guards did their best to avoid my eye. While their heli settled, I warned the Marine lieutenant of consequences should word of this fiasco leak.

I doubt I overawed him, but perhaps taking pity on me, he agreed. When they were finally gone I turned on my heel and hurried back to Officers' Quarters. The door to Sleak's cabin was ajar.

Seated at Sleak's console, Tolliver said only, "Nothing yet, sir. Thank you for arranging a stimulating work break. We were just admiring—"

I growled, "I don't want to hear it." I shut the door, returned to my cabin. I tossed and turned for hours before drifting off at dawn.

"He must have left a clue somewhere." Tousled and bleary, I glowered at Ibarez and Tolliver.

"I went through everything, even his sister's letters." Tolliver seemed weary, too. "Ms. Bien is checking his puter files one more time."

"Don't you—" I forced down an unreasoning anger. "Did you find any notes, anything at all?"

"Of course, like anyone would leave. Lunch appointments, figures jotted. Nothing special."

"What kind of figures?"

His voice grew testy. "One note looked like logistics for transporting plebes up to Station next term. The others, I have no idea. Would you like to see them?"

I checked my watch. "Let it wait 'til after breakfast."

Darwin Sleak's death made no sense. He'd been angry with me, had asked for a transfer because I'd set Tolliver to investigate his accounts. But Edgar had found nothing to incriminate Sleak, and the man wouldn't destroy himself out of pique.

Tolliver had frightened me by sealing the base, but I had to admit his actions made some sense. The Navy mustn't wash its dirty laundry in public. Because my name was involved, the mediamen would look for a scandal connected to the suicide, or even invent one.

I sighed. My lieutenant's body was in the cooler, and must be dealt with. In addition, I didn't look forward to breaking in his replacement when I myself was still a novice. Beyond that, I was tired, I had rocket-lag, and I missed Annie. At least now that I was groundside I could visit her, as soon as matters were under control.

At breakfast assembly I sipped moodily at my coffee, watching the scrubbed and shining cadets. No one at my table commented on Lieutenant Sleak's empty place.

On the way out, Lieutenant Bien caught me alone. "The quartermaster has indent requests, and there are daily systems reports for Mr. Sleak."

"What do you want me to do about it?" Her look of resignation infuriated me. With an effort I contained myself. "Sorry, Ms. Bien. Pass the word Mr. Sleak is on special detail. All reports and requests go to you."

"Aye aye, sir. And the barrel?"

That was the first lieutenant's chore. I hesitated. "Take it to Tolliver, he's senior."

I walked through the compound to my office, shut the door. I paced, gnawing at the mystery of Sleak's death. We'd found no clues in his apartment. Perhaps there were none to find, and the man had simply succumbed to depression. If so, a simple announcement would suffice. I sat at my desk, played at drafting a statement. Deep in my stomach a knot began to form.

At length I erased my scribblings, buzzed the outer desk. "Tell Ms. Bien I want her." I waited impatiently until she knocked. "You stayed late in Mr. Sleak's cabin. What did you find on his puter?"

"Nothing much, sir. Notes, letters, reports. About what I expected to find."

"No hint of a problem?"

"No, sir. Check for yourself. I locked his files under your personal security code."

Two hours later, we'd found nothing out of the ordinary. Finally I gave it up. I dismissed Ms. Bien to her other duties, sat back to brood.

By lunchtime I decided I wanted the incident done with, mediamen or no. I snapped on my holo to draft a statement.

Sergeant Kinders knocked. "Weekly reports are ready to be sent to Admiralty, sir. Shall I—"

"Send them." The damned reports didn't matter, no one read them. As far as Admiralty was concerned, I was on my own, as Commandant Kearsey had been. I was free to spend or misspend my budget, cashier errant cadets, train them as I saw fit. Unless, of course, I failed to coddle Senator Boland. Then, Admiral Duhaney called me to account. Admiralty would do better giving me some reasonable guidelines rather than letting politics—

Guidelines. Very well. If Duhaney wanted to meddle in Academy I'd give him something to meddle with. "Mr. Kinders!"

The door opened. "Yes?"

"Put in a call to Admiral Duhaney. It's urgent."

"Aye aye, sir." He disappeared. I paced my office in relief. I'd tell Duhaney the truth. Let him figure out what to make of the problem. And let the announcement come from his office, not mine. The mediamen would withhold—

I cursed, flung open the door. "Cancel that call, Sarge."

Sergeant Kinders looked up, his face noncommittal. "Aye aye, sir."

"I can't tell him over the air, for the same reason Tolliver couldn't report—" I stopped short, studied his face. "How much do you know?"

"Officially? Nothing. But something's happened to Mr. Sleak, that's obvious."

I had to trust my own staff. "He killed himself in his cabin. I have to go see the Admiral." Another bout with the harsh acceleration, and I would miss seeing Annie. But there was no other way, unless . . . "On second thought, I'll draft a message. Call in a middy." I fumbled for a name, any name. "Mr., uh, Thayer."

An hour later I put the chip in a pocket case, gave it to the red-haired youngster waiting at-ease in front of my desk. "See Sarge for your travel orders. Go to Lunapolis Admiralty, announce yourself at Admiral Duhaney's office. You're not to surrender this chip except personally to him." Without that precaution, my notice might get lost in the stacks of reports Admiralty received daily. "These orders may not be counter-manded. You understand?"

The boy's eyes sparkled with excitement. "Aye aye, sir!"

"Dismissed." I watched him stride out. His eagerness was under-standable; it was his first trip aloft without supervision. And when his errand was done, he'd have some hours in Lunapolis, perhaps even over-night. An inquisitive young middy could augment his education, in its seedier warrens.

I leaned back. One way or another, Sleak's death would be handled. That aside, the man had to be replaced; Terrestrial Academy was under-staffed with three lieutenants, to say nothing of only two. Aboard ship, on a long, dreary interstellar cruise, I would make do, or promote a midship-man. In home system I had only to call BuPers. Even with a staffing freeze, they'd give me whoever I wanted.

Who, then? I thought briefly of Alexi Tamarov, decided that even if his mind had cleared, I'd interfered enough in his life and brought him only harm.

We wanted someone with a special understanding, a special affinity for Naval traditions. A disciplinarian, who might transmit his high standards to future generations. No one I knew fitted the bill. I would have to leave it to BuPers. If I tolerated Ardwell Crossburn, I could work with anyone.

That afternoon I called the clinic, asked for Annie. She was out on the grounds. Tired and irritable, I waited in my office for Admiral Duhaney's call until I was nearly late to dinner.

The cadets stood smartly for my entrance. I strode past the tables, noticed Jerence Branstead with his bunkmates. I sang out, "Gentlemen, be seated." Chairs scraped, and conversation resumed.

Edgar Tolliver seemed to have caught up on his sleep; his wit was in full flower. I ignored a sly reference to the visit of the marines, but when he made another I leaned close. "No more, Mr. Tolliver. Granted, I made a fool of myself. But you're done rubbing it in."

His eyebrow raised. "Rubbing it in? Not at all, sir. If I, ah, dwell on the incident, it's because I enjoyed the relief from our dull Academy life." He managed to keep his face straight.

"Dull, is it?" He'd pushed me over the brink. "Very well, I'll give you some diversions. Finish your report on the indents, the one that irritated Mr. Sleak so. I want it on my desk within a week. And for amusement, you can supervise the morning runs for a month or so." That would roust him out of bed at least an hour early, every day. He wasn't a middy, subject to demerits, but he'd learn it was risky to goad a Captain, even shoreside. He ought to have known that by now.

"Aye aye, sir." He seemed unperturbed. Perhaps Tolliver was an early riser; I realized that after a year of close contact with the man, I didn't know.

"A call for you, sir." The mess steward, at my shoulder.

"Yes?" I leaned against the entranceway, blocking the room's muted roar with my free hand.

"Duhaney, here. Your chip arrived an hour ago."

"Yes, sir."

"You were right, it would make an unfortunate incident, especially after the death of that boy on Farside. We don't want any problem with enlistments just now. I'll arrange matters from here. Say nothing. I'll send some people down for the, ah, package."

"The what?"

"The package!" His voice sharpened. "The one you wrote about. I'll have it dealt with up here. We'll reassign some personnel and handle it in a routine manner."

Unbelieving, I blurted, "You want to ferry the—the . . ." I couldn't refer to the late Lieutenant Sleak as a "package." It was an obscenity. "You want to transfer the entire problem to Lunapolis, as a personnel assignment?"

"Damn it, Seafort, isn't that what you wanted? Why else did you dump it in my lap?"

"I—yes, sir."

"Give me a day or two. I'll send a heli to take the package to London Shuttleport. The paperwork will be backdated."

Suddenly it seemed all wrong. "Sir, if there's an inquiry, won't it look, I mean, I—" I was as tongue-tied as young Adam Tenere.

"Not to worry, Seafort. Security is tight. Remember, um, last month's false alarm over the mistaken fish sighting. We have these matters well in hand." He rang off.

Well, he was right; they'd managed to cover up the sighting. There had been only minor interest from the zines, whose commentators asked why our radionics were so inaccurate. I trudged back to my table.

"Good news, I trust?" Tolliver was at his most suave.

"Actually, yes." I tore viciously at a roll.

Behind me, a crash of dishes; a clumsy cadet had dropped his tray. Demerits, unless his sergeant was in a forgiving mood. Catcalls and whistles erupted from nearby. I jumped to my feet, stalked to the table whose cadets had jeered. "Sergeant Olvira! Put them all on report!" Conversation hushed throughout the mess hall. "How long ago did they take the oath, Sarge? If you can't straighten them out, I'll find an instructor who can!"

The Marine stood, assumed the at-ease position. "I'm sorry, Commandant. I'll see that they don't trouble you further."

"You'd damn well better. This is a disgrace! I want these hoodlums in my office first thing tom—"

"Excuse me, sir." Tolliver's voice was urgent.

I wheeled. "Get back to your table, Lieutenant. If these—"

"It can't wait." He interposed his shoulder between me and Sergeant Olvira. "Please. Right now."

Astounded, I followed him a few steps toward our table. "What's so damned important it—"

"Get hold of yourself!" Tolliver's mouth was set. His tone was so low I had to strain to hear.

"No more insolence, or I'll have you cashiered!"

"That's your decision, sir. But while I'm your aide, I'll protect you even from yourself. The business with the Marines was nothing. Right now you're making a total fool of yourself in public!"

Slowly I became aware of the overwhelming silence. I took a deep breath, and then another. With shaky legs I turned again to Sergeant Olvira. I strove to make my tone casual. "Sarge, it's not decent for them to laugh when a cadet drops a tray. Every mate's misfortune is their own. Speak to them about it, please." I turned back to my own table.

Lieutenant Bien eyed me, turned away. Lord God, what was wrong with me? I'd thrown a tantrum worse than any I'd ever seen from a plebe. Missing a night's sleep was no excuse; I'd learned to manage without. I muttered to Tolliver, "Thanks."

His tone was still low. "There's Sergeant Olvira too. I'll have a word with him after dinner, if you like."

"Yes." I closed my eyes, feeling my ears burn. If proof was needed that I was unfit for my duties, I'd just provided it.

"Pardon me, sir. Another call."

I whirled. "Now who?"

The steward smiled apologetically. "I have no idea, sir."

I might as well carry a stereochip caller, like a civilian. "Very well." I stalked to the doorway, took the caller. I snapped, "Seafort!"

"Nicky? I told dem not to be bothering you."

"Annie."

"They said you called."

"Yes, hon. How are you?"

A pause. "I don . . . don't know, Nicky. Times I feel good, other times I'm all confused. I think about . . ." Her voice trailed off.

"I understand."

"About what they did to me, in Centraltown." Her tone was determined.

I closed my eyes, leaned against the wall, my relief almost too much to bear. It was the first time Annie had ever spoken of her brutal rape.

"Are you okay, Nicky?"

"Yes, except I miss you."

She giggled. "Good, I want you to be missin' me. Day you don't, I be in trouble."

"Wait 'til you see our apartment, Annie. It's huge. And there are all sorts of shops across the Commons, in Devon."

She snickered. "Bet I know something else that's huge."

"Annie!" Despite myself, I blushed.

"Nicky? . . ."

"Yes, hon."

A sob. "I love you." The line went dead.

With heavy step, I returned to my place. I waited for dessert, aching for the solitude of my apartment. I topped off my coffee, relishing its warmth. The bowl of pudding came.

"Sir, excuse me." The mess steward.

"Now what?"

He said warily, "Another call."

I stared at my pudding. "Almighty Lord God in His heaven."

"I'm sorry. I didn't mean to—"

"And His angels! Amen." I stalked to the caller. "Seafort!" My tone was savage.

"Sergeant Obutu reporting, sir." She seemed distant, as she was. "I hope I haven't disturbed you."

"You have, and it had better be important!"

"That's for you to judge, sir. Cadet Arnweil was sent to Lieutenant Paulson this evening. To the barrel."

Too bad, but I couldn't do anything about it. "I'll read the Log later. Why bother me about—"

"Sergeant Radz sent him. And Kyle Drew just pulled his tenth demerit. He's to report to Mr. Paulson in the morning." Drew? He had enough misery, after his accident.

I paused. "Sergeant, who issued the demerits?"

Her formality matched my own. "I believe most of them came from Sergeant Radz, sir."

I let the silence stretch.

"The Stritz boy too, sir. The one with the low grades, in Kuhn's barracks. He's on punishment detail for a month."

"Why?"

"To improve his grades."

Something was going wrong. Sergeant Radz had felt remorse over Edwards's death, but couldn't accept his responsibility for the cadets' plummeting morale. He saw his role as toughening his youngsters into proper Naval officers. Apparently, so did Stritz's drillmaster, Sergeant Kuhn.

"Very well, I'll deal with it as soon as I get back."

A pause. "Aye aye, sir. I'll log off Cadet Drew's demerits when he reports back from Mr. Paulson."

Deftly done, without a hint of criticism. I sighed. "Tell Sergeant Radz he's to cancel Drew's demerits and see that no one else reaches ten before—"

"Aye aye, sir. Are you quite sure that's what you want?"

I gripped the caller tightly, forced myself to relax. This woman knew what she was about. "What would you suggest, Sarge?"

"I don't know, sir. But I wouldn't think undercutting Sergeant Radz in front of his barracks is the answer."

Damn it, she was right. Well, the alternative was letting Kyle Drew be caned. So be it, unless—

"Send the cadets groundside. All three of them."

"Surely there's a better way than washing them out."

I growled, "I didn't say I'd wash them out; just transfer them here. Do it before Mr. Drew has to report to the barrel." That would get the boy off the hook, without undercutting Radz too obviously. I hung up the caller, trudged one more time to my table, where all waited for me to dismiss the assembly.

Tolliver saw me to the door. "I'll be along after a word with Sergeant Olvira."

"No. Come with me." We walked in silence to my apartment. Safely inside, I flung off my jacket, threw myself on my couch. "Tolliver, should I resign?"

"I beg your pardon?" His eyebrow lifted.

"I'm out of control. Look at me."

Unbidden, he sat. "You're tired. We're not as young as we used to be."

"Goofjuice. Tantrums aside, I don't know what I'm doing. I veer between harsh discipline and coddling them."

"So, you're erratic. You're a Captain."

I snarled, "None of your middy humor, Edgar. Not now."

Tolliver shrugged. "You're having a bad day. Don't make too much of it." He stood. "If that's all, I'll smooth Sergeant Olvira's feathers. I'm sure he didn't enjoy being chewed out in front of his cadets."

"Sit. I haven't dismissed you." It sounded more petulant than I'd intended. "Sorry. Problems on Farside; a couple of the barracks sergeants are riding roughshod over their joeys. It's gotten out of hand."

"What will you do about it?"

"I don't know. That's why I'm the wrong man for the job." I brooded. "How soon can you finish your expense and deliveries report?"

"The audit? You gave me a week. I could do it faster, if I didn't have to supervise morning runs." His expression was bland.

"Drop everything else, finish the report. As soon as you're done I'm sending you aloft. The staff is—I need a moderating influence."

"I'm hardly the one for that."

I said gruffly, "You did well enough in *Victoria*'s wardroom." Tolliver, as Midshipman, had soothed the burgeoning hostilities among my junior officers. I realized, with a pang, that my long-nursed resentment of his hazing might be somewhat unreasonable as well. "That's all, Edgar. Get some sleep."

"Right. Aye aye, sir. I'll see Olvira first."

"I'll deal with him. No, don't argue about it!" After he was gone, I sat on the couch, head in my hands, trying not to think of the ordeal ahead. Finally, after an hour, I stood slowly, reached for my jacket.

I strode from Officers' Quarters across the compound to the cadet dorms, taking salutes from passing middies. The night air was chill; I increased my pace.

Sergeant Olvira ran Wilhaven Barracks, the third along the neatly bordered walk. I heard laughter from inside as I bounded up the steps.

A cadet saw me, shouted, "Attention!" They rushed into a line, stood with spines stiffened. Some wore jackets, others were in shirts and ties. A few were in undershorts only. Bunks were rumpled, holovids spread out and opened. A typical barracks evening, the relaxed cadets finishing their work before Lights Out.

"At ease." I looked around. "Where's your sergeant?"

A boy with a corporal's stripe said tentatively, "I think he's in his quarters, sir."

"My compliments, and would he please join us."

"Aye aye, sir." The cadet slipped on his boots, hurried out.

We waited in silence. After a moment, footsteps returned. "Sergeant Olvira reporting as—"

"As you were, Sarge." I took a position in the center of the aisle, addressed the cadets. "Someday you will command sailors, who have a right to expect your best. Let this be a lesson to you." I turned to Olvira, spoke for all to hear. "Sergeant, I tender my apology for the rude and unwarranted remarks I made in dining hall tonight. They show I am unable to control my temper, which I will endeavor to correct in future. I am sorry."

Every eye was fastened on me. I swallowed bile, turned to the line of cadets. "The only thing worse than misbehavior to a fellow officer is failure to acknowledge it. My discourtesy to your sergeant is not excused by your laughing at a fellow cadet, whose embarrassment at dropping a tray in the Commandant's presence can only be imagined. I rebuke you, as I rebuke myself for my response. That is all." With what dignity I could muster, I strode out.

That night I slept, free of dreams, a deep refreshing slumber. In the morning I hauled myself out of bed, showered, went to breakfast, settled in my office. I buzzed Sergeant Kinder. "Any word from Admiral Duhaney?"

"Not since last night, sir."

Well, he had said it would take a day or two. I thought of Lieutenant Sleak, in the sickbay cooler awaiting transshipment. His life, taken in despair, would end in travesty.

"I'm sorry," he had said. Would that he had waited long enough to add a few words of explanation.

I tapped my desk. Not only had we lost Sleak, I intended to reassign Tolliver to Farside. We needed a new lieutenant, and flank. I took up the caller. "Get me BuPers."

After a short wait I found myself speaking to Captain Higbee, the same official who'd refused to reassign Ardwell Crossburn. Lamely, I explained that Lieutenant Sleak was to be transferred aloft at Admiral Duhaney's orders, and I needed another officer. It was almost true.

"Do you have anyone in mind?" Higbee sounded preoccupied.

"No."

"Very well, I'll find you someone. You'll hear from me." He rang off.

I spent the morning skimming through reports. Shortly before lunch the caller buzzed.

Sergeant Kinders. "Midshipman Keene is down from Farside. He's escorting three cadets."

"Very well." In my pique of the night before, I'd failed to make arrangements for them. Just as I'd failed to call off the invasion of the Marines. Early senility, perhaps. "Send them in."

They came stiffly to attention before my desk, Thomas Keene proud with responsibility, the three young cadets subdued and wary.

"Did they give you any trouble on the way down, Mr. Keene?"

"No, sir."

"Very well." I thought for a moment. "Thank you. I suppose you're anxious to get back?"

"Not rea—yes, sir."

I felt magnanimous. "I suppose not. The acceleration must be terrible for a man of your advanced age." Keene was barely eighteen. "Well, take two days leave, if you'd like. You could see London."

His eyes lit up. "Thank you, sir!"

"Dismissed." When he'd left I turned to the waiting cadets. "At ease. You must be Stritz."

"Yes, sir. Johan Stritz. You met me in my barracks." I concentrated, recalled the wiry, muscular boy who'd slipped into the dorm during my reverie. The cadet's forehead gleamed; he was frightened.

"I won't bite, Mr. Stritz." I turned to Arnweil, my voice gruff. "How do you feel?"

"I'm all right, sir."

"Can you sit at mess?"

Kevin's face went red. "Yes, sir. I guess Mr. Paulson went easy on me."

I turned to Kyle Drew. As often as the name had been in our deliberations, I'd seen him only once, on the Hull. His face was sallow, his cheeks sunken. Puberty was barely upon him. At fifteen, a hard burden to bear.

"So you're Drew." Inane, but I could think of nothing else to say.

"Yes, sir." He shifted nervously.

I studied the three of them. I hadn't thought the matter through beyond calling them down to Devon, out of harm's way. I'd have to assign them to barracks. "Do you know why you're here?"

Kyle Drew. "Because we can't hold our own. We foul up." His tone was bitter.

Arnweil added, "To see if you'll give us another chance before washing us out."

"Who told you that?"

"Sergeant Radz, sir."

Damn the man. I blurted, "No, you're here to—" I hesitated. By bringing them back to Devon I'd consigned them to classes they'd already passed, to plebe dorms. They would assume I judged them failures, and they'd act the part. But what else was I to do?

I improvised, "You're here as—as part of an experimental program. Some cadets seem to do better with individualized instruction, and I want to see why." Johan Stritz gawked. "I'll bunk you in one of the dorms. You'll exercise with your bunkmates. Your academic work at Farside will be converted to individual study projects."

Kyle Drew said hesitantly, "Pardon, sir, but I don't understand. What do we . . . do? I mean, during the day?"

A good question, to which I had no answer. But of course they mustn't know that. Decisively I said, "That's the whole point. You're assigned to me. You'll accompany me back and forth to Farside and work at—at duties I assign from time to time. In my office." I was perspiring. "That's enough for now. Report to Sergeant Kinders. He's to assign you a barracks. To Sergeant Ibarez," I added. Ramon Ibarez would provide the nurturing Radz could not.

As the door closed behind them I sat, stunned. What in heaven's name had I done? I'd babbled as if demented about programs that didn't exist, independent studies that had never been authorized, duties I would have to invent before I could assign. And under my personal supervision, no less.

Effectively, I'd taken three troubled youngsters out of Academy and made them my personal responsibility. Worse, I'd shattered the tradition that cadets were so insignificant as to be beneath an officer's notice. How could these joeys respect me if they knew me so well?

11

By evening, I'd gotten Arnweil, Drew and Stritz settled into barracks. The next day I arranged for Sergeant Kinders to assign them tasks to keep them occupied. As it happened, they were rather useful now, as we were short an officer. The middies, whom we otherwise used to run errands or help with chores, were helping fill in with Lieutenant Sleak's responsibilities.

The following morning a heli landed on the pad, and Darwin Sleak's remains were quietly hustled out of Academy. I accompanied the sad bundle strapped to the dolly, offering a silent prayer as I walked. Whatever the cost of announcing his death, I knew we had done wrong to conceal it, and the fact that the Admiral had decided on the course did not excuse my part in it. After, I returned to my office.

My three cadets took meals with their plebe barracks; I was relieved not to have them underfoot. I was uncomfortably aware that for all my words of reassurance, I'd shunted them aside the moment our interview was done.

The following day I managed not to see them at breakfast and lunch, but by dinner I could stand it no longer. I signaled the mess steward. "Three more places, if you please." With Sleak gone and Tolliver absent, we were hardly crowded.

The places set, I had the steward fetch my three cadets from Sergeant Ibarez's table. They approached with embarrassment, Kevin Arnweil in the lead. Lieutenant Bien made as if to speak, looked away. In living memory, no cadet had ever been summoned to the Commandant's table, not even for a rebuke. Tradition.

"Sit, gentlemen. From now on you'll take dinner with us." Arnweil sat shyly alongside Sandra Ekrit, the two other boys found a place nearby. The three huddled together as if for warmth in the disapproving chill.

I spooned my soup, waiting for someone to break the ice. At first, no one spoke. Then Midshipman Ekrit deliberately turned her face from the cadets, resumed her conversation with Lieutenant Bien. Arnweil went red, concentrated on his bowl. Johan Stritz whispered something to Kyle Drew, who played with his fork. Drew, after a moment, glanced sheepishly at Sergeant Olvira. "Good evening, sir. I mean, Sarge."

"Good evening." The sergeant's tone was wintry. He swivelled to Midshipman Thayer. "Was Lunapolis all you expected?"

Anton Thayer grinned. "Yes, I—"

No. It wouldn't do. I looked across to Stritz. "How old are you, Johan?"

"Fifteen, sir."

"You were having trouble with Nav, as I recollect. How are you doing now?"

"A little better, sir."

"Good." My tone sharpened. "I believe Midshipman Ekrit did well at Nav." I turned to the first middy. "Isn't that so?"

"Yes, sir." Warily, she studied my expression.

"Then you won't mind giving Mr. Stritz a hand in his studies."

Her distaste was apparent. "Of course not, sir."

"And since you won't know when Johan needs help, you're confined to base until his grades improve."

"I—"

"And your manners."

The midshipman looked down to her plate. "Pardon me for offending you, sir."

I smiled coldly. "You didn't offend me, Midshipman, though I'm sure Mr. Stritz feels affront. Of course, as a cadet he can't express it."

She said in a small voice, "I apologize, sir. And to you, Cadet."

I'd accomplished my purpose; time to let up. I smiled at Anton Thayer, gestured to Arnweil. "Tell Kevin about your trip to Lunapolis, Mr. Thayer. Did you go Outside for the light show?"

Lieutenant Bien probed my face as halting conversation resumed. I looked back, impassive. If necessary, I would make an example of her as well. Perhaps she understood; eventually, she turned to Kyle Drew and began to chat.

After dinner I returned to my office, fuming at the callousness of my staff. I'd invited the cadets to break bread with us, and my officers owed them the same courtesy as any guest, tradition or no.

The caller buzzed. "BuPers, sir."

A click. "Please hold for Captain Higbee, sir." The line went silent. Waiting, I tapped knuckles against my teeth. True, lieutenants and midshipmen alike assumed cadets were less than nothing. But even as a cadet I'd known officers who saw the person inside the creased gray uniform. Midshipman Jeffrey Thorne, for example. He'd shown me kindness, had taken me into his world of risk and adventure, had been my mentor and friend.

"Seafort? I have a lieutenant for you. Brann, age fifty. He's recovering from a fall; light duties would suit him perfectly."

"Very well."

"He was on the Vega run for several years, and isn't very happy about going shoreside. But that's his worry. When he's well, we'll see about transferring him out."

Brann wouldn't fit in at Academy, supervising frisky, healthy youths, resenting his own disability. What I really needed was a younger man, one with enthusiasm.

Higbee's tone became more guarded. "Your Mr. Sleak is on Lunapolis, by the way. Assigned to the Admiral's staff." I grimaced, but said nothing. "I'll transfer Brann's file to your puter and send him his travel orders."

"No."

"You can expect him—what?"

"I don't want him."

"I asked if you had someone in mind, and you didn't. We've been through this before, Seafort. Unless he has unsatisfactory ratings, you're stuck—"

I took a deep breath. "Don't bother sending him, I'll just ship him back."

"I'm senior to you, Mr. Seafort, please keep that in mind. And I'm acting with the authority of Admiral Duhaney."

I snarled, "Very well, in that case, reassign me Lieutenant Sleak!" There was silence. "In fact, I have a mind to give him a commendation. It would make a nice press release. The Admiral loves press releases, they stimulate enrollment."

Higbee's tone was cautious. "What do you want, Captain?"

"I don't know. I want someone—someone who . . ." Someone like Jeff. "Tell me, whatever happened to a Thorne, Jeffrey? Graduated in '88."

"I haven't the faintest idea, and in any event we can't pull someone off—"

"Very well, I'll make do with Sleak."

A long pause. "I'll get back to you."

I put my head in my hands. Higbee would ring through to Admiral Duhaney, whose patience with me was exhausted. Perhaps he'd relieve me. It was just as well. The Commandancy called for tact and political skills I could never master.

I brooded. Men like Sergeant Radz strove to do their duty, and were excellent officers in their own fashion. But competence had to be tempered with kindness. I myself was incapable of it; I lashed out indiscriminately, regretting my impetuosity only when it was too late. The cadets didn't need coddling, they needed . . . a hand. Sometimes, all one could give them was understanding. I sat in the dusk, remembering.

Jeffrey Thorne looked away, his expression pained. "I'm sorry, Nick. I didn't mean for it to end this way."

I ignored his apology, echoed the word of greatest import. "End, sir?"

The midshipman scuffed the deck. "I have to watch myself for a while; any more trouble and they'll throw me ashore. Mr. Zorn warned me." His foot scuffed at the deck. "Even talking to you like this, I can't risk it anymore."

I felt the girders of my world snatched away. "Yes, sir."

"Seafort, you're second year now; soon you'll make middy. You don't need me."

I flared, "You don't know what I need!" Immediately I added, "I'm sorry, Mr. Thorne. Please excuse me." Friend or not, he was an officer and I was but a cadet.

"Oh, Nicky." He waved it away. For a moment he flashed the captivating smile that had brought about my humiliation and disgrace. "Anyway, no more missions. I told them it was all my fault."

"I know, sir." My eyes stung. "But it wasn't. I didn't have to go with you."

"Sure you did." He rested his hand on my shoulder. "I'm sorry, Seafort. I let you down. You weren't supposed to get a caning."

"I'm all right."

"Yes, you are. Do you understand that?"

"Of course. It hurts, but—"

"No, listen to me. You're all right, Seafort. Inside."

For some reason, I felt a desolation. "What do you mean?"

Thorne thrust his hands in his pockets, looked away. "It's just . . . you don't have many friends, do you?"

"There's Robbie, and Arlene, lots of—"

"Joeys you really talk to?"

I swallowed. "What is there to talk about?"

He came close, looked directly into my eyes. "You tell me, Nick."

I shrugged. "Father and I—we didn't speak a lot."

"But you feel the need, at times."

I looked to the deck.

"You're lonely, Nick. I am too, sometimes, but you seem to have an inner strength. You'll get through."

"Will I?" The cry sprang from me.

"Yes. It would be easier if you could . . . share, I suppose. Don't look at me like that. You give, when your friends need it. I saw you once, when Rovere was upset about Sarge chewing him out. The way you diverted him, until he got over his sulk. But I'm not talking about giving . . ." Again he trailed off.

"Say it, sir." My plea sounded almost a command. I held my breath until I saw he took no offense.

Thorne fidgeted. "Opening up. Sharing yourself. People can't help you unless you let them in." He looked away. "I wouldn't press, but I don't know if we'll get another chance."

"I'm all right, I—"

His look was one of sadness.

"I don't know how," I blurted. "I never have. Once I had a friend, Jason—" The memories flared, and I thrust them down. "I'm all right, sir. Really."

The young middy smiled. "Well, we had some good missions."

My return smile was tremulous. "Yes, sir."

"Hang on, Cadet. You'll get through." A quick squeeze, and he was gone.

I watched him stride down the corridor, never looking back. I thought of Father, and felt a chill.

After breakfast I left my apartment and wandered the compound. On the gunnery range, cadets practiced with their ancient laser simulator, while a few were allowed to focus an actual laser cannon locked to low intensity. Later, outside the suiting room, I watched cadets stumble through their suiting drills. Today, none turned green from the gas and clawed at his helmet.

I wandered toward my office, brooding. Perhaps I should schedule a surprise inspection. Tolliver or Bien could help make the rounds. Was I considering it merely to alleviate my own boredom? Well, even so, the cadets could use—

"Cadet Arnweil reporting, sir!"

I whirled. "Don't sneak up behind me, you young—what do you want?"

The boy snapped a salute, tugged his gray jacket into place. "Sergeant Kinders's compliments, sir, and there's a visitor at the gate asking—"

"Parents aren't allowed entry. Have the guards send him away."

"—asking for you personally, sir." He stopped to catch his breath.

"Who is it?"

"A Mr. . . . ." He fished for the name. "Mr. O'Neill, sir."

Did we have a cadet by that name? I wasn't sure. "Tell the guard whoever it is should call for an appointment." I strode back to my office.

Sergeant Kinders looked up from his caller. "Oh, there you are, sir. Captain Higbee from BuPers on the line."

"Very well, I'll take it." I went into my private office, sat at the desk.

A click. "Seafort? I have a Thorne, Jeffrey R., lieutenant, four years seniority. A year on U.N.S. *Targon*, staff at Lunapolis Admiralty, now at Callisto Base."

"I want him."

"His enlistment is up in six months. Policy is not to transfer—"

"He'll reenlist, he's career Navy." Why hadn't I thought of Thorne before? His good humor, his occasional irreverence to tradition would be ideal. "He's the one."

Animosity leaked through Higbee's polite veneer. "I may not be able to get him for you."

If I'd stroked him, I wouldn't be in my predicament. Even knowing that, I couldn't contain myself. "Mr. Higbee, I don't know how to play this game. I'm no politician. But there's two or three people I could ring who do. One by himself might not have enough influence, but I'll bet that all of them together could clip your wings. Shall we see who has more pull, you or I?" I was astounded at my insolence. It verged on mutiny.

A pause. I wondered who I could call, other than the Admiral. The only person of influence I knew was Senator Boland, and he would merely laugh and hang up.

"Very well, you'll have Thorne in a few days. It's of no consequence." Higbee made no attempt to conceal his anger. "I'll look forward to assisting you again." He rang off abruptly.

Another enemy. I was so good at making them. Now I'd have to watch every new appointment like a hawk. I sighed, then relaxed. It didn't matter. I was getting Jeff Thorne.

Again the caller buzzed. "Yes?" I bit back anger. "The guardhouse, sir. A visitor is insisting—"

"A Mr. O'Neill? We don't take unannounced—"

"Dr. O'Neill, not Mister."

Lord God. The clinic. "Send him to my office immediately. Do you have a middy to escort him?"

"I'll use one of your special cadets."

I grunted. My special cadets. Well, I'd created that problem for my-self.

I waited with an attempt at patience, but gave up after only a few minutes. I hurried out to the corridor, met O'Neill and Drew at the main door. "I'm terribly sorry. I didn't recognize your name."

"No matter." Well dressed, receding hairline, thin-faced. He shook hands, shot me a probing glance. "I thought it best to see you in person. Have you somewhere to talk?"

"My office."

He waited until we were seated with the door closed. "Mr. Seafort, this is an unfortunate situa—"

"What happened?"

"I don't know how to tell you." He hesitated. "You have to under-stand, the practice of medicine is not an exact—"

I came to my feet, gripped the back of my chair. "For God's sake, man, spit it out!"

He said warily, "She's gone."

"Annie's dead?" My stomach went hollow.

"No, gone from the clinic." He saw my face, hurried on. "I mean, procedures normally ensure . . . it's not as if we run a prison, you under-stand. I want to assure you that normally—"

"I don't care about normal. What about my wife?"

His forehead shone with perspiration. "Yesterday afternoon she left the grounds and never came back."

"You let her walk out, in her condition?"

"Almost all our patients are voluntary. Mrs. Seafort has free use of the grounds."

"But she's not on your grounds."

"One of our patients had his family visit. Afterward your wife walked them to the gate, strolled out when they did. We didn't even know how she'd left until we replayed the tapes."

"What was she wearing?"

"A light jumpsuit."

"Money?"

"As far as we know she had none. All her expenses were billed to your account."

My fists bunched.

"The police are looking. We called them within hours."

"Did you check the squatters' shacks outside the clinic?"

"When the police came. We couldn't go out alone."

"Of course not. You might have found her."

"I understand your anger, Mr. Seafort. That's why I came in person."

I ignored that. "Was she upset?"

"Her chart shows that she's been moody, of late. But that's natural, at her stage. Eventually her mood swings will lessen, and she may be quite placid as long as she takes her meds. But for now—"

"She's gone. Without money or proper clothing."

"Yes." He hesitated, blurted, "It may not be as bad as all that. Your wife's, er, background . . . she may be more skilled than most at coping with—"

I stood, my voice odd. "Background?"

"Well, after all, she is a trannie. They can handle the most appalling—"

I was on my feet. "Lord God damn you!" I could strangle him. I was young enough, strong enough. He was within reach.

"Captain, many papers have been written about the peculiar transpop subculture. It's not—"

I roared, "KINDERS! GET IN HERE!"

Within seconds the door popped open, and the Sergeant dashed in, eyes wide with alarm.

"It's not insult, only fact that she could well survive situations that—"

With effort, I made my voice steady. "Dr. Richard O'Neill, before witness I do call challenge on you to defend your honor! Let me know the name of your second. Choice of—"

O'Neill didn't move, and his voice was precise. "Though our clinic is private, we receive funds from the municipal government. As it happens, I am classified as a civil servant and therefore exempt from the dueling statutes."

I leaned across my desk, beside myself. "You pompous fool, find my wife, however you have to do it! If she dies, I'll kill you myself, if I end up in a penal colony."

Dr. O'Neill was pale. "As I said, I understand your anger. Even though your threats are actionable, I won't file a complaint unless—"

"Kinders, show him off the base, and that means NOW!"

The sergeant didn't bat an eye. "Aye aye, sir." He crossed the room, bent over O'Neill, took his arm. "Come this way, sir. Right away, please."

I paced the office in mounting fury, until finally I flung open the door. "Call Tolliver!"

I waited until my aide cautiously peered in. "I hear you're on the warpath."

"Annie's missing. She walked out of the clinic."

His manner changed in an instant. "My God. I'm sorry." He pulled up a chair, sat without my bidding. "What do you want me to do?"

"She sneaked out yesterday, and there's no trace of her." I faced the window, grappled with a sudden difficulty in speaking.

"They'll find her, sir. It's just a matter of time." He pursed his lips, thought. "You could help."

"Go look for her, you mean?"

"No, of course not. Where would you search that they haven't tried? But you could take advantage of your popularity for once. Light a fire under the jerries."

"I could do that." I turned. "Get the number of the local station."

His sardonic smile returned. "That wouldn't be your style, sir. Try the Commissioner of Police. The Mayor. Hell, call the Secretary-General; he'd take a call from you. Anyone would."

"Except Admiral Duhaney."

"Well, he knows you." When he saw my eyes his smile vanished. "Sorry, I'm out of line. How high do you want to start?"

"The Police Commissioner, if I can get through."

Tolliver rose. "Give me a few minutes."

Half an hour later, I hung up, the Commissioner's assurances ringing in my ears. They would make every effort, highest priority, etc. I sat, biting my knuckles. Somehow, it sounded like a brush-off.

I passed the rest of the day in an agony of anticipation. I snatched up the caller every time it buzzed, dreading a catastrophe, praying that Annie had been found.

No word.

At dinner I was silent. No one at my table had been told about Annie, but they knew my moods enough not to bother me. Subdued conversation detoured around me while I played with my food.

Two days passed in endless agony. I signed reports, caned a hapless cadet who'd been caught outside the fence, ordered a cabin made ready for Lieutenant Thorne. Admiralty called, requesting me to attend the commissioning of U.N.S. *Wellington*, two weeks hence. I agreed. By then Annie would be found. She had to be.

By midafternoon of the third day I was nearly beside myself. Several times I called the clinic, to see if Annie had returned on her own. I plodded mechanically through my duties.

"Captain?"

I swung round so fast I almost fell out of my chair. "What, Edgar?"

"I think I found something."

After a moment I realized that Tolliver wasn't speaking of Annie. I forced myself to concentrate. "Go on."

"Remember when Sergeant Ibarez was keeping Jerence Branstead away from his mates? He had him recheck serial numbers in the suiting room. I looked them over."

"So?" At the moment I didn't give a damn about suits, or the cadets who wore them.

"Branstead's tallies match the suiting room manifest, but they don't check against the invoices in the puter. It may mean something."

"Is the number of suits correct?"

"Seems to be. It's an odd discrepancy, though."

"It happens all the time. An order is diverted from one ship to another. Forget about it."

"Aye aye, sir. Why don't I just forget about the whole audit, while I'm at it?"

"Tolliver!" My voice was dangerous.

Eyes blazing, he stood his ground. "You told me the bloody audit was important. I've gone without sleep, worked until the room spun to get out this damned report. The first time I have something that doesn't check out, you tell me to forget it. Make up your bloody mind!"

I retreated before his fury. "I'm sorry. I'm thinking of Annie. Do whatever you want."

"Aye aye, sir," he said, barely mollified. "Any word yet?"

"Nothing." I hesitated. "Edgar, what should I do?"

"What can you do? Wait it out."

"She's alone out there."

"You don't know that."

"What do you mean?"

His tone was gentle. "Sir, she's home."

My fists tightened. "That's not her home anymore. It can't be."

"That's how you and I see it." He left the rest unsaid.

"Those damned drugs . . ."

He shook his head. "Perhaps it was better in the old days, when they left people unbalanced. Even if they were schizo and glitched."

I waved it aside. "I want my wife, not your theories."

"Yes, sir, I'm with you on that. Wait it out. It's not as if you could go looking for her."

My head came up.

After a moment I said, "Why not?"

12

Tolliver objected vigorously to my leaving, and was apoplectic when I suggested going alone. To placate him, I agreed to take a middy. He picked Adam Tenere, who was groundside with dispatches. Well, the boy was well intentioned; I'd just have to be cautious in spaceport corridors.

To the annoyance of the steward, I was on my feet the moment the suborbital landed. Adam at my side, I fumed while the ramp swung ponderously from the gate. Outside, New York was already darkening.

Was there any point going to the clinic at this hour? Better to check into our hotel, start fresh in the morning. My Academy schedule was no immediate concern; I'd canceled all appointments, leaving Tolliver to greet Jeffrey Thorne and look after the paperwork at Devon.

No, a hotel would drive me cabin-crazy. I needed to see the clinic, put myself in Annie's place.

After losing several helicabs I gave up waiting my turn and shoved like everyone else, only to end up with a cabby who argued for five minutes before consenting to fly to the Bronx.

I settled back in my seat and glowered at Adam's attempts at conversation. At last, we set down on the visitor's lot, as far from the fenced perimeter as the cabby could manage.

"Sign us in at the Sheraton, Adam. I'll meet you later."

"Aye aye, sir. Can't I come—"

"No."

The clinic door opened at my first knock; I'd been on camera from the moment the heli had landed. At night, security would be especially tight.

The orderly at the desk looked up with scant effort to conceal his boredom. "Captain Seafort? I'm Jose Gierra. Dr. O'Neill was waiting, but he left for home an hour ago."

"My flight was delayed." I set down my duffel. "Show me Annie's room, please."

"Sorry. The rules say only the supervising physician can approve a visit. Come back tomorr—"

I was already striding to the ward door. "I'm not visiting, I'm inspecting."

"You need an escort in the ward."

"Fine! Escort me!" I opened the door as he dived, too late, for the automatic lock.

The orderly panted as he caught up with me. "Easy, joey. This job ain't no zark."

We strode along the corridor past silent darkened rooms.

Annie's cubicle was as I'd remembered: spartan, tidy, white. Her few clothes were stored neatly in the tiny closet. The sheets were tucked under the mattress with hospital precision.

I opened the bedside drawer; a brush, a comb, a chipcase. Annie's holovid lay on the chair. I inserted a chip. A romance holodrama, of the type she loved. I looked for a chip on which she might have left a note.

"There's nothing to find. The jerries looked four days ago."

I yearned to knock out his teeth. Instead, I asked politely, "Are you married, Mr. Gierra?"

"Sure."

I sat on the bed. "What's her name?"

"Connie."

"Would you care if she were killed?"

His fists bunched. "Of course."

"What if Connie were wandering out there, where the gangs could jump her?"

"Yeah, but she's no trannie."

My face showed no expression.

After a moment his sullenness faded. Slowly he lowered himself into the guest chair. "I'm sorry, Captain. You got every right to worry."

"Sorry I snarled at you."

"No matter." He gestured to the closet. "We looked for clues, but found nothing. The jerries came, asked a few questions. Truth is they wouldn't bother if you weren't famous. Another lost trann—lost patient is the least of their troubles."

"If you had to find Connie in a hurry, what would you do?"

"I'd want to search, same as you. But not at night."

"You people come in to work, don't you?"

"By heli, during the day. That's why Dr. O'Neill couldn't wait. Another few minutes and he'd have been stuck here for the night."

"We once took the Gray Line tour through Manhattan." A lifetime ago, Amanda and I. "It wasn't that bad."

He snorted. "Manhattan, on an armored bus, in daylight. The Crypsnbloods on the streets 'll eat them downtown grodes, they ever stray this far."

"I have to find my wife, Mr. Gierra."

"You Navy types go armed?"

"Not groundside."

"Well, there you are. You might try in the morning."

I stood. "If a cab won't come for me, where can I get one?"

"Across the river. Or maybe they'd land at the jerryhouse on One seventy-fifth; the block around it is cleared."

"Could I walk?"

"Ever try walking in the Bronx? You have no idea what it's like. They'd leave your carcass to rot."

"I've got to find my wife."

"Maybe in daylight, if you're lucky. Believe me, Mr. Seafort. Don't even think of going out tonight."

I sank back on the bed, shook my head. "Why build a clinic in an armed camp?"

"We been on this site for years. It wasn't so bad 'til the city abandoned the housing projects. When they went trannie, that was the end."

Annie was out there, somewhere.

"Captain, stay in your wife's room 'til morning. I'm sure O'Neill won't flare jets over it, after he let her walk out."

"All right." I had little choice. "Thanks, Mr. Gierra."

"Joe. I'm sorry I gave you face." He stood. "I'm on all night. Tomorrow I'll show you the neighborhood."

"I'd appreciate that."

I undressed for bed, eyes on Annie's few clothes in the closet. I yearned to press her head to my chest. When I lay down in the dark, her pillow proved a poor substitute.

I slept like the dead. In the morning I woke to an insistent hand on my shoulder.

"Captain? Care for breakfast?"

I groaned, opening an eye. "Give me a couple of minutes." I ducked into the head. Joe Gierra was waiting in the corridor when I came out knotting my tie. "Where can I make a call?"

"In the cafeteria." He steered me along the corridor.

I rang the Sheraton, waited several rings.

Adam sounded sleepy. "You never showed up, sir. The clinic operator said you were staying in Mrs.—"

"I'll be out for a while. I'll call around noon."

"Aye aye, sir. May I come wi—"

"No." I rang off.

I chewed on a roll. "How do you get home, Joe?"

"Helicab, usually. There's a few armored ground taxis left, but they usually work the Holdouts."

"The what?"

"The families who lived here originally. The Bronx was part of civilization, once. When the last subways stopped most everybody left, but a few diehards bricked up their windows and carried on. Their children still live here. They aren't Uppies, but they have their own shops, their own way of life." He tore a piece of syntho bacon, dabbed it in egg yoke.

"But . . . what do they do?"

"Same as anyone, I guess. Try to survive. They go out in groups, armed to the teeth, and only in the daytime. Their convoys bring in supplies every week or so. They use ground cabs when they can get them."

"What a life."

"Me, I'll take helicabs, even if they cost a few unibucks more. I don't want to get caught in a tin can if the Crypsnbloods come out."

I finished my third cup of coffee. Each moment it became less difficult to keep my eyes open.

"Come on, Captain. I'll show you the gate."

Someone had alerted Dr. O'Neill to my presence. When we dropped off my duffel at the desk he popped out of his office. "Captain, I called the stationhouse just a few minutes ago. Still no word of Mrs. Seafort. I don't recommend you go out alone."

"I'll keep it in mind." It was all I could do to maintain a pretense of civility. "Mr. Gierra?"

A few moments later we were at the gate. He pointed. "These shacks run all around the old stadium walls. Maybe a squatter saw her leave. You can ask."

"Right."

"When you get past the shacks, One sixty-first runs that way, east and west." He pointed. "Best to stay off it."

"Thanks, Joe." As the guard clicked open the gate, Gierra hesitated, thrust out his hand. I shook it.

I strode toward the nearest shacks a half block away, stumbling over broken asphalt barely discernible under waving weeds.

"Hey!"

I turned. Joe Gierra trotted after. He stopped, shrugged as if embarrassed. "I just thought . . . Hell. I might as well go with you. Two's safer."

"It's not neces—"

"She was a good joe, your lady. One of the nicer ones." He buttoned his jacket. "C'mon, before I change my mind."

I smiled, feeling as if the sun had broken through the morning haze.

We trudged toward a ragged line of huts built from the scrap of a crumbling civilization: broken alumalloy panels, crumbling brick mortared with mud. Not a soul could be seen, even in midmorning.

At the first hovel, I tapped on the dented door. Silence. "Are they abandoned?"

Joe snorted. "Are you kidding? When we put out the garbage . . ."

I moved to the next shack, knocked again. "Please talk to us. We won't hurt you."

The door flew open. A haggard crone in a filthy jumpsuit. In her hand, a knife glinted.

"I'm looking for—"

"Get away!" Her voice was like a nail on slate.

"My name is Captain Seafort. My—"

She lunged. As I reeled back she darted into the hut and slammed the door.

"Jesus, Lord Christ!" I didn't know I'd spoken aloud until I saw Gierra's face.

We crossed the haphazard lane and knocked at another shack. The door opened at once, as if the occupants had been waiting. Perhaps they had. Two husky youths, in their early twenties. One leaned on a club. "Whatcha wan'?"

"My wife was in the clinic. I'm trying to find her. I have a pic—"

"Ain' seen her, and wouldn' tell ya if I did. Prong yaself!" The door slammed shut.

I said with feeling, "Bastards."

"You'll get the same from all of them, Captain."

"They're all this bad?"

"No. These are the civilized ones." He spun, yelled, "We got blades, joey! Don't even think about it!" A sullen urchin hefted his rock, spat, ducked out of sight.

I whispered, "Did you really bring a knife?"

"No, I didn't plan on coming with you."

I tried another door. A woman with ragged children clinging to her knees peered at my holo, shook her head. "Ain' seen her. If she been, she gone. No point lookin'."

"Did someone get her?" I felt a chill.

"Must of. No one comes out here. Even us isn't safe." She picked up the smallest child, bared her breast, pleaded, "Go 'way, mister."

"Thank you, ma'am." She'd been the most civil of the lot.

I pointed past the end of the lane. "What's that way?"

"The real street. Abandoned stores, old apartments."

"Let's try it."

"Too far. Let's look around the other end of the fence."

"All right." I'd walk the street by myself, after.

We retraced our steps. Joe stopped. "This is too risky. I'll go back for a club or a blade. It'll just take a minute."

Reluctantly, I walked him back to the gate. I checked my watch, anxious not to waste precious daylight. I said, "Meet me on the south side of the compound. I'll start at the shacks nearest the fence."

He strode off, and I made my way to the ragged huts. A whiff of something foul; I wrinkled my nose. Perhaps Tolliver had been right; best to go back to London and let the jerries do their work. These people—

"Whatchew wan'?"

I whirled. Three men, two of them bearded. The third was flushed as if from exercise or fever. He held one hand behind his back.

"I'm looking for someone."

"Girl?"

"You know about her?" My voice was eager.

Their leader looked me over, rubbed his scraggly beard. "How much ya got?"

I hardened my tone. "Enough. Where is she?"

He pointed to the side lane. "Dat way."

The path was deserted. "Wait until my friend gets back." I peered, hoping to see Joe.

"Prong yo' frien'." Fever Face leered through broken teeth.

"Bugger off!" My snarl surprised even me. I thrust my hand in a pocket. "Mess with me, you be dead!" They hesitated. "G'wan!"

Scraggly Beard flashed a hand signal. I turned to Fever Face. Smiling, I took a casual step forward and kicked him in the groin.

He squalled, fell to his knees, revealing the laser pistol he'd hidden behind his back. As the third joey lunged for it I stomped on his hand. He howled, scrambled to his feet nursing his hand as I snatched up the gun.

I jammed the pistol in my pocket. Lord God knew if it had a charge.

Scraggly Beard hurled a rock. I gasped as it slammed into my side. He hauled Fever Face to his feet. I braced for a new attack, but they disappeared around the corner.

Joe Gierra was right; I couldn't search alone. I would need Adam Tenere, or a police escort. A Naval gunship might come in handy.

A sound, as feral shapes emerged from a nearby shack. Teens. One twisted a rusty chain; another beckoned with a huge and filthy knife. The third dangled a splintered club. I turned to run, stumbled as the club caught me behind the leg. I needed a rock, a pipe, anything. I clawed in my pocket, pulled out the pistol.

"Get away! I'll use it!" The charge was so far down the low battery light didn't even blink.

"Ain't no good, sailorboy! Empty!" The boy's shirt was no more than rags.

"Leave me alone, damn you!"

The chain boy howled as he leaped. I hurled the pistol at his face. A spurt of blood. He dropped, clawing at his eyes.

His companion charged. His club caught me on the side of the head. Blinking away stars, I clung to his neck. He reeked.

"Leggo me, gayfag!" The boy tried to pull away, but my legs were unsteady. I hung on, weaponless.

The last attacker circled, his knife twitching. He lunged. I whirled the joey I held so he was between me and the blade.

With a shriek, the boy I clutched dropped his club, stood trembling. As if unutterably weary, he rested his head on my shoulder. His legs buckled and he slid slowly to the ground. The third attacker backed away, eyes wide. Blood dripped from the knife in his mate's side. I gagged on the stench, rubbed my aching head.

"Frazzing sailaboy!" The remaining youth snatched a fallen club, charged. I caught the blow on my arm. A white blaze of pain.

I dug in, slammed my shoulder into his chest. He went down, rolled clear, sprang to his feet. I fled.

He was scant feet behind me. I dodged aside, crashed through the door of an abandoned hovel. I needed a club, a brick, anything. I stumbled over a broken table, smashed it into the wall. It disintegrated. I snatched a table leg.

The maddened youth charged through the doorway. As he raised his club I reared back, swung at his face with all my might. A crunch. His body flipped backward. His legs flew up and caught me in the gut. I lost my balance, slammed my head against the wall.

13

My skull ached abominably. I pried open my eyes, saw only black. Was I blind? I groaned, probed the painful lump on the side of my head. I lay against a wall. I'd been in a fight. Running. Chains. Clubs.

Crawling on hands and knees, I groped for the door. Fabric, on a stiff cold form. Something jagged and bony. And sticky. With a cry I pulled my hands free, rubbed them frantically on my jacket, the floor, anything I could find.

I knew what I'd touched.

Blind or no, I had to get out. I clawed to my feet, stretched out my hands, stumbled over debris. Where was the bloody door? If I had to touch that . . . that thing again . . .

A breath of cool air thrust through the fetid stench. Shakily, I stood and sniffed, trying to sense its direction.

Where in God's own hell was the door? Hands outstretched, I lurched like an automaton. I collided with something hard that smashed my lip and nose. Cursing, I nursed my throbbing face. The edge of the damned door had passed between my outstretched hands. Dabbing at a trickle of blood, I tottered into the welcome air.

Why hadn't Joe Gierra returned? If I called aloud, he might hear and help. But others might also hear. Perhaps they watched me even now. Help me, Lord God. Not for my sake, but Annie's. She has no one else.

A dim glow, as if in the distance.

I rubbed my eyes.

Lights.

With a rush of orientation I realized I'd lain unconscious until night. The distant lights must be Manhattan's Uppie towers.

If so, the clinic should be . . . that way. No, I couldn't remember which direction I'd taken. I could think it through, if I didn't panic.

A dog howled. My skin prickled.

Voices, quite close. I stiffened to immobility. Shapes passed.

Without warning, I sneezed. Someone screamed. The thud of pounding feet. Silence. My teeth bared in a feral grin. The squatters were as fearful of me as I of them.

As my eyes became accustomed to the night I saw lights flickering through imperfect walls. The shacks were occupied. I squinted, decided I could detect the end of the lane. I trotted toward it, fell flat on my face. Cursing, I scrambled to my feet. Why had I been so stupid as to go out alone, without lights or a caller?

A heli droned far overhead. Its searchlight played on the broken asphalt. Jerries? How could I attract their attention? Not by noise; they'd never hear. Did they have heat seekers? No use, every living body would set them off. I needed a light. Break into a squatter's shack, find something for a torch. My lips curled in a savage smile.

The blow smashed me in the back, hurled me to the ground. Paralyzed, I gasped for air. Hands pawed at me. My breath returned in a convulsive sob.

Someone pulled my jacket loose, flipped me over. Hands tugged at my boot, opening the snaps.

I yanked back my free leg, kicked at a shadowy face. The form toppled. I heaved myself to my knees. A whistling sound; I ducked. The club missed by an inch.

I ran as if from Satan himself. I caromed off a wall, found the lane again, turned a corner. A stone twisted under my loose boot; I hopped a few steps, ran again, my ankle sending warning stabs of pain. The voices faded.

I blundered into a pile of garbage. A cat shrieked; so did I. Jesus, Lord God. Reeling, I fetched up against an abandoned electricar, realized I was in a regular city street.

"Annie!" My shout rent the air. "I'm here for you. Come out, for God's sake!"

Running steps. I came to my senses, ducked behind the car, scuttled away low to the ground.

Where in God's name was I headed? The lights to my right must be Manhattan. Was that west? No, south. I was running . . . east. Into darkness.

I stopped, leaned against a building, tried again to catch my breath.

The clinic was on One sixty-first. I strained to see its lights; without them I'd never find my way. Hide until morning, then. In daylight I'd have a better chance; these savages knew their streets as I could not. I peered down the block, searching for shelter.

Ahead, a flickering light. Civilization? Behind me, a can clattered. I bolted toward the sanctuary of the light.

Some instinct made me slow as I neared. Stooped figures cavorted around a fire, in a vision reminiscent of Hieronymus Bosch. One toted a chair, another a bottle. A third held a bugle high over his head, cackling and cawing. A few of the dancers were naked.

A spit was propped across the blaze. On the spit, a dog. A bald creature in women's clothes capered in a dizzy circle, shrieking unintelligibly.

Pace by pace, I retreated, my heart hammering. Behind me, a growl. I spun on my heel. Two red eyes, over a toothy mouth. I screamed. The creature backed away. So did I, toward the fire, where the dangers were human.

The beast snarled again. Perhaps it was only a dog, but I didn't stay to find out. I sprinted toward the flame and the gamboling tribe. The wild dance wavered. Someone seized a brand, another a knife. I bolted past them into the campsite, sent the bald woman sprawling, leaped over a seated figure, and was gone into the night.

Favoring my aching ankle I galloped down the center of the road. I glanced over my shoulder. Naked revelers, a maddened hound, and the demons of hell pursued me. I was outdistancing all but the dog. A sprawl of gutted cars; I swerved left.

The shouts behind me redoubled. I risked another look. The beast loped ahead of the rest, determined, tongue hanging. I stopped to seize a brick. As the animal lunged I hurled my missile. The dog yelped, skittered away. Again I turned and ran, breath sobbing in my throat. The dog limped after me. Behind him came the calls of the humans.

I cantered on in darkness, my boot loose and flapping, a persistent hound and cavorting dancers in tow. Where were the jerries when you needed them? The nearest station was . . .

One seventy-fifth, Joe Gierra had said. I turned a corner, swerved left, charged on.

Rocks bounced at my feet; the campfire lads had reached the corner too. Soon I'd be too weary to run, too tired to care. I had to save at least some strength for when they cornered me.

In the black of the night a bugle sounded a charge. Its notes echoed along down the broad, silent avenue, over and again.

Doors opened. Boys and young men poured into the road. Two more dogs joined the chase as the bugle sounded anew. I'd blundered into a fox hunt, and I was the fox.

Hands clawed; I tore through them and staggered on.

One sixty-fifth. Ten more blocks, but I wouldn't make it. My breath came ragged. Onward I ran, closing my eyes to maintain the rhythm . . .

* * *

"Move it, Seafort!" Sergeant Tallor reached forward with his baton.

"Aye aye, sir." I lurched along the Farside track until I'd gained several steps. Sarge could easily have caught me, but I knew he wouldn't increase his pace just to touch me. He was always fair. Still, I had to maintain my distance; one tap with his baton and I'd be sent for a caning. It befell one or another of us, not every day, but often enough. I wasn't sure, but I suspected they'd been slowly increasing the pace.

Two laps to go. Robbie Rovere was half a length ahead, alongside Corporal Tolliver.

Could I hold out? In the months I'd been at Farside I'd felt my stamina increase, and I'd already been made to turn in my slacks and jacket for the next larger size. I wasn't sure, but I thought my voice had deepened another notch too. Perhaps it was the food.

Sergeant Tallor was gaining again. I could sprint, probably even catch the stragglers a dozen meters ahead of me, but if I used my little reserve of energy I'd collapse before the last lap.

I stumbled, lost my pace. Tallor's steps neared. Damn! No choice now. I dashed ahead, stopped only when I had left him a quarter turn behind. Now, I had only to hang on.

I turned into the last lap. Behind me, Sarge's inexorable footsteps. My lungs heaved. It wasn't fair. I'd been caned only last week. Lightly, it was true. Track canings were always light. But the humiliation was unbearable.

I staggered on. His step came closer. "Move on, boy."

I nodded, too bereft of breath to acknowledge the warning. The distance between us closed. He reached with the baton. I lurched forward, avoided it by inches.

Again he neared. If only I hadn't stumbled, the lap before. Now I couldn't last even the remaining quarter lap.

The baton reached out—

And I went down. "Ow!" I rolled in the gravel. "My foot!" I clutched my leg. "Oh, God, my ankle!"

Sarge knelt by my side. "Don't blaspheme." He pushed my hands away, felt the joint. "Can you move it? How about this way?"

I sobbed, "It hurts. I think I twisted it."

"That happens. You'll be all right." He blew his whistle to attract the attention of Sergeant Swopes.

I lay on the gravel track while the two conferred over my sweaty form. "Nothing's broken, Nick. We'll have the med tech check you just to be sure."

"Okay, Sarge."

Swopes reached down, offered a hand. "I don't think you need the stretcher, do you?" I came tremulously to my feet. "Lean on me." I did so. Hobbling and hopping, I made my way to the infirmary.

Bone diagnostics found no damage; the tech wrapped my foot in icy towels for an hour, then sent me back to my dorm. I showered and changed. By the time I caught up to my mates at lunch I was hardly limping.

During afternoon classes I managed to avoid the instructors' disapproval, though my mind wandered. Sergeant Swopes let me off tray duty for the night. I ate listlessly. After dinner we trudged back to barracks for Free Hour before Lights Out. I lay on my bed.

"You all right?"

I looked up, smiled. "Sure, Arlene."

She sat alongside me, whispered, "See Peterson? He pulled a fast one tonight."

"What do you mean?" I leaned close.

"Were you in his Nav class? He got caught passing a note, and Vasquez gave him a demerit."

"So?"

She looked disgusted. "That made ten, dummy. He had to see Zorn."

"Yeah, he got caned. That's why he's lying on his stomach."

"And after, he went to the Commandant's office."

I nodded. The unfortunate cadet would knock on the Commandant's hatch, say the ritual words to the duty officer. "Cadet Peterson reporting, sir. Lieutenant Zorn's compliments, and would you please cancel ten demerits."

Sanders slipped off the bed, sat on the floor, her mouth close to my ear. "I saw him in the shower tonight. He wasn't caned. No marks, not even red."

I whispered, "Maybe Zorn let him off."

She snorted. "Do they ever let a cadet off?"

I shook my head, puzzled. "How did he get out of it?"

"Don't you see? He never reported to Zorn. He just waited and went to the Commandant to have his demerits canceled."

I whistled softly at Peterson's audacity. If they caught him . . . "What'll you do about it?"

Her look was scornful. "Me? It's his affair, not mine. And pardon the pun, but it's *his* arse if they catch him."

"Geez."

After she wandered off I stared at Peterson, looked away, disappointed. I'd liked him.

The chime sounded, warning the end of Free Hour. We made ready for bed.

As the bulbs dimmed for Lights Out, the hatch opened. Sergeant Swopes surveyed us in our beds. When he spoke his voice was somber. "Cadet Peterson, out of your bunk."

The boy complied at once. He wore only his shorts. "Yes, Sarge?"

"Put on your pants and shirt."

"Aye aye, sir." He grabbed his clothes. I noticed he was careful not to turn his back to Sarge.

"And your shoes."

Half dressed, Peterson waited by his bunk. Sarge walked up and down the aisle, looking at each of us in turn before he turned back to Peterson. "Report to the Commandant's office at once."

"Aye aye, sir." He started toward the hatch.

"With your duffel."

"Aye—what?"

"You heard me. Move."

Cadet Peterson thrust his remaining clothes in the duffel, scurried out the hatch.

Sergeant Swopes walked down the aisle to Peterson's bed, sat on the end rail, a shadowy figure in the dim light. After a moment, he spoke to the opposite bulkhead.

"Your lives are committed to the United Nations Naval Service. The Service is worthy of you. It is our hope that you will be worthy of it. To that end we exercise you, train you, teach you the skills and crafts you must know."

He paused. The barracks was utterly silent.

"None of you would tolerate a cadet cheating his bunkmates. You know you must stand together, rely on each other without reserve, to survive the rigors of space. Likewise, your mates must be able to depend on your courage, your intelligence, your honesty."

He stood. "You must also learn that not only your bunkmates rely on your integrity. The entire Naval Service is as one with you. Captains, admirals, lieutenants, and middies. Officers and men.

Cooks and engineers. Your word is your bond, to each of them. It must always be so."

He paused, until the tension was agony, sat again on the bed. "You must not tolerate deceit. Not in me, not in yourselves. What is deceit? If I pull surprise inspection and you kick a loose sock under your bunk, that's fair. It's your responsibility to appear ready, mine to find the sock. But, if I ask, 'Cadet, is there a sock underneath your bunk?' you must respond with the truth. Dishonesty violates your oath of enlistment, but worse, it violates your integrity, and you will have become something you cannot long endure."

Somewhere, a sob caught in a throat.

"What Cadet Peterson did today was despicable, but the cancer has been excised. Whether it will reoccur is up to you. You are teens, and I am adult, but together we are the Navy. You, by your acts, will decide what kind of Navy that shall be."

He stood once more. "Does anyone have anything to say?" The room was silent. "Anyone?" He walked to the hatch, slid it open.

A voice wavered. "Yes, sir. I do."

He didn't turn. Still facing the hatch he said, "Yes, Seafort?"

"I lied today, when I said I hurt my ankle. I fell on purpose."

A long silence. "Come with me." He passed through the hatch. In nothing but my shorts, trembling, I faced him in his cabin.

"Why, Seafort?"

"Sergeant Tallor was about to baton me."

He nodded. "You were that afraid of the barrel?"

My eyes stung. "Not afraid, exactly. I just—no excuse, Sarge."

"Belay that. The truth."

"I couldn't run any faster. I was looking for a way out, and I couldn't think of anything else. I panicked." My ears flamed.

"You threw away your integrity to avoid a few strokes from Mr. Zorn."

"I—yes, sir." If only I could crawl under the hatch. If he would just look away.

"I see." He went to his file, pulled out a folder. "Read it."

I opened the file. On the left, my picture. On the right various reports, exam grades. On top, a note, dated today. "Cadet Seafort pretended injury today to avoid the baton. Action withheld for the moment."

I closed the folder. "You knew." I forced myself to meet his eye. "Then why didn't you send me with Peterson, sir?"

"There was hope you'd redeem yourself."

I swallowed, too miserable to speak. "What are you going to do to me, Sarge?"

"Me? Nothing. It's up to Tallor." He gestured to the hatch. "Get dressed and report to him."

"Right now?"

"That's what I said."

Fifteen minutes later I was knocking on Sergeant Tallor's hatch, barely in control of my dread. "Cadet Seafort reporting, Sarge."

"It took you long enough."

I blushed scarlet. "You know?"

"Yes."

"I'm—" It seemed so inadequate. "I'm sorry."

"But the damage is done. Do I need to lecture you?"

I looked up. "No, sir. I understand what I've done."

"Is it any different from what Peterson did?"

Of course it was. Peterson had actually lied, pretended to have been caned. I'd just . . . I looked at the bulkhead, past it to Father and home. Maybe, after they expelled me, I could learn courage in those rocky Welsh pastures. Perhaps even honesty, someday.

"No, sir. It's the same. I deserve the same punishment."

His tone was sharp. "That's for me to decide."

"Yes, sir."

He sat on his bunk, shaking his head. "Would a caning do you any good?"

I blurted, "Maybe nothing would." At his surprised look I rushed on, "I shouldn't even be here, at Academy. I missed Final Cull. They knew I wasn't qualified. Cane me, or get rid of me, Sarge. Do something, so I won't hurt the others."

"Easy, Seafort."

I bit back tears. "It's true."

"Very well." He thought for endless moments. "No caning."

Relief and despair battled within me. "Why not?"

"You understand what you've done, and either you'll do it again or you'll mature. You won't learn anything from the barrel."

"You'll punish me, though?" My tone was hopeful.

"Four demerits. And pot detail, every night for a month. It's hard work, but it won't occupy your mind. You'll have time to think."

"Thank you, sir."

"That's all."

When I was halfway through the hatch he stopped me. "I wouldn't have batonned you, Nicky."

"I couldn't run a whit faster, and you kept getting closer!"

"But I hadn't touched you, and I wasn't going to. You were giving your best."

I cried, "How was I to know that?"

"You were to trust me, and the Service. As I want to trust you."

I wiped my eyes. "Why did you come so close, then?"

"I was trying for your Yall."

I understood at last. Since we'd arrived at Academy they'd exhorted us to "give your all" at one thing or another. It was an Academy catchphrase, giving the "Academy All," or Yall.

"I picked up the pace but you hung on. I picked it up again and still you managed. When you're running, focus on each step, one at a time, as if it's the only one. Don't worry about the others to come. You have more endurance than you think. That's what I wanted you to learn."

"Sarge, I'm sorry. Please, I mean it!"

"I believe you, Cadet. Dismissed."

I slunk back to my dorm.

"Git 'im! He goin' for the jerries!"

My breath rasped. One sixty-ninth; six blocks more. I risked another glance back. One joey pedaled a rusty bicycle, a few others had rollerboards.

The boy on the bicycle pedaled furiously, swinging a heavy chain. He yowled, "Meat t'night! You be dinnah!"

I veered onto the sidewalk, but it was littered with broken furniture and debris. I yelped as my foot twisted again and I nearly lost my loose boot. I swerved back to the street. The rider came at me, chain whistling.

I stopped short, sprang under the blur of the chain. The rider crashed to the pavement. I ran on, mist seeping across my vision. I couldn't keep going.

"Yes you can, Seafort."

Not five more blocks, Sarge. Honest.

"Another few steps, boy."

Dutifully, I did as I was bidden. He'd take care of me. They always would.

One seventy-second street. Eons later, One seventy-third. Most of the mob had given up. A few grinning youths loped along, waiting for me to falter.

Surely the station would be floodlit. Ahead all was dark, but to the east, a glow. Please, Lord God. Joe told me 175th. Don't make me run crosstown. I can't, even for Annie.

Somehow, I reached the corner. Where's the frazzing jerryhouse?

There. The next block east, lit against the night. Encircled by a high chain-link fence, the station seemed a fortress. Surrounding buildings had been cleared away so it stood in a great open square.

Gasping, I staggered to the fence. Two youths closed in on me, taunting. "He wanna fin' jerries!" A hand snatched at my shirt.

The snap of a laser. My attacker dropped. I flinched, realized the shot had come from the station. The other youths dodged across the street into the dark.

No gate. Exhausted, I grasped the fence to hold myself upright. A sizzle.

I shrieked with pain, nursed my scorched hand. Across the street, jeers of laughter. Weeping, I lurched along the sidewalk. A high gate. Thank Lord God.

I flicked a finger at the bar. No charge. I rattled it with my good hand, looking for a buzzer, a camera. "Help me!" I'd intended a shout, barely managed a croak.

A speaker I hadn't noticed, on the top of the gatepost. "Off the gate, trannie! We're closed until morning."

A rock crashed into the fence. The hunters, behind me.

"They're after me!"

"We'll cover you to the corner, then you're on your own."

"I'm Nicholas Seafort! *OPEN THE FRAZZING GATE!*"

"Dey no help!" A youth more daring than the rest scuttled to the center of the street, hefting a brick. "I eat you!"

A new voice, tinny in the speaker. "It's him, the one Commander Chai said to watch for! Open the gate!"

"Comeon, sailaboy!" A brick spun toward me, struck a glancing blow on my forehead.

I stumbled, and the world spun.

"You be dinnah!"

Black.

"Are you all right, sir?"

I lay on my back, cold cloth on my forehead. A bright lit room. I focused on the young face looming over me, the blue uniform. "You're a jerry?"

A momentary frown. "I'm a police officer, yes, sir. Patrolman Wesley De Broek."

"I'm in the stationhouse?"

"Fifth Consolidated Precinct, One seventy-fifth Street Station."

I lay gathering my wits. "Help me sit."

The young patrolman put one arm behind my neck. "Easy, Captain. You've had a rough time."

"I'm all right." I think.

"I'll tell Commander Chai you're awake."

"Wait a minute." I took stock. My hand was swathed in gauze. Shirt ripped across the front. No jacket.

Across the room was a wall mirror. I peered at it. Good Lord. On my forehead, a blue lump. My nose was bloodied, my lip swollen. I giggled. "Just like the cover of *Holoworld*."

"They made a mess of you, sir. You're lucky, though. Some of the Holdouts, after the trannies are done with them . . ."

"I see why you don't open the gate."

"Yes. Well." He looked embarrassed. "No one imagined you'd stroll to the stationhouse in the middle of the night. Jensik figured the word was out, and the trannies were playing with us."

"I see."

"We knew you were out there somewhere. Some Brit lieutenant's called half a dozen times. He's been raising hell."

Ah, Tolliver. I didn't know you cared.

I limped to a chair. "Mr. De Broek, this place . . ." My gesture took in the whole district. "The government's lost control. Why don't they abandon the area or send in the military?"

Patrolman De Broek stuck his hands in his pockets, stared out the reinforced window. "I have no say in that, sir. In my opinion, we should shut down the stationhouse. Give the Bronx to the trannies, fall back to Manhattan. If we consolidate our strength, we can hold some of downtown. Under the towers, at least."

"Why don't they?"

"The Holdouts still have their voting cards, as long as they scrape up the taxes. With land values fallen to nothing, they can afford to hang on to their cards. It's their only hope of even minimal police protection."

"Can you do anything for them?"

"During the day we fly patrols over their stores. We even hold most of the roads. At night, you see how it is."

"Surely you have enough firepower to—"

"Our heat seekers and smart bombs could kill anything that moves. But unless we're prepared to blast our way out, we'll lose a heli, like last November. Three officers killed." De Broek rubbed his face. "Some of what we see is . . . beyond belief. Even for me, and I've been a jerry six years." He went silent.

"My wife is out there." She had to be. The alternative was unbearable.

"I'd better get the Commander."

I lay back, weary and aching.

The Precinct Commander hurried in. "Thank heaven you're well." He held out his hand in a politician's handshake. "Stay with us until morning if you like, or we can escort you out now. What would you like?"

"Find my wife."

"We'll try. As you know, this isn't the Garden of Eden." He waited a moment. "As for tonight . . . ?"

I sighed. Until I knew Annie's fate I would have no peace, but I couldn't find her trail. The transpops wouldn't help; they banded together against all outsiders.

There was nothing I could do for her; I saw that now. And my cadets awaited. When all was said and done, I had duty.

Hon, I loved you. I'm sorry I was so weak.

I'd hoped Annie's picture, her shy smile, might pierce their sullen hostility. But she was nothing to them, or to the police. No one cherished her but I.

I, and—

I looked up, lips dry. "Take me to the Midtown Sheraton."

The Precinct Commander turned to De Broek. "Call up a heli. Drop him at his hotel."

I got to my feet, carefully. "My duffel's still at the clinic. We'll stop to get it."

We landed inside the clinic fence. De Broek jumped out to fetch my gear.

A figure ran toward us from the gate. "Is that you, sir?" Adam Tenere swung up on the step, hair disheveled. "Thank Lord God! I didn't know what to do, I called Mr. Tolliver and—" He ground to a halt, saluted. "Midshipman Tenere reporting!"

His eyes widened as he took in my bloody shirt, my bandaged hand. "Sir, are you—I know you told me to stay at the hotel but I was so . . ."

I snarled, "Finish a bloody sentence!"

"I was so worried for you," he said in a small voice.

I looked away, cleared my throat. "Forgive me. It's been a . . . trying night."

De Broek loped back to the heli, my duffel slung over his shoulder. Adam gave way.

De Broek climbed in. "Is this joey coming along?"

"It seems so." I slid over. "Let's go."

While we flew over the darkened city, I let Adam help me change into a clean shirt. Nonetheless, my appearance tested the urbanity of the jaded skytel clerks. Jacketless, bandaged, I limped through the penthouse lobby. Well, it couldn't be helped. I settled into my tub for a long soak.

With fresh gauze on my abrasions I emerged feeling almost myself, though desperately tired. "Hand me the caller, Adam." I eased myself into a chair.

I waited for my connection. "This is Captain Seafort. Get Admiral Duhaney, flank."

"Captain Helgar has the watch, sir. The Admiral's in his apartment, asleep."

"Wake him."

I wasn't sure if the gasp came from Adam or the lieutenant.

"I can't, except for impending fleet action. I'll give you Captain Helgar."

Helgar was senior to me and would bottle my call until morning. Precious hours wasted. I snarled, "I said Duhaney, not Helgar! Get him on the line or I'll have your job, if not your skin! NOW!"

The line clicked. I gripped the caller, wondering if I'd just thrown away what was left of my career. Duhaney had reason enough to cashier me even without this latest provocation. Restlessly, I tapped the chair arm.

Half a minute. Then, "Duhaney." His voice was groggy.

"Nick Seafort."

"I know. Lieutenant Sprey nearly wet his pants. This had better be important."

I blurted, "Sir, I'm in trouble and need help."

His tone changed immediately. "What is it, Seafort?"

"My wife." Quickly I explained about Annie. "I walked off my job without authorization, to try to find her. Lieutenant Tolliver's covering the base."

"What can we do to help?"

"First, authorize my absence. I'm AWOL, and I don't want it in the holos. I can't expect my cadets to toe the line if I don't."

"Done. Christ, Seafort, she's your wife. Of course you went after her." He paused for thought. "Why not tell the holozines? With her picture on the public news screens, someone might spot her."

"Sir, it's worse out there than you think. A newsflash would set off a manhunt. Someone might hold her for ransom, or kill her." If she weren't already dead.

"Very well, it's your choice. What else?"

"I need help finding her. I have someone in mind, but staff transfers are frozen. Will you—"

"Anyone you want. Tell BuPers."

I gulped. "Sir, I don't know how to thank you."

"Stroke Senator Boland, once in a while. Is that too much, Captain?"

A silence. "I'm sorry, sir."

He snorted. "Whatever you did, he hasn't mentioned his son again. You pulled a fast one, I'm sure of it. Someday I'll find out how."

"I'll tell you now, if you ask."

A chuckle. "No, I'm sure you followed orders, in your own style. I prefer not to know the details. Can I go back to sleep now, Nick?"

"Yes, sir, of course."

His voice softened. "About your wife, you have my best wishes. And my prayers."

"Thank you, sir." I forced out the words.

"Good ni—"

"Admiral!"

His tone was startled. "Yes?"

I gripped the caller, took a long breath. "Something you should know, before you leave me in charge of Academy." Sergeant Darwin T. Swopes stood in the aisle, his eyes somber. I raised my eyes to his.

"Get on with it."

I said, "Captain Higbee, in BuPers. I didn't like the replacement he chose for Lieutenant Sleak, so I told him I had influence, that I would destroy him if he didn't cooperate." I held the caller to my cheek, waited for the explosion.

He sighed. "They trained you too well, Nick Seafort."

"I don't understand, sir."

He hesitated, as if groping for words. "Try to see it as two Navies, son. The one they told you about, the Navy you're in. It protects the star lanes and mobilizes its resources to fight fish. The other one, that I'm a part of, fights for appropriations and commissions new warships. What they told you about honor, and truth, and integrity, that's valid for your Navy. It's never applied to mine. We're political, lad. Always have been, always will be. We admit Senators' sons, keep the bureaucrats content, requisition the supplies and arm the warships so you and your heroes can do the fighting."

"Sir, I—"

"Let me finish. That's the way it is in Washington, in London, in the corridors of the U.N. If you want equipment, you fight for it, or pay what has to be paid. If you want someone on staff, you pull him in with whatever it takes. Higbee complained to me three days ago. I told him to stay out of my hair. I figured if you had the balls to browbeat him, you'd get your staff. If you didn't, you shouldn't have been put in charge of Academy in the first place."

The silence stretched. He added, "Nick, you don't need to join my Navy, I just want you to know about it. Do what you have to, and don't punish yourself with guilt. It's how the system works."

"Aye aye, sir." It was all I could say.

"Good night." He rang off.

"*Satisfactory, Cadet.*"

My head snapped up. "What, Sarge?"

Adam gaped. "I didn't say anything, sir."

"Not you. Mr.—" I bit off the rest. I'd made fool enough of myself for one day. "Adam, before you go to bed, call Naval Liaison. I want a groundcar and a heli standing by. And another jacket; I only brought one. Have them see to it."

"Aye aye, sir. It's four in the morning, sir, I don't know if they'll—"

"Someone will answer. The Navy never sleeps."

Alone, I undressed, lay on the bed, turned down the lights, dreading my next task. After a moment I took the caller once more, rang through to Admiralty. "BuPers, please." I waited while the connection was made. My heart beat faster.

"BuPers. Lieutenant Dervis, duty officer."

My voice rang with confidence. "This is Captain Nicholas E. Seafort, calling at the order of Fleet Admiral Duhaney. Triple A Priority, Immediate Action. I need a man transferred groundside from U.N.S. *Waterloo*; she's in home system. Start a shuttle out to him within the hour. I want him at Von Walthers by tomorrow afternoon."

"Who's your man?"

My heart was pounding. Through unwilling lips I said, "His name is Eddie Boss. Seaman first class."

14

I stirred restlessly in the shuttleport caller booth. "I know what I'm doing, Edgar."

"He has no reason to trust you, sir, or want to help."

"I'll handle it. Meanwhile, you're in charge. I've got the Admiral's stamp on that."

"No matter to me, sir. I already had your okay."

Tolliver was right. Acting under orders, he was relieved of responsibility.

"The special cadets. Arnweil, Kyle Drew, and Stritz."

"Yes, sir?"

"You may be aware . . ." I sighed. No reason not to admit it, especially to Tolliver. "I have no idea what to do with them."

"I'll keep them busy running errands, but the plan was for them to be with you."

"Not where I'm going."

"You're due at the *Wellington* ceremonies next week. Why not take them along? Give them something to look forward to."

"Are you out of your mind? Raw cadets with the Navy brass, at a commissioning?"

"Why not?"

"Because . . . because—"

"You said that."

"I'll think about it." A woman approached the booth, stared meaningfully at the caller. I waved her away.

"Yes, sir. Pity I can't tell them now, so they'll know they're not just your errand boys."

"*All* cadets are errand boys." I paused. "Very well, tell them."

"As you wish, sir. I trust you'll go armed this time?"

"Yes." With a pistol, perhaps. No more. The object was to seek help, not fight a war with the transpops. "Is your report done?"

"I'm waiting for an answer from United Suit and Tank."

"Has Jeff Thorne come down?"

"Due this afternoon. I'm sending a middy to meet him in London."

"Very well. Give him my best. I'll see him when—when this is over."

"Godspeed, sir." We rang off.

I replaced the caller, limped to the counter. Adam jumped up from his seat to join me.

"Gate twelve is this way, sir."

"I can read," I growled.

"Yes, sir. If your foot's bothering you I can fetch him."

"I'm no invalid." Everyone had treated me as one, from the moment I'd taken command. Sending Adam to meet me at Earthport Station, as if I couldn't find my own way. He'd nearly made me an invalid himself.

I limped another few steps, past an empty waiting area. I sighed. "Very well, I'll wait here. You'll have no trouble recognizing him. He's no taller than you, but twice your bulk. If you have any doubt, just call out his name." I took a seat in the passenger lounge.

"Aye aye, sir. Shall I get you a holozine?"

"Go!" I didn't need a blanket or a pillow, either. Certainly not a bloody nursemaid.

I brooded. In a few minutes I'd have to look again on Eddie Boss. The young seaman's sneering face rose before my eyes. Arms that could snap a spine. His scornful gap-toothed smile. His—

I sighed again. Eddie had done wrong, but he was no monster. Plucked from the streets of Lower New York as part of an ill-advised transpop resettlement project, he'd been abandoned on *Challenger* with Annie and me. If I closed my eyes I could recall his huge hand reaching out to touch mine with awe, after I'd sworn to teach him to read.

I conjured Eddie at my polished conference table, laboring to form the difficult words. And I thought of how, moments after he'd taken the oath as a seaman, he'd slammed Chris Dakko to the deck when the Uppie lad had refused his own oath. I could see him—

Enough. I wanted to see him no more.

—in *Challenger*'s mess, hesitant, squirming with embarrassment. Would I teach him Uppie speech, Uppie manners, so he wouldn't have to die a scorned trannie?

We'd worked for weeks. Slowly, he'd mastered civilized diction, struggled to refine his unsophisticated ways. At last, he succeeded.

And then he'd brought me Annie, to do the same for her.

"Midshipman Tenere reporting, sir."

I wrenched myself back to the shuttleport lounge. "Very well, Mr. Ten—"

The sailor came to attention, his seaman's whites stiff and starched. His face was expressionless. "Seaman Boss reporting, sir."

"As you were, both of you." The midshipman relaxed; Eddie Boss did not.

"The shuttle was early, sir. It came in at—"

"Be silent, Middy. Hello, Mr. Boss."

The muscular young sailor grunted. He maintained eyes front.

I temporized. "Mr. Boss, did they tell you why you were brought down?"

"No." The response required a "sir," but I wouldn't make an issue of it.

"I asked for you. I need help."

His face twisted. "Do I have a choice, Captain?"

Good question. I could order him to comply, but what use would his enforced assistance be? Anyway, could I order him to risk his life on my private errand? "Yes, you have a choice."

"I choose no."

Adam stirred indignantly. "You're talking to a Captain!"

"I know who he be." Eddie's tone was surly.

The middy bristled. "Mind your manners, sailor! This is—"

"Mr. Tenere, leave us." I knew the boy was only trying to do his job. It was a junior officer's responsibility to keep discipline among the ranks.

"Aye aye, sir." With a look of reproach the middy retreated beyond earshot.

"Mr. Boss—" I stopped, tasting bile. Whatever it took, I would do. "Annie is gone, Eddie. She walked out of a hospital. If she's still alive, she's on the streets. We have to find her."

"I don't. You do."

I said softly, "Doesn't she mean anything to you?"

"Annie Wells? The trannie bitch who married some Uppie Cap'n? She don' mean nothin' ta me!"

"Eddie!"

"She don't. You neid—neither."

My knees were unsteady. I sat abruptly. "Eddie, I can't do it without you. Look what happened when I tried." I raised a bandaged hand to the bruises on my face.

His grin was malicious. "I see it, I feel zarky."

I took a deep breath. "Is it . . . Is this about Centraltown? My sending you away?"

"Nah, you think ol' Eddie care 'bout dat? 'Bout bein' put on some big ship, headin' God Hisself know where, away from alla res', away from her?" He waved it away. "With a file says, take this joe outa system, his Cap'n don' like him, so I get to mop frazzin decks alla way home?" He reverted to a parody of his most polished diction. "Think that matters to me, Captain Seafort, sir?" His face was dark.

"Eddie, when I found you with her, I was beside myself." I stared through the window at the baggage carts. "I didn't understand." I forced myself to face him. "But now I do. It wasn't the same, for you. You knew her long before I did. Trannie—transpop culture isn't like mine. Sex is more casual, more for fun. What I saw as betrayal, you saw as—as—"

"It weren't nothin'," he whispered. "Not a damn thing, Cap'n. We be tribe, man. Tribe doin' it allatime! Boys and girls, boys and boys, girls an— it don' matter none, in tribe!"

"Eddie, help me."

His faced hardened. "Nah. I ain' goin' trannie no mo'."

"I'll beg, if I must. Please."

His mouth lit with a cruel smile. "Yeah, I like dat. Beg ol' Eddie, see what he do."

Annie, even this, I love you so. I slipped out of the chair, dropped to my knees, oblivious of the passing throng. My eyes bored into his. "Eddie, I beg you. Help me find—"

He yanked me to my feet. "Don' do dat, Cap'n! Not for no man!" His eyes glistened. "Don' crawl fo' ol' Eddie. Never!"

"Help me," I whispered.

He turned aside, slammed his fist into the bulkhead. It shivered. "God, I wanted ta hate you!" he cried. "Allatime in dat ship, see yo' face, smash it, but allatime it come back, allatime lookin' at me, like when I ask you learn me read. Those eyes, sad, but somethin' else, like you look at Annie, later. God damn, I wanta hate you!" His voice sank. Almost inaudibly, "I couldn'."

"Oh, Eddie."

For a moment his shoulders slumped. Then he straightened, spun around. "Not fo' you! Fo' her, 'cause she tribe! You unnerstan'?"

My heart leaped. "Whatever you say."

He nodded. "Fo' her." He picked up his duffel, and we started for the corridor. Eddie's fingers closed around my arm. "Fo' her, mos'ly. Jus' a little fo' you."

He couldn't touch the Captain. If the young middy loping our way saw it, he could execute Eddie on the spot. Still, I smiled, gently pressed Eddie's hand. "A little is enough."

Eddie hoisted his bulk out of the heli. I followed to the clinic gate. "She walked out with some visitors, and disappeared."

The sailor squinted at the squatter shacks, but said nothing.

"If we stay here at night, go out each morning—"

Eddie shook his head. "Nah. We don' look here."

"But this is—"

"She be here, she dead." He spoke with authority.

"How can you know?"

"Mira!" His wave encompassed the stadium, the foul streets, the ragged children. "Them be Bronks. Crypsnbloods. Can't you tell? Bronks get her, she gone. Don' bother lookin' no more."

"She's dead?" My tone was bleak.

"I din' say that. Jus', if a Bronk get a Hat . . ."

I shook my head in bewilderment. "Hat?"

"Cap'n, Annie and I be from 'Hattan. Bronks 'n Hats ain' the same. Joeys here, dey eat anythin'. Even their dead, sometime. You think Annie an' me be garbage like Bronks?"

"Of course not," I said with fervor, recalling the urine stains Eddie's transpops had left on my corridor decks, the befouled cabins. "No. The difference is obvious."

He peered at me with suspicion. "Maybe," he conceded, "you Uppies so far up, you can't tell." He spat with contempt at the squatters' hovels. "Dey jus' garbage, man. Come on." He turned away.

Exchanging glances with the astonished middy, I followed. "Where to?"

He spoke as if to a child. "Home, Cap'n. 'Hattan. Annie'd know dem Bronks wanna kill her. So natch she try go home to Mace. If she alive, dat where she be." Annoyed, he rattled the clinic gate. "Open up, joey! I got a Cap'n wid me."

"Eddie, how could she get back to Manhattan? The transpops tried to kill me on sight. I barely made it a mile."

He grinned sourly. "But you ain't trannie, Cap'n. Annie smart. Stay low, move at night. She a Hat, better 'n any Bronk. Use her head, she get past 'em."

My tone was meek. "Where do we start?"

"Dunno. Fin' Mace tribe, first thing. Might be better I go alone." We crossed the wide expanse of lawn.

"I want to help."

"You don' know tribes. On other han', you be famous joe, on alla news screens. I hear trannies even got special name fo' you. Might help, dey see yo' face. Okay, come along, but get me outa dis billysuit. Can't go onna streets innit."

"What about me?"

He grinned his gap-toothed smile. "You too pretty in whites, Cap'n.

Work blues, maybe, like you was goin' out on the hull ta supervise. But 'less you look Navy, dey won' believe it be you." He stopped, scratched his head.

"What should the middy wear?"

"Him? I ain' takin' care a no boy if we wanta fin' Annie." He seemed unaware of Adam's outrage.

"All right." I rang the entrance bell. "Let's hope they have something your size."

"Too small be allri'. Look more trannie."

I made my needs known at the clinic desk. While we waited I asked, "What about all I taught you, Eddie? How to talk, and the rest. It's all gone?"

He favored me with a long, contemplative look. "My speech is jus'— just fine, Captain, when I use it. I didn't want to be a trannie no more. You say do it. Okay. But you tell me to go trannie, I gotta be trannie inside too."

I reddened. "Sorry I asked, Mr. Boss."

"Don' matter. Sir."

I left him to his thoughts.

From the pilot's seat Midshipman Tenere said, "I'll be there at noon, sir. If you don't show up, noon the day after." He twisted to face me. "Sir, think again. Every sailor going through New York gets a packet warning that groundside travel is dangerous."

Eddie snorted derisively.

"I'm not worried for myself, sir, I'll get the groundcar through, but—"

"Just be at Thirty-fourth and Broadway." I patted the pocket of my blues, felt the reassuring bulge of the pistol. My other pocket held two recharge packs. A change of clothes, a light and shaving gear were all I'd carry. "Ready, Mr. Boss?"

The seaman nodded. "Dark comin'. Bes' be gettin' on wid it."

Reluctantly, the midshipman started the engines. As we lifted from the Sheraton rooftop, Eddie lifted his lumpy bag. After leaving the clinic we'd stopped at a grocery. Eddie had picked out a couple of dozen cans of meat and vegetables, and a few instameals. At the hotel he stuffed them in a pillowcase. Then, outside on the roof, he'd taken a firm grip on the open end of the sack, and twice smashed it against the cement wall.

"What was that for?"

He grinned his gap-toothed smile. "My cansa be too pretty, dey won' think I be trannie."

Now, as the heli swooped, Eddie turned to the middy. "Bes' yo . . ." He scratched his head, started again. "Mr. Tenere, when you set down, we jump out, you take off real quick. Okay, sir?" The boy nodded. The huge sailor muttered, "Gettin' night now. Never know, Maces and Broads might be dancin'."

Adam came in fast and low. At the last moment he flared, dropped us in the center of the street with a thump. Before I had time to speak Eddie flung open his door, leaped out, hauled me from my seat. He slammed the door. "Outaheah, Navyboy!" Adam lifted instantly.

To my surprise, the streets were deserted. When I'd taken the Gray Line tour, people had been everywhere. Of course that had been midafternoon, and a bit farther uptown.

"Now what do we—"

"Move, man, 'fore some Broad diss ya!" Eddie propelled me toward the crumbling facades. I thrust his hand away, but hurried to keep pace. We moved cautiously down the desolate street. Where I would have pressed against the wall for safety, Eddie stayed close to the curb, staying clear of open doorways. I did likewise.

"Who are we watching for? There's no one here."

He snorted with derision. "It gettin' nighttime, what you expec'? Broads be out plenny inna day. Maybe dance wid us, come dark."

"Broads?"

Eddie favored me with his gap-toothed grin. "Fine time be askin' dat. Broads be trannies live here. Annie 'n me, we Maces. Dis' be Broad turf." We neared the corner.

"How do you know?"

"Don' you listen, Cap'n?" He pointed to the rusting street sign: BROADWAY. "Where else Broads be? Lesgo!" He slung his bag of foodstuffs over his shoulder, sprinted across the street.

We crouched behind the shelter of a gutted electricar. The sign read Thirty . . . it could have been an eight or a nine.

"Next block, lotta buildin's down. Too open. You see anyone, keep quiet, grab my arm." He rose cautiously. My hackles rising, I followed.

"Why didn't we just land at Thirty-fourth?"

"Not so loud." He studied the windows above, finally relaxed. "Ol' Eddie come down outa sky in a heli in middle a Mace turf, anyone gonna listen he say he be trannie? Trannie wuzbe, maybe, but no trannie still."

"I don't under—"

"You wanna find Annie, dey gotta help. No trannie gon' tell nothin' ta no Navyboy come down inna frazzin' heli. Dis way we walk in, natural. Get ready ta run."

He took a breath, sprinted past a lot filled with the rubble of a collapsed building. We came to a storefront with boarded windows. The doorway was sealed with crumpled sheets of siding. Eddie surveyed it, grunted with satisfaction. "Alrigh' here to corner." He straightened. "But better I had somep'n." His gaze fastened on a battered speed sign. He shambled toward it, put down his bag, and took a firm grip on the sign pole. He heaved. The steel post bent only slightly.

"I have a pistol."

"Pistol okay, you wanna diss someone. Scare 'em off, you wan' a pole." He considered the unyielding post. "It's in kinda deep. But maybe—" He grasped the pole, hauled on it until his muscles bulged. It bowed a few degrees. With a grunt of anger Eddie threw himself at the pole, forced it the other way.

I wandered back to the rubble-filled lot. Was there some board, a piece of wood or metal?

"How'm I gonna watch fo' you, jus' walk away?" Eddie had abandoned his battered post.

"I just thought—"

"Never min', let's go. We fin' something." We retreated toward the boarded building. "Two blocks, come to Mace—"

Suddenly we were face-to-face with a gaunt woman and a bearded man, at the boarded door. The man gripped a bat.

I gawked. Eddie thrust me behind him, twirled the sack over his head, lunged forward. The woman screamed. The man took a wild swing with the bat. Eddie dodged the blow. The man shoved the woman back to the door, bared his lips, flexed his bat.

My hand went to my pocket, and the pistol. Eddie snapped, "No, you get us killed." He took a menacing step forward.

The man blurted, "Fadeout be cool."

Eddie hesitated, lowered his sack. "Evenup?"

"You ain' no Broad. Outaheah."

"Outaheah evenup."

The man looked to his woman. She nodded. "Zark." He backed a step to the door.

"Cool," said Eddie. Cautiously, they took a step apart, then another. The bearded man pulled aside the sheeting. He and his woman backed into the doorway and disappeared.

"Run." Eddie's tone was urgent. We dashed across the intersection without checking for hazards. In the middle of the next block Eddie crouched by an abandoned car.

I asked, "Won't he call for help?"

"Nah, he say fadeout cool."

"But what does that—"

Eddie's exasperation showed. "We was ready ta dance. He ask fadeout. Mean we split, no rumb. I made him say evenup too." He searched my face for a sign of understanding. "Evenup, no geteven. Long as we get outa Broad turf, we okay. He won' call tribe."

Eddie peered over the car, decided it was safe to proceed. We hurried on. "Daytime, Maces 'n Broads, even Subs c'n talk, sometimes trayfo. But joey was righ', we on his turf, don' belong." He slowed. "So I din' hurt him none."

I grinned, thinking of the bat the man had wielded.

As if reading my mind Eddie shot me a sidewise look. "You don' know nothin' 'bout ol' Eddie, you think a little bat stop 'im." Still, he looked over his shoulder one more time, for safety.

The litter-strewn avenue stretched into hazy distance. I could see little difference from one tribal block to the next, but nothing recalled the bizarre campfire I'd encountered near the Bronx clinic. Here, no shacks leaned against one another in haphazard lanes of rubble. Tall, neglected buildings brooded above us, but at least they still stood. Maybe someday, money and attention could resurrect the central city.

"C'mon, Cap'n. One mo' block, Mace turf."

"What's a Mace? You keep using that—"

"I showya. Nex' block be Mace."

I glanced around, appalled. "Annie was born here?" A horrid thought.

"Yeah, Annie an' alla resta us." He stomped down the street, muttering under his breath. Then he brightened. "Deke gone on ship, but Sam 'n Boney 'll 'member ol' Eddie. Don' worry none, Cap'n. I talk fo' you." His step lengthened.

"Where to?"

He pointed. "Corna." He straightened, walked proud past the remaining buildings. "I showya where Annie 'n me . . ." He stopped short.

The sack slid from his fingers.

"Eddie?" I gripped his arm; he shook me off as a fly.

He charged into the debris-filled lot. For a moment he stared at nothing. Then he snatched up a rock, hurled it across the rubble. "Maces! WHERE YOU BE?" His agonized cry echoed in the dusk.

I retrieved his sack, picked my way across cement and brick. Eddie hunkered on his knees, scrabbling through crumbled stone.

"What's happened?"

"Mace gone!" His eyes held something akin to madness.

"We must be in the wrong place."

He stabbed at the rubble. "Here, I tolya! We Maces!"

"What's a Mace? I already asked you onc—"

"Tribe! Where we live. Like, Broads live on Broad!"

I stood, turned slowly, searching the empty block. "What was here?"

His finger jabbed at the open space. "I born dis spot. I maybe thirteen, Ma die in rumb wid Broads. Righ' there!" He pointed to the corner. "We a big tribe, hunners of us. I Boss on four flo'."

At last I had a glimmer. "Eddie, this was the old Macy's?"

"I keep tell'n' ya." A tear trickled. "Cap'n, where dey be? What hap'n my Maces?"

"Dey be gone."

We whirled. Four figures, crossing the lot. The leader was male, lean, hard. A ragged jacket. With him were two other men, and a woman.

Eddie leaped to his feet as if galvanized. "Whatchew wan'?"

"Naw, wha *chew* wan'? You on my turf." The leader's tone was sharp. I swallowed. My hand moved to my side.

The leader barely looked my way. "Prolly fif'y of us Rocks be watchin'. C'n ya take fif'y, sailorboy?"

"Where be Maces?" Eddie took a step forward.

The Rock smiled meanly. "Innifo!"

Eddie opened the sack. "Cansa. Two."

"Prong ya frazzin' cansa." The Rock snickered. "Two minutes, offa Rock turf. Else ya diss." He turned on his heel.

"Rock turf?" Eddie's eyes were wild.

"Eddie—"

"Rock turf?" Eddie's sack lashed out, smashed the leader on the temple. The Rock reeled. Instantly, knives appeared in his mates' hands.

Eddie spat as he advanced, sack whirling. I clawed for my pistol, but the two men were already in retreat. The woman, more intrepid, leaped on Eddie's back. He shrugged her off. She scrambled to her feet; Eddie's fist shot out, caught her alongside the jaw. She dropped.

A retreating figure turned. "You meat, joeyboy! Rocks comin' out now!" He cupped hands to mouth. "Aiyee!"

At the cry Eddie sprang forward. The Rock tribesman turned and ran. Eddie followed a few steps, spun around to see the Rock leader stagger to his feet. Eddie thundered back. His second blow smashed the dazed Rock across the back of the head. The man dropped and lay still. Eddie swung again.

"No, Eddie!" The downed Rock lay inert. I clawed at Eddie's arm.

He raised the sack, clubbed the fallen tribesman yet again. The sack dripped red.

"Stop!" I thrust between him and his victim.

"Mace turf! Was, is, will be! Always!" He stared down at the body, kicked it savagely. After a moment he sagged. His expression lapsed into misery.

"Eddie, get us out of here!"

"Mace gone." He stood dumbly, as if paralyzed.

"Who are those people?"

"Rocks. Useta live uptown in Rockcenta, 'til got pushout."

"We can't stay." I prodded him. "Is there a caller somewhere? We need Adam and the heli."

Eddie looked back at the corpse. "Rocks was never much inna rumb."

"Eddie!"

"All righ'. We go Three Four, eas'."

"Why not back where—"

"Rocks." He pointed across the street. I chilled; men, women, even children, were gathering outside the crumbling buildings. They were ominously quiet.

Eddie seemed to throw off his daze. "Move!" He hurried me along Thirty-fourth Street. Behind us, voices.

"Eddie, the whole tribe is—"

"Who care." Nonetheless, he increased his pace. After a moment he said grudgingly, "Better getcha pistol ready. All Rock places, here." His eyes roamed, lit suddenly. " 'Xcept maybe there." He pointed across the street to a storefront covered with heavy metal plates. "Pedro Chang, useta be. My—a neut." He veered across the street.

The Rocks followed. Unlike the rabble who'd chased me to the precinct house, they kept together, seemed in no hurry to close in. I asked, "Will he help?"

"Dunno." Eddie tried the solid door. His foot thudded into a steel plate.

I said, "Those locks won't help much against a laser."

"No lasers inna street. Recharges too hard ta get, an' Unies dissya onna spot if ya got one." He hammered on the door. "Chang! Openup!" He waited, tried again. The Rock tribesmen were closing in.

Behind the door, a cough. "Close."

"Eddieboss nee' trayfo, man!"

"Eddie be gone three, fo' year. Jerry sen' him outboun'."

A stone thudded into the boarded window. I flinched, drew my pis-

tol, set it to high. Across the street the mob waited. Clubs, spears, children
lugging bricks.

"C'mon, Changman, let us in!"

A fit of coughing behind the door. "Innifo?"

"Cansa. Dozen."

I braced myself against the wall, aimed with both hands.

The sound of metal on metal. A lock turned, then another. The door
opened a cautious inch. A wizened face peered between heavy chains.
Another stone whizzed past.

"Who—Eddie? I din' think—" The door slammed in our faces. I
cursed, but almost immediately the door reopened, this time fully. Eddie's
brawny hand shot out, hauled me inside. The door swung shut against a
hail of stones. The old man scurried to secure his chains.

I blinked. A light mounted on a Valdez permabattery pierced the
gloom. The dusty store was filled with boxes, piles, odd assortments of
goods. Cans of foodstuffs were stacked on sagging shelves meant to hold
lighter stock. Heavy winter clothing was stacked high on chairs. A scent of
spices lingered.

"Hola, Pedro."

The old man scowled at Eddie. "You din' say no bringalong."

"Cansa be his." Outside, banging on the door.

"You got. Gimme."

Reluctantly, Eddie handed over the sack.

"Why he widya?"

"I—" Eddie seemed at a loss. "He be my Cap'n."

The old man looked my way, cackled. "Cap'n of what?"

"Navyboy." Eddie drew himself up. "Like me."

"You was sent outboun' when Unies gotcha."

"I be joinup."

"Outaheah, you try swind ol' Chang." The man Eddie had called a
neut shook his head decisively. "Trannie joinup? Nevah hearda no—"

Some metal object rapped on the boarded windows. They were
braced with iron struts; for the moment we were safe. Chang scuttled to
the panels, shouted, "Go way! Don' mess wid Chang!"

A voice from outside. "Give us Maceboy. Wan' venge."

Chang reared back. "I dunno no Rock venge on Mace. You comeon
ol' Chang, he show you venge!" That brought a silence. Chang nodded
with satisfaction, said softly, "Dey ain' goin' nowhere."

After a moment he trotted back from the window, looked me over,
snorted with derision. "Cap'n, hah!"

"Mr. Boss, who is—"

The sailor scowled. "Dis be Pedro Chang, neut I tolya 'bout. He gone glitch wid old. Usetabe, had mo' chips innis head 'n any six trannies."

Pedro Chang drew himself up to his meager height. "Glitch, he say? Wan' me believe trannie joinup inna Navy an' come back fro' outboun', bringin' Cap'n widim? Who glitch?"

I moved closer to the light. "Look at me. At my uniform."

Chang came close, peered up at my face. "No joeyboy swind Pedro Telamon Chang." He padded slowly around me, grumbling. "Neuts gotta be smarter 'n alla tribe. Rock or Mace or Broad, don' matta. Traytaman gotta be tough." He came close, fingered my tunic. "Navy weave, yeah, but any joe could get. An' Cap'n threads be white. I got holozines."

I didn't move but my voice was as ice. "Take your hands off me." Chang's fingers hesitated, fell back. "A Captain wears what he pleases. I wouldn't wear dress whites in a thrustersuit. Or here."

He clicked his teeth. "Oh, high and mighty, is he. Jus' like Uppie."

"Do you read, old man? Are you smart enough to remember pictures? Do you even have a holovid?"

Chang glared at me, spat.

I hefted my pistol, strode to the door. "Eddie, come along! I'll take my chances out there." I twisted at the locks. "We have at least fifteen charges, maybe—"

"They kill you, Captain Nicholas Seafort." The old man's voice was changed. "You slaughter fifteen, maybe more, if you get to the recharge in ya pocket. Then the rest club you to death."

"You fraud!" I clawed at the chain. "What's happened to that thick dialect, now? I don't need you, I don't want to know you."

Chang ducked under my arm, rebolted a lock. "I don' put nothin' on. I talk trannie 'cause I be one. Jus' 'cause I c'n talk more Uppie if I try, no reason you look down on me." His rheumy blue eyes found mine.

"I don't care what—" I swallowed. "All right."

Chang swiveled to Eddie. "So dat mean you be Navyboy. If Cap'n marry trannie, I guess trannieboy c'n be joinup." His gaze returned to me. "Allatime you on news screens. Course I knew ya, righ' from start. Alla trannies watch screen, high up on tower, but they think stories ain' real. Now, what you doin' inna street?"

"My wife, Annie Wells. She was a Mace. We're looking—"

"Was, is, willbe. Trannie stay trannie inside."

Eddie rumbled, "You don' know, ol' man."

Chang trotted up to Eddie, jabbed his finger in the seaman's brawny chest. "When Maceboy came cryin' dat his Ma be dead, an' wan' venge on the Broad dat done her, was it 'ol' man' you call me, or Mista Chang, hah?

When I trayfo Broad's name so you diss the righ' one, even widout you had innifo, was I 'ol' man'?"

Eddie reddened. "All righ', din' mean nothin'."

"Glitched, I be? Maybe I slap yo' face fo' you, Maceboy. I did it when you little, an' raz ol' Chang."

The sailor shuffled his feet. "Din' mean nothin', I said. An' don' go slappin' no one. I ain' joeykit no mo'."

"An' I be Pedro Chang, the one frien' dat Maceboy had." After a moment his expression softened. "Could be still, Maceboy had manners."

Eddie forced his knotted fists to relax. "Don' flare. Frien' what I need, now."

"Ah. Now we talk." The old man scurried to the chairs, transferred clothing onto other piles, bade us sit. "Why you look for Annie?"

I said, "She disappeared from a clinic in the Bronx where she was getting hormone treatments. She's wandering around somewhere, confused and miserable."

"If she be alive."

I forced myself to acknowledge the thought. "If she's alive."

"No good, dem Bronks catch her. Can' trayfo, can' even talk widem. Glitched, alladem."

"Eddie says she'd try to go hom—come here."

"If she could."

Eddie clutched at Chang's bony arm. "Wha happen ta Mace?"

The old man slapped at Eddie's fingers with annoyance. "Don' hol' on, you ain' no babykit." He trotted across the room, rummaged in a bin, emerged with a teapot. He plugged it into the permabattery, poured water from a plastic jug on the floor. "Mace Three Four got tore down two year back. Walls goin' bad, chunks fallin' on street. Jerries come in, by hunners. Bulldozers. Maces tried ta hold on, got some of themself killed."

From the drawer of a battered desk Chang emerged with teabags. "Less'n a week, dey all onna street."

Voices from outside. "Hey, Changman! You neut or Mace?"

Chang looked disgusted. "Rocks don' know bein' patient." He shuffled to the door, spoke through it. "I talkin' wid Maces. You wait 'n see, like I tolya. Filmatleven!"

"We ain' got all—"

"You ain' got nothin'! Wanna see if ol' Chang still got nitro, jus' waitamin!" Footsteps retreated. Chang grinned through stained teeth.

"Where my Mace go?" Eddie asked.

"The Rocks wouldn' give passby widout innifo. Maces din' have—"

My voice was sharp. "What's innifo? Everyone keeps saying that."

The old man put three cups on the dusty table. "Trannie word. Wha's innifo?"

"I just asked you!"

"An' I tolya." Seeing my puzzlement he repeated slowly, "Wha's innifo *me*? Can' tray widout innifo."

"They wanted—bribes?"

"Course. If Maces wanna cross Rock turf, need innifo. Dat trannie way. But they din' have lotta trayfo lef', pushed outa Macestore. So they fight their way crosstown, past Rocks, past Unies even."

Eddie leaned forward, eyes riveted on the wizened old man. "Did they make it?"

"Dunno, for sure. Rocks din' stop 'em. Heard they got past Unies, heard maybe they push out Easters, but maybe Mace all dead, who know? No one eva came back." He poured scant portions of tea into our cups. After a moment he reconsidered, poured again until they were full.

"Mr. Chang, did Annie come to you?"

"I din' see her."

Eddie growled, "Ya waitin' fa innifo?"

Chang snapped erect. "I givin' you good tea I c'n trayfo cansa or even a holovid. Don' you talk me no innifo!"

"Fadeout. Din' mean nothin'."

"'Sides, I already got all your innifo." Chang squatted by our sack, lifted out a can. "Real meat, good. Vegs, okay." He sifted through the sack. "You bring good trayfo, boy."

Eddie said dryly, "That was the idea."

"Oh, listen ta sailorboy talk Uppie!"

"Cap'n taught me."

"Sen' you school, hah?"

Eddie averted his gaze, said with care, "The Captain taught me himself. On ship."

"Captains don' do that."

"This Captain does."

Pedro Chang trotted to my chair. He stood over me, arms folded, studying my face. At length he nodded. "Okay, you looked after Eddieboss, I help you some. Not too much, I be a Neut." Before I could ask, he said, "Neut means, don' take sides. What'd you do ta get them fizzed?"

Eddie said, "I dissed a Rock. Maybe two."

Chang sucked air through yellowed teeth. "Can't fix dat, take too much innifo. I gotta give you back."

I said, "Is there another exit?"

"Rocks watchin' all ways out. They not so stupid as Maceboy think."

Chang perched on the table, sipped at his tea. "But ol' Chang smart traytaman. Maybe trayfo."

"What is—"

"Trade for," they said simultaneously. Eddie turned back to Chang. "Like you say, we ain' got innifo, 'xcept what we gave ya."

"Them Rocks won' give up venge for cansa. Dunno what ta offa." Chang rubbed his chin. Finally he brightened. "Chang don' offa' nothin'. Askem." He took up a cudgel, crossed to the door, hammered on it. "Rocks! You wan' talk to Chang or no?"

Cautious footsteps. "You got nitro?"

"You need to fin' out, o' we jus' talk?"

"We wan' Maceboy."

"I know dat. One Maceboy, one Rock, talk in Chang house. No rumb."

"Jus' a min."

Time passed. Chang leaned against his door, eyes bright. Finally the voice came again. "Alri', but two Rocks. Jus' talk, no rumb, cool?"

"Chang put his word. Go for Rocks too."

"Zark. Openup."

Chang said softly, "Inna back, both of you, 'til I call."

"C'mon, Cap'n." Eddie was out of his chair. "Cuppa?" He pointed at the tea.

The trader said, "Leave it. Rocks know you here."

Eddie led me to the curtained doorway. The apartment behind was scrupulously clean. In one corner was a carelessly made bed. The wall was lined floor to ceiling with old books printed on real paper. A corridor led back to a heavily barred door.

Straining to hear, I thrust an inch of the curtain aside.

Bolts scraped. Pedro's tone held dignity as an ill-kempt woman entered. "Welcome to Chang house, Tresa."

A tribesman pushed past her. "Nevamin' fancy talk, we wan' Mace!"

"We talk, maybe you get."

He growled, "Talk too much, maybe we take!"

Chang bristled. "You give word, no rumb. How much innifo Rocks' word?"

The woman was indignant. "Rocks' word good! Fadeout, Butchie."

Eddie whispered, "Sheet. Rocks' word don' mean nothin'."

"Okay okay, sit an' drink Chang coffee." The old man busied himself with the pot. "Why you wan' Maceboy?"

Tresa said, "Arno lyin' inna street, head all smash. Wan' Mace fo' evenup!"

"Arno allatime bigmouth. Was askin' ta get diss."

"Nah, he jus' talkin', an Mace whomp him wid sack a rocks."

Eddie hissed, "Not jus' talkin'. He call it Rock turf—"

I jabbed him in the ribs; he lapsed into dark muttering.

Chang poured into metal cups, handed them around. He turned to the woman. "Trayfo evenup?"

"Din' ya hear Butchie tellya venge?"

"Okay okay, Chang be neut, he giveya Maceboy, ya wannim."

I stiffened. "You said he was your frien—"

Eddie shook his head, whispered, "Chang ain' givin' me ta Rocks."

"How do you know?"

"He give us tea." It made no sense, but I kept silent.

"What kinda trayfo, afta he diss Arno?" Butchie's laugh was raucous. "Alla Chang store, fo' evenup?"

"Know better'n dat, Butchie. Trayfo wha'?"

"We don' tray Arno's venge fo' no cansa."

Chang didn't hesitate. "Okay, okay, Rocks knows what dey wan'. No trayfo. Finish coffee, outaheah."

Tresa was thoughtful. "Maybe trayfo evenup, one way."

Chang waited.

"I saw Uppie joey hadda laser. Trayfo cansa an' tea an' laser, fo' evenup."

The old man reared back. "Laser pistol, evenup fo' one frazzy Rockboy? Laser be whole Rock tribe, an' a few Unies fo' change."

"You sayin' Rocks ain' worth—"

"I sayin' none a tribes got lasers! Rocks got laser, be bossman onna street!"

Butchie muttered, "C'n rumb wid Broads, we gotta laser. Wid Subs, even."

Exasperated, Tresa snapped, "Keep shut, Butchie! I can' tray wid Chang, you sayin' dat."

Pedro shook his head. "Can' trayfo laser. Uppie still got it."

Tresa nodded as if he hadn't spoken. "Laser, three recharge. An' cansa. Evenup fo' Arno."

Chang folded his arms. "Nah, if Chang get laser he keep it, giveya Maceboy."

"You stayin' Neut?" Butchie's tone was ominous.

"Wid laser in his pocket, Chang be Neut, Rock, anythin' he want!"

Tresa's tone was plaintive. "You say cominheah ta trayfo. Now you won'!"

"I neva tolya no laser. Uppie got laser, maybe won' giveya. Askem, be bes'.'" Chang trotted to our curtain, yanked it open. Before he turned away, one shrewd eye winked. "C'mon out, talk wid Rocks."

He might have given us warning. Warily, I stepped out of the alcove. Eddie followed.

"You meat, Maceboy!" Butchie.

"Dogs prong ya motha!" Eddie's muscles rippled. "Frazzin' Arno was on Mace turf—"

"Nuffadat!" Chang's growl cut across the rising tension. "Here fo' talk, no rumb. Put word, bothyas did!"

Reluctantly, they subsided. Chang placed his chair between the warring parties, addressed me. "Cap'n, you wanna givem laser, evenup Mace fo' Rock?"

His gaze gave no hint of the expected answer. I thought for a long moment. The laser was our only protection, and Naval Stores wouldn't be pleased at the paperwork involved in its loss. On the other hand, Chang was a skilled negotiator. Should I seem eager, or no? They wanted Eddie's life, and I couldn't allow that. If I guessed wrong, the war would escalate. I glanced at the sullen Rocks. If only Eddie hadn't . . .

I flicked a finger at Eddie. "Give up my weapon, to help that trannie scum?" My voice was cold. "You're glitched, old man. Anyone goes for my laser, I'll fry the lot of you!"

Eddie's fists bunched. "Don' you go callin'—"

"Shut your mouth, joeyboy!"

Chang said, "Gotta put you out, if no. Den dey gonna getcha."

I snapped, "They'll burn first!"

"Rocks wan' Maceboy 'n you, both. Or trayfo—"

"Talk English, you old fool! And forget about trading with trash like those two!"

The Rocks were on their feet.

"Whoa, whoa, whoa." Chang patted the Rocks toward their chairs, pushed at Eddie's unyielding form. "No rumb in Chang house. Uppie thinks like Uppie, whatcha 'xpec'? He won' give laser fo' evenup."

Tresa hawked and spat. "Uppie, you gon fry us Rocks? How many, 'fore resta tribe on ya? An' afta, what, skinya, maybe?"

My smile was nasty. "Try me, bitchgirl."

Chang padded toward me, hands held out in a placating manner. "Okay, okay, Cap'n. Maybe you no unnerstan', lotsa Rock tribe inna street, not jus' two three. If rumb start, don' matter how many it take, dey gonna getya. Bes' you trayfo."

I thrust him away, hoping he wouldn't fall. "We should have cleared the streets years ago! I'll stay here until my bodyguards come looking. There's plenty of food."

Chang bent over the Rock negotiators, spoke in a low tone. "Lemme talk widim. Ol' Chang be traytaman, maybe c'n trayfo."

Tresa's tone was hoarse. "Nevamin' no trayfo, give us Uppie!"

Chang patted her shoulder. "Maybe I talk, he lissen. But gotta talk solo."

Tresa stalked to the door, spat once again. "Bigmouth Uppies think ya own the worl'! One day we get allayas!" She let Chang unlock.

The trader pushed Butchie gently toward the door. "Letcha know. Filmatleven." As soon as the Rocks were gone he rebolted the locks.

"Mr. Chang, I'm sorry if I—"

"Gottem now!" His eyes danced. "Cap'n oughta be traytaman, let Chang sail starship!" He trotted across the store, turned the teapot high. "We givem time, hour maybe. Den we deal." He veered around Eddie, who hadn't budged.

"Trannie scum?" The seaman's eyes blazed.

"Mr. Boss, I didn't—"

The old trader poked at Eddie's chest. "Stupid Maceboy, chewin' on Cap'n fo' save yo' life! When crybaby joey teen came knock'n Chang door, din' I teach him smarts? Hah! Chang and Cap'n know, even if Maceboy don'."

"Know what?" Eddie's tone was menacing.

"Yo' Cap'n—" He spoke with dignity. "Your Captain knew Rocks won' tray if they be too mad at Eddie. So he makem mad at hisself. Make all us mad. Now dey forget 'bout you, an' tray."

The sailor glowered. "How I know he din' mean it? How I know 'bout anything he say? My frien', once. Teach me read, talk. Den he sen' me—" Eddie stopped short, muttered, "Dunno."

"He still you' friend, silly young Maceboy."

"How you know?"

"'Cause he gonna give me laser ta save you." Chang held out his hand. "An' 'cause ol' Chang can' be traytaman, not knowin' insidea joes."

I slipped the laser from my pocket, placed it in his hand. My eyes turned to Eddie.

The sailor shuffled his feet. After a moment he turned away. "Can' figure out nothin, no mo'." His tone couldn't conceal his relief.

When Chang judged the time right, he called back the Rock tribesmen. He dismissed with scorn Tresa's demand for more booty. She countered by offering safe passage for me alone; Chang wouldn't hear of it. "Came togetha, leave togetha," was all he'd say.

Finally they settled on Chang's initial goal: a trade of my laser and recharge packs for our free passage through Rock territory, in the morning.

"An no venge," the old man admonished. "Evenups, bothadem."

Grudgingly, they agreed.

"Speakfo?"

"Alla Rocks. I be bitchboss, ya know dat. I say even, is evenup!" She spat at Eddie's feet. "But nex' time, Maceboy, ya be meat!"

Eddie growled, but between my fingers digging into his forearm and Chang's warning glare, he said nothing.

When they had gone I asked, "Will they keep the deal after they get the laser?"

Chang's eyes flashed. "Transpops ain' like Uppies. Word be good. Dey don' have much else."

I let it be.

Chang puttered about his quarters, disappeared into the cellar, and reemerged with a handful of cans. Humming to himself, he began to cook over the hotpad. The aroma of savory chicken wafted through the store. At length he beckoned us into his apartment, sat us at a rickety table that reminded me of Father's. We supped on chicken stew with pop-rolls fresh out of the self-heating package, and more of Chang's precious tea.

Afterward he showed us the lavatory. To my surprise, it had running water and was fairly clean. Somehow, I'd expected an unspeakable midden.

We lay down in Chang's apartment on mattresses he'd had Eddie haul down from an upper floor. He refused my offer of help. Apparently the trader's trust wasn't enough to reveal whatever stocks he concealed in the neglected, boarded building.

Exhausted from tension, I dozed, but at first sleep avoided me. Finally I succumbed.

In the dark a hand shook me awake. I had no idea of the time. "Why—"

"Shh." The old man led me past Eddie's snores through the curtain, into the store. I followed, bleary-eyed, to the counter where the pot steamed, sat where he directed. The tea was dark and rich, a flavor I couldn't identify.

He waited until I sipped through the steam. His voice was soft. "What happen 'tween you an' Eddieboy?"

"Happened? I don't—"

"Nonna this makes sense." The trader perched on the edge of his chair, cup balanced on his lap. "A Captain don't wander streets with a transpop sailor, and sailor don't look at him like he love an' hate him at same time."

I looked away. "It's nothing I care to speak of."

"You owe me innifo, I save his life." He puttered with the pot. "But, okay okay, I talk instead."

He blew across his tea, reflective.

"Chang had wife once, long time go. She good girl. But no babies." He shrugged. "Ain' easy be a Neut in trannietown. Can' show no favors. Like, if you kept laser, I'd a had to give you to Rocks. No choice.

"But if a Maceboy joey come to Chang's door, eyes all red, actin' as much a man as he can, wantin' ta trayfo name of the Broad who diss his mama, a Neut can help little bit. A Neut can maybe see he makes it through first winter, 'til he strong enough be on his own. Maybe even think what a son woulda looked like, he'd had one."

Chang stared into his tea. After a moment, "Okay, okay, Eddie all grown, no baby now. Still, traytaman can think, wonder why Captain whose face be on alla holos wan' dis particular joey ta help him fin' wife."

Silence stretched while I breathed the hot welcome steam. When I spoke, I addressed the wall. "On a ship like *Challenger*, at first you see Eddie as one of a hundred angry transpop faces." I sipped at the tea. "But later, when you're trapped on a derelict vessel knowing no help will reach you, and a joeyboy asks you to make him into something better than he was, you work with him day after day, watching him struggle with the words . . ."

Chang was silent.

"You want so much for him to succeed, you become one with him. He's too old to be a son. A brother, perhaps. You're rescued, and he stays in the Navy and ships out with you again. He's strong and loyal and one of the few people you trust. You're desperate to keep your wife safe. So when civil authority starts to crumble, you have him guard her."

My words came faster. "Then something happens between them, and you rush him off-planet, and because you left her alone she's raped and beaten and her mind is snatched from her. You want to hate the boy but can't, because it's your fault, not his, and the voice you can't silence tells you so, over and over, in the terrible truth of the night."

We drank of our tea.

After a moment Chang said, "He had no one, after his mama. Girls now and then, is all. When jerries took him with the other young ones, I think he was glad." His clouded eyes sought mine. "Ol' Chang traytaman and Uppie Captain, we be his mama."

"I've done him more harm than you can imagine."

"No, you give him someone to respec'. He need that."

I snorted. "Respect? After what I—"

"Revere, maybe. Don' look so surprise I know dat word, you think I got all those books, don' look in 'em?" He waved it away. "Nevamin'. I wan' my innifo."

"I can send you money, whatever—"

His wiry hand gripped my knee with surprising strength. "You keep yo' coin, it don' mean nothin' ta Chang. Want ta pay yo' innifo, gimme Uppie word."

I laughed, a harsh sound. "You said what an Uppie's word is worth."

"That ain' what Navy say. 'An officer's word is his bond.' "

I flushed. "What do you want?"

"Take care of ol' Eddieboss, bes' you can."

"I can't be sure—"

"Bes' you can, I tolya. I don' ask more." He got to his feet, showing his age for the first time. "He be like brother, once? You don' walk away from brother." He took the empty cup from my lap. "Chang din' walk away from Maceboy ask help." He pounded his frail chest. "Eight year, maybe, ol' Chang keep boy like son, in here." His look was iron. "I wan' my innifo. You give or no, as you wan'."

With dignity he padded to the curtain, passed through it. For a long time I sat hunched in the chair in the dim light of the battery lamp. At last, I tiptoed back to bed.

15

In the morning Chang tucked the laser pistol in his pocket, unbolted the door, and slipped outside. Half an hour later he returned, a satisfied look on his wrinkled face. "Okay okay, Maceboy. Outaheah, 'fore Rocks say Chang ain' Neut." He scuttled across the store, found our sack of foodstuffs. "Don' go eas' on Three Four, Unies too strong. Rocks take you up one block, you trayfo passby wid Broads."

Eddie frowned. "Wrong way. We need ta—"

"You need ta listena ol' Chang, little Mace. Go back way you came, to Four Two Square. Talk ta Subs, dey let ta walk crosstown unner."

"You glitched fo' sure, Changman. Broads'll ask innifo, we ain' got. An' Subs—"

Chang thrust out the sack. "Cansa be good nuff fo' Broads." He hesitated, fished in the sack, removed two cans of meat. "These be innifo Chang. Broads won' know I took 'em, anyway." He handed Eddie the remainder of his sack. "Jusasec." He disappeared behind the curtain. It was several minutes before he reappeared, a box in his hand. "Uppie Cap'n carry it fo' Subs. Dey wan' more 'n cansa."

"What's this?" I asked. It was heavy.

"Batteries. Valdez permas. Subs allatime trayfo permas, nobody know why." He shrugged. "Don' badmouth no Sub, dey rumb fo' dat. With innifo, maybe dey let you through." He opened the door, said, "Outaheah, bothyas."

Eddie looked down, shambled to the door.

My tone was formal. "Mr. Boss, this is an order."

"Huh?" Eddie struggled to change identity. "Yes, sir?"

"Before you go, hug him."

Chang bristled. "Frazzin' Maceboy try touch Chang, I stick him wid—"

"Do it, Mr. Boss." I folded my arms.

Chang backed away. "I'm a Neut, no one touch a—"

Sheepishly, Eddie enfolded the trader in his arms. After a moment, Chang was still.

I picked up my bundle of clothes, opened the door. "Fare thee well, sir. Lord God be with you."

The old man pushed Eddie to the entrance. "Try that again, joeyboy, Chang cut you good! Outaheah! Work to do!" His eyes glistened.

Eddie grinned. "We be gone." He shut the door behind us.

I blinked in the sun. The street was full of people. Some sat with trays of merchandise, others stood around, talking. Down the block, children played. "Lord God!"

"Kinda different." Eddie pointed. "But trash, mosta what they got. Ol' Changman has the only—"

"Lesgo, Maceboy." Three men. One of them was Butchie.

"Okay." Eddie seemed unafraid. "Nor', to Four Two."

"Righ'," They bracketed us, escort or guards, I wasn't sure which.

One of the men fell in alongside us as we walked. To my amazement he chatted sociably with Eddie. Unlike the previous night, streets were crowded with transpops, some with their families.

I said quietly, "Eddie, why didn't we come in the daytime?"

"Tolya. Trannies see us in heli, who gonna help? Even Chang maybe wouldn' let us in."

From block to block we were passed uneasily through the tribal territories until at last we approached an open plaza.

"Where are we, Mr. Boss?"

"Four Two Square."

I looked up. "Isn't that a skytel? We could go in, get a heli—"

Eddie laughed. "In, fro' street? You see door, a window even?"

"A tour bus, or—"

"Likely shoot us soon as talk." Eddie dismissed the idea.

We ventured into the square. In its center the ruins of a tall building clawed skyward. Across the street, crumbling steps disappeared into the ground.

"What's that?"

"Dunno. Sub tribe live there."

"Surely there's a better—"

"Only way we fin' Annie is if she with Maces. How you wanna get crosstown, in heli?"

"You don't even know where your Maces are!"

"Yeah, but we fin' em." Eddie sounded confident. "Maces won' scurry roun' like no mouse. Dey gone eas', tribes'll know." His face darkened. "First, gotta go down."

I hesitated at the gaping cavern. "Couldn't we walk across on Forty—"

"Too far, too many Mids. An' dey don' give passby fo' innifo. C'mon."

He took a tentative step downward, then another. "Yo, Sub!" His bellow echoed in the darkness. No answer.

The broken stairwell led to a rubble-strewn landing. Below, another staircase. Well, in for a pence . . . I trotted down, gripping my box. "Anyone here?"

"Easy, Cap'n." The foot of the staircase was a black cavern.

I squinted. "Where are your bloody Subs?"

A voice in my ear. "We here."

"Jesus!" I jumped half a meter, dropped my bundle. "Lord God in—"

A snicker. "Whatchew wan', Uppie?"

"Who are you?"

"I be joey what belong down here. You be joey what don'."

"Ooh, he got a trannie frien'!"

"No rumb," blurted Eddie. "Innifo!"

"Too lay' fa innifo. We gotcha, now." Hands seized my arms, pried loose my box.

Eddie squalled, "You frazzin'—" A thud. He gasped, and his words came painfully. "Tha's righ', whomp on someone can' see ya! Jus like a Sub!" He cried out again, groaned.

"Let him alone!" I tried to pull loose. "We came looking for you!" A fist drove into my stomach. I doubled over, retching. Hands grabbed, hustled us through the darkness.

When I could breathe again, I found myself surrounded by tribesmen in a large tunnel lit by dull overhead bulbs. Eddie lay slumped in an alcove.

My captors were heavily festooned with earrings and chains, their clothing a hodgepodge of lurid colors. Men and women alike had their hair tied with bands at the sides and back. Some sat cross-legged eating from metal plates at a communal pot that simmered over a hotpad; others jabbered among themselves. Ancient broken furniture was strewn about.

"Where are we?"

No one answered. I leaned against the concrete wall, nursing my aching stomach. "Where's my box?" Again, silence. I decided I was already lost, cast caution to the winds. "Animals!"

One youth looked my way. "Uppie talk. Think all trannies be—"

I spat. "I've seen trannies, real ones. Broads and Maces. Mids. You Subs are trash, not trannies!" It brought a few of them to their feet.

Eddie groaned, rolled to his knees. Someone kicked him. He lashed out at the foot, missed.

"Fadeout, Subs!" Across the cavern, a figure waited. "Lettim talk."

My fists bunched. "Who are you?"

"Alwyn be I, Boss Sub, 'til some joey call me out." His eyes roved, as if seeking a challenge. He found none. "An' you?"

"Nicholas Seafort. Captain."

"Jump off yo' tour bus, didja?"

"We came to find you. We brought—"

"Batteries. Nice a yas. C'n always use 'em." Alwyn beckoned to a scrawny girl. "Tell Jossie an' alla res', come mira. Few minutes we gonna diss an Uppie."

"Righ'." The girl scampered off.

"Shouldn'a come down, joey." He came close. Young, muscular, his dress was somehow different from the rest. Fewer colors, more patterns.

"They told us you take innifo, for passby. We—"

"Dey?"

I pushed down my smoldering anger. "A trader. He gave us batteries for you."

"We take innifo when we wan'. No one tell us. You coulda took a heli steada playin' wid trannies. Now you got youself diss."

"We need your help. I'm looking for my wife, a transpop girl. Mace." How could I get through to him?

He swung to the others. "Says his bitch a trannie!" It brought jeers.

Bitch? I surged forward. "She's my wife, damn you!" Someone shoved me back; I slapped the hand away.

Alwyn's voice rose. "Lissenup, Sub!" It brought quiet. "Don' matter why he come. Law be, no one in sub but Subs, less'n we okay firs'!" Murmurs of agreement. "Anyone speak fo' Uppie?" Silence. "Then he—"

"I do!" Eddie struggled to his feet. "Leave 'im 'lone! I brought 'im. Diss me, you wan' blood!" Three Subs tackled him, brought him down amid curses and blows.

"You be nex', joeyboy," Alwyn told him. "Afta Uppie."

The sound of running steps. A dozen more tribesmen crowded near. Lord God, help me. I need time, for Annie.

The Sub leader whipped out a wicked blade, held up a hand for silence. "Uppie, this be why we diss ya. Like you say, we trash." He overrode grumbles of discontent. "But we got lives, jus' like you. We make kidjoes, same way Uppies do. An' Subs die, same as you, jus' fasta!"

He pointed upward. "Onna street, no hosp, no job, no teachin'. Looks like alla 'Hattan goin' like Bronx, nothin' but Crypsnbloods. We can' stop dat. But look 'roun, Uppie! We got food for any Sub who wan', and for frien' if Sub bring down. We got beds, onna track. We got Sub turf, Sub law. I be Sub Boss 'til someone call me out. Here, we say who come in, who don'."

"You kill strangers on sight and call it law?"

"Justice. You Uppies killin' us day by day. I come to yo' skytel, ask help, what I get?"

Somehow I had to divert him. I could think of no way. "Alwyn—"

He crouched, gripping the knife. "You be meat, Uppie." He took a step.

I backed into the wall. Despair overcame the last of my sense. My voice rang out. "Alwyn Boss Sub, I call you out! Rumb fo' boss!"

His jaw dropped. "Uppie can'—"

"Gimme blade!" In a fury I lashed out, shoved him across the room. "Law, you say? Rumb wid Cap'n unner Sub law!"

"A Cap'n talk trannie?" Alwyn's gaze held what might even have been respect.

"I be trannie, joey; we all be!" My voice grated. "Ain' no diff when Lor' call us out!" I spat at Alwyn's feet. "C'mon, rumb!"

"You win, an' stay Sub?"

"Long as I wan'. Same as you!"

His mouth twitched in a grudging smile. "Righ', same as. Jossie, give Cap'n shiv!"

The young girl thrust a knife into my hand.

Alwyn feinted. I dodged aside, ran to a steel beam in the center of the tunnel. He followed. Around us a wary circle formed.

We thrust and parried, neither drawing blood. Sarge, what was it you taught us? Crouch, palm upward? I tried.

Across the cavern Eddie struggled to his feet, tribesmen clinging. With a roar he shook them off, jumped onto a table. It shuddered, but held.

"Mira, trannies! He ain' no Uppie Cap'n!" Eddie stomped at grasping hands. "He the one onna joinup sheet!"

What in the name of . . . ? Alwyn, as puzzled as I, raised his hand. I nodded, stepped back.

Eddie's voice dripped contempt. "Subs too glitch to know why news screen allatime talkin' about joinup?"

"Say fish, outdere!" A teen. "Jus' a scare story."

"An' who foun' fish?"

"Some ship—"

"His ship!" Eddie's shout echoed. "He no cap'n, *HE DA FISHER-MAN!*"

Into the hush, Eddie spoke more softly. "He's da one what come back in dead ship, save Hope Nation! He da Fisherman Cap'n!"

Alwyn tapped his sheath, slid the knife in for me to see. I nodded. He came close, examined my face. "Swind?" His tone was cautious. "Fisherman be real? Not jus' inna holos?"

I was too enraged to care. "Look at a frazzing poster; it's my face they used! I'm Nick Seafort!"

He shook his head. "Don' need. Same face." His hand darted out, grazed my shoulder, pulled back as if scorched.

"What was that for?"

Alwyn grinned. "How many trannie c'n say touch Fisherman?"

I snarled, "How many trannies c'n say wan' diss Fisherman! You still scum! Puttin' down shiv don' change nothin'!"

He swallowed. "Doin' by law, is all. Evenup?" He held out his hand.

I slapped it away. "You wan' evenup, new law. Else, g'wan, rumb wid me, Subs get new boss."

Alwyn rubbed his stinging hand, spoke with dignity. "New Boss? Subs c'n do dat, anytime dey wan'. I make mistake wantin' ta diss Fisherman, so Subs fin' better boss." He drew his knife, extended it blade first. "G'wan. Alwyn die proud."

"Captain." Eddie jumped down from the table.

"I know." I took the knife, pressed it to Alwyn's breast. He didn't flinch. After a moment I reversed it, held it to my own. "G'wan. Life for life!"

Slowly his hand came up. His fist closed around the hilt. I held my breath as the point pricked my tunic.

His hand fell. "Fisherman Cap'n, be you frien' wid Sub?"

"Frien'." My hand crept out. "An' tribe." In hushed silence, we clasped. Eddie sighed.

"What new law you wan'?"

"Joey come down see Subs, not reason enough ta diss 'im."

"How dey gonna respec—"

"Diss whoever ya wan' if they attack ya. Else, no."

After a moment he turned to the others. "Law?"

Grudging murmurs, then general assent.

"Tribe say okay. Now, whatchew wan' wid Subs, Fisherman?"

My legs were shaky. I moved casually to a bench. "We brought innifo for passby east."

"Talk Uppie, Fisherman. I'll unnastan'. You go eas', den what?"

"Get past the Unies, find my wife."

"Unies bad grodes. Easters too."

"I'll get through. I have to."

"Okay." He raised his voice. "We help Fisherman go eas'. Jossie, Lo, bring innifo Unies. An' fo' Easters."

"How much?"

"All!"

She beckoned another youth. "C'mon!" They disappeared.

Alwyn whispered to a tribesman, who nodded. A few moments later the Sub lugged in my box of batteries. "Yours, Fisherman."

"Innifo for Sub."

"Don' need no innifo fro' tribe."

"Gift, then." I held out the box. He accepted it. I asked, "Why perm-abatteries?"

Alwyn grinned. "Showyas." He called for lights, led us up a flight of stairs, through a long, dim cavern.

"What is this place?"

"Sub's way, dey called it. Usta ride in, 'fore helis 'n Uppies. Give it up, 'bout three life back. Track gone, mostly. We tryin' ta fix."

"How many tunnels are yours?"

"Lotsa, in 'Hat. We block off some part. Bad tribes."

"Where we going?"

"Secret place." He stopped, waited for Eddie and a throng of tribesmen to catch up. "Onna street, gotta trayfo passby. Dis better."

As the corridor gave way to a wider tunnel, Alwyn jumped down onto the roadbed, disappeared into the dark. Uneasy, I followed.

He waited just around a bend. "Go eas', you say." He shone his light into the tunnel.

An ancient electricar, of sorts. Its lamps gleamed bright. Alwyn climbed in, held a hand, hoisted me up. "Shuttle, dis be. Four Two Square, Grandcen. Back 'n for'." With hoots and laughter other Subs crowded aboard. I searched, found Eddie chattering with excited tribesmen at the opposite end.

"The subway was abandoned."

"Yeah, long time. But wid 'nough permas . . ." Alwyn opened a compartment door. Inside, he pressed a lever, with care. The car lurched. Slowly, with a screech of rusty wheels, it slid forward.

"We got dis track workin'," he shouted over the racket. "By ourself. Not all trannies be stupe."

"I didn't—"

"Or trash."

"I'm sorry. I was angry."

He shrugged. "You jus' Fisherman, not real trannie."

At last the shuttle ground to a halt, and the Subs piled out. At street level I turned to wave, but Alwyn was gone.

Eddie and I emerged into daylight with an honor guard of Subs. While we waited Jossie bargained passage with the Easter transpops.

She said, "Mace joeys be south, mile. Dey pushout Efdears."

"Who?"

"Efdear Dri'. For groun'car."

"Tolya Maces made it 'cross!" Eddie was jubilant.

I asked, "Anyone hear of a Mace girl who came crosstown, a week ago?"

Jossie jabbered with our guides. "Dunno. Hear maybe six Unies be diss inna night, on Three Four."

"Dat's Annie!" Eddie's eyes glowed. "She see Mace gone, askaroun', someone tell. So she go eas'."

I said, unbelieving, "Annie killed six transpops?"

"If dey in her way. You dunno Annie, Captain. Never did. On ship, in Centraltown, she lost. Here, she home. Ain' no Bronk, no Unie gonna stop 'er."

"Good Lord."

The last mile was like a dream; we strode through sunlit streets with a guard of Subs and Easters.

We crossed a narrow access road, passed ravaged apartment buildings that recalled the devastated Bronx. To our left was the East River, bounded by a crumbling, fenced highway along which occasional groundcars still jounced. A rusted entrance sign proclaimed: F.D.R. DRIVE.

As we progressed, our Easter guards grew more alert, kept hands near their weapons. One of them pointed ahead, said, "Two block mo', Easter turf." He hesitated. " 'Xcept last block, look out fo' rumb."

"Whyfo?"

"Frazzin' Maces wannit. Rumb ever' week or so, pushem back."

Eddie bristled. I gripped his arm, shook my head. He growled, "Tolya at clinic, can't be sailor 'n trannie same time."

"You're a sailor seconded for special duty, Mr. Boss. I know these were your people, but . . ."

"No 'but', sir. Still my people, was, willbe."

"You started a riot with the Rocks, Mr. Boss. We won't have another." He didn't answer.

The last block of Easter turf was a scene of appalling devastation. The apartments that once graced the riverside were gutted. Those that hadn't been torched were near collapse, stripped bare of even their windows.

"Why do you fight over—that?"

"Weren' dat bad, 'fore Mace. Dey try push us out, we push back."

"Mace live here?" Eddie was scandalized.

"Here, inna river, who know." The Easter spat. "All Maces is glitch."

"Be silent, Mr. Boss!" I was barely in time.

The Easter tribesmen led us cautiously to the disputed block. "We wait. If ya come out, we take ya back."

Eddie and I went on, through sidewalks strewn with rubble. The area seemed deserted.

We reached a corner. A ragamuffin teen leaned against a post under a gutted apartment, fingering a whistle chained around his neck. He jeered, "Whazzis, a Navyboy tribe? Ya pushback Easters?"

Eddie growled, "You Mace?"

"Offa my turf. Move yo' frazzin' ass 'fore it meat!"

Eddie picked him up, slammed him against the pole.

"Leggo me!" The boy snatched his whistle. Eddie twisted it out of his hand, yanked hard, snapped the cord. The boy yelped, rubbing his neck.

Eddie growled, "You be Mace, joeyboy?"

"Go prong—"

Eddie's hand lashed out, slapped him hard.

The boy squealed, "We be Mace!"

"Easy, Mr. Boss."

"Learn him manners!" Eddie thrust the whistle into the youngster's hand. "Call Sam 'n Boney! Call Rafe!"

"Go—" He stopped short at the look in Eddie's eye. He blew three short blasts.

I watched the street, bracing for trouble.

For almost a full minute, no one came. Suddenly three figures leaped from a low window. Two carried knives, one a studded club.

"Back, Cap'n!" Eddie twisted the teen's arm, held him as a shield. "Wanna rumb, Maces? Rumb wi' Eddieboss?" He squinted at a scrawny tribesman barely out of his teens. "Boney, dat you? Ya growed!"

"Outaheah, Easter!" They circled. A club lashed out; I ducked back.

Eddie shoved the boy into the street, snatched the club from the attacker's hand. "Was it some Easter save Boney's ass in rumb with Broads, back when? Mira, joey! I be Eddieboss!" He lowered the club. "I look' allova, fin' Maces! Ya know Eddie!"

The teen yelled, "He whomp on me, no reas'!"

"Hol' it!" Boney held up a hand, peered suspiciously. "Eddie wen' outboun'."

"I come back." Eddie's gap-toothed grin warmed his face. "Home 'gain!"

"Who bringalong?"

"Cap'n, lookin' fo Anniegirl."

The Maces exchanged glances.

I couldn't contain myself. "Where is she?"

"Din' know," Boney said to Eddie, as if in appeal. "Mace bitchgirl come back inna nigh', say she been outboun', see Fish, go nudder place, marry a Cap'n. All glitch fo' sure." He shook his head. "Din' mean nothin', Eddie. Don' wan' no troub.'"

"What'd you do to her?" My voice was hoarse.

"Din' do nothin, Cap'n!" Boney seemed eager to please. "Din' hurt none, jus' din' help."

Scowling, Eddie took a step toward the tribesmen. They retreated. "Take Cap'n ta Annie rightaway fas'!"

"Sure, Eddie." Boney collared the boy. "Fin' Sam, tell'm Eddieboss back!" He pointed to the alley. "Onna grounflo'. Mos'ly she stay in dere."

I swallowed. "Is it safe, Eddie?"

"G'wan, Cap'n. Dey know we Mace, now."

I ran down the alley, disappeared around the building. A rotted doorway gaped. I peered inside. Broken furniture, trash, an appalling stench.

My wife crouched in the corner, hands over her ears. "G'way, allyas! Don' care 'bout no rumb, no Unies. Don' care!"

"Annie . . ."

She didn't hear. I took a deep breath, said more loudly, "Annie, I've been searching for you."

Slowly, she came around, raised her head. "Whatcha doon here, Nicky?"

"I came to take you home."

"I be Macebitch." She whimpered; the sound tore at my soul.

"You be wife, Anniegirl, fo'ever an' mo'."

For a second, she smiled, then she shook her head. "You be no trannie."

"I be what I haveta be, ta bringya widme."

Her eyes explored mine. "Don' wanna go, Nicky."

"What you want, Annie? This?" My wave took in the filthy room.

"Dunno what I wan'!"

"That's why I came for you." I crossed, squatted at her side. "You're sick from the drugs. Come home."

"We don' got home!"

"I'll take you to Father, then. Away from cities."

"Cities is what I know. I be Mace."

"Not no more, Anniegirl." The voice in the doorway spoke with authority. "You be like me. Nothin' now."

"Eddie!" She scrambled to her feet.

He set down his club. "We ain' trannie, ain' Uppie. If ya home ain' wid him, where?"

Her face twisted. "If I ain' Mace, I do what, Eddieboss? Die?"

He shook his head. "Go wid him. He love you."

"Annie—" My voice was hoarse.

She ignored me. "What kin' lovin', drag me 'notha planet, leave me fo' grodes prong me 'til dey done, drag me back here, throw me in frazzin' hosp?" She slid down the wall, her face in her hands.

Eddie took a slow breath. His words were careful. "None of that was his fault."

"Whose, den? Who sent ya 'way?"

"My faul', prongin' you when I had no righ'."

"We tribe!"

"Not no more." He crossed the room, hauled her to her feet. "Go with Cap'n now. Bes'."

"Wid Nicky?" She twisted around, studied me as a foreign object. "I wan'—wan'—"

With a cry, she spun again, wrapped herself around Eddie, buried her head in his chest.

He stood motionless, arms at his sides. As Annie began to weep, his eyes came up to meet mine.

I nodded.

Slowly, he enveloped her in his broad strong arms, rocked her. "Cap'n the man fo' you, Anniegirl. Hasta be. But I be here, long as he let me. I be here."

In the awful quiet of the room I whispered an impotent echo. "I be here."

True to Alwyn's word, the Subs provided an escort back to civilization. Twenty Subs and a handful of Mace led us uptown along the river to the new U.N. enclave. Annie clung dazedly to Eddie. She let me take her other hand.

At the U.N. we merged with the lines of tourists passing through the electric fences. Though the government seldom acknowledged transpops as a constituency, under the open access policy even they were allowed in the International Lobby.

I called the Sheraton, told Adam to pick us up. When I asked the Subs how they'd make it home safely, they just laughed. We left them, and waited on the rooftop.

* * *

I took Annie to our suite. She was docile, as she'd been since leaving the crumbling apartment.

I helped her bathe away the grime of the streets, spoke gently about my search. It seemed to please her. She told me nothing of her own escapades, and I was afraid to pry.

At the hotel, our dinner was overcooked and tasteless, and made more bothersome by the fact that I was approached for autographs. At the end, I signed for the meal with indifference.

Annie was safe.

I booked the three of us on the morning suborbital for London and went to bed, exhausted. Annie rested her head on my chest, willing to be cuddled. Just before I slept she squeezed my shoulder and murmured, "Maybe time make it different, Nicky."

As Cardiff neared I switched off the autopilot and guided the heli by my own hand. I'd never before flown home, but once I spotted the Bridgend road I followed it through twisting hills until I spotted a pasture and a stone house, set near the foundations of an ancient barn.

Father would consider setting a heli down in his yard a prideful ostentation, so I landed in a meadow across the road. Annie jumped out before Eddie could help her. "This where you from, Nicky?" Her cheeks were flushed.

"Not exactly. The house, over there."

She giggled. "Tha's what I meant." She looked about. "Feels funny, no streets. Kinda like Centraltown."

"Not quite as untamed." I took the duffel Eddie handed down. "Better let me do the talking, when we go in. Father . . ." I hesitated. "He'll treat you well once he knows you, but he's suspicious of city folk." We started up the lane.

"How long we stayin', Nicky?"

I'd already told her, but repeated it patiently. "We'll see how you do. I may go back to Academy and let you recuperate with Father."

"He ain' . . . isn't gonna like me."

How to explain? "If he sounds harsh, remember it's his way. I'm his only son, and he talks to me in the same manner." I wished he'd been home when I tried to call. Though my own welcome was never in doubt, I hoped he wouldn't rebuff Eddie and my wife. If he got on his religious high horse and lectured them I'd have to find some way to intervene.

Annie put her hand through Eddie's arm. "He give me trouble, Eddie take care of him, woncha?" She might have been teasing. Perhaps not.

The sailor gently disengaged his hand from hers, fell back as we strolled to the house. I was grateful.

As the sagging gate creaked I felt a twinge of guilt. Time and again I'd promised Father I'd fix it, and always it was left for last. This time I'd take care of it.

As always, the door was unlocked; Father kept nothing to interest thieves. "Father?" I went in. We'd wait in the kitchen until he got back from shopping.

A teacup and saucer sat unwashed in the sink. He would wash them before taking the daily bus to town; no chore must be left undone. I looked into his bedroom; the bed was neatly made. I checked the lavatory, the storeroom.

"Nicky?" She met me at the door. I brushed past, a growing unease quickening my step.

I found him facedown by the woodpile behind the house. He'd been getting wood for the stove. It had been several days. Dogs and other wild things had worried at him.

I knelt beside him, tried to take his hand. I couldn't force myself to do it; the body was too far gone. I forced down my gorge, sought some prayer that would please him. What came to mind was, *"For in death there is no remembrance of thee: in the grave who shall give thee thanks?"*

It was so grotesquely inappropriate that I bent my head in shame, conjured Father's stern visage from the days when I memorized my boyhood verses. I barely noticed Annie's soft hand squeeze my shoulder.

At last I whispered, *"I have set the Lord always before me: because he is at my right hand, I shall not be moved. Therefore my heart is glad, and my glory rejoiceth: my flesh also shall rest in hope. For thou wilt not leave my soul in hell."* I looked up. "He'd like that verse, if he didn't think it too prideful." I crouched on my knees, oblivious of the damp earth staining my trousers.

"Nicky." She dropped behind me, circled me with her arms.

I pressed her birdlike hands to my chest, those hands that had killed six Unie transpops who stood in her way. With revulsion I thrust away the thought. She was Annie Wells. My wife.

After a while I went to a neighbor, called the coroner. When the van with its flashing lights had carried Father from his house I sat at the rickety table in the bare kitchen, nursing a lukewarm cup of tea.

The old copper teapot needed polishing; I'd have to put it on my list, along with the gate.

"Don't cry, Nicky."

"I'm not." I brushed my sleeve across my eyes. "Where's Eddie?"

"Outside, straightening the wood."

Without a word I rushed out to the woodpile, flung myself at Eddie's crouching form. "Get away from that!"

"Jus' picking up what he drop—"

"I see what you're doing! Leave it alone!" I swept the firewood from his arms, battered at his massive chest.

Eddie regarded me stolidly. "Whompin' ol' Eddie ain' gonna bring him back, Cap'n."

"Don't talk back to me, you trannie—" I checked myself, too late. "Go in the house!"

I busied myself with the wood. Presently I understood I'd been arranging and rearranging the logs, trying to refashion the bundle Father had dropped, exactly as he'd left it. I slumped against the woodpile, hugged myself, rocking back and forth.

In the pasture, birds chirped their discoveries.

After a time I shivered, thrust my hands in my pockets, walked slowly back to the house.

"Sit down with me, please." I pulled out chairs for them. "Mr. Boss, I have no excuse. I'm sorry."

"For callin' me trannie? It's what I am."

"It's not a nice word."

"Nah, we use it alla time." He shifted, and the chair creaked.

"The tribes do, but I have no right."

For a second a wan smile flashed. "Why not? You a Sub now."

. Annie giggled. Her hand stroked his arm.

"Pedro Chang made me realize . . ." I trailed off, lost in reverie. "I have no friends left, Eddie. Derek Carr is light-years away, if he lives. Alexi is learning to manage on his own again. Other than them . . ."

"Cap'n—"

"Once, I sent you away. Would you stay with me, now?"

"You don' need no trannie frien'." At first I thought it was sarcasm, but then I saw the anguish in his face.

"Please." It was all I could manage.

We buried Father two days later, at the bleak cemetery on the hill. A cold drizzle saw him to his grave. A few acquaintances, the butcher, the greengrocer, paid their respects while a minister read from the Book.

I stood shivering in my dress whites. Annie leaned on Eddie. When the service was done I trod across the rocky ground to Jason's grave, but could find no tears, even for him. Afterward, chilled, we rode back to the house. I kindled a fire. Annie snuggled at my knees.

"I wish I could stay." I stared into the flames.

The sailor stirred. "Where you gotta go, Captain?"

"They expect me at *Wellington* for the commissioning. We'll have to leave soon."

"You taking Annie to a ship?" He sounded uneasy.

"No, of course not. You'll stay at Academy."

Annie said with force, "I don' wan' go there."

"Why not? They'd take good care—"

"I don' belong!"

For her sake, I tried to suppress my frustration. From her perspective, she was right. Officers and cadets would be scrupulously polite to the Commandant's wife, but she'd have no one to talk to, no one who understood. On the other hand, where else could she—

"Stay here, then." I waved away their surprise. "It's why we came. And the house is mine now."

"I can't stay here alone, I go glitch!" She seized Eddie's arm.

"Not alone, Annie." I looked to Eddie Boss.

"You leavin' me wid her again?" He looked frightened.

"Annie needs someone to—"

"Not widout you!" He scrambled to his feet.

After a moment I understood. "Come outside, Mr. Boss."

We huddled in the lee of the shed. "Cap'n, ain' good idea put me alone wid Annie!"

"Someone has to protect her." From herself, perhaps.

"In Academy, den!" He stomped his foot, turned away. Finally, scarlet, he blurted, "I ain gon' touch her, Cap'n! Swear! Won' touch her never!"

I closed my eyes, remembered her hand seizing his for comfort. "Look after her, Mr. Boss. And if need be . . ." I forced the words. "If need be, touch her. Give peace to my wife."

I hurried back to the house.

Part 3

November, in the year of our Lord 2201

16

"The important thing is, you found her." Tolliver's expression was somber. "She'll heal in time."

I couldn't describe Annie squatting in the shack, nor tell him of her dependence on Eddie. "What's come up while I was away?"

"The usual. Two cadets caned, the latest biweekly test scores are on your puter, the new simulator's been delayed again. One other thing. I heard from United Suit and Tank about those serial numbers that didn't check."

"When Branstead was doing inventories?"

"Yes. U.T. and S. says the numbers on our list match the suits they shipped. So I asked them to help identify the numbers on the suiting room manifest." He waited.

"I'm in no mood for games. Spit it out."

"Aye aye, sir. United Suit and Tank says they're old numbers."

"What are you talking about?"

"Sorry, sir. Not old numbers, old suits. Refurbished."

My weary mind tried to grapple. "How can that be?"

"One explanation comes to mind. The new suits were, um, diverted, and old ones substituted." Tolliver waited for a response, leaned forward. "Let me make it clearer. Someone sold the new equipment we paid for, and sent us junk."

"Who?"

"It's the quartermaster's job to check new inventory."

"Sergeant whatzisname? Serenco?"

"Yes, sir."

"What does he say?"

"I wasn't about to tackle that without your presence, sir. Too touchy."

I growled, "That never stopped you before." Childish, but so be it.

Tolliver rose to the challenge. "Very well, I'll deal with him on my own."

"No, let me think on it." I got to my feet. "Anything else?"

"Your friend Mr. Thorne arrived last week. I assigned him a flat." He gathered his notes. "Don't forget you leave for *Wellington* in five days."

"I just got back." I sighed. "I really don't like the idea of bringing cadets to a commissioning. Let's drop that idea."

"After you had me tell them? Forget it."

"I'm Commandant here, not you!"

Tolliver crossed his arms. "You break the news to them, then." I bristled, but he overrode me. "If you'd seen Kevin Arnweil's face, you'd understand. Have you ever seen him smile?"

"He doesn't smile much."

"Now he does."

I sighed again, my ire fading. "They haven't earned special privileges, you know. I really should bring the cadet with the best grades."

"Go ahead. One more won't make a difference."

"Oh, sure. Like a mother duck with—"

"And a middy to take care of them."

"Good Lord." I waved it away. "I'll think about it."

Tolliver stood. "My condolences about your father, Mr. Seafort."

"Thank you. Dismissed."

I sat for a while, brooding about the U.T. and S. suits. It was no small thing to accuse a staff sergeant of dishonesty; if I was wrong, our relations would be poisoned. Despite Tolliver's suggestion, the discrepancy in numbers might be accidental.

I could decide later. In the meantime, it would do me good to look up Jeff Thorne. For the first time in ages, my spirits lifted. I left my office. In the anteroom Kevin Arnweil stood hopefully. His glance flickered to my bruised face, and away. Like the others, he dared make no comment.

"I'll be back soon." I tried to ignore Kevin's crestfallen look, stopped at the outer door. "Come along, Mr. Arnweil. I'll introduce you to our new second lieutenant."

"Aye aye, sir." He scurried to my side.

We crossed the quadrangle. "I've known Mr. Thorne ever since I was a cadet."

"Yes, sir."

"He was a middy at the time."

"Yes, sir." He kept pace alongside.

I gave it up. Arnweil could no more imagine me as a cadet than himself as Captain.

Tolliver had bunked Jeff Thorne in Officers' Quarters, but, thankfully, not in the apartment of his predecessor Mr. Sleak. That would have been too much. Despite myself, my heart beat faster as we neared his apartment. Would he take me on another mission, someday? To raid the galley, unbeknownst to all?

I knocked, waited. "Mr. Thorne?"

No answer. "Jeff?"

Nothing. Kevin Arnweil shifted uncomfortably. I sighed. "Another time, I guess. You'll meet him soon enough." I started back to the office, the cadet at my heels.

The depth of my disappointment surprised me. On the spur of the moment I asked, "When you were aloft, did you hear of any middies, ah, leading cadets on unauthorized missions?"

"I . . ." He swallowed. "I guess, I— No, sir."

I stopped short. "Forgive me. That came out badly."

"Aye aye, sir."

"I wasn't asking you to inform."

"Oh, no, sir!" He seemed desperate to please.

"I just meant, I wondered if they still, I mean, I don't know if you'd even be aware—" I clamped my mouth shut. Adam Tenere's babbling held nothing on mine.

"I'm sorry, I always get it wrong." Arnweil smoothed his black locks with a nervous gesture.

"Belay that!" We walked the rest of the way in silence. No point trying to explain; I'd done enough damage.

At the outer door he blurted, "I'm sorry I didn't answer you right, sir."

"It wasn't your fault." I'd already apologized, what else did the young twit want? I crossed to my desk, came to a halt. "Damn it to hell!" I turned back to the anteroom.

"Kevin, come along." I stalked out into the cool afternoon, turned toward the front gate.

The cadet trotted to keep up with my stride. "About what you asked, sir, I could probably think of—"

"I don't want to hear it."

"Sorry, sir."

After a time my pace slowed. I turned from the path, crossed the tree-lined lawn, found a secluded spot. I took off my jacket, loosened my tie while Kevin watched in consternation. I sat back against the tree, patted the ground. "Sit."

I took time to assemble my thoughts. "Kevin, I made a fool of myself, asking you the wrong question. Let me tell you a story. I was a plebe at Farside, probably more scared than you are now. My cadet corporal was down on me, I had almost no friends, I imagined I'd wash out at any moment."

Arnweil contemplated me, saying nothing.

"There was a boy, a middy." I looked into the distance. The words came hard. "He was everything I wasn't. Handsome, likable. He didn't have to bully; he had natural authority. Ever meet someone like that?" I didn't wait for an answer. "Even though I was a mere cadet, he took me aside for talks as if I mattered to him. Late at night he would haul me from barracks on the pretext of hazing, but once we were out of sight we'd round up some others and do crazy things. Spying belowdecks. Raiding the emergency rations in the suiting room. We even reprogrammed the console in Nav class."

I risked a glance. Kevin was engrossed by a blade of grass.

"It ended suddenly when we got caught. I took a caning. But I sometimes realize . . ." I cleared my throat. "If it weren't for him, I couldn't have gotten through. I mean, you can get so lonely." I had to stop, at that.

The boy's tone was urgent. "You don't have to talk about those things, sir."

"Lonely." Annie in Cardiff, her future unsure, only Eddie to guide her. I shook my head. No, this was about the past, wasn't it? "They throw the courses at you, and discipline, and traditions, and sometimes it's too much to take."

She might never come back to me. Even Father's meager comfort was gone. I had no one, not even Lord God. Nothing but my duty, and I was failing at that.

"So, you see, I was just wond—" I tried again. "What that middy did meant so much to me. It's over, as far as my own life, but I needed to know whether it goes on still. If it does . . ."

"Sir, I—"

"It would mean a lot, just to know." Abruptly I got to my feet, faced away. My eyes burned. Damned air, full of pollutants.

After a time I picked up my jacket. "Come, let's go back."

"Aye aye, sir." This time our pace was slower. I walked with hands in pockets, glad of the confession, even if Arnweil hadn't understood a word I'd said. Shy crocuses peeked from carefully tilled flower beds. Someday, I would go home to Cardiff, whether Annie was there, or not. I would till and mend fences, search for elusive peace.

"I wasn't part of it." Kevin was subdued. "Doing things."

"That's all right, lad. I just needed to explain."

"Dustin Edwards . . . we signed up together. We thought—" His voice wavered. "Now that he's gone, there's no one."

"I understand."

"Some of the middies, they're nice. Mr. Keene, Mr. Tenere." His step slowed. "None of them notice me, the way you talked about."

"I'm sorry, I—"

He took a deep breath. "I lied a little, before. There's stories you hear, in barracks. Middies trying to get through the guards, to the gravitrons. I don't know if they bring cadets along."

"Ah." I studied the impatiens. Their colors seemed to brighten.

"Three joes got caught putting jelly in the toes of training suits. I heard it wasn't the first time."

"Terrible."

He saw in my eyes that which didn't match my words. He offered a tentative smile. "Yes, sir."

My tone was gruff. "Thank you." We walked on in silence, paused at the Admin Building door.

"Shall I wait inside for orders, sir?"

"Well . . ." I smiled. I was Commandant, and could do as I liked. "No, take the afternoon off. Get a haircut. Do whatever you wish." Unheard of. A cadet's every moment was regimented, and rightly so.

"Aye aye, sir." He saluted, waited for dismissal.

I opened the door, hesitated. Annie was still in Cardiff, Father was still gone. Lord God's face was still turned from me.

Nothing had changed. Yet somehow my load was lighter.

It was barely a week since I'd last taken my place in the dining hall, but it seemed ages. I ate slowly, thinking about Tolliver's investigation. After Cardiff, Academy problems seemed unreal, and I had to force myself to concentrate. At table, Kevin Arnweil offered me a shy smile, was rewarded with a frown from Sergeant Olvira. I winked.

After dinner Tolliver accompanied me to my office, past Arnweil and Kyle Drew, who'd been assigned late evening duty in the anteroom. They stood, saluted.

I closed the door. "How should I deal with Quartermaster Serenco?"

"Why not just ask him, sir?"

"Oh, come on! 'Good afternoon, Sarge. By the way, have you stolen our training suits?' "

"Something along those lines. 'There's a discrepancy in suit numbers. Can you help us explain it?' "

I bit back an angry reply. It might be the easiest approach after all. "Very well. Have him report in the morning."

"Right. Do you want me present?"

"Yes." Tolliver had the facts at hand, and I didn't. "By the way, Jeff Thorne wasn't at dinner. Know where I can find him?"

Tolliver's tone was cold. "Since when is it my duty to keep track of the Commandant's favorites?"

"Tolliver!"

"We traded shifts. He went to town. Seems he stayed late."

"Why?"

My aide rose to his feet. "Ask Jeff Thorne, not me!" He flung open the door, snapped a wrathful salute, stalked out.

I gaped. For all his foibles, this was unlike Tolliver. Had the two argued? It was important they get along; I intended to send Edgar aloft, so I could spend time groundside. I'd expected Jeff to be his mainstay at Farside.

I brooded at the console. Annie, in Cardiff, pressed heavily on my mind. I had done her so much harm; far better had I left her to proceed to Detour with the others of her tribe. Why was my life filled with misery and death? So much of it could have been avoided, had I been more aware, more competent. Perhaps even Lieutenant Sleak might have been saved.

At least I had Jeff Thorne. He'd help, even if only by offering a sympathetic ear. When would our paths finally cross?

After a time I found myself yawning. I turned off the console. I checked my desk one last time, turned off the light.

"—voice down. He'll hear us!"

I froze with my hand on the knob. Now what were the cadets up to?

". . . don't know how you feel? I think about it every day!" A high-pitched voice. Kyle Drew. I leaned my head against the door, the better to hear.

"I never said it was your fault." Arnweil's tone was sullen.

"You don't have to, Kevin."

"Who asked you to bring it up again? He's gone. You can't change that, I can't—" Arnweil's voice caught.

For a moment, silence.

Kyle. "Don't look at me like that! I can't stand it! I'd switch places with him in a second if I could. I dream about it every night."

An anguished whisper. "So do I."

A long time passed. Kevin Arnweil muttered, "Dus and I joined up together. We were close. It was a miracle when they put us in the same dorm."

"You don't know how close." Kyle giggled. "That time he got ba-tonned, you walked like it was you."

"Don't make fun of us, you frazzing little—"

"I wasn't!" The scrape of a chair. "Kevin, I'm so damn jeal—" Silence. "I'm sorry. I just wanted you to know. If there was anything I could do—I'm sorry. I miss him too."

Arnweil sounded weary. "Thanks. You didn't do it on purpose."

Kyle's answer was so low I could barely hear. "What does that matter?"

I leaned against the door. Preoccupied with Nav grades, with laser training and calisthenics, we did nothing for our joeys' aching souls. I thought again of Jeff Thorne, and what he'd meant. He would understand how to help.

I tiptoed back to my desk, groped in the dark for the caller. "Ring Sergeant Kinders for me, please."

Arnweil, his voice all business. "Aye aye, sir."

Kinders answered on the first ring. "Sarge, have Lieutenant Thorne report to my office after breakfast."

"Aye aye, sir."

No, damn it, that wasn't what I wanted. A summons from the Commandant would only emphasize our difference in rank, when I wanted to meet him as an old friend. "Belay that, Sarge." How to—"Mr. Kinders, you're familiar with town?"

"Somewhat, sir. I've lived here for—"

"If an officer were off the grounds, where would you find him? Are there restaurants, pubs?" It occurred to me I'd never left the Academy grounds other than by heli.

"Yes, sir." He hesitated. "Is it Lieutenant Thorne you're . . . ?"

"Yes."

"I saw him in the Athenia Tavern a couple of nights ago."

"Thank you." A few minutes later I was memorizing directions from the guard at the gate. I crossed the commons into the center of town.

The Athenia was on a side street about half a mile distant. I didn't mind the walk; it gave me time to clear my head, compose myself.

Above the entrance was a huge holo projecting a distorted, romanticized view of the Solar System. As best I could tell, the ship that captured that view would be close enough to the Sun to melt its holocamera.

Inside, a jangle of laughter amid stale fumes of drink.

"A table, Captain?" The maître d'.

"I'm looking for—" My eye roved to the booths in the dining room, spotted a Naval uniform. I looked closer, recognized Midshipman Thayer with a civilian. He caught my eye. I grimaced, waved him back to his seat.

"No table, thanks." I turned toward the door. "I thought one of my lieutenants might be . . ." I trailed off. "Never mind."

"There's a young man in the vidroom."

It wouldn't be Thorne. Still, I poked my head in. Someone was in the Arcvid helmet, surrounded by admiring teens. The uniform was unkempt, the body flabby. A drink teetered on the console.

"I've got the bastards!" The young man spun the thrusters savagely, rotating his ship in the enhanced sensory environment of his helmet. A replica on the blue console screen followed his motion. He slapped at the fire control; three of the enemy ships disintegrated. The console flashed a bright green. "Level sixteen! Prepare for attack!"

The teen nudged me. "No one ever gets to sixteen!"

I watched, drawn into the game despite myself. Despite Jason's avid encouragement, I'd always crashed at level four. The player in the helmet spun and fired at his attackers with consummate skill. In moments he was at seventeen. By eighteen, the attackers' speed was simply too great; he went out in a blaze of unreturned fire.

The player slid off his helmet.

"Jeff?" Dismay rose from deep within my throat.

Thorne blinked in the light of the vidroom. "Ah. Our Commandant." He brought himself together in a mockery of an Academy salute. "Lieutenant Jeffrey Thorne reporting, sir."

His shirt was awry; he needed a shave. I stared, at a loss for words.

Thorne chuckled. It was not a pleasant sound. "I'm a bit hungover. Had rather a good time last night." The watching joeys poked each other and grinned.

"Drinking?" Fatuous, but I couldn't help it.

He met my gaze. "Oh, yes. But off base, on my own time. It's never been more than that."

"I wasn't accusing—I just wanted to say hello."

"Hello, then." A silence stretched. At last he said grudgingly, "I have a table."

"It's not—perhaps another time."

"I don't mind." His smile was sour. "Those joeykits want the console. I tie it up for hours." He led me to the dining room.

We sat.

"Sorry, I should have changed clothes. On Callisto Base it didn't seem to matter."

"Here it does." My tone was blunt. "You're supposed to set an example for the cadets."

"I don't hold myself out as an example, Commandant."

"Once, you did."

Silence. He swallowed. "A long time ago."

"What's happened since?"

"I grew up."

A waiter came with menus. I shook my head; Thorne waved his away. "Another gin."

I said, "Mr. Thorne, what's wrong?"

His expression was faintly hostile. "Nothing. In a few months my enlistment runs out and I'll be off."

Enough was enough. I stood. "What you do on your free time is none of my business. But on duty you will conform to Academy standards. And there'll be no more switching watches!"

"Aye aye, sir, fair enough."

"Mr. Tolliver will show you the ropes. Have you any questions?" Hearing no answer, I turned for the door.

"Just one." For a moment he sounded like the Jeff Thorne of old. "What other revenge will you take?"

My fists bunched as I wheeled about. "You're speaking to a superior!"

His voice cut like a knife. "Don't I know! You transferred me to gloat over it!" Conversation hushed; the waiter took a hesitant step our way. Thorne waved him off.

"How could you think such a thing?" My voice was unsteady.

"Why else take someone with my record?" His eyes bored into mine.

"What record?"

"Oh, you've learned deceit, now? As a cadet you were the boy who wouldn't lie!"

"As a middy, you were the boy I revered!" I could have bitten my tongue off, but it was too late. My ears flamed. I managed to meet his eye. "What's on your record, Mr. Thorne?"

"All right, we'll pretend you didn't look. Sit down; I don't mind humiliating myself." He kicked out my chair. Everyone's eyes on me, I sat again.

He said, "I served two years as Academy middy, you remember. Just as you were leaving they posted me to U.N.S. *Targon.* Another year, this time as first middy."

He swirled the liquor around the rim of his glass, drank it all in a gulp. "It wasn't a bad time. Good training, and I made friends." His eyes wandered to the starched tablecloth.

"They rotated me to Lunapolis, to Admiralty. Running petty errands for Captains on leave. It went on month after month. Accommodations detail, they called it. Unambitious middies and bootlicking lieutenants.

My requests for transfer were ignored." His mouth twisted. "You know what happened then."

"I don't, Jeff." I felt a chill.

"Lieutenant Tryx was transferred out. It was too much trouble to break in a replacement. They promoted me. Not because I'd earned it, but because it was . . . convenient." He spat the word. "Higbee, in BuPers, told me so himself."

The bastard. "Go on."

"I'd trained as an officer in the U.N.N.S., not as a bloody hotel concierge! Sure, aboard ship, when a Captain asks you to do a favor, no one minds. But this went on for months. Years!" He swilled the dregs of his drink, waved for another.

"What happened?" My voice was soft.

He leaned into my face, said thickly, "I'm no procurer!" He watched my face, as if he expected me to contradict him. His eyes fell to some fold of the cloth. "U.N.S. *Vespa* came in, with Captain Reegis. I made the usual offer, anything I can do to be of service, et cetera. Where the hell is my drink? Waiter!"

"You've had a lot, Mr.—"

"And I'll have more, if I choose." Thorne looked about, subsided when he saw the waiter hurrying with a fresh glass. At length he said, "Reegis wanted a woman, preferably blond, and uninhibited."

"Good Lord."

"Oh, it wasn't the first time I'd been asked, and I always accommodated. This time . . ." He sought refuge in the clear cold liquor. "You see, they wouldn't give me a transfer; I was too good at my job. I felt . . . trapped. So instead of making the usual call to a seedy hotel, I rang Mrs. Duhaney. I knew the Admiral was groundside. I told her Captain Reegis was having a party, and sent her to Reegis' hotel room. Mrs. Duhaney's hair happens to be blond."

"My God, Jeff!"

"I figured they'd cashier me. Well, that was fine if they wouldn't let me in the real Navy." He sipped his drink once more. "Instead, they sent me to Callisto."

"The most remote—"

"You have no idea, Nick." His troubled eyes met mine. "There's . . . nothing at all." He brooded. "Except Arcvid." He flashed a twisted smile. "I took to the Arcworld immediately. It embraced me, whenever I got another lousy rating on my fitness reports. I'm—I was the base champion."

"Jeff, I'm sor—"

"Arcvid's just like life, Nick. You can't win. Sometimes you evade defeat for a long, long time. Once I reached level twenty-three." When he looked up, his expression was bleak. "But Arcvid always gets you, in the end." His eyes lost their focus. He whispered, "Always."

The waiter approached; I waved him back. "He's had enough. Come, Mr. Thorne, I'll take you home."

He stood uncertainly, leaned on the table for support. "Home is where the heart is. Where's that, Captain Seafort?" He laughed.

I threw money on the table, got his arm over my shoulder.

No taxi in sight. I resigned myself to a long walk supporting my half-conscious lieutenant, but the cold night air seemed to brace him. Once, as we neared the commons, he said, "I read all the zines they sent. Saw your pictures."

"Watch where you put your feet."

"Callisto was hell." He stumbled, caught himself. "Knowing you made it much worse."

"How?" I maneuvered him past a tree.

"An example to the cadets, you called it? There I was, consigned to that abyss, and always your holo accusing me, an example of what I could have become. I hated you."

"They wasted you."

"Did you hear what I said? I hated you." I could find no reply. A moment later he dropped to his knees and was sick. After a time, he wiped his mouth, got unsteadily to his feet. "Sorry." He lurched on. "With luck I won't remember any of this in the morning."

I saw him to his apartment. He closed the door without a word. I went to bed, and lay unsleeping until well past dawn.

"Sergeant Serenco reporting, sir." The quartermaster marched in smartly, came to attention in front of my desk. Edgar Tolliver stood at my left, hands clasped behind his back.

"As you were, Sergeant. Please be seated." My tone seemed too formal; I tried to sound more relaxed. "We've been running some equipment checks, Sarge. All routine, but a few gaps need correcting."

"Gaps, sir?" Serenco's guileless blue eyes met mine. "I don't quite understand."

"For example, the training suits." I punched up the figures. "Look, inventory numbers don't match."

"With what, sir? This is the first I've heard of suit numbers." He turned to Tolliver. "Is that why you've been going through my manifests, Lieutenant? Why didn't you come ask me, like any—"

"Because it's—"

"Be silent, Tolliver! Sarge, I told him not to." So much for the tactful inquiry I'd intended. "Purchasing and inventory are a shambles. I wanted an investigation."

Serenco's blue eyes flashed as he got to his feet. "You may have my resignation. I won't have my honesty questioned just because I've done things the way the old Commandant—"

I shouted, "I didn't give you permission to stand!" I slammed my fist against the table. "You'll obey orders like everyone else! Sit!" When he'd complied, I forced my tone to be calm. "No one questions your honesty. I had Mr. Tolliver check on procurement and inventories. A few minor matters have come up and we—"

"Minor? Hauled before the Commandant and his first lieutenant like an errant—"

"Interrupt again and I will by Lord God have your resignation, or worse!" I got to my feet. "I run this place, Serenco. I'll do what I want! Now, how soon can you check on these figures?"

"I have no idea." His fury was barely under restraint. "First, I need a copy of what you found. Then, maybe—" He saw my expression. "Two days, three perhaps. I may have to ask our suppliers."

"You have until I'm back from *Wellington*. By then Mr. Tolliver will have a list of other questions. Dismissed."

When he'd gone, Tolliver crossed to the chair he'd vacated, dropped into it without permission. "Yes, I'm glad I waited. You handled him much more tactfully than—"

"Belay that." I paced, fuming. "I don't give a damn about suit numbers, but his manner . . . interrupting the Commandant! Quarreling! What's happened to discipline?"

"You're shoreside, sir. Shipboard discipline is much more—"

"And he's a Marine sergeant!" I threw myself on the couch. "He's as insolent as you are!"

Tolliver raised an eyebrow. "Bad night, sir?"

"Don't patronize me." Slowly, my anger abated: "I didn't sleep well." I brooded. "The damned impudence."

"Don't complain; you're his role model." He withstood my glare. "Which reminds me: I called BuPers. Higbee is . . . irked."

I sighed. "I would imagine." In obtaining Eddie's transfer I'd been, um, inflammatory.

"What was it you said to him? No, it might give me ideas. Anyway, I arranged an orderly for you."

I sat upright. "I told you when we first took this job I didn't want—"

"Yes, but you changed your mind." He raised a hand to forestall me. "How else would you like to explain Mr. Boss, if someone asks?"

"Lord God." I'd forgotten.

"You had pull enough to yank him groundside at short notice, but if he's to be assigned here permanently, he needs a regular berth."

"Very well." I smiled weakly. "Thank you."

"All part of the job, sir." He stood. "Anything else, before I go?"

"No. Yes, one thing." I sat behind my desk. "Why did you call Jeff Thorne my favorite?"

"I withdraw the remark. I was—"

"Answer!"

Tolliver hesitated. "It's the only explanation that came to mind, considering what I've seen of his attitude."

"Damn it, Edgar, you knew him!"

"Oh, yes. Thorne despised me, though I doubt he even remembers." He shrugged. "Was there something more to him, or did time soften your memories?"

"He had—" No. Tolliver could never understand. "We were friends. Not the way it sounds. I admired him greatly. He had a way about him. I thought he'd inspire the cadets."

"Yes, I'm sure the cadets will appreciate Arcvid lessons instead—"

"DISMISSED!"

This time, he didn't argue.

"Be seated." At every table, chairs scraped. I took my place at lunch. Jeff Thorne sat across, next to Midshipman Sandra Ekrit. His expression was carefully neutral. Whether it concealed a hangover, I couldn't tell. His hair was well brushed, his uniform clean and pressed.

Between bites I studied the florid face, searching for the young Thorne I remembered. Not yet thirty, he bore twenty extra pounds and a manner from which all gaiety had been extinguished.

I was ragged from sleepless hours interspersed with nightmares. Father had been in some of them. The morning's conversation with Sergeant Serenco had left a foul taste. Still, I made an effort to draw Thorne into conversation. At length, defeated, I lapsed into bitter silence, wishing I had never sent for him. Edgar Tolliver watched with barely concealed amusement.

A cadet hurried toward me, out of breath. "Cadet Kyle Drew reporting, sir. Mr. Kinders says, a call, from Cardiff."

I threw down my napkin, strode to the door, willing myself not to break into a gallop. "Annie?"

"It's me, Captain. Eddie Boss." The line whistled and crackled; the voice seemed light-years distant.

"What's wrong?"

"Today's the second day. She won't eat, just lies in bed cryin'." He sounded anxious. "I dunno—don't know if I should let her be or not."

"No, take her—" I paused. Where? To a hospital? Back to the dreaded clinic? "What does she want, Eddie?"

"Lie around all day feelin' sorry for herself, what she want!"

"She's had a rough time, Mr. Boss."

"Yeah, sir, but she not the only one. Time to think 'bout other stuff. Move on." He didn't sound sympathetic.

"Well . . ." I sighed. "Is she taking liquids?"

"Lotsa tea. Thassall she want."

"Wait another day. If she doesn't start eating, call a taxi and bring her to Academy. You know how to use the trains?"

"I ain' no—I'm not glitched, Captain." His voice betrayed injured dignity. "I can find out the schedule."

"Very well. Call if you need—want help." I rang off.

Tolliver raised an eyebrow. I shook my head. Nonetheless, I was worried. If Annie grew malnourished—

"Excuse me, sir."

"What is it, Ms. Ekrit?" My tone held an edge.

"As you ordered, I've been tutoring Cadet Stritz. His biweeklies are up."

"Very well." I tore at a roll.

"I was hoping, uh, that is . . ." She braced herself. "You confined me to base until his grades improved, sir. I thought . . . I mean, would you consider . . ."

"Don't we teach middies how to finish a sentence?" I shook my head. "Jeff, you had my nose against the bulkhead for an hour when I did that."

Thorne's voice was soft. "Yes, sir, but you weren't speaking to the Commandant at the time."

I scowled at Ms. Ekrit. "Until the cadet's grades improved, I said, and your manners."

"Yes, sir."

"Ask after his next biweeklies." Two weeks on base was nothing. Aboard ship, she might be confined to a tiny wardroom. "If his scores hold I'll let you off."

"Thank you, sir." If she felt any disappointment, she wisely concealed it.

After lunch Jeff Thorne casually pushed back his chair. "May I walk with you?"

"If you wish." We set out across the compound to Officers' Quarters.

He was silent awhile. "About last night, I seem to remember an awkward conversation."

"You hoped you wouldn't."

"If I was rude, I'm sorry."

"You were, but it was the liquor talking." I tried to sound agreeable.

"Let me tell you what wasn't the liquor." Thorne stopped, faced me. "Did BuPers mention that I'm up in five months?"

"Yes, but I knew you'd reenlist."

"I won't." His eyes met mine. "Time for a career change."

My tone was harsh. "Because you blew a chance at advancement?"

"No. Because—" His eyes clouded. "Never mind."

"Belay that!" I startled a passing cadet. "Why, Mr. Thorne?"

His tone was defiant. "'Reenlistment is at the sole decision of an individual officer, and no superior may attempt to force or influence his choice.' Section one hundred two, paragraph—"

"This is me! Nick Seafort!" A gaggle of cadets approached.

His expression soured. "Yes, the hero of—"

I shouted, "Do I look like a bloody hero?" The cadets gawked. I wheeled on them. "What do you joeys—"

Thorne's voice was brisk. "Run along, lads. This is a private conversation and you shouldn't be overhearing!"

"Aye aye, sir!" With hurried salutes they detoured and scurried off.

"I'm a fraud, Thorne! I blundered my way as Captain of *Hibernia*. On *Challenger*, a fish saved us. At Hope Nation I committed treason!" I slammed my fist into my thigh. "I hear enough of that guff in the holos, I won't have it from you!"

"Steady, Commandant." He spoke quietly.

"I won't have it!"

"All right, you're no hero." Seeing no one, he took my arm and led me off the path. "Easy, Mr. Seafort."

His voice was so like the middy I'd worshiped at Farside, I bit back a sob. "Sandra Ekrit, back there. She didn't like dining with cadets, so I grounded her. I have no restraint, Jeff. I need you to do what I cannot!"

He snorted. "She'll manage a couple of weeks confined—"

"You have no idea the bridges I burned to get you! Higbee will never forget. I actually threatened him, and he's my superior!"

"Good, he deserves it."

"You don't understand." I turned away once more.

"I understand you're near a nervous breakdown, sir."

My eyes darted to his, away again. "I'm fine. Never mind that."

"Come to my apartment, Mr. Seafort." It might have been an order. Numb, I let him lead the way.

Inside, he closed the door to his bedroom, but not before I saw the clothes strewn about. He rummaged in a cabinet, emerged with a bottle.

"Don't drink now, Mr. Thorne. Please."

"Not for me. For you." He poured a stiff shot of gin, added ice from the tiny cooler. "Sit." He handed me the glass.

I swirled it, took a sip, grimaced. "I'm all right." I waited for him to take a chair. "All right, I have no legal right to ask why you won't reenlist. But . . ." I brooded. "I need to know."

His wave took in himself, the untidy apartment. "I'm no good as an officer. Those stories we were raised on, of honor, gallantry. They don't describe the real Navy. I don't fit."

I said, "You were the finest officer I've ever known."

"That's goofjuice!"

The drink spilled over my hand as I slammed it on the table. "Do you have any idea what you meant to me?"

"All right, so you looked up to me. Misplaced hero worship. How can you forget the caning I got you?"

"The galley raid? What does that matter?"

He got to his feet, his expression bitter. "I've regretted that idiocy for years! I took you where I couldn't cover for you, betrayed you to—"

"Don't be a fool, Lieutenant." I busied myself blotting the table with a napkin, sipping what was left of my drink.

"Nick, whatever inspiration I offered you is long gone. My foolishness with Mrs. Duhaney proves that. So do my ratings at Callisto."

I nursed my drink, wondering how to reach him. "Outside, with the cadets just now. Why did you interrupt me?"

"You were going to—sorry, it's not my place to say."

"Say it."

"You were about to lash out at them, and they'd done nothing."

"So what? They were just cadets."

"You can't believe that!" He studied my face.

"Neither can you." I swallowed the dregs of my gin. "That's why I want you."

We sat in silence. After a time he stirred. "I wish I'd served with you, sir."

"You might have stopped me from damning myself. No, don't ask, I won't talk about it."

He leaned back, his voice tired. After a time he said, "What happened to our hopes?"

"They're victims of maturity." I stood. "Thanks for the drink. As you can see, I'm at my wit's end. I need you, Jeff."

"It's too late. Even if I wanted, I could never get another decent posting." He saw my eyes, went red. "I'm terribly sorry, I didn't mean it like that. A posting with you is all I could ask for. But I truly thought you called me down to retaliate for that old galley incident. I—it seems I was wrong."

"Please reenlist."

"I'll think about it, sir."

For once I knew to leave well enough alone.

17

Restless, I peered out the porthole. At least two other shuttles waited ahead of us for access to *Wellington's* locks. I sighed, dreading the endless conversation I'd face with politicians and brass, all denizens of Admiral Duhaney's "other" Navy.

Behind me the cadets fidgeted. Midshipman Tenere whispered to Johan Stritz and giggled. I fixed them with a laser glance, and they quieted instantly. "If I come to regret I brought you, I'll make you sorry!"

Robert Boland sat up straighter, still pale from his recent bout of nausea. Stritz and Arnweil stared at their laps. Jerence Branstead blushed. After a moment, Adam beckoned, and they slipped out of their seats to wander back to the large porthole.

I took a slow breath, tried to relax. It wasn't the middy's fault we were delayed. I tried to concentrate on my holozine, gave it up.

Why had I brought them to such an important ceremony? Had it really been necessary to give such a munificent reward to Branstead and Boland, our high achievers? A few words of praise, a week's freedom from kitchen and barracks chores, would have sufficed. What would my colleagues think of including untrained children in a state function?

No matter. My accepting the Commandancy had been a mistake. If I could figure how to abandon my post without disgracing the Navy, I'd resign in an instant. All I wanted now was to help Annie heal.

Our shuttle's turn came at last. As we crowded into the mated locks I tugged at my dress whites, straightened my tie. The hatch slid closed behind us.

This was a formal occasion; I cleared my throat, said into the speaker, "Captain Nicholas Seafort and party request permission to come aboard."

"Permission granted, sir. Welcome to U.N.S. *Wellington.*" The hatch slid open. "ATTENTION!"

A double row of sailors stiffened at their lieutenant's bellow. Several other officers resplendent in crisp whites came to attention, saluting smartly. Cadet Boland sucked in his breath at the spectacle. Jerence Branstead was less impressed; he'd spent nine months aboard *Victoria* on the way home from Hope Nation. He knew what lieutenants looked like.

"Lieutenant Hollis, sir. Welcome aboard." He gestured to the ladder.

"Captain Pritcher will stay on the bridge until the last of the mediamen board. Admiral Duhaney is with Senator Boland and the other guests in the lounge. Where shall I escort you?"

Not to the lounge, and the politicians. "I'll pay my respects to the Captain, if he'll see me."

"I'm sure he will, sir." He eyed Adam Tenere and the unexpected cadets, but his tone remained polite. "And, the rest of your, er, party?"

I couldn't risk sending them to the lounge; Lord God knew how the cadets might embarrass me, or Academy. And if Adam took it in mind to scamper around a corridor bend . . . "They'll come with me."

We trailed the lieutenant along a spotless corridor. The silent machinery, the unblemished decks, the hint of fresh oil in the recycled air all testified to *Wellington's* recent departure from Lunapolis shipyards. She'd completed her deep-space trials only two weeks ago.

While Hollis knocked at the bridge hatch I lined the cadets along the corridor bulkhead, out of the way. "Wait here until I'm through."

"Captain Seafort, sir." Hollis stood aside as I entered.

Captain Pritcher rose, a cold smile flitting across his sallow face. "Dismissed, Lieutenant. Captain Seafort, a pleasure to meet you."

I saluted; he was senior to me by a number of years. "Good afternoon, sir." My eyes greedily roamed the bridge. The huge simulscreen on the fore bulkhead blazed with the lights of a billion stars. The consoles blinked their steady reassurance.

"A rough trip aloft, Mr. Seafort?" He stared at the bruises that marked my encounter with the Crypsnbloods.

I blushed. "No, sir." Best not to say more.

His voice was flinty. "We'll start the speeches in an hour or so; everybody wants to have their say. Deputy Secretary-General Franjee will do the commissioning, but first we'll put the ship through her paces for the civilians."

"I'm sure they'll be impressed," I said.

"They'd better be, for what *Wellington* cost." His smile was bleak. "I have the crew drilling as smartly as can be expected, considering every man aboard is transferred from another ship."

Pritcher must have his hands full. Breaking in new hands was hard enough, but familiarizing an entire crew with the quirks of a new ship was a task I didn't envy him.

I searched for something to say. "Where will they send you, sir?" I already knew.

"We'll join the Home Fleet."

A coveted assignment. Pritcher and his officers would avoid the stultifying tedium of a long Fuse to a distant colony, and they'd never be more than a few days from shore leave.

"She seems a good ship, sir."

"Six banks of midships lasers, the latest model fusion drive. We'll be conducting a tour as part of the ceremonies." His unsmiling eyes met mine. "I suppose I could have someone escort you through the ship now, if you like."

I gave the expected reply. "No, sir, though I appreciate the offer. I'll wait."

"Very well. There are refreshments in the Level 2 lounge." It was a dismissal.

"Thank you, Captain. Good luck, and congratulations." He didn't bother to return my salute.

Now I had no choice but to join the politicians. Trailing a middy and cadets, I made my way down to the Level 2 lounge. Outside the hatch I paused. "Are you recovered, Mr. Boland?"

He blushed scarlet. "Yes, sir. The gravity helps a lot."

"Very well." I frowned at each of them in turn. "You're about to mingle with the top brass, so speak only in answer to a direct question. Don't offer any opinions, don't interrupt, and behave yourselves as gentlemen. Adam, keep them in line." I smoothed my jacket and went in.

"Ah, there you are, Nick." If Admiral Duhaney was put out by my recent escapades it didn't show in his tone. Then again, the drink in his hand may have been a mellowing influence. Though alcohol was contraband aboard a U.N.N.S. vessel, a major ceremony such as commissioning was an exception. After all there were civilians present and, more important, the media.

"Hello, sir."

"Let me introduce you to the Deputy SecGen. He's got a lock on the top spot if De Vala ever retires." He looked over my shoulder. "Cadets, hmm? Peculiar idea, bringing them." He squinted. "Is that Boland's son, by the wall? Now that's smart thinking, Nick!" He clapped me on the shoulder. "His father will be pleased."

My tone was stiff. "The boy earned it. His grades were—"

"Of course." Duhaney smiled. "That's the way." He patted my shoulder again.

A familiar voice, behind me. "Excuse me, sir."

I flared, "Now what?" Adam Tenere should have the sense not to bother me when I was with the Admiral.

The middy took a step back, forcing me to follow. His voice dropped. "Cadet Boland is nauseous again. I can escort him to the head and leave the others, or send him off by himself, or leave with all of them. I didn't know what—"

"Don't annoy me with—" I caught myself; it was a reasonable question. "I don't want you marching out with a flock of cadets, and you can't leave them unattended with the brass. There's a head just off the corridor; point Boland toward it and stay here with the others." I turned back to Admiral Duhaney. "The Boland boy scored first out of—"

"Oh, come along, let's meet Franjee. Over there, with McPhee from *Holoworld*, and the others."

I had no choice but to follow the Admiral to the cluster of civilians at the far bulkhead.

"Mr. Secretary, may I present Captain—"

"Seafort. I'd know you anywhere, even without your famous scar." The short, dark-skinned Deputy SecGen extended his hand. "Thanks to your exploits we should have met long ago, but I understand you're shy of publicity."

"Yes, sir, I—"

"Not that you managed to avoid it; you were plastered across the holos yet again, when you brought *Victoria* home. So, young man, tell me: when are we going to steer you into politics?" Others in his clique smiled. Several gave me appraising glances.

Not during this lifetime. Self-contempt or no, I wouldn't sink so far. I struggled for a polite answer. "My duty is to the Navy, sir."

"Yes, but enlistments end, and life goes on. When you're ready, talk to me, or Richard here. The Supranationalists could use you."

"I'll keep it in mind." Desperately, I seized on Senator Boland. "Good to see you, sir."

"And you, Commandant." As we moved away his eyes met mine, revealing nothing of his feelings.

I flushed. When last we'd spoken I'd threatened to resign if he so much as called my office. I searched for some appropriate, inane comment.

Richard Boland saved me the trouble. "She's a great ship, isn't she?" His gesture took in the spacious lounge. "I've often thought, if chance hadn't led me along another path, that I'd have wanted to serve in the Navy."

I tried not to show my scorn. Life wasn't a matter of chance, but hard work and perseverance. I'd dedicated myself to a Naval career from the time I was ten, devouring the holozines, studying my math, dreaming and planning with Jason. Had Boland truly wanted a Naval career, he could have done likewise.

I sought a peaceable reply. "At least you'll achieve your ambition through your son, sir."

"His ambition," Boland corrected. He smiled, but his eyes were sharp. "Quite a surprise to see him walk in with you. It would have been nice to know he was coming."

I stiffened. "I'm sure it would have." I'd be happy to notify a cadet's parents when he was assigned to travel. The day hell froze.

Boland's tone was still affable. "By the way, Commandant, that odd personnel matter has been settled."

For a moment I thought he was referring to my problems with Jeff Thorne, but that made no sense. It must be Darwin Sleak, Lord God rest his soul. "He's had decent burial?"

"At Lunapolis." He hesitated. "You handled that well. A mysterious death would have catapulted you onto the front pages, though few in your position would object to that. Calling Duhaney was a smooth way to handle it."

It had been Tolliver's idea. On my own, I'd have blundered into a scandal. "I'm out of my depth in such things."

A new voice intervened. "Ah, Richard, keeping our young hero to yourself?"

"No, Brett, just chatting." Boland moved slightly, made a place for Senator Wyvern.

"They'll want interviews, Captain," Wyvern's chuckle held a hint of malice. "The media can get at Franjee anytime; if they don't call him, he seeks them out. You're fresh meat."

"Not if I can help it."

"Ah, but you can't. That's my point." His manner changed subtly. "On that subject, I have some advice for you. Let's step outside for a moment. Somewhere quiet."

I checked my watch. "They'll be starting in a few minutes."

"And we'll be done by then." He guided me to the hatch. I would have shaken him off, but I'd already made too many enemies for Academy's good.

The corridor seemed inordinately quiet, after the babble of the crowded reception. We wandered toward the corridor bend. I stopped. My cadets were still in the lounge supervised only by Adam, and Lord God knew what he was capable of. I sighed; I never should have brought them. "Advice, you said?"

"Yes." Wyvern's smile faded, and something hard took its place. "You know, the mediamen will press you with questions; you've avoided them too long."

"I'll do my best—"

"They'll ask about your illustrious career, your amazing escapes."

I shook my head. What was his point? "I still don't—"

"They might ask about your lunatic wife slumming in New York—"

"Senator!"

"—and the trannie sailor she prongs while you play the martinet at Academy."

The corridor lurched. My knuckles ached. I stared unseeing, realized that when I'd missed his jaw I'd slammed my fist into the bulkhead. Wyvern waved me away as he backed off. "Don't try that again, Seafort."

"You bastard!" My face was white.

"Better prepare for it, boy. Or maybe they'll ask why you were skulking the streets pretending you're a transpop instead of attending to your duty. Find any nice trannie bitches down there?"

I pinned him against the bulkhead. "Wyvern, I'll kill you!"

"But they'd still ask."

"They don't know about those things!"

"Ah, my boy, I agree. The point is, they will. I can guarantee it."

My rage withered slowly to defeat. I sagged, released his collar. "Why? What do you want of me?"

"Hardly a thing. Just one report, discarded."

"What are you talking about?"

"Your quartermaster, and that fool of a lieutenant who won't let the matter drop. Tell him to forget about it."

I gaped. "Sergeant Serenco? Tolliver? How does that concern you?"

"That's another matter you may forget."

"The man is stealing us blind! Why should I let him get away with—"

"It's a political matter."

"Tell me, damn you!"

His voice came as a hiss. "Because he's my nephew! My niece should never have married him, but now he's family. I'll see to it the loss is covered in next year's appropriation."

"I won't have a thief go unpunished!"

His face turned ugly. "You'd damn well better, or your wife and her lover will be the celebrities of the day!"

My fingers itched to close around his neck. Oh, Annie. For your sake, look what I must do.

No! Get thee behind me, Satan.

"Do your worst, Wyvern!" I turned toward the lounge.

"I will. It will destroy you, and of course her. And Serenco will still get off; I have enough influence to fix that."

I stalked down the corridor, slowed before I reached the bend. Annie, forgive me. I can't let him do it.

"What if I let the matter be?" My voice was unsteady.

"Your word that you'll take no action on my beloved nephew, in return for mine that I won't leak the story. Don't give me that look, Commandant. I'm a politician; if my promise wasn't good, nobody would ever deal."

I could hardly hear myself speak. "All right."

"It's arranged, then?" He knew better than to offer his hand.

"Yes." Soon, Annie. The moment I reached groundside, I would resign. Then Wyvern would have no reason to destroy my wife. I doubted he'd do it out of spite; he was too clever a politician to waste his power. I felt a strange relief, now that my course was decided.

I'd been concerned it would be a slight on the Navy to resign so soon after I'd been appointed Commandant. Now, if I stayed, I'd be nothing but a liability. I'll come home, love. At long last.

Almost light-headed, I headed for the bar seeking refreshment, anything that would remove the taste of our conversation.

"Ladies and gentlemen, distinguished guests, your attention, please." A lieutenant in crisp whites at the hatch, his every word recorded by two mediamen with holocameras. The cabin quieted. "On behalf of Captain Pritcher, we welcome you to U.N.S. *Wellington*. The commissioning will take place on the bridge, but first we invite you to observe several Naval exercises."

He paused. "The first will be a Battle Stations drill. You may observe from the engine room or from Level 1, near the bridge. The crew has not been told the order or timing of these maneuvers."

I corraled my cadets, shepherded them with the other guests to the ladder. Robert Boland's expression was strained. I leaned close, caught the acrid whiff of vomit. "Are you all right, boy?" The last thing we needed was for him to make a spectacle of himself.

He grimaced. "Yes, sir, I think that was the last of it. I'm sorry for the trouble. I'll take the pills next time." He looked away.

I said gruffly, "It's all right, boy. I've been sick too."

He hesitated. "Do I get demerits, sir?"

"One, for even asking." The boy should know better, and if he didn't—

We climbed the ladder, filed along the Level 1 corridor behind the Deputy SecGen. I cleared my throat. "Canceled, Mr. Boland. But mind your manners."

"Aye aye, sir."

Alarms shrieked. "Battle Stations!" Captain Pritcher, on ship's speakers. "All hands to Battle Stations!" I blanched, even knowing it was just the anticipated drill. Mediamen aimed their holocameras at midshipmen sprinting to their assigned posts at gunnery, in the comm room, on the bridge. Scant seconds later the first ratings raced up the ladder to the laser control compartment.

A middy dived through the bridge hatchway seconds before the hatch slammed shut. *Wellington's* bridge was now an impenetrable fortress. Captain Pritcher silenced the alarms, put his caller on shipwide frequency.

"Aft lock reporting secure, sir!"

"Engine room secure, sir! Full power available!"

"Hydroponics secure, sir! Compartment is sealed from ship's air."

Throughout the great warship, emergency hatches slid shut, isolating each section of the vessel for the safety of all. If a sector were penetrated, it alone would decompress.

"Lasers up and ready, sir!" Now, the ship could fight back.

"Comm room fully manned." We could call for help.

One by one the remaining compartments called in: recycling, damage control, galley, sickbay. When the last confirmation came I stole a surreptitious glance at my watch. Not bad, for a new crew. And response times would improve as she settled in to duty, if Pritcher was worth his salt.

"What do you think, Mr. Duhaney?" Deputy SecGen Franjee looked to the Admiral.

"Very smartly done, sir." Duhaney sounded confident. "Twenty seconds faster than last week." Odd; I'd been standing just across from the Admiral and hadn't seen him check the time.

A few moments passed, then Captain Pritcher's dry voice. "All hands stand down, except laser control." He cleared his throat. "Our next demonstration will take place in the laser control compartment on Level 1."

Dutifully, we crowded into the laser room. It bristled with consoles and screens. Two rows of alert ratings, uniforms gleaming, waited at their places. An officer stepped forward. "Good afternoon, Mr. Franjee and other distinguished guests. We're about to conduct a laser firing drill, held regularly on any ship of the line. Today we will fire at real, not simulated, targets. They'll be released by ship's officers from our two launches."

Perhaps the boats would be manned by middies, overjoyed at the rare opportunity to command. Or perhaps, with the brass watching, Captain Pritcher had put more seasoned lieutenants in charge.

The officer keyed his caller. "Laser compartment to bridge. Ready, sir."

"Very well, lasers are activated." A green light flashed at the laser console; the Captain had released the safeties that normally prohibited ship's lasers from firing. "Mr. Johanski, Sanders, begin, please!"

I peered over the tech's shoulder. Live fire drills were a nuisance to set up, and the vessels releasing targets always risked a laser tech misreading them for a target in the heat of competition. On the other hand, a real hit was more satisfying to the gunner than a simulated one, thereby raising his learning curve.

The first target accelerated toward *Wellington*. The tech in front of me dialed up his magnification, graphed the trajectory on his trackball.

With only two launchers releasing targets, the crews knew there would be only two points of origin, and therefore the approximate trajectories. That meant—

"Commence fire!"

All was still except for the sporadic slap of hands on the fire pads. Because of the watching brass the techs were unusually restrained. No muttered curses, cries of satisfaction, calls of encouragement, broke the silence.

From time to time an alarm blared as a missile cleared the ship's defenses. The puter's impersonal voice announced simulated damage. "Penetration amidships, Level 2! Hull damage to hold, port side!"

The incoming salvos became more ragged, degenerating into sporadic individual fire, much harder for *Wellington's* defenders to track. I nodded my approval; Captain Pritcher had made it a fair test. Many Captains would have set up an easy drill with the Admiral and the media watching. But the exercise simulated missile and laser fire, not attacks by the fish that were our most likely enemy.

"Port bow lasers destroyed!" An unlucky hit. The port bow laser console went black as the ship's puter disabled it.

"Two are on me, Charlie, get the son of a bitch!"

The gunnery officer hurried across the aisle to stand behind the anxious young tech. I grinned. This was more like it. Laser fire was a cooperative effort; two consoles working together could get a crossfire on an incoming, and take it out while protecting each other's flanks. It was tense work, and the tech's cry for help was artlessly natural. Had I been his gunnie, though, I'd have stood back. A lieutenant staring over his shoulder would only make the sailor more nervous.

The perspiring tech's fingers danced across his console. The electronic circuitry under his hands was of awesome complexity, yet all boiled down to human, not putronic intelligence.

Puters were intelligent, puters were faster, but only a human could make a good decision on insufficient data while a possibly lethal object streaked across his screen. We could program puters to recognize any known threat, but what about the unknown? What would Darla, *Hibernia's* puter, have made of the fish that emerged from behind the derelict *Telstar?* Would *Hibernia* have survived to make her way home with the news?

Speed wasn't everything.

Judgment was.

Five bells chimed; the lights dimmed momentarily and brightened. The tech I was watching slapped his firing button on a target in the crosshairs, let out his breath in a long sigh of satisfaction.

"All consoles cease fire!" The gunnery lieutenant turned to the politicians and officers crowded in the laser compartment. "In the exercise you just witnessed, the intensity of incoming fire approximated a full fleet engagement. *Wellington* took only eleven hits, while destroying two hundred twelve incoming missiles." A patter of applause interrupted his speech.

As the visitors filed out of the cabin I focused on the silent consoles. Simulated or no, it was the last time I would see a ship under fire.

Secretary Franjee beamed. "What do you think, Commandant? You've seen more action than most."

Caught off guard, I stammered some meaningless words of praise. The Secretary stepped into the corridor. I hesitated at the hatch, stole one more look at the techs and their consoles. True, there'd been over two hundred incoming. But eleven hits would have crippled *Wellington*, perhaps destroyed her.

Though I wouldn't tell the SecGen, our transpop crewmen on *Challenger* had performed better, after our endless simulation drills. Captain Pritcher's dry voice echoed in the speakers. "The final exercise will take place in the engine room." Senator Boland sighed, grinned ruefully at Franjee. Captain Pritcher had the dignitaries trooping about from stern to aft. I beckoned to my waiting cadets.

We followed the others down to Level 2, waited for the civilians to proceed.

Alarms shrieked. "General Quarters! All hands to General Quarters!"

Once again, the thud of running feet. We pressed to the side of the ladder; a rating grinned as he hurtled past, two steps at a time. General Quarters was but one stage of readiness below Battle Stations; emergency hatches remained open and the Captain didn't release the laser safeties, but all crewmen dashed to their duty stations forthwith, and remained there for the duration.

"Just part of the program," Admiral Duhaney told the Deputy SecGen. His tone was reassuring.

"How can you know?" demanded Senator Wyvern. A good question. A General Quarters drill was no different from the real thing. The call must be instantly obeyed; only the Captain knew why he sounded the signal.

"I'll check, if you'd like." Duhaney was eager to pacify his constituents. "If it isn't a drill, I'll have Pritcher announce it on the caller immediately. You gentlemen go on down to Level 3." He trotted back up the ladder like an obliging middy.

He couldn't have reached the bridge before the speaker came to life. "All hands stand down!" Wyvern sighed, muttered under his breath. I grinned maliciously; maybe Pritcher would give the Senator a heart attack. We reached Level 3, trudged past the recycling chambers to the engine room.

"FIRE IN THE RECYCLERS! ALL HANDS TO FIRE STATIONS!" The Captain's tone was taut. "Break out Level 3 hoses!"

I shoved Kyle Drew out of the way as fire crews raced past, their faces grim. Corridor hatches slid shut, isolating the endangered section. A whir and a click indicated the overhead air vents had closed, isolating each section to its own air. Automatically I scanned the bulkheads for canned air storage bins.

Senator Boland nudged me in the ribs. "Isn't Pritcher overdoing it a bit?"

My voice was tense. "If it's a drill." A mediaman shouldered me aside for a better shot of a crewman dragging the bulkhead hose along the corridor. Adam Tenere sucked in his breath, drew back a fist. I managed to snag his arm. "Easy, boy."

"He shoved you, sir!"

I found Adam's outrage reassuring. "He needed to film and I was in his way."

"But you're Captain!"

The hose buckled, sprang to life as *Wellington's* puter opened the valves. I patted Adam's shoulder, smiled. "The contact rules apply to Naval personnel, not groundsiders."

"I know, sir." The middy took a deep breath, forced himself to relax. Then he stepped forward casually, as if to watch the crewmen at work. He planted his back squarely in front of the mediaman's holocamera.

I frowned, but held my peace. In a day or so none of this would matter; I'd be home with Annie.

A middy appeared at the hatch, thumbed the ship's caller. "Recycling chamber to bridge. No sign of fire, sir."

The Captain's voice was dry. "Very well, stand down."

The corridor hatches slid open. Our party of politicians paused to watch the crewmen fold their hoses. One crewman muttered to his mate, "Why don't he just pipe Abandon Ship and get us outa here?" I pretended not to hear.

Ten minutes later we gathered in the outer chamber of the engine room for the last exercise.

The Captain's dry voice came over the speakers. "Ladies and gentlemen, here on the bridge our officers will calculate a Fuse to Vega. We'll copy the data to your engine-room screens. When calculations are confirmed, we will ready *Wellington* for Fusion." He paused. "Those of you with commitments at home will be relieved to know we will not actually complete the Fuse."

The politicians laughed dutifully. A trip to Vega would involve a Fuse of months, with only occasional stops for nav checks.

"Engine Room, prepare to Fuse."

"Aye aye, sir." The Chief Engineer's response was immediate. "Bring Three on-line, reduce all auxiliary output." Engine-room ratings worked their consoles while sailors below watched the drive for signs of trouble.

Secretary Franjee broke off a conversation with a man from Holoworld. "What's happening, Mr. Seafort?"

I pointed to the console. "Right now the Chief is bringing full power on-line to prepare for Fuse. On the bridge they're running nav coordinates."

The mediaman asked, "How do you know what they're doing?"

"For one thing, the calculations show on that screen." I pointed.

"Why can't they run the calculations down here?" the Secretary asked.

"I suppose they could, sir." It would save middies hours of dread under the Captain's stern eye. But calculations were done from the bridge; that was the Navy way. After all, the Pilot's place was on the bridge and he was responsible for the accuracy of the Fuse.

Figures flashed across the screen. Two levels above, a midshipman sweated at his console, no doubt aware of the watching brass.

The puter could run all our calculations faster than any human hand. But the Navy's first rule was: never trust the machinery. All nav calculations, all safety readouts, were confirmed by the officers on watch. Too many lives were at stake to risk the vagaries of malfunctioning circuits.

Even massive built-in redundancy couldn't protect a ship against glitches in programming, such as we'd found on *Hibernia*.

"I have coordinates, ma'am." In the speaker, the young middy's voice sounded confident.

Mr. Franjee checked his watch. "Now what, Mr. Seafort?"

"He's passing them to the Pilot. They'll be done in a moment, sir." I tried to sympathize with the Secretary's frustration. All he saw was flashing lights, figures that meant nothing. The Captain would have been wiser to eliminate this drill.

"Pilot?" The Captain's dry tone.

"Confirmed to four decimal places, sir."

"Very well. Harlan?"

The puter. "A match to five decimal places, Captain."

"Very well."

I said, "Now, they'll feed the coor—"

The figures flashed onto our consoles. Captain Pritcher rasped, "All hands, prepare to Fuse!"

"It's just a simulated Fuse, so they won't actually—"

The Chief Engineer roared, "Prepare for Fuse!" He punched in a code on his console. A green light flashed, indicating the Fusion safeties were disabled. He entered Fusion codes.

I pictured the actions on *Wellington's* unseen bridge. The Captain would check the coordinates one final time. His hand would hover over the screen. Then, were we actually to Fuse, his hand would trace a line down his screen to the BEGIN FUSE position.

A bell chimed. "Engine room, Fuse!"

Secretary Franjee looked alarmed. "I thought you said they wouldn't—"

As the Chief slapped the go-pad, machinery hummed and the lights dimmed slightly. "Engine room to bridge. Fusion drive is ignited!"

"It's just a simulation, sir. Though a very realistic one."

N-waves danced on the small screen, next to lines showing expected output. Techs at the nearby consoles struggled to match the two lines exactly. Such simulations were used routinely in training.

"Stations, report!"

"N-wave generation within parameters!"

"Main turbine, no overheat."

"Pumping, normal and no overheat."

Mr. Franjee shifted from foot to foot. "All very well, but how long does it go on?"

"I'm sure they'll stop in a moment."

"Temperature beginning to climb, Chief."

"What's your wave at?"

"Fifty-five percent."

"Get me a match at sixty."

The Secretary looked mystified. I said quietly, "He's matching output to intended coordinates. The simulation's set at sixty percent generation, that is, sixty percent of the N-wave strength necessary to Fuse."

The Chief's eyes never left his console. "That's correct, sir, except that it's not a simulation. We're generating real waves."

I staggered as if struck. "You're what?"

"All today's exercises are real, no simulations. We're holding the wave output down to sixty percent. Don't worry, if we overheat I can shut—"

"Real waves?"

The Secretary cleared his throat. "Captain Seafort, what does—"

I waved him silent. "Chief, disengage your engines, flank! You're caterwauling!"

"Sorry, I have no idea what that means."

"Broadcasting N-waves. You'll attract fish!"

His tone was soothing. "It's only for a few minutes, sir. Ships Fuse all the time, I'm sure it won't—"

"Give me your caller!"

"Begging your pardon, sir, I can't just now. We're engaged."

Senator Wyvern watched with amusement. "Problems, Seafort?"

"Yes, I—" No point in explaining, especially to him.

Pritcher. "Engine Room, go to sixty-five, hold the wave line for ten minutes, then disengage."

The Chief took up his caller. "Aye aye, sir. Sixty-five percent confirmed."

I thrust through the crowd, slapped open the corridor hatch. "Excuse me. Adam, watch the bloody cadets!"

Senator Boland gave me room to pass. "Captain, where are you going?"

"Topside!" I strode down the corridor, increased my pace to a sprint before I reached the bend. I tore up the ladder to Level 2, circled the well.

Abandoned on *Challenger* light-years from home, our caterwauling had attracted the deadly fish. On Hope Nation's Orbiting Station I'd deliberately set disabled ships to run their drives at low power, to summon all the fish I could to our remote outpost before I blew the Station.

Wellington was doing likewise, in home system.

I pounded up the steps, tore along the corridor to the bridge. The hatch was sealed; I hammered on the tough alumalloy.

The camera swiveled; after a moment the hatch slid open. A young lieutenant sat bent over her console to the right of the Captain's chair, conferring with a middy.

"Captain Seafort reporting. Permission to enter bridge!"

Pritcher swiveled. "Granted."

Admiral Duhaney was perched on the edge of the Captain's console. "What's the matter, Seafort?"

"Shut off the drives before you call the fish!"

Pritcher's face remained expressionless, except for one lifted eyebrow. "I beg your pardon? Was that an order?"

Damn it, the man was senior. "No, sir, of course not." I tried to make my words conciliatory. "Perhaps you don't realize fish can hear your N-waves. If you generate without Fusing—"

"Yes, I know, your report calls it caterwauling. An interesting concept. But even if it's proved, a few minutes test won't call Fish from—"

I wheeled. "Admiral, for God's sake. Have him turn off the engines! You have civilians aboard."

"Seafort, you're overreaching." Duhaney's eyes were cold.

"If you'd been there, seen what they can do—"

"Behave yourself!" The Admiral came to his feet, crossed the few feet between us. His finger jabbed at my chest. "You had your chance for a ship, we almost begged you to take one! *Wellington* is Pritcher's. He's in charge."

"Aye aye, sir. But do you understand that the waves we're throwing are exactly the ones I proposed in the automated bomb to attract fish?"

The Admiral paused. "Exactly?"

"Well, the fish respond even more violently to skewed N-waves than true. But—"

Captain Pritcher snapped, "Our waveline is true. Look at the graph!" With an effort, he made his voice more civil. "Besides, Seafort, we're in home system. Our ships Fuse from here to one colony or another every week, if not every day. One short test won't make a difference. With the Deputy SecGen aboard, I want it to look right."

My shoulders slumped; it was useless. "Yes, sir. As the Admiral said, you're in charge. Sorry I burst in on you."

He sounded only slightly mollified. "Very well."

Duhaney was tentative. "Harry, do you think maybe we should . . ."

"I'll wrap it up shortly, sir. I just wanted them to see how well our techs can hold a line."

"Whatever you say; you have the conn."

His authority confirmed, Pritcher could afford to be magnanimous. "Engine Room, prepare for Defuse." He replaced the caller. "Oh, by the way, Captain Seafort, my lieutenant tells me you've met."

The young woman looked up from her console.

I whispered, "Arlene?"

Her voice was shy. "Lieutenant Sanders reporting, sir." Our eyes met, locked.

Pritcher's dry voice cut into my daze. "Lieutenant, please escort Captain Seafort back to the lounge."

"Aye aye, sir." She rose at once.

Like an automaton, I saluted Pritcher and the Admiral, followed Arlene from the bridge. The hatch slid closed behind us.

Her soft voice seemed hesitant. "Good to meet you again, sir." Automatically, we moved to the ladder, started down to Level 2.

The speaker crackled. "Engine Room, Defuse. Ladies and gentlemen, that concludes our exercise."

"Arlene . . ." I swallowed hard. "How have you been?"

"I've done fine, sir, though for a while I thought I'd never get beyond middy."

I looked to either side; the Level 2 corridor was deserted. Tentatively, I held out a hand. Shyly, she put hers in it.

I had been so young, so hopeful, so innocent.

I moved closer, smelled the fresh clean scent of her hair.

So young.

Sergeant Swopes growled, "Full inspection this afternoon. Word is the Commandant himself may take it. One crease out of place, one speck of dust, and I'll stuff whoever is responsible in the recycler! Is that understood?"

"Yes, sir!" Our chorus was immediate. Despite his warning I wasn't worried. By now we were seasoned second-year cadets, and knew the tricks to passing an inspection. More exciting were the rumors that some hundred cadets had been chosen for promotion. I hoped against hope I would be one of them, but knew how unlikely that was.

Academy had no set graduation date. A cadet remained under the tutelage of his sergeants until he was deemed ready, no matter how long it took. When we took the oath we'd been warned that we could stay cadets for our entire five-year enlistment, and there were rumors it had actually happened, though no one knew of such a case.

After Sarge left, we set about the boring task of getting our dorm ready: mopping, dusting, cleaning ourselves and our environment. Corporal Tolliver strutted about giving unnecessary orders, while making sure not to neglect his own work. He would suffer with the rest of us if our dorm were cited.

As per a long-standing arrangement I did our boots while Arlene made both our beds; I normally made my own, but we relied on her superior skills for the starched creases of an inspection, while I had the knack of turning the toe of a boot into an ebony mirror.

Hours later, I tugged at my jacket one last time, smoothed back my hair yet again. At the hatch, Robbie Rovere called out, "They just left Armstrong, headed this way!"

"Get ready!" Tolliver's warning was unnecessary. We took our places in two lines, waiting to stiffen to attention as the hatch opened.

"Good luck!" Arlene made the crossed fingers sign; I grinned tightly as I replied in kind.

"ATTENTION!" Tolliver's bellow rang through the dorm. We jumped, backs ramrod-straight, eyes front.

Sergeant Swopes entered first, saw us already in place, stepped aside.

I sucked in my breath. It *was* Commandant Kearsey. Lord God help us if anything went wrong.

His inspection was thorough. Running his hand over Donover's locker, he rubbed his fingers as if brushing off dust, but said nothing. The inspection party disappeared into the head, reemerged shortly.

Kearsey nodded to Sarge. "Very well, Mr. Swopes. Passed."

"Thank you, sir."

The Commandant paused at the hatch. "Some of you may have heard scuttlebutt that a promotion list is out. It isn't." A collective, almost inaudible sigh swept the room. "And it won't be, until Free Hour this evening. You'll find it in the corridor." With that, he left.

Silence held for a full half minute. Then the barracks erupted with cheers. Robbie pounded my shoulder, hugged Arlene. "Some of us have to be on it! Maybe me, or you. We'll be out of here!"

"Don't get your hopes—" It was too late. Robbie cartwheeled down the aisle, narrowly missing Tolliver, who aimed a halfhearted kick in his direction.

The day passed in an agony of anticipation. I dreamed through

Nav class, earned a sharp rebuke from Mr. Reeves. After that I did my best to concentrate; even if my name was on the list it could easily be removed.

Dinner came and went. If I ate at all, I had no recollection. Milk, perhaps. Or possibly the napkin.

Sergeant Swopes appeared not to notice our odd behavior. It must have taken effort, as Donover dropped a cup of coffee on himself, and Robbie Rovere tripped noisily over his chair.

"Think it's posted yet?" Arlene matched her step to mine.

"Free Hour. Another hour and a half."

"I know when Free Hour is," she said, nettled. She moved on ahead.

"Dumb, Seafort." Tolliver's tone was mocking. "You blew it. Maybe she had the hots for you!"

I whirled, shoved him against the bulkhead. "Watch your mouth! She's a bunkie!"

"Get your hands off—"

Robbie's voice was cold. "I heard that, Tolliver. You're disgusting."

Tolliver's look swiveled from one to the other of us. "Easy, joeys. I didn't mean it." He pushed my hands away. "Watch it, or Sarge'll see you."

I didn't care if I took demerits for disrespect to a corporal. Even by barracks standards, Tolliver had been obscene. Arlene Sanders and I were bunkmates, closer than even brother and sister. The thought of pronging her made my stomach churn. How could I? We shared a dorm, even a shower.

Slowly my anger dissipated. I smiled sourly, sought a reply. "Forget about Sarge. Just hope I don't tell Sanders." Arlene's prowess at hand combat was formidable.

Back at the dorm we spread out our homework, as usual preferring our beds to the study rooms. By unspoken understanding, Sergeant Swopes didn't disturb us during study hour, and we were free to assume whatever relaxed posture we wished. I usually curled up on my side, holo in front of me. Some sat cross-legged on their bunks, others lounged on the deck. Robbie Rovere usually lay on the deck, legs up across his bed.

Though all was quiet, I doubted that much study actually took place. For my own part, I gave up after half an hour, switched off the holo.

I knew I wouldn't be graduated just yet; I hadn't scored well in the last round of tests. But even if I stayed, it meant new bunkmates, perhaps even a new sergeant, as depleted dorms were consolidated and merged.

At last the bell chimed, signaling Free Hour. Two cadets dashed for the hatch. Others stood more nonchalantly, stretched, wandered out to the corridor as if for a walk.

I lay on my bunk, arm over my eyes, depressed. Sooner or later I would pass the postings on the way to class, take a look. There was no hurry.

"Coming, Nicky?"

I uncovered my face. "You go ahead. Maybe later."

She sat on my bunk, slipped on her crisp gray jacket. "I'm scared. Let's look together."

I snorted. "You scared? Right." Arlene Sanders took no guff from any joey in the barracks. Still, once, back in the Training Fuser, she had lost her nerve. Maybe it was possible. "Okay."

I got up, joined her in a stroll to the list posted on the corridor bulkhead. Cadets from several barracks pushed and shoved their way through. Someone whooped.

We shouldered into the crowd. I peered at the two columns, too far away to see anything useful. Someone jostled. I lashed out with my elbow.

"Easy joeys, take your turn!" Midshipman Thorne's voice commanded obedience, and the pushing and shoving lessened. By unspoken agreement we formed ourselves into lines; those in front scanned the list, turned away crestfallen or with unconcealed joy.

Corporal Tolliver was several places ahead of us. He reached the list, ran his finger down the column. He froze, turned slowly. I tried to read his face. He took off his cap, flung it down the corridor against the bulkhead. His grin made him seem almost human. "Yes! I'm out of here, Seafort!"

Arlene's voice was flat. "Congratulations."

Tolliver didn't seem to hear. He ran to the bulkhead, scooped up his cap, flung it again. It sailed past Mr. Thorne's nose, but the middy just smiled. "Careful, Tolliver. You still have Last Night to get through."

"Yes, sir." The prospect of the traditional hazing didn't seem to phase him.

The boy at the head of our line turned. Robbie Rovere. His lip trembled. He made a manful effort, lost his battle. Quickly he wiped a tear with his sleeve. "I didn't make it."

"Oh, Robbie." I sought a consolation. "We'll be together, anyway."

"Yeah." He scuffed the deck. "Maybe next time, huh?" He turned away abruptly, but Arlene's hand darted out, pulled him close. She threw an arm around his shoulder. "You're okay, joey. Kearsey's a blind old fool, everyone knows that."

Lord Jesus. I jabbed Arlene in the ribs. If anyone heard . . .

"You'll make it next time," she said.

"Thanks." Robbie twisted loose, hurried toward the dorm. He almost blundered into Midshipman Jenks, come to watch the comedy. Annoyed, the middy thrust him away.

Only two cadets separated us from our fate; we pushed forward until it was our turn. Arlene's finger ran down the list, reaches the S's. A small sound escaped her.

I said, "You made it!" I threw my arms around her, danced for joy.

She whimpered, turned it into a laugh. "Oh, Nicky, I was so frightened!"

"I'll bet you were the first they picked." I pounded her back, grinning like a fool.

"Move it, you two!" Someone yanked at my arm.

I retreated, but Arlene held me back. "Aren't you even going to look, Nicky?"

"What's the point?" To please her, I searched the list again. "There's no way I—"

My name.

Dumbfounded, I fell back from the list. "I'm—Lord God, I made it!" No, it had to be a mistake. I thrust back into the crowd, looked once more. "Seafort, Nicholas E." I scanned it again, unbelieving. What miracle was this?

"I made middy." It sounded preposterous. I eased my way out of the crowd, passed Jeff Thorne. As I did so Midshipman Jenks stuck out his foot, and I would have gone down if Thorne hadn't caught me.

Back in the dorm I fell onto my bed, raised my hand, inspected the gray wool of my jacket. Now I would trade it for blue. I propped myself up on an arm. "Hey. What was the effective date?"

Sanders grinned. "Go back and look for yourself. I made your bed, what else do you want?"

I sighed, swung my feet off the bed.

"Tomorrow, noon."

"Really?" I hadn't imagined it would be so soon.

Her tone grew wary. "It means tonight is Last Night."

All midshipmen and officers hazed cadets; it was part of the system. But hazing on Last Night could be merciless. I swallowed a foreboding. Whatever they did, by tomorrow it would be over.

Nine in our dorm were to graduate, but the mood was subdued. Friendships would be broken, familiar bunkies exchanged for the unknown. I found myself wishing my name weren't on the list. I felt shame for my cowardice.

They came for us after Lights Out.

Flashlights searched out our faces. Led by Jenks, the middies hauled Reston and Lorca out of bed, ordered them into the corridor. We waited, most of us awake, straining to pierce the silence of the night. Perhaps, in the distance, I heard someone cry out. I couldn't be sure.

An hour passed and I began to doze.

Arlene screamed. I flung myself upright. She thrashed in her bunk, trying to free herself from the drenched sheets. Chunks of ice skittered across the deck. A grinning middy kicked the bucket across the aisle, pulled at Arlene's soaking top.

"You bastards!" I jumped out of bed, shoved the middies aside. "Leave her alone!" I was wearing only my shorts.

Someone caught my arm. I swung and missed; the middy twisted my arm behind my back.

Arlene sobbed in fright and humiliation. I lashed out with my bare foot, caught Jenks in the shin. "You frazzing asshole!"

"What a mouth on that one!" Jenks picked up the empty bucket, plopped it on my head. I shook it off. "Let's teach him manners." The middy glanced around. "Into the head."

Some brave soul muttered, "Leave him alone!"

Jenks wheeled, his flashlight searching. "Louder, please?" No one answered.

Two middies dragged me kicking into the head. They were bigger and heavier; I couldn't pull loose. Pinned against the sink, I awaited my fate.

Jenks paused at the hatchway. "Corporal Tolliver, join us."

Hazing or no, it was an order and Tolliver had no choice. He appeared in the hatchway, tugged at his shorts. "Yes, sir?"

"Just a moment." Jenks was curt. "Hold on to little Nicky," he told my captors, turning on the sink tap full blast. "Manners, Seafort.

You can't be a middy without knowing manners." He held the bar of soap as they forced my head down, pawed at my mouth.

My struggles did me no good. Finally, bruised and humiliated, I held still, tolerated the foul rasp of the soap.

Jenks was thorough in his ministrations. He paused only when two of his henchmen appeared in the hatchway with a hot water bottle. He pointed to Tolliver, whispered to a crony. They seized the cadet corporal, dragged him unceremoniously into a toilet stall. I gagged, tried to spit soap, had my head dunked for my pains.

Behind me there echoed a cry of anguish.

My new uniform seemed strange and out of place, though nothing but the color had changed. They moved us immediately to a new dorm; naturally we middies couldn't bunk with mere cadets. Youngsters who only yesterday were our friends saluted self-consciously; we responded with equal embarrassment.

Few middies were assigned to Academy itself; most of us were to be posted elsewhere. We waited our destiny with trepidation, and as days passed more of us left for coveted ships of the line. Arlene and I were among those who remained.

Jeff Thorne stopped by one day. As a middy posted to Farside, he bunked in the wardroom, not with us. "You survived Last Night."

"Barely." At times I could still taste the soap.

"I'm sorry. Jenks is an ass, but he's a senior ass."

"It's not your fault, sir."

"Jeff, now."

I grinned shyly. "Yes, si—it's hard to change."

"I remember." He put out his hand. "Tomorrow, I'm off to *Targon.* I came to wish you luck. You too, Sanders."

I shook hands. "Thanks. You—" I hesitated. It didn't matter; Arlene was a bunkie. "You meant a lot to me, Mr. Thorne."

His tone was gruff. "I wish we could have done more. We never got to the gravitrons."

"No one ever does." We smiled.

"As for the rest, I'm sorry." He clapped me on the shoulder, and was gone.

Our orders came two days later. I was to go to *Helsinki,* Arlene to *Freiheit.* We would join our ships at Earthport Station, after four days leave in Lunapolis.

Leave? We stared at each other. For two years we'd been shepherded to meals, to barracks, to exercise, to haircuts. We had barely an hour of our own.

Now we were midshipmen, granted our majority by statute of the General Assembly itself. While civilians of our age were still subject to the dictates of their parents, barred from adult entertainments and pleasures, we were free to drink, go where we desired, even drive electricars if we knew how.

A heady thought.

Five of us took the Farside shuttle to Earthport Station, and thence to Lunapolis. I don't know about the other new middies, but a lump formed in my throat as I peered through the porthole for one last look at the domes of Academy. At the moment, I loved it all, even Sergeant Swopes. Well, perhaps not all. Not Jenks.

Hours later we took our seats on the connecting shuttle for Lunapolis. We all had plans; mine included a tour of the First Warrens and of the Spaceflight Museum. We could have booked rooms in one of the less expensive hotels, but Arlene and I signed into Naval barracks. Though we were now on salary, we had no savings to squander. I'd had to draw against advance pay for my leave.

By the first night I exhausted the tourist sights I thought would last a week. The Museum of Spaceflight consisted mostly of replicas, and I'd seen more vintage craft in my years at Academy than in the exhibits. First Warrens were fascinating, though. I struggled to picture the early settlers living in such primitive conditions.

I spent my second day of leave in a bar, and my second night curled over a toilet, retching until there was nothing more to bring up. I passed my third day battling a monumental headache and an overwhelming sense of shame; by evening I sought out the Reunification Church and prayed forgiveness for my folly.

It was the fourth day, my last, that I summoned the courage to explore the lower warrens.

Like any city, Lunapolis had its good districts. Old Lunapolis wasn't one of them. Dives beyond description offered vices I'd dreamed of in the privacy of my sheets, as well as others I'd hadn't dared to imagine. The health officer's lecture ringing in my ears, I studiously avoided most establishments, ended up alone in a seedy café that my young eyes saw as worldly.

I ordered dinner, boldly agreed to wine. I had no experience with liquors, and let the waiter choose. What I was served bore a strong resemblance to bulkhead cleanser. Nonetheless, I sipped it in manly fashion. Presently, a young woman drifted past my table, stopped to say hello. Shortly after, she was sitting across from me, chatting comfortably. Lynette.

After dinner she took me for a walk. I'd read of a certain type of woman, in histories. I prepared to refuse, indignantly, her demand for money. To my relief, she asked for none. Instead, she put her arm through mine, whispered her desires in my ear. I stared unbelievingly. Did people really do those things?

I had no apartment, and bringing Lynette back to Naval barracks was unthinkable. With little more than a reproachful look she galvanized me into thumbing through my wallet. I tossed bills onto the hotel counter with desperate bravado. The room was as dingy as its location had promised, but Lynette didn't seem to mind. "You and me are the whole world, Nicky. Nothing else is real."

She planted me in a chair, draped herself in my lap, nestled close. I kissed her shyly while she fondled me, whispered of the bliss to come. She put my hands where she wanted them.

At her urging I stripped off my wonderful new uniform, trying to pretend I was back in barracks, that no one but fellow cadets observed my exposed skin. Lynette took off her halter, pressed her hardened nipples against my hairless chest.

A few moments after, I slipped between cold sheets, aflame with fantasies. Lynette pressed close, and I strove to please her. Somehow, her twists and turns were always in the wrong direction. I locked my arms around her, pulled her tight, but to no avail. My lust faded to insignificant proportions. I closed my eyes, willing away the shame.

At first I thought Lynette was trying to excite me anew, and I struggled to cooperate. That seemed to please her, but despite my passionate desire, my tumescence faded to naught. Now her fingers grew cruel, jabbing at my groin, dispelling what little excitement remained.

"Is that how a man acts?" Her voice was cruel.

"I'm—I need—stop that!" I caught her wrist, pulled it away.

"If I knew you were so tiny I wouldn't have bothered. How old are you, joey? Thirteen?"

I twisted away, lay with my back to her, nursing unspeakable hurt. Along with the shame came remorse that I had failed her. "I'm sorry, Lynette. Give me a minute, I'll be all right."

She seemed to calm. Presently she stroked me again. "All right, honey. It's okay. Don't cry." Gratefully I turned back to her arms. For many minutes she was patient, until at last I began to respond. In her eagerness she kissed too hard, bit my lip. I yelped, jerked my face away, tried to concentrate. My hands roamed her body, settled on her breasts. She went inert as a rag doll.

After a moment, I stopped. It was no use; perhaps our chemistry was wrong. I sat up. "I'm sorry. I'll go."

"Running away?" Her voice held disbelief.

"No." I fished for my shorts. "Just going."

She sat up. "Your daddy's in Wales, you said? How would he feel if he knew you were with me?"

About the way I felt, just now. I grabbed my shirt.

"Know something, little boy? The one thing that would disgust him more than you lying here sweating is you not even being man enough to do it!" Her eyes blazed. "There's nothing down there, joey! You're a blank!"

"Why are you doing this?" I jammed my feet into my shoes.

"You'll never be good enough, not for any woman! Try men!"

I slapped at her. She pulled her head out of the way; my fingers barely grazed her cheek.

"Go home, joeyboy! Play with it until you learn how!"

I snatched my jacket and tie, ran to the door. Somehow I got it unbolted, fled down the hall, fumbled at the corridor hatch.

A shrill voice pursued me. "Freak! Do you have a vagina hidden down there?" Her breath came in short rasps as she followed me into the hallway. "You're useless!"

I glanced back, frozen in the agony of my degradation.

Her face was contorted with passion, her lips full. She rubbed her hand against her crotch. "Faggot freak!"

I dashed blindly through the dirty corridors as if Satan himself were behind me. Perhaps he was.

Long hours later, I stumbled back to Naval barracks, my feet aching from the unnoticed miles I'd plodded. By now I was past tears, past caring, past life itself. I averted my eyes, certain everyone could read the humiliation in my face, and its cause.

I tapped in my hatch code, slipped into my cabin. I leaned against the hatchway, eyes shut. I tried not to weep, failed. Clawing off my sweat-soaked clothes, I dropped on the bed, jumped off immediately. I wasn't fit for bed. I fled into the head, turned on the shower, stood gratefully under its steaming warmth. Endless minutes passed while I tried to wash away the woman's foul imprecations.

Why had she destroyed me? Could I have deserved that? The hot spray of water caressed me. Despite myself, my body began to relax. Finally, reluctantly, I took a deep breath, turned off the tap, toweled myself dry.

Celibacy wouldn't be so terrible; someday I might even get used to it. In the meantime there was U.N.S. *Helsinki;* duty would help.

A towel wrapped around my waist, I stepped into the bedroom. Far too miserable to sleep, at least I could pray, and perhaps, before morning, find peace.

Someone pounded at the hatch. I ignored it; in my new life I'd be a hermit. Anything else was unthinkable.

More hammering. If I refused to answer, they'd go away.

"Nicky?"

Damn it, Arlene. Not now. Not even you. I flung myself onto the bed, buried my head in the pillow.

After a time she went away, and I was left alone with Lynette. The vile words echoed. "Freak! Play with it! Try men!" I tossed and turned, sat to retrieve the Bible from my duffel. Sitting on the edge of the bed, I leafed through its familiar pages. Father, forgive me. I was foolish, and I despise myself.

Keep thee from the evil woman, from the flattery of the tongue of a strange woman.

Please, Lord. I repent. Let me forget.

For by means of a whorish woman a man is brought to a piece of bread.

I let the Book fall closed. A lump of bread. For the sake of lust, I have reduced myself to that.

Another knock. "Nicky?"

I sighed. She'd knock again every few minutes, unless I spoke. "Not now, Arlene."

"Just for a minute."

Cursing under my breath I crossed to the hatch, flung it open. "Now what?"

Cadet Sanders—Midshipman Sanders, now—grinned at the towel around my waist. "I like your style. Quite a uniform." Her eyes danced, her breath smelled of sweet wine.

"What do you want?"

She studied my face. "Headache?"

"For God's sake, Arlene! Have your say and let me alone!"

She drew herself up. "Prong yourself! I came to say farewell; wine makes me foolish. Skip it!"

"You stupid bitch!"

Her slap rocked me back on my heels. My hand shot to my stinging face.

"What an ass you are, Nicky! I hate you!" She stalked off.

I paced my room, rubbing my face, cursing a steady stream of obscenities. Passing the chair I gave it a savage kick, spent the next minutes hopping and clutching my throbbing toes. Finally, exasperated, humiliated and in misery, I thrust myself into bed and turned out the light.

For weeks I tossed and turned. At last I gave up, turned on the light, learned that less than an hour had passed.

Damn it, Arlene, why did you have to stir me up? So what if I forgot my manners? I've had the most awful day of my life, and—

No, it wasn't my most awful day. That had been spent kneeling over a blanket on the cold damp grass, in a stadium far, far away.

"Geez, you have a temper, Nicky."

Oh, shut up, Jason, you're dead and gone. I miss you, but don't nag.

"All right." The voice faded.

No, Jase, come back!

Silence. I hunched over my knees, bowed my head, weeping. I'm sorry. I didn't mean it.

The reply was as if a whisper. *"You talking to me or her?"*

You. No, her. Both of you.

Silence.

I reached for my clothes. Moments later, I slipped through the hatch, started down the hall, realized I didn't know her room number. Why was life so bloody complicated? I plodded to the front desk, waited for the rating to look up from his holo.

"Midshipman Sanders; what room?"

His eyebrow raised. "We don't give out rooms."

I spoke with someone else's voice. "You do tonight!"

He stared, found something in my eyes that persuaded him. "Three fifteen."

I climbed the stairs two at a time, hurried to her door. All right, I'd abase myself. She meant that much to me, or had once. For old times' sake, she deserved it.

I knocked. No answer. "Arlene?"

I waited, heard no sound. I swallowed. "I understand, Arlene. Whatever you think of me, you're right. I'm sorry." It was so inadequate, I could say no more. I crept away.

I opened the stairwell door, bumped into someone coming through the other way. "Sorry, I—"

"What are you doing here?"

"I went to your room. Where were you?"

Arlene's voice was small. "At your room, knocking. You wouldn't answer."

"What did you want?"

I held up a hand to forestall her answer. "I came to apologize. I'm a fool, and cursing you was"—I turned away—"despicable." I forced myself to meet her eye.

She said, "I don't know what came over me, telling you off. I just wanted to say good-bye. In barracks I acted tough, but inside, I feel sentimental. Lonely. I—Nicky, don't turn away, let me see! Your eyes, I've never seen you look—why are you crying?"

I mumbled, "It's nothing."

"Oh, Nicky." She drew my head against her shoulder. Grateful beyond words, I succumbed to her caress. After a moment, I straightened, wiped my eyes. "It's been an awful day."

"Tell me."

I couldn't possibly. Still, the urge to confess was almost unbearable. I could talk about some of it, perhaps. Not the worst parts. "Not here." I led her to my room.

Arlene perched on my bed, cross-legged, as time and again she had on Farside. "Tell me."

I began with the casual conversation at my restaurant table. Bit by bit, as if drawn by a magnet, the story tumbled forth. I thought to pass over the details, found I could not. At the end I lay on my side, eyes shut tight, humiliated.

I expected consolation, but her tone was hard as nails. "Can you find her again?"

"Why?"

"I'll kill her."

Awed, I looked up, found her eyes. She meant it. I muttered, "I deserved it."

"Don't be an idiot." She jumped to her feet, paced, stopped to slam the bulkhead with her fist. "The Molesters, they call themselves. A sex cult. The men find young girls, the women boys. They . . . humiliate them. It's how they get their zarks."

I turned on my back. "How do you know?"

She colored. "When the middies had me standing regs, one of

them thought it would scare me." She swore fluently. "The worst hazing we ever had wasn't that awful."

"No."

"The bitch wanted to scar you forever."

A whisper. "She did."

Arlene pushed me aside without thinking, sat. "Now you'll think of her every time. Have you ever had sex?"

"Arlene!"

"Just asking. I have. Last year, twice. With joes from a second-year dorm."

"Lord God in heaven."

"Forget I asked. It's no big thing." She patted my forehead. "Jesus, Nick."

A long moment passed. My voice was muffled. "Tonight was the first time." I studied the far bulkhead, my cheeks on fire.

Arlene looked at her watch. "I report in six hours. So little time."

"I know. Get some sleep."

"That's not what I meant." She began to unbutton her tunic.

"What are you doing?"

"Taking off my clothes. It's better that way."

I sat quickly. "Stop it! Not with you, and anyway I couldn't, after tonight."

"Why not with me?"

"You don't do it with bunkies!"

"We're not, anymore. I'm *Freiheit* and you're *Helsinki,* remember?" She slipped out of her slacks.

I cried, "Arlene, I can't! Don't make me try, I'm begging you."

She hesitated, leaned over to brush her cheek against my chest. "If that's what you want. But I'm lonely. Can I stay, just to talk?"

I cast about for a way to refuse without doing her more hurt. I found none. "All right." Somehow, the night would pass.

A while later we nestled in the dark under the covers. "Poor Robbie. He wanted so much to make middy." Her voice was soft.

"They won't keep him long."

"I know." She sighed. "He cried, after Lights Out."

"I heard too."

"Hold me, Nicky."

An hour passed. I dozed in the comfort of her warmth. Then, abruptly, I woke. "Arlene, what are you—"

"Don't talk." She snuggled closer. "You're decent, Nicky. You're kind, under that righteous pose. Anyone can see that." Her soft fingers stroked my flank.

"Oh, Arlene, if only it were true." Still, grateful, I offered a shy kiss.

Her voice held wonder. "I think I love you, Nicky." Her lips met mine. I delved into her mouth, and presently, elsewhere.

Arlene's fingers brushed my Captain's bars. "Who would have thought, sir? So soon."

I closed my eyes, tried to shake away the despair. "It didn't happen like the holo stories. Not remotely."

"I know." As if recalling her surroundings she took a step back, cleared her throat. "I can see it in your eyes."

"I'm all right." My tone was gruff. "Tell me about yourself." We cleared the ladder well, started down to Level 3.

Her laugh was light and brittle. "They bounced me all over the Navy. *Freiheit,* then *Bolivar,* then Admiralty. Now here."

We climbed down to Level 2. "When did you make Lieutenant?"

"Four years ago. A fluke, really; if Captain Voorhees hadn't—"

The alarms shrieked. "BATTLE STATIONS! ALL HANDS TO BATTLE STATIONS!" Pritcher's voice echoed in the speakers.

Arlene Sanders stamped her foot. "What's the matter with the man? We've all had enough!" She started up the ladder.

"He wants to impress the brass. If they—"

The Captain's tone was ragged. "Battle Stations! This is no drill!"

"Oh, Jesus!" Arlene tore up the ladder to Level 2. For a second, I gaped. Then I raced after.

Swiftly as she ran, Arlene was only a step ahead when she charged through the bridge hatch. I dived past just as the Captain slapped the emergency close. The hatch slammed, isolating us from the rest of the ship. The middy of the watch was nowhere to be seen; only the Captain, Admiral Duhaney, Arlene and I.

Arlene dived for her console, flipped to the plotting screen. "Lieutenant Sanders repor—"

"Three of them!" Pritcher's voice quavered. He waved at the simulscreen. "In the training holos the fish didn't seem so . . . so big . . ."

Reports crackled from the speaker. "Comm room manned and ready, sir!"

"Engine room secure, sir! Full power available for thrusters!"

Duhaney clutched the back of the Captain's chair. "Harry, take us out of here!"

Pritcher seemed not to hear. "They can't show up so soon, even if they Fuse faster than we do!"

"Hydroponics secure!"

"Three encroachments confirmed, Captain." Arlene.

"Lasers up and ready, sir!"

"Distances a hundred meters and closing, the second is half a kilometer." She spun up her magnification. "Just a moment on the third."

"Harry—"

"Shut up, I'm thinking!" Pritcher pounded the console.

Admiral Duhaney looked astonished but fell silent.

Icy tentacles gripped my stomach. On the simulscreen, a fish off the port bow seemed close enough to touch. Slowly, it began to form a tentacle.

"Third fish two kilometers, closing fast." Arlene hesitated. "Captain, we're ready to open fire." She waited. "Sir, may I give the order?"

Duhaney stirred. "Harry, say something!"

I looked over the Captain's shoulder to his console. The laser safeties were still on lock. Pritcher's hands grasped the armrests of his black leather chair.

Casually, I stepped between Pritcher and the simulscreen, bent to see his face. His eyes were glazed.

My tone was soft. "Captain Pritcher, get hold of yourself. Defend your ship!"

No answer.

"Mr. Pritcher, *please!*"

He whispered. "The size of them. They're . . . monstrous."

"Laser control to bridge. Targets acquired."

I cleared my throat, spoke in a normal voice. "Captain, may we clear the safeties?"

"Harry, order a Fuse!" Duhaney.

"Belay that!"

Duhaney whirled at my voice.

"Our coordinates are set for Vega, Admiral. Even if we plot new ones we're too close to Earth to Fuse safely." We risked meltdown, if not worse.

An alarm clanged. Harlan, the puter. "Two encroachments at six kilometers!"

Pritcher whispered; I bent close to hear. ". . . can't be here so soon . . . can't . . ."

The fish alongside twirled its tentacle, ready to throw its acid into our hull.

I swung to Arlene. "Relieve him. I'm not a member of the ship's company; I can't."

Her eyes searched mine, troubled. "They'll hang me, Nick!"

"The Admiral's here! Ask him!"

The tentacle twirled faster.

"Harry, Fuse the ship!" Duhaney was hoarse.

I snapped, "Will you take command, Admiral?"

"What?"

"You heard me. Take the ship!"

"I can't—I mean, I haven't served shipboard for years, not since—"

"Then shut up!" I leaned over Pritcher's shoulder, slapped the laser safeties off, and committed mutiny.

It was a rule so absolute, so ancient, that it needed no restatement. A ship had but one Captain. Rebellion against his authority merited death. And a Captain represented not just civil authority, but the will of Lord God Himself.

There is no power but of God: the powers that be are ordained of God . . . they that resist shall receive to themselves damnation.

So be it. Now I was twice damned.

I thumbed the caller to shipwide frequency. "This is Nicholas Seafort, Captain, U.N.N.S., transmitting the orders of Captain Pritcher." Stating it any other way would only cause confusion.

"Lasers, fire as you bear!" Almost instantly, the lights dimmed, brightened.

"Two squirts, port thrusters. Middy of the watch, get your arse to the bridge! You too, Pilot!" The Pilot was best trained for the tight maneuvering ahead.

The speaker crackled. "We got him!"

I squinted. The fish alongside spewed protoplasm from numerous holes. Its tentacle had stopped twirling. "Go for the nearest first! Fire at will!"

Duhaney said tentatively, "Nick, are you sure you want—"

"Captain Pritcher, Engine room reporting—"

"What is it, Engine room? Pritcher's busy."

"Secretary Franjee wants me to ask who's in charge and will we Fuse to safety."

I snapped, "We've no time for civilians!" I spun the dial. "Comm Room, get off a signal to Fleet Ops. *Wellington* under attack, coordinates . . . you have our position?"

"Yes, sir."

"Laser room reporting, second target Fused to safety!"

A hammering at the hatchway. I swiveled the camera, saw a middy, slapped open the hatch. "Midshipman Rives report—"

"Comm Room, report to Admiralty we have five fish, one dead, the others closing fast."

The puter blared. "Encroachment seventy meters! Another at two hundred fifty meters!"

The frantic middy saluted Captain Pritcher. "Sir, I got caught behind the section six hatch, there were half a dozen locks between—"

Pritcher gave the middy an agreeable nod. "No hurry, Mr. Rives. Is Mr. Franjee ready for the commissioning?" A fleck of spittle glistened on his chin.

I growled, "Belay that, boy! Comm Room, repeat until they acknowledge, and make that *seven* fish. Ask if there's any help nearby!" There wasn't, I knew. *Wellington* was positioned alone, to emphasize her magnificent splendor. "Laser Control, acquire new targets! Harlan, help plot laser coordinates."

Harlan's voice was cold. "You have no authority aboard *Wellington*, Mr. Seafort. Only Captain Pritcher can—"

"Listen here, puter—"

"Let me, sir." Arlene's tone was urgent. "Harlan, I'm Lieutenant Sanders, officer of the watch. Acknowledge."

"Acknowledged. Of course I know you, that's not the—"

"Acquire targets, puter. Do whatever else—"

"No, Arlene!"

"—Captain Seafort asks."

Too late. She'd be hanged at my side. No time to think of it now. "Arlene, plot a Fuse."

"Where to, sir?" Arlene's face was pale.

It didn't matter; Fusion was a final resort, and might well destroy the ship, if we commenced so close to Earth's mass. "Uh—one point one four AUs should be far enough. Keep us clear of encroachments." If we Defused into space occupied by a planetary body, we'd never know. They'd notice the result on Earth, though, even without a telescope. "Midshipman! Help her calculate."

"Aye aye—I mean, Captain Seafort? What's the matter with Capt—"

"Do what you're told!"

The youngster bent to Arlene's console.

Alarms. Harlan. "Ms. Sanders, eleven new encroachments, one amidships at eighty meters, the others—" I switched off the buzzer. A moment of blessed peace.

"Laser Room, get the midships fish before he throws inside our range!" A warship's guns could depress inward to within a few degrees of its hull, but no farther, else an excited tech might skewer his own ship's sensors.

The aft fish was also ready to throw; he'd Defused with a tentacle already formed. Once the protoplasm separated it would become a much harder target.

"Opening hatch for the Pilot!" Arlene didn't wait for approval.

"Pilot Arnaud reporting." A young man, gaunt. "Who has the conn?"

"Seafort, at the moment." Duhaney.

The Pilot dived for his console, taking in the simulscreen. "Suggest we maneuver to port, that'll give us a few extra sec—"

The tentacle separated from the fish, swirled toward us. I shouted, "Damage Control, stand by for breach! All hands to suits!" Damn my stupidity; that should have been my first order.

"Christ, they're swarming all over!"

"Laser Room, be silent!" How dare they babble on bridge frequency?

The puter. "Two fish closing astern!"

"Where did they come from?" I grabbed the caller. "Laser room, fire on the fish astern!" I whirled to Arlene. "I need a Fusion plot!"

"Working on it, sir." Arlene's fingers flew. "Just another couple of . . . there! We're eighteen minutes from Fusion safety, at flank speed. Mr. Arnaud, confirm!"

"Belay that, Pilot! Stay with the thrusters, keep the fish away from us." I hesitated. "Head us toward Fusion safety if you can."

"Son of a bitch, they're Fusing as we hit them! Sorry, sir, Laser Control here. They Fuse away and reappear, or maybe it's new ones. We keep losing them!"

"Harlan, confirm Fusion plot."

The puter's reply seemed instantaneous. "Plot confirmed to two decimals, divergence at—"

"Close enough. Engine Room, acknowledge coordinates, stand by to Fuse!"

With *Wellington's* mass, Fusing from our current position might well mean death. But if our end seemed inevitable I'd cast *Wellington* to Lord God's mercy, rather than that of the fish.

"Bridge, I need the Captain's personal order to prepare—"

"He's, ah, indisposed, Chief."

"I'm following procedures. I don't care who's—"

I snarled, "Acknowledge *this instant*, or I'll execute you for mutiny in the face of the enemy!"

The speaker was silent for but a moment. "Aye aye, Bridge, standing by."

"Fuse, for God's sake!" Admiral Duhaney jabbed his finger at the simulscreen. "Take the risk. There must be a dozen fish out—"

"Fourteen, at the moment." My hand shot to the simulscreen controls, halted. "Harlan, focus aft!"

Suddenly I was viewing the tapered drive tubes. I recoiled; the fish were so close they seemed within the cabin. The skin of one of them seemed to agitate. Protoplasm spewed from a glowing hole made by one of our lasers. The alien drifted away, propelled by the force of its own death. Meanwhile its companion had begun to grow a tentacle. I looked closer, blanched. The creature's skin swirled in a pattern I remembered all too well.

"Master-at-arms, break out weapons! Prepare to repel boarders astern. Chief, get all civilians topside, flank. The fish is launching outriders."

Duhaney yanked at my arm. "Answer me, Seafort! Why haven't you Fused?"

I shook him off. "Comm Room, did you get off your message?"

"Yes, sir. Fleet Ops says to stand by for instructions. The nearest armed sloop can reach us in two hours."

"No! Tell them not to send the sloop, we'll fight or try to escape!" I swiveled to the Admiral. "If all else fails I'll Fuse, but—"

"The Deputy SecGen's aboard! Once the fish melt our tubes, we're done. Get us out of here!"

"Where to? Do you think—"

"Obey orders, Seafort!"

I couldn't fight the fish and the Admiral as well. I slammed my fist on the console. "You still don't understand! What brought them here?"

His mouth worked in rage.

I shouted, "Months ago I urged you to build a caterwaul bomb, but you did nothing while fish closed in on home system. Do you get it yet, Admiral? *THEY HEAR US FUSE!*" I snatched off my cap, hurled it to the deck. The young middy recoiled, white-faced.

Again the speaker crackled. "Bridge, the fish launched those outrider beasts! They're bypassing the drive shaft, going for our stern lasers!"

I ignored the caller. "We can run, but not far enough to gain any time, and they'll hear and follow. So will every other fish in the Solar System."

"You had coordinates for Vega. Damn it, you still have!"

"*Wellington* isn't stocked for an interstellar cruise. If we aim for a far target and Defuse short, Lord God knows where we'll end up, and we'll be alone. If we stay on course to Vega, we'll be eating each other before we're a month out!"

We eyed each other, both in a rage.

I spun around my chair. "Take over! Fuse wherever in hell you want!" I thumbed the caller. "Engine Room, stand by for orders from the Admiral." I grabbed Duhaney's hand, slapped the caller into it, strode to the hatch. "Fuse! Save yourself the trouble of hanging me." I struck open the hatch.

"Seafort!" The Admiral's voice was unsteady. "I—Jesus, don't leave the bridge."

"Take the conn, or give it to Sanders!"

"Please . . . for God's sake! I told you I'm not seagoing Navy. I don't—it's been too long!"

New alarms shrieked. "STERN PORT LASER DISABLED! HULL DAMAGE, LEVEL 3. DECOMPRESSION IMMINENT!" Arlene reached across, silenced the clamor.

"Nick, please." Duhaney was pale.

Arlene's eyes met mine. More lives were at stake than my own. I swung back to the console. "Captain Pritcher, can you take over?"

The Captain smiled. "Oh, yes, quite." He turned to the middy. "Deactivate lasers. Stand down from Battle Stations." The middy stared. Pritcher reached to Duhaney for the caller.

I didn't hesitate. "Midshipman Rives, escort the Captain to his quarters, by force if necessary."

The boy's eyes were saucers. He gulped. "Aye aye, sir." He leaned over Pritcher, spoke softly in his ear. The Captain shook his head. The boy glanced at me, whispered again.

I pried the caller from the Admiral's limp hand. "Midshipman Tenere, report with your cadets to the Master-at-arms! Harlan, open corridor hatches for them. Master-at-arms, issue my midshipman laser pistols."

I swiveled back to Harlan. "Status report for all stations!"

"Engine room fully operational, Captain. Comm room—"

"Cancel. Status regarding attackers, summary."

"Eleven fish in area. Level 3 portside hull sensors inoperative. Attack assumed in progress by outriders from fish astern. Amidships—"

"What's the stern fish doing now?"

"It's inert, assumed dead. Amidships we have four to six fish, Defusing and Fusing again at irregular intervals. Update, now three fish. New encroachments astern! Total of twelve surrounding ship."

"Pilot, turn us about, our stern lasers are gone!" At my left the middy argued quietly with Captain Pritcher.

The Pilot's bony hands flicked the thrusters. "We're no bloody rowboat, it takes time to—"

"I know." *Wellington's* middy was still urging his Captain. "Mr. Tenere, report to the bridge!"

"HULL BREACH! DECOMPRESSION SECTION THREE! HULL—" I flicked off the alarms.

I pray You, Lord God. Help us.

"Comm Room reporting. Signal from Fleet Ops to Captain Pritcher. From Vice Admiral Llewelin Stykes, officer of the watch. 'Take all necessary evasive action. Seek further instructions from Admiral Duhaney on board your vessel.' End message."

I gazed at Duhaney, said nothing.

The Admiral flushed. "They're playing it safe."

"He must have political ambitions, sir." My courtesy was elaborate.

"Master-at-arms calling bridge! Two outriders burned their way into section three! I have them on camera. I've got four men in there with lasers. Damn, they're fast!"

"Laser Room, fire on the stern fish the moment your midships lasers bear."

"Another few degrees, sir."

A cry from the speaker. "My men are down! It rolled right over them. Christ!"

"Hold the corridor hatches to either side of section three!" If the aliens had the run of the ship . . .

"Aye aye, sir, trying. How do we fight these things?"

"Burn them, full laser charge. Their mothership is dead. If you get the two . . ."

"Right." He rang off.

"Harlan, status!"

"Two more fish disabled, one Fused. Eight attackers, three alongside, remainder closing astern."

The Pilot fired the port thrusters with a savage squirt. "Two can play at that!" Ponderously, *Wellington* turned.

I watched the screen. Three fish within throwing distance. With our aft lasers disabled, we couldn't protect our stern. If I allowed damage to the tubes, we were done. My hand hovered over the Fusion controls.

The fish nearest our stern released a burst of propellant from its blowhole, and drifted closer to the drive shaft. Responding ever faster to her thrusters, *Wellington* turned on her axis, withdrawing her stern from the advancing form.

Harlan's tone was urgent. "Armed party approaching, not ship's company. I've sealed the hatch."

"Arlene, let them in." In the simulscreen, one of the sternside fish had swung into range. As I watched, half a dozen lasers pierced it.

"Aye aye, sir." Sanders got up, slapped open the hatch.

"Midshipman Tenere reporting, with the cadets." Kevin Arnweil, Kyle Drew and the rest crowded onto the bridge. Jerence Branstead was white-faced.

I said, "Captain Pritcher is ill and disrupting the bridge. Take him to his cabin. Now!"

"Aye aye, sir." Adam swallowed, approached the Captain with a resolute face. "Sir, get up, please."

"Midshipman Rives, place yourself under arrest in the wardroom."

"Aye aye, sir. I tried, he just wouldn't let—"

I shouted, "Off the bridge!" Ashen, the boy scurried out of sight.

"Boland, take Mr. Pritcher's arm!" Adam's tone brooked no argument. "Arnweil, help him!"

In a moment, the cadets had hustled *Wellington*'s Captain off his bridge. Arlene stared somberly into her console.

I slipped into the sacred Captain's seat. "Harlan, status update."

"Six fish, two of them astern, one a kilometer off the port bow. The remaining three amidships, starboard side. One is alongside laser bank three, closing fast."

"Pilot?"

He licked his lips, eyes glued to his screen. "The engine room is critical."

"I agree."

"I'll try some spin on the vertical axis . . ." Again he fired our thrusters.

"Master-at-arms calling bridge! The section two hatch is heating. We have our lasers trained on it."

"Fire the instant you see a target."

"Amen. That is, aye aye, sir. I have another armed party at the hatch to four."

"The outriders can just as easily burn through our bulkheads as our hatches."

"Yes, sir, but I can't be everywhere. The camera shows them skittering back and forth in there. If they go for the bulkheads we should get a sensor alarm."

"Where are the civilians? Franjee, the Senators?"

"We moved them to Level 2 mess hall. I have a detail guarding them."

"Very well, keep me posted."

"Laser Room reporting. Two fish amidships destroyed!"

I glanced at the screen. If no more came, we might just make it. My hand eased off the Fusion control.

"Harlan, are any more Defusing?"

He sniffed. "I'd tell you if there were."

I bit back a reply; no point in arguing with a puter.

I snapped off the caller, and paced.

All I had to worry about was decompression in section three, two aliens roaming our corridors, and four fish maneuvering Outside. No cause for alarm. My teeth bared in a travesty of a grin.

I was ready to order the master-at-arms to unseal the section three hatch and attack, when the outriders saved us the trouble. They burned through to section four, where withering fire from the master-at-arm's company turned them to smoking stains on the deck.

"Class A decontamination in effect! Every man to the sickbay for inoculation the moment he's desuited!" I rekeyed the caller. "Continuous fire at remaining fish!"

While we disposed of the last four fish, I tensed for new alarms at any moment.

But the screen was quiet.

Admiral Duhaney sat in the chair I'd vacated. His fingers worked the fabric of his jacket.

After half an hour with no new fish, I began to breathe easier. In an hour, I stood down from Battle Stations. The crew needed a rest; before the skirmish, Captain Pritcher had worked them for hours drilling for the brass.

"Pilot, plot a course for Lunapolis." *Wellington* remained functional, but her damage needed repair.

"Aye aye, sir." His fingers worked the keys. The moment coordinates were confirmed I had him fire thrusters at full power, heedless of the waste of propellant.

18

I took up the caller. "Attention, passengers and crew. *Wellington* has beaten back an attack by some fifteen fish. We sustained hull damage, decompression of one section, and three dead. We are returning to Earthport Station for repairs. Admiralty has been notified. Lieutenant Hollis, report to the bridge."

My eye fell on Duhaney. I looked away. One more duty, before the ignominious end to my career. I said into the caller, "U.N.S. *Wellington* has proven herself a proud ship of the line. With Secretary Franjee's permission, commissioning will be held on the bridge in two hours." I replaced the caller in its socket.

As my adrenaline ebbed, I became conscious of the electric silence of the bridge. Finally, I stood. "Ms. Sanders, I surrender the ship to lawful authority. Lieutenant Hollis will take the conn. Admiral, what is your wish?"

He barked, "Say what you mean."

"I face court-martial. Shall I report to the brig?"

"I—God!" He hesitated. "Yes. Wait, not until the commissioning. Christ, what a position you've put me in."

I waited.

"You went too far, Seafort. Not just with Pritcher. You refused my orders, in front of the others. It was mutiny." He raised his eyes to mine. "Yes, we'll try you. As quietly as we can, for the Navy's sake."

Good. Better that than Wyvern's way. "Aye aye, sir."

"Just a moment, please." Arlene Sanders's voice was soft, but its edge compelled our attention.

"This doesn't concern you, Lieutenant."

She stood. "Begging your pardon, Admiral, it does. Think twice before court-martialing Nick."

Duhaney's eyes flashed dangerously. "That sounds close to a threat, young lady."

"No, sir, just a fact. Even if you're so morally low as to execute him after he saved you, I'm a witness. They'll interrogate me under drugs, so I can't lie to protect him. But I don't have to."

Duhaney raised an eyebrow, said only, "Go on."

"You dithered after Mr. Pritcher became ill. I was the ship's officer at hand, so Nick asked me to relieve my Captain. I couldn't. I'm a coward, and now I know it."

"Arlene—"

"Shut up, Nick. I mean, Captain, sir." She faced Duhaney, her jaw set. "In desperation Nicky asked you to take the conn, and you also refused. That left him senior officer present, and he took over. True, he wasn't a member of the ship's company, but that's a technicality, and you know it."

"Are you finished, Lieutenant?"

"Nearly, sir. With *Wellington's* Captain in a funk, you pestered Nick to make wrong decisions. That's what I'll testify. At the trial I won't be under drugs. I'll tell the truth, but my manner will say all that's necessary about your behavior, as well as Nick's."

What in God's heaven was Arlene doing? Challenging the Admiral just to save me? I couldn't allow it. I opened my mouth to speak.

No. To save herself. She faced death for concurring in my mutiny. I closed my mouth, held my breath. Lord, help her save herself, at least.

Duhaney shook his head, as if amused. "You dare threaten me, Lieutenant?"

"Not threaten, sir. Warn. Yes, I dare. I don't want to be part of a Navy that destroys Nick Seafort." She turned away quickly, ran her hand across her eyes. My brow wrinkled. Could it be for me, after all? She turned back. "Make your choice, sir. We'll both have to live with it."

I clutched the chair, my knees weak. Perhaps the aftermath of action.

Duhaney seemed more curious than outraged. "What would you have me do?"

"Cover for him. He effectively relieved Pritcher, and you made no objection, therefore you concurred. You're Admiral of the Fleet, and have authority to authorize it."

"So your bargain is, I leave Seafort be, and—"

"No, sir, no bargain. You do as you wish. I'm advising you of my testimony."

Glowering, he wheeled on me. "She's another of your ilk. You trained her?"

"No, sir. *With* her. Ms. Sanders always had the makings of a fine officer." I knew my endorsement was worse than silence, but I couldn't say less.

Lieutenant Hollis knocked at the hatch.

The Admiral growled, "Get out, both of you. I'll think it over."

"Aye aye, sir."

The bridge hatch slid closed behind us. After the frenzied action of our engagement, the corridor seemed strangely still. Arlene strode ahead of me to the ladder.

Thanks to her preposterous defense, I might escape the death I merited. But only because Duhaney was a politician, not a fighting sailor like his predecessor, Admiral Brentley. The Admiral had heard Arlene's threat as an offer to deal, and responded accordingly.

So now I could go back to Academy, saddled with my superior's displeasure, but with no other penalty save that of Lord God. I would concentrate on training my cadets for battles such as we'd just survived.

No. I'd forgotten about Senator Wyvern. My career was still done. For a moment I mourned its loss, then remembered *Wellington's* three crewmen who'd died fighting the aliens. Compared to their sacrifice, mine would be nothing. I closed my eyes, offered prayer for their souls.

At the foot of the ladder I paused, said lamely, "Arlene—Lieutenant—you shouldn't have antagonized him for me. I didn't need—"

"For you?" Her eyes reflected loathing. "For me, Captain Seafort. As penance."

"I don't—look, however you see it, I'm grateful beyond words. Seeing you today meant . . ." Tentatively, I put out my hand.

"Don't touch me! Even as Captain you haven't that right!"

I pulled my fingers back as if burned. Her eyes blazed. "I don't want ever to see you again. What you did to me was unspeakable!"

"What did I—"

"Asking me to relieve my Captain, in front of an Admiral? I'm not the wonderful Nick Seafort; they'd have hanged me without a moment's thought!" She stamped her foot. "You forced me to make the wrong choice between duty and death. We're not all heroes! I can't help my cowardice. You should have known when you put me to the test that I couldn't choose to die!"

"That's not—why would I think that of you?"

"Remember the airlock that malfunctioned in the Training Fuser? That day, I turned to jelly."

"Arlene, please. I never thought—"

"From now on, when I face you, I have to face myself! Get out of my sight, Nick Seafort. Get out of my life!" Without a salute she ran down the ladder, and out of view.

Stunned, I sagged against the bulkhead. I'd meant no harm. Meeting her again had been a ray of hope in the darkness of my soul. And now . . .

After a time I roused myself to join the others in the Level 2 mess hall. As I crossed the hatchway, conversation stopped cold. A barrage of flashes blinded me. Within seconds, half a dozen mediamen surrounded me, holocamera whirring, recorders thrust in my face.

"When did you realize Captain Pritcher lost his mind?"

"How does it feel to—"

"Look this way!"

"—a hero yet again?"

"Are the fish after you personally? Did you—"

"Should Pritcher be court-martialed? Will you testify?"

"—warn Pritcher about the caterwauling?"

"*BELAY THAT!*" My bellow stopped them in their tracks. I swiped at a holocamera. "Get that recorder out of my face!"

For a moment it worked. Senator Boland's eye held a glint of amusement. Then they pressed forward as if I hadn't spoken. "Was Pritcher glitched before the cruise? Did he—"

I turned in disgust, but they danced around me in full frenzy. "Was he crying when—tell us how it felt to—know you were sailing with a coward?"

I spun on my heel. "Captain Pritcher is a fine officer! He reacted to an unexpected fright the way any of you would. He's no coward!"

"Then why take over? Wasn't he disabled?"

I looked to Boland for sympathy, got a shrug, and glared at the nearest mediaman. "Ghouls! Captain Pritcher is ill and miserable. What will your headlines do to him? You're here to cover the commissioning; make your report out of that!"

The holoreporter grimaced. "Hey, joey, this is a bigger story. We can't ignore it."

"You'd destroy Pritcher for a day's story?"

"I'd do *anything* for top of the hour!" The others nodded agreement.

By relieving Pritcher I'd virtually ruined him; if there was any chance to salvage his career I had to divert the vicious publicity. My thoughts whirled. If they had something else to focus on, something of equal interest . . . But what could compare to the spectacle of a Captain cracking under fire?

I tried to contain my revulsion. "What about me?"

"You're the hero as usual, joey, but you've ducked every question we've ever asked. What can we write about you?"

"I'll trade. Me for Pritcher."

The mediaman perked up. "An interview? When?"

"Now, and again after the commissioning, if need be."

One of his colleagues intervened. "Not a five-minute jam. You'd have to open up."

"We'll be hours heading back to Lunapolis; I'll give you as long as you ask. But only if you kill the Pritcher story."

The second reporter looked to the others. "What do you think?"

I saw skepticism, nods of agreement. "It's all or none," I said. "Make up your minds." I poured a cup of hot coffee, turned a chair to face them. It was the least I could do for Pritcher. I, too, was locked in my cabin, sick and afraid.

One by one, they gathered round. The silent cameras spun. A mediaman cleared his throat. "What happened on the bridge today, Captain Seafort?"

"I assisted Captain Pritcher in a skirmish against the fish. We prevailed."

"Tell us your feelings about the fish."

I swallowed bile. A small payment on the punishment due me. "The fish? Well, obviously they're a great menace. What I've found odd about them is . . ."

The ceremony was an anticlimax, but I found it moving. If there was any doubt the Navy needed battlewagons such as *Wellington*, the attack had dispelled it.

Secretary Franjee spoke earnestly for the cameras; the mediamen dutifully recorded the commissioning. When it was over and the symbolic toasts drunk, I rounded up Adam and the cadets and took them to the lounge.

Walking the Level 2 corridor I marveled anew at the Navy's resourcefulness. Barely three hours after the attack, emergency hull patches were in place, the Level 2 corridor scrubbed and decontaminated, and shipboard life almost back to normal.

Almost, but not quite. Captain Pritcher lay sedated in his bunk, and three young seamen were no longer among the ship's company.

The risk of infection was too great to allow the bodies to remain in sickbay; *Wellington's* dead sailors were jettisoned from the aft airlock with little ceremony, and the lock itself decontaminated. The viral epidemics that had decimated *Portia* and other ships after invasion were taken seriously now; passengers and crew alike had lined up for inoculations.

In the lounge, Jerence Branstead piled his plate with delicacies. I repressed an urge to rebuke him; in perspective, it mattered not a bit. The other cadets clustered eagerly at the buffet.

"A word, sir?"

I turned, found myself face-to-face with Secretary Franjee. "Of course."

"I'm no tactician, Mr. Seafort. They send the fleet here, order it there, and I have no choice but to concur. But I'd like your opinion. Was it wise to gather so much of the top brass several hours from Lunapolis and the fleet's assistance?"

"I'm not part of—"

"Just between us, Captain, to go no further. Tell me."

I hesitated. Admiral Duhaney was no strategist, not a man to direct the fleet's operations. He'd proven that again on *Wellington's* bridge. And Lord God only knew how Pritcher had passed the psych tests; perhaps he too was someone's nephew. Or perhaps the tests couldn't calibrate the horror of a clash with the fish. On *Challenger's* bridge I'd yearned to close my mind to them as Pritcher had done. Now I had the ear of a politician with power to change the policies that had led to today's tragedy.

I took a deep breath. "As I said, sir, I'm not keyed in to fleet tactics; I'm just Academy Commandant. Still, it would seem . . ." Across the room, my eyes caught Duhaney's. He shifted his gaze.

I need have no loyalty to men like Duhaney. Ships might founder, sailors die, due to their fumbling and foolish decisions. I owed it to my compatriots to prevent that. Yet again I hesitated.

I was Navy, Franjee was not. That was all I need remember. "Hind-sight is too easily mistaken for wisdom, sir. Naval decisions are made by men such as you and myself. We're fallible, but we do our best. *Wellington* was to take her place in the Home Fleet; it made sense to have the ceremony near her assigned post."

He searched my face. "And the risks?"

"Only three fish have ever been seen in home system. As a society, we've made the decision to combat them, not to cower and hide. There was no reason to think *Wellington* would be in greater danger here than moored at Earthport Station. Except . . ."

"Yes?"

I could have bitten off my tongue, but it was too late. Well, I'd already made my thoughts more than obvious, racing from the engine room to the bridge. "Except for caterwauling. I think that was unwise, and I've always said so. I'm sure fleet policy will be modified, now that we've had a graphic demonstration."

"Is that all you'll say?"

I felt almost at peace. "Yes, sir, it's all I know to say. If the Navy has problems, it also has procedures to correct them." Procedures like the court-martial I so richly deserved. In any event, I wouldn't wash the

Navy's linen in the sight of civilians. Whatever foul crimes I'd committed, at least I was above betrayal.

Franjee let it be. After a few words of praise on my handling of *Wellington*, he drifted away. Within moments his place was taken by Richard Boland. The Senator made no pretense at small talk. "Captain, I have a request."

I waited for him to continue, yearning for a drink.

"Since our, ah, conversation a few months ago you'll notice I've done as you asked. I haven't inquired about Robert, either directly or through Admiralty." Yes, I'd noticed, assuming almost daily that his restraint would end, and I'd be forced to resign. I braced myself for another interference.

"Mr. Seafort, please don't interpret this as pressure. But, considering the nightmare we've all been through, and the fact that my son is no more than twenty feet away, would you take it amiss if I spoke to him?"

My hostility vanished. "For as long as you like." My tone was gruff. "He probably needs it more than you do; he's had a rough day."

"I'm grateful." He seemed to mean it.

"He'll relax more if I leave the room." I moved toward the hatch.

"No, if anyone deserves drinks and a peaceful meal, it's you. We'll wander outside, if you'll let him."

"Thank you." I snapped my fingers, beckoned to Adam Tenere, gave orders to let Robert Boland go with his father. I closed my eyes. Would that I could go with mine.

Hours later, we docked at Earthport Station.

I allowed the mediamen one last round of photos—a deal was a deal—and booked a shuttle groundside. Only my letter of resignation awaited.

It was early the next morning when we reached Devon. I saw the exhausted cadets to their dorms, gave Robert Boland an extra clap of assurance. Adam walked me back to Officers' Quarters. For most of the way we were silent.

"Is that how it is on a ship of the line, sir? Mostly quiet, then the alarms?"

He had no business speaking to me, unbidden, but now we were comrades in battle. "Some sailors can't take the boredom of Fusion," I told him. "Other than stand watch, there's nothing to do except what you make for yourself. But it's not a peaceful boredom; you never know when the siren will shriek, or why. Decompression, engine failure, the fish . . . The Navy's not for everyone."

"It's for me." He spoke with certainty. "Sir, the speakers were broadcasting most of the time you were on the bridge. Your orders—we all heard them."

"So?" I reeled with exhaustion.

"I—nothing, sir. I mean . . . someday, if . . ." He pounded his side. "On the bridge. I want to be like that." His voice grew embarrassed. "Like you."

I wheeled. "You may be stupid enough to think that, Mr. Tenere, but don't ever say it again in my presence!"

"But—aye aye, sir!"

"Go to bed!" I stalked off.

In my apartment, I flipped on my console while I undressed. No word from Eddie Boss; presumably that meant Annie was well. I'd call him later, to confirm. I glanced at the other messages, but the screen wavered. I flicked it off, fell into the dark.

19

I dressed slowly for my last day in the United Nations Naval Service. Every act, even combing my hair, seemed fraught with significance. I selected a fresh-pressed jacket, resisted the temptation to don dress whites. Before leaving my apartment I thumbed the caller. "Page Mr. Tolliver to my office after breakfast."

I left to take a final walk around the grounds. The sun was barely above the treetops, but squads of ruddy-faced cadets were already concluding their morning exercises. I strode briskly to the gate, paralleled the long fence through the tree-shaded lawn. Not far from here, I'd sat with young Jerence Branstead during changeover. Once, I'd promised his father Harmon that I'd watch over him. After today I could do nothing to keep the pledge. In any event Jerence needed little help. He'd earned the second highest scores on the base.

I followed the track south to the classroom quadrangle. Many years ago, I'd left, thinking I was seeing them for the last time. Now, at last, it was to be so. I'd leave in ignominy, but I'd have time for Annie. Perhaps, in Father's house, I could repair the ruin of our marriage.

I stopped at an empty classroom. On the spur of the moment I stepped in, peered at the hallway pictures. Here, on my visit during Final Cull, I'd encountered two nervous young cadets, and met Sergeant Ibarez. What a hash I'd made of things since.

I checked my watch, and left. Today, it wouldn't do to be late.

I swung open the mess-hall door, and two hundred fresh-scrubbed cadets stood as one. "You may be seated!" I strode to my table.

Adam Tenere and the two lieutenants held their salute until I returned it. I pulled out my chair. "Good morning."

"Morning, sir." Jeff Thorne stared down at his plate.

Sandra Ekrit half ran to the table. "Sorry, Commandant. I was delayed."

"No problem. One demerit."

Tolliver regarded me with curiosity. "I hear there's a special issue of *Holoworld* this afternoon."

"I've no idea what you're talking about."

"Odd, since you're on the cover." He passed me the rolls. "You never stop, it seems. Congratulations on your latest exploit."

"Change the subject." My tone allowed no argument. "What was the Code Two you left on my console last night? I was too tired to decipher."

Tolliver glanced at the middies and the staff sergeants sharing our table. "Yes, I used the cipher. It wasn't for general distribution."

"But I no longer care." I realized I'd spoken the words aloud. Well, no matter. "Go ahead."

"I have a reply from the, ah, sergeant regarding that inventory question. A great deal of verbiage. Everything is as it should be. His reply completely ignores the serial numbers. Meanwhile, I ran some estimates on food purchases based on the figures from five years ago."

"Drop it."

"Aye aye, sir. Sorry, I always seem to be one command behind."

Jeff Thorne bristled. "Mr. Tolliver, would you have me answer you in the manner you speak to Captain Seafort?"

Tolliver rose to the occasion. "Certainly. I should get as I give." Nonetheless, he looked abashed.

Across the table, Sandra Ekrit toyed at her food, her expression sullen. I said with malice, "Perhaps two more demerits would improve your attitude, Ms. Ekrit?"

Her tone was reckless. "Perhaps they would, sir. I have no way to please you."

I gaped at the two lieutenants, astonished at her audacity.

Tolliver said, "I'll handle it. Middy, report to my cabin after the meal!"

"Aye aye—"

"Edgar, I'll need you at my office. Let Jeff instill sense and manners in this—this person. Ms. Ekrit, leave my table! Wait for Mr. Thorne outside his quarters. Regardless of what he gives you, six demerits."

"Aye aye, sir." Her rebellion doused, she fled to her fate.

I wheeled on Tolliver. "That's a result of your insolence. Blame yourself, not her."

"Regardless, she's still a middy talking to a Captain! The nerve—"

Jeff Thorne's voice was as oil poured on troubled waters. "She's having a bad day." His eye held a glint of humor. "We all do, at times."

I subsided, grumbling. Whether or not Thorne chose to cane Midshipman Ekrit, her manner would improve. Jeff had the knack. Once, when I'd been surly, he'd stood me against a bulkhead and . . . I blushed at the memory.

Downing a tasteless breakfast, I brooded on Sandra Ekrit. After a time I shrugged. It was no more than we could expect, demanding adult behavior and judgment from adolescents. Would the Navy be better to enlist its officers at a later age, as once had been the norm?

No, Britannia had ruled the waves for two glorious centuries, and they'd enlisted midshipman younger than ours. And there was the risk of melanoma T that demanded early exposure to N-waves. What was the answer, then?

Musing, I sipped my coffee.

"Midshipman Lea, sit up. One demerit." Billy jerked upright. Furtively, I straightened in my seat, kept my eyes glued to my holovid as if in rapt attention. I hated Law and Regs, but it was part of continuing education, now that I was a middy on *Helsinki.*

Lieutenant Jarewski paced the confines of the comm room, favoring his weak leg. "Brewster, chain of command. Detail."

"Aye aye, sir." Midshipman Tommy Brewster jumped to his feet. "The chain of command runs from the highest ranking line officer to the lowest. It—"

"And if it's broken? By death, for example."

"It automatically relinks, sir. Until the dead officer is replaced, the subordinate reports one link higher."

"That's obvious." Jarewski passed his bleak eye over each of us in turn. "And what if communication is lost?"

"Then the highest—"

"Not you, Mr. Brewster. Seafort, who's dreaming about leave in Earthport with a holo star."

I jumped to my feet, frantically trying to remember the question. "Yes, sir. If, uh, communication is lost the highest available rank takes command."

"Such as a doctor."

"I—" It was heresy to contradict a lieutenant, but I'd learned better than to agree with Mr. Jarewski's false postulates, however casually stated. "Pardon me, no, sir. A doctor isn't a line officer. I should have said, the highest available line officer."

"Such as yourself, Mr. Seafort?"

"A lieutenant at least, sir. I'm a midshipman." Resentful and reckless, I added, "Just vermin."

He'd been about to call on someone else. Now, he just smiled. "And I imagined you were an officer and a gentleman. Do explain your remark."

I wasn't going to get away with it. I did the best I could. "I'm sorry, sir, I was repeating what I'd been told. I assumed a superior officer must be correct." I put on my most innocent expression.

Billy Lea shook his head ruefully, aware that I'd sent myself to the barrel.

The lieutenant's eyes narrowed, but he said only, "An admirable supposition, Midshipman. Yet, what if your superior isn't correct? What if he's dead wrong?"

"I still have to obey him, sir."

"Why? He might get you killed."

"He's my superior officer. I have no choice but to obey."

"Ah." Jarewski limped back to his desk. I waited to sit down, marveling at my good fortune.

Not quite yet. "Always, Cadet Seafort?"

"Yes, sir." I waited for dismissal, realized my trap, blurted just in time, "Unless I'm prepared to relieve him."

His mouth closed, opened again. "On what grounds, Cadet?"

It had become an interrogation. "Mental or physical disability, sir. Those are the only grounds."

"Cite."

I wracked my brain. "Section One hundred and . . ." I was lost. "I can't remember the number, sir, but I can quote it, more or less."

With a smile that sent a chill down my damp back, Jarewski sat on the edge of his desk. "Do so."

"An officer may be relieved of command by his superior for any reason, and by a co-equal or subordinate officer under his command when observed disabled and unfit for duty by reason of mental illness or physical sickness or injury."

"You're referring to Section one twenty-one point four. Are those the only grounds?"

"Yes, sir."

"Well, Mr. Midshipman Vermin. Or rather, Midshipman Seafort." Off the desk now, approaching my chair. "Three demerits. One for insolence, one for being silly enough to provoke me without need, and one for not reading the chapters I assigned. Sit down."

"Aye aye, sir."

He wasn't done with me. "Tomorrow I'll expect you to correct your error."

My encounter had left me with nine demerits. The next one would send me to the barrel; I had to work at least one of them off immediately. I sweated over the exercise bars, knowing I'd been foolish to call Mr. Jarewski's attention. But, nearly seventeen, I'd begun to chafe under the wardroom's unyielding restrictions. I was filling out, my voice deepening, and was reaching for some station, I knew not what.

First Midshipman Arvan Hager found me in the exercise room. He lounged against the bulkhead while I worked. "Who'd you piss off, Nick?"

"Lieutenant Jarewski." I was into sit-ups at the moment, and found it hard to talk.

"How?"

I told him.

"That was notably stupid." His tone modulated the sting his words might otherwise carry. "Even considering the chip on your shoulder."

"I don't have—yes, Mr. Hager." I was in enough trouble as it was.

My sullenness earned a momentary frown. After a moment he said, "What's bothering you, Nicky?"

"Nothing." I finished the series of sit-ups, lay back with a sigh. I was allowed a full minute. His question nagged at me. Suddenly I battled raging resentment. "Nothing, except people calling me 'Nicky' and treating me like a child."

"You are a child!" His voice had a snap. "You're proving it even now."

"Yes, SIR, Mr. Hager."

He didn't waste time with words; instead he crossed the cabin, hauled me to my feet, and slapped me, hard. I yelped. "Seafort, I like you, but at times you're a total ass!"

To my shame, I found myself crying. I spun to face the bulkhead.

I hoped he would leave, slamming the hatch behind him. But after a moment of quiet, he came to my side. "Sorry, Nick—Midshipman Seafort. Perhaps I overreacted."

"You're first," I mumbled. Any midshipman was subject to the discipline of the senior middy, who ran the wardroom. It had always been thus. I couldn't object, unless I was prepared to offer the traditional challenge. I wasn't ready for that, yet.

"It's just that your sullenness gets under my skin. Have they been riding you?"

I said tightly, "I'm fine, sir."

"No, you're not. Tell me about it."

I wiped at my eyes, trying not to lose control yet again. "There are times I hate this place. I have no freedom, no choices . . ."

"*Helsinki*'s like any ship."

So I'd heard, and was regretting my choice of career.

"Who called you vermin?"

I hesitated, not wanting to carry tales. "Mr. Jenks." Alfred Jenks, nephew of an Admiral, had been promoted from Academy midshipman to lieutenant and posted to *Helsinki*. Mr. Hager was stuck with the situation, as was I. Somehow, that made it all right to tell.

Hager shrugged. "Consider the source," was all he said. I smiled weakly. "Come find me after your shower, Nick. We'll talk."

Later, ashamed of my outburst, I tried my best to be congenial with him. I had few enough friends.

"Are you ready for Law tomorrow?"

"I haven't looked it up yet." If I had to scan the whole manual . . . Well, there was always key word search.

Hager looked about, made sure we weren't overheard. "Try Chapter Six."

"Thanks." I'd skimmed it, and couldn't remember anything about . . . "Oh!"

"You've got it now?"

"Yes, sir. But that just restates one twenty-one point four."

"God, don't tell Jarewski that." It was a mark of Arvan Hager's sense that he left it for me to untangle.

"We'll begin with Mr. Seafort." The Lieutenant rested his bad leg across the other.

"Aye aye, sir." I got to my feet. "Yesterday I forgot about sixty-four point three. I thought it just restated one twenty-one point four. The difference is that to relieve under one twenty-one you have to be in the presence of the commander, and under sixty-four you do not."

He looked surprised. "Very good, Cadet." I blushed, treasuring the unexpected praise. "Right to the heart of it. In fact, under sixty-four, you MAY not be present. It's designed for a different set of circumstances." He waved me to my seat.

Limping back and forth, Jarewski described sixty-four as a relief valve, in case a dreadful error by a distant commander was consigning the fleet to disaster. The penalties for misuse were draconian, but they were also theoretical.

In the history of the Navy, no one had ever sixty-foured a superior.

Arvan Hager found me on the way to dinner. "How was class, Nick?" Not "Nicky." I noticed the change.

"Jarewski wants a paper on when sixty-four might be used," I said, my tone resigned.

"That's easy. Never." His vehemence set me back. "It's an incitement to mutiny. If I'm ever on a sixty-four court-martial board, I'll vote guilty, regardless of the circumstances."

"But—"

"The Navy is about obedience, not rebellion. No one has a right to take over the fleet. Hasn't discipline taught you a thing?"

This time I knew better than to argue.

The next day Mr. Jarewski tore my defense of my paper to shreds. Nonetheless, he graded it an A. Who could figure a lieutenant's mind?

When class was done, I waited until the others had left. "About the other day, sir. I apologize for my attitude."

"Thank you." He eyed me, said not unkindly, "Will you take some advice, Seafort?"

"Yes, sir."

"Be patient," he said. "Adolescence ends."

Breakfast over, I crossed the compound to my office, perhaps for the last time, ignoring a lump in my throat.

I skimmed files until Tolliver arrived. He flipped a salute, headed for his accustomed chair. "Now that we're private, let me show you what I found. Mind if I turn on your console? That thieving son of a bitch took—"

"I told you to drop it."

"When do you want to discuss it, then? Serenco's response is goof-juice; we've got enough to go to the Solicitor Gen—"

"Forget the whole matter. Destroy the records of your inquiry, and mention it to no one."

For a moment he was still. Then he rose, leaned on my desk, studied my face. "By God, they got to you."

"Dismissed, Lieutenant."

He turned to go, made it as far as the door. Still inside, he slammed it shut, stalked back to my desk. "What did they offer you? Flag rank? Or was it the old 'No scandals during wartime'? I thought if anyone would see this through, it was you!"

I came out of my chair. "How dare you!" With an effort I controlled my rage. "Acknowledge your orders!"

"Why? At least in a court-martial the drugs will bring out the truth!"
He made a gesture of appeal, cut it short. His expression was bitter. "God,
I'm a fool. I keep wanting to trust you."

The caller buzzed. I ignored it. "No need. I'm resigning, as of today."

"All your talk about setting an examp—you're what?"

"I called you to help draft the letter. No discussion, Edgar."

He sank slowly in his chair. "You mean this, sir?"

"Yes."

"Don't." His voice held something I'd never heard before. Entreaty.

"I must, and I won't explain. The stated reason will be that I'm ill
from overwork. I want it sent this afternoon."

A knock. Sergeant Kinders, through the door. "Sir, you have a call—"

"No calls, Sarge."

"Aye aye, sir. It's Admiral Duhaney."

"Christ." For a moment I reveled in the blasphemy. "Sorry. Amen."

"Shall I leave, sir?" Tolliver.

"No need." I put the call on the speaker. "Seafort here."

The Admiral's voice was brisk. "Just wanted to tell you the official
line. Pritcher was suffering from dehydration and flu, and he's recovering.
That's it. He won't keep *Wellington*, of course. Perhaps another ship, later
on."

"I hope so. It was his first sight of the fish, and they—"

"Don't tell me my job, Commandant Seafort."

"Aye aye, sir."

"That's all." He hesitated, then rushed on. "No, by God, that's not all.
I haven't slept since I got back to Lunapolis. I kept thinking about those
monsters, and how you handled them. And about your insolence."

"Sir, I'm sor—"

"Be silent! I tossed half the night realizing what a fool I was, lectur-
ing you. Two Navies, I said, thinking you were an innocent at politics. Ha!
You put us pros to shame."

"I don't know what you're talking about!"

Tolliver stood, whispered, "I'd better leave."

"Sit."

"Seafort, I don't care what the Sanders woman said; what you did was
mutiny, plain and simple. I may have been mistaken but I was the Admiral; you owed it to me to obey!"

"Sir, I—"

"And you knew it too, so you hurried below to put your face on the
cover of every bloody holozine on the racks. The hero of *Wellington*,
they're calling you! You know damn well I can't court-martial you now.

Well, you got away with it, laddie. For the moment. And what I think of you won't bear repeating."

"Sir, that's not the way it was. I did it for Capt—"

The line went dead.

Ears flaming, I sat with my head in my hands.

Edgar Tolliver said softly, "I don't know what happened, but he's wrong."

"Don't be an idiot. You just said you feel the same way."

"Oh, belay that. You are an innocent. You're the only person I know who cares nothing for self-advancement. You're so undevious you should fall flat on your face, but somehow you don't. You make it hard for even me to hate you."

"Why, thank you, Lieutenant."

"Sorry, it's no time for my—for sarcasm. Why must you resign?"

"I won't discuss it."

"It has to do with *Wellington*, that much is obvious." He studied me. "The Admiral tried to stop you from dealing with Serenco. You should have spit in his eye, but didn't, so he must have something on you. But, what? You have no pride in yourself."

"Tolliver—"

"So instead you resign. What does that solve? Now Serenco will rob the coffers with impunity." He bit his knuckle, frowning. "It all comes down to what they have on you."

He was too close, and his blundering would do untold damage. "Not Duhaney."

"Who, then?"

"I can't tell you. And the reason . . ." I hesitated, threw caution to the winds; we'd been through too much together. "Annie." I started to say more, choked.

"Sir . . ."

After a moment I found my voice. "It doesn't matter. I should have retired long ago, when we brought *Victoria* home." I cleared my throat. "Now, about the letter. I won't allow my resignation to create a scandal; that's the last service I can do the Navy. How do I handle it?"

"Is there any way to change your mind?"

"No."

He brooded. "Be elsewhere when it's released. Where the mediamen can't get to you."

"Hide?"

"I wouldn't call it that. Send the letter from Farside."

I shook my head. No point in going aloft just so that . . . Still, it made sense. I could leave for Lunapolis or Earthport Station whenever I chose. If necessary, I could even lie low at Farside Base until the publicity ebbed. And I'd avoid frenzied mediamen jumping the Academy fence for a picture or a story.

"It'll look strange, my running up to Farside without notice."

"We ship almost a hundred cadets aloft day after tomorrow. What would be more natural than going with them?"

"It would delay my letter two days."

"You send it now, effective Wednesday."

"Very well." I leaned back. "As a courtesy I should address it to Duhaney."

"After the way he spoke to you? Send it to BuPers."

I allowed myself that small satisfaction. "From: Nicholas E. Seafort, Commandant, U.N.N.S. Academy. To: Captain Francis Higbee, BuPers. This is to inform you . . ." It took me no more than a moment. When I was done Tolliver snapped off his holovid, his expression somber.

The caller buzzed. I snatched it. "Now what?"

Sergeant Kinders. "You said to hold your calls, but I thought you'd want me to put Senator Boland through."

I grimaced at Tolliver. "Should I bother?"

"Are you still Commandant?"

"Unfortunately." I thumbed the caller. "Seafort."

Senator Richard Boland's voice echoed in the speaker. "Good morning, Captain. You're recovered from our adventure?"

I snapped, "Is that what you call it?"

"Well, whatever. Congratulations, by the way. They just delivered my *Weekly Holoreview*. You handled them well."

"I'm quite busy, Senator. Is there anything else?"

He sounded jovial. "No, not really, I'll let you go. Oh, one other matter. That topic my colleague brought up with you aboard *Wellington*. It's settled."

"What in hell does that mean?"

Tolliver raised an eyebrow, but I ignored him. It no longer mattered; in hours my resignation would be in Higbee's hands.

Boland's voice sharpened. "I'm trying to tell you to disregard his threats. Go ahead and nail your quartermaster's hide to the wall. I'll handle Wyvern." Too late, I dived for the speaker switch and transferred the call to my handset.

"How did you . . . there are things I can't talk—I mean—" Tolliver watched me sputter, with avid interest.

"Nick, don't worry about that oily son of a bitch. He found your pressure point, but he has a few of his own. As far as you're concerned, he's out of the picture."

"I made a—a bargain," I said quietly.

"Yes, I know. I have his authority to tell you the deal is void, and Mrs. Seafort will be left alone. Go about your business as you would have."

I put down the caller, laid my head on the table. Tolliver . . . the letter . . . Annie . . . My office spun slowly about me.

Tolliver said, "Sir, are you all right?"

I bestirred myself, took up the caller. "Are you sure, Senator?"

"He won't breathe a word, Seafort. Trust me on this."

"Mr. Boland, why are you helping me? Is there a favor—"

"Because I want to." He chuckled and rang off.

"Jesus, Lord Christ." I found myself on my feet, paced, blundered into the end table. "It seems . . . seems . . ."

"That's all right, sir. I'll leave you alone. Ring when you're ready."

"Thank you." It was all I could manage.

"And my holovid must have malfunctioned. That letter is destroyed, whatever it was."

I could only nod.

After he'd left I walked the office, my legs inexplicably shaky. How did the Senator find out, and why had he intervened? I returned to my desk, sat staring out the window.

The caller buzzed once; I ignored it. After a full hour of wracking my brain, I had the answer.

As I reached for the intercom I sighed, hating what I had to do. "Mr. Kinders!" The sergeant came to the doorway. I gave him his orders, paced with growing impatience until a knock came.

The youngster marched in, identified himself, stiffened to attention. His uniform was crisp, as it should be. The shoes gleamed. I'd expected no less. The boy's ears still stuck out, he still had the lankiness of an awkward puppy, but his face held confidence and pride. I'd have to be careful.

I studied him. "The Commandant doesn't involve himself in cadet discipline unless the offense is appalling, as is yours."

"Please, sir, what did I do?"

I slapped him; he yelped. "Don't speak unless you're bidden, or have you forgotten even that?"

"No, sir! Aye aye, sir!"

"Cadet Boland, do you know why you're here?"

"No, sir!"

I forced myself to ignore the tear that trickled down the boy's cheek.

"In the Navy, tradition is all. Beyond the regs, some matters are so ingrained as to be universally understood. Wardroom etiquette, shoreside customs, honor, the legacies of those who've gone before. It was Sergeant Ibarez' job to teach you, and he's failed."

I waited, but he didn't dare speak.

I said quietly, "Robert, how did you find out?"

"About what, sir?"

I slapped him again. The boy gave up all pretense of standing at attention; he hugged himself, crying silently.

"Answer!"

"I was sick from the free fall, even after we boarded *Wellington!*" A torrent of words. "Mr. Tenere sent me around the corridor to the head. When I came out, I heard your voice. I intended to excuse myself and go past, but you sounded so angry, I . . ."

"You snooped to listen."

"I thought I'd go back into the head until you were done, but then I heard Senator Wyvern. He's been in Dad's house lots of times." The boy swallowed, wiped his face. "I couldn't help it, I was afraid to open the hatch to go back in, you might hear me. So I just—I listened."

"That's despicable." My mind flashed back to a time, eons past, when I'd skulked in *Hibernia's* corridors to overhear the whispered conversations of my crew. I thrust down the memory. It was my task to make my cadets better than myself.

I perched on the end of my desk, spoke quietly. "Robert, you violated the Navy's honor as well as your own. No, not by listening; though that was bad enough. Your offense was in going to your father."

He whispered, "I only wanted to help. Wyvern was hurting you so."

"You took a Naval affair to outsiders. That's unforgivable, no matter what the circumstances. You've disgraced yourself."

"It was for you." He looked away, eyes streaming.

"That excuses nothing. I handled the matter in a way I found acceptable, and you betrayed me. It's the worst offense I've seen since I became Commandant. I'm prepared to expel you this very afternoon, unless I have your solemn word as a prospective officer that you will never do such a thing again. Naval affairs are for the Navy to handle."

He blanched, and his lower lip quivered. "Sir, I—"

"Take your time, Mr. Boland."

"I promise." His words were barely audible.

"Very well; I'm pleased with your decision. Now, your punishment. Hang your jacket over the chair." I waited. "Bend over my desk. Cross your hands under your chin." I grasped the cane lying against the corner wall, stood behind the anguished cadet. "Mr. Boland, this is for dishonoring the Navy." My cane lashed down on his buttocks with the crack of a shot. His body jerked.

When at last I was finished I sent the sobbing boy back to his barracks. I set down the cane, viewed it with distaste.

Surely there was a better way. What was gained, flogging children for their indiscretions? Had we slipped back into barbarism? Still, the Rebellious Ages had brought such horrors that society had recoiled, determined not to lose more generations to sin, sloth, dissipation.

But why couldn't a child be raised with love rather than pain? Wouldn't I have been the better, had I been so cherished?

Father's visage floated before me. "The Book, Nicholas."

I know, sir. "*Withhold not correction from the child: for if thou beatest him with the rod, he shall not die. Thou shalt beat him with the rod, and shalt deliver his soul from hell.*"

I sighed. I was no freethinker, and such matters were beyond me.

Edgar Tolliver and I walked the close-trimmed path as the sun beat down with dazzling brightness. I said, "It's hard to make the transition."

"It must be like a second life." He was still on good behavior.

"Edgar, don't misunderstand. I want to resign, to live quietly with Annie. It's just—"

"You wanted to do it with honor."

"Yes, I—no, not honor, I have none left. There's no vileness to which I haven't stooped. But if I resign, it should be in such a way the Navy isn't besmirched."

"Well, if you wanted to resign, putting yourself on the cover of eleven holozines wasn't a great start." Back to his normal self. I felt better.

"So, now what?"

"Finish what you started with Serenco."

"And then?" Absently, I took a midshipman's salute.

"Carry on. Go aloft to Farside."

"That was so I could resign quietly!"

"Don't forget the Naval Affairs Committee visits soon. You might want to start getting the base ready."

Not only that, but I had the majority of my cadets at Farside, and by tomorrow less than two hundred would be left at Devon. My duty was aloft.

In silence, we neared the mess hall. Regardless of Tolliver's advice, I was free to run Academy as I wished. I'd send Jeff Thorne and Tolliver to Farside, stay here with the remaining cadets. Walk in the spring sunshine,

instead of scurrying through cold Lunar warrens. Visit Annie whenever I
wanted.

I sighed, as my dream faded. "When do the transports leave?"

As Commandant I'd gone aloft several times, but I'd never organized
a shift of plebes from Devon to Farside. Traveling alone, I had only to
order a heli to London and fly a shuttle to Earthport Station, where transport would meet me.

Resettling a gaggle of cadets to Farside was organized havoc. Eventually I gave up, and stayed out of the way to let the experienced drill
sergeants do their work. They began with rigorous dorm inspections, followed by extra laundry call so the youngsters' duffels would be filled with
clean clothes.

In each dorm, a sergeant demonstrated how to pack. After his excited
charges had filled their duffels, he opened them one at a time, liberally
sprinkling demerits. Then the duffels were repacked to his satisfaction.

Meanwhile, Sergeant Kinders and Ms. Obutu at Farside scheduled
the fleet of transport helis that would airlift a hundred cadets to the spaceport.

Letting a throng of boisterous youngsters mingle with civilian passengers at London Shuttleport would be asking for trouble. We had to make
prior arrangements with the shuttleport for a private gate.

A hundred cadets and their vigilant sergeants were too great a load
for even the largest civilian shuttle; that meant arranging one of
U.N.A.F.'s military craft. Here, interservice rivalry raised its head. Glad I
could finally make myself useful, I contacted the colonel in charge of
U.N.A.F. transport. My name was enough to assure that the shuttle would
arrive when needed.

And that was just groundside.

By the time everything was double-checked to my satisfaction my
nerves were raw. Late that evening, I sat wearily at my desk with Edgar.
"Farside has enough food on hand?"

"For the third time, yes. And oxygen, and toilet pa—"

"Tolliver!"

"Yes, sir, enough food, though it isn't easy putting through indents
when your quartermaster is in the brig. I had to—"

"When do they come for him?"

"Tomorrow afternoon. You sent Serenco to formal court-martial, so
they'll take him to Portsmouth, where they'll do the polygraph and truth
drugs."

"Serves him right." The drugs left one dizzy and nauseous for days, but the truth would emerge. I thrust it out of my mind. "What have I forgotten?"

"Nothing." He stretched. "Ibarez says moving four hundred at a crack is the real fun. Actually, I don't think you'll have much to worry about; they all have their serg—whoops!"

I flinched. "Now what?"

"The special cadets. They're supposed to be your personal charges. Do you want them traveling with the others, or—"

"I'm not a nursemaid!"

"Of course not, you're Commandant of Academy. It's not your job to worry about a few mere cadets, even though you said you'd—"

I sighed. "What do you suggest, First Lieutenant Tolliver?"

"Take them with you, or give up the ridiculous pretense that they're your personal wards."

"It wasn't ridiculous, just the only way I could think to . . . oh, all right. Book seats on our shuttle."

"Aye aye, sir. Do you want Tenere along?"

"No, let Adam help with the main flock. If you and Jeff Thorne aren't enough to tend three runny-nosed cadets, I'll fire the pair of you."

"That might help. Anything else?"

I growled, "Good night."

The next morning we fed the cadets a light breakfast and set on our way. Casual inspection wouldn't reveal any difference between the cadets we took aloft and those we left behind, though test scores and training evaluations would tell a truer story.

After a few last-minute instructions to the Devon staff I boarded the heli with my officers. My eyebrow lifted. "What are you doing here, Mr. Keene? You're supposed to be on a transport with Sergeant Radz."

The boy blushed red to the tips of his ears. "Yes, sir. He told me to, ah, go—come with you."

I strapped down; we lifted immediately. "Were those his words?"

Keene looked unhappy. "No, sir. Not quite."

"Pray continue."

The boy's face fell. "He said to go annoy the Commandant the way I was bothering his cadets." Passively, he awaited the inevitable demerits.

Johan Stritz nudged Kyle Drew; the two exchanged glances in which glee was barely suppressed. I ignored them; it wasn't often cadets got to see a middy squirm.

"I see." Two thousand feet below us the hills drifted past. "Begin annoying me, Mr. Keene."

"Aye aye, sir. I was just trying to be helpful."

"I can imagine." I let him be.

We landed at London just ahead of our first transport, as I'd intended. Sergeant Ibarez seemed almost nonchalant as he directed his charges to the waiting area. Among them I noticed Robert Boland. His gait was stiff from the caning I'd administered. If he saw me, he gave no sign.

I gave in to Tolliver's urging and waited in the Naval Liaison lounge, though I had no idea why my presence might make it harder for cadets to follow instructions. Sometimes Edgar could be quite irrational.

Tolliver, as senior lieutenant, sent Jeff Thorne from time to time to see if embarkation was going according to plan. I was glad of the respite. When I'd asked Thorne if he had come to a decision about reenlistment, his manner had turned surly.

At length Tolliver suggested we board our shuttle.

"The cadets are safely out of my sight?" I didn't feel gracious.

He was at his most bland. "You could have overruled me. I thought a comfortable lounge, a drink—"

I muttered something under my breath.

"What, sir?"

"You should have told me to go bother Sergeant Radz, the way I was annoying you."

Tolliver only smiled, but Midshipman Keene blushed furiously. I clapped the boy on the back. "Let's get out of their hair." We walked across the pad to the waiting shuttle.

Acceleration. Ache. A long wait.

We deboarded at Earthport Station, trudged down the endless service corridor to our transfer shuttle. The cadets would follow on a larger transport. A waste of resources, but I made no objection; travel with a cabinful of excited plebes would lacerate what remained of my nerves.

The U.N.A.F. pilot greeted me indifferently; I pretended not to notice.

The jaunt to Academy Base took over two hours. As setdown neared I watched my three cadets; they seemed at ease. Well, it wasn't their first trip aloft.

I leaned across the aisle to Johan Stritz. "So. How does it feel to be back at Farside?"

"Feel? Fine, sir." He licked his lips.

"The truth."

"Aye aye, sir. I mean, I'm sorry." His eyes flicked to his mates, as if for support. He rubbed the arm of his seat. "I—I don't know how to feel, exactly. Sergeant Radz and I . . . he was kind of . . . I'm sorry."

"Criticizing your betters, Cadet?" My tone was sharp.

"May I have a word with you, sir?" Tolliver, in the seat forward.

"Go ahead."

"Privately." Without waiting, he unbuckled and went to the rear. I followed. "Now what's the problem?"

"That boy!" His finger stabbed at Johan Stritz. "You hauled him out of his barracks for a special program that didn't exist. You haven't spent—damn it, let me finish!—spent ten minutes alone with him for all the time you had him. You won't let him give you a polite answer about how he feels, but when he admits the truth you chew him out. Go ahead and cane him, if that's what you're after!"

"I spent plenty of time with those cadets! I took them—"

"Did you talk with them? Ever?"

"Of course I did. I had Adam—" I swallowed. "I talked with Kevin, just last week."

"How does Stritz feel about your 'special program'?"

I was silent a long moment. "I don't know."

He said nothing.

"Edgar, what should I do?"

"Do as you please." Suddenly he seemed tired. "I just know I hate bullying."

"You bullied me enough, in the dorms!" What was wrong with me, bringing that up now?

"So you say. Maybe I did. Have we learned nothing over the years?"

"No." Disturbed by what I'd revealed by the one syllable, I blurted, "I've learned I'm worse than ever I imagined." I left him, returned to my seat. "Mr. Stritz . . . Johan—"

The speaker crackled. "We'll be setting down shortly. Those of you who wish to suit as a precaution, do so now." The main transport, half an hour behind us, would be full of suited cadets fogging the inside of their visors with excitement, but our own VIP shuttle would dock directly at the pressured gate.

"Should we suit, sir?"

"Go ahead, just to be safe." I ignored my own suit in the rack above. Let Lord God take me, if that was His wish. I'd evaded His justice long enough.

While Thorne and Tolliver held back in the lock, I stepped forward to take the salutes of Lieutenant Bien and the midshipmen she'd gathered to fill out the welcoming party.

"Welcome aboard, sir."

"Thank you." I forced congeniality into my tone. "Are you ready for an onslaught of plebes?"

"Mr. Radz has them in hand, sir. He's at the main lock. When they're all desuited, shall I assemble them for greeting?"

"I'll see them at dinner. Mr. Keene, settle your middies into the wardroom. Report to Mr. Tolliver for new assignments this evening. I'll see you three cadets in my office now—no, make it an hour." Time to drop my duffel in my cabin, freshen up, walk off some of my restlessness.

A few minutes later I wandered through the barracks area. Everything appeared exactly as it had on my last visit; I didn't know why I'd expected otherwise.

The classroom warrens. I found nothing of interest. Back past the barracks, but there I encountered the first squads of plebes, duffels shouldered, on their way to their new dorms.

To avoid them I ducked into a service corridor, off-limits to cadets. Somewhat disoriented, I struck out toward the Administrative wing.

Around a corner, Lieutenant Jeff Thorne stood, hands in pockets.

He came to attention, saluted casually.

"As you were." My tone was not overfriendly. I made an effort to soften it. "What are you doing here?"

"Thinking about the last time I was in this passage."

"When was that, Jeff?"

He didn't answer directly. "I never thought I'd come back. Did you?"

"After we graduated? No." I leaned against the bulkhead. "It feels . . . odd."

His bitterness welled. "Worse than that. It reminds me of things I'd—rather not recall."

"What are they?"

His eyes swiveled. "Isn't that prying, Commandant?"

I was suddenly tired of reaching out. "Yes. I'll stop. Carry on." I moved toward the hatch.

"Wait." It sounded like an appeal. "It reminds me of—hope, I guess. Or innocence. What I expected from life."

Despite myself, I was moved. "Jeff, it's not too late."

"You think not?" A scornful smile.

"Yes!" I took his arm. "Not for *you*, at any rate! You've betrayed no one but yourself."

He disengaged my hand. "What are you saying, sir?"

"You feel sorry for yourself because you failed to live up to your potential. I've failed Lord God Himself—do you know what I'd give to trade places with you?"

"I apologize."

"Don't be sorry, get hold of yourself!" Was I talking to him, or to myself? "Groundside, when Sandra Ekrit was insolent at table. Did you cane her?"

"Yes and no. We talked. When I was done, I gave her one stroke. I think she might have been happier with more."

"See? You have a natural instinct for handling cadets, and middies too. I've told you that before."

"But I'm lost." He grimaced. "Arcvid, gin, forcing myself out of bed to face another day—"

I wanted to shake him. "Be what you were! What you are!"

He was quiet a long moment. "Do you think I could?"

For a time neither of us spoke. At length I said, "Do you know when I was here last?"

"Farside?"

"No, this corridor."

He shrugged. "Cadets weren't allowed."

"Unless a midshipman took him on a mission . . ."

Bewilderment. Then recognition dawned. "The gravitrons. We never even came close. Old Ridley had the guard."

"And Robbie Rovere stumbled into me, and I went rolling down the ladder. The rest of you disappeared so quick . . ." I smiled. "I've never scrambled up a flight of stairs so fast. All Ridley saw was a blur."

"We deserted you." His face darkened. "As I did later in the mess hall. If you'd been caught . . ."

"But I wasn't." Not that time. "We lived to roam again. Don't forget, when they caught me in the mess hall, you tried to take the blame. I learned something from you, that day."

His eyes shimmered. "What was that, sir?"

Suddenly my voice was strained. "Your courage, in coming forward. Jeff, I've done many things—terrible things, and my soul is forfeit. But I've never betrayed my mates; thanks to your example, at least I've kept that." I had to turn away.

"Easy, sir." His tone was gentle.

"I'm all right." I started slowly for the hatch. "Jeff, get over your regrets. You have a great deal to give the youngsters."

"And give up Arcvid? Sorry, a joke. What I mean is . . . I'll think about it, sir. That's all I can promise." He grimaced. "Maybe here, without the pubs . . . we'll see."

My mood somber, I went directly to my office, found my three charges waiting. I ushered them into my inner sanctum. They wouldn't normally see it unless for extraordinary punishment.

"You may sit."

I laced my fingers, not knowing how to begin. Wasn't it best to avoid the indignity, say nothing, just send them back to barracks?

Father's visage was stern. *"There is no shame to confessing error. Only in committing it."* Yes, Father. Why then did I dread admitting my follies to you, despite the relief it brought?

Kyle Drew squirmed, subsided at my frown.

"I owe you all an apology." My eyes grew heavy with the need to look away. I did not.

Kevin Arnweil ventured, "What for, sir?"

"I've done nothing to help, after bringing you all groundside." I met his eye. "Kevin, you were in shock after Cadet Edwards died. You weren't coping, and I thought Sarge was making it worse." As if ashamed, he looked to the deck.

"And you, Kyle. How could we make you understand Dustin's death was our fault, not yours? I can imagine the guilt you feel, that it was your helmet that opened his."

Drew stared into his lap, his mouth firmly shut.

"Johan. You got off on the wrong foot. I thought somehow I could help you, and the others. But I didn't."

It was Arnweil who finally spoke, hesitantly. "Sir, are you washing us out?"

"Of course not!" I stood, paced helplessly. "I had to tell you . . . I—I don't know how to help. I intended to give you my time, help you through your troubles. Instead I made you into errand boys, or ignored you. All that's left is to apologize."

The silence stretched.

Kevin Arnweil blurted, "You didn't ignore me, sir."

"Rubbish. The only time I spoke with you was when we tried to find Mr. Thorne."

"Yes, sir. Right after that. We walked, and you told me what it was like for you as a cadet."

"That was nothing."

"For you, perhaps." The boy's expression was almost defiant. "It was good to hear someone else had been through it." His cheeks flamed.

"Oh, I remember how a cadet feels." I gestured. "My second year, Commandant Kearsey put me across that very desk to cane me. In his office I felt the terror you must feel at having to speak to me. But that's why I'm the wrong person for you."

Stritz blurted. "Please don't send us back to Devon." I gaped, but he raced on. "It's our fault too! We keep quiet around you, so as not to make you mad. We don't give you a chance." He looked to the others. "You know it's true."

Kyle Drew studied my face, risked speech. "I guess I was kind of disappointed, waiting around for messages to take the sergeants. I thought you're always learning things at Academy. Besides the books, I mean. Like, flying helis." He brightened. "But at least I got to see *Wellington.*"

"You deserve more." My tone was gruff.

"Are you sending us back to barracks, sir?"

That's exactly what I'd had in mind, but now it would seem a punishment for being frank. Again, I'd trapped myself. I made the best of it. "Not if you'll give me another chance. I'll try new rules. You're free to ask questions, or to tell me what's on your mind. Sergeant Obutu will get you back on track with assignments."

It wasn't enough; I needed more. "You may do your homework in my cabin before bunking in the dorm." Good Lord. What was I *doing*? "I'll help you with it." I added lamely, "I'll try not to let you down again."

They said nothing. I could imagine what they were thinking. The Commandant had gone quite mad, and they now had to spend their entire day with him.

"That's all." I hesitated. "Unless anyone has anything to add." Heresy. Pure heresy. They were *cadets!*

20

That evening I caught Tolliver on the way to the mess hall dome. "I apologized to Stritz and the others."

"Oh, wonderful."

"Now what's the matter?"

He shrugged. "Better than snarling at them, I suppose. Best if you could find a distance and keep it. A Captain doesn't apologize."

"This one does. He needs to." I increased my pace. "I was wrong to give them special treatment in the first place." He made no reply.

Tolliver stood aside for me to enter. Five hundred cadets rose as one. I took my place. "Where's Lieutenant Bien?"

Tolliver. "She left on the transport, sir."

"Why?"

"I gave you the leave roster last week. You approved it yourself."

After dinner, I again walked the warrens in restless anxiety. Sandra Ekrit and Midshipman Anton Thayer, on some errand, stood aside, salutes held until I'd passed. Hands in pockets, I strode on.

I turned, went through a service corridor. It led . . . where? The laundry? I had no interest in that. I detoured down a ladder halfway through the corridor. It led me deep into the bowels of Farside, on the service level where the technicians and ratings who manned our machinery were housed.

I bypassed the gravitron chamber where a tech stood watch day and night, went instead to the outer fusion control room. A bored tech sat reading a holo. No matter; our power station was fully automated and his watch was excruciating boredom.

He jumped to attention.

"As you were, mister."

"Aye aye, sir. Is there anything I can do for you?"

"No." I pointed at the splotched deck. "What's that, spilled coffee? Have someone clean it up." Perhaps I should run inspections for staff as well as cadets.

"Aye aye, sir."

I climbed the ladder back to the main level, went to my cabin to sleep.

* * *

A few evenings later, I sat in my office reviewing memos at my console. A report from Portsmouth: Quartermaster Serenco had confessed to stealing over a hundred thousand unidollars and was remanded for trial. No mention of his relationship with Senator Wyvern; apparently that was part of Boland's deal. I sighed, tried to put it out of my mind.

Memorandum from Admiralty: the caterwauling bomb was being passed to Naval Engineering for preliminary design. At last the wheels were rolling, however slow. Another note. Captain Pritcher was reassigned as Admiralty Chief of Protocol, directly under Admiral Duhaney. Captain Tenere, Adam's father, would take *Wellington*.

I read the message from Eddie twice. Annie was eating again. He had found my old bicycle in the shed, fixed it up, and bought a sturdier one for himself. He and Annie biked into town for supplies each day.

Thank you, Lord. At least that goes well.

Kyle Drew knocked, came shyly into my office. "Am I interrupting, sir?"

"Not if I'm alone, you know that." In the days since our last conversation I'd encouraged my cadets to unbend, and I'd managed not to wither them with a disapproving glare when they did. Awkward, for all of us. I checked my watch. "Isn't it nearly time for bed?"

"Yes, sir." His voice cracked, and he blushed. "I have a few Engineering problems left for tomorrow. May I do them here?"

"Quietly." After a moment I added, "Unless you need help."

"Aye aye, sir."

I thumbed through a few more files while Kyle tapped industriously at his holo. "Why here, rather than the dorm?" I asked.

"I'll go, if you'd like. It's just . . ." He flushed. "It's not very friendly there, sir. Since we were assigned to you."

I should have known. By taking the three under my wing I'd made outcasts of them. Well, it was still better than washing them out, and that had been the alternative.

I freshened my coffee, went back to my files. After a while I noticed the boy crossing and uncrossing his legs, muttering under his breath.

"Need to visit the head, Cadet?" My tone was sharp.

He was startled. "No, sir."

"Stop fussing, then." I dictated a few notes. I'd need to talk to Tolliver about appointing a new quartermaster; if we left it to Higbee at BuPers, Lord God knew whom he'd send.

Kyle Drew sighed.

I glowered. "Get out if you can't keep quiet!"

Immediately he gathered his chips. "I'm sor—"

"Belay that." As Tolliver said, I couldn't find a distance and keep it. "What's wrong, Kyle?"

"I'm sorry, sir. I can't get this stuff." He laid his holovid on my desk. "*Basics of Electrical Engineering.* Ergs and ohms and watts."

"It takes study." I tried to sound sympathetic.

"Why do we have to know this goofjuice? Engine-room gauges tell you if you're in the red." He checked my face, afraid he'd gone too far.

"The Navy wants to make you an educated man, not a gauge reader."

"I know a watt is a measure of power, which we call 'P,' and voltage is a measure of electromagnetic force, and we call it 'E.' But all those formulas . . . I get lost."

I leaned back with a smile. "That's easy, lad. There are just two formulas you need to remember. Say after me: 'Twinkle twinkle, little star; Power equals I squared R.' " Kyle gaped, but repeated the jingle dutifully.

"You know that 'I' is current measured in amps. 'R' is resistance measured in, uh, ohms. Now, voltage—'E'—equals 'I' times 'R.' You can derive the other formulas from that, right? 'I' equals 'E' over 'R.' 'R' equals, um, 'E' over 'I.' " I stopped while I was ahead.

He looked at me with wonder. "How did you learn that, sir?"

I basked in the glow of his admiration. "Don't they still teach the rhymes? Go back to your problems, see if you can get them now."

As a cadet I'd labored for weeks at memorizing the merciless formulas. Two years later, on *Hibernia,* crusty Chief McAndrews had discovered my ignorance when I was assigned engine-room watch. On a practice drill I'd misplotted a Fuse to set us inside the B'n Auba Zone, so close to the Sun that no vessel, no matter how small, could escape.

Rather than chewing me out and sending me back to the books, he'd taught me the mnemonic, and begun to rectify my ignorance. Thank you, Chief.

For a time Kyle and I worked peaceably at our tasks. The companionable silence mellowed me; I felt almost light-headed.

The gawky youngster stretched. "Thanks a lot, sir, that'll really help my weeklies." He flashed a grin that lit his sallow face.

His relief seemed to affect me; I felt a burden lift. It was as if I were pounds lighter. "I'm glad. Better get back to barracks before Lights Out." I lifted my cup for another sip, and slopped steaming coffee over my shirt. "Damn!"

"Aye aye, sir." Kyle stood. With a startled look he waved his arms as if to catch his balance. "Whoa!"

Alarms shrilled. As I spun to my console the puter came to life.

"MALFUNCTION IN THE GRAVITRON CONTROLS! COMMENCING SYSTEM SHUTDOWN! POWER DIVERTED!"

Something was terribly wrong.

I grabbed the caller. "Emergency close all corridor hatches! All hands stand by for suitup! Tolliver, Thorne, to the Commandant's office!"

"SYSTEM DISCONNECT COMPLETE! LUNAR GRAVITY PREVAILS. COMMENCING DIAGNOSTIC RUN!"

"What in hell?" I jumped to my feet, banged my skull on the overhead. I caromed down to my desk, managed to anchor myself. Kyle Drew watched, mouth ajar.

The caller panel lit like a Christmas tree. I rubbed my aching forehead.

Jeffrey Thorne poked his head into my office. Grinning, he entered with the slow-sailing lope characteristic of Lunar gravity. "They did it!" he sounded exultant.

"Did what? Who?"

"The middies finally got to the gravitrons!" His eyes sparkled.

"That's nonsense, they've never . . ." I reached to the console, thumbed the caller. "Gravitron Control Room!" I waited.

A knock. Tolliver, taking careful Lunar steps. Sergeant Kina Obutu was close behind.

"We tried for years, all of us!" Thorne's face was flushed. "They made it at last!"

Kyle Drew's face widened into a grin.

Little pitchers. I frowned. "Cadet, back to barracks."

"Aye aye—"

Tolliver. "He can't, sir. You have all the hatches closed. It took me forever to key in the codes."

"Very we—"

The caller buzzed. "Gravitron Tech Siever reporting, sir. I'm in the power station at the moment. The little bastards recoded my hatch. I can't get in!"

"What happened?"

"A cadet came with a message. The engine-room caller wasn't working, and would I go help—"

"What did he look like?"

"Long blond hair, bushy eyebrows, how should I know? They're all the same!"

Sergeant Obutu muttered, "A wig? None of them have long blond—"

"Sir, even after I figure out how to get in it'll take a good hour to restart—"

I grated, "Have Maintenance burn through your hatch. Get the bloody gravitrons up and running!"

Savagely, I punched a caller button.

"Sergeant Radz here, sir. We've lost pow—"

"I know, damn it!" I spun to Thorne, almost launching myself from my chair. "Find out who did it! Have them thrashed and expelled!"

"Let me use my judgment, sir. I'll handle it." Thorne sounded solemn.

"Not this time, you won't. Send them home! Better yet, send them to court-martial!" I stood to pace, thought better of it.

Ms. Obutu coughed. "It's only a prank, sir."

"Only a—" I stared at the alarms, fuming. Lord knows what harm they'd caused. Thank heaven it had been late in the evening. As it was, they'd caused me to spill hot coffee all over myself, and even now I couldn't get to my feet without risking ballistic flight. The gall of those middies, skulking around off-limits corridors, raising havoc in the night. When I was their age I knew better than to—than . . .

Jeff Thorne stared at me fixedly. When he was sure Kyle's eye was elsewhere, he winked.

After a moment the corners of my mouth twitched. "All right, Thorne, straighten out this mess as you see fit." I hoped he'd have the sense to apply the cane, if nothing else. Long-sought triumph or no, the middies must be taught that all things come at a cost.

I swiveled to Tolliver. "There'll be chaos in the dorms tonight. Pillow fights, or horseplay. Maybe worse. Pass the word to let them be." I shrugged off his surprise. "In the history of Academy, no middy ever reached the gravitrons. Very well, let them celebrate."

Kyle Drew grinned like an idiot. I snapped, "Don't get ideas, joey. It isn't funny."

It really wasn't. But even the Lunar gravity couldn't explain my light-heartedness.

"I really must protest." Ardwell Crossburn wore the stubborn look I'd come to know too well. "The damage they caused. We didn't get the gravitrons back on-line until past—"

"Why not?" I demanded. Crossburn was maintenance officer, and after Lieutenant Sleak's death he'd taken the base's Systems responsibilities as well. All too seriously, it now seemed.

Across the conference table, Jeff Thorne rolled his eyes. Tolliver looked solemn.

"The techs had to burn through the hatch, as you know. Mind you, at the cost of a new hatchplate. Then they had to unscramble the gravitron passwords those criminals had changed. I'm astounded Thorne won't tell me who they are." The man was a fool; he had only to observe which three middies were walking with uncomfortably stiff gait.

Crossburn had gone red. "It's most odd, your letting them off. I must say, most odd indee—"

I came to my feet. "You must say? You dare judge me?"

"Not at all. The comment was in a, ah, private capacity." His tone turned sullen. "I won't speak of it, if you insist. But my advice is to cashier whoever's responsible before the Naval Affairs Committee learns next week—"

I slammed my holovid on the table. The shattered lensplate skittered to the deck. "Mr. Crossburn, pack your gear! I want you off base this very day!"

Crossburn was smug. "Without me you don't have enough officers for five hundred cadets. Mr. Kearsey issued a base regulation on that. Anyway, I'm not needed at Devon and my responsibilities here—"

"Jeff Thorne will take your duties. Don't go to Devon. Report to Captain Higbee at BuPers in Lunapolis."

"And what would you like me to tell him? Everything I know?" Crossburn had thrown caution to the winds.

My tone was glacial. "Tell him you're no longer employed at Naval Academy. Get out! Now, before I call Mr. Tenere to help!" Adam had recent experience in removing uncooperative superiors. I wondered if he'd find a posting anywhere, if I allowed that into his record.

Crossburn threw his notes onto the table. "You'll hear about this, sir. I'm not done—" He saw my expression, and fled.

For a moment all was silent.

"Very instructive, sir. I must remember that technique next time a middy—"

"Edgar, shut up!" He was truly impossible; why did I put up with him?

Jeff Thorne asked in a plaintive tone, "What, exactly, does a systems and maintenance officer do?"

I growled, "There's a manual someplace. Read it."

Tolliver said helpfully, "His main duty is keeping the middies away from the gravitr—"

"EDGAR!"

"Yes, sir. Perhaps we ought to get back to business." He pondered his notes while I stalked the cabin, working off my ire. He said, "Your former associate Crossburn had one good point. The annual Naval Affairs visit next week. They'll expect red-carpet treatment, as usual."

I stopped in midstride. "How?"

"One of Mr. Duhaney's assistants was most helpful on that point. For one thing, we serve them decent food. Steaks, not synthos."

"Take care of it." My mind was still on Crossburn. I should have gotten rid of him months ago. Thank heaven I'd done it now, before he buttonholed some Senator with his ubiquitous black diary.

"I'll order up some fancy fruits and vegetables. Just for the VIP tables, of course."

A bad example for our cadets; in the Navy all ranks were fed alike. It couldn't be helped. Duhaney would have a stroke if I didn't cultivate the Naval Affairs Committee.

"And wine. I can—"

"No." I resumed my pacing.

"Aye aye, sir. These Senators vote our budget. Let them stay thirsty."

I growled, "If they don't like it, let them stay home. No wine."

"Jeff, help me, he's in one of his moods again. Sir, it's only for a week." Tolliver made a note. "I'll bunk with Mr. Thorne for the duration; Ms. Bien can join the middies in the wardroom. That will leave enough cabins empty, if you take two guests in your suite like Commandant Kearsey did."

Only eight Senators. But that didn't count their innumerable aides. We'd have to move some of the techs to provide quarters belowdecks. An inconvenience, but . . .

"This year, only four of them are bringing family. I'll arrange for middies to watch the children. They can—"

"No!"

"Beg your pardon, sir?"

"This isn't the Lunapolis Sheraton! No children!"

"Be reasonable. You can't tell them who to bring and—"

"Who runs this place?" I threw myself into my chair.

"I'm not quite sure, sir." Tolliver regarded me gravely. "Do we get hints?"

Jeff Thorne intervened before I could explode. "I don't mind moving, sir. It's in everyone's interest to please the Committee."

I stared balefully at my shattered holovid. It had been my favorite reader since cadet days. "I'm not turning this place into a shambles for a gaggle of politicians and their families! Cancel the visit!" I picked pieces of lens off the carpet.

Tolliver leaned back, folded his arms. "You really can't do that, you know. Perhaps we should break for lunch?"

"Don't treat me like—damn it!" I sucked blood from my pricked finger. "Get this mess out of—" I took a deep breath. "All right, let them come. But no special food, we'll feed them out of stores."

"Aye aye, sir." Tolliver sounded resigned.

I wrapped my finger in a handkerchief, muttered under my breath. My officers and I would all be dislodged, our schedules disrupted . . .

No. I wouldn't have it. "And you'll stay in your own quarters."

"That'll leave us six places short, sir."

"Eight. I don't take boarders." For a moment I relished his surprise. "Send Krane Barracks to the Training Station a week early. That will free thirty places."

Tolliver gaped. "A dorm? We can't bunk spouses and aides and children in a communal cabin!"

"That's the Navy way. We do it all the time." I opened the hatch.

"But they're not—"

I said sweetly, "Isn't it what they're here to inspect?"

By dinner I had calmed myself, but after reflection, I decided to leave matters where they stood. Political visits to Devon were one thing, unwelcome as they were. Senatorial jaunts to Farside were altogether too disruptive, budget or no. Maybe my actions would discourage them. However, I took the precaution of warning Tolliver not to mention our new arrangements to Admiral Duhaney's office.

During the next week I busied myself with paperwork. I had recommendations to write for graduating cadets, supply indents to approve, a new inventory program to outline so that Mr. Serenco's defalcations would not reoccur. Occasionally, in the evenings, I called down to Cardiff. Annie seemed well, but remote.

The day before the Committee was to arrive, I addressed the cadets about to leave for the Training Station. My goal was to impress on them the need for care without actually threatening dire consequences should they misbehave. I wanted no more deaths on my conscience, and with VIPs looking over our shoulders an accident now would be politically disastrous.

I wasn't sure if they heard me, but at least they stayed awake.

Tolliver and I walked back from the main lock.

"You have someone cleaning the dorm, Edgar?"

"Mr. Diego, with two ratings. Not that they're needed."

I agreed glumly. Sergeant Radz would have made sure the barracks was left spotless.

I was having doubts about my decision to house the VIPs in Krane Hall. I resolved to think it through again, though a change of orders would make me look indecisive.

In the morning a flurry of outgoing reports occupied my mind. By lunchtime the Senatorial party had arrived in a U.N.A.F. transport, and the die was cast.

I rounded up my officers, greeted our guests effusively at the lock, and let Tolliver show them to their quarters. For the remainder of the afternoon I managed to be too busy to deal with visitors.

Kevin Arnweil fell in beside me on the way to dinner. "Evening, sir. I finished the trig we worked on last night."

"Good."

"Mr. Sties said it was excellent. Should I tell him half the grade is yours?" Well. The youngster had a sense of humor. If I hadn't forced myself to unbend with my special charges, I'd never have known.

"No, thanks. I have no desire to be half a midshipman next year."

Kevin grinned with delight. I felt a twinge of guilt; a kind word from me meant so much to the lonely joeys I'd put under my wing.

"Sir, the word is that you're making Robbie Boland's father sleep in a barracks."

We turned into the main corridor. "Is something wrong with that?"

His answer was quick. "Oh, no, sir. Barracks is—fine."

"Good." As we passed through the mess-hall hatch I called out, "Be seated."

Normally the Krane cadets sat toward the rear of the hall, but I'd had their unused tables moved closer to the front for the VIPs. Tonight and for the rest of the week my officers and I would dine with our visitors; Thorne had braced the middies to be on their best behavior.

I took a deep breath, pasted a welcoming smile on my face as I approached the long table. "Good evening. Sorry I couldn't be with you today."

Hostile expressions, from men and women alike. "Do you know where they took our gear?" Senator Dorothy Wade, of Ontario. "I tried all afternoon to reach you!"

"Is there a mix-up, Senator?" My voice was bland.

"Our rooms. Your idiot lieutenant"—Tolliver, at the opposite end of the table, affected not to hear—"took us to a barracks by mistake." Next to her, an aide listened with smug satisfaction.

Johan Stritz's face went red; he quickly covered his mouth with a napkin. I felt a moment's panic. If he were sick in the company of—then I saw his shoulders shake. Kyle Drew nudged him ungently in the ribs.

I'd gone too far; even my cadets were laughing at me. Best to give the Senators the cabins they deserved, even if it meant ousting my officers on short notice. Blame it on Tolliver; he wouldn't mind. "I'm sorry, I was tied up all afternoon with—"

Senator Myemkin set down his fork. "Really, Mr. Seafort, someone's made an error. They've crowded us into—"

Mrs. Wade said sharply, "There's not even a plug for a full-size holo-screen!"

Myemkin's tone was mild. "Doris, let me handle—"

She overrode him. "And the bathrooms! They're unspeakable!"

I stopped short. "They're not clean?" Someone's head would roll.

"What does that have to do with it? They're stalls, lined up in a row. It's an insult!"

What had I done? I'd have to give them better accommodations, immediately. "Mrs. Wade, please don't take offense. The heads in Krane Hall are like all the cadet dorms. I'll change—"

Her shrill voice echoed through the hall. "They're fit for animals and trannies! We're decent people!"

The mess hall went absolutely still. Slowly, I folded the napkin. "I'm terribly sorry your accommodations don't suit you, ma'am." Tolliver caught my eye, as if in reminder that I'd been warned.

Thanks to the hushed silence, my humiliation would be public. My gaze swept the dining hall. Cadets, oblivious of their sergeants' scowls, sat twisted to face the drama. On their faces were odd expressions. Embarrassment. Shame.

No, anger.

I stood, made sure my voice was just loud enough for all to hear. "I regret Farside doesn't have quarters befitting your station. Obviously you can't stay . . ." Again I looked at the rows of cadets, and stumbled to a halt.

Their outrage was directed at her, not me.

Trannies? Animals? How could I agree with her allegations, in the hearing of these well-scrubbed, starched youngsters? We'd told them over and again that living in close quarters without a shred of privacy was an honor. Ms. Wade's epithets applied to them as well as me.

My tone was firm. "Krane Barracks is the only housing we have available. Our cadets find it an honor to be assigned to them, or any other barracks in Farside. Can you imagine how hard they struggled—" I bit off the rest. What did these folk know of Academy tradition? "However, there's a solution."

Richard Boland cleared his throat. "What can you do for us?"

"I'll make ready your shuttle, Senator. Anyone who finds our accommodations unacceptable may leave tonight for Lunapolis." Tolliver put his head in his hands.

"But the inspec—"

"We'll meet groundside, when it suits my schedule. I understand there are excellent hotels outside the Devon gates." I threw down my napkin. "I find I'm not hungry, and I have urgent work to do. If you will excuse me." I stalked from the hall.

My caller was disconnected, my office hatch closed. I paced the cabin, increasingly distraught. Why hadn't I controlled my temper just this once? At the least, Duhaney would dismiss me as Commandant this very night, as soon as the Senators' furious calls reached him. His contempt for me was already beyond tolerance, thanks to the interviews I'd given on *Wellington.*

The personal cost didn't bother me; now I was free to go home to Cardiff. But my outburst had done incalculable harm to Academy, and to my cadets. I wondered if my successor could ever repair it.

A knock. Sergeant Obutu.

"No calls, no interruptions!"

"Yes, but Mr. Tolliver says—aye aye, sir."

I resumed my pacing, kicked an offending chair out of the way. Animals. Trannies. So what if I'd been provoked? Hadn't I learned to take worse in wardroom hazing?

Another knock. "Sarge, if you so much as come near—oh, it's you." Johan Stritz.

"Sorry, sir. Yesterday you said I should come to do my Nav problems . . ."

"Stay out. I don't have time to—" No, you fool! "Johan, that was uncalled for. Sit and do your work."

"Aye aye, sir." He took a chair, flicked on his holovid. I resumed my pacing.

"You should have seen them after you left, sir. They—"

"Mind your own business." I stalked the office, muttering under my breath. If I took no calls until morning, Duhaney would have to wait until then to let me know I was cashiered. During the night I could creep down to Devon on our remaining shuttle. At least I wouldn't hear the Senators gloat over their revenge.

I could only imagine what had been said about me.

No, I could do more than that. "Tell me."

Eagerly he put down his holovid. "That old grode Wade called—" He saw my expression. "Sorry. Ms. Wade, I meant. You're a muscle-brained adventurer. A sexist Neanderthal who enjoys humiliating his betters. And Senator Myemkin said you were an unprincipled—"

Another knock. I flung open the hatch. "How many times do I—"

Jeff Thorne. "Yes, I know you weren't to be bothered, but this shouldn't wait."

"Tell the whole lot of them to go to hell! I don't care what they want now!"

He stared, then comprehension dawned. "The politicians? No, this is more serious."

"Let the new Commandant handle it." Grudgingly, I stood aside for him to enter. "Make it fast."

"I don't think Stritz should be here."

"Get on with it!"

"Aye aye, sir. You're not going to like this. Olvira found two second-year joeys—" He seemed at a loss for words. "Sorry. They were pronging each other."

"It happens, sometimes." Arlene Sanders had told me as much, long ago in Lunapolis.

"Sir, they're both in his dorm."

Aghast, I said, "Bunkies?"

"Yes, sir. Tanya Guevire and the Chambers boy." He saw my expression, rushed on. "I know, I feel the same way. They're waiting outside my cabin right now, but I thought it deserved a visit to your office."

"Don't bother! Send them home tonight!"

"Sir, that's a bit extreme. They—"

"I want them out!"

His tone was patient. "It's morally repugnant, but—"

"Damn it, how can the middies crowd into a wardroom if everyone's wondering who's pronging whom! Disgusting! Call the Pilot, have him get the shuttle ready. They're both expelled."

"But—"

I snarled, "Can't you obey a simple order?"

"Yes, sir. Aye, aye, sir. I'd like you to listen first."

"Get—" I reached inward, found some last measure of control. "All right."

"Thank you. We both know it's wrong. But that's what we're here to teach them. I'll see to it neither ever dreams again of having sex with a bunkie. You have my promise."

"They're mates, damn it." It wasn't just that the sex was morally repulsive. Our joeys had to learn that the Navy was as one, that we didn't go around pronging our brothers. I thought of Arlene, and felt a hot flush of shame. I glared at Stritz. "What are you looking at?"

He snatched up his holovid. "Nothing, sir."

Thorne waited.

I sighed. "I don't want to see them. Make it a good one, Jeff. See that they can't sit down for a week."

"Aye aye, sir. Thank you for changing your mind." He saluted, left before I could reverse myself.

I'd turned Academy into a madhouse. Cadets were humping in the corridors, a party of outraged Senators roamed Krane barracks, everyone, including me, questioned orders, and I was preparing to empty my desk while a cadet who should long since have been washed out sat where he didn't belong, pretending he was engrossed in his holovid.

Law and order.

I snorted. At least Ardwell Crossburn was gone. His little black book would haved steamed before he was done writing tonight's events.

Another knock. I whirled, looking for something to throw. Kina Obutu. "I know, sir, but it's Senator Boland. Are you sure you . . ."

"All right, put him on." I took the caller.

"He's right here." She stood aside.

"Well?" It was far too late for civility.

"The vote was five to three, Captain. We stay." He glanced at Stritz, turned away unconcerned. He raised an eyebrow. "Your novel hospitality is . . . refreshing."

His dry manner extinguished my temper. At a loss for words, I crossed to my desk, laid my head in my arms. Should I laugh or cry? Perhaps both. "Senator, things . . . got out of hand."

"Really? With you, I'm never quite sure." He sat. "My colleague is somewhat abrasive."

"She set me off, but I accept the blame. My replacement will smooth things over, I'm sure."

"You mean when Duhaney finds out what you've done? That's why I'm here, actually. I've been delegated to make the call, on behalf of all of us."

"Ms. Obutu's caller is on her desk."

Boland locked his fingers behind his neck. "I think the circuit is busy. In fact, I'm sure of it. Tomorrow, I'll have left Duhaney a message. That should hold them for a few days." In a leisurely manner he got to his feet. "Silly old bitch." He paused at the hatch. "Oh, by the way."

I snapped shut my hanging jaw. "Yes?"

"I told you once I'd have liked to serve in the Navy, if I hadn't gone into politics. Is this your way of giving me the chance?"

I fumbled for a reply, but he was gone.

Kyle Drew and Johan Stritz came jauntily into my office, cheeks flushed. Stritz flipped me a casual salute. "May I sit? They're worse than plebes, sir. It took both of us to get Mr. Myemkin suited. Kyle almost had to sit on him."

I smiled wanly. In the two days since I'd made mortal enemies of the VIPs, I'd had the two cadets help shepherd them around the base. Aides and Senators were continually losing themselves in the maze of warrens.

I studied Johan's rosy face. The boy was coming along. The day before, he had made friends with Senator Rudolpho's twin daughters. Audaciously, he'd knocked on the wardroom hatch to ask permission for the twins to look inside, knowing the frustrated middies couldn't blame him for carrying out official duties. Today the twins were presumably out with their parents and the rest of the party, on a daring fifty-yard stroll to the Hull. Thorne and Tolliver would keep them safe.

Still no call from Duhaney. Senator Boland's message must have been pigeonholed, if he'd sent it at all.

Kyle hesitated. "Sir, do you have time to help me with Law tonight? I'd ask Mr. Keene, but he's busy with the Senators."

I patted the empty seat by my desk. "Now would be better, Drew." I sighed. Even in my private office, the boys felt all too at home.

Worse, I was starting to like them.

21

I was briefing Ngu Bien on Systems and Maintenance when Sergeant Obutu knocked. "Sir, it's the Admiral."

In the week since the Naval Affairs Committee had left, I'd heard nothing. If Duhaney wanted retribution, surely he wouldn't have waited so long.

"Very well." I warily took the caller.

"Seafort?" His voice was jovial. "Higbee's been complaining again. Some Crossburn fellow. You gave him his walking papers without authorization."

"I do a lot without authorization, sir." He knew it better than I.

"Yes, but you're not supposed to admit it. I put him on headquarters staff for now."

Good God. I'd created a monster.

"Listen, I apologize for my remarks about your being a politician. It seems you're better than even I realized."

"What are you talking about?"

"The Committee, Seafort. You know the impression you made."

I gulped. "Yes, sir, I'm sor—"

"Boland couldn't stop raving. Letting them sit in on classes, that was a masterstroke. And who was it put them through fish simulator firing drill for a whole morning, you?" No, it was Olvira. "Myemkin said he hadn't been so tired in his life, but he understood for the first time why we take our drills so seriously."

I regarded the caller as if it were a snake. "Sir, are you, uh, joking with me? Aren't they—"

"They showed me the preliminary draft. Looks like we'll see our first real budget increase in years. One dissenter, but she was overruled seven to one. They're even giving us funds to upgrade the barracks next year."

"There's nothing wrong with—"

"I have to run, Seafort, another damnfool ceremony at U.N.A.F."

I blurted, "Sir, what about the caterwauling bomb I—"

"It's coming along, Commandant. Good work." He rang off.

I sat dumbfounded.

Everything I tried to do well turned out badly.

It was only fitting that what I tried to do badly turned out well.

I dressed quickly, returned to my office to meet Sergeant Radz. On the caller he'd said it was urgent. Ms. Obutu, whom I'd also summoned, sat in the outer room, yawning.

"What's up, Sarge?" I beckoned to a chair.

"A few minutes ago I heard noises through the bulkhead. It's after midnight; they should all be asleep. I found two cadets in the head going at it full blast."

"Again? Are they all sex-crazed?" One revolting incident was enough. "This time we'll make an example—"

"No, sir, not that. They were trying to pound each other into the deck. A real donnybrook. I flung one of them halfway across the barracks, collared the other. He's in my cabin now."

"Good Lord. What was it about?"

"I don't know. I came here before asking." For the first time Radz showed a trace of anger. "My choice would be to send them both to the barrel, and ask after. But last time you didn't like the way I—"

"Stow that!" I stood, turned aside to pace. Everyone's nerves seemed to be on edge. Mine, the sergeant's, even the cadets'. It was my own fault; the Commandant set the tone. "Send them up. I'll deal with them."

"Aye aye, sir." He saluted, strode to the hatch.

I paced anew. I'd been far too lenient of late. I'd let off the middies, forgiven illicit sex, allowed Stritz and the others all sorts of familiarities. Time to toughen—

A knock.

"Enter!"

The boy limped in, drew himself to attention as best he could. His right eye had begun to swell shut; his lip still oozed blood. "Cadet Jerence Branstead reporting, sir."

"You!"

"Yes, sir."

"What in God's own hell have you been up to?"

He mumbled, "A fight."

"Stand straight! Speak up!"

"Aye aye, sir." He complied, winced from the pain. "We were fighting."

"I know; you're bleeding all over my deck!" He licked at his lip. "Stand easy, if it hurts that much."

"I'm all right, he just kicked me kind of . . ."

"Who? Better yet, why?"

"Cadet Ochard, sir." He hesitated. "Please, sir, I'd rather not talk about it."

"Four demerits, you insolent young—" I strode to the cane. "By Lord God, you'll learn to obey before I'm done with you! Exactly what was this fracas about?"

"I—he said I was your—your . . ." The boy's jaw quivered. He made a manful effort at control.

My anger dissolved. "All right, lad." I led him to the couch, gave him my handkerchief. When I thought he was able, I prodded. "Well?"

"He said I got into the Navy by—by sucking up to you, on *Victoria*. Except, that wasn't how he said it." His breath came in a sob. "I work hard, Captain Seafort. Honest, I do. My coming home with you had nothing to do with my scores. It's true, isn't it?" His eyes flickered to mine. "Didn't I earn them?"

"Of course." My voice was tight.

"Sarge wouldn't give—I mean, if he did, being in the Navy wouldn't mean . . ."

"None of the instructors would dare. Not for me, or anyone."

"Yessir. Some of the joes are always on me about it. Tonight, I had enough."

I shook my head. If it weren't that, they'd have found another pretext. Wolves always sense the vulnerable ones.

My voice hardened. "You expect sympathy, joey? No, what you get is a caning. You sat in a cabin for weeks resisting a vial of goofjuice, and now you fall apart because a boy calls you a toady!"

"Not just a toady, a—" He compressed his lips.

"It's all right, you can say it. My bedmate, I assume. Children's nonsense."

"They're my mates!" An anguished cry.

"All the more reason to hold your temper. How in heaven do you think you'll cope with wardroom hazing if you can't—"

The caller buzzed. "Sir, priority call from Earthport Station." Sergeant Obutu.

"Later, I'm in the middle of—"

"Captain, pick up the caller!" Her voice brooked no argument.

Speechless, I thumbed the caller onto the speakers. "Yes, what—"

"—ERGENCY BROADCAST TO ALL SHIPS, ALL PERSONNEL! REPEAT: LUNAPOLIS BASE HAS BEEN BOMBED, EXTENT OF DAMAGE UN—"

"Lord God!" I stood frozen.

"—ADMIRALTY BASE DOESN'T RESPOND. SHIPYARDS AT EARTHPORT STATION UNDER ATTACK. AT LEAST SEVENTY-FIVE FISH ARE—"

"*Captain Tsong on* Invincible. I'm taking—"

"—OUR LASER BANKS. ANY SHIP WITHIN RANGE, PLEASE ASSIST. WE'RE—"

"*Get off this channel; we need it! Until the chain of command is reestablished I'm senior. All vessels moored to Earthport Station, cast off immediately! About a hundred fish have Defused above Earth's atmosphere!*"

A hundred? Lord, save us. If—

"Sir, should I—" Jerence was white.

"Shut up!" I bent close to the speaker, strained to hear.

"*How the hell would I know,* Wellington? *They're not on a social call, that's certain. Take your position and stay off the chan—*"

"Mayday! U.N.S. *Aztec*! We can't beat off attack, they've breached our hull! Mayday! Coordinates—"

I rasped, "Jerence, back to barracks! Move!"

"Aye aye, sir!" He saluted and was gone.

I keyed the caller to general frequency. "Tolliver! Thorne! To my office, flank!"

"*Gibraltar* to *Invincible*! We killed six, but a dozen more Defused alongside. We're coming up on *Aztec*, will try to help."

The caller buzzed. Sergeant Obutu. "I'm sending Cadet Ochard back to his dorm."

"Who? Yes, of course. Have all cadets report to barracks, flank."

"They're already in bed, sir. It's the middle of the night." The calm of her voice was a warm, gentle wave.

"Very well. Send Tolliver and Thorne in. And you too." I'd want her placid good sense. "Put someone on our landing radar. Wake a tech or one of the sergeants. If anything shows overhead, sound the alarms."

"Aye aye, sir."

"Turn off all outside lights. And no outgoing radio." If by any chance we'd escaped notice of the fish, best to do nothing to attract them.

I turned back to the speaker, as the hatch opened.

"Lieutenant Thorne reporting."

"Listen!"

Tolliver raced in, out of breath. "Hope this is important; I was dreaming of—"

"Quiet, Edgar!" I pulled up another chair. Kina Obutu came in, with cups and a pot of coffee; bless her. I poured a steaming cup, took a sip. "Lunapolis has gone off the air. We have no central command."

Tolliver. "U.N. Headquarters will take over. Or London."

"Groundsiders. We need Fleet Ops."

Sergeant Obutu said, "It may take a while to reorganize. London Admiralty normally relays through Earthport Station, and if the Station's under heavy attack . . ."

Thorne bit at his knuckles. "What's Admiralty supposed to do about it? We can't defend everywhere at once."

"I know that. They have to assign—"

"—OUTSIDE THE HULL! THEY'RE BURNING THROUGH! WE'VE ALL GONE TO SUITS—"

"—*Fusing to safety. We'll reestablish contact when—*"

"—most of the city under several feet of water. The asteroid struck the gulf fifty miles southeast of Galveston. We need helis, medical—"

"Do something!" I set down my coffee to pace.

We huddled at the caller while disaster swept through home system. Five ships were lost outright; thirteen others were damaged but still fighting. Four ships of the line were clear of gravitation and Fused out of the Solar System.

Fish came in droves. According to the scattered reports, almost three hundred aliens roamed home system. Earthport Station fought desperately to survive; if it fell, Earth's vast interstellar commerce would die with it.

Why hadn't the fish struck at Farside? Was it because only an occasional shuttle without fusion drives docked here? Thank Lord God that Radz and his Krane cadets were back from the Training Station.

I muttered, "Maybe we should get everyone suited. If the fish show . . ."

Tolliver. "There's nothing on radar."

"Sooner or later, they'll come for us. They've knocked out Lunapolis and they're swarming around the Station."

Kina Obutu said gently, "Do we really want middies and Sergeants running to help five hundred teens change tanks every couple of hours?"

"Suits without helmets, then." Thorne. "Call a suit drill. Have them practice putting helmets on and off."

Tolliver's eyebrow raised. "In the middle of the night?"

"You'd rather not tell them we're under attack?"

I said, "No one's attacked us yet." Yet I was certain they would, in time. "We'd panic our joeys, Thorne. They're still children."

Tolliver said, "U.N.N.S. cadets can face—"

I waved vaguely at the bulkhead. "They belong at home with their mothers. What right had we to pretend they're adults, take them off-planet to . . ." It seemed too much trouble to continue.

"Farside can't be defended." Tolliver tapped the console. "We have no laser cannon. Even the Trainers are unarmed."

Sergeant Obutu's voice was soft. "Even with weapons, middies and cadets can't hold against an alien armada. What about making a run for groundside?"

"In what, the transport shuttle?" Again I paced. "We only have one, and it's not built for reentry. I doubt the fish would let us transfer at Earthport Station."

She flushed at my sarcasm, but persisted. "We could orbit just above Earth's atmosphere. At least we'd have a chance to maneuver."

"Our transport can't hold more than fifty. Who would we leave behind?" That brought a silence.

"So, we wait?" Thorne.

"Yes. There's nothing else to—"

The speaker blared again. "—narrowly missing Vancouver. Fires are burning out of control in—"

"—FISH OUTRIDERS IN SECTIONS FIVE THROUGH NINE. WE'LL TRY TO HOLD OUT ON THE BRIDGE."

Thorne leaned over my desk, his face inches from mine. "Captain, this may be their last night! Tell them!"

I raised an eyebrow. "Was that an order?"

He blushed. "No. Sorry."

"If it's their last night, would you have them spend it in terror? I'll make an announcement tomorrow, if the fish haven't shown by then."

The voice from the speaker was light-years distant. "Admiral Iskander, speaking from London. We're gathering situation reports, but it's already clear we're under all-out attack."

"Observant of you!" Tolliver's fists bunched.

"Be silent!"

"—til we know enough to develop an overall strategy, every Station, every base, must defend itself independently. Ships in squadrons, follow the orders of your flotilla commander. All vessels within five hours of Earth proceed immediately toward Earth's outer atmosphere where fish are massing. Further orders will fol—"

"—SEVENTY-FIVE OR MORE. NEARLY A HUNDRED STILL SURROUND THE STATION, AND WE LOST OUR TOPSIDE LASERS ABOUT AN HOUR—"

"*Mayday! Mayday!*"

Tolliver was grim. "It'll be a short war, Captain. They've taken out the Navy."

"Not all of it. We still—"

"—assume Callisto Base is destroyed. That leaves the Naval Station on Deimos as the only—"

"Fiske here, in *Electra*. Am I senior?"

"—Coordinates twelve, two-sixty, fifty-four—"

"—*massing over East Asia! For the moment they're ignoring us, but we need help, they're too many for the lasers to take*—"

Thorne looked up. "Tolliver's right. We've lost."

"Maybe they'll leave us." On Hope Nation, they'd sometimes withdrawn for no discernible reason. "Once we have time to organize . . ." Wearily, I turned the volume down. If only I'd made my point clearer to Admiralty, we'd have a caterwaul bomb in production.

We sat in silence.

"In a way, it's a relief," Thorne said. My jaw dropped. He added, "We all have to go someday. Now I know it'll be soon."

Oddly, I understood. Whether the fish came tonight or days from now, soon I would face my reckoning with Him. "Even Hell seems preferable to the wait." I didn't realize I'd spoken aloud.

"That's rot, Captain!" Tolliver's contempt was withering. "The renowned Nick Seafort giving up? You've never done that!"

I growled, "What should I do, take command of the Hull?" I waved toward the mockup half buried in the Lunar dust. "We've no ships, no weapons, no place to hide. Sooner or later we'll run out of supplies!"

"Think of something! You always have!" Abruptly he turned away.

Thorne said, "As you pointed out, we're unarmed." When he spoke again his tone was wry. "Now if you don't mind, I'll go to the lounge. I'm of a mood for Arcvid."

Tolliver snarled, "That's what I'd expect of a loser like you!"

I snapped, "Apologize, Edgar. At once." Tolliver murmured something inaudible.

Thorne shrugged. "I don't mind, Captain. He's right. Back when we were cadets and middies, I didn't understand. Mr. Tolliver, I wish you well. Commandant, I think if—if things had worked out differently . . ." For a moment he sounded shy. "I'd have tried to redeem myself for you."

"Thank you." I rubbed my eyes. Hours ago—or minutes—I'd been ready to cane Jerence for brawling. Now our very civilization was crumbling. "Mr. Thorne, go to your Arcvid. Ms. Obutu, you're free to leave. You too, Tolliver."

Jeff Thorne hesitated. "I could stay, if you like."

"I'll call if I need you."

"Do that." He left.

Tolliver waited until we were alone. "Shall I get your suit, sir?"

"No. I won't be needing it."

"If the fish . . ." He grasped my intent, and stopped.

"Aye aye, sir. Will you sleep?"

"I'll wait by the caller." My cabin held nothing. "Leave me be!" Glowering, I watched him go.

I shut the hatch, turned low the lights, sat hunched at the console, scanning channel after channel.

"—onto Lunapolis. We've lost thousands. Admiralty warrens decompressed but there may be survivors. Our puters are off-line. If the fish hold off awhile we can—"

"—*have a rock! Must be two hundred of them around it. Am tracking*—"

"—estimates nearly six hundred fish altogether—"

The fish had scored a complete surprise, and had gained overwhelming strategic superiority. They . . .

Annie! My wife was abandoned in Cardiff, while fish gathered above, shepherding rocks to destroy her.

And I was helpless. I swallowed my impotent rage.

Why did they attack like frenzied sharks? No one knew. I supposed it no longer mattered.

The anguished reports from the speaker faded into distance.

WHY HADN'T I MADE THEM LISTEN?

A distant call. "Be alert for distress call from U.N.A.F. shuttle 382AF or its lifepods. Admiral Georges De Marney, recently returned from Hope Nation, was en route from London Spaceport to assume command—"

A knock. I raised my head.

"Me, sir." Jeff Thorne. For a moment, he hesitated, then his shoulders squared. "I don't know what I was thinking. My place is here."

"In my office?" I waved at the furnishings. "You want the job?"

"No, sir." He smiled at my sally. "You handle it well. My duty is to help."

I looked away, ashamed. His tone recalled a young midshipman I'd once known. "Jeff—"

"Yes, sir." He came to the desk. "Remember when I told you Arcvid's like life? We're at level twenty-three. The ships come too fast. We're about to lose the board." Despite his words, his eyes were animated. "Let's see if we can make another level or two, sir."

"God, Jeff!" My voice was raw. "If only we could!"

"Let's start by closing our decompression hatches; that'll buy time even if a bomb hits."

"The concussion alone would kill us."

"Depends how close it strikes, right?" He gestured toward the barracks. "We want to save as many joeys as we can."

I was silent a moment. Then I stood, offered my hand. "Welcome back, Mr. Thorne."

His fingers clasped mine. "Thank you, sir."

"I wish I'd let them give me a ship. What a mission we could fly, you and I." I smiled, but in truth I was nearly out of my mind with frustration. I needed to do something, anything. Attack a fish with my bare hands. If they came to me I'd . . . My smile faded. Using what, a hand laser?

Anyway, I had no way to attract fish; Farside had no ships to call them.

"Sir, may I close the hatches?"

Static. "—for a broadcast by Secretary General Rafael De Vala."

I bent closer to the speaker.

"Citizens, members of our Armed and Naval Forces. Home system is under intense attack by the aliens known as the fish. Hundreds circle Earth itself. Galveston and nearby towns have been swamped by a tidal wave.

"As we learned at Hope Nation, the fish will use any means to subdue us. They may hit us with a lethal virus. They may try to bomb our cities. They may attack in ways we can't anticipate. There are unconfirmed reports they've already landed on the surface of Earth."

I sat heavily, rested my head in my hands.

"Lunapolis is destroyed, and with it, Fleet Operations Command. We're reorganizing command at Admiralty in London, but meanwhile—" The SecGen's voice wavered, then resumed.

"—though many elements of the fleet remain unharmed, our forces are scattered, our communications disrupted. Fish attack our groundside and satellite lasers in ever-increasing numbers."

Remote-controlled lasers couldn't fight them off. Even the fleet wasn't enough.

"U.N. Armed Forces across the planet are to engage the aliens wherever they try to land. Admiralty sends the following signal to all Naval units: 'All ships withdraw from engagement, and take up position in geosynchronous orbit over North America and Europe. At all costs we will defend our industrial base.'"

He faltered. "Admiralty sends the following message. 'To all ships and forces, everywhere: The United Nations expects every man to do his duty.'"

The speaker went silent.

"He abandoned Asia and Africa!" Thorne was stunned.

"Half the fleet is lost, maybe more! Should we protect African jungle, or the Boeing-McDonnell plants?"

"But . . ."

I sighed. "Go close the hatches, Jeff. There's not much else we can do." If only we had the caterwaul bomb.

"Aye aye, sir." He trod to the console in the outer office, tapped the control keys.

I sat wretchedly, as calls poured over the speaker.

If I took our shuttle, I could get to the fish at Earthport Station.

But the shuttle had no weapons.

Ram the bastards. I'd done it before.

They'd overwhelm me before I had a chance to do much damage. There were myriads of fish, and only one of me.

Time and again I'd refused a ship. Now I was on the far side of the moon, on a training base with no attack weapons.

"Groundside lasers broke it up! Only small pieces left!"

"—N.S. *Targon*. I've got to take the chance and Fuse. They're after our—"

"If anyone can hear me, this is Captain Roman de Ville, in a lifepod drifting inward toward the Sun. Three fish are Outside. One of them is swinging a—"

Please, God. Help us.

Thorne returned.

"Jeff, I want to be alone."

His face fell. "Yes, sir. I'll check the barracks."

"Good." Opening hatches to work his way along the warrens would give me time to ponder my folly.

I'd been the only person who had enough encounters with fish to comprehend their true menace, the one person with influence to persuade Admiral Duhaney to speed manufacture of the caterwaul bomb. I could have made them listen, made them prepare. But rather than annoy the Admiral, I'd worried about my petty career. And doomed the human race.

Lord God, what will I say to You, when the time comes? Do You have someplace worse than Hell to consign me?

"—whatever you can to hold them off. You've GOT to buy us time!"

Buy time for what? The fleet was devastated; we'd need years to rebuild, even if the fish retreated.

"—lost with all hands. U.N.S. *Victoria* was the fastship brought home some months ago by Captain Nicholas Sea—"

"—*need time to evacuate the cities, if nothing else! Attack, I told you! I don't care what odds—*"

I became aware of a sharp ache in my hand. I'd scraped my knuckles when I slammed them into the console.

I wrapped my handkerchief across my aching fingers. Had it all come to a hopeless effort to evacuate our vulnerable cities?

In any event, we hadn't enough transports or time to empty cities like New York. And evacuation would start with the influential Uppies; joeys such as Pedro Chang and his tribesmen would be forgotten.

Lord, let me do something. Given time, luck, weapons, I could kill fish. I'd nuked hundreds of them swarming around Orbit Station. I'd fought them in the Ventura Mountains, burned them with *Wellington*'s lasers. I'd even skewered one with *Challenger*'s prow in a desperate effort at revenge.

"—OVER THE MIDWESTERN UNITED STATES! ALL SHIPS, TRY TO BREAK UP THEIR FORMATION! EXPECT A LARGE GROUP WITH A ROCK TO DEFUSE AT ANY—"

I shut off the speaker.

An hour passed, perhaps more. I roused myself, sat staring, opened the desk drawer.

"I'm sorry," Lieutenant Sleak had said to the holocamera, at Devon.

I understood, at last. When he'd uncovered Sergeant Serenco's embezzlement, he blamed his own incompetence as a supervisor. He'd felt it his duty to prevent, or at least discover, Serenco's misdeeds, and the shame had been too great to bear. And so he'd taken his pistol from the drawer.

Oh, yes, I understood.

There's nothing left, you see. I have no way to defend my children, no way to draw the aliens away from Earth. I've no way to destroy them even if I could call them.

I've no way to atone.

I gripped the pistol, thumbed the safety. "I'm sorry."

The empty office made no answer.

I set the pistol to point-blank range, pressed it to my temple. What else could I do? We couldn't repel fish from an unarmed training camp. I had nothing but a base full of cadets, a transport too small to carry more than a handful to safety. And the Training Station, with *Trafalgar* and a few Fusers. All were unarmed. It was hopeless.

Unless . . .

I sat bolt upright. After a time the pistol fell from my hand.

It could be done.

But, Lord, the cost.

Part 4

January, in the year of our Lord 2202

22

I rushed to the head, splashed water on my cheeks, stared at the wild face in the mirror.

Back at my console, I opened the decompression hatches throughout the base. I keyed the alarm for General Quarters, thumbed my caller.

"ALL CADETS, ALL STAFF, ALL OFFICERS, ASSEMBLE AT THE MESS HALL, FLANK! TAKE NO MORE THAN ONE MINUTE TO DRESS!"

Ignoring my own orders, I straightened my tie, brushed my hair, smoothed my jacket. Before I left the office, I stooped, picked up the pistol.

During my long, last walk to the mess hall I practiced my calm. No one must suspect.

Edgar Tolliver sprinted down the corridor. "Have they come? What's happened?"

"Not yet." I slid open the mess-hall hatch.

"STAND TO!"

Officers and men, middies and cadets, snapped to attention. I holstered the pistol, strode through the crowd. Boys and girls stood stiffly, cheeks flushed, uniforms awry, hair uncombed. "At ease!"

They complied. For a moment I felt a wistful pride. I would have liked to take them to graduation, and beyond.

For a long time I gazed. Then I began.

"I've decided to take a number of cadets on special mission to the Training Station. You'll be supervised by midshipmen. We leave immediately. Ordinarily I would select candidates based on skills and training, but there are reports that fish have been sighted in home system. Therefore, I will take only volunteers."

Absolute silence. Kina Obutu shook her head sadly. I blushed. As casually as possible I added, "There may be some danger. However, volunteers will receive credit for two months of Nav." Somehow, despite the obscenity of what I'd said, I managed to hold their gaze.

A hand shot in the air, then another.

Tolliver moved to my side, puzzlement battling anger. I said quietly, "Be silent. That's an order."

I looked to the closest raised hand. "Step forward. Name?"

"Rafe Slater, sir." His voice hadn't yet broken.

I forced a reply. "Report to the suiting room."

"Aye aye, sir. Excuse me, should I get my duffel?"

"No." I nodded to the next upraised hand. "Name?"

"Vasily Karnyenkov."

"Very well. Who else?"

A sharp tug at my jacket. Tolliver. "Where do you think you're taking them?"

I thrust him away. "Next?"

"Jacques Theroux, sir."

I frowned. "Your name's familiar. How do I know you?"

"I don't know, sir."

"Report to the lock." I looked around; only a few hands waved.

"You don't even remember!" Tolliver's words came in a hiss.

"I told you to be silent."

"You threw another boy off at Cull, for Theroux."

Did I? That was so long past. A damnation ago.

"Sergeant Ibarez!"

He hurried forward.

"Go to the lock, help the cadets suit up, send them to board the shuttle."

"Aye aye, sir." No questions.

I searched for more volunteers.

"Robert Boland, sir."

"I know." I stared through him. "Very wel—No. refused." The others might be mere names, but I knew too well what the boy meant to his father.

"Sir, please!" His tone was anguished. "You told me I paid for my offense."

"That's not it; it's that I don't want you!" My voice was the harsher for knowing I was unjust.

He whispered, "Please, I'm first in my class in Nav! Let me go!"

I looked around the room. Cadets shifted uneasily from foot to foot, anxious to avoid my glance.

A man chose his own fate. "Very well. So be it."

"Johan Stritz, sir." He stood proudly. Behind him, Kyle Drew and Kevin Arnweil waited their turn.

Why, Lord? They're my special charges. Could you not spare . . .

I made my voice hard. "Very well." One by one, I accepted all three. "Loren Reitzman, sir." I frowned, then recalled. The boy who'd balked at the oath of enlistment. He'd had a week of misery, then buckled down to the business of being a cadet. We'd had no further trouble. Would he crack again?

"Very well." The cadet trotted off to the suiting room. A tall, gawky girl raised her hand tremulously, gave her name. I nodded; she ran off.

"Jerence Branstead, sir." His bruised features appealed.

I swallowed. I accepted the Boland boy, and all the others. How could I not take him?

No. Lord help me, I could not. I'd sworn to his father to keep him safe, when he'd entrusted the boy to my care on Hope Nation. Even though my word was without value, I would spare at least one child.

I raised my gaze. "No. Refused."

He blurted, "Sir, I know what I'm doing! Please let me come!"

"BE SILENT! I FORBID IT!"

Shamefaced, Jerence crept from my sight.

"Elena Von Siel, sir!"

I nodded heavily. "Very well."

A black-haired dark youngster. "Omar Benghadi." The girl at his side raised her hand tentatively, brought it down. She looked away.

I knew him from somewhere. He fidgeted while I stared through him, racking my brain. Nothing. "Very well. Go with the others."

The girl watched him disappear, her fists clenching. Abruptly her hand shot into the air. "Alicia Johns, sir!"

So young, so vulnerable. I made my voice flat. "Very well." Who were they?

I had it. The young pair I'd met on an idle visit to the Devon classrooms a few days before my appointment; the meeting had led to my chat with Sergeant Ibarez.

I turned to my work.

When the last hand was acknowledged forty-three cadets had volunteered. Were they enough? I could draft just a few, for—

No. That was too great an abomination, even for me.

My voice rang out. "You other cadets! Return to your barracks. Your officers will be along shortly. Dismissed!"

Some sheepish, others relieved, they herded toward the hatch.

I couldn't leave on that note. I called, "Those who didn't volunteer need have no shame. I wish you well." I bit off the rest; it sounded too like farewell.

"Midshipmen, step forward!"

Self-consciously, the seven young officers clustered around. Thomas Keene, Adam Tenere, Sandra Ekrit. Others I hardly knew: Guthrie Smith and Tommy Tsai. Red-haired Anton Thayer. Eduard Diego.

"You're all coming with us. Mr. Keene, have your joeys report to the shuttle immediately." Should I have given them a choice, like the cadets? No. They were officers.

I was proud that their discipline held. No questions. First Midshipman Keene said only, "Aye aye, sir." He turned to the others. "Let's go."

In a moment no one was left in the hall but the shuttle Pilot, my two lieutenants, the drill sergeants, and a few techs. I beckoned them close.

"Pilot Trayn, you'll take us to the Training Station. Get the shuttle ready. The rest of you, listen carefully. As I told the cadets, there are fish in home system." The Pilot paused at the hatch to listen. "They've done great harm, and it's possible they'll come here. Keep the outside lights off, stay off the radio. Lord God willing, help will arrive." Pilot Trayn nodded, went out to the corridor.

"Lieutenant Thorne is in charge until . . . while I'm gone. You sergeants, follow his orders. If the fish come . . ." Something seemed wrong with my throat. "Get your joeys suited, try to keep them alive as best you can. Perhaps the fish will do their destruction and leave."

"What about you, sir?" Ms. Obutu.

"I'll be at the Training Station." I was careful to say no more; someone might still obstruct me. "That's all. Dismissed."

Sergeant Radz hesitated. "Commandant . . ."

"Yes?"

"Godspeed, sir."

"Thank you."

He snapped a parade-ground salute, turned and strode out. My eyes filled. Kina Obutu lingered for a word; I shook my head.

"Am I relieved?" Tolliver.

"What?"

"You put Thorne in charge. What will you have me do?"

"Go with me."

His tone was bitter. "I thought so. I'm at your orders."

I said gently, "It wasn't an order, First Lieutenant Tolliver."

"What are you up to this time?"

"I can't tell you."

"The last time you said that you nuked a bloody Station!"

"There's none here to nuke."

"I'll go. We started together. It's fitting that we end together. I'll meet you at the shuttle." I wondered how much he'd guessed.

* * *

I checked and rechecked my suit. Though earlier I'd been ready to welcome decompression, now I had to stay alive until my task was done.

I tested my helmet clamps one last time, looked to Ibarez. "Is everyone boarded?"

"Yes, sir. Am I to come along?"

He was an experienced hand, but he had a barracks, and his flock mustn't be abandoned. "No. Go back to your joeys."

"Aye aye, sir." He hesitated, gestured to the lock. "Odd mood they were in. Even though they sense something's wrong they were jostling like puppies to go aboard."

"Children think they're immortal."

"Yes." His expression sobered. "That's why we're here. To protect them until they learn otherwise."

I stepped into the lock.

Outside, all was still. I tried to adjust my vision to the pinpoints of a billion stars.

I loped across the Lunar dust, waited impatiently while the shuttle lock cycled. Every moment meant lives lost on Earth.

Inside, I brushed past Tolliver and strapped down in the front row. I keyed to suit frequency. "Edgar, tell the Pilot we're ready for liftoff."

"He's not here, sir."

"He's had plenty of time to get ready!" I keyed to base frequency. "Find Mr. Thorne." I fretted while the precious minutes passed.

"Lieutenant Jeffrey Thorne repo—"

"Get my Pilot suited and out here!"

"Isn't he with you, sir? I haven't seen him any—"

"Find him! Move!"

"Aye aye, sir." The line went dead.

Tolliver took a seat across the aisle. "You seem in some haste." His tone was dry.

"None of your lip, Tolliver!"

"No, sir. Of course not. Is there a schedule we have to meet? I only ask as your second in command."

No need to explain; he'd find out all too soon. "We're sitting ducks if the fish come!" I drummed on the seat arm. "Where's the bloody Pilot?"

As if in answer my radio crackled. "Thorne, here. Mr. Trayn is nowhere to be found. We can roust the cadets and search cabin by cabin until—"

"When he shows, brig him! Tolliver, let's go!" I scrambled out of my seat, launched myself toward the cockpit. I took the copilot's seat, waited for Tolliver to buckle in alongside. "Help me lift this bucket."

He said mildly, "We're not rated for—"

"Remember the Venturas shuttle on Hope Nation? Compared to that, this is child's play. You have to *work* to foul up a Lunar launch."

"I see. In that case, would you take the Pilot's seat?"

I ignored him and flicked switches, waited for the puter to self-check. The vessel was fully fueled, as I knew it would be. I pumped a few liters of propellant through the fuel tubes, watched the gauges wiggle.

A dry, mechanical voice. "Beginning preflight checklist. Port thrusters indicate full tanks. Starb—"

I glanced skyward though the porthole. "No time. Cancel the checklist." A methodical check would consume almost a half hour.

Console lights shifted. "Discontinuing launch at your order."

"No, damn it, prepare to launch!"

"Beginning preflight checklist. Port thrusters indicate—"

I cursed silently. "Puter, prepare for launch without checklist."

"Standing orders require checklist prior to—"

"Cancel standing orders! I'm the Commandant!"

"Only the Pilot may do that. I'm a U.N.A.F. shuttle, not subject to Naval command."

I slammed my gloved fist on the console. "What are you laughing at, Edgar?"

"Nothing, sir."

"Puter, log me on as Pilot."

"U.N.A.F. authorization code?"

"As Base Commandant I relieve the Pilot and appoint myself. Tolliver, is there a manual shutoff to this idiot?"

"I have no idea." He bent to the dash. "Don't see one."

"Power down!" I flicked the switches. One by one the console lights extinguished.

Tolliver said mildly, "It'd take less time to let him run his—"

"We don't need the puter to turn on power." I switched on the engines.

"We need him to plot a course to—"

"Not to lift off." The hell with regs. "All we need is orbital velocity, and the nose pointed away from the ground."

"Right. I'm glad we're doing this by the book."

"By the way, you have the conn." I leaned back. "Oh, don't gape, we both know you have a surer hand." I braced for the mild acceleration.

There was no reason a U.N.A.F. shuttle couldn't launch manually. I recited that, as a mantra, while our engines shuddered and the frustrated pull of the moon thrust me into my seat.

At last Tolliver silenced our motors. I peered out at the Lunar surface far below.

"If you see the Training Station, let me know."

"Don't be silly, it wouldn't be—" I realized he was in one of his moods. Though I'd warned him not to lapse into insolence, I felt oddly relieved. "Turn on the Station beacon by remote." I watched the radar screen, half expecting fish to Defuse at our side.

"Is there a chance the puter would tell us the way?"

"I'd rather walk." Nonetheless, I switched the puter on, waited for its circuit check. "Plot a course to the Naval Training Station."

A pause of at least a second. "Voice ID indicates you are Nicholas Seafort, U.N.N.S. Do you confirm?"

"Yes."

"Who is the Pilot?"

"I am." Another few seconds and I'd do the plot by hand.

"Your name isn't in my Pilot registry."

"All right, have it your way. There's no Pilot aboard."

"A licensed Pilot must be in the cockpit of a U.N.A.F. shuttle prior to launch."

"But we're aloft, and he doesn't seem to be here. Will you plot our course, or does your bloody program call for us to starve until our orbit decays?" Dosmen are all alike. They never program flexibility.

The puter's voice took on a firmer note. "Emergency procedures now in effect. I'm plotting course to Naval Training Station, will initiate automatic course corrections."

"Why, thank you." I knew I ought to recheck the figures by hand, but for once I let it go. My mind was too full.

Figures flashed across the screen. A moment later our side thrusters fired briefly, orienting us toward the Station.

"You're welcome," the puter said. "On return I will file a complaint with U.N.A.F. Transport concerning your violation of regulations, Base Commander Seafort."

By then I wouldn't care. Still, I wasn't about to take any bilge from an animated circuit board. "Puter, on our return I will file a complaint with U.N.A.F. Transport concerning violations of regs by this shuttle."

A puff of propellant; our turn eased. The main engines ignited. "My files show no record of a complaint ever being filed by a human against a puter."

"Then this will be the first. Tolliver, duck back and make sure everyone's all right. Don't be long. I need you to watch for fish."

"Aye aye, sir." He ducked back into the cabin.

Silence, for several billion nanoseconds. A slight hesitation in the mechanical voice. "Query: what would be the consequence if a puter were found in violation of regs?"

Ah. "I'm Navy, not U.N.A.F., so it's not my decision. I would expect complete power-down, and personality dissolve." Heartless, but I was irked. Time and again, on ship or Station, a snotty puter had aggravated me beyond endurance.

Tolliver slipped back into the cockpit. "No one's gravsick, at any rate."

"Good." Perhaps I could let the cadets unclamp their helmets, even walk around. They'd be a long time in suits. But a fish might Defuse alongside without notice, and if it threw, we'd decompress faster than our clumsier youngsters could resuit.

"Commandant Seafort, no violation of regs was intended."

"Be silent, puter. Use your circuits to scan for fish. Alert us for anything within five hundred kilometers."

"Acknowledged, Captain." He subsided.

I flicked on the caller, scanned Naval and emergency channels. To my surprise, the U.N. was broadcasting bad news as well as the occasional good.

In some aspects the situation had worsened. More ships had been lost, more rocks hurled at our cities. On the other hand, we'd reestablished a clear chain of command, and banks of groundside lasers had burst several rocks hurled by the fish into Earth's gravity well.

Though the Admiralty warrens of Lunapolis were devastated, many decompression hatches had slammed shut in time. It appeared most of our brass had survived, though communication was sporadic. Admiral Duhaney, through a multiship relay, had transferred fleet command to London. It was for the best; he was no battle commander.

Until we reached the Station there was little to do but listen. I switched frequencies back and forth.

"U.N.A.F. lasers on the outskirts of Beijing are gone. Nonetheless Beijing command reports—"

"—landed outside Kiev—"

"—*locked in the comm room! The hatch is smoking! For God's sake someone help us it's coming*—"

"—thirteen settling over Brasilia. Groundside lasers have—"

U.N. military command reported two hundred fifty kills. Yet some six hundred fish continued to Fuse in and out of home system, attacking our fleet, raining destruction on our cities.

Tolliver. "We should report to Admiralty, sir."

"It would serve no purpose." If I told them where I was headed, they'd ask why.

The puter came to life. "Seven encroachments, at outer limit of search zone. Presumed hostile."

My mind snapped back to the shuttle. "Where?"

"Coordinates two five two—"

"Never mind that, just tell me where!" What did I want him to do, point?

"Just short of the Lunar horizon, Captain."

"What's in that direction?" I peered.

"Aliens, as I've said. And Earthport Station. I can contact Station Control and inquire what other objects might be in their zone of—"

"No." I tried to gnaw at my knuckle, bumped my hand against my closed helmet. "How far is the Training Station from Earthport?"

"Calculating. Assuming no orbit corrections by either body, eleven hundred point five one kilometers as of this moment."

Too close for comfort. No one knew what else the fish could sense, in addition to N-waves. If they learned of our presence, how long before they showed up to annihilate us?

I thrust the thought aside. Nothing I could do about it.

"*Bolivar* to London Command! They're Fusing away by the dozen! We're winning!"

"*—lost our tubes, but otherwise we're all right. Only seven of them out there and—*"

"*—urge you to let us disengage from over North America. There's so many fish we're not doing a damn bit of good. Earthport needs us, so does—*"

I flicked to another frequency.

"Deputy SecGen Franjee has landed in London to establish an alternative command in case U.N. Headquarters is, uh, disabled. UNESCO Director Johanson has issued an advisory warning against any public gatherings during the next month due to the risk of virus . . ."

I muttered something.

"Pardon, sir?" Tolliver

I repeated, "No need to worry about virus. We don't have a month."

"How do you know? They've only hit a few cities, even if the death toll—"

"Didn't you hear? They're Fusing out in large numbers, for more rocks."

"You can't be sure—"

"I know. The bastards have found a weapon that works." I switched back to fleet channel. "I thought that rusty chipboard told us we'd only be an hour!"

The puter spoke with injured dignity. "Forty-seven minutes since I gave you our ETA, Base Commandant."

"We dock in thirteen minutes?"

"In thirteen minutes we begin docking maneuvers. Estimate ten minutes of fuel-conservative maneuvering for close approach, five for mooring and airlock mate."

"No time. Just get us close enough to throw a line; we'll go hand over hand. And don't waste time saving propellant."

"Regulations prohib—"

"Did you hear me, puter?"

Another full second. "Acknowledged, Base Commander." He seemed anxious to avoid further quarrel.

"—masses of fish Defused over Bombay, with an asteroid. A few minutes ago they dropped it on . . . dear Jesus, all we can see is a fireball; there must be hundreds of thousands dead—" The voice broke in a sob.

"You were right, sir."

I made no answer.

Despite the agony of Bombay, Earth had so far been lucky; no other great city had been hit. If New York or London were targeted, deaths would be in the millions.

All I could do was wait. And plan ahead. "Mr. Tenere and Mr. Keene to the cockpit!"

Moments later the two middies appeared, clinging to the bulkhead straps in free fall.

"Check every cadet's helmet clamps, then pump out the ship. Use emergency overrides to open both inner and outer hatches." They listened intently. "You'll find grappling lines in the lock. When we're at rest relative to the Station one of you—Mr. Tenere—take a line across. Secure it and wait with Lieutenant Tolliver for Mr. Keene to send the cadets over. When the Station lock is full, cycle them inside and come out for more."

"Aye aye, sir."

"Mr. Keene, get the cadets ready."

"Aye aye, sir. What are we doing? Is this a training—"

"Two demerits. Any other questions?"

"No, sir!" He beat a retreat.

Edgar Tolliver studied the gloves of his suit. "Indulge my curiosity. Is there a reason you won't explain what you're up to? What harm in telling them? Or me, for that matter?"

I said hoarsely, "I'll bear the responsibility."

"For what? If anything happens to you . . ."

"Watch for the Station, Edgar."

He sighed.

The puter. "You'll find it about seven degrees to port, distance thirty kilometers."

I peered into the endless night, thought I saw a patch where no stars shone. "Any fish nearby?"

The puter's tone held reproach. "I'd have told you. Your standing orders—"

"Skip it."

"I will approach with my lock facing the Training Station, at a distance of twenty meters."

"Very well, Shuttle. As soon as we've crossed over, withdraw to three hundred meters." I'd need room to dock the Fusers.

A silence. "Usually I have a Pilot. It's not often I take my own conn." His tone was wistful.

My gloved fingers drummed against the instrument panel. "How soon?"

"Approximately five minutes fifteen point three two sec—"

"Tolliver, make sure he doesn't ram the Station." I twisted out of my seat.

"There isn't the slightest danger of contact with—"

"Adam! Mr. Keene! Are you ready? Get your cadets lined up!"

Some of our youngsters had trained on lines strung to the Hull outside Farside, others had not. I had no idea if any of my volunteers had been through their Station training; in my eagerness I hadn't bothered to ask. Well, it didn't matter all that much. They needed only to make their way across to the Station lock; I wouldn't send them clambering Outside after that.

When it was time, Adam gauged his distance to the Station, launched himself with the shuttle's line secured to his waist. Moments later he had it tied to the stanchion just outside the lock. Tolliver crossed next, to help on the Station side.

Under my irascible scrutiny Thomas Keene placed each youngster's hands in the correct position, and eased him out the shuttle lock. Endless minutes later the last of the cadets had crossed to Tolliver's outstretched

822

hand without mishap. Next, the middies. Anton Thayer grinned, swung across the line with agile grace. Sandra Ekrit followed. Then Diego.

Keene and I were last. A moment after I detached the mooring line, the shuttle's side thrusters squirted a cloudy spray of propellant that instantly turned to crystals of ice. The shuttle drifted clear.

Tolliver, Keene and I cycled through the lock, to find middies and cadets milling aimlessly in the corridor. I frowned.

"Adam, run to the control cabin, check the air gauges." The sooner we got our cadets out of suits, the better.

The eleven Fusers were docked in a line extending around the disk. The Station had but two locks. We'd have to bring the Fusers around, a pair at a time. I keyed my radio. "Mr. Tolliver, go Outside and mate the closest Fuser to the forward bay."

Should I send Keene or Adam for the next boat? I knew Tenere could handle the thrusters, but Keene was first middy; if he was incompetent, better to learn it now. "Mr. Keene, dock the second ship at the aft bay." The boy's eyes lit with pleasure; for a few brief moments he'd be in charge of a vessel, however tiny. "Anton, give him a hand."

Tolliver and the two middies cycled through the lock. They would clamber around the rim of the Station disk until they reached the Fusers. Adam and I had done the same on our visit months before.

My suit radio crackled. "Midshipman Tenere reporting, sir. The Station console shows breathable air. I'll start checking cabin gauges."

"Don't bother. Come back."

"But—aye aye, sir."

"You cadets, take off your suits. No, form a single line, first. Midshipmen, you too, over there. We're about to conduct a special exercise." Very special. I spoke as calmly as I could.

"One midshipman and five cadets will man each trainer. I'll direct, from *Trafalgar*." Thanks to the legacy of the Screaming Boy, I would be able to call each Fuser, but their single-frequency radios could contact only my command vessel.

I unclamped my helmet.

We had middies enough to launch seven trainers, though I had cadets for eight. I'd assumed the Pilot would take a boat, but he'd heard me mention the attacking fish, and had hidden until we departed.

I myself had to be aboard *Trafalgar*, and I needed Tolliver with me; I couldn't run the Mothership and direct all the trainers by myself.

Even eight Fusers might not be enough. How could I risk it with seven? But how could I put a trainer in the hands of unsupervised cadets?

A bump, barely perceptible, as the lock seals kissed. Tolliver had docked. In other circumstances I'd tease him about the jolt; middies were taught only a perfect mating was acceptable. During my simulation drills on *Hibernia*, I'd writhed in humiliation at my lieutenant's sarcastic mirth.

The outer airlock hatch shut; Tolliver was cycling through. I clawed free from my suit. "Ms. Ekrit, take the first five cadets onto Fuser One. Show them where to sit. They should all be able to read an instrument panel, at least. I want you clear of the lock in five minutes."

"Aye aye, sir. To where?"

"A half kilometer should be enough. Be ready to dodge if another trainer drifts out of control." With middies and cadets at the helm, Lord God knew what havoc we might engender.

"Aye aye, sir. Will we maintain close formation after—"

"Get aboard, Middy!" A sullen look flashed, but she obeyed.

"Ready for orders, sir."

I jumped at the sound. "Where did you come from, Mr. Keene? I told you to—"

"I docked at the aft bay, sir."

I hadn't felt the bump. "Very well," I said, grudging his competence. "You five, go along with Mr. Keene. Slater, into the lock; you can pull off your suit after." I turned to Adam and Tolliver. "As soon as the locks are clear, bring two more Fusers alongside."

Soon the second pair of Fusers were mated to the Station. Fresh-faced Tommy Tsai took Fuser Three. A handful of cadets followed him aboard. As they filed past I put out my arm, blocked Kyle Drew. My hand rested on the lanky cadet's neck, pulled his forehead against my chest. "Godspeed, boy." I had to look away.

His voice was bright. "I'll be all right, sir." He hefted the helmet slung under his arm.

"I know you will."

He stepped into the lock.

Please, Lord. Give me strength to do my duty.

"Fuser Two to Commandant. We're half a kilometer out." Thomas Keene, but how had he reached me? My suit radio wasn't set to Fuser band. After a moment I realized the midshipman had been smart enough to use his own suit radio to contact mine.

"Very well, Mr. Keene. Radio silence until further orders."

Back to work.

Redheaded Anton Thayer, the boy I'd found cavorting on his graduation day, took the fourth Fuser. Johan Stritz strode eagerly into the lock, along with four other cadets whose names I couldn't recollect.

I paced anxiously until boats Three and Four untied and cast off.

Tolliver and Adam cycled through the aft lock for two more. Vital time was wasting; Lord God knew what harm the fish had done while I dithered here on the Station.

Several cadets still hadn't finished pulling off their suits. One clumsy lad had his suit half off but still wore his helmet. Plebes; I should never have brought them. No matter. They'd have time to desuit aboard their Fusers.

I was suddenly aware of the silence. I set my suit radio to scan Naval frequencies.

"—above Lunapolis. So far I don't see a rock but if we get too close—"

"We will fight them on the beaches, we will fight them in the cities—"

Guthrie Smith was the next middy in line. Once, he'd been caned for fighting with a cadet in an attempt to enforce discipline. I hoped he'd learned better. "Get ready, boy."

The hatch to Five opened. With Midshipman Smith went Loren Reitzman, the ungainly lad who'd balked at his oath. Four others, whom I barely knew.

A bump. Tolliver, mating the sixth Fuser.

"Edgar, as soon as the locks are clear take Adam out for another two—"

My suit speaker crackled. "U.N.A.F. Shuttle 20123 to Naval Base Commandant Seafort. Query: do orders given while you were aboard apply after you've departed?"

"Shuttle, stay off the caller! I have—"

"Very well, I'll assume they do not." The speaker went dead.

"Tolliver, dock yours at the forward—damn it!" I keyed the radio. "What orders, Shuttle?"

"You directed me to alert you of any fish within five hundred kilometers. At that time you were still—"

"How many? Where?"

"Two. Distance seven kilometers, closing slowly. They appeared moments ago, so I assume they arrived by Fusion. They do not respond to—"

"Mr. Diego! Move your cadets into Six, flank!"

"Aye aye, sir!" The middy grabbed the first cadet, thrust the black-haired youth toward the aft lock. Benghadi, I recalled. The next two cadets ran after. A youngster from the back of the line darted forward, inserted herself behind them. "I'll go, sir. Please let me!"

"Who are you—all right, move!"

"Alicia Johns, sir! Thank you!" In mess hall, she'd volunteered the moment he had. Mates.

"Tolliver, how soon can we dock the next two Fusers?"

In my radio, the lieutenant's voice was tight. "Three minutes for mine, but both locks are still engaged."

"Mr. Smith, break away from the fore lock! Now!"

It was an agonizing minute before the response. "Aye aye, sir. Sorry, I was seating the cadets. They don't—"

"Move!"

"I am, sir! Lock is cycled, rocking the seals loose . . . I have break-away!"

"Clear the lock area, Tolliver's coming round!"

"Aye aye, sir. I'll wait for orders at half a kilometer like you told Ms. Ekrit."

"Good lad, Guthrie. Adam, Edgar, get moving!"

"*U.N.A.F. shuttle to Station. Three more fish within the search zone.*"

"How far?"

"*One of them is at three point six kilometers, the other two at fifty meters.*"

Fifty meters? Lord Christ. I'd told the cadets to desuit. If a fish threw now, and melted our hull—

"Tolliver here." Edgar's breath came fast; clambering over the disk was hard work. "No fish in sight. Ask him, fifty meters from where?"

"Shuttle, did you hear?" A thump, from the aft lock. Midshipman Diego was breaking free without waiting for orders.

"*Yes, I monitor all channels used by—*"

"Where?"

"*Fifty meters from me, of course. All reckoning is assumed egocentric unless—*"

"Where the hell are you, Shuttle?"

"*Three hundred meters from the Station, as you ordered.*" The puter's tone was injured.

Still too close. A fish might be upon us before we could launch the next Fusers.

"Guthrie Smith reporting, sir. There are fish near the shutt—"

"Quiet, Middy!" I would give Adam Tenere one of the last two train-ers. My plan had been to put unsupervised cadets in the eighth, but now we'd have no time to talk them through breakaway. Could they handle it alone?

"Any of you had Station training?"

A girl stepped forward, said proudly, "I have, sir. Tanya Guevire."

Guevire? Hadn't someone found her in bed with—No time for that.

"I've had training, sir." I caught my breath. Kevin Arnweil, who'd seen his friend Dustin die on the Hull.

Lord, You make it so hard. "Anyone else? Very well. Kevin, you're in charge of Nav. Ms. Guevire will pilot. As soon as—"

"Captain, two fish between us and the shuttle!" Tolliver's calm held, but barely. "I'm on my way with Fuser Seven. Adam just reached Eigh— it's squirting this way! I'm—God, I hate those things!"

"Edgar, take Seven to the forward lock! Adam, thrust to the aft lock. Don't bother trying to mate. Decompress your craft now!" Adam was slower at mating than Tolliver, and if a fish caught his Fuser at the lock the rest of us would die for naught.

I stumbled as I thrust a leg into my suit. "All unsuited cadets to the fore airlock with Arnweil and Guevire! Everyone else to the aft lock. Check your helmet clamps!" They all rushed to comply. The boy who'd never removed his helmet ran to the aft lock, thrust his legs into his suit. He wouldn't have enough time to finish; I propelled him to the fore lock, turned to Guevire.

"Tanya, as soon as your hatch is sealed, run to the console and rock your Fuser loose. Remember how?"

"Portside thrusters. Fore, aft, fore, aft. If the seal doesn't break, both at once for—"

"You've got it." I clamped my helmet tight.

Adam Tenere, his voice taut with tension. "Sir, my mooring line is unhooked; I'll be right there. What should I do if that fish comes at me?"

"Try to evade, or abandon ship at once if it throws at you." I grimaced; I'd wish nobody the death he faced.

"Shuttle!"

"Yes, Base Comm—"

"Turn on your lights! Begin maneuvers. Full spin, X axis. Hold for one minute, then commence spin on Y axis!"

A second's pause. *"That might attract the fish. I am charged with self-preservation unless—"*

"This is an Unless! Do it, or . . ." I groped. "By God, mister, I'll have your circuits up for court-martial!"

I heard Tolliver snort. Well, I couldn't think of anything better.

"Commencing maneuvers." The shuttle.

A bump, not gentle. "I'm docking Fuser Seven, Captain." Tolliver. "I'll have—come on, damn you!"

"Edgar, the second you're mated, come in and help me transfer the suited cadets to Fuser Eight!"

"Will do, but that bloody fish is still nosing around Adam. About sixty meters distant."

I made a final check of my suit. Another bump, from Outside. The lock light flashed; Tolliver had mated. The slim youngster I'd pushed to the forward lock zipped his last suit seal, twisted his helmet clamps just as our inner hatch slid open. "Into the trainer, all of you!"

I herded the six cadets to the lock. In the confusion the boy who'd resuited evaded my arm, dashed instead to the aft lock. Well, he was suited and we'd need him for the last Fuser.

The forward lock shut, cycling the cadets to Seven.

I slapped open the aft hatch. "Everybody in!"

A girl hesitated in the corridor. "Fish are out there!"

"Get in the lock!"

"Not with those things outside!"

I lunged at her; she backed away.

"Come along!" I stepped into the lock, where Tolliver and the remaining eight cadets crowded.

Adam, in my helmet. "Sir, this bloody fish is squirting toward the Station!"

No time to deal with the terrified girl. With the fish approaching we might not have time to launch Fuser Eight.

I slapped the lock shut. "Hang on to the safeties!" I yanked the emergency release. The outer hatch popped open; I felt myself pulled out by the rush of escaping air. One boy lost his grip on the safety bar; I managed to grab his arm while hanging on to the safety with my other hand.

"Adam!" I leaned out into space.

"Right here, sir! Stay clear until I get this thing stopped." Fuser Eight drifted closer, huge from the perspective of a suited figure in its path. I ducked back into the lock.

The middy. "Cabin air is blown, sir. I have my hatch open."

"Base Commandant, four fish are within fifty meters. May I break off maneuver and retreat?"

"All right, Shuttle. See if they follow. If not, reengage."

"That's not the purpose of retreat." The puter's tone was plaintive.

Two quick squirts from Adam's forward thrusters. Fuser Eight came to rest relative to the Station. "Adam, throw a line!" I waited for him to appear in the Fuser's gaping lock.

I cursed. He was taking too long. Someone would have to jump across, help speed things up. Could I launch myself and manage not to miss the Fuser? If I guessed wrong . . . I braced myself against the lock.

Adam clambered into the Fuser lock, a magnetic line draped over his arm. He uncoiled it, swung twice, let go.

The line would miss our lock by at least a meter. If the magnetic disk struck cleanly it would cling to the Station's hull. Otherwise Adam would have to reel it in and try again.

With the maddening slowness of free fall, the line sailed toward the hull. I gripped the safety bar, leaned out as far as I could.

The disk struck the hull a glancing blow and recoiled.

I lunged.

The line caressed my fingers, slipped free. "HOLD ME!" I let go the bar, grabbed at the drifting line. Momentum carried me outside the lock. Adrenaline clutched my stomach. My fingers closed around the line just as a hand grasped my ankle.

"Next time, warn me!" Tolliver grunted with effort as he hauled me back.

I twisted, clamped the disk securely to the hull. "You, cross the line!" I shoved a cadet forward. He placed one hand on the line, then the other. A deep breath, a sob. Eyes screwed shut, he worked his way across. Adam Tenere pulled him into the Fuser.

A young voice, in my ear, surprisingly firm. "Cadet Guevire reporting from Fuser Seven. Am breaking away as per orders."

"Acknowledged, Cadet." I grabbed a boy's arm. "Next!"

"A FISH!" Adam's shriek almost deafened me. The midshipman stabbed wildly with his gloved finger. An alien form drifted just within the horizon of the disk.

"Move, boy!" I put a cadet's hand on the line, thrust him into space.

He grabbed the line with his other hand, kicked as if fighting nonexistent gravity. All that it did was disorient him.

"Hold still! Swing one arm across and—"

The boy tried to comply, missed with his right hand after he'd already let go with his left. The momentum of his lunge propelled him from the line. He snatched at it and missed. Ever so slowly, he drifted away.

He began to scream.

I strained to reach him, but he was too far from the airlock. If I swung onto the line, reached out with my foot—no, the bloody line was too loose. No way to lever myself round.

"I'll get him, sir!" Adam Tenere launched himself across, swinging like a monkey.

"Tighten the line!" I reached for it, forgot I was in free fall, almost propelled myself out of the lock. I grasped Tolliver's shoulder, steadied myself until I got hold of our end of the line. Together, hanging on to the safeties, Tolliver and I hauled the line tighter.

"Easy, sir! We'll pull in the Fuser!"

"Too much mass!" The Fuser was more likely to yank us out of the lock, or pull my arm out of its socket.

"*Base Commandant—*"

Adam swarmed across the line.

"*—do I calculate correctly that your intention is to avoid contact with the fish?*"

"Shut up, puter!"

"*I could assist.*"

"Shut—how? Adam, hurry!"

"*With thrusters at full, my inertia would be greater than that of the fish.*"

"So? Cadet, stop that infernal noise, the middy's coming for you!"

"*I could*"—a millisecond pause—"*muscle the fish aside, as it were.*"

I glanced at the fish, saw a tentacle form. Adam neared the frantic cadet. At what would the fish throw? The Fuser? Adam? The Station?

"Shuttle, the acid may melt your hull."

"*I'm aware. As long as my thrusters are untouched, hull breach will not affect my operation.*" The puter sounded quite calm.

"Do it!" I felt a flash of guilt.

"*Coming around.*" The shuttle's bow was blunted, unlike that of a starship. The puter couldn't skewer the fish, but he could ram, unless the fish Fused to safety.

Adam gripped the line, forced his legs up and out to the windmilling cadet.

I peered into the night. Had the shuttle's lights grown closer?

"Got him!" Adam pulled his knees tight as the boy swarmed up his body. The moment the cadet's hand touched the line Adam swung back, straddled the line, closed his legs across it. The cadet lapsed into blessed silence, punctuated by gasps for breath.

The fish let go. The mass of protoplasm sailed across the void. Toward the Station.

It would miss the lock, miss the Fuser. Adam shoved the hysterical boy toward the trainer's waiting hatch. I thrust another cadet out my lock. "Grab hold!" The youngster did so. I couldn't make out his features. Or hers. "The rest of you, get across before that beast throws again!"

Two cadets dived simultaneously for the line. I hauled one back, catching a glimpse of blond hair, dampened from the humid suit. Jacques Theroux, the Parisian I'd added at Final Cull. I let go of his arm after his mate had pushed clear.

With the ease of long practice Midshipman Tenere swung himself around the kicking cadets so he was behind them on the line. "How many more, sir? I'll help them over."

Four left. We'd need one on *Trafalgar*. I'd hoped to launch another trainer, but with the fish this close—

I hauled a youngster to the edge of the lock, said to a cadet, "You'll go as soon as those two are clear."

In majestic silence the U.N.A.F. transport sailed across the vacuum. A spray of propellant glittered in its taillights.

The nearby fish had grown another tentacle. Slowly, it began to swing.

"Tolliver, how far around the disk is *Trafalgar?*"

"About halfway. Closer from the west. Shall I go for it?"

"Wait until this Fuser's clear."

The two cadets struggled to Eight's hatch, helped each other aboard. I shouted, "Go!"

The cadet grabbed the line and launched himself.

Adam made to follow; I held him back for a last word. "Don't bother sealing your lock. I'll unclamp your line the instant you're aboard. Thrust at full power until you're clear of these monsters. I'll send orders from—"

"He's throwing!"

I whirled, or tried to, tangled myself in my own feet. By the time I recovered, the tentacle had broken free.

The acid sailed toward us. For a moment I thought it would splatter against our lock. Then I realized it would not. "CADET! COME BACK!"

The boy looked up. He froze, halfway across the line.

The mass of protoplasm spun lazily.

Behind him the shuttle sailed across the void.

The cadet moaned, flinched.

The twirling mass of protoplasm slapped him from waist to helmet, knocked him off the mooring line. A sizzle. With horror I realized the sound came through the boy's suit radio.

An agonized shriek, a puff of air. Silence. I gagged.

The line to Fuser Eight parted.

The shuttle glided across our horizon. Its prow rammed into the fish. The fish convulsed. Together they floated past the disk.

I was exultant. "Shuttle, come around and go for another!"

No answer.

"Puter?"

The shuttle's tailbeams flickered silently into the galactic night.

"Captain, Midshipman Keene. Permission to Fuse to safety!"

I roused myself. "Is a fish alongside?"

"No, sir. They don't seem to care much about the Fusers. But two more just popped into sight alongside the Station."

I keyed my suit caller to broadcast across a band that encompassed all my fleet. "No one is to Fuse! Stay in the area unless you have a fish within one hundred meters!"

"Aye aye—"

"Shuttle, respond!" No answer. I gave it up. "Fuser Eight! Throw us another line!"

A voice trembling with excitement. "Looking, sir! I'm Theroux. Am I allowed to answer? Mr. Tenere isn't—"

"Yes. Have someone take the conn!"

Tolliver gripped my arm, pointed. A fish drifted slowly toward Fuser Eight.

I shouted, "Belay that line, Eight! Close your lock. Fire portside thrusters, fore and aft together, five seconds! Move away from the fish!" I turned to Tolliver. "We've got to launch *Trafalgar!*"

Adam Tenere gauged the distance to Eight. "Let me jump, sir!" He seemed on the verge of tears.

A squirt of propellant, and the Fuser began to recede. "Too late, Middy." Apparently the cadet helmsman hadn't ignited both thrusters at the same moment; the tiny ship drifted in a lazy circle. I wondered if Tenere mourned the independent command he'd lost.

Adam cried, "There's only four of them! They'll need help!"

I felt a moment's shame. "Everyone out of the lock." I hung on to the safety bar, kicked free, twisted almost double so my boots touched the hull outside the Station lock. I let go with one hand, flicked on my magneboots.

I was clamped to the hull, but I was bent almost backward. Surely someone could design a better way to step out of an airlock. Straining my back and leg muscles, I managed to straighten. Now I stood on the hull at right angles to the lock. I grasped a safety, took a cadet's outstretched arm. For a moment he flailed, but quieted to let me set him on the hull. I reached down and snapped on his boot magnets.

Tolliver hoisted himself out. Below him Adam Tenere guided another cadet out; Tolliver handed her up to me. "Where are the fish?"

"Everywhere." No time to look.

Another moment and we were all on the outer hull. Tolliver pointed. "*Trafalgar*'s there." Beyond the horizon of the disk.

Walking to the horizon on the tiny Training Station wasn't the herculean task it would be on Earthport, or even Hope Nation's Orbit Station. Nonetheless, a Captain often provided his middies a dose of healthy exercise by having them help with tasks on the ship's hull. It was hard work to unclamp each boot at every step. Leading three clumsy cadets made the going even slower.

Someone sobbed. From the pitch of his voice I guessed it was a cadet, but couldn't tell which. I wanted to join him.

The outer edge of the Station disk was relatively free of obstacles. We'd save distance by taking the shorter route across the surface of the disk, but the flat surface bristled with antennas, dishes, and sensing devices; our fastest route was the rounded circumference.

None of us spoke. I grabbed a cadet's arm, flicked off his magneboots, slogged forward as fast as I could. The youngster clutched my wrist in justifiable terror; if I let go of him he'd drift helplessly until caught, or until the fish sensed him.

Tolliver quickly followed my example. After a moment, so did Adam. Painstakingly we made our way across the rim of the disk, each with a cadet in tow.

"Sir, where are you?" Sandra Ekrit.

"On the rim. Shut up!" A step, then another.

"But—aye aye, sir."

"My God. Look!" Tolliver.

The fish to our port side was no more than forty meters distant. While I watched it squirted propellant from its blowhole, floated toward the flat of the disk. Its nose touched. A gentle spray of propellant held the fish against the Station's hull. It wiggled back and forth in a nuzzling motion.

Lights from within, where none had been before. The hull was breached. I tried to run, almost lost my balance. Without jumpsuits or safety lines, our only means of progress was step after careful step.

"Sir, I can walk, they showed me how."

I ignored the boy. Another step. "Where the hell is *Trafalgar*?"

"Fifty meters or so."

The fish's skin became indistinct, began to swirl. Outriders! I spun ninety degrees to starboard, yanked the cadet after me.

"Adam, over the side!" In three steps I was at the edge of the Station's rim. A shape grew on the fish's swirling skin, began to emerge. I stepped over onto the flat of the disk. Tolliver and Adam scrambled after.

We were now on the opposite side of the disk from the fish. In free fall, up was where you wanted it to be. I oriented myself. Here, toward the disk edge, the surface was less cluttered. Farther toward the center, auxiliary solar panels spread like the wings of mounted butterflies.

Adam screamed.

I jerked with fear, let go my cadet. The youngster convulsed, wrapped himself around my neck.

Adam scrambled back toward the rim. I fought to free myself from the cadet's viselike grip. His wrist rubbed against my helmet clamps.

"Don't go that way, Adam! The fish!" I tugged at the cadet's smothering arm with one hand, reached for Adam with the other.

Tenere screamed again, eyes riveted on something past my shoulder. I turned.

A cadet, his suit ragged and in places gone, floated idly. After a time I realized I was staring at what had been skin.

"Adam, get hold—"

The middy vomited into his face mask.

He was in trouble. If his air line plugged he'd suffocate inside three minutes; the suit itself held barely enough air for a few breaths, and it would be so foul the boy would try not to breathe it. On top of which, he was blind.

I clawed at the frantic cadet on my back; he paid no mind. In desperation I elbowed him in the stomach. It loosened his grip just enough for me to pry him loose. I wrenched his leg down, flicked on his magneboot, stepped back before he could seize me again.

Adam stood frozen to the hull. His gloved hands scrabbled at his helmet. I slapped them away. Sounds of choking.

"Tolliver, help the others!" I reached down, unclamped Adam's boots, got a grip around his waist. Holding him under my arm like a sack of potatoes, I unclamped my own boot, lunged forward across the flat of the disk. I angled toward the rim. Clamp. Unclamp. Adam flailed.

Beyond the edge of the disk, metal, barely visible in the dark of night. Adam's kicks grew more desperate.

My motion seemed agonizingly slow. "Hang on, we're almost there!" His limbs twisted.

The tail of a ship crept closer. The indistinct metal resolved into fusion tubes. Was it *Trafalgar* or another of the Fusers? Adam's foot lashed out, caught my knee. My breath hissed in pain.

Another step. Christ, why hadn't I brought a jumpsuit? Adam clawed at his helmet.

Two more steps. I clambered past the fusion tubes.

Trafalgar's tubes.

Thank you, Lord. Two more steps. The mooring line was knee high. Rather than try to climb over, I shifted Adam to my other arm, transferred my boot to the ship itself. *Trafalgar*'s hull was laced with footgrips, much easier for an experienced sailor than clamping each boot. But I didn't dare try them; one misstep and we'd lose contact.

Twenty meters to the aft lock. I'd never make it in time; by now Adam barely moved. I bent, flicked off my boots, caught the boy in a scissors grip between my legs, grabbed the nearest footgrip with my free hand.

Like a crab, I scuttled across the surface of the hull. Fifteen meters. Ten.

Frantic with haste, I slapped open the airlock, hurled Adam inside, slammed my hand against the closer. The lock began to pump. I glanced at the gauge; ship air was at one atmosphere. No time to confirm on the bridge console. I straddled the inert middy, hands poised on his helmet clamps.

The light flashed; the inner hatch slid open. I tore the clamps free, yanked off Adam's helmet.

His face was blue.

I rolled him onto his stomach, waited for a breath. If he'd aspirated the vomit—

Tentatively I pressed my palm against his back. A breath. Another. Adam twisted onto his side, gagged until I thought he'd never stop. Finally, another breath. His eyes streamed.

I dragged him into the cabin, dashed back into the lock, slapped it closed. The moment the outer lock slid open I surged out, cannoned into Tolliver. I reeled in pain, marveling that I hadn't cracked my helmet.

"You all right, sir? Take this joey." He thrust a cadet at me, clambered back the way he'd come.

"Where are—" I closed my eyes, willing away the hurt. Robert Boland's voice piped, "The other cadets are on the hull, sir. I'm sorry I hung on to you. I was—"

"Hold on to the safety bar! Don't touch anything!" I was gone.

I risked the footgrips, stumbled my way across the hull. Tolliver had left his two cadets a few meters past the mooring line. With dreamlike slowness I neared them.

From my vantage point on the hull I could look over the Station rim. A motion caught my eye. I squinted through the fog of my overworked suit.

The metal plates of the rim seemed to ripple. My stomach contracted.

I churned my way toward Tolliver, met him near the mooring line.

I grabbed a cadet's arm; Tolliver let go, turned his attention to the second figure.

The tall, gawky cadet twisted loose from my grip. "I can do it, I know how!"

"Hey, come—"

She slipped her boot into a grip, launched forward, caught the next grip, slipped her first boot loose, glided ahead.

I gave up; I'd barely catch her, much less be of help. I reached to Tolliver, snatched the other arm of his cadet. Lifting the youth like a toddler between his parents, we clambered to the lock.

I looked over my shoulder to the Station rim. Deck plates swirled, abruptly dissolved. Something emerged, changed shape to fit the hole. My breath hissed.

We reached the lock.

"Lord Christ!" Tolliver's tone made my hair rise.

Frantically he slapped the hatch control.

Behind us, an alien outrider quivered on the rim of the Station. Specks and odd shapes swirled on its surface. My heart slammed against my ribs. The airlock hatch shut, blocking the view. I couldn't get enough breath. Were my tanks running low? My gauges glowed green.

The inner hatch slid open. Adam lay facedown on the deck. Forgetting we had no gravity, I tried to run to the console. I sailed helplessly across the cabin. I was panicking like a plebe.

I fetched up against the far bulkhead, grabbed a handhold. I flicked on my magneboots, lowered my feet and hobbled across the deck as fast as I could. Sliding into the Pilot's seat, I threw a strap across to hold me and jabbed at power switches with clumsy, gloved fingers.

Tolliver peered out the porthole. "The damn thing's sitting on the rim, quivering. Christ, we're still moored! We—I'll have to go out and—"

I panted, "I'll tear us loose." The console lights glowed; *Trafalgar* had maneuvering power. I fired the port thrusters.

"You'll crumple the lock!" The mooring line was fed through the stanchion just outside the airlock.

"Our stanchion's rated higher than the line." I flicked on the simul-screens. The beast seemed to stare at us, though I could find no eyes. Once more I fired thrusters. The line snapped taut, held.

Tolliver punched open the inner hatch. "I'll go out and untie us."

I slapped the hatch override. "No time!" My ears roared; I couldn't breathe. "My air." It came out a croak. "Something's wrong with my suit!" The cabin swam.

Tolliver flung himself to the console. He thrust my arm aside, peered at my gauges, then at my face. "Your air's fine, you're hyperventilating! Pull your helmet!"

In a fury I tore at the clamps; they came loose and the helmet bounced off the deck. "Watch that demon out there!" If the outrider jumped to our hull we were done for. Again I fired thrusters at full power. The ship lurched, but the line refused to part.

"The outrider's moving! Break us free!"

The alien flowed along the rim toward our mooring line.

I took a deep breath, fired a short squirt from the starboard thrusters. We lurched toward the Station.

Tolliver screamed, "WRONG WAY!"

"I know!" For two more seconds I let us drift closer. Our line slackened. On the Station hull, the alien gathered itself.

I fired port thrusters at full power, added stern thrusters to boot.

The alien leaped across the chasm.

A crack sounded through the bones of the ship. Our broken line recoiled against the Station hull. I jammed down the thruster levers, as if forcing them through the console would add to our speed.

We slipped away from the Station.

The alien drifted closer.

Unbreathing, I willed our thrusters to carry us away. Ever so slowly we gathered speed, but the creature floated within feet of our lock.

Finally, our velocities matched. Then the gap began to widen. The alien receded, until it was but a quivering blot against the uncaring stars.

23

"Jesus, Son of God." I let out my breath, released the thrusters.

Tolliver sagged against the porthole. "Amen."

My hands fiddled at the console; in a moment, the gravitrons began to hum. I felt weight settle on my frame. Across the cabin Tolliver hugged himself.

Adam Tenere lay on the deck, lost in a private hell.

"It's all right, lad, pull yourself together." My voice cracked.

A cadet stirred. "Sir, are we—what should we do?" Robert Boland.

It seemed a great effort to think. "Open your helmets."

On the console a comm light blinked. I switched frequencies.

"Mid—Midshipman Thayer reporting, sir! Are you there? Wha—what do we do now?" Close to hysteria.

Stop stammering, for one thing. I made no response.

Robert Boland squinted out a porthole. "I don't see any—"

"Speak when you're spoken to!" Tolliver's voice was thick.

Time to take control. Laboriously, I sat up straighter. My muscles ached as if I'd just run the Academy track.

I keyed the caller to Four. "Mr. Thayer, any fish in your vicinity?"

"I—no, sir. Not right here."

I made my voice casual. "Good. Take a moment to organize your boat. See who's had engine-room training, set two cadets at the Fuser console. Put another at Nav, the last one at radionics." I groped for something familiar. "I'll grade you on the results, so do your best. Report back when you're done."

"Aye aye, sir." Thayer sounded more steady.

Now my own ship. I had Tolliver, Adam, Boland, and . . . who? I was supposed to know these things. "Call off by rank."

"First Lieutenant Edgar Tolliver reporting, sir." His tone had a sharp edge.

Adam Tenere made no response. His eyes were shut.

Tolliver hauled the midshipman to his feet, shook him like a rag doll. "Report to the Captain, or by God I'll—"

"*BELAY THAT!*"

My throat was raw. Tolliver retreated. The middy stared at the deck plates.

I got to my feet, came close. "Adam, I need you."

"I—can't." A sob caught.

"Of course you can." As my hand came up he flinched, but I only took his chin in my palm and lifted. "Report, Mr. Tenere."

Liquid eyes stared into mine. Then, he shuddered. "Midshipman Adam Tenere reporting, sir."

"Very well." My hand rested on his shoulder, squeezed once.

"I'm sor—" He bit it off. I turned away, feeling a Judas for my encouragement. "Continue."

"Cadet Robert Boland, sir."

"Cadet Rene Salette."

Still facing the bulkhead, the last cadet mumbled something inaudible.

"Speak up!"

He braced his shoulders, took a deep breath, and turned. "Cadet Jerence Branstead reporting, sir."

For a moment my mouth worked. I launched myself across the cabin, slammed him against the bulkhead. "How did you get here?" My slap spun him sideways, gave him no opportunity to answer. "I forbade it! Why, damn you?"

"I—sir, I—" His eyes teared.

Another slap, like a rifle shot. He squealed, "No excuse, sir!"

I raised my hand in fury. It came down hard, on a shoulder that had interposed itself. Tolliver was between us, hands thrust deep in his pockets. I flailed at the youngster I'd sworn to save. Again the shoulder blocked me.

"Tolliver, I told you he wasn't to be allowed—"

Jerence cried, "Sergeant Ibarez left the hall before you turned me down. That's how I knew I could get aboard!"

The mists began to recede. I looked down at my cocked fist, willed it open. My legs seemed shaky. "That will be all, Mr. Tolliver. I'm—myself, now."

He muttered, "How reassuring." He stood aside, unmoved by my laser glare.

The speaker squawked. "Midshipman Tsai, sir. What are our orders?"

I keyed the caller. "Just a moment." I skewered Branstead. "You. I expected better." His face was red, whether from my blows or shame I couldn't know. "You're unfit—" With an effort I stopped myself from saying worse.

"Tolliver, get him out of my sight. Assign all of them stations." I strode back to the console. "All right, Mr. Tsai. Report."

"Very well, all boats stand by for further orders." My uniform was soaked. A precious hour had slipped past, but my Fusers were organized. The hardest to deal with had been the four unnerved cadets in Fuser Eight. None were adequately trained for their mission. I should have chosen experienced cadets instead of calling for volunteers. And I should have . . . No matter. Add it to the multitude of regrets that comprised my life.

With luck, Eight would be able to manage. If necessary, we'd instruct them, switch by switch, how to work the controls.

"Adam. Nav drill."

He roused himself. "Aye aye, sir."

I took my time explaining. It was important that he fully grasped the problem.

The middy's eyes grew wide. "But, sir, that would—I mean, you can't—"

"Mr. Tenere!"

He flinched. "Yes, sir. I mean, I'm—Aye aye, sir!"

"How long will it take to set up coordinates?"

"For all of them? It shouldn't be too—twenty minutes, sir?"

"Very well. I'll be in the comm room." I eased myself out of my chair. Though I could speak to Robert Boland from my console, Adam would work better if I wasn't staring over his shoulder.

"Don't get up, Mr. Boland." I took a place at the comm console, reached for the controls, pulled back my hand. Might as well allow him to help; why else had I brought him? "Merge the incoming Naval comm frequencies."

Perhaps the fish were withdrawing, or at least tempering their attack.

"Aye aye, sir." His hands flitted to the keys. "To earphones?"

He'd learn the truth soon enough, in any event. "No. To the speaker."

A blare of reports permeated the tiny chamber.

"—huge tidal wave rolling across the Sea of Japan—"

"If we don't Fuse now it'll be too late! Sir, let me save my ship!"

"—fish massing over the atmosphere, we're standing back, we have to. There's no way—"

"MAYDAY MAYDAY MAYDAY MAYDAY MAYDAY—"

Reports poured in. Many fish had withdrawn, as the tide from a tsunami. I was certain they would return. When they came . . .

"Acting Fleet Ops to all capital ships. We will retrea—er, regroup the

*fleet around Deimos. Maneuver to begin in thirty minutes. All ships move
at flank speed to positions from which you can Fuse. Prepare Fuse coordinates for—"*

"NO!" I snatched the caller, spun the frequency dial. "BELAY
THAT! DON'T FUSE!"

Boland's jaw dropped.

*"Stay off this channel, whoever you are. Repeat, all ships are to
Fuse—"*

"Captain Nicholas Seafort in U.N.S. *Trafalgar*. Sir, if you Fuse in a
coordinated maneuver you'll lose the fleet!"

A new voice came on the speaker. *"Admiral Richard Seville, acting
FleetOpsCinc. Get the hell off my frequency and maintain radio silence!"*

"Aye aye—no, sir, I can't! For God's sake, Admiral, countermand
your order." I was beside myself.

Adam Tenere appeared in the doorway. "Sir, I have coordinates—"

I spun to the middy. "Are you sure? Absolutely sure?"

"Yes, sir, I'm sure. But—"

"Send each Fuser its coordinates, to execute at my command. Don't
forget our own engine room. And get Tolliver in here." Adam disappeared.
A moment later the lieutenant strode in.

"Edgar, walk the cadets on Fuser Eight through the steps. First their
engine room, then the console. Tell me when they're ready."

"Aye aye, sir. But Jerence is alone in the engine room. If you're about
to move us, I should—"

"Adam will be there to handle it. Move, Edgar!"

I tried again. "Admiral, the fish will return en masse at any moment.
If you Fuse to Deimos they'll follow and wipe out the fleet!"

Seville's reply indicated he'd run out of patience. *"How the bloody
hell do you know what a fish will do?"*

Captain's intuition, or the grace of Lord God. I couldn't tell him that;
I groped for a rationale. "I was at Hope Nation. I saw their tactics."

He snorted. *"Hope Nation survived because those weren't their tactics. The fish never came back en masse. We're under heavy attack, but
their numbers are diminishing. We'll try to finish them off with groundside
lasers and preserve the remainder of the fleet for—"*

"Emergency bulletin from U.N. Command. They've just told me
Melbourne, Australia was struck by a—by a—" The voice caught. "At
11:15 P.M. Greenwich time a huge meteorite or other object hit the city
center. First reports indicate there is nothing left. Of the city. Of the . . .
people."

I couldn't help myself. I sank to my knees. Lord God, gather those souls into Your arms. Show them Your mercy. I know what You think of me; I ask nothing for myself. Soon, now, I'll go willingly to Your judgment. Please, don't take more innocents.

After a moment I struggled to my feet.

Ignoring Robert Boland's frozen horror, I keyed the caller to all my Fusers' frequencies. "This is Commandant Seafort. We've sent you a set of Fusion coordinates. On my command, bring your fusion drives on-line as you've been taught. Remember, we'll have a substantial radio time lag after you Defuse. Be ready for further orders."

"Aye aye, sir." A voice tremulous with fear.

"Orders received and understood, Capt—"

"Yes, sir. I mean, aye aye, sir."

"Orders received, Commandant Seafort."

When the last boat had acknowledged, I drummed my fingers, waiting for Tolliver to finish instructing Fuser Eight.

"HELP ME!" The anguished cry rattled my speaker.

Befuddled, I stared at the frequency indicator. It wasn't on a Fuser channel.

"THEY'RE COMING! OH, GOD!"

I spun the dial. "Jerence, is that you?"

His voice was husky. "No, sir."

"GOHHHHDD! GET AWAY FROM ME!" Panting.

Cadet Boland. "That's a suit frequency, sir."

But who neglected to desuit, in one of the Fusers?

Lord God, have mercy. The girl who'd run away, at the Station. I didn't even know her name.

I spun my dial. "Cadet, hide behind a—"

A shriek of agony, abruptly cut short.

"Eight is ready, sir." Tolliver. "As ready as they—"

I grabbed the caller. "Execute!" I ran my finger down the line on my screen.

The stars vanished. Seconds later the cutoff alert flashed, and I Defused, flinching unnecessarily. Had the explosion come, I would never have felt it.

"Boland, Tolliver! Encroachments?"

"Yes, sir, one!" Robert had it first; he had faster reaction time.

"Forty thousand kilometers, sir." Tolliver. "She transponds as Fuser Eight."

It was why I'd flinched on Defusing. I'd had Adam send identical coordinates to Eight and our own engine room. Absolutely forbidden by

Naval doctrine, though the one percent inherent inaccuracy of Fusion made the risk of collision almost infinitesimal. But doctrine was doctrine, and so I'd flinched, just in case.

"*Trafalgar* to Seven. Respond." I ticked off the seconds. Seven and her cadets were now five million miles outward of *Trafalgar*'s new position. The reply would take almost half a minute.

We'd all started from Lunar orbit; one AU, or some ninety-three million miles from the Sun. Now *Trafalgar* was near the tail of a string of Fusers, spread between one AU and point two five AU. Fuser Eight, with Jacques Theroux and four other unsupervised cadets, was nearest the Training Station. The rest of the Fusers, except for Seven, were inward of us.

"Fuser Seven to *Trafalgar*. Cadet Tanya Guevire, in the comm room."

"Very well. Who's on thruster controls?"

Another maddening minute. "Cadet Arnweil."

"Put him on." Again I waited. If only we were bunched closer.

"Cadet Arnweil reporting, sir."

What I had in mind would take coordination. Five co-equal cadets probably couldn't achieve it. On the other hand . . . "Kevin, you've done well. I'm appointing you Cadet Corporal. Tell the others. You are to commence a fusion drive test at sixty percent power, random coordinates."

Tolliver's eyes widened.

"Kevin, the test may attract fish. Watch the screens carefully. Use your thrusters to avoid the fish, but do NOT, repeat—"

"Thank you, sir!" his response seemed bizarre until I remembered the time lag. He was responding to my earlier praise, not my warning that he'd summon fish.

"—do NOT Fuse if fish begin to arrive. You need to estimate how long you'll be able to avoid them, and let me know thirty seconds before that time. You'll say, 'Fuser Seven discontinuing test.' A half minute after you notify me, stop testing. The fish should—"

"Won't that attract fish, sir?"

I roared, "Damn it, don't interrupt! Remember the time lag!"

Tolliver glowered. "What infamy have I helped you with?"

I wheeled on him, a threat in my eyes. "Don't speak, Lieutenant."

For a moment he wavered. Then, "Aye aye, sir." He made no effort to conceal his fury.

Kevin Arnweil, chastened. "Orders acknowledged, sir. I apologize."

My voice was soothing. "It was an error of enthusiasm. Yes, you might attract fish, but I want—need you to take the risk. Evade them like . . ." I searched for an example. "Like you would in Arcvid. You

MUST keep testing for thirty seconds after you give the quit signal. Acknowledge."

An interminable minute. Tolliver's eyes bored into my side.

"Acknowledged, sir. If they get too close to avoid, may we Fuse?"

"That will only make them follow you. If all else fails, use your lifepod." I forced the next words through unwilling lips. "The pod's too small for the fish to see. You'll be safe there until we come for you." Tolliver stirred. "But I don't want to lose a Fuser," I added quickly. "Execute."

Tolliver snarled, "Are you *trying* to kill them?"

I made no answer, switched channels to Fuser Six, several million kilometers inward. "Stand by to test fusion drive at sixty percent power. Do not begin until I give you the signal to execute. Once you begin—"

Tolliver wouldn't be denied. "Why'd you tell Arnweil he'd be safe in a lifepod?"

"If he thought it would keep him safe, he'd Fuse clear of the fish long before he had to. I want Seven calling fish."

"They're at point nine AU. That's too close to Earth for—"

"We'll pass their fish inward to Six. You're disobeying orders, and I'm short of time." I clicked the caller. "Six, *Trafalgar* resuming orders. Once you begin testing . . ." I repeated what I'd told Seven.

Tolliver. "All right, you send a few fish down the line, and probably lose a Fuser and five cadets in the process. What happens when the fish reach Fuser One, at twenty-five million miles?"

I said, "The fish are organic. Maybe they'll have trouble that close in. It's hot."

He spluttered, "That's the great Seafort plan? Pull them close to the Sun and see what happens? Christ!"

"Don't blaspheme."

"The fish won't follow so close. They must have SOME survival instincts!"

The speaker crackled. "Fish, sir. Two of them!" Cadet Corporal Arnweil, in Seven.

I changed the subject before Tolliver could think it through. "Edgar, get on the horn. Pass the standby orders down the line to Five." I switched back to Arnweil. "Acknowledged, Seven. Take evasive action if they come near. Keep testing." I left Tolliver at the console, strode to the comm room.

"Mr. Boland, listen for a signal from Seven. Do you know the frequencies?"

"Yes, sir." He pointed to the screen, on which he'd posted all the Fuser channels.

I smiled. In a comm-room drill, Sarge would be outraged by the visual aid. "Very well. Listen to Seven, but set your outgoing to Six. If you hear 'Fuser Seven discontinuing test,' then transmit—write it down—'*Trafalgar* to Six: commence test. Execute.'"

Boland tapped himself a note. "Aye aye, sir." A sheen of sweat dampened his forehead.

"Captain! This is Arnweil. We've got half a dozen now. One was just a few meters off, before I squirted away. May we turn off the drive?"

I took the caller. "Corporal Arnweil, get this straight. Don't stop until your area is swarming with fish. Dozens, not just two or three. You have plenty of propellant and your Fuser has so little mass that the thrusters will flit you around like a top. You can keep clear of them."

I switched to Admiralty frequency.

"*—huge rock, but it's breaking up! Jesus, that must have been a hundred miles across! There are dozens of fish around it, they're—*"

"Captain Seafort to FleetOpsCinc. Urgent." I gripped the caller.

"—U.N.S. *Potemkin* to Admiralty. Do you want us to reengage the fish that brought the rock? We can—"

"Negative, *Potemkin*. Fuse on signal with the rest of the fleet. Countdown is three minutes."

"*Mayflower* to FleetOpsCinc. We got the bloody fish but one tube's melted; I can't join the fleet at Deimos. Is Lunapolis still under attack?"

I pounded the console. "Why won't the bastard answer me?"

Cadet Robert Boland cleared his throat. "Sir, the—"

"Don't interrupt."

"—time lag." He looked guilty. "Aye aye, sir."

I swallowed, loosened my death grip on the caller. "I forgot." The words came hard. "Let that be a lesson to you. When you're on the bridge you'll have to calculate—" I broke off.

"Admiral Seville to Seafort. What now?"

I reddened; his tone said it all. "Sir, I'm trying to draw the fish by caterwauling. Please hold off Fusing the fleet." I waited out the seconds to his reply, hoping against hope.

"You can't help, Seafort. *Trafalgar's* unarmed. That rock we broke up may have been their last try. We'll regroup around Deimos. And if any fish follow, we'll—"

"Sir, don't call the fish to Deimos, I need them here! I'm begging you, give me a chanc—"

"—blow them out of the Solar System. We'll have all the concentrated firepower of—what's that? Christ. *Potemkin*, engage over South Atlantic as fast as you can. There's a squad of fish bringing a rock into—"

"Sir, for Lord God's sake, don't—"

Robert Boland said plaintively, "They won't listen."

"Shut up!" If the fleet Fused, all my efforts would be in vain. I waited, clutching the caller.

"SEAFORT, GET OFF MY CHANNEL! THAT'S AN ORDER!"

I recoiled from his blast.

Then I snapped.

Before I had time to assess my folly I shouted, "Captain Nicholas Seafort on U.N.S. *Trafalgar* to all ships, top priority! On behalf of the Government of the United Nations I hereby relieve Admiral Richard Seville from fleet command!"

Tolliver came thudding into the cabin, aghast.

Now, even if I survived my holocaust, they would have done with me. I raced on, to certain death. "I hereby assume emergency command of the Home Theater of Operations. U.N.N.S. Regs Section—" Lord Christ, what was it? "—sixty-four point two. Uh, three."

"Oh, no!" Tolliver; a cry of dismay.

"All ships, hold your positions, stand and fight! Maneuver by thrusters only! Ignore further orders from groundside, and do not Fuse!"

"You lunatic, you sixty-foured him?" Tolliver. "How could you? You had no grounds! For God's sake, why?"

"—Captain Valdez on *Iberia*, to Seafort. What the hell are you pulling?"

"Admiral Seville to Seafort. You are relieved from—"

"Seafort to *Iberia*. As Theater Commander, I order you to stand and fight, or retreat by thruster. No other option for any ship in Home Theater of Operations. Ignore contrary instructions until the emergency abates!"

As I set down the caller it took an effort to control my voice. "It's come, Tolliver. Armageddon. For us or the fish."

"Christ, you're cracking!"

I laid my hand on the arm of the chair to still it. "No, I'm just—yes, perhaps I am. I don't think it matters."

"Damn it, you always play your cards too close. This time I can't read you! I've got to relieve you, or burn you for mutiny. No other option, as you put it." His hand crept to his holster.

The speaker crackled. Kevin Arnweil in Seven. "Sir, two dozen fish. I can't hold them off much longer! I've got to send you the—oh, God that was close! Maybe another minute—"

I reached for the caller, pulled back my hand. "Do it, Edgar." I was panting, from exertion or lack of air. Or fear.

Our eyes met.

Slowly Tolliver drew the laser. "I'm sorry, Nicky. Captain. I have no choi—Ay!" He tumbled to his knees, the pistol slipping from his fingers.

"Leave my Commandant alone!" The voice was shrill. Jerence Branstead let fall the chair with which he'd clubbed his lieutenant. He snatched the laser from the deck, scampered clear. "You let him be, you—you—" His chin quivered.

"Give it back." Tolliver lurched to his feet. "The Captain's sick. I won't hurt him. I'm going to relieve—"

"No you're not!" Jerence brandished the pistol. "I'm a good shot; Dad taught me back on Hope Nation. And I read the regs! Get away!"

"Please, what's a sixty-four?" Robert Boland.

"Jerence, the laser." I held out my hand. "Look it up, Mr. Boland, you're supposed to know. NOW, Branstead!" Jerence let go the weapon.

"Aye aye, sir." Boland punched commands into his console, calling up the U.N.N.S. Regulations and Code of Conduct, revision of 2087, embedded in every ship's Log.

"Fuser Seven discontinuing test. Oh, God, hurry! So many fish!"

Boland hesitated, his eyes flitting between me and Tolliver. I slammed the heel of my hand into the boy's shoulder. "They're your mates! Help them."

Cadet Boland snatched the caller. "Fuser Six, commence test! Execute!" I waited out the lag.

Eduard Diego, fear in his voice. "Fuser Six to *Trafalgar*, aye aye."

Boland turned back to the keyboard, skimmed through the regs.

"Captain Foss of *Potemkin*, to Seafort. State your grounds for assuming command. You're junior to us all, aren't you?"

"Section sixty-four." Unthinking, Boland read aloud. I reached over to his console, flicked on the caller.

> "When a commander in the Theater of Operations has data essential to the preservation of the main body of Naval forces, and communication with his superiors is restricted through no act or omission of his own, he may relieve his superior and assume command of all forces in the theater for the duration of the emergency."

Boland stopped.
"Go on."

> "In order that authority not be divided or contested, the superior must allow the temporary usurpation of his authority.

No challenge may be made to the assumption of command by any other officer under said superior, or any officer not in the theater.

"However,"—Boland's voice faltered—"upon conclusion of the emergency the relieving officer must show by incontrovertible and conclusive evidence that his usurpation of authority was essential to preserve the main body of Naval forces."

I switched off the caller. "Well, Edgar?"

Robert looked up, his eyes troubled. "Sir, there's more."

"I know. Read it aloud. It may satisfy Mr. Tolliver."

Boland whispered, *"The penalty for wrongful usurpation of authority is death. Any such sentence, once imposed, may not be appealed, commuted, or pardoned."*

Tolliver's eyes were bitter. "You're dead, Nick. Nothing can save you." He sagged. "I'm at your orders, Commander."

He had no choice.

24

Fuser Six was close enough to *Trafalgar* for our sensors to detect. It caterwauled for fifteen minutes, attracting thirty-five fish before Midshipman Diego begged for permission to stop, forgetting he had his own authority in my orders. I passed the fish to Midshipman Guthrie Smith, in Five.

Robert Boland huddled with Jerence Branstead at the far console. Rene Salette made herself invisible in the engine room. Tolliver, fielding calls from the fleet, was in a state of barely controlled fury.

Guthrie Smith. "Sir, may—please, may I keep talking with you? I'm—"

I knew the word he was loath to use. "Yes, of course, Guthrie. Just remember the lag."

"Six to *Trafalgar*. They're going, except for—oh, thank Lord God!" Midshipman Diego caught a sob. "There's the last of them. That was horrid!"

"Steady, Mr. Diego." I thrust down words of rebuke. He was an officer, but throughout the fleet older men fought similar terror. Captain Pritcher had crumpled at less.

"Five to *Trafalgar*! Fish! Dozens of them! Jesus!"

"Move about, Guthrie! Use your thrusters!" It would take almost half a minute for my words to reach him.

Smith shouted, "All around me! Taking evasive action. They're—" The voice cut off.

After a moment Robert Boland asked, "May I call them, sir?"

"Yes."

A minute passed, ample time for a response. Any longer and the fish might disperse. Heavily, I picked up the caller. "*Trafalgar* to Two. Execute." Two was far inward of us, fifty million miles closer to the sun. Over eight minutes for a response to my message. Please, Lord. Let the fish follow.

Still no answer from Five. Had Loren Reitzman cried out for his father, for the schoolmates he'd abandoned to take the oath at my urging? Had Guthrie Smith perished with his hand on the thrusters, trying frantically to escape the aliens?

I wrenched my mind from the speculation. For a while more, I needed my sanity.

At last, a response from Two crackled in the speaker. First Midshipman Thomas Keene. "Aye aye, sir. Executing Fusion test."

"London Admiralty to *Trafalgar*. Stand by for relay from Admiral Duhaney in Lunapolis."

The speaker wheezed and crackled. "Nick, are you out of your mind, taking command? The fleet's in chaos!"

"Sorry, sir, it's done. I have to see it through."

The Admiral's voice hardened. "You know perfectly well sixty-four is a dead letter. In two hundred years it's never—"

"It's as dead as the rest of the Regs, sir. Or as alive."

"Don't quibble! And properly speaking, you're not even in the theater of oper—"

"*Lusitania to* Trafalgar. *Permission to Fuse; they're all around and I can't break loose! Three lasers are down!*"

My voice was heavy. "To *Lusitania*. I'm sorry, Captain. The only sound they must hear—"

"*We'll go under, Mr. Seafort!*"

It would be so easy to make an exception, but I owed a debt to Smith, to Reitzman and the others. "*Lusitania*, do NOT Fuse. Take evasive action. Godspeed."

Duhaney's tone quivered with outrage. "Seafort, I never thought of you as a damned sea lawyer. I can't stop you, but I'll bloody well remember at your court-martial. I'll be on the board myself!"

"Admiral, I'm busy and you're distracting me."

Tolliver gasped. Even for me, that was a bit much.

"Seafort! At least tell us what you're doing!"

"Caterwauling. We're distracting the fish from your fleet."

"You're not armed! What can you—"

"But I have my Fusers. Over and out."

Tolliver said through clenched teeth, "What CAN we do, Commandant?"

"You, for one, can obey orders."

"Of course. I'll follow the example you set."

In the resulting frigid silence I checked the computations on my screen one last time. Tolliver busied himself with calls from the harried fleet.

*   *   *

To my surprise, all but a few scattered ships accepted my self-declared authority. Well, it was there in black and white, if one bothered to read the Regs.

It was time.

Fuser Eight had only the four inexperienced cadets. She had to be first. "*Trafalgar* to Eight, respond."

"Cadet Theroux here, sir." The boy's voice held a quaver.

"These are your new Fusion coordinates. Twenty-five, eighteen . . ." I took my time, made sure the cadet had them right. "After you Defuse, I want you to test your fusion drive immediately. Lock your drive into sixty-five percent for fifteen minutes with a random unlock code."

"Aye aye, sir. But, sir, if we lock in the code we can't end the test early if the fish attack."

I made very sure my answer was on Eight's frequency only. "They won't attack you, Cadet. I'm having three boats Fuse at once. That will confuse the enemy's senses. But you MUST lock in your drive. If you stop testing you'll endanger the other trainers."

Tolliver, in a growl. "Poppycock!"

"Aye aye, sir." Theroux. "What do we do after the fifteen minutes?"

"Fuse back to here. Reverse coordinates."

He sounded relieved. "Thank you, sir."

Tolliver stared at the coordinates on my screen.

"Fuser Eight, prepare to—"

"Belay that!" Tolliver snapped off my caller. "Sir, run the calculations again! You're Defusing them inside the B'n Auba Zone!"

I said, "Use the coordinates we have."

"Don't you understand? Eight will be so close to the Sun she'll never be able to Fuse clear!" Tolliver was nearly beside himself.

I said the hardest words I'd ever said in my life. "I know."

Before anyone could move I keyed the caller. "Fuser Eight, execute."

"Aye aye, sir. Executing." The ship disappeared from our screens.

For a moment all was still.

Tolliver leaned so that his head was close to mine. "Oh, you vile bastard."

My voice was ragged. "Tolliver, I—"

He spat full in my face.

I sat as if made of stone. Warm spittle dribbled down my cheek.

I hoped he would do it again.

He busied himself at his console. I didn't dare speak.

"Why, sir?" Robert Boland appealed for understanding. "Why our own mates?"

"There's no other way."

"But—"

"Be silent, Cadet Boland."

Keene's voice in the speakers, his voice four minutes old. "Fuser Two reporting. My God, that's a lot of fish, sir! More than I've ever seen. More than maybe you've seen, even at Hope Nation. They're Fusing in on all sides. I'm trying to get around the main mass . . ."

"*Potemkin to Acting FleetOpsCinc Seafort. We and* Hibernia *engaged a mass of fish trying to drop a rock over the Atlantic. A whole bunch of them suddenly Fused away. I don't know whether it was our attack that—*"

Keene. "Over a hundred of them now! They see me. They keep trying to—Holy God, what a blast!" The middy's voice trembled with excitement. "Sir, one of them Fused into another! It knocked out visuals right off the screen! If we'd been any closer—get away from me, you son of a bitch!"

Minutes inched past. Boland stared at his screen. Jerence lay slumped in his seat, drained.

"Too many for us! I'm discontinuing—God, it'll be four minutes before you—sir, I can't hold that long! I'm—THEY'RE GOING AWAY! Oh, blessed God!"

Eight had done its work.

"Mr. Boland, try again to reach Fuser Eight." It was a pointless order; even if the fish hadn't destroyed the frail Fuser, her radio had little chance of penetrating the solar haze.

After a moment of static I asked, "Who's aboard her?"

Tolliver found his voice. "Cadet Jacques Theroux. Cadet Vasily Karnyenkov. Cadet Sera Thau. Cadet Kathryn Janes."

I'm sorry, Jacques. And all of you. You'll never know, but you saved Mr. Keene. I need his skills more than yours.

"Pray for them." I cannot. It would be blasphemy.

It was Boland who answered. "Aye aye, sir."

Like an obscene parody of God, I chose who was to live and die.

I had Fuser Seven entice the fish. After a time, I ordered them passed along to Four.

"Captain, I have one question." Tolliver's voice was formal.

I was grateful that he acknowledged my existence. "Yes, of course."

"You're sending cadets to their deaths. How do you know it's working?"

"Working?"

"That the fish are dying."

"They must be." I struggled with the monstrous concept that I'd murdered my cadets for naught.

"You don't know that."

"But—" It had to be so. "Even if fish can survive ten thousand degrees, Fusion follows the laws of physics. The fish are caught just like a ship."

"We don't know that either. They—"

"Captain, permission to discontinue test!" Anton Thayer, in Four, his voice a fearful shout.

"Fuser One, execute!" It would take six minutes for my order to wing inward. I spun the dial. "Mr. Thayer, you must test for six minutes before you shut down. Do your best to evade."

Tolliver persisted. "Before you kill any more of us, how can you be sure the fish follow the last call?"

I thrust away the argument. "We're caterwauling. They *have* to follow. Once they're caught—"

"We have instincts, so must they. How could they survive without knowing not to Fuse near a star?"

"Leave me alone!" He was unfair; how could I know such things? I stalked out, paused at the bridge, turned instead to the rear corridor and the engine room.

"Everything all right, Mr. Tenere?"

Adam looked up from his console. "Yes, sir." Behind him, Cadet Rene Salette anxiously watched her gauges.

I turned to go.

He blurted, "Please, sir—I mean, could you—" He pounded his leg with clenched fist, turned red. A deep breath. "Sir, please, what's happening?"

I raised an eyebrow. "You too, Mr. Tenere?"

"I'm sorry!"

I relented. The usual discipline didn't apply. Perhaps it never does. "We're passing the fish along a great conga line from here to the Sun."

"What happens when they get near the Sun?"

"They die."

The boy's face lit with hope. "It's that easy? We can really beat them?"

I retreated to the hatch. "That easy," I said.

Robert Boland raced out of the comm room. "Sir, Mr. Tolliver's compliments, and would you—

"Belay that." I didn't care anymore.

"We heard from Ms. Ekrit in One. She says she has fish, they're endangering her ship and she's going to discontinue testing unless you answer."

Cursing, I ran to the comm room. "Tolliver, tell her she'll be hanged if she disobeys in the face of the enemy. She may discontinue in exactly"—I checked my watch—"four minutes. Not before."

Tolliver was grim. "Aye aye, sir." He knew cowardice when he saw it.

Boland stood with me in the corridor, uncertain. I pointed to the comm room. "Back to work." Head down, he brushed past.

Four minutes, before I must pass my next sentence of death. I dropped into my seat, plotted coordinates over and again until I was sure I had them right. Then I picked up the caller.

"*Trafalgar* to Fuser Seven, respond."

It had to be Seven. Kevin Arnweil had twice managed to avoid destruction while his ship caterwauled, but the five unsupervised cadets were still the weakest link in my chain. Their luck couldn't last.

I had to use them before it was too late.

Seven was closer; only twenty-four seconds for my voice to reach them.

"Fuser Seven responding. Cadet Kevin Arnweil reporting, sir." By the book. The boy had come far from the youngster who wailed over the stiffened body of his friend Dustin.

"Mr. Arnweil, you're to Fuse once more." I swallowed, then continued smoothly. "These coordinates will put you just outside the B'n Auba Zone, near the Sun." A small deceit. My eyes locked on the console, to avoid meeting any others.

"As soon as you Defuse, you're to test again. Set the puter to lock your fusion motors . . ." Painstakingly, I gave him the instructions I'd given the others. "Confirm, please." I checked my watch. "Quickly."

Tolliver watched from the second officer's chair, his eyes boring into my back.

We had but two minutes left, before Sandra Ekrit would stop caterwauling. At last, Kevin's response. "Ready to execute. Please, sir, could another ship call the fish if we can't get away from them?"

I gripped the caller. "Of course, Kevin. One will be standing by. Just let us know."

Tolliver stalked from the cabin.

"Very well, exec—Kevin, you remember Dustin Edwards?" I didn't know why I blurted that.

A long moment, while the last grains of time slipped through the hourglass. "Of course, sir. All the time."

"I do too," I said gently. "Execute."

Five Fusers left, and Lord God knew how many fish. "Mr. Boland, general call on fleet circuits. Each ship in Home Theater of Operations is to report the number of fish in their sector."

The boy made as if to rise. "Aye aye, sir. Shall I tell Mr. Tolliver you asked him to do it?"

"You make the call on our behalf."

His chest swelled with pride. "Aye aye, sir!"

"Fuser One to *Trafalgar*, Midshipman Ekrit reporting. The fish are gone!"

So she'd survived. "Prepare to repeat testing maneuver in approximately eight minutes. We'll send the signal to execute."

It would be a while before she acknowledged.

It was *Trafalgar*'s turn to summon the aliens.

"Carry on, Mr. Boland." I left the comm room, settled myself in the bridge, placed my hands on the thrusters. "Mr. Tenere, we're going to caterwaul at sixty percent. Don't stop before I give the order."

The middy's voice was strained. "Aye aye, sir. Ready at your command." No protest. I felt strangely grateful.

"Commence." I tensed, eyes glued to the screens.

Edgar Tolliver slipped into the second officer's seat. "I would have liked someday to see Vega."

I grunted.

He asked casually, "Do you know how much I hate you, at times?"

"Only at times?"

"Yes, but this is one of them." His stare was defiant.

I wiped imaginary spittle off my cheek. "I know."

He flushed. "You deserved that."

"No, Edgar. Much more."

The speaker blared. "Fuser One to *Trafalgar*." Sandra Ekrit. "Sir, we barely survived the last attack. Whatever you're trying doesn't work. I can't hear what you're telling the other boats but—"

"Obey orders, Midshipman!" I forgot the damned time lag.

"—sending the fish in a circle from one Fuser to another will just get us all killed for nothing!" Her voice rose. "Sir, as chief officer I can't endanger the boat—"

Tolliver's voice cracked like a whip. "Fish, a thousand kilometers!"

"I see them." My back was stiff from tension, but there was nothing we need do. Not at a thousand kilometers.

Alarms clanged. Tolliver grated, "Seven, eight . . . eleven fish! Port, very close, aft, two hundred meters—"

I slammed down the port thrusters. The screen reeled.

"More of them at—"

They were upon us, and I had no Fuser ready to call them away.

I tried to plan while maneuvering. Either seemed too much effort; together it was impossible.

"Look at the bastards!" Tolliver.

I fired thrusters with desperate urgency, trying to maneuver the ungainly vessel like an electricar. If I wasn't careful I could drive the ship into one fish while trying to escape another. If I did, we were finished.

Tolliver's hand tugged at my arm. "Please. Let me!"

I recalled Hope Nation, and a missile leaping toward our heli. "Now!" His hands leaped for the controls.

I grabbed the caller. Eduard Diego was closest, in Six. "*Trafalgar* to Fuser Six! On my command, Fuse to the following coordinates." I punched up Sandra Ekrit's location at twenty-five million miles, outside the B'n Auba Zone. I read off the string of numbers.

"When you Defuse, immediately commence Fusion test at sixty percent, and continue for eight minutes. Acknowledge."

His reply would take nearly a minute. The stars spun crazily under Tolliver's evasive maneuvers.

I switched back to Fuser One's frequency. I had a weak link to repair. "Very well, Ms. Ekrit, you're right. Fuse back to us and wait for further orders." I fed her the coordinates. "Acknowledge and execute." I spun to Tolliver. "I'll need about half a minute's notice to the Diego boy. How many are there now?"

"Look at the frazzing screen!"

A reproach died in my lips. The simulscreen was blotted by dozens of encroachments, many breathtakingly close. Each moment brought more. Tolliver maneuvered to starboard of the main mass, but, as in Arcvid, the enemy could pop onto our screens anywhere without warning.

The delayed response from Six. "Midshipman Diego reporting. Orders acknowledged. Standing by to Fuse. Please, sir, don't make us—" A second's hesitation. "Standing by, sir."

How many fish? Sixty. No, eighty at least. If we—"LORD GOD PRESERVE US!" I flung my arms over my face. A blowhole filled our screen. Tolliver slammed our nose thrusters to full, but our inertia was considerable.

A knock at the hatch. "Sir, Cadet Boland reporting. They—"

"Hang on!"

We glided toward the fish. I braced myself for collision. Damn it, why hadn't we gone to suits? Without them we'd have no—

Meters from our prow, the fish disappeared. I gaped.

Tolliver grinned tightly. "It doesn't like our hydrozine." Our forward thrusters had squirted directly into it.

I took a much-needed breath. "Go on, Cadet."

The words tumbled out of Boland's mouth. "I talked to the warships and they gave me numbers, about eight hundred fish still in the theater but maybe some ships are reporting the same ones, can I go now, please?"

I glanced over my shoulder. The boy's glazed eyes were riveted to the screen.

"Dismissed, Robert."

Tolliver spun us to port. "Sir, you'd better tell Mr. Diego . . ." His voice faltered.

I reached out, shut off hysterical alarms, gazed in awe at the screen.

U.N.S. *Trafalgar* floated within a vast armada of fish. A kilometer from us drifted a sub-planetary body, so huge I would have lost perspective except for the attending aliens, some two hundred of them. A few squirted propellant from their blowholes, and glided toward us.

"Christsir what now?"

As if I had all the time in the world, my hand crept to the caller. "Nothing, Edgar. Don't move us." When I spoke my voice was hushed. "*Trafalgar* to Six. Midshipman Diego, execute. Confirm and execute!" I reached out, slid my finger down the line down the screen, turning off our fusion drive.

Mechanically Adam Tenere, in the Engine Room, said, "Confirm Defuse, aye aye."

"They're still coming." Cautiously, Tolliver fired a gentle squirt. We drifted astern, backing away from a dozen fish.

"In a few seconds they'll hear Mr. Diego." The mass of fish was staggering. Could Fuser Six hold out until I could arrange another boat to call the alien flotilla?

A screen light blinked out. Then another. I held my breath. More pinpoints of light went dark.

The fish were leaving.

A new blip, twenty thousand kilometers distant. More fish arriving, or—my fingers punched the keys, querying our puter. Metal.

A familiar voice. "Fuser One to Trafalgar, Midshipman Ekrit reporting. Sir, I'm sorry if—"

"Belay that, Middy, no time." I ground my knuckle into my forehead, searching for a way. "Ms. Ekrit, Fusers Four and Seven report false readings from their external fusion tube gauges. Our testing may have melted the wires. Who's in your engine room?"

"Two cadets, sir. Bonhomme and Farija."

"Send them Outside—no, I can't rely on them. Do you see any fish at the moment?"

"Only near you, sir. They're forty thousand kilometers from us."

"If I sent you out to do a visual, how fast could you get back in?"

"I'm pretty good on the footholds, sir." Her tone was confident.

"We need to know if the sensors are reliable. Get suited. Put all your cadets at the bridge console except the two in the engine room. I'll stay on Fuser frequency; they can communicate with you via suit channel."

"Aye aye, sir. What am I looking for?"

"Any evidence of bad connections or overheating. You can't Fuse with bad sensors."

"Yes, sir. Give me a minute to finish suiting. Sir, am I in trouble for countermanding your order? I was senior officer present and—"

A Fuser was a boat, not a ship, and she wasn't a Captain. She should have known that. "No, Ms. Ekrit. I didn't realize your problem. Hurry, will you? I need to send you back toward Earthport Station."

"Aye aye, sir. Going to suit frequency."

I closed my eyes, pictured her screwing tight her helmet, checking her suit clamps. Turning toward the lock. Slapping open the inner hatch. Reaching for the pump control.

"Commandant Seafort to Fuser One. Can you hear me? Identify yourself."

In a moment, a nervous voice. "Yes, sir. Cadet Wallace Freid, sir. Cadet Chambers is with me. And Cadet Zorn."

"Where is Ms. Ekrit?"

"The outer hatch just opened, sir. She's Outside."

Damn. I'd waited too long. "Can she hear us?"

"I don't think so, sir. Not unless I press the intercom bar."

"Call the two cadets from the engine room. Hurry."

A muffled instruction. A moment's wait. "The other cadets are here now, sir."

SEAFORT'S CHALLENGE

858

"As your Commandant, I relieve Ms. Ekrit as your superior officer. Do you understand what I said?"

Tolliver whispered, "Watch the time, sir. Diego must be in trouble by now." The screen was nearly empty of fish.

"Relieve? You mean she's not a midshipman anymore?"

"She's no longer in command. You report directly to me, and not to her. Acknowledge."

"I understand, sir."

"All of you!" I waited for the murmurs of assent. "Very well, tell Ms. Ekrit I said she's to come in immediately, never mind the sensor."

"Aye aye, sir." A pause. "She's coming; she told us to ask why." I shook my head. Still questioning orders.

"Look at your console. See the hatch overrides?"

"No, sir."

"Left upper corner, two blue switches."

"Yes, sir. I see them now."

"Turn on the inner hatch override. Acknowledge."

"Aye aye, sir. Done. But she won't be able to—"

"Is she back in the lock?"

"She's just entering now, sir."

"When you hear the pump, flip the outer hatch override."

"But she'll be trapped—"

I screamed, "Obey orders, Cadet Freid!"

"Yessir. The hatch just closed. I can hear a motor, it must be the pump. I turned on the override, sir."

"Very well. Copy the following Fusion coordinates." Grimly, I passed along the lethal figures I'd first given Seven, then Eight. I said to Tolliver, "Deceit. Always more deceit."

"Justified, this time." His voice was a growl. "It was outright mutiny."

"And what I'm about to do?"

His face was grim. "Not justified. Under any circumstances."

I took the caller, once again the Angel of Death. "Fuser One, the instant you Defuse, lock in your fusion drive for fifteen minutes and start testing immediately. Remember how? Good. You'll be all right. I'm having three other ships Fuse at the same moment. The fish won't know what to do." By now the falsehood tripped glibly off my tongue.

"Aye aye, sir." Wallace Freid sounded more excited than afraid. "Ms. Ekrit is pounding on the hatch. What should I say?"

"Nothing. I'll deal with her later. Until then, let her wait in the lock."

A lonely death, helpless, disregarded by her shipmates. I flipped a blue switch in my mind, overriding the thought.

"She's very angry."

"Think of it as revenge for the middies' hazing."

His voice was more cheerful. "Aye aye, sir!"

"Mr. Freid, execute."

Fuser One vanished.

We sat in somber silence. I took the caller. "Mr. Boland, check again with the fleet, and have Fuser Six stand by for further orders."

"Aye aye, sir."

"Tolliver, how are the others?"

"Fine, under the circumstances. Jerence Branstead hasn't said much since he came at me."

"He was right, you know. After I sixty-foured the Admiral you were duty-bound to obey."

He shrugged. "I doubt anyone would object if I relieved you."

"Do it!" Let death be on someone else's head.

"No. I've changed sides for the last time. I suppose they'll hang me with you." He smiled, but not with his eyes. "You'll be remembered, sir."

I whispered, *"I was a derision to all my people; and their song all the day."*

"What? Are you all right, sir?"

"Was I ever?" I took up the caller. *"Trafalgar* to Fuser Three. Respond." I waited for Tommy Tsai.

Tolliver's look was grim. "Sir, wait for Boland's report from the fleet. For all we know, the fish follow us until the last call and then go back to attacking Earth."

"They can't. The caterwauling drives them crazy." I spoke without conviction.

"FUSER THREE TO *TRAFALGAR,* CADET KYLE DREW REPORTING. MR. TSAI IS IN THE ENGINE ROOM." The boy's voice was shrill. I turned down the volume.

"Copy the following orders, and inform Mr. Tsai."

Tolliver persisted, "Damn it, you don't know for certain, and you've already killed nineteen cadets!"

Help me, Lord, I know not what to do.

At last I stirred. "Tolliver, call Mr. Tsai and cancel Three's orders."

"They'll be delighted. What now?"

"Plot coordinates for *Trafalgar* to the vicinity of Two." In seconds, we'd be millions of miles inward.

"Aye aye, sir." His fingers were already working. "We mustn't Fuse, remember? We'll attract them."

"That's all right. It won't be for long." We Fused.

I stared impatiently at the blank simulscreen until we Defused. Now I could speak to Midshipman Keene without lag. "Edgar, plot coordinates for Two to nineteen point five million miles."

Gritting his teeth, he bent to the keyboard. I switched frequencies. "*Trafalgar* to Fuser Two. Mr. Keene, turn your heat shields to full, and Fuse to these coordinates, on my order." I read them from Tolliver's screen.

The midshipman's voice came crisp and sure. "Aye aye, sir. What then?"

The contrast to Sandra Ekrit brought a catch to my voice. Well, she was punished.

"The coordinates put you a million miles short of the B'n Auba Zone." I made my tone casual. "For a ship of your mass, the Zone extends to seventeen million miles, so there's plenty of leeway. In a few minutes I'll send your return coordinates." My eyes seemed to blur. I rubbed them. It only helped for a moment.

I rushed on. "After you Defuse, commence a test at sixty-five percent power."

"Aye aye, sir." For all Keene's response, I might have asked him to pick up a holochip from the deck.

A fish appeared, kilometers away. I ignored it, my throat aching. "Mr. Keene, after you begin the test, orient toward the Sun and fire your stern thrusters continuously at full power until you reach seventeen and a half million miles."

I waited for him to object. At length he said, "Aye aye, sir. Let me read back those coordinates, please."

I confirmed them. "Don't stop transmitting to us. Tell us how many fish come to you, and what they do afterward. Watch to see if they Fuse to safety. Remember to transmit constantly."

"Aye aye, sir. Anything else?"

Tolliver swung his chair, his voice low. "Tell him the truth."

"What truth is that, Mr. Tolliver?"

"What you're asking of him!"

"I can't take—take the chance." I found it difficult to speak.

"For decency's sake, you must!"

"If he refuses, how will we know what happens to the fish?"

"Thomas will do what you order!"

I said thinly, "You'd bet the human race on that?"

For a moment Tolliver was silent. Then, "Yes. Otherwise, we're worse than the fish."

I picked up the caller.

"Nick, let him sacrifice himself for you. Don't send him to death with a lie. For the sake of your soul!"

He'd undone me. "Mr. Keene, execute!" I broke from my chair, ran to the comm room console.

I had no soul.

25

Robert Boland said, "Sir, no answer from Mr. Diego in Six. I tried three times."

"All right, go help Mr. Tolliver."

I sat alone in the comm room, listening to static on Fuser Two's frequency.

Keene's new position put him sixteen million miles closer to the Sun than *Trafalgar*. Drained of all emotion, I watched the seconds drag across the clock.

"May I come in, sir?" Jerence Branstead, shifting from foot to foot. "Mr. Tenere gave me permission. If it's all right with you."

"What do you want?"

"Just to talk." His eyes appealed.

I shook my head.

"To be with you," he blurted. "Please!"

"Behave yourself. Go back to your post."

"I wouldn't—aye aye, sir." Dejected, he made his retreat.

How dare he. A cadet, pestering his Captain? What were things coming to?

Armageddon.

No wonder Jerence was unnerved.

The speaker came to life. "Fuser Two to Commandant Seafort on *Trafalgar*. Midshipman Thomas Keene reporting." The middy's voice was crisp and formal, as it would be on a drill, with the Captain frowning from the bridge. "We've Fused to new position. Orienting ship."

Silence. If I spoke, how long for him to hear? I was too tired to calculate. A minute and a quarter, more or less.

An age passed. Then, "We're caterwauling at sixty-five percent. No fish yet. Accelerating toward the Sun. Our thrusters combined with gravitational pull will give us a hell of a velocity." For a moment his voice wavered. "Sorry, I didn't mean to be flippant. No fish yet."

I unbuttoned my jacket. The heat would be awesome.

It was necessary. Tolliver was right.

"God, the Sun is huge from here! Our heat shields are on full, and cabin temperature hasn't risen much, but it feels hot. Probably my imagination. No fish."

I'd denied him honor.

"Still no aliens. Aiming directly toward the Sun helps the heat shields, I think. Less hull for the radiation to—whoops! A fish. A big one, close."

I'd denied him truth.

"Its skin is changing, sir. Darkening. It's squirting toward me, I'll try evasives. The side thrusters don't work very well."

Why should one more betrayal matter? I'd hurt everyone I'd ever known. Even poor Jerence, just now. A boy frightened out of his wits, and trying to hide it.

Like Keene.

"Sir, I commend Cadet Elena Von Siel, who managed the Fuse. And Rafe Slater, who's on comm. We're falling faster now. I've adjusted the gravitrons; we're not uncomfortable yet. Another fish, some distance off. Whoa. Two others. No . . . Hey, one Fused away!"

Christ, no.

"I've got a fish close, skin dark red, with an oddly shaped blotch. If it manages to throw, we'll be"—he hesitated—"off the air, I think. Five more fish. Seven. Here they come, sir! Commandant, my cadets are frightened. I've told them it's all right."

I closed my eyes.

"Dozens of fish, now. They orient themselves toward my fusion tubes. The red one is trying to throw, but it can't seem to form a pseudopod. Solar gravity, I guess. Just a minute, sir."

Silence.

My knees trembled. I tried to still them, could not.

"Sorry, sir. Cadet Frow lost control of himself. I left the conn to give him a sedative. I know it was against orders, but the problem was . . . distracting."

Lord, take them gently. Please. Please please please.

My deceit seemed a mercy, now.

"Sir, reports from the fleet!"

I hissed, "Not now, Boland." He crept to the corner, sat waiting.

"The red one just moved closer. It's . . . convulsing? Wow, it's gone. Just Fused away." A long pause. "I don't blame it. Sorry, please excuse that. A lot more fish now, sir, almost too many to count."

I summoned my voice. "You're doing fine, Mr. Keene. I'll have you up for lieutenant as soon—as soon as you get home."

"THE RED ONE'S BACK!" Keene's voice trembled with excitement. "Sir, they can't stay away. Praise Lord God, we have them!" I stood, hair rising on my neck. "They can't get away! That red fish isn't as close this time, but I see it clearly and it's the same one! I don't—it's all right, Mr. Slater, anytime now he'll give the order to Fuse. A cold shower, after we get home. Sorry, sir."

My hand crept to the caller. I dialed the bridge. "Mr. Branstead to the comm room."

"Sir, we're at eighteen five million miles and accelerating. Comm room says about a hundred sixty fish. The number keeps growing. A while back some were Fusing away, but none anymore. And they aren't throwing at us. Either they're unable or they're confused by the caterwauling." A pause. "And the heat. Our shields may not take much more."

I came to my senses. Perhaps there was time. "Your commendations noted, Mr. Keene. And yourself, especially."

"Cadet Branstead reporting, Cap—" The boy's voice quavered. I beckoned, opened my arms. He plunged into them, buried his head in my chest.

From the speaker, static.

"Commandant, I've sent the cadets to the outer cabin and had them turn off their speaker. My father's name is Raphael Keene, from the Midlands district. You have his address, of course. Please tell him I was thinking of him. Holy God! Hundreds of fish, with a huge rock! It's a miracle they didn't Fuse into us!"

Oh, Thomas.

Keene's voice was fervent. "Sir, they're shriveling! Steam bursts out their blowholes! It's working, sir! That's what you needed to know, and why you sent us."

The transmission was breaking up. He spoke ever faster. "I liked Academy, I really did. Hazing didn't bother . . . much. I'm sorry if I failed you as first middy. My favorite course was Astrophysics . . . must have changed the textbooks since . . . took the course . . . essor Hoskins taught us quite clearly the B'n Auba Zone is a constant . . . twenty point three million miles and doesn't change . . . gardless of the mass of ship."

I shouted into the caller, clutching it with both hands around the tousled bundle buried in my chest. "Forgive me, Mr. Keene! Please! I only meant—I'm sorry! Mr. Keene, I'm so sorry!"

". . . easily three hundred of them, all shriveling, no one left in the comm room to cou . . . terrible heat . . . breaking up and we . . ."

Static.

"Mr. Keene, I'm sorry!" I was still begging absolution when Jerence tugged the silent caller from my hand.

26

"How many of us left?"

Jerence sat very close, his head resting on my arm. "I don't know, sir. Bobby was in charge."

Boland said, "Sir, we have Mr. Thayer in Three, and Mr. Tsai in Four."

"That's all?"

"And us."

"Yes, of course."

I switched frequencies. "*Trafalgar* to Four. Here are your orders." Again I went through the ritual. "Acknowledge."

Fuser Four was ten million miles outward; nearly two minutes until a reply from Midshipman Tsai. I asked, "Mr. Boland, what word from the fleet?"

"Hundreds of aliens, sir. More keep Fusing in. They hit Denver with a rock. Rotterdam's gone too. The tidal wave—Holland's in bad trouble. And fish have landed near Cairo."

Two Fusers and *Trafalgar*. Not nearly enough. Our effort would fail.

"Sir, ships keep asking what to do. What do I tell them?"

It shouldn't come from the boy. I switched to fleet frequency.

"—to Seafort. If you're in charge, answer, or we'll assume you're—!"

"—*last only another couple of minutes and then I'm going to Fuse, I don't care what his bloody orders—*"

"—IN OUR ENGINE ROOM! WE'RE GOING TO LIFEPODS!"

I keyed the caller. "Nicholas Seafort, Acting FleetOpsCinc, to all ships." I glanced at my watch. "We're calling the fish away from Earth and the fleet. You should already be seeing results. No vessel is to Fuse for two hours. Unless I issue further orders, command will then revert to Admiralty London and you may Fuse at will. For now, *Trafalgar* remains in command. I now initiate radio silence for two hours."

For eternity. I switched off the caller.

I should have told them how the fish were being destroyed; it would have given them heart. But I couldn't bear to admit what I'd done. After we were gone, they'd figure it out. Or perhaps they would not.

Jerence searched my face. Ignoring him, I hurried down to the engine room.

Midshipman Tenere's eyes were troubled.

"Adam, you and Selette be ready to test at sixty-five percent, then Fuse, and test again. We may repeat that several times."

"Aye aye, sir." He hesitated. "Sir, what's happening to the Fusers?"

A lie sprang to my lips, died unuttered. Face-to-face, I couldn't manage it. "We're losing them. One by one they're calling fish."

"To where?"

"The Sun." Seeing his face I couldn't leave it at that. "They're magnificent, Adam. They're heroes."

The maturity of his answer came as a shock. "Does it matter, now they're dead?"

"Be ready for Fuse," I said curtly. "Whatever you do, don't let our tubes overheat."

I turned, and had almost reached the safety of the corridor when his voice pierced me. "Sir, forgive me, I know it's not my place . . . sir, you're doing the right thing."

"How dare you!"

His tone held resolve. "You were right, sir. We have to stop them. I just wanted—you to know that."

I managed not to strike him, slapped the hatch shut, stalked back to the comm room in a blazing fury, in time to hear Midshipman Thayer's distant reply.

"Fuser Four to *Trafalgar*, orders acknowledged."

A good lad, Anton Thayer. "Execute."

In a few moments, Four began to caterwaul.

"Tolliver!"

He ducked around the bulkhead and appeared in the comm room hatchway. "Yes, sir?"

"Once we start caterwauling we'll get a lot of fish. Be ready to Fuse a short way out of the main mass."

"You know better than that. Minimum Fuse is seven hundred thousand—"

"Run it like a nav drill!" We routinely taught middies to plot two Fuses, out and back, to reach a point closer than the minimum Fuse. The maneuver, though a good teaching tool, was rarely used because the margin of error made results erratic.

There was little I could do until Tolliver finished his calculations, except prepare Tommy Tsai. "*Trafalgar* to Three. Respond." I waited out the lag.

"Captain?" Jerence was subdued. "Was it true, what Robbie said? Are they going to hang you?"

I said gruffly, "No. They won't."

"You'll be acquitted? You had cause?"

"No."

After a long moment my meaning reached him. He clutched my arm, forgetting all he'd been taught. "After the last Fuser it's—it's—"

Cruelly, I waited him out.

"—our turn." He licked his lips. I nodded.

"Fuser Three to *Trafalgar*. Cadet Kyle Drew reporting."

"Enter the following Fusion coordinates, Mr. Drew." I read them off. "After you Defuse . . ." I went through the ghastly instructions. "Acknowledge and wait for my order to execute."

Another lag. I turned back to Jerence. "I ordered you not to go. I wanted to save you." Ashamed, I had to look away. Lord God had rebuked me for playing favorites.

"I thought you were mad at me, that I wasn't good enough."

"None of you knew what I was asking, or you'd have known better than—"

"I understood!" He added, "Don't you remember? You were about to give me a licking when the reports came in. I knew about the fish!"

I said, unbelieving, "And you came? Even if you had to sneak aboard?"

"I wanted to be with you." His bruised face wrinkled. "You protected me, always. And if you were going into danger—" He spun away, his voice muffled. "I wanted to help . . . for you."

"Oh, Jerence." I let my hand stray to his shoulder.

A new voice on the caller. Johan Stritz. "Fuser Four to *Trafalgar*, too many fish! Over a hundred, and they—oh, God, Commandant! Please! Help us now!"

"Engine Room, sixty percent Fusion!" I changed frequency. "Fuser Four, discontinue test!"

We would gather fish as long as we could, then send them to Three. That would doom young Tommy Tsai. And Kyle Drew. He'd bear no more guilt for shattering Dustin Edwards's helmet.

"Tolliver, hurry with those coordinates. Stand by to maneuver!"

I sat brooding until Tolliver's voice crackled in the speaker. "Coordinates are ready. I think you want to stand by to help."

I stood. "Jerence, I'm sorry."

"I don't want us to die."

I tried to grasp his sentiment. Only the assurance of death, of Lord God's most awful hell, sustained me.

For the last time, I took the bridge of a U.N.N.S. starship. Tolliver's eyes met mine. Sensing something of the formality of the moment, he rose to salute me.

"Carry on, Mr. Tolliver."

"Seven fish, so far." He pointed at the screen. None were near.

Alarms clanged; *Trafalgar* lurched.

"Close. God, sir, if we only had a laser." The screen was filling with encroachments.

I asked, "How many now?"

"That's your bloody job!"

Chastened, I made a rough estimate. No more than sixty.

"JESUS!" A fish loomed. Tolliver rammed down a starboard thruster. A snap, as the lever broke in half.

"God damned half-arsed Naval consoles—" His hands danced from thruster to thruster.

He pushed up the jagged stub, quieting the thruster. "The lever still works."

"A hundred ten fish!" Was there no end to them? Within the mass, a small asteroid, a hundred meters in diameter. "Edgar, we'll have to Fuse in a—"

Lights flashed from one end of the screen to the other, each indicating a fish. He shouted, "NOW!"

I jabbed my finger down the control. The stars blanked. Two seconds later I slapped the Defuse. I called up our return coordinates. Again I Fused.

No encroachments within throwing range but the screen was white with fish—

An immense explosion. The air inside our ship slammed against the hull, popping my ears with the sudden change in pressure. The simulscreen went black.

"WHAT HAPPENED?" I could barely hear.

"A fish must have Fused inside another."

"No, the explosion was too big—" Then I had it. "Rocks! They must have Fused one into—"

"I can't see with the screen out!"

I punched in the alternate circuit. It restored most of the screen, but our starboard fore sensor was gone. *Trafalgar* was half blind. Tolliver swiveled on our linear axis so our port sensor faced the fish. Over half of the accumulated mass had been obliterated when their rocks met.

As I watched, other fish Defused to take their place.

"Tolliver, you'll have to handle them alone."

"Where do you think you're going?"

"Outside. We have spare sensors in the rack in the—"

"You idiot, what if I have to Fuse?"

"Then you'll lose me. And a cadet." I keyed the caller. "Rene Salette, get your suit on, flank!" When we'd raced to board the Mothership, it was she who'd skittered expertly along the hull footholds.

I ran to the lock, grabbed my suit off the rack, fumbled into the legs. Rene was already sealing her helmet. I cursed as my foot caught in the webbing. No time to be clumsy now. I thrust one arm inside, struggled with the other.

"Here, sir." Jerence Branstead helped me insert my arm. While I grappled with my helmet, he dived into his own suit, faster than I'd have thought possible.

"You're staying here." I snapped the clamps.

He thrust in his arms, reached for his helmet. "Please, sir, don't make me disobey again. I'm still a cadet."

I swallowed, nodded reluctant assent. The three of us entered the lock. I slapped shut the hatch, opened the lock's supply rack. I'd only need one spare; no other sensors had faced the blast. Still, best to bring two, in case we inadvertently let one loose and it floated off. "Hold this!" I dumped the first replacement in Rene's arms. I clutched the tools and spare sensor.

The airlock pump took forever. Too late, I remembered to check my suit air. Enough. If I didn't slow down and follow procedures, I'd get someone killed. I snorted at the irony.

"Captain, hurry! We're picking up fish like fleas on—"

"Hold your water, Tolliver." I slapped open the outer hatch.

Jerence gasped. A dozen fish, plainly visible.

"Move!" We clambered onto the hull. "Don't miss any footholds."

The girl pointed aft. "Which one is it? There?"

"No, forward." Agile, she swung around, slipped her foot into a hold, drifted forward along the line of footholds in dreamlike slow motion. I did my best to follow.

Urgency sped our steps. In a minute we'd reached the sensor mount. My breath rasped in my helmet, clouding the faceplate as fast as the suit could clear it.

"Captain, move! One of them is only seventy meters—"

As I watched, the fish drifted closer.

My wrench fumbled at the mount. Jerence said quietly, "Sir, if you let me, it'll go faster."

Astounded, I looked up, saw calm confidence. I handed him the wrench. Still in the same foothold, he knelt, turned the bolts easily. He slipped it into his suit pouch. After a moment, another bolt. He grinned, ignoring the looming fish. "These are like the motor mounts on my electrobike. I used to tear it apart all the time. Dad hated—" His face clouded. "Dad." Harmon Branstead had stayed on undefended Hope Nation.

Tolliver fired our port thrusters. The fish receded slowly.

As soon as Jerence pulled the last bolt Rene Salette changed footholds, carefully dropped to her knees, extended the spare sensor. "Here."

Jerence fitted it into place. I stooped, unclamped the line, fastened it to the new sensor while Jerence turned the nuts.

"*SEAFORT, LOOK OUT!*" Tolliver, his voice ragged.

I looked up, froze. A fish, no more than seven meters away, bow on to us, drifting ever closer.

"*I CAN'T THRUST TO STARBOARD, ANOTHER ONE'S TOO NEAR! GET THE HELL INSIDE—*"

"Leave it!" I pulled Jerence to his feet. The fish's skin swirled.

Rene scampered along the hull. Jerence stared, mesmerized. I thrust him past me toward the sanctuary of the lock.

"*GET IN! GET IN!*" Tolliver was hoarse with frustration.

The fish's skin went indistinct. Abruptly a outrider was pulsing on its surface.

Rene clambered toward the lock. As she groped for a foothold the alien flung itself across the gap. It wrapped itself around her faceplate. Her foot came loose from the hold. She shrieked. Together, they floated off the hull.

"Please oh God please not like this help me—"

Branstead tugged on my arm until he finally penetrated my funk. "Come on, sir! The lock!"

Beyond us, the girl's shape seemed to waver. A yelp, and the radio went silent.

I took another step, still clutching the tools and spare sensor.

Jerence tugged at my arm. "Hurry, it's coming!"

The fish had drifted almost close enough to touch. Its nose came within a meter of where I stood.

"*Captain, we have to Fuse NOW! Get in the lock!*"

The fish had no eyes, no mouth, no discernible features. The skin at its prow began to swirl. In seconds another outrider would emerge.

Jerence tried again to pull me to safety. I shrugged free, all the rage in the cosmos exploding within me. I set my boot in the foothold, inches from the fish. "BE GONE, THING OF SATAN!"

The alien's translucent skin parted. The form of an outrider began to appear.

"ENOUGH!" My voice broke. "LUCIFER! IN THE NAME OF LORD GOD ALMIGHTY, I BANISH THEE!" In a frenzy I swung the sensor over my head, plunged it into the widening, swirling surface. My foot twisted. I slipped to my knees.

The fish convulsed. Almost instantly a blowhole tore open. A swirl of propellant streamed over my head, shot past the curved hull of the Mothership.

The fish receded, its colors a violent swirl.

Jerence tugged. I lost my balance, and my foothold. I floated helplessly while he hauled me toward the waiting lock. He steered me in, pushed me to the inner bulkhead. I made no effort to grasp it. Jerence swung himself in, slapped the hatch closed.

His hands scrabbled at the caller. "Sir, we're inside!"

The stars blinked out.

Unresisting, I let Jerence Branstead strip off my suit. When he was done I stood for a moment, walked with toddler's steps to the bridge. I found my seat.

"Sir—" Tolliver's eyes searched my face. "You—I've never—" He said nothing more.

I gazed at the screen. Could there be so many fish in the universe? Hundreds upon hundreds. Their blips punctuated the screen like . . . I knew not what.

Jerence crept into the cabin, took a seat, stared at me as if in awe. I studied the screen. Lights began blinking out, reappearing closer, searching for our drive tubes.

I found it hard to form words. "Time, now. Fuser Three."

Tolliver said, softly, "Captain . . ."

"Time to kill Tommy and Kyle." I reached for the caller, couldn't close my hand around it.

Tolliver was far away, "He's in shock. Get the medkit!"

I brought the caller to my lips. "Captain Seafort to Fuser Three." What was it I had to tell them? Something about fish.

"Christ, Captain, hang on. I've got to—" Tolliver's hands slammed the thruster controls.

Jerence skidded back onto the bridge.

Tommy Tsai, Tommy Keene. It was my task to kill Tommys. I smiled.

"Fuser Three here. Midshipman Tsai reporting."

Jerence held my right arm. Tolliver abandoned his controls, brought the medgun toward me. My left hand lashed out, snatched it away, smashed it on the edge of the console. "Not yet, Mr. Tolliver." My eyes made him recoil. "It still has to be done, you see. And the guilt has to be mine."

"Sir, you're—"

"Insane. Yes, I know. It doesn't matter."

Jerence sobbed. I took up the caller.

With a curse Tolliver worked the thrusters, spun us away from a looming fish. The lurching screen made me dizzy.

"Tommy . . . Mr. Midshipman Tsai. It's your time." I smiled at Tolliver, spewed my villainy to Fuser Three. "Execute."

"Aye aye, executing. Sir, will the fish attack us?"

It would take a long time for my reply to find him. "Not if you lock in your fusion motors. Mr. Keene is testing, and Mr. Diego. Together you'll confuse them."

Eternity passed.

One by one the lights of the fish began to blink out.

"We sent Tommy a lot of them." My tone was conversational.

No one replied. Jerence wiped his eyes.

I took the caller. "Fuser Four, respond."

I hummed. We had a few minutes, until Fuser Three's work was done. "Edgar, this time we'll have to caterwaul a good while. Better set up more coordinates."

Tolliver reached for the medkit. "Sir, you're not well. Let me give—"

"No, thank you. Tend to your duties."

He stared into my eyes. At length he nodded, subdued.

"Fuser Four. Midshipman Anton Thayer responding."

"Jerence, don't cry. It distracts me."

The boy jumped. "Aye aye, sir." To my surprise, he stopped.

"Mr. Thayer, stand by to Fuse and test again." I gave Jerence a reassuring pat. "It will be the last time."

I waited out the lag, nodding satisfaction.

Midshipman Thayer's voice was troubled. *"Commandant, what are we doing? How does this help?"*

"We're confusing fish so they'll Fuse home." I began to tremble. After a time, it ceased. "Take care if fish come close, and don't forget to lock in your drive for the test." My head ached. I wasn't sure if it had just begun, or had been aching all my life.

Waiting out the lag, I said, "What's wrong, Jerence?"

"Nothing, sir." The boy swallowed. "You're doing fine."

It wasn't his place to tell me that.

"We'll lock in the motors, sir. Standing by to execute on your order."

I marveled at how well Thayer had managed the transition from cadet to middy. Foolish, to think of disciplining him over a mere pillow fight.

The last Fuser, before our own turn. I let relief wash over me. "Mr. Tolliver, begin testing at sixty-five percent." That was the loudest we could call without risking the tubes.

"Aye aye, sir." Tolliver passed the order. "Captain, I want to Fuse sooner this time, before they surround us."

"No, we're summoning them. They need a point to aim at."

"Let me Fuse out and back. We'll last longer."

My thoughts were fuzzy. "Very well. You're in charge of evasives."

Fish popped onto the screen.

I leaned back as if viewing a holodrama. Encroachment lights flashed, a few at first, then by the dozen. Tolliver Fused; we were alone in the deep. Immediately he Fused back. We emerged nearly a million kilometers from our start. A bad roll of the dice from Fusion's margin of error.

After a time, the fish found us.

Some two hundred, now. Rocks were scattered among them. Lord God knew from whence we summoned the aliens. In the last hours, we'd caterwauled longer and louder than had ever been done.

Hundreds of lights. Explosions. We Fused.

I contemplated our silent, dreamlike dance through the cosmos. Perhaps it was His cosmic joke, to fight the evil of the fish through the evil in me. It satisfied me to be His instrument, even in this.

"Captain. Captain!"

I struggled back. "What, Mr. Tolliver?"

"Look at them! We can't avoid all—" He cursed, sent us spinning, Fused again. "We've called at least five hundred of them, maybe more. If we don't survive we can't pass them on to Four!"

I leaned back. Our time was not yet. Fish still swam.

We Fused clear. The relief of blank screens. Back.

"Lord Jesus!" Again, we'd Defused into a vast mass of fish. Tolliver slammed his hand against the console screen; the stars vanished once again.

His hands trembled. "I can't take any more! Enough!"

"TAKE US BACK BEFORE THEY DISPERSE!" I pounded the console, catching my palm on the broken lever. Cursing, I sucked at blood, punched in new coordinates. Our return Fuse put us near the edge of the huge flickering mass.

"You'll get us killed for nothing! Give the order to Thayer!"

"Not yet." I watched the ever-increasing lights.

"It has to be now! We're almost out of propellant!"

I checked; he was telling the truth.

Reluctantly, I gave the order. "Mr. Thayer. *Trafalgar* to Fuser Four. Fuse and commence test! Acknowledge."

Three fish squirted toward us. Tolliver looked up, cursed, used the last of his prepared coordinates.

I asked, "How far are we?"

"From the fish? About two million miles."

"Go back. I want to see."

"Wait until the order gets to Thayer."

"That's less than a minute. Go back."

Tolliver sighed. "Aye aye, sir." He took his time preparing coordinates, but I knew it was useless to complain. He'd only use the interruption to delay further. At last, he was ready, and we Fused.

Fish swarmed.

"Thayer didn't caterwaul!"

"Be patient," I said.

"We Fused here. They'll have heard that."

As if to prove his point, a fish Defused alongside. Tolliver reacted instinctively, slamming the starboard thrusters to full. We veered away. The fish followed. Two others appeared, one directly astern.

"Captain, you waited too—"

The fish disappeared.

Thank you, Anton.

A few lights blinked out. Then dozens.

The middy and cadets in Four would be engulfed by fish trapped by the vast Solar gravity, wilting in the unbearable heat.

Try to understand, Anton. I had to do it.

I waited. At last the screen was empty of fish. I calculated the coordinates we'd need.

"Tolliver."

"Yes, sir." Still shaken, he stared at the console.

"Go below to the engine room. Mr. Tenere may recognize the final coordinates."

"He'll obey."

"Go below. Just in case."

"Aye aye, sir." Obediently, he left his chair. At the hatch, he hesitated. "Sir, what I said before, about hating you—"

I was unconcerned. Nothing Tolliver said could harm me now.

"I want you to know, I don't hate you. What you've done . . . sir, it's beyond love or hate. You're saving the—"

"GET OUT!!" I'd been mistaken. He could hurt me.

I picked up the caller. Suddenly the speaker crackled to life. Freak radio waves, pierced the veil of Solar radiation, cluttered with static.

Anton Thayer, on Four. A sob.

"Sir, they're all around us! You said we'd be safe!"

I swallowed.

"Captain Seafort . . ." The middy's voice was sick with hurt and wonder. *"YOU LIED!"*

The speaker crackled static.

I sat still for a terribly long time, blood from my palm dripping on the console. At last, I picked up the caller. "Engine Room, sixty percent Fusion power."

Midshipman Adam Tenere, his tone firm. "Sixty percent, aye aye." The line on the screen began to pulse.

I waited. Thayer's voice echoed in the silent cabin.

I readied our final coordinates: eighteen million miles. As soon as fish responded to our call, I'd go immediately to perdition. I couldn't risk freeing them if they attacked our tubes.

Come to me, spawn of Lucifer.

I stared at the screen until my eyes watered.

Nothing. On the console, the Fusion line wavered.

"Mr. Tenere, check your gauges!"

"Aye aye, sir. Sixty percent."

I cursed. "Increase to sixty-five!"

"Sixty-five, aye aye."

I waited, forcing a semblance of calm. No fish.

Our drive was malfunctioning. Yet it had just Fused us ten times or more. "Adam, what in God's hell is wrong down there?"

It was Tolliver who answered. "Nothing, sir. We're caterwauling."

"No we're not! There isn't a single—"

"Come check for yourself. We're heating. I know there's power going out!"

"Comm room to bridge, Cadet Boland reporting. Sir, I've—"

I switched off the speaker. Come to me, you bastards.

No fish.

I snatched the caller. "Seventy percent!"

Adam. "Sir, we'll melt—"

I yelled, "Seventy percent, you mutineer!"

"Aye aye, sir. Seventy percent." The line on my console leaped. We couldn't maintain seventy for long, I knew.

Nothing.

"God damn you, come to me!" My outburst startled Jerence; he drew back.

Robert Boland burst into the hatchway. "Sir, the fleet! They're calling from all over home system. No one sees any fish. They're gone!"

I shrieked, "OUT!" He recoiled.

"They'll come!" I spun to Jerence, my eyes wild. "They have to!"

He backed away.

I shouted into the caller, "Come to me when I call you! *I'M THE FISHERMAN!*"

Jerence turned and ran.

"Captain, we'll melt the tubes!"

"Throttle down to sixty-five, but no less!"

The cursed screen remained blank.

I cried, "Damn you, God! DON'T DO THIS TO ME!"

Nothing.

The Lord's revenge; He would even deny me oblivion.

Father's visage swam. Grim lessons, across the kitchen table: *"Nicholas, Satan's deceit knows no bounds."*

You almost had me there, Lucifer. But I know we're calling from the wrong place.

I rechecked coordinates. "Engine Room, Fuse and resume caterwauling!" I ran my finger down the screen.

The stars refused to blink.

"Fuse, damn you!" I hammered my fist on the console, caught the jagged edge of the broken throttle. Blood sprayed. Welcome agony flowed up my arm.

Faces appeared in the hatch. I appealed, "Can't you see? We have to Fuse!"

The screens remained dark.

I pounded the broken lever over and again until my palm was ragged.

"Fuse! I'm begging you! Don't make me live."

They came closer.

"Fuse!"

A gentle hand fell on my shoulder.

"Fuse!" My voice broke.

27

I woke in an unfamiliar cabin. I ran a numb hand across my eyes; a bandage scratched my face.

Tolliver looked up.

"Where am I?"

"*Prince of Wales*, sir. The first lieutenant's cabin."

"How did . . ."

"They met us, yesterday. You were still sedated."

My mind veered away from the bridge, and my failure.

"The fish?"

"None anywhere. That last great caterwaul of ours, before we pitched them to Fuser Three . . ."

"Where are we headed?"

He said simply, "Home."

"Court-martial." Then, surcease. I could wait, if I must.

"Yes." A knock; the hatch opened. A starched midshipman with a tray. He saluted, and left.

"How soon?"

"We dock tomorrow. Earthport has only two undamaged bays for the entire fleet, but they want you groundside."

"Thanks be to God."

He hitched his chair closer. "What do you mean, sir?"

"They'll help me end."

"You're that anxious to die, Nick?"

"Not anxious. Desperate."

"The guilt you spoke of."

"Edgar, it's unbearable."

"I understand." His look was one of pity. "But you can't confess. Not all."

"Don't be silly. I want—"

"Think, sir." He crossed to the hatch, made sure it was sealed. His voice dropped. "What do you intend to tell them?"

"That I stole command of the fleet. That I tricked cadets into volunteering, betrayed them with lies, sent them to—"

"Captain!"

His tone brought me to a halt.

"Imagine you're the father of a fifteen-year-old. Kyle Drew, let's say. Proudly, you sent him to Academy. Now you get a fax. Your son was roasted in a Fuser spinning toward the Sun. He didn't sacrifice himself bravely; his Commandant tricked him into it. All you have left is that memory."

"It's truth."

"Truth is too cruel!" He leaned forward until his head almost touched mine. "Our cadets were heroes. Do you understand? Heroes!"

"I can't live with betrayal! Confession is—"

"They volunteered for a suicide mission, every last one of them!" He grasped my lapels. "You have no choice. Demented or no, you can't be so vicious as to deny their families that consolation."

"But you know, and Robert. Jerence. Adam Tenere. It will come out."

"I've already explained to them. They won't be charged, Captain; command was yours. So no P and D for them." He eyed me. "Confess what you must, but not what you did to the cadets. That's obscene."

I shook my head. "The truth, before I die. Just once."

Tolliver's eyes glistened. "Nick, you'd do that to Thomas Keene?"

I cried, "In Keene's case it was so! He went knowing!"

"What about the others? You'll tell their parents they died fools, not heroes?"

My voice was hoarse. "Don't do this to me! I don't have the strength."

"You know the truth. I know. That's enough."

I whispered, "Edgar, I beseech you. It's the only consolation I'll ever know."

With the finality of a judge, he shook his head.

I let them clothe me in my dress whites, lead me silently through crowded corridors to the forward lock. Every man in *Prince of Wales* had found excuse to be present, to see the notorious Nicholas Seafort one last time.

Stone-faced, I showed them nothing.

We cycled through to Earthport Station, strode along patched corridors to the waiting shuttle. I took my seat, fumbled uselessly at the belts with my injured hand, allowed them to strap me in.

They lodged me at Portsmouth, where I'd sent Sergeant Serenco for trial. The next day Admiral Duhaney, lips pursed, himself handed me the indictment. The formality of his salute startled me, but I returned it crisply.

I saw no one else except Captain Jason Tenere, appointed my counsel. He told me of the crowds massed in the streets outside, hoping for a glimpse of me.

Captain Tenere ignored my instructions to plead guilty. Over my outraged protest, he entered a plea of innocence. I tried to dismiss him, demanded to speak for myself, but the Court refused. I would have to undergo trial. Because of my attempted plea, I was spared the misery of the drugs.

The trial lasted two weeks.

Entering and leaving the courtroom I endured the bright lights of the holocameras and the forest of mikes thrust in my face.

I refused to speak on my own behalf.

Cadet Boland was one of many called. Young, proud, he stood before the bar in crisp grays, a splendid specimen of the Navy to come. If it weren't for the obscenity of his testimony, even I would have been moved. He spoke earnestly of my intent to join my victims in immolation, and of the vast hordes of fish we had summoned and passed down the line.

One by one, Captains in the Home Fleet waited their turn to attest to the hopelessness of their situation, before we'd begun to caterwaul.

Even Admiral Duhaney made his appearance, acknowledging that I'd submitted a caterwaul bomb proposal and begged him to speed its development.

By the time an aide to Admiral Seville came forth, to testify regarding the welter of unconfirmed reports and pleas for help that had inundated London Admiralty, I suspected the worst. The Navy was gathering around one of its own.

When it came to pass, my acquittal didn't shock me. Holding my nausea in check, I stood at stolid attention while the President of the Court extolled my resourcefulness and heroism, and cited the incontrovertible and conclusive evidence that it was necessary for me to relieve Admiral Seville to preserve the fleet.

After, they sent me back to Admiralty House.

Lord God wasn't done toying with me.

A week later, they summoned me to Duhaney's London office. I went, my resignation typed and ready in my pocket.

The Admiral's aide showed me in. Senator Richard Boland was present; I hadn't expected him. Well, no matter. I saluted, held attention until released.

I listened to what the Senator proposed, refused at once.

"Good heavens, man, you're a natural," Senator Boland said. "You saved the world. As a candidate you're unstoppable!"

"You're mistaken." I peered down from the window to the pedestrians scurrying in the warm afternoon sun.

"No, I'm not. You don't know politics, Seafort. You'll be—"

"I'm stoppable. In fact, I'm stopped."

The Senator crossed glances with Duhaney. "What do you mean?"

"I resign the Commandancy of Naval Academy. And I resign from the Naval Service of the United Nations." I unfolded my formal paper, laid it on the desk.

Duhaney gaped. "Resign? Don't be ridiculous, Seafort. If you won't help us in the legislature, the Navy needs you. Your image is invaluable, and we have a fleet to rebuild, the aliens' home planet to find—"

"No."

"Let me remind you," he said with asperity, "you have no choice. Captain or Midshipman, you serve where you're assigned."

"True. I'll admit freely at court-martial that I refuse your orders."

"Court-martial?" His tone was unbelieving.

"Yes. Let me go, or try me all over again."

"Is it because of how I spoke to you on *Trafalgar*? You were right, we were confus—"

"You misunderstand. I'm done, for my own reasons."

Duhaney said, "All right, perhaps we shouldn't push you into politics, no matter how much it would benefit the Navy. But you can't resign; you have your duty. Your honor must rise to that."

I walked toward his desk, spread my hands on its gleaming surface, leaned close. My voice made even my own hackles rise. "Duhaney, if you again use the word honor in connection with my name, I'll kill you with my bare hands." I held his gaze until he could not.

The Senator studied me with interest. "What will you do, Seafort, without the Navy, without politics?"

"Do? It's none of your concern. We've nothing further to say to each other." I crossed to the door.

"Mr. Seafort, thank you for saving my son."

I'd tried to kill his son. I strode to the door, and to purgatory.

Epilogue

That wasn't the last of it, but in the end they had to let me go.

I rode the ancient electric railway to Cardiff, but with Father gone, nothing was the same. Eddie and Annie met me at the cottage door. Their anxious pretense at welcome set my nerves on edge. After a time Annie noticed my discomfort when her hand strayed to Eddie's for a reassuring touch. On the few occasions she ventured to stroke my shoulder I responded with rigid indifference.

We endured the mutual misery for three days. I brooded, and visited Jason's grave. Then I left.

I took a flat in Devon near Academy, but word of my presence soon spread, and I had no peace.

I wandered Britain, looking for I knew not what. When recognized, I fled.

One bleak day my path led me to the Neo-Benedictine order at Lancaster. My interview with Abbot Ryson was difficult; he seemed to take a visceral dislike to me. Nonetheless, something in my recital moved him to admit me as a novice. Three weeks later I took vows of chastity and obedience, and moved into the cloister bringing only the clothes I wore.

Father Ryson had warned that monastery life would be hard. I didn't mind. Testing my vow of obedience, he obliged me to weeks of absolute silence, a requirement normally reserved for punishment or as a mark of disfavor.

The silence eased my way. Each morning I rose, filed with the brothers to matins, prayed on my knees on the cold stone floor. After, I toiled in the bakery where I learned how to knead the dough for three risings, preparing the sweet hot rolls that graced our meals.

At night, I went to my bed in the tiny room called a cell, but which wasn't such. I said rote prayers while making ready for sleep. The ritual words gave a certain remembered comfort, but I couldn't feel the presence of God.

At least they helped me not to think.

Kneading dough helped me not to think.

Cleaning latrines helped me not to think, a duty from which Father Ryson eventually relieved me, over my bitter protest.

A parishioner recognized me at services, and for a time public services were unusually well attended. I focused my gaze on the stone floor, managing not to see the pointing fingers, not to hear the murmurs. Once a congregant brought a holocamera to services, but, thank You, Lord God, was bustled out by two burly monks before he could torment me further.

Not thinking is difficult, when you've spent your life training to be a more precise thinker. Failing at it only makes me try harder. I've opted for confession, now a voluntary rite. Weekly I confide my sins to Abbot Ryson, whom I elected my confessor.

Among my sins is the self-absorption that requires me to think of who I am and what I've done.

Perhaps as penance, Father Ryson has required me to set down the history of my life in such detail as it takes for me to adjudge it complete.

And so, these many months, I've sat in my tiny, scrubbed cell after the day's baking, and scratched with an old-fashioned pen onto real paper these recollections of my life. Written ostensibly to Abbot Ryson, they are actually addressed to You, Lord God, as if You could not read that which is inscribed in blood in my heart.

With the detached observation that has always been my burden, I've described my self-ordained slide down the greased chute to hell. It started, perhaps, with the undeserved pride that made me offer myself to the Navy, and the foolish complacency that allowed me to stake my soul on the certainty that I could fulfill my oath.

I slid further by lying to myself on the occasion I saved Vax Holser from the penalties of his disobedience, when he refused to abandon me on *Telstar*. At the time I pretended it was an act of mercy, but now, I know better. It was dereliction of duty.

I slid faster, until I could skirt my oath of obedience merely to save Midshipman Philip Tyre a caning. Gliding ever onward, I found myself able to refuse an order from my superior Admiral Tremaine to take on the passengers he had disembarked.

Could I ever have stopped, saved myself? Truly, I don't know.

By then it had become so easy, You see. I confess: duty had replaced You as my beacon. To protect my ship, my people, I knowingly swore Elena Bartel no harm, then shot her through the heart, exploding beyond pretense the myth that my oath, my covenant with You, was a thing I valued.

What matter, after such folly, that I lied glibly to my superiors about Vax Holser's conduct at Orbit Station? By now I was sliding with breathless speed, the breeze against my face ever warmer.

And so we come to my ultimate folly, wherein I tricked obedient boys and rosy budding girls into casting away their lives to save my planet from the alien fish.

Would they have given themselves willingly?

I don't know. I never gave them the chance.

Was what I did necessary?

In a sense, yes. Because I had no faith that You would save Your people, Your Church, Your creation. In my arrogance I believed that my acts alone could draw away the fish.

But at night, when I compose myself for sleep and lie tossing until the early hours of the morn, I commune with Kevin Arnweil and Kyle Drew and Jacques Theroux, and so many others. At times, Midshipman Thomas Keene sits charred at my bedside, to vanish when I wake.

I see them, please forgive me, at matins when my mind should be on the prayers I chant, and when I should not, of all times, be forced to *think*.

I see them now, when I prepare to lay down my pen and attend to vespers.

I am damned. That is as it should be, for what I have done is damnable.

But yet . . .

In the silence of the night I sit at the side of my bed, robe thrown over my bare shoulders, and I wonder . . .

How is it that I know that You are a God of mercy, a God of love, yet, nonetheless, I know equally well You must not forgive me?

You see, if You could forgive the frightful evil I've done, then, Lord God, I'm sorry, I could not believe in You. For the sake of the children, if naught else, You must mete justice, and I, of all men, have earned punishment.

But after I return to bed, and lie sleepless through the waning night, sometimes a still, small voice wonders, Oh, Lord God, surely You knew what You were doing, when You fitted my cog into the complex interwoven gears of Your creation?

You made me what I was, and You provided the circumstances by which I threw myself from Grace. It was You who made it appear that my world and its people could not be saved unless I led those bright trusting children to their doom.

And then, I ask:

Lord God?

Lord, why hast Thou forsaken me?

Afterword

So ends the as yet unpublished autobiography of my friend and mentor Captain Nicholas Ewing Seafort, U.N.N.S. These painfully frank pages are the only record he has made of his accomplishments.

Though his story ends here, history's judgment of Mr. Seafort is less harsh than his own. As we all know, ten years after he completed these writings, he emerged from seclusion and plunged himself into the world of politics, drawn by a plea for help from an old friend.

Allying himself with the Boland organization, Seafort was elected to the U.N. Senate with virtually no opposition. From the start he demonstrated the unswerving, selfless honesty that was ever after his trademark. His divorce from Annie Wells Seafort, later Annie Boss, had left him alone and desolate, a condition he endured for several years until his marriage to Arlene Sanders in the rotunda of the U.N.

Most biographers have underestimated the effect of Abbot Ryson's harsh mercy on the tormented ex-Captain in his care.

Drawing on Seafort's unbroken relationship with Lord God, Ryson evoked from him the depths of his anguish, and its cause. The means by which Nick Seafort unburdened his tortured soul and became reconciled to his past is unknown. But ever after, he would brook no evasion, no dishonesty, not the most insignificant white lie.

This characteristic made his company uncomfortable for some, but wiser men, and I, found it reassuring.

During his term as SecGen, Mr. Seafort staunchly supported the Navy while it rebuilt from its debacle with the fish. Yet, at the same time, he moved firmly and decisively to quell the Navy's chronic nepotism. Today's Naval meritocracy is a direct result of his efforts.

Nicky Seafort was utterly inept at traditional political skills. He tolerated no diplomatic lies or convenient subterfuge. In the Port of London scandals, it was his unflinching honesty and refusal to disavow blame that led to the fall of his government and his personal disgrace. Had he been less blunt about his failure to oversee Senator Wade's misdealings, his administration might well have survived the March 2224 vote of confidence.

Over time, the public and the Senate have come to appreciate Seafort's refusal to exculpate himself. His admissions are now admired as a mark of integrity and honor, and there are those who have called for him to cast aside his premature retirement and enter again the public arena. His urgent need for privacy, his troubled nature, and his distrust of power make that event unlikely.

It is hard, in times of relative tranquillity, to recall the turmoil and uncertainty of those perilous days when fish roamed unchecked and the colonies struggled to recast their relationship with the home world.

Today, unmanned Caterwaul Stations in permanent Solar orbit safeguard the security of mankind. It would seem the threat from the fish has ended, but the Stations remain sentinels of our vigilance, serviced by Nick Seafort's beloved Navy.

I met Captain Seafort again on several occasions when business brought me to Earth or politics took him to Hope Nation. When together, we often reminisced about living friends and long-departed comrades, and those young days when our destinies lay ahead.

Despite the honors and achievements of later years, Captain Seafort once remarked that never in his life did he feel as fulfilled as when first we'd met, while he served as senior midshipman on U.N.S. *Hibernia*, on our first hopeful voyage to the stars.

> Derek, Lord Carr
> First Staadholder
> Commonweal of Hope Nation
> October, in the year of our Lord 2225